Narcissa

BY LANCE TOOKS

DOUBLEDAY
GRAPHIC NOVELS
New York

PUBLISHED BY DOUBLEDAY
a division of Random House, Inc.
1540 Broadway, New York, New York, 10036

DOUBLEDAY GRAPHIC NOVELS
and its colophon are trademarks of Random House, Inc.
and DOUBLEDAY and its colophon are registered trademarks of Random House, Inc.

Images on pages 82–83 are used courtesy of the Spanish Council. Images on pages 101–2 are used courtesy of Konemann Staff, from *Andalusia*, 2000.

This graphic novel is a work of fiction. Any references to real people, events, establishment organizations, or locales are intended only to give the fiction a sense of reality and authenticity. Other names, characters, and incidents are either the product of the author's imagination or are used fictitiously, as are those fictionalized events and incidents that involve real persons.

Book design by Lance Tooks

Cataloging-in-Publication Data is on file with the Library of Congress.

ISBN 0-385-50342-3

Printed in the United States of America

October 2002
First Edition

10 9 8 7 6 5 4 3 2 1

To Deborah Cowell, who made this book possible

To Hazel and Kimmy, who made this author possible

To Suni, contigo mañana es possible

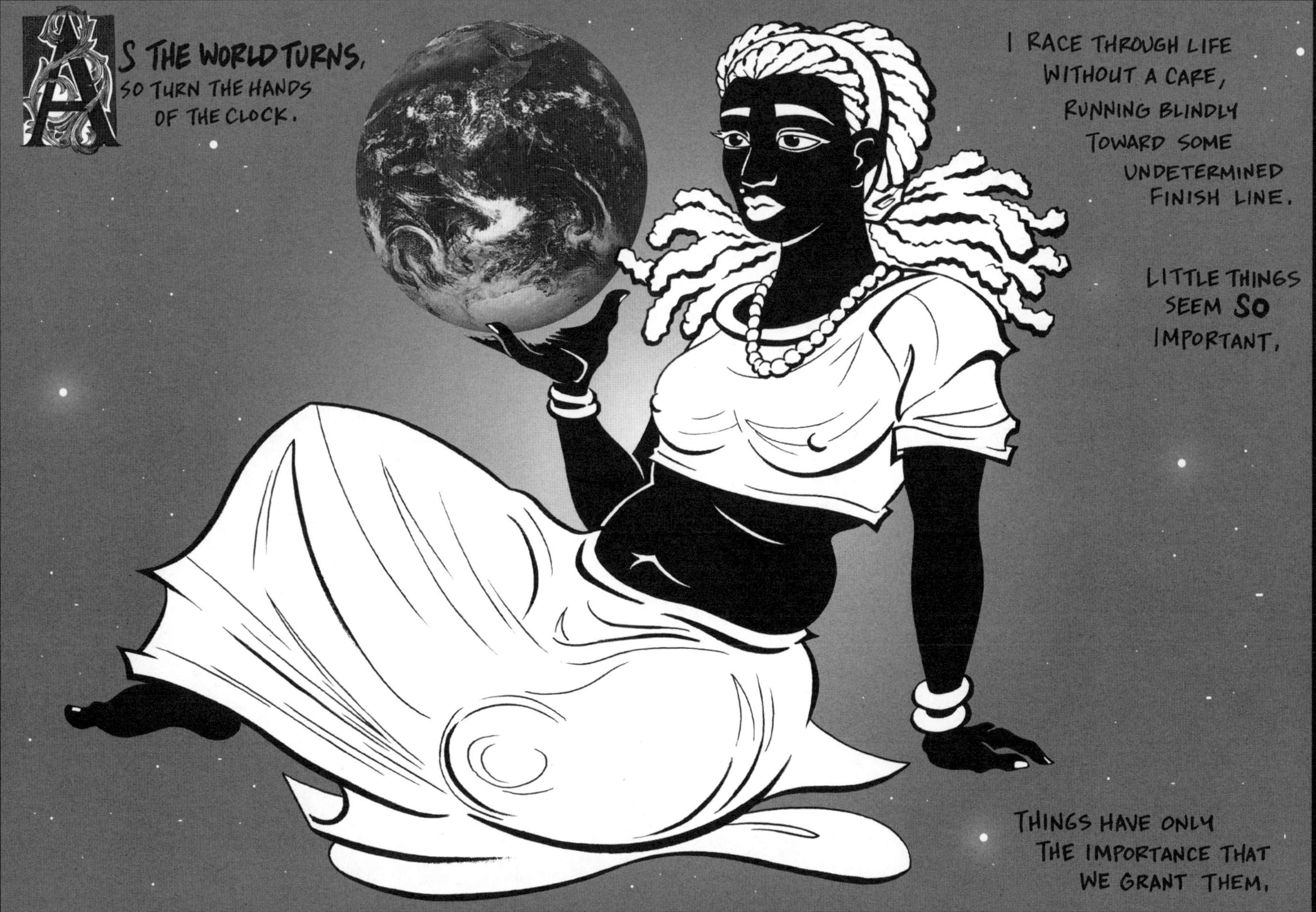
AS THE WORLD TURNS,
SO TURN THE HANDS OF THE CLOCK.
I RACE THROUGH LIFE WITHOUT A CARE, RUNNING BLINDLY TOWARD SOME UNDETERMINED FINISH LINE.
LITTLE THINGS SEEM SO IMPORTANT,
THINGS HAVE ONLY THE IMPORTANCE THAT WE GRANT THEM,

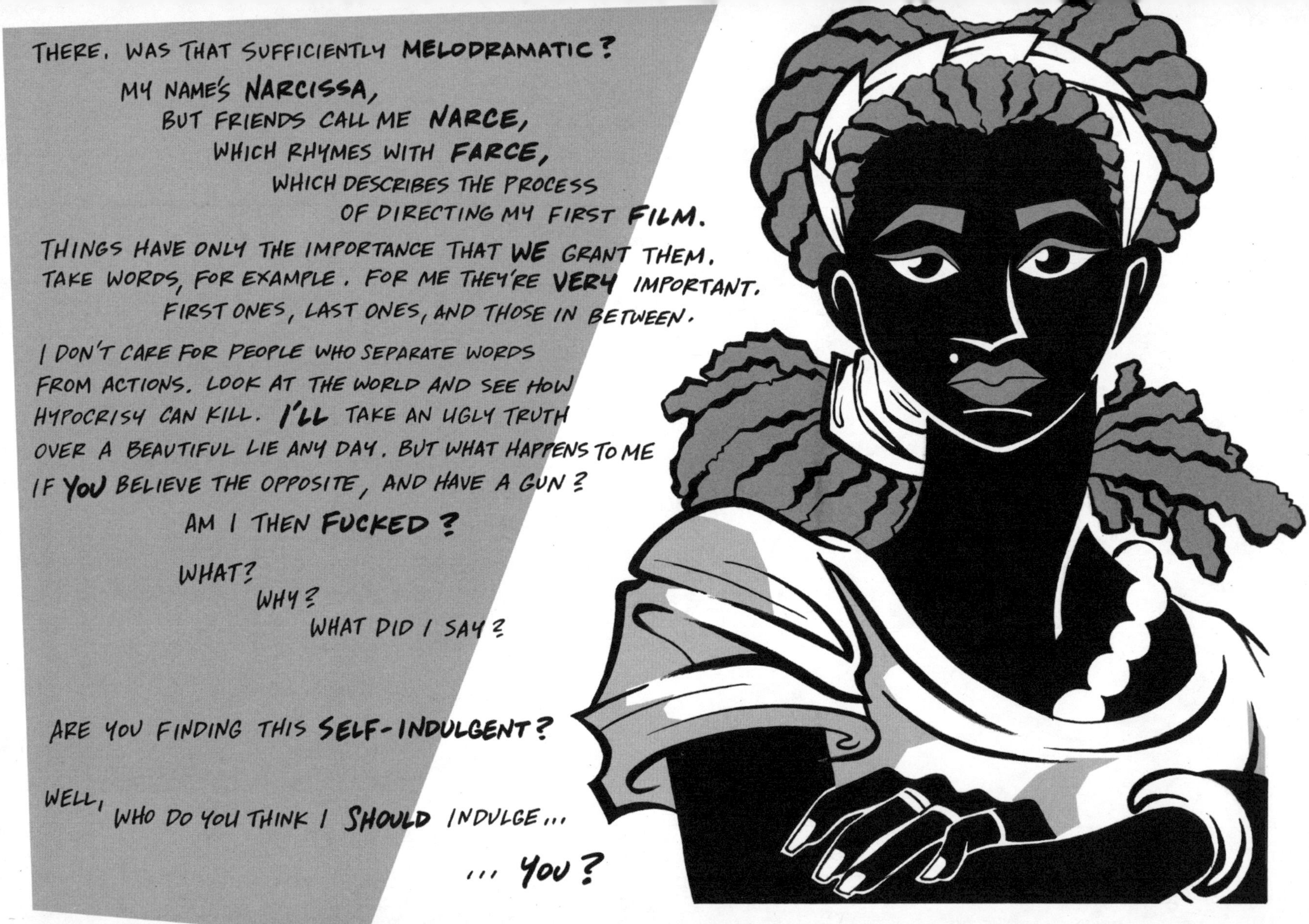
THERE. WAS THAT SUFFICIENTLY MELODRAMATIC?
MY NAME'S NARCISSA,
BUT FRIENDS CALL ME NARCE,
WHICH RHYMES WITH FARCE,
WHICH DESCRIBES THE PROCESS
OF DIRECTING MY FIRST FILM.
THINGS HAVE ONLY THE IMPORTANCE THAT WE GRANT THEM.
TAKE WORDS, FOR EXAMPLE. FOR ME THEY'RE VERY IMPORTANT.
FIRST ONES, LAST ONES, AND THOSE IN BETWEEN.
I DON'T CARE FOR PEOPLE WHO SEPARATE WORDS FROM ACTIONS. LOOK AT THE WORLD AND SEE HOW HYPOCRISY CAN KILL. I'LL TAKE AN UGLY TRUTH OVER A BEAUTIFUL LIE ANY DAY. BUT WHAT HAPPENS TO ME IF YOU BELIEVE THE OPPOSITE, AND HAVE A GUN?
AM I THEN FUCKED?
WHAT?
WHY?
WHAT DID I SAY?
ARE YOU FINDING THIS SELF-INDULGENT?
WELL, WHO DO YOU THINK I SHOULD INDULGE...
... YOU?

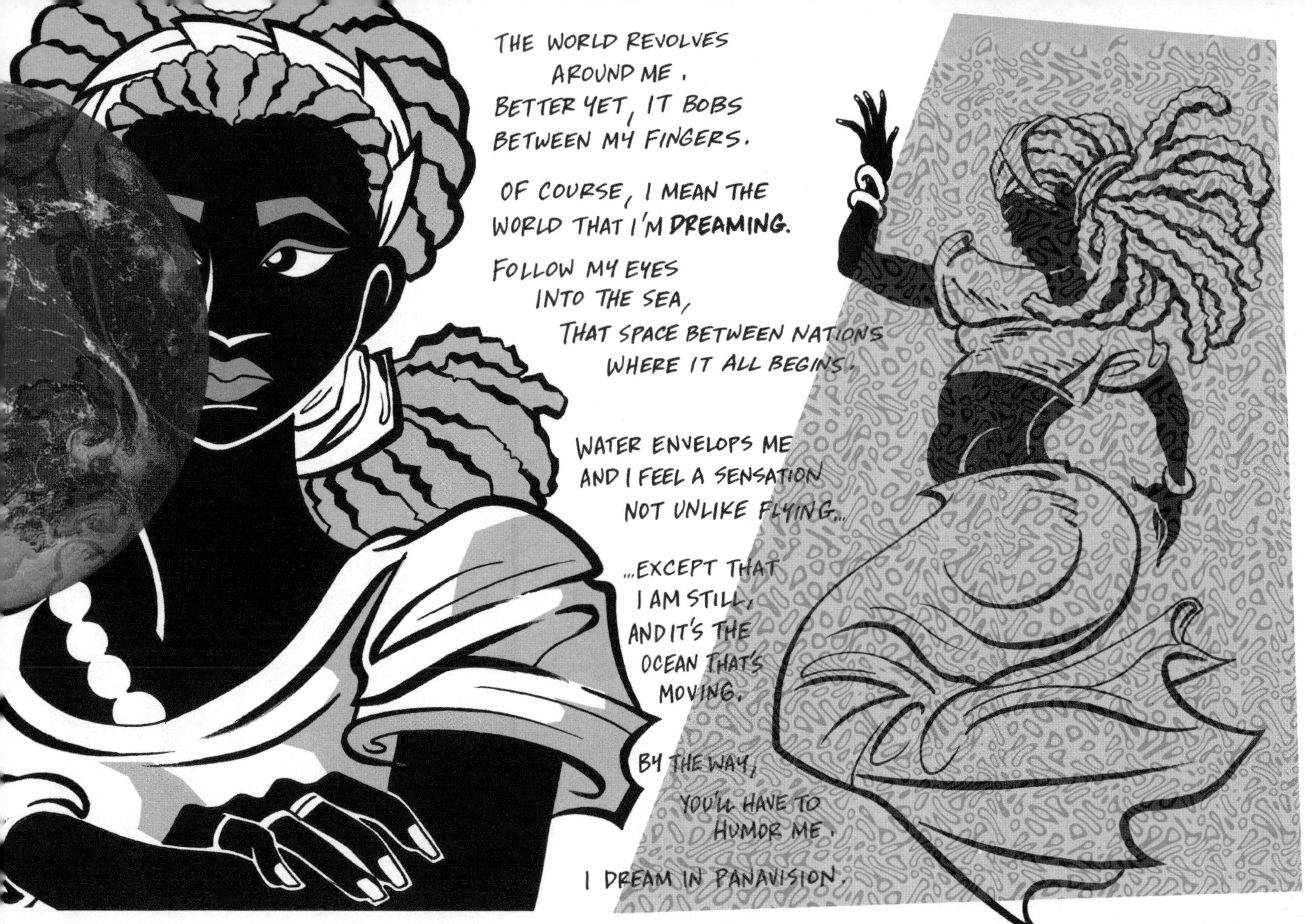
THE WORLD REVOLVES AROUND ME.
BETTER YET, IT BOBS BETWEEN MY FINGERS.
OF COURSE, I MEAN THE WORLD THAT I'M **DREAMING.**
FOLLOW MY EYES INTO THE SEA, THAT SPACE BETWEEN NATIONS WHERE IT ALL BEGINS.
WATER ENVELOPS ME AND I FEEL A SENSATION NOT UNLIKE FLYING...
...EXCEPT THAT I AM STILL, AND IT'S THE OCEAN THAT'S MOVING.
BY THE WAY, YOU'LL HAVE TO HUMOR ME.
I DREAM IN PANAVISION.

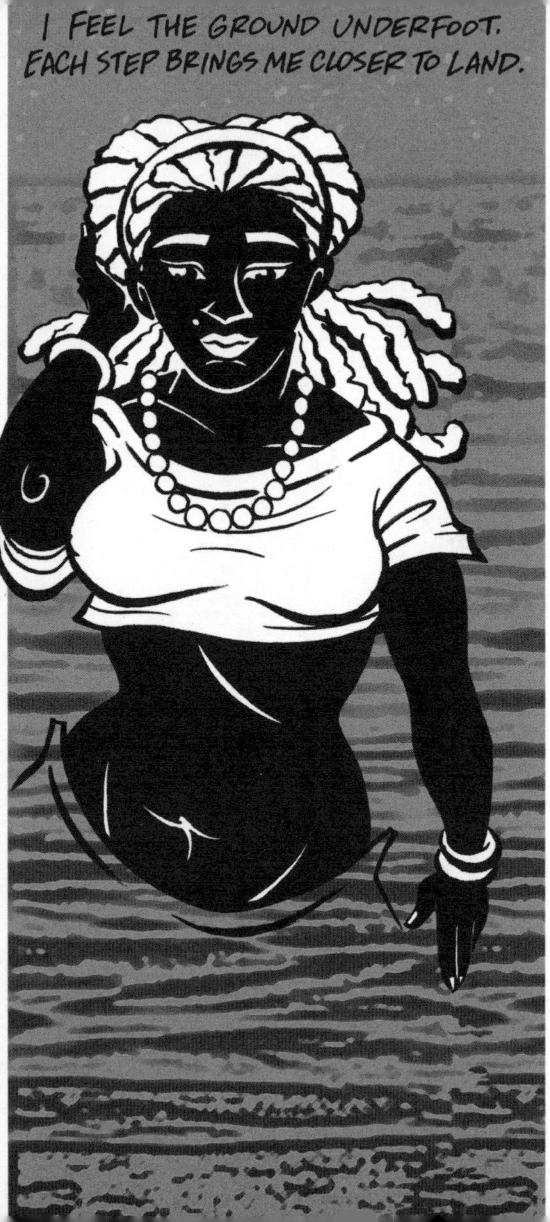
I FEEL THE GROUND UNDERFOOT.
EACH STEP BRINGS ME CLOSER TO LAND.

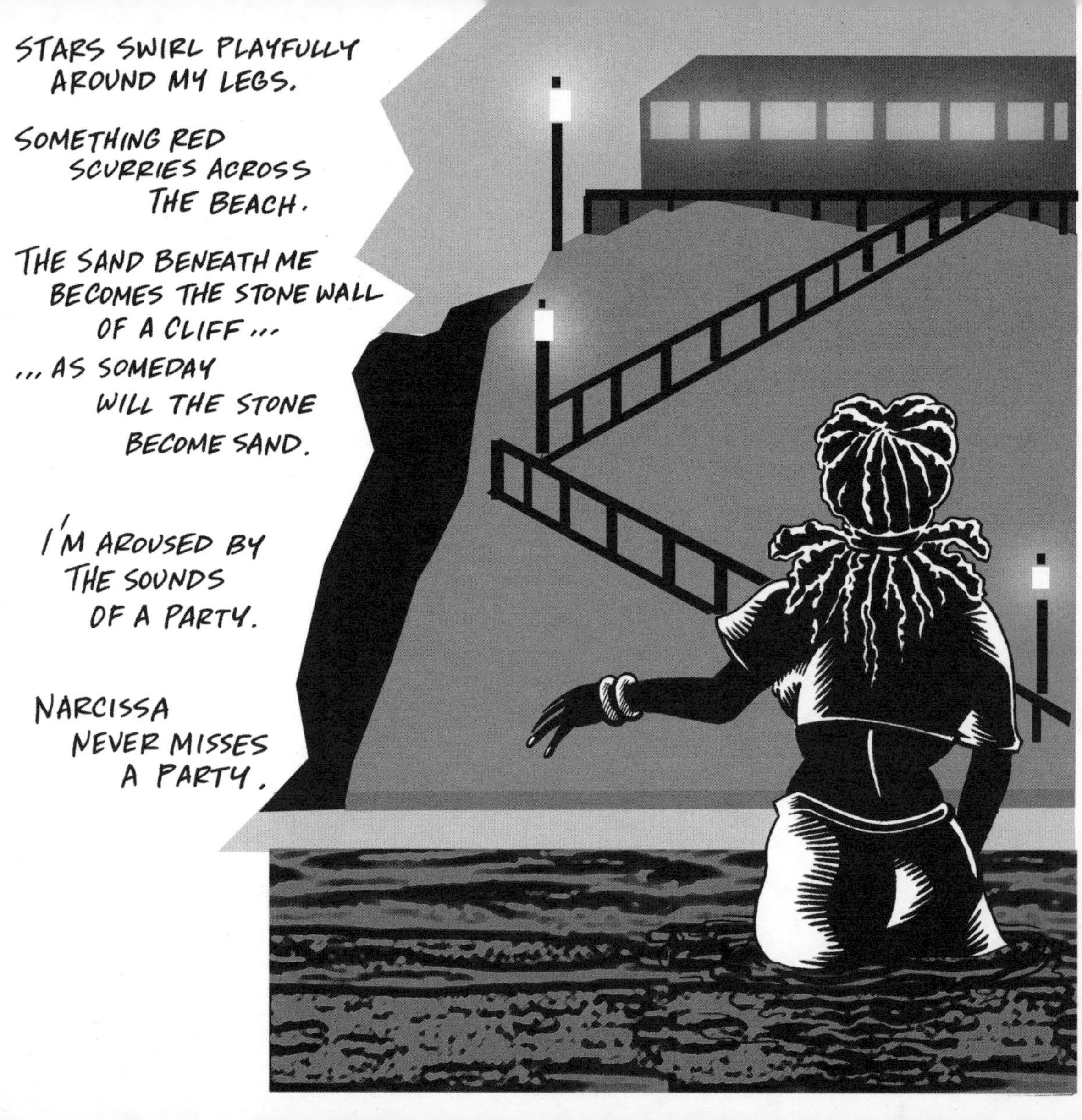
STARS SWIRL PLAYFULLY AROUND MY LEGS.
SOMETHING RED SCURRIES ACROSS THE BEACH.
THE SAND BENEATH ME BECOMES THE STONE WALL OF A CLIFF ...
... AS SOMEDAY WILL THE STONE BECOME SAND.
I'M AROUSED BY THE SOUNDS OF A PARTY.
NARCISSA NEVER MISSES A PARTY.

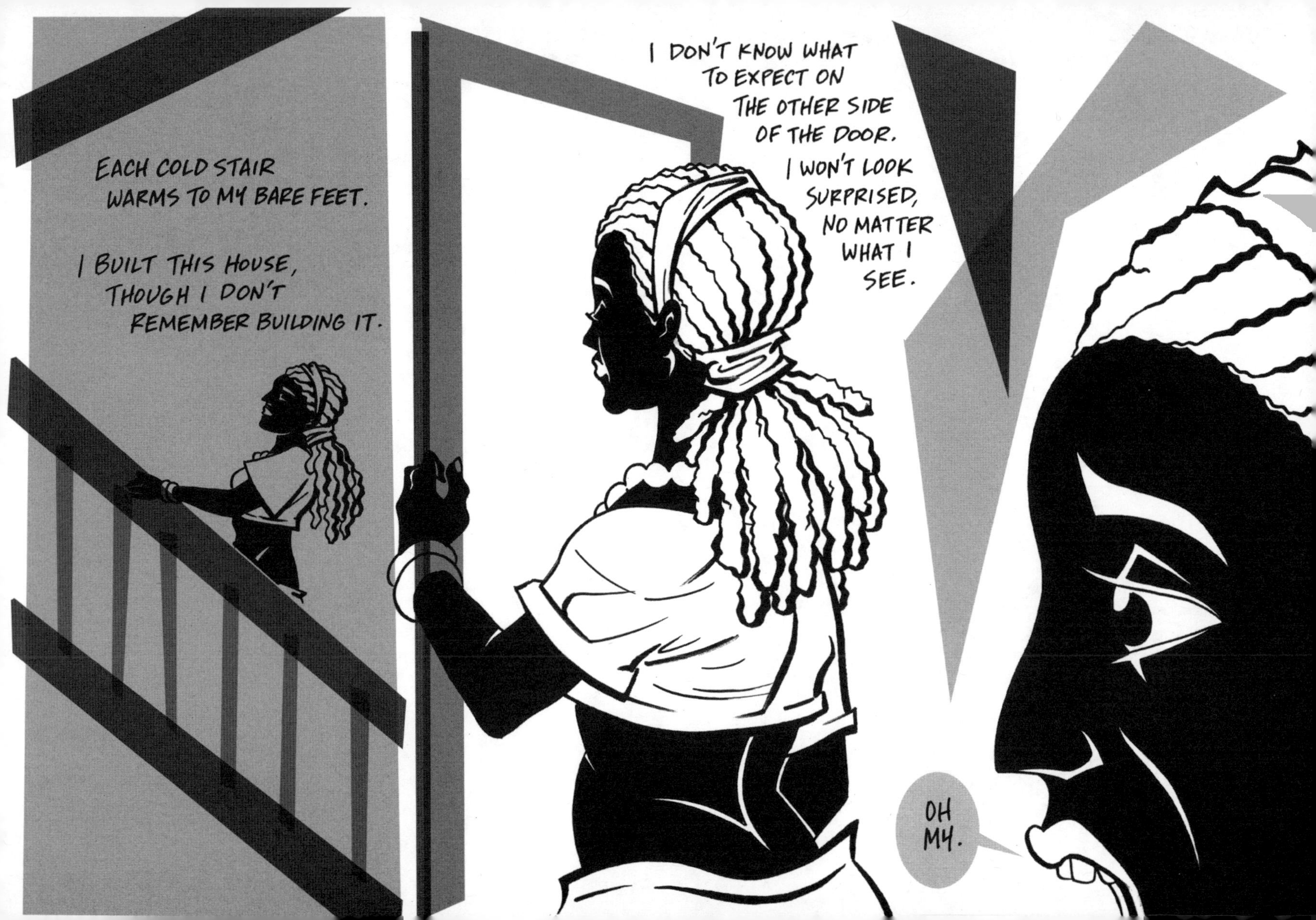
EACH COLD STAIR WARMS TO MY BARE FEET.
I BUILT THIS HOUSE, THOUGH I DON'T REMEMBER BUILDING IT.
I DON'T KNOW WHAT TO EXPECT ON THE OTHER SIDE OF THE DOOR.
I WON'T LOOK SURPRISED, NO MATTER WHAT I SEE.
OH MY.

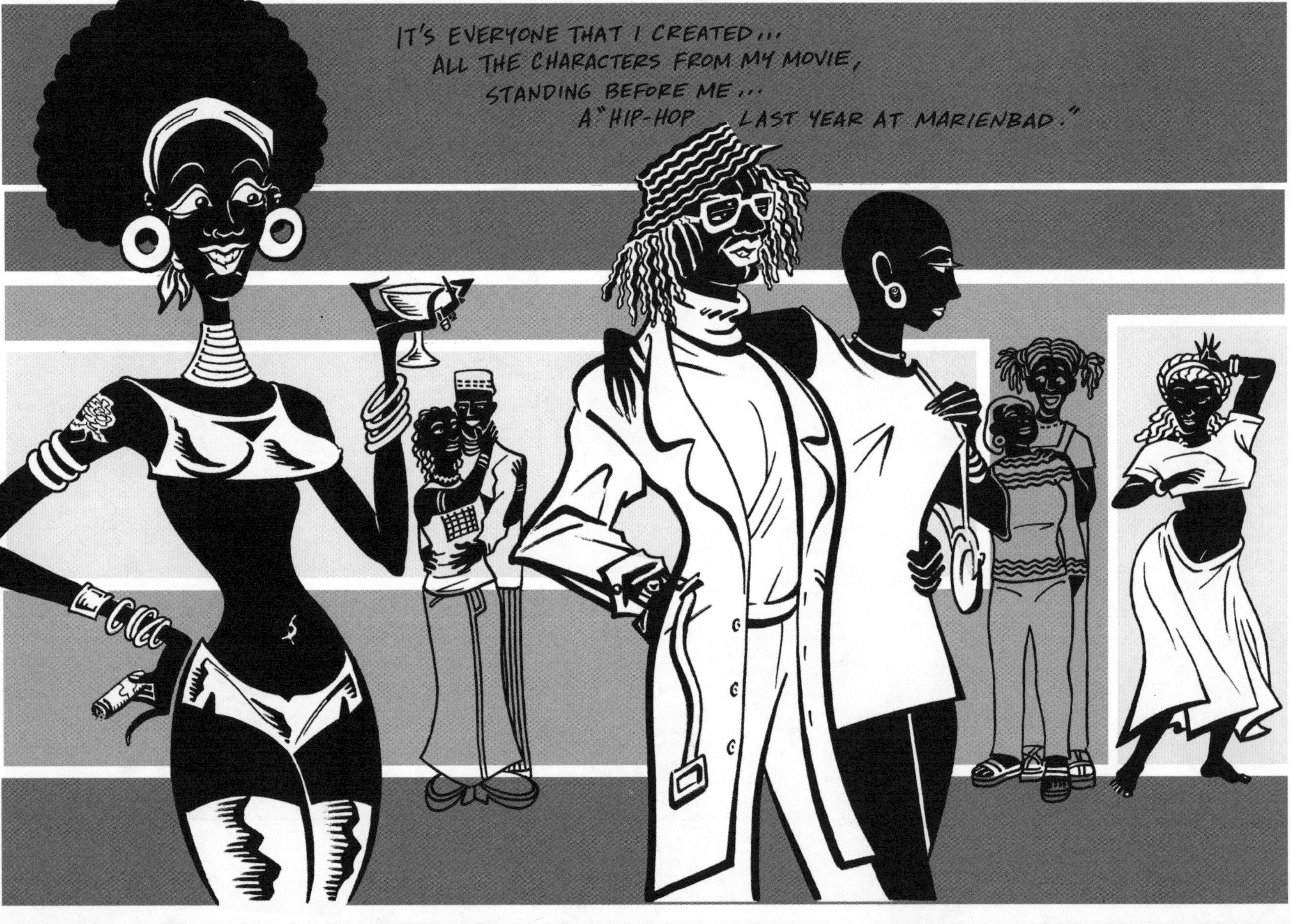
IT'S EVERYONE THAT I CREATED...
ALL THE CHARACTERS FROM MY MOVIE,
STANDING BEFORE ME...
A "HIP-HOP LAST YEAR AT MARIENBAD."

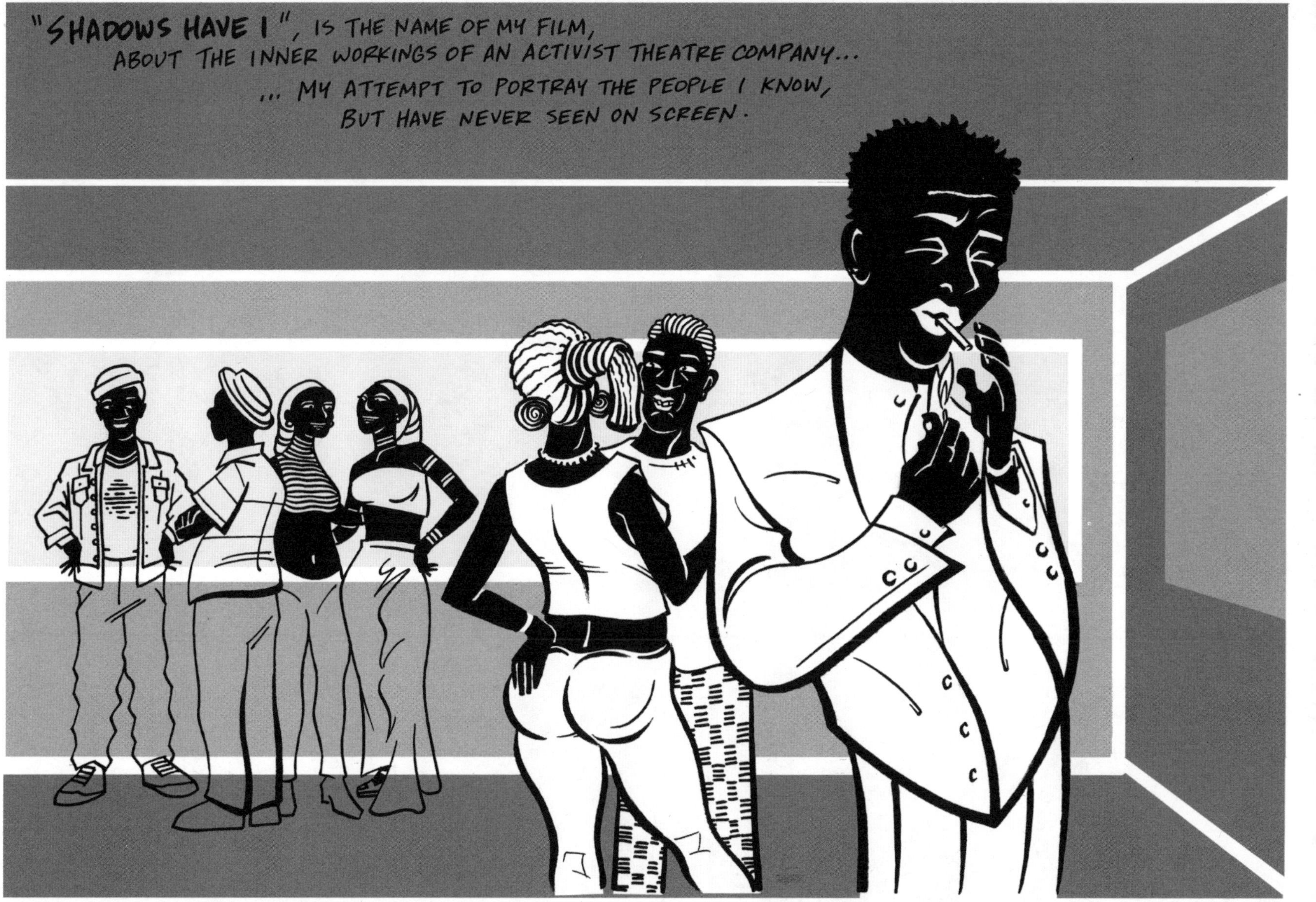
"SHADOWS HAVE I", IS THE NAME OF MY FILM,
ABOUT THE INNER WORKINGS OF AN ACTIVIST THEATRE COMPANY...
... MY ATTEMPT TO PORTRAY THE PEOPLE I KNOW,
BUT HAVE NEVER SEEN ON SCREEN.

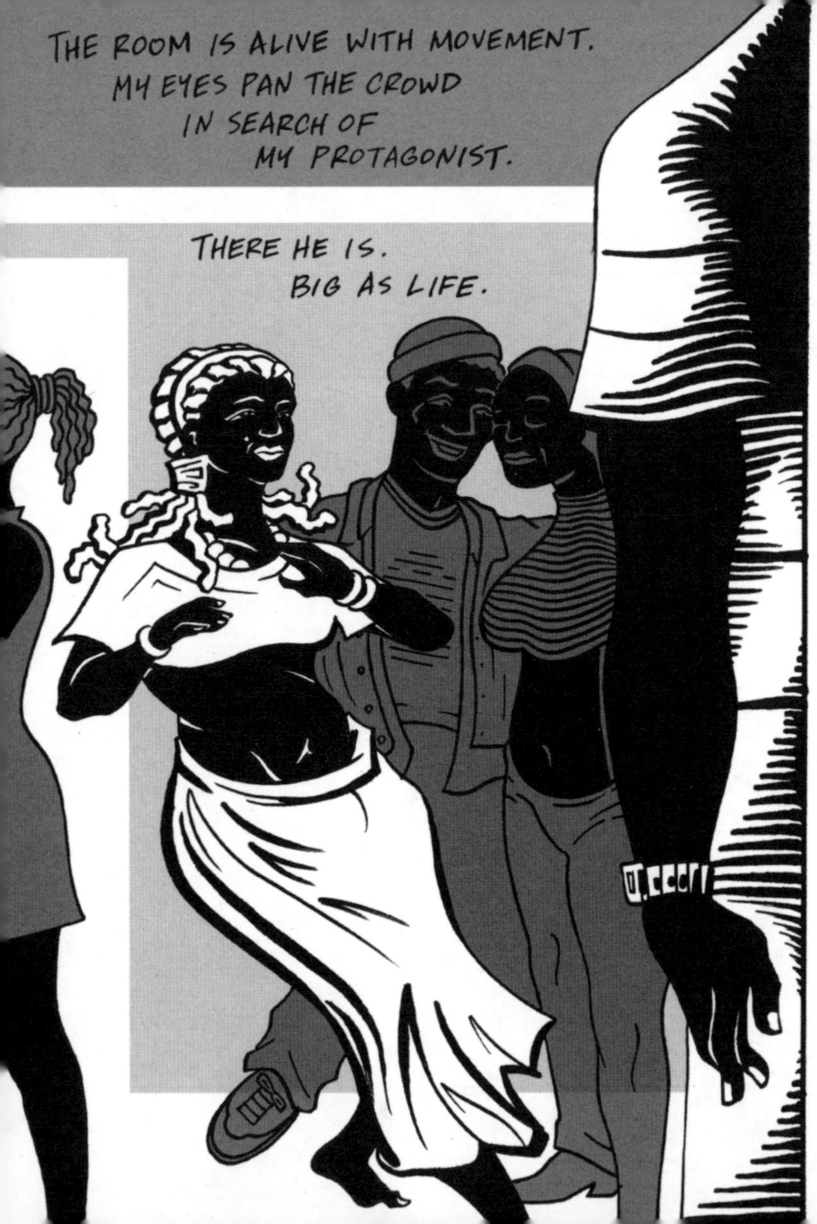
THE ROOM IS ALIVE WITH MOVEMENT. MY EYES PAN THE CROWD IN SEARCH OF MY PROTAGONIST.
THERE HE IS. BIG AS LIFE.

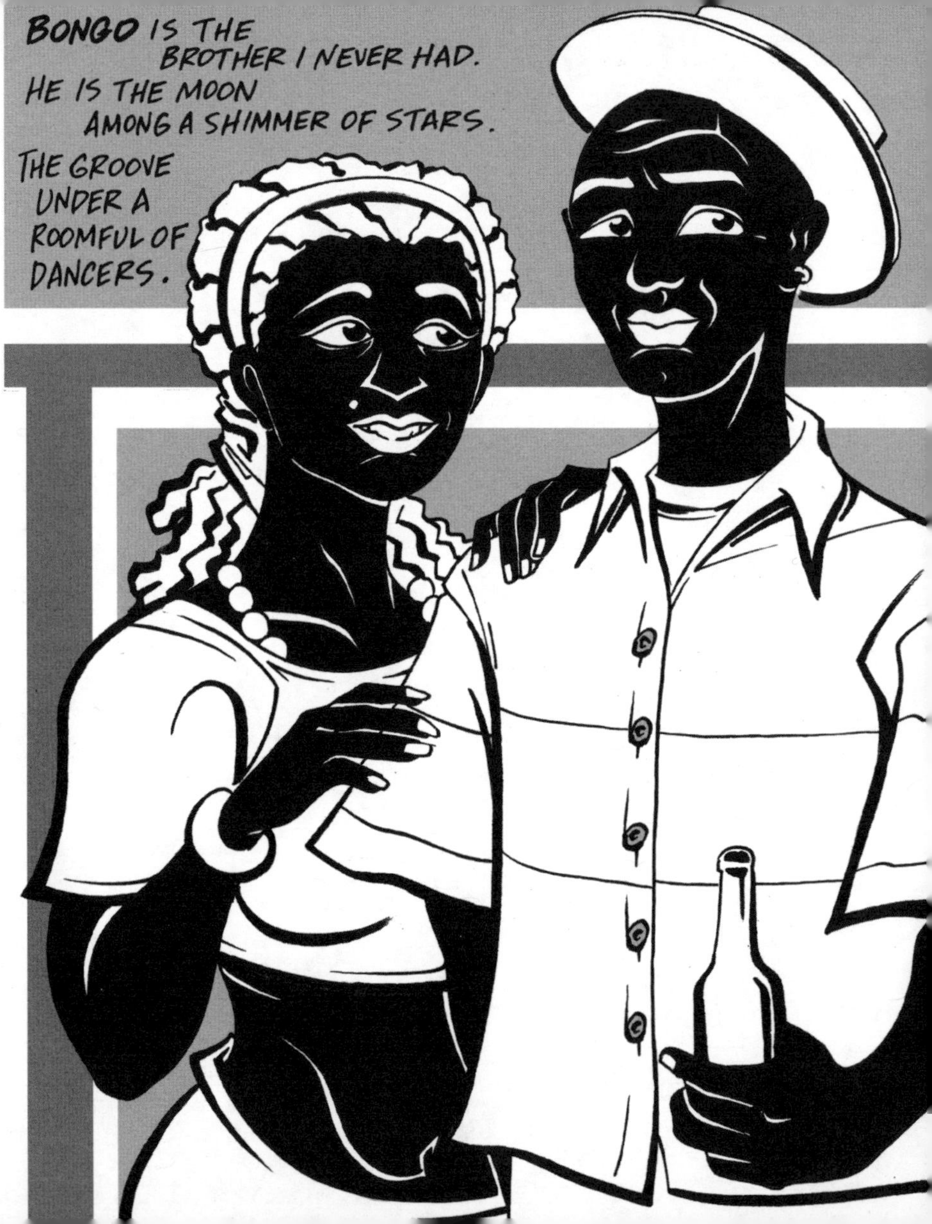
BONGO IS THE BROTHER I NEVER HAD. HE IS THE MOON AMONG A SHIMMER OF STARS.
THE GROOVE UNDER A ROOMFUL OF DANCERS.

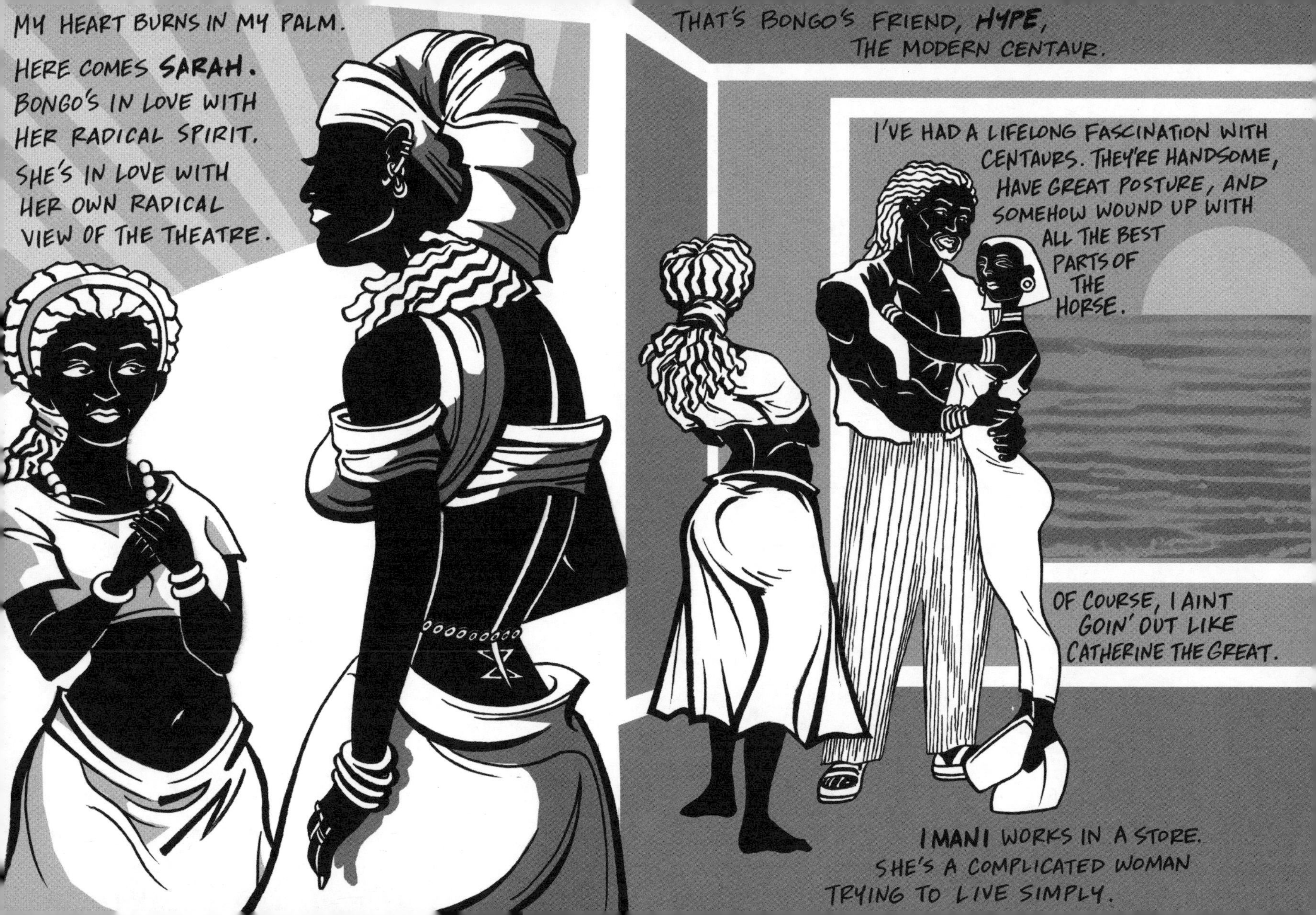
MY HEART BURNS IN MY PALM.
HERE COMES SARAH. BONGO'S IN LOVE WITH HER RADICAL SPIRIT.
SHE'S IN LOVE WITH HER OWN RADICAL VIEW OF THE THEATRE.
THAT'S BONGO'S FRIEND, HYPE, THE MODERN CENTAUR.
I'VE HAD A LIFELONG FASCINATION WITH CENTAURS. THEY'RE HANDSOME, HAVE GREAT POSTURE, AND SOMEHOW WOUND UP WITH ALL THE BEST PARTS OF THE HORSE.
OF COURSE, I AINT GOIN' OUT LIKE CATHERINE THE GREAT.
IMANI WORKS IN A STORE. SHE'S A COMPLICATED WOMAN TRYING TO LIVE SIMPLY.

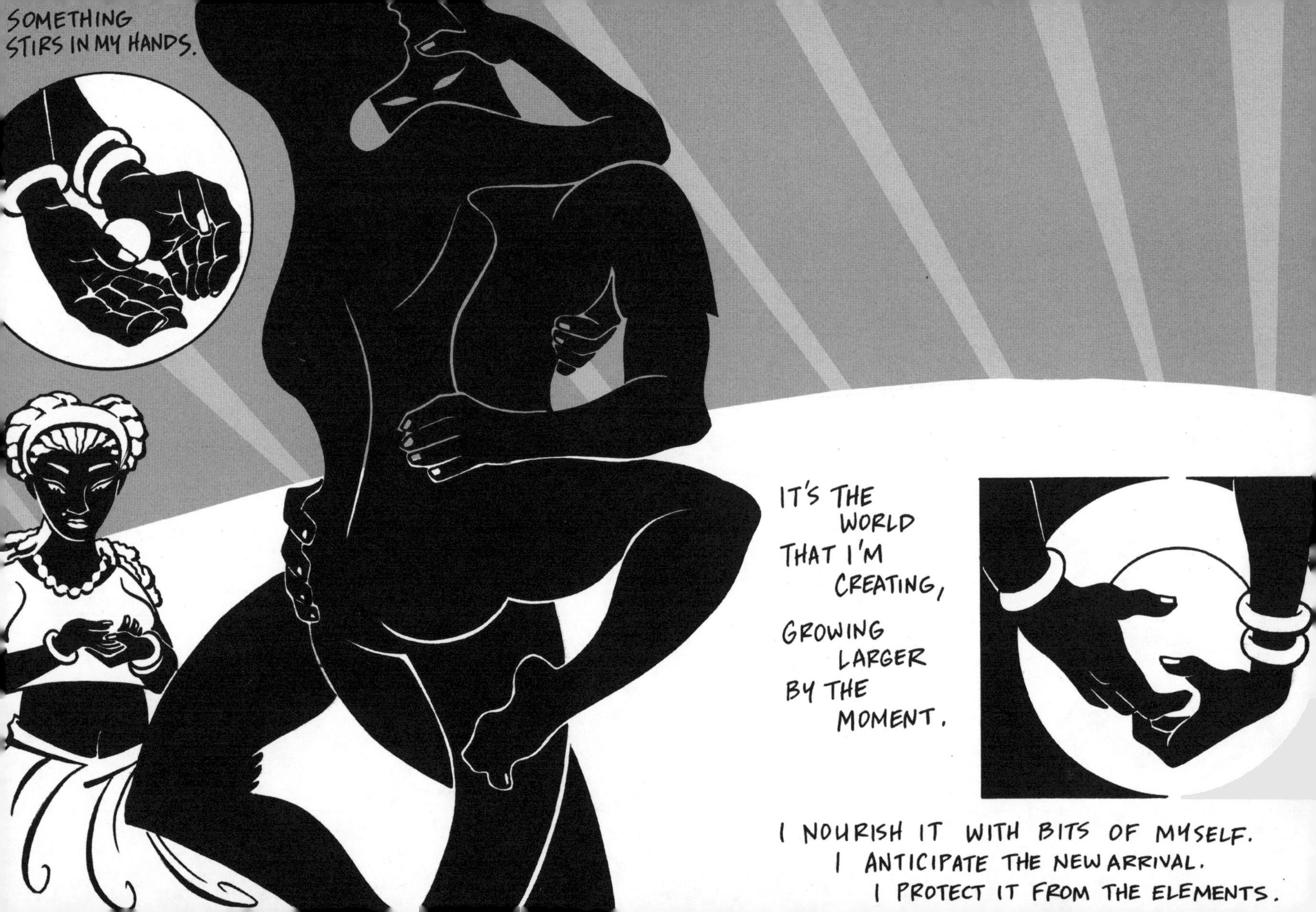
SOMETHING STIRS IN MY HANDS.
IT'S THE WORLD THAT I'M CREATING,
GROWING LARGER BY THE MOMENT.
I NOURISH IT WITH BITS OF MYSELF.
I ANTICIPATE THE NEW ARRIVAL.
I PROTECT IT FROM THE ELEMENTS.

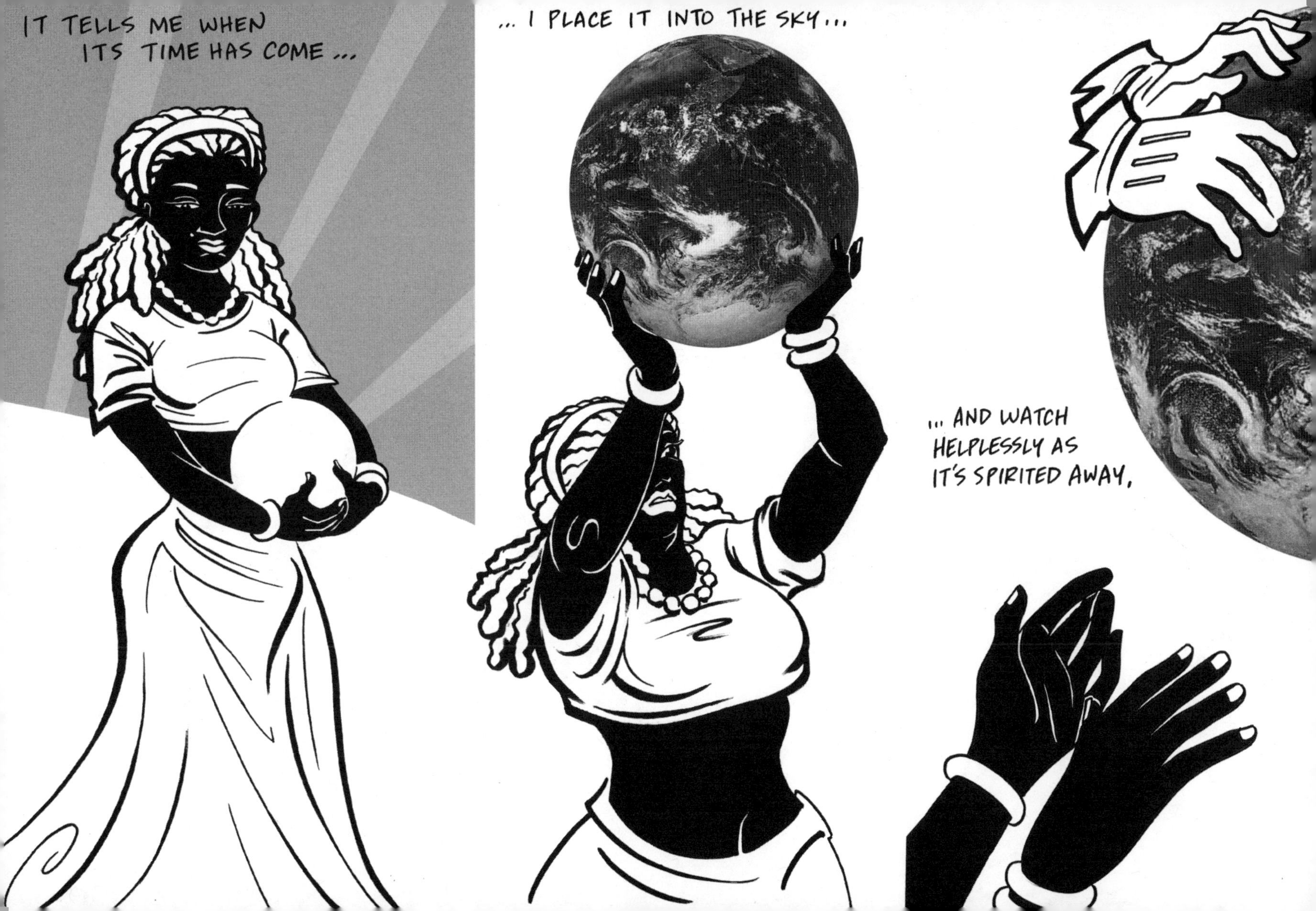
IT TELLS ME WHEN ITS TIME HAS COME ...
... I PLACE IT INTO THE SKY...
... AND WATCH HELPLESSLY AS IT'S SPIRITED AWAY,

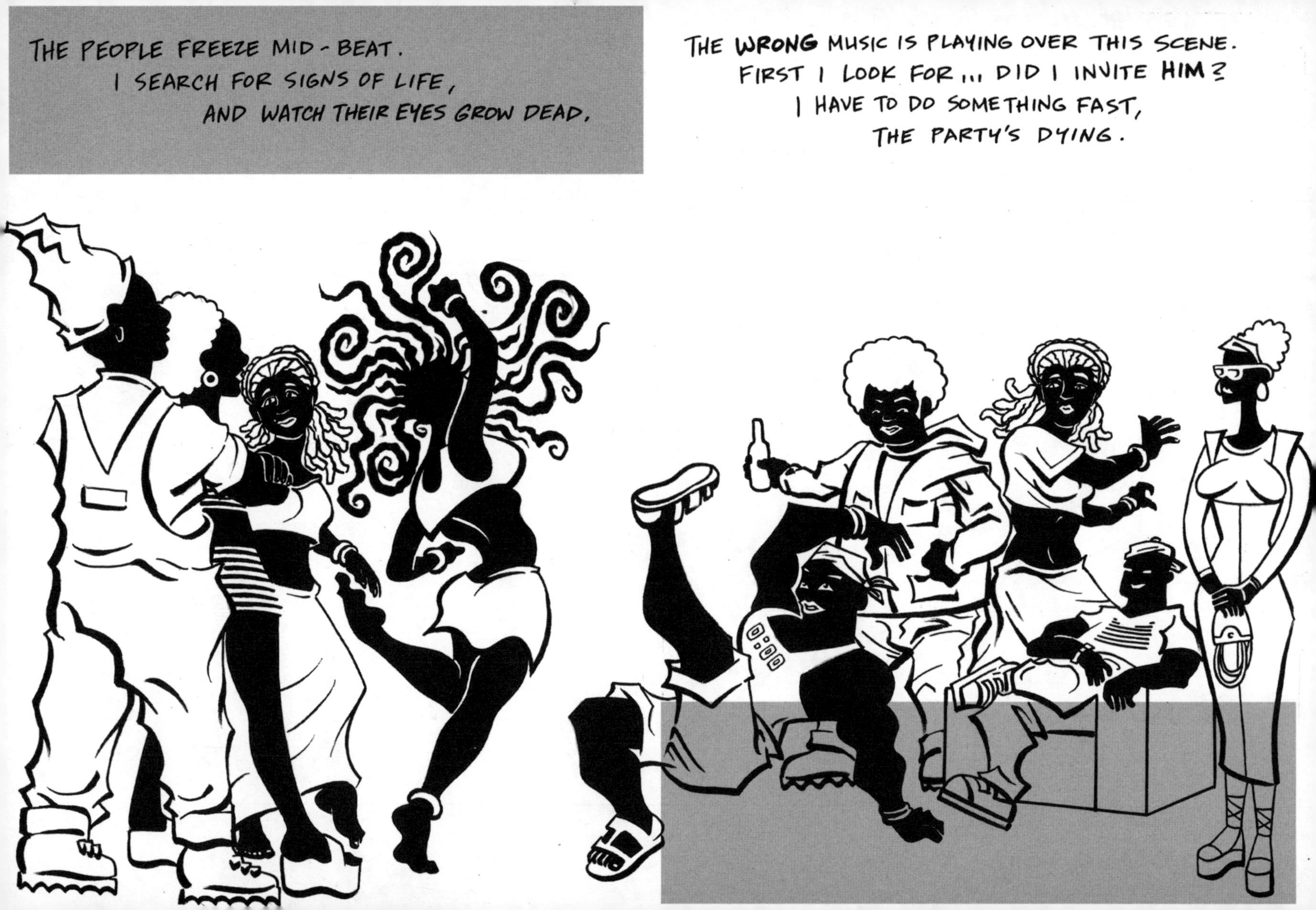
THE PEOPLE FREEZE MID-BEAT.
I SEARCH FOR SIGNS OF LIFE,
AND WATCH THEIR EYES GROW DEAD.
THE WRONG MUSIC IS PLAYING OVER THIS SCENE.
FIRST I LOOK FOR... DID I INVITE HIM?
I HAVE TO DO SOMETHING FAST,
THE PARTY'S DYING.

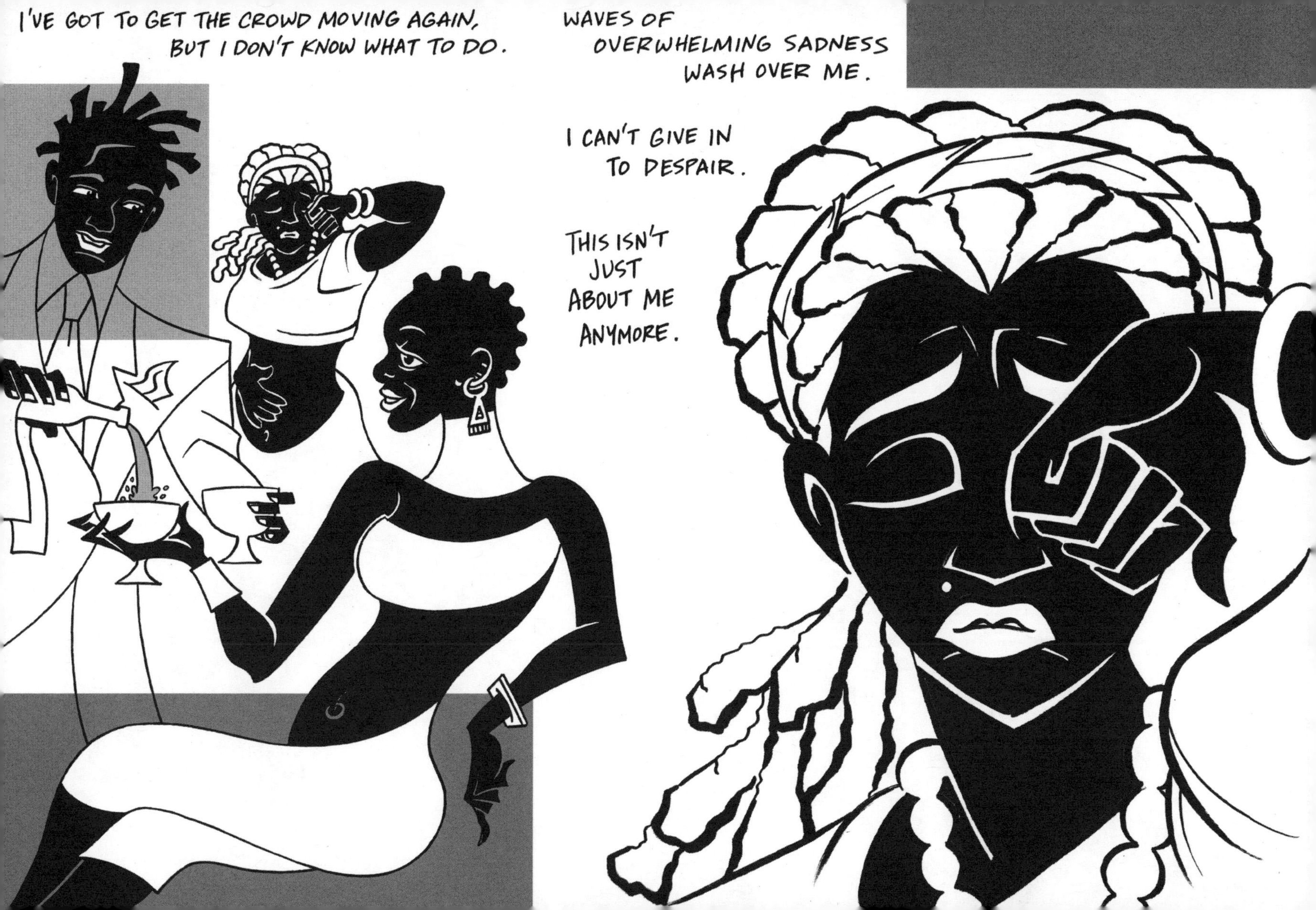
I'VE GOT TO GET THE CROWD MOVING AGAIN, BUT I DON'T KNOW WHAT TO DO.
WAVES OF OVERWHELMING SADNESS WASH OVER ME.
I CAN'T GIVE IN TO DESPAIR.
THIS ISN'T JUST ABOUT ME ANYMORE.

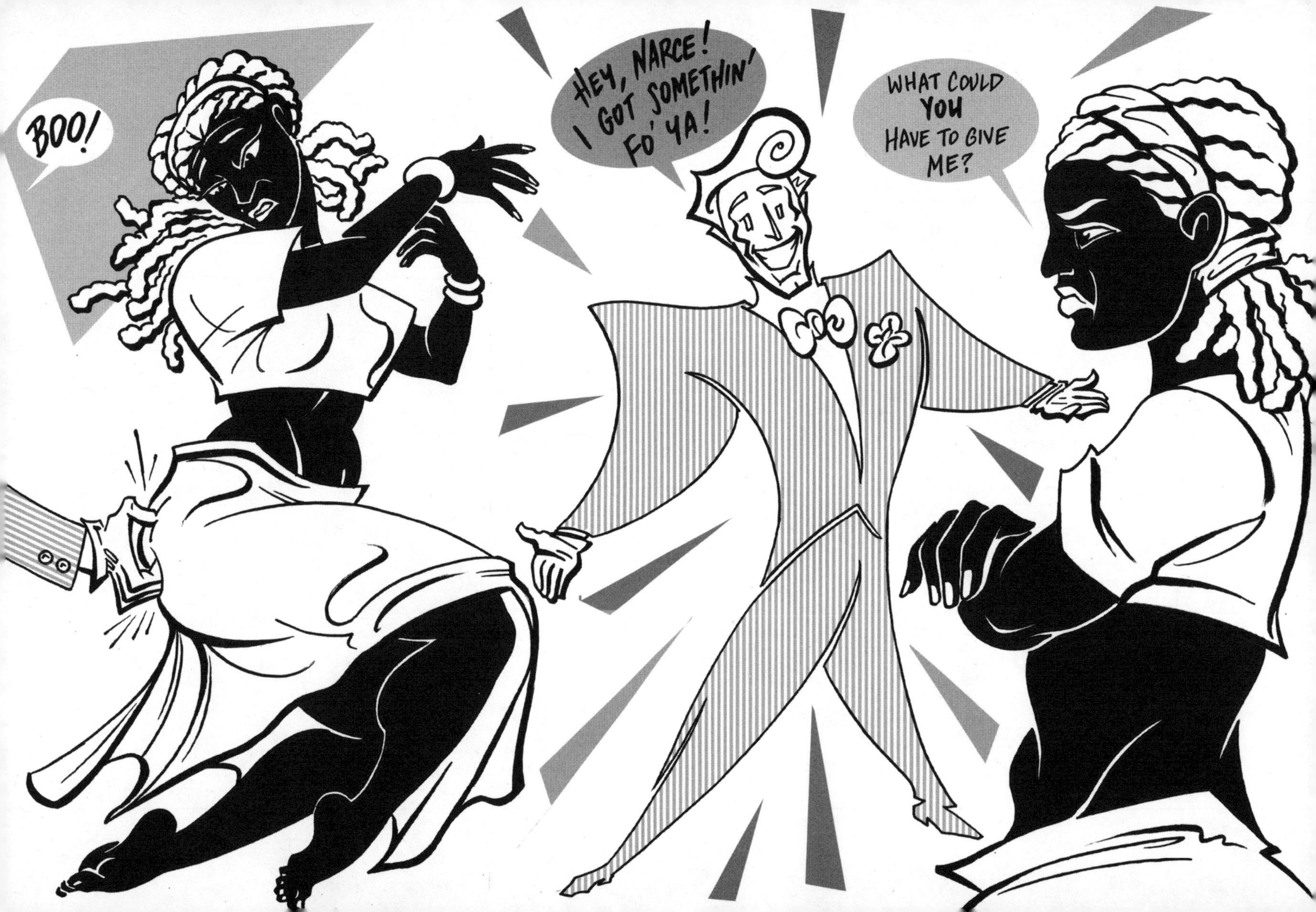
BOO!
HEY, NARCE! I GOT SOMETHIN' FO' YA!
WHAT COULD YOU HAVE TO GIVE ME?

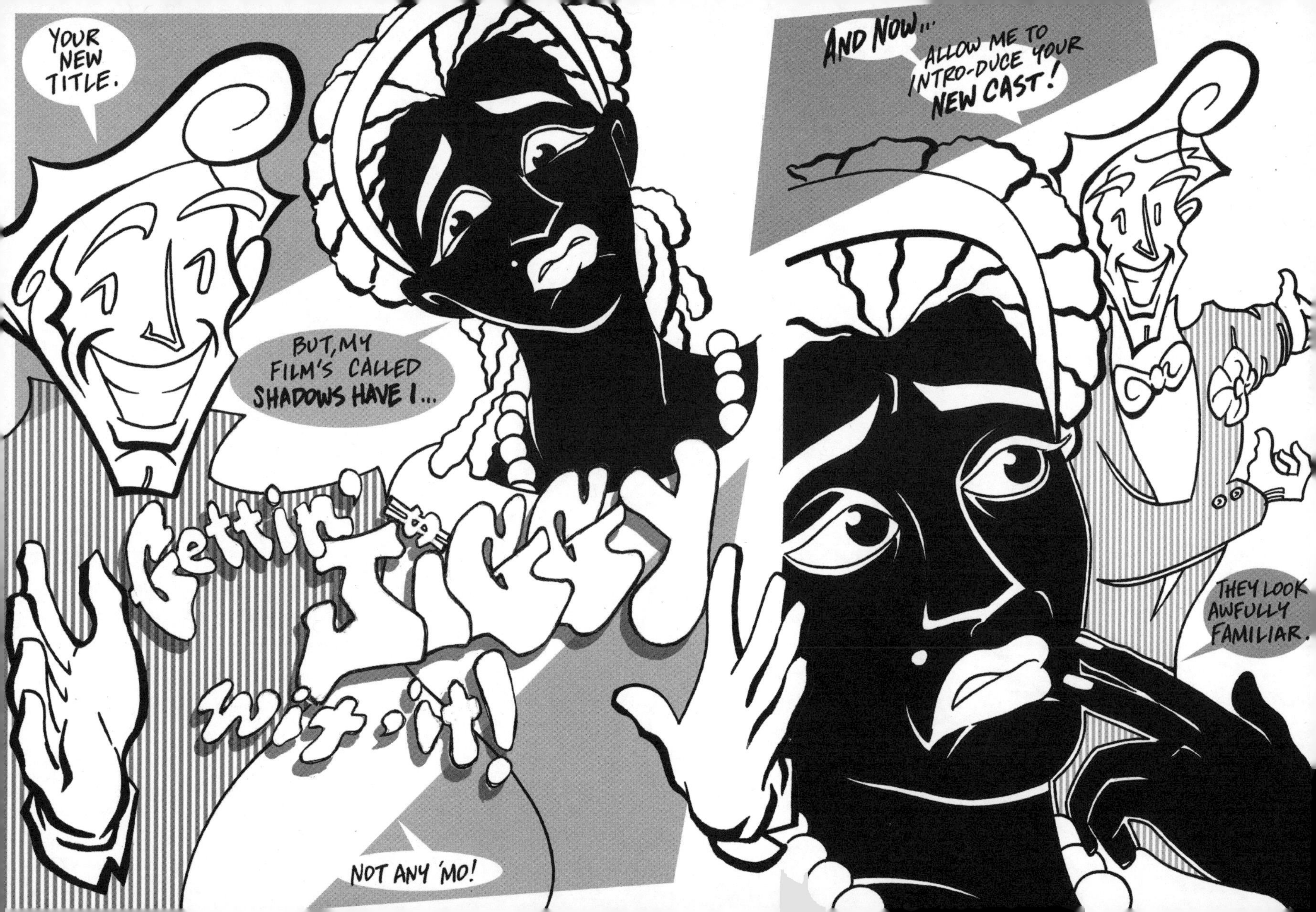
YOUR NEW TITLE.
BUT, MY FILM'S CALLED SHADOWS HAVE I...
Gettin' Jiggy Wit-it!
NOT ANY 'MO!
AND NOW... ALLOW ME TO INTRO-DUCE YOUR NEW CAST!
THEY LOOK AWFULLY FAMILIAR.

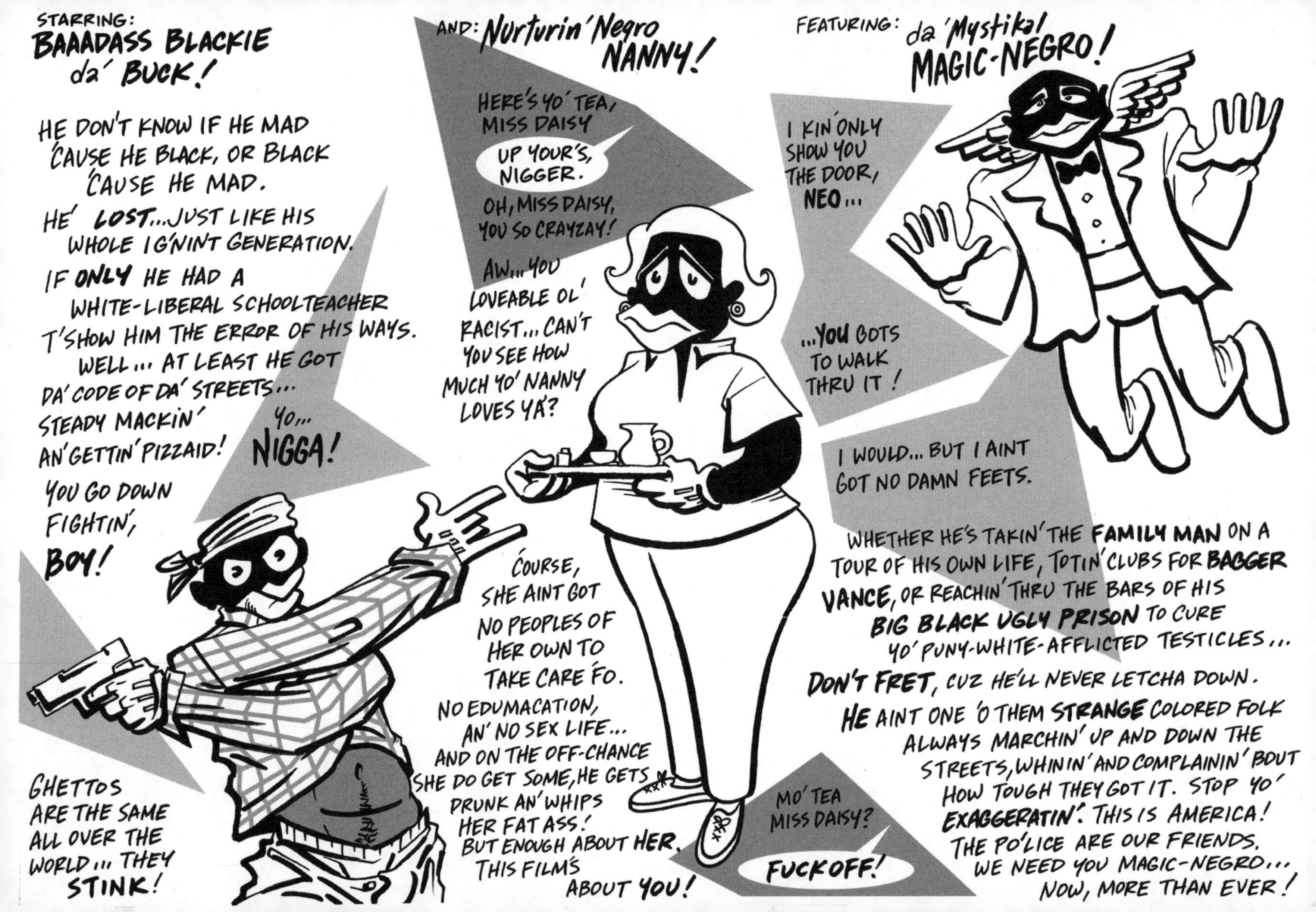
STARRING:
BAAADASS BLACKIE da' BUCK!
HE DON'T KNOW IF HE MAD 'CAUSE HE BLACK, OR BLACK 'CAUSE HE MAD.
HE' LOST... JUST LIKE HIS WHOLE IG'NINT GENERATION.
IF ONLY HE HAD A WHITE-LIBERAL SCHOOLTEACHER T'SHOW HIM THE ERROR OF HIS WAYS.
WELL... AT LEAST HE GOT DA' CODE OF DA' STREETS... STEADY MACKIN' AN' GETTIN' PIZZAID!
YO... NIGGA!
YOU GO DOWN FIGHTIN', BOY!
GHETTOS ARE THE SAME ALL OVER THE WORLD... THEY STINK!
AND: Nurturin' Negro NANNY!
HERE'S YO' TEA, MISS DAISY
UP YOUR'S, NIGGER.
OH, MISS DAISY, YOU SO CRAYZAY!
AW... YOU LOVEABLE OL' RACIST... CAN'T YOU SEE HOW MUCH YO' NANNY LOVES YA?
'COURSE, SHE AINT GOT NO PEOPLES OF HER OWN TO TAKE CARE 'FO.
NO EDUMACATION, AN' NO SEX LIFE... AND ON THE OFF-CHANCE SHE DO GET SOME, HE GETS DRUNK AN' WHIPS HER FAT ASS!
BUT ENOUGH ABOUT HER. THIS FILM'S ABOUT YOU!
MO' TEA MISS DAISY?
FUCKOFF!
FEATURING: da 'Mystikal MAGIC-NEGRO!
I KIN' ONLY SHOW YOU THE DOOR, NEO...
...YOU GOTS TO WALK THRU IT!
I WOULD... BUT I AINT GOT NO DAMN FEETS.
WHETHER HE'S TAKIN' THE FAMILY MAN ON A TOUR OF HIS OWN LIFE, TOTIN' CLUBS FOR BAGGER VANCE, OR REACHIN' THRU THE BARS OF HIS BIG BLACK UGLY PRISON TO CURE YO' PUNY-WHITE-AFFLICTED TESTICLES...
DON'T FRET, CUZ HE'LL NEVER LETCHA DOWN.
HE AINT ONE 'O THEM STRANGE COLORED FOLK ALWAYS MARCHIN' UP AND DOWN THE STREETS, WHININ' AND COMPLAININ' BOUT HOW TOUGH THEY GOT IT. STOP YO' EXAGGERATIN'. THIS IS AMERICA! THE PO'LICE ARE OUR FRIENDS. WE NEED YOU MAGIC-NEGRO... NOW, MORE THAN EVER!

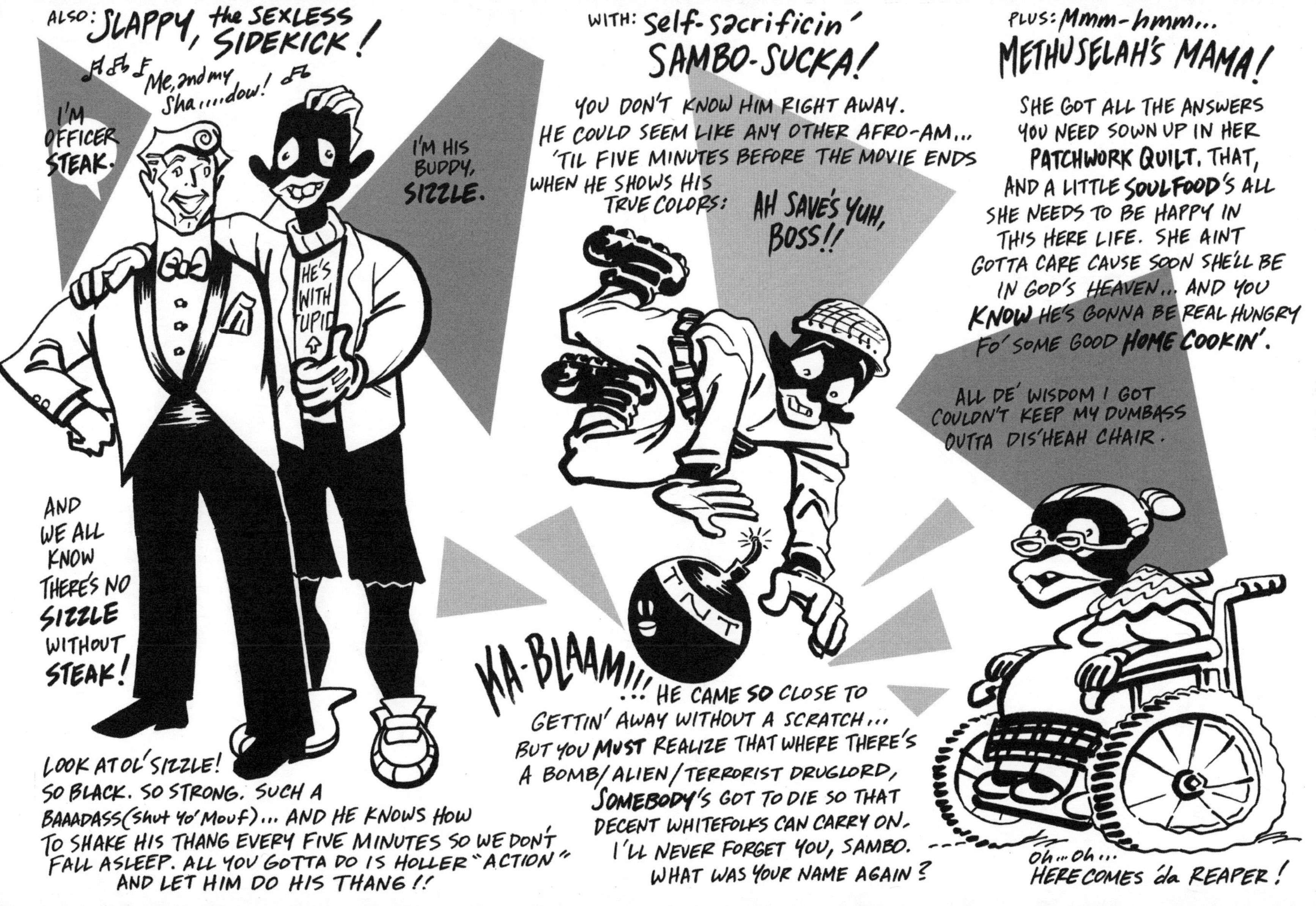

ALSO: SLAPPY, the SEXLESS SIDEKICK!
Me, and my Sha....dow!
I'M OFFICER STEAK.
I'M HIS BUDDY, SIZZLE.
HE'S WITH STUPID
AND WE ALL KNOW THERE'S NO SIZZLE WITHOUT STEAK!
LOOK AT OL' SIZZLE! SO BLACK. SO STRONG. SUCH A BAAADASS(shut yo' mouf)... AND HE KNOWS HOW TO SHAKE HIS THANG EVERY FIVE MINUTES SO WE DON'T FALL ASLEEP. ALL YOU GOTTA DO IS HOLLER "ACTION" AND LET HIM DO HIS THANG!!
WITH: Self-sacrificin' SAMBO-SUCKA!
YOU DON'T KNOW HIM RIGHT AWAY. HE COULD SEEM LIKE ANY OTHER AFRO-AM... 'TIL FIVE MINUTES BEFORE THE MOVIE ENDS WHEN HE SHOWS HIS TRUE COLORS:
AH SAVE'S YUH, BOSS!!
TNT
KA-BLAAM!!!... HE CAME SO CLOSE TO GETTIN' AWAY WITHOUT A SCRATCH... BUT YOU MUST REALIZE THAT WHERE THERE'S A BOMB/ALIEN/TERRORIST DRUGLORD, SOMEBODY'S GOT TO DIE SO THAT DECENT WHITEFOLKS CAN CARRY ON.
I'LL NEVER FORGET YOU, SAMBO. WHAT WAS YOUR NAME AGAIN?
PLUS: Mmm-hmm... METHUSELAH'S MAMA!
SHE GOT ALL THE ANSWERS YOU NEED SOWN UP IN HER PATCHWORK QUILT. THAT, AND A LITTLE SOULFOOD'S ALL SHE NEEDS TO BE HAPPY IN THIS HERE LIFE. SHE AINT GOTTA CARE CAUSE SOON SHE'LL BE IN GOD'S HEAVEN... AND YOU KNOW HE'S GONNA BE REAL HUNGRY FO' SOME GOOD HOME COOKIN'.
ALL DE' WISDOM I GOT COULDN'T KEEP MY DUMBASS OUTTA DIS'HEAH CHAIR.
Oh...Oh... HERE COMES 'da REAPER!

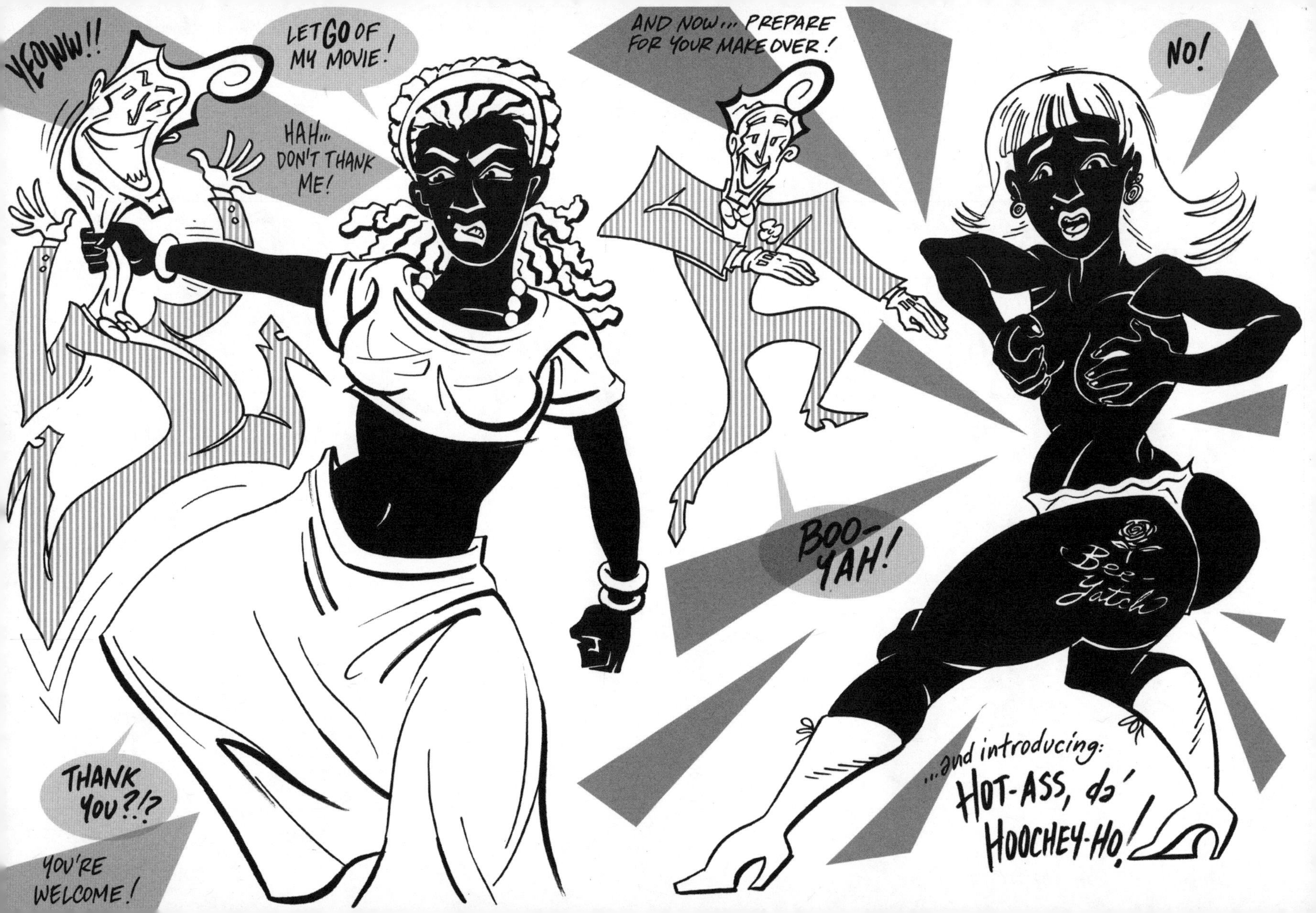
YEOWW!!
LET GO OF MY MOVIE!
HAH... DON'T THANK ME!
THANK YOU?!?
YOU'RE WELCOME!
AND NOW... PREPARE FOR YOUR MAKE OVER!
NO!
BOO-YAH!
Bee-Yatch
...and introducing:
HOT-ASS, da' HOOCHEY-HO!

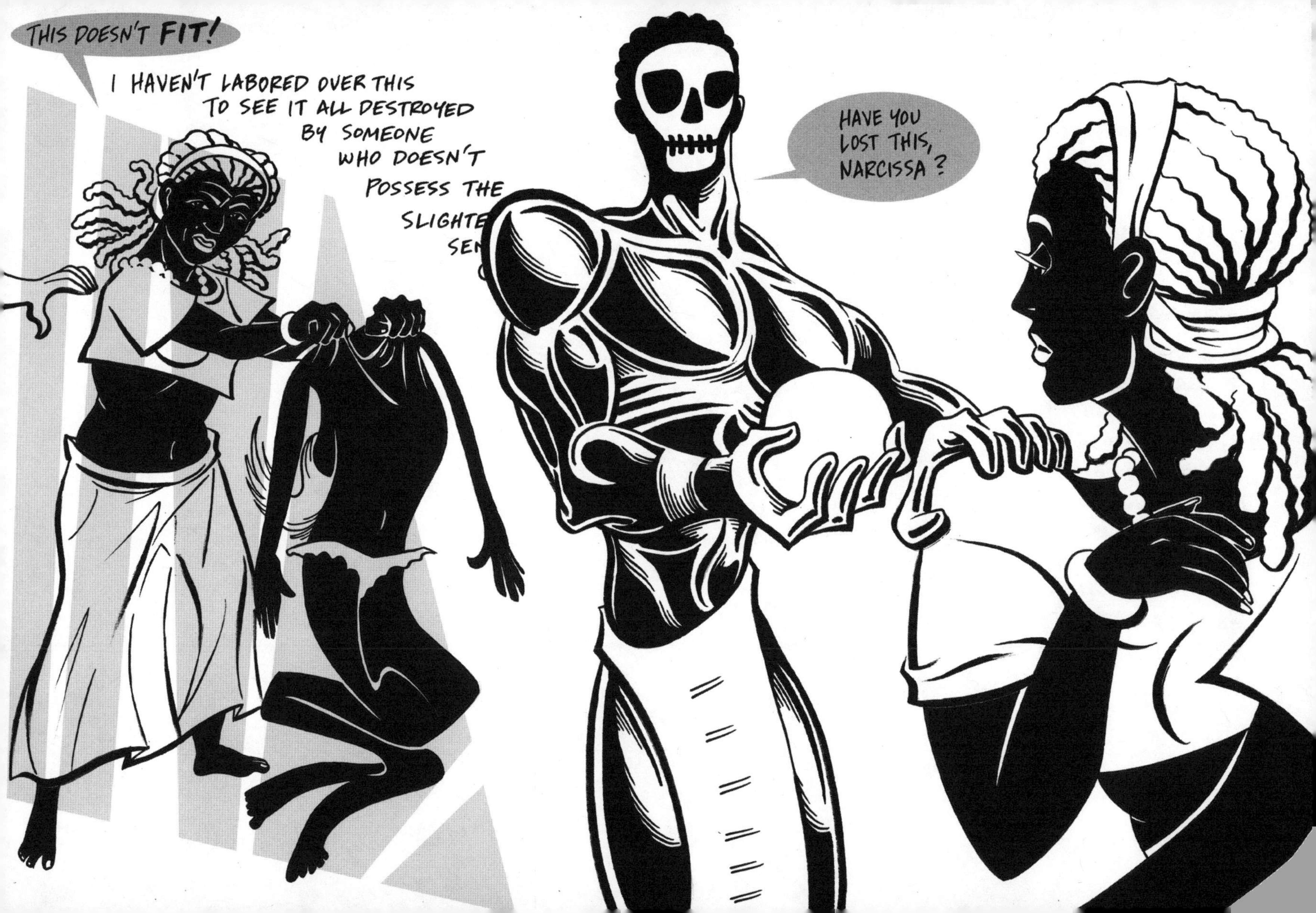
THIS DOESN'T FIT!
I HAVEN'T LABORED OVER THIS TO SEE IT ALL DESTROYED BY SOMEONE WHO DOESN'T POSSESS THE SLIGHTE
HAVE YOU LOST THIS, NARCISSA ?

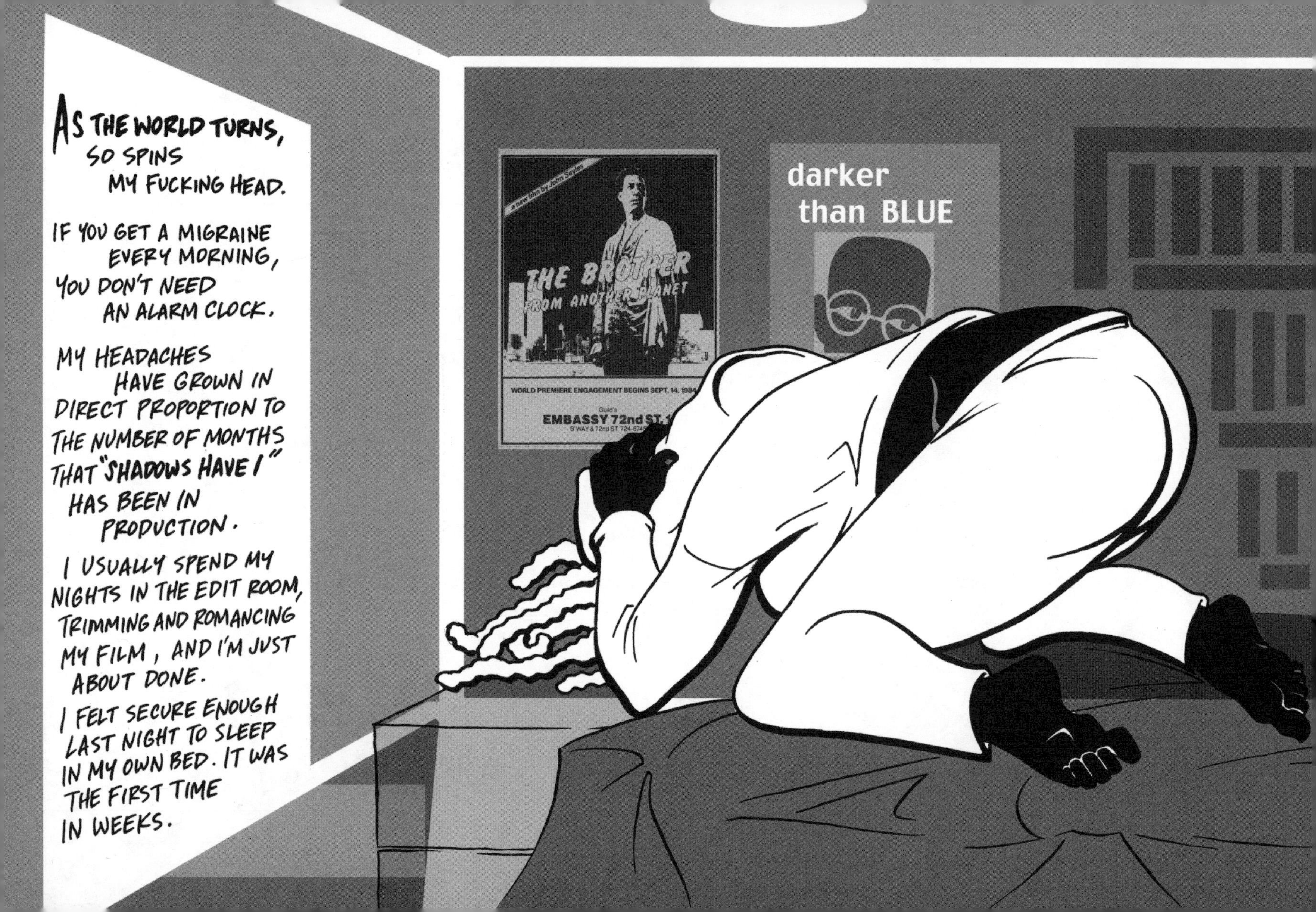
AS THE WORLD TURNS, SO SPINS MY FUCKING HEAD.
IF YOU GET A MIGRAINE EVERY MORNING, YOU DON'T NEED AN ALARM CLOCK.
MY HEADACHES HAVE GROWN IN DIRECT PROPORTION TO THE NUMBER OF MONTHS THAT "SHADOWS HAVE I" HAS BEEN IN PRODUCTION.
I USUALLY SPEND MY NIGHTS IN THE EDIT ROOM, TRIMMING AND ROMANCING MY FILM, AND I'M JUST ABOUT DONE.
I FELT SECURE ENOUGH LAST NIGHT TO SLEEP IN MY OWN BED. IT WAS THE FIRST TIME IN WEEKS.
a new film by John Sayles
THE BROTHER FROM ANOTHER PLANET
WORLD PREMIERE ENGAGEMENT BEGINS SEPT. 14, 1984
Guild's
EMBASSY 72nd ST.
darker than BLUE

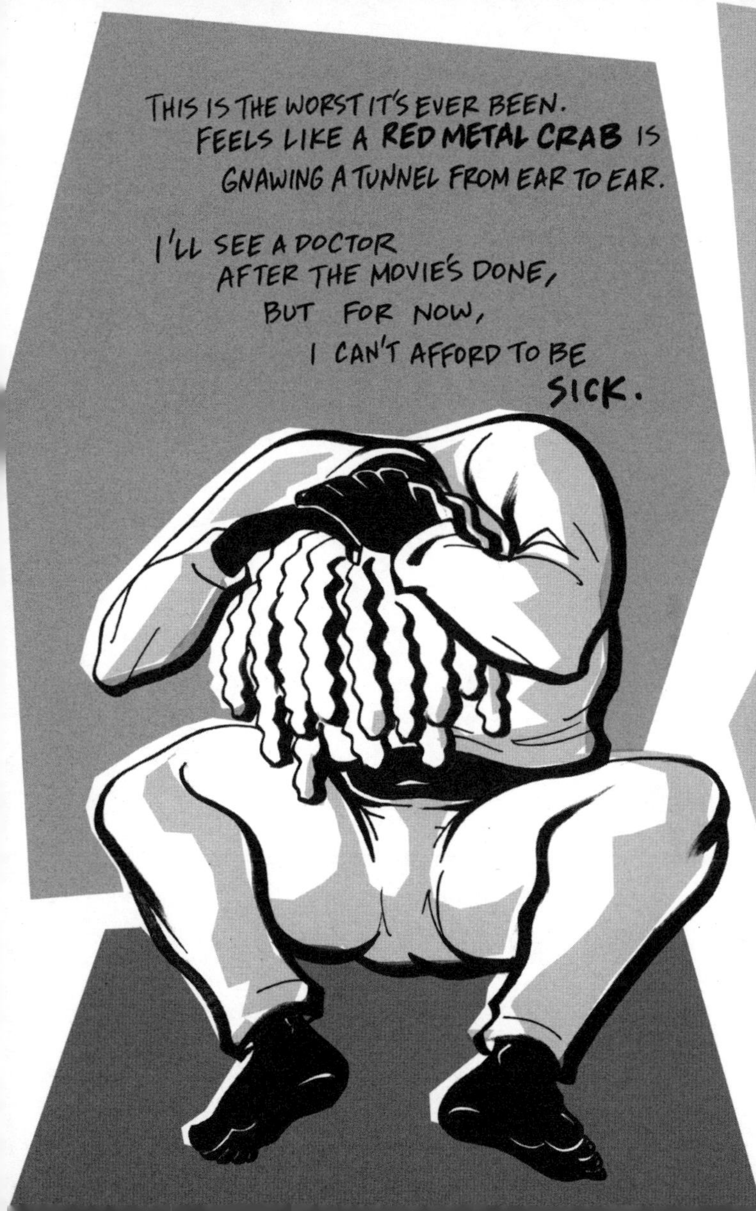
THIS IS THE WORST IT'S EVER BEEN.
FEELS LIKE A **RED METAL CRAB** IS GNAWING A TUNNEL FROM EAR TO EAR.
I'LL SEE A DOCTOR AFTER THE MOVIE'S DONE, BUT FOR NOW, I CAN'T AFFORD TO BE **SICK**.

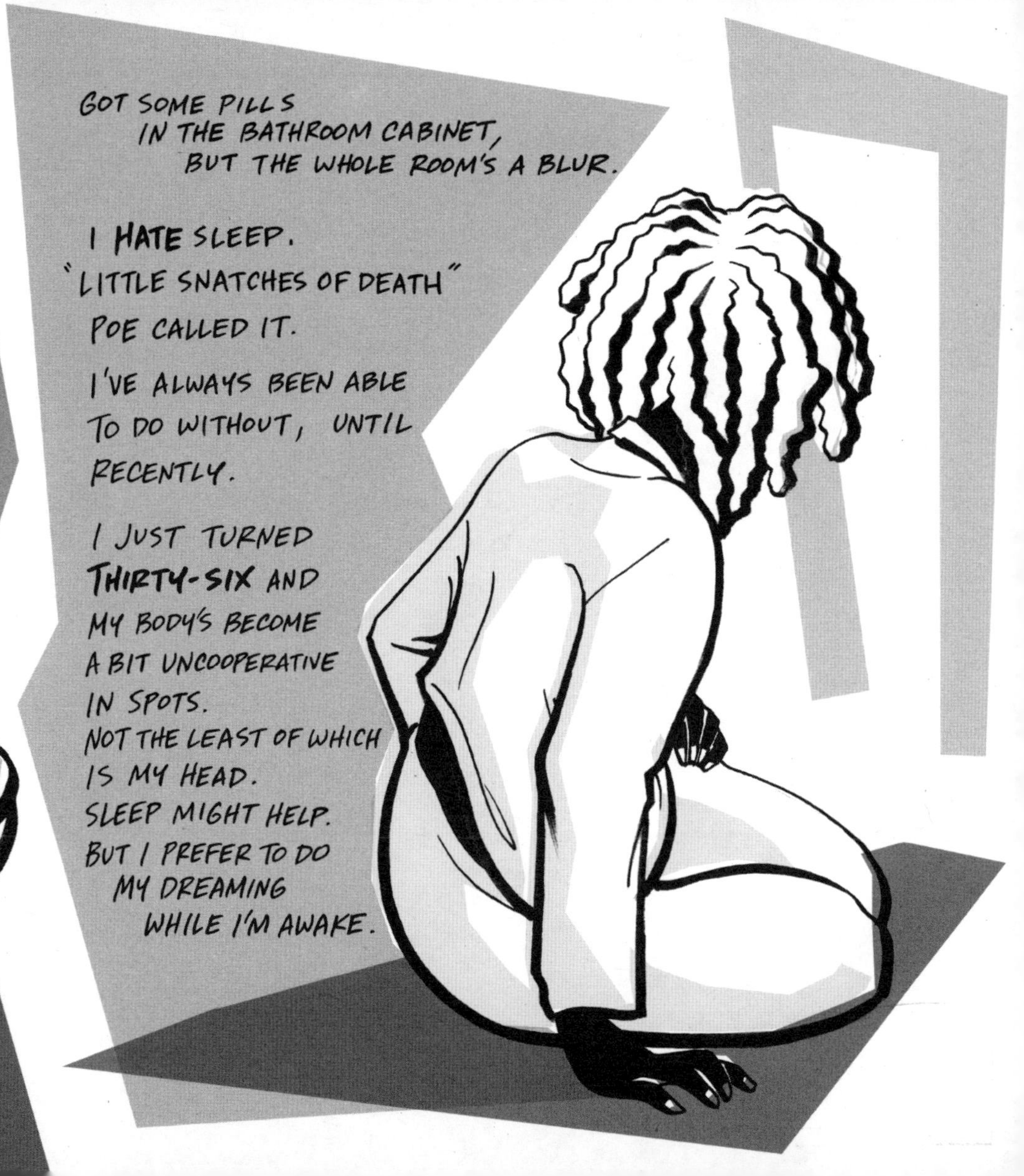
GOT SOME PILLS IN THE BATHROOM CABINET, BUT THE WHOLE ROOM'S A BLUR.
I **HATE** SLEEP. "LITTLE SNATCHES OF DEATH" POE CALLED IT.
I'VE ALWAYS BEEN ABLE TO DO WITHOUT, UNTIL RECENTLY.
I JUST TURNED **THIRTY-SIX** AND MY BODY'S BECOME A BIT UNCOOPERATIVE IN SPOTS.
NOT THE LEAST OF WHICH IS MY HEAD.
SLEEP MIGHT HELP.
BUT I PREFER TO DO MY DREAMING WHILE I'M AWAKE.

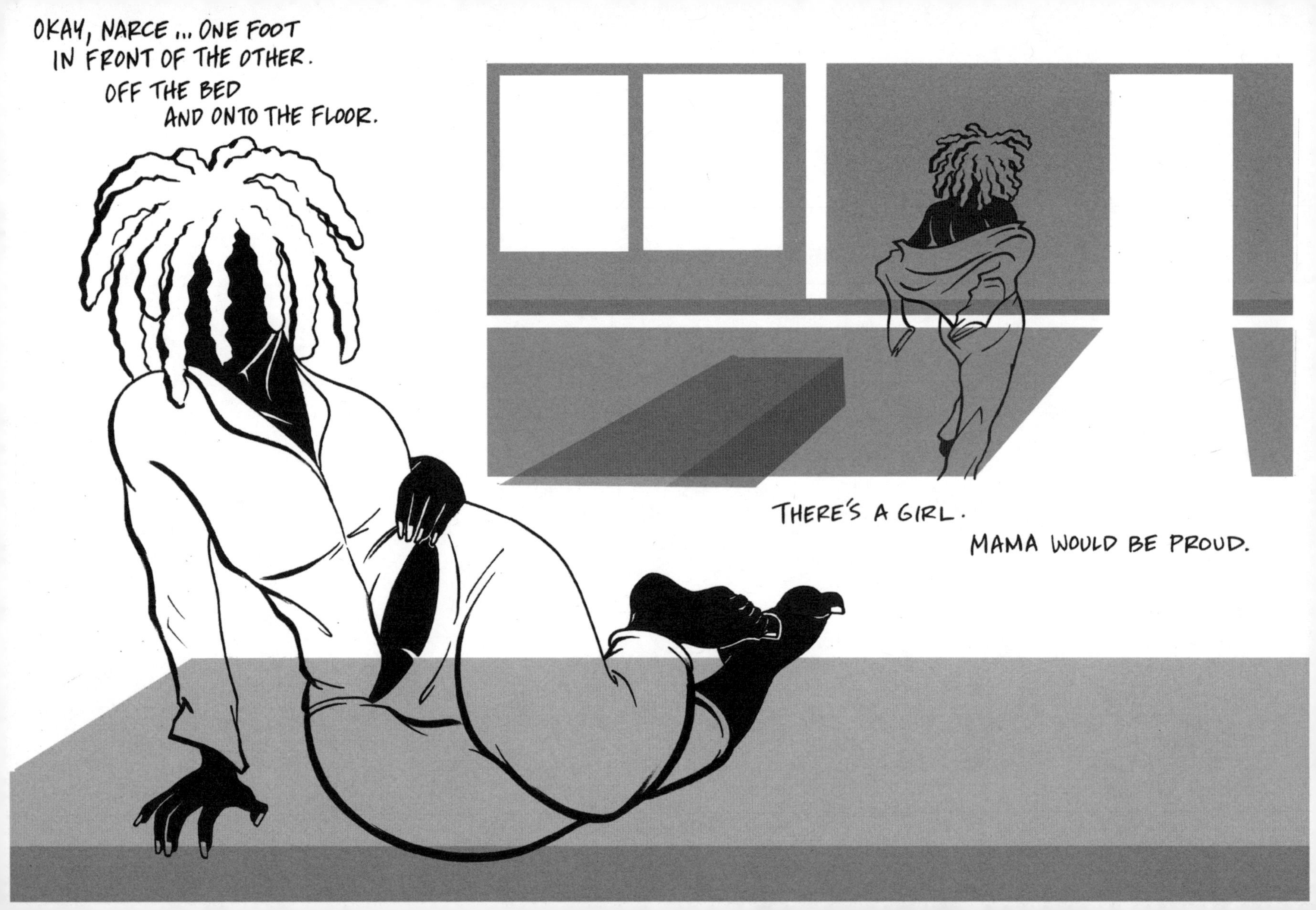
OKAY, NARCE ... ONE FOOT IN FRONT OF THE OTHER.
OFF THE BED AND ONTO THE FLOOR.
THERE'S A GIRL.
MAMA WOULD BE PROUD.

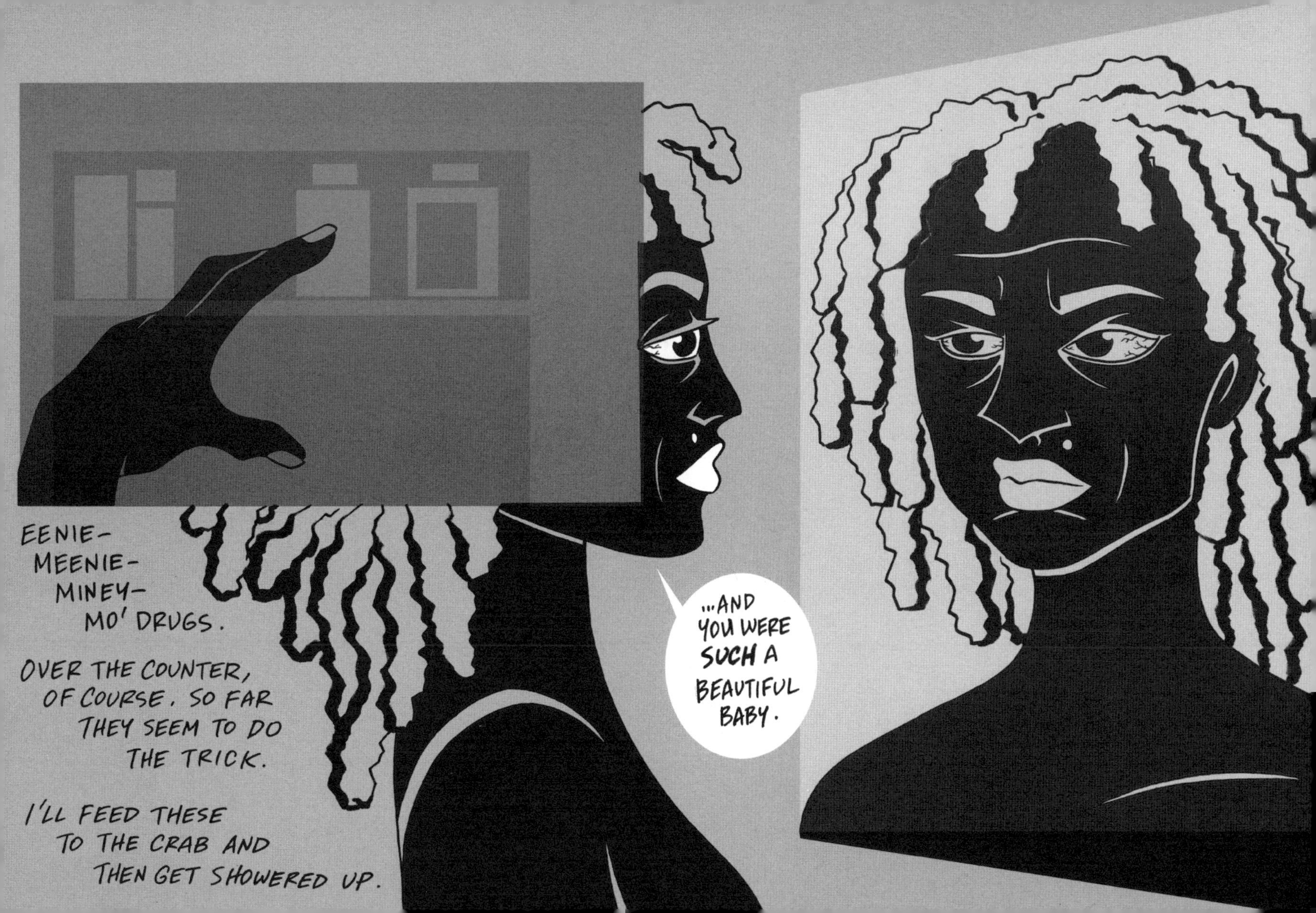
EENIE-MEENIE-MINEY-MO' DRUGS.
OVER THE COUNTER, OF COURSE. SO FAR THEY SEEM TO DO THE TRICK.
I'LL FEED THESE TO THE CRAB AND THEN GET SHOWERED UP.
...AND YOU WERE SUCH A BEAUTIFUL BABY.

DIDN'T MEAN TO GET MY DREDS WET...

THEY TAKE FOREVER TO DRY.

BEEN SO LONG SINCE I WASHED 'EM THOUGH.

BETWEEN THE PILLS AND THE WATER, I'M STARTING TO FEEL A LITTLE BETTER...

...STARTING TO.

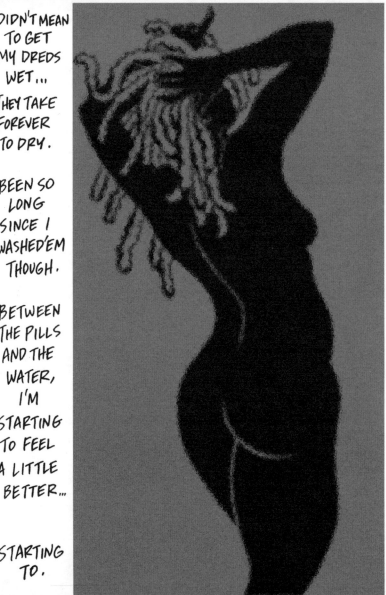

A MESSAGE ? BEFORE I HEAR THE FIRST WORD, I KNOW IT'S BAD NEWS.

NARCE... IT'S ME, LUCY. YOU GOTTA GET IN HERE, NOW.

SIMON'S **RE-CUTTING** THE FILM! **NARCE!**

WHERE THE FUCK ARE YOU ?

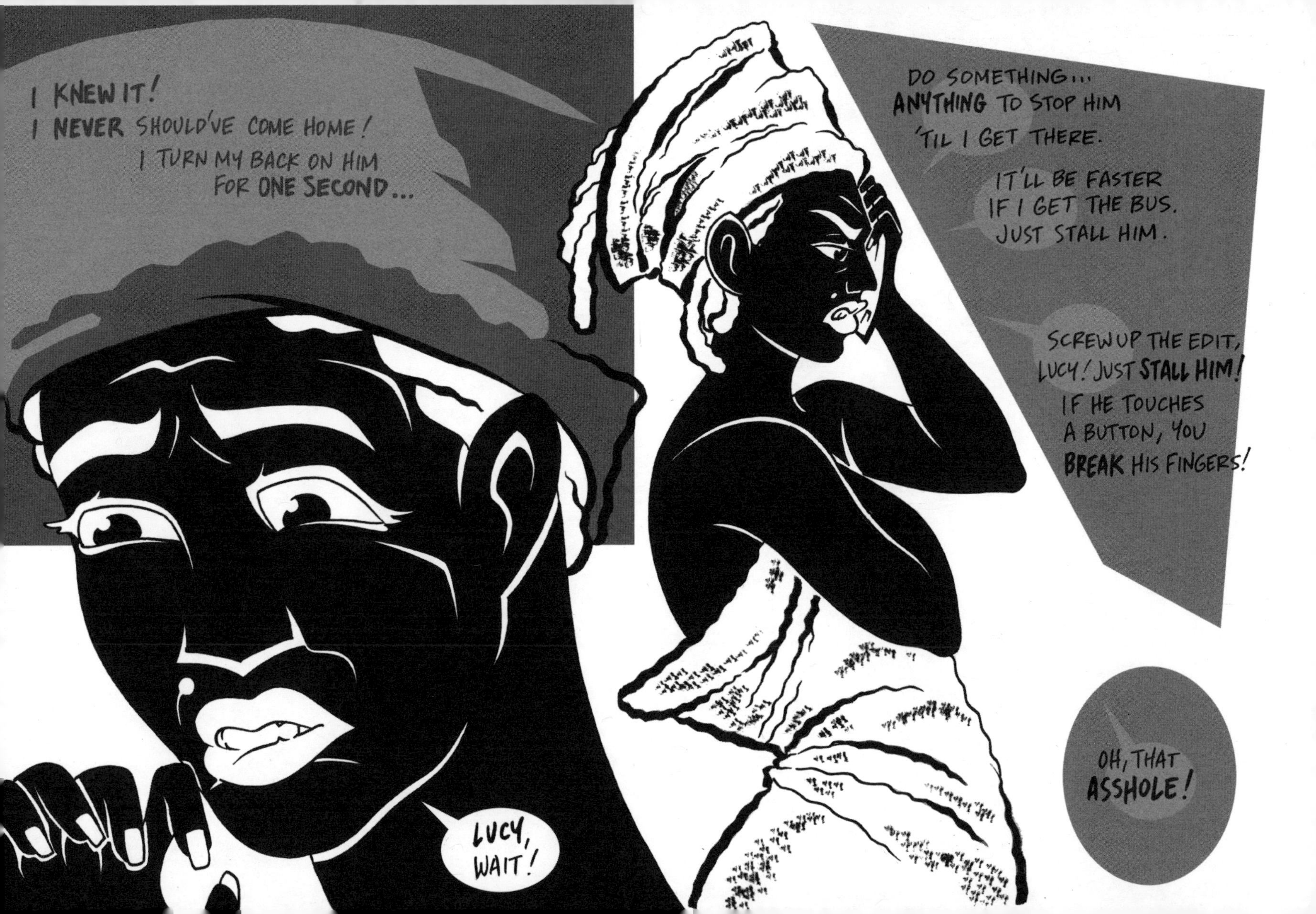
I KNEW IT!
I NEVER SHOULD'VE COME HOME!
I TURN MY BACK ON HIM FOR ONE SECOND...
LUCY, WAIT!
DO SOMETHING... ANYTHING TO STOP HIM 'TIL I GET THERE.
IT'LL BE FASTER IF I GET THE BUS. JUST STALL HIM.
SCREW UP THE EDIT, LUCY! JUST STALL HIM!
IF HE TOUCHES A BUTTON, YOU BREAK HIS FINGERS!
OH, THAT ASSHOLE!

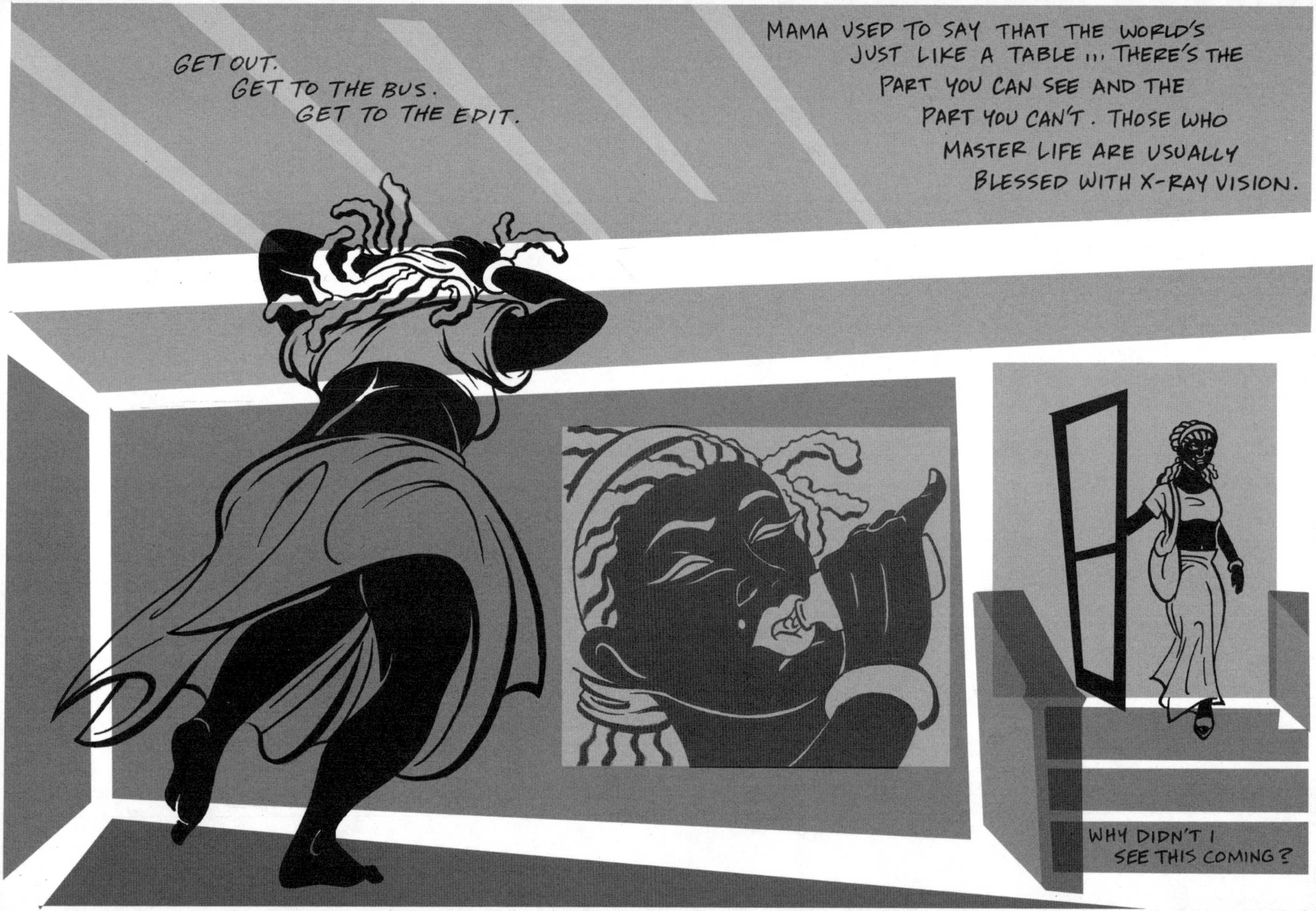
MAMA USED TO SAY THAT THE WORLD'S JUST LIKE A TABLE ... THERE'S THE PART YOU CAN SEE AND THE PART YOU CAN'T. THOSE WHO MASTER LIFE ARE USUALLY BLESSED WITH X-RAY VISION.
GET OUT.
GET TO THE BUS.
GET TO THE EDIT.
WHY DIDN'T I SEE THIS COMING?

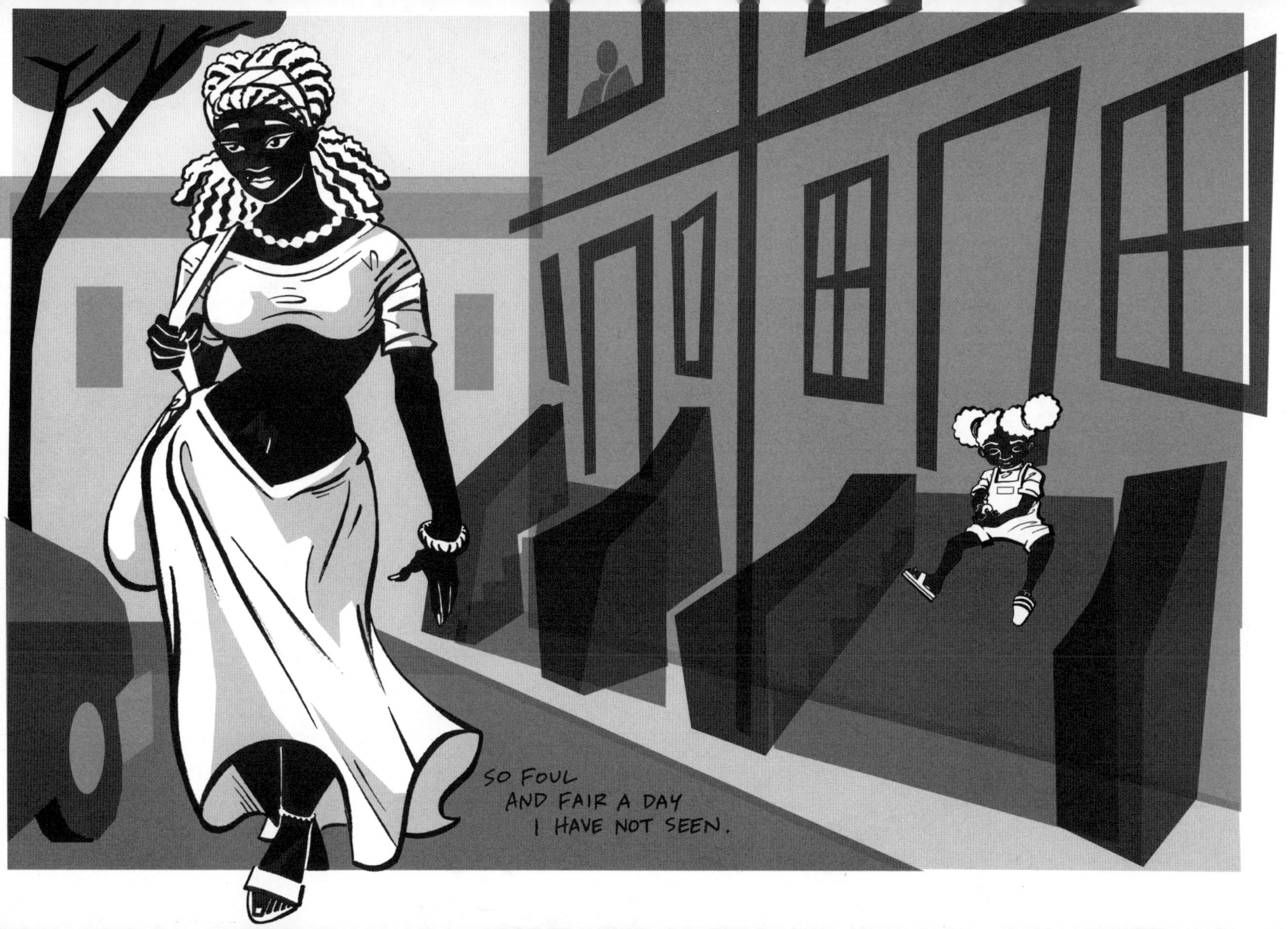
SO FOUL
AND FAIR A DAY
I HAVE NOT SEEN.

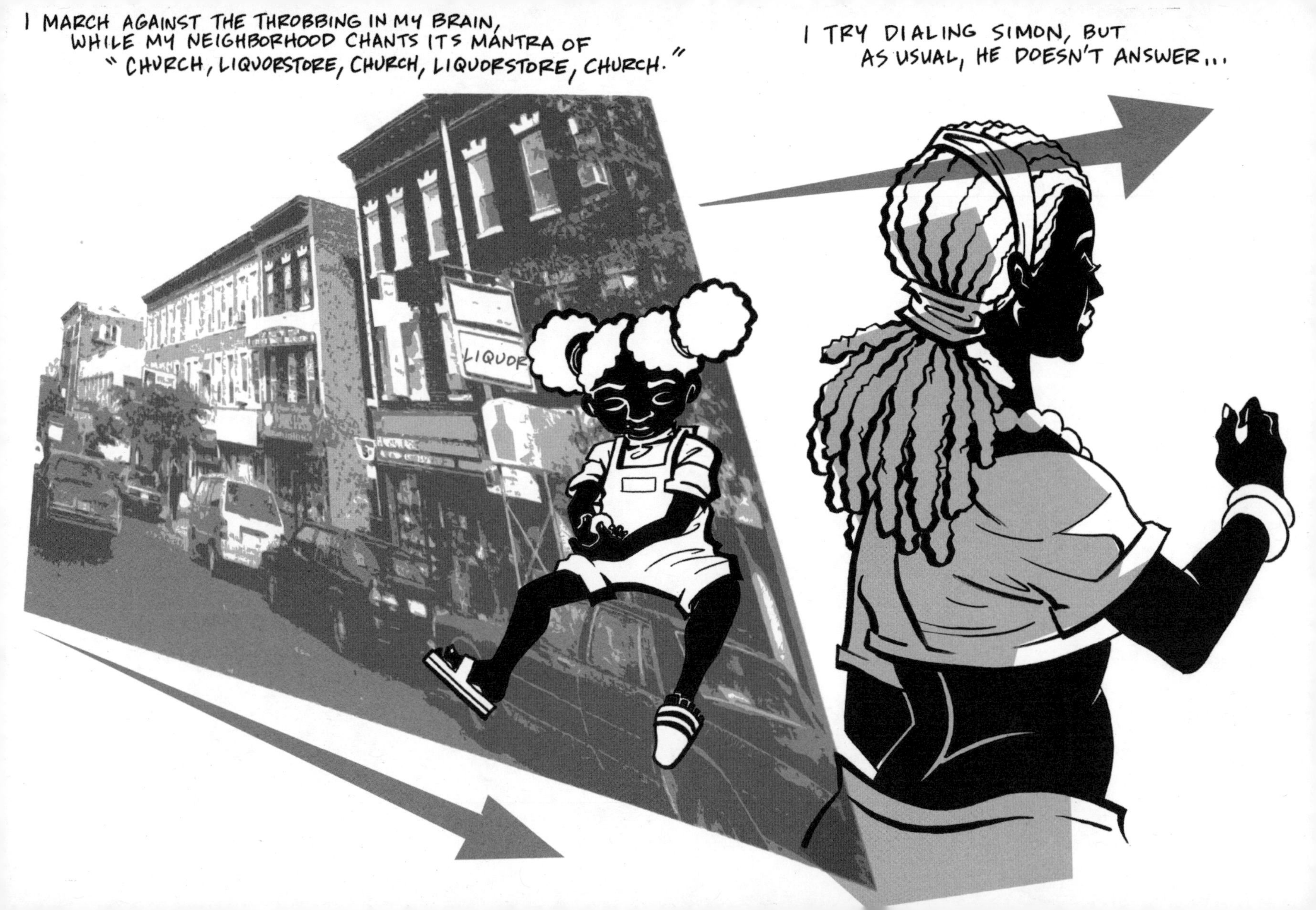
I MARCH AGAINST THE THROBBING IN MY BRAIN, WHILE MY NEIGHBORHOOD CHANTS ITS MANTRA OF "CHURCH, LIQUORSTORE, CHURCH, LIQUORSTORE, CHURCH."
LIQUOR
I TRY DIALING SIMON, BUT AS USUAL, HE DOESN'T ANSWER...

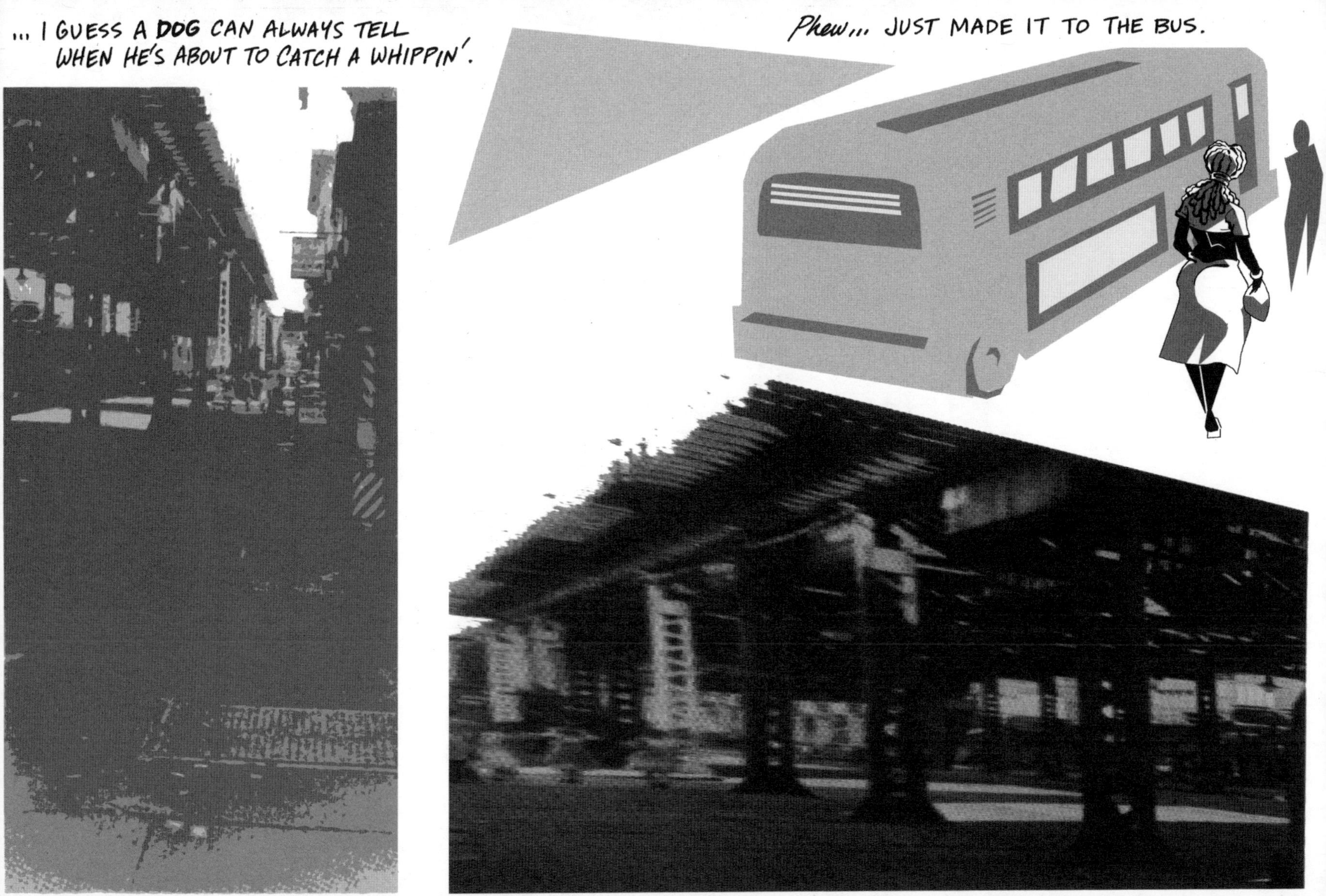
... I GUESS A DOG CAN ALWAYS TELL WHEN HE'S ABOUT TO CATCH A WHIPPIN'.
Phew... JUST MADE IT TO THE BUS.

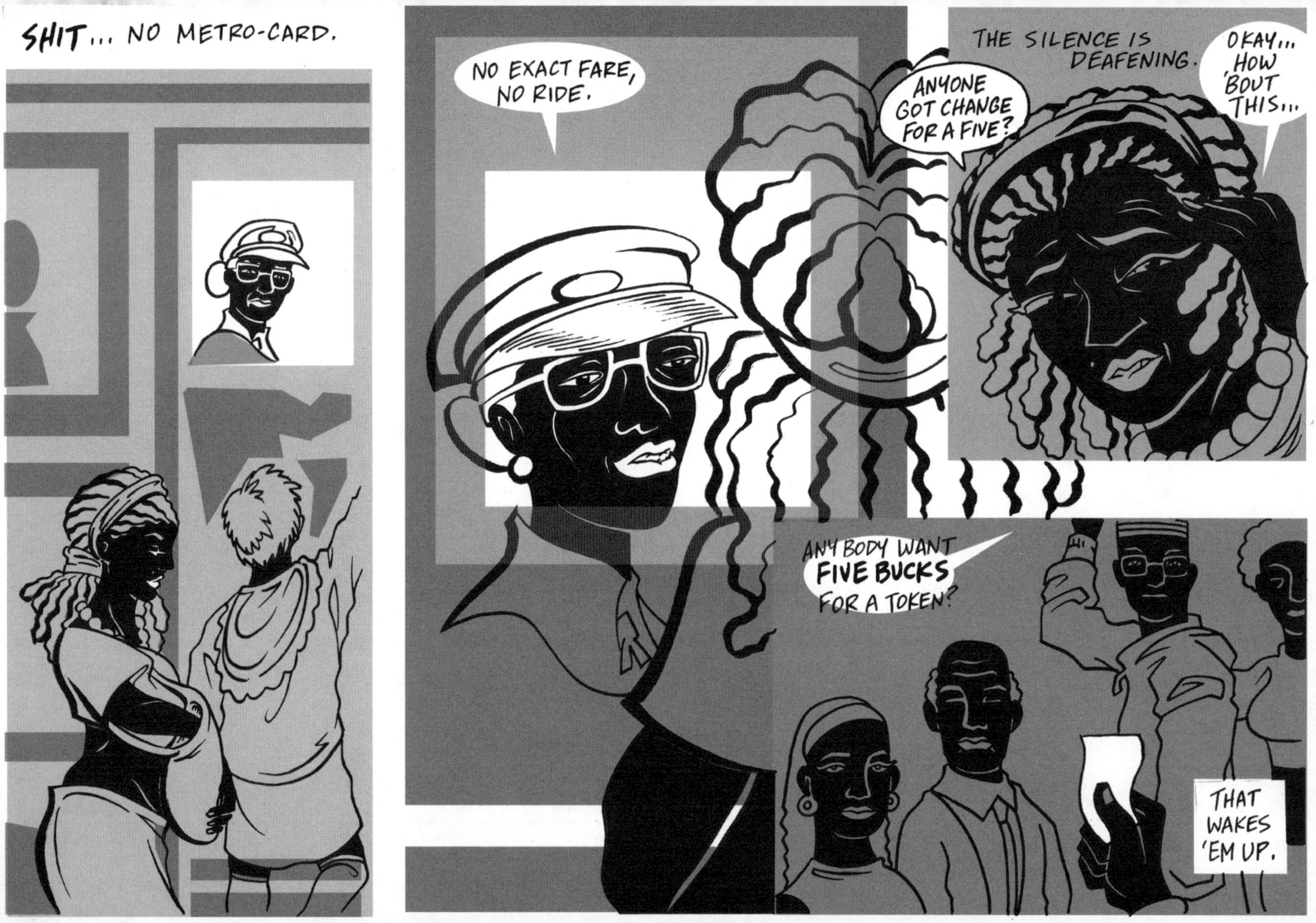
SHIT... NO METRO-CARD.
NO EXACT FARE, NO RIDE.
ANYONE GOT CHANGE FOR A FIVE?
THE SILENCE IS DEAFENING.
OKAY... HOW 'BOUT THIS...
ANYBODY WANT **FIVE BUCKS** FOR A TOKEN?
THAT WAKES 'EM UP.

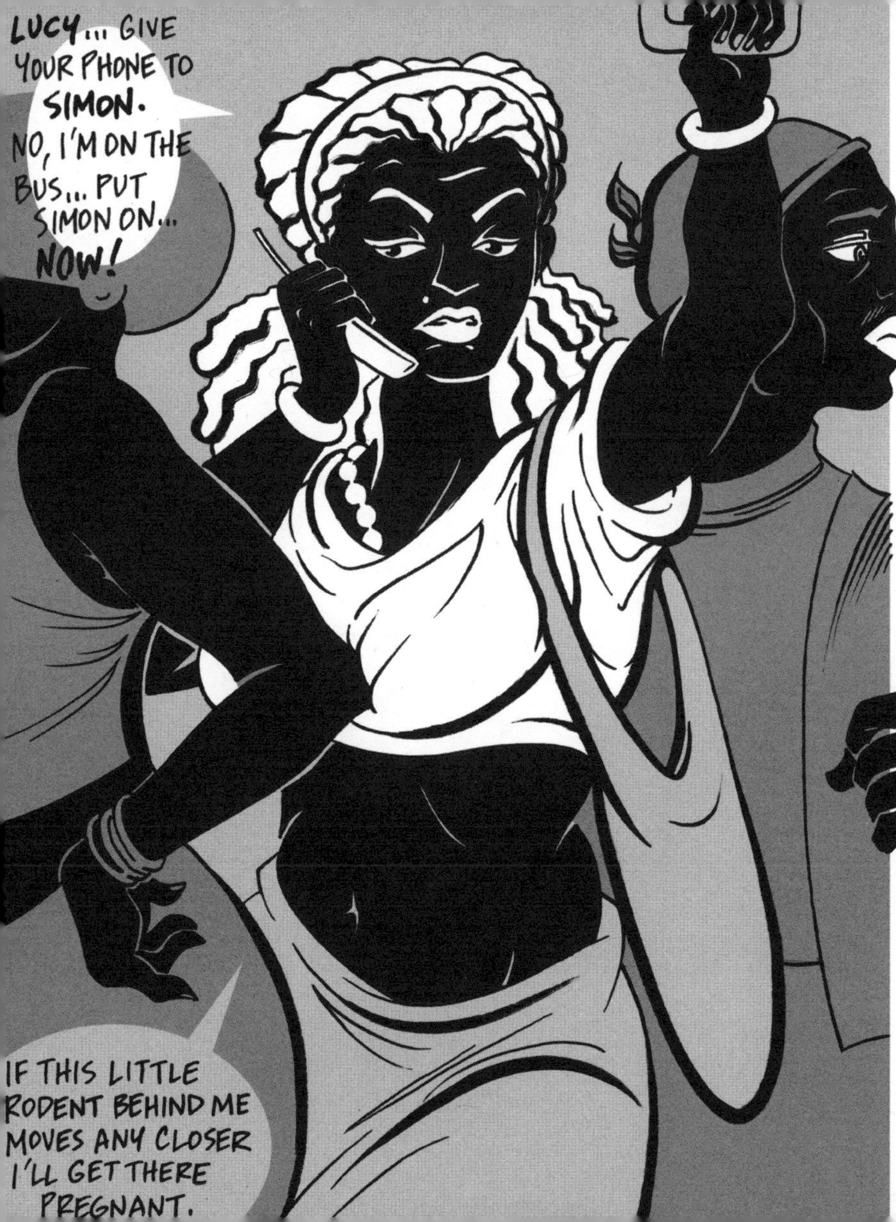

LUCY... GIVE YOUR PHONE TO SIMON. NO, I'M ON THE BUS... PUT SIMON ON... NOW!
IF THIS LITTLE RODENT BEHIND ME MOVES ANY CLOSER I'LL GET THERE PREGNANT.

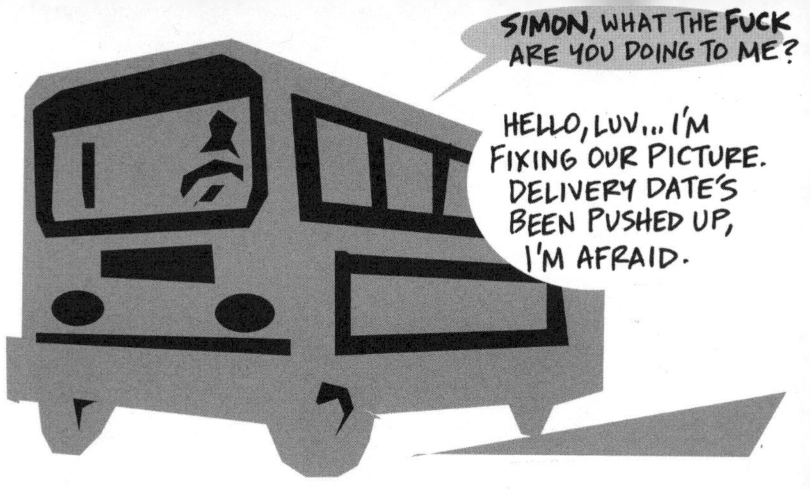

SIMON, WHAT THE FUCK ARE YOU DOING TO ME?
HELLO, LUV... I'M FIXING OUR PICTURE. DELIVERY DATE'S BEEN PUSHED UP, I'M AFRAID.

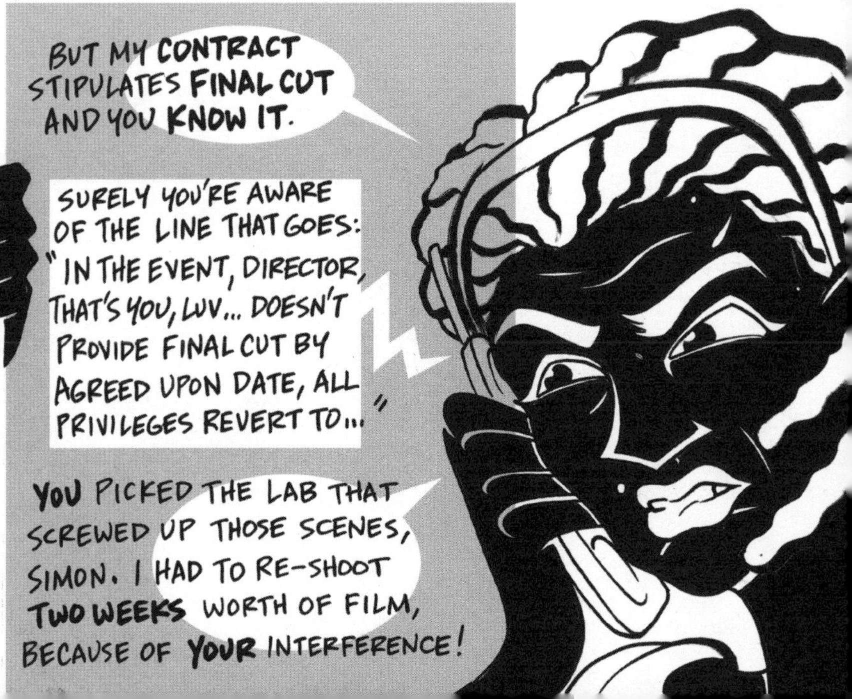

BUT MY CONTRACT STIPULATES FINAL CUT AND YOU KNOW IT.
SURELY YOU'RE AWARE OF THE LINE THAT GOES: "IN THE EVENT, DIRECTOR, THAT'S YOU, LUV... DOESN'T PROVIDE FINAL CUT BY AGREED UPON DATE, ALL PRIVILEGES REVERT TO..."
YOU PICKED THE LAB THAT SCREWED UP THOSE SCENES, SIMON. I HAD TO RE-SHOOT TWO WEEKS WORTH OF FILM, BECAUSE OF YOUR INTERFERENCE!

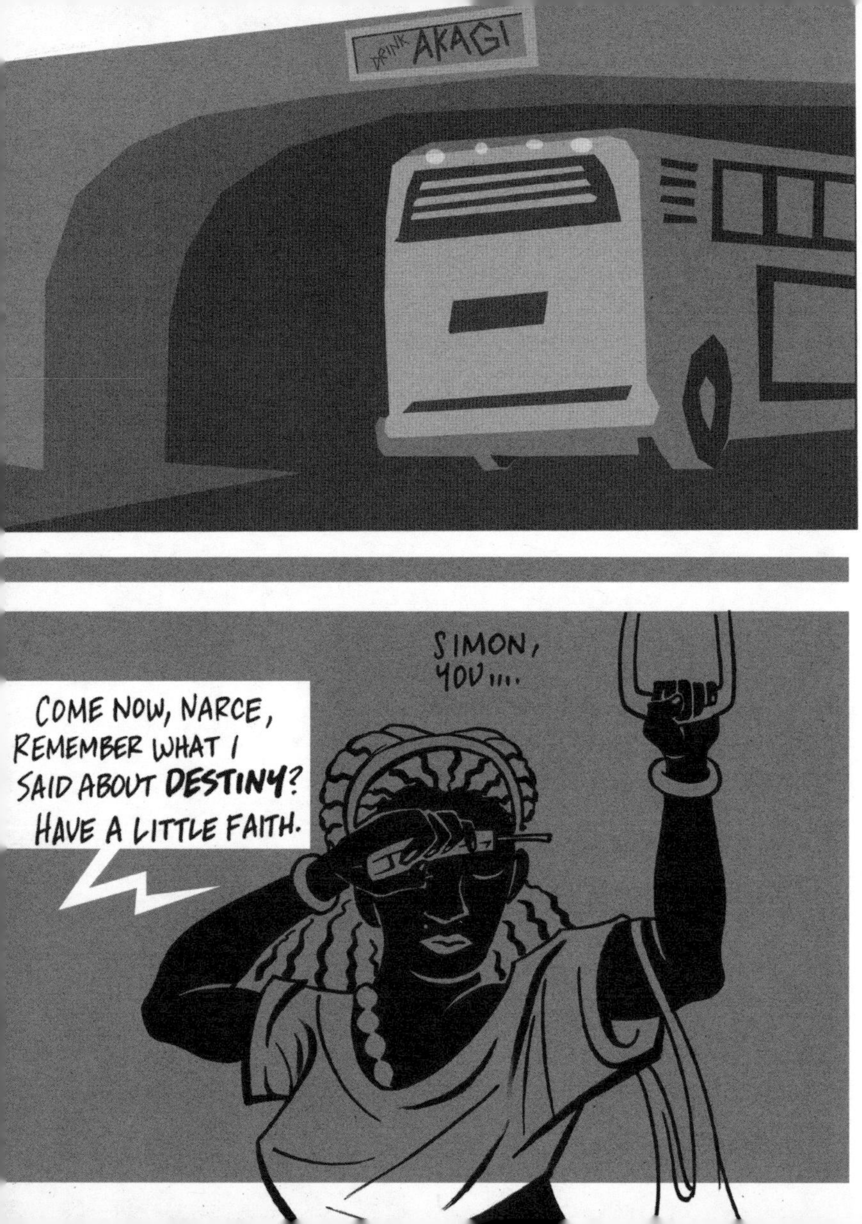
DRINK AKAGI
SIMON, YOU....
COME NOW, NARCE, REMEMBER WHAT I SAID ABOUT **DESTINY**? HAVE A LITTLE FAITH.

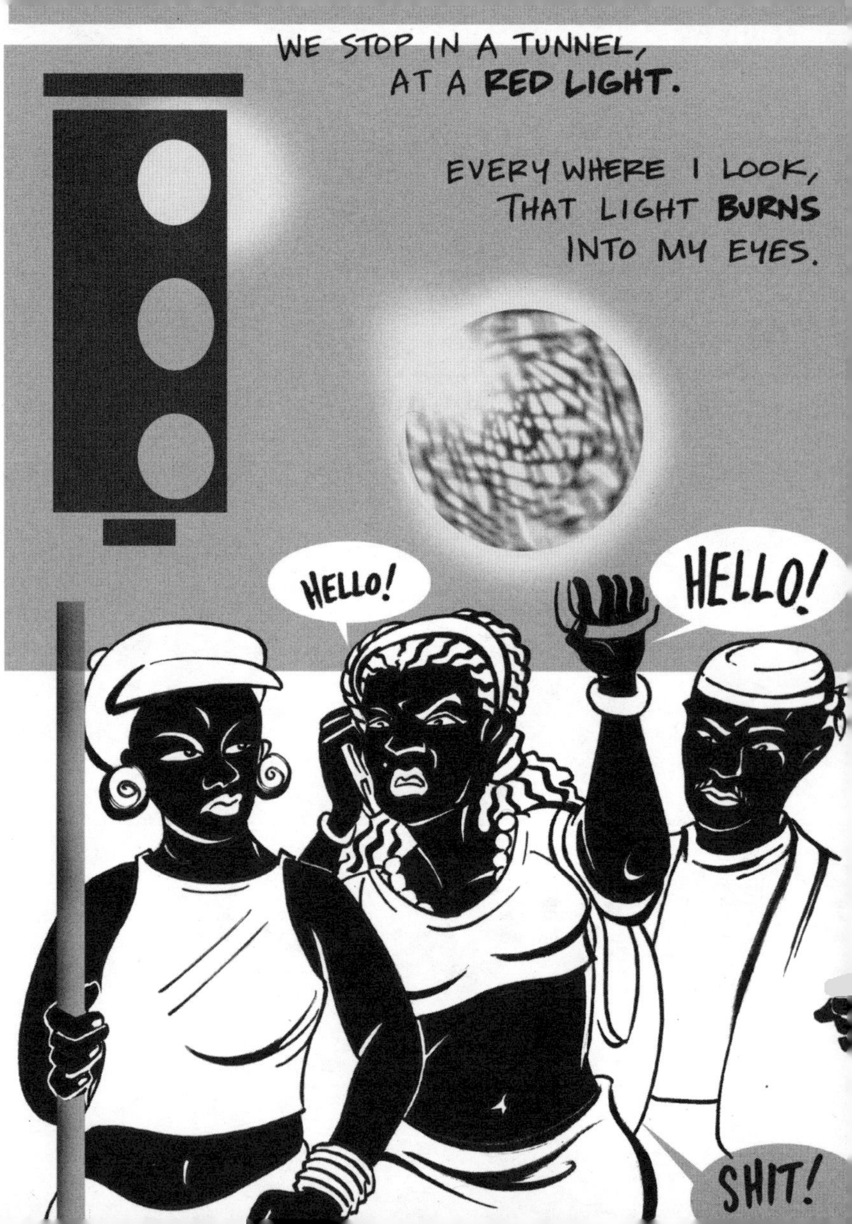
WE STOP IN A TUNNEL, AT A **RED LIGHT.**
EVERY WHERE I LOOK, THAT LIGHT **BURNS** INTO MY EYES.
HELLO!
HELLO!
SHIT!

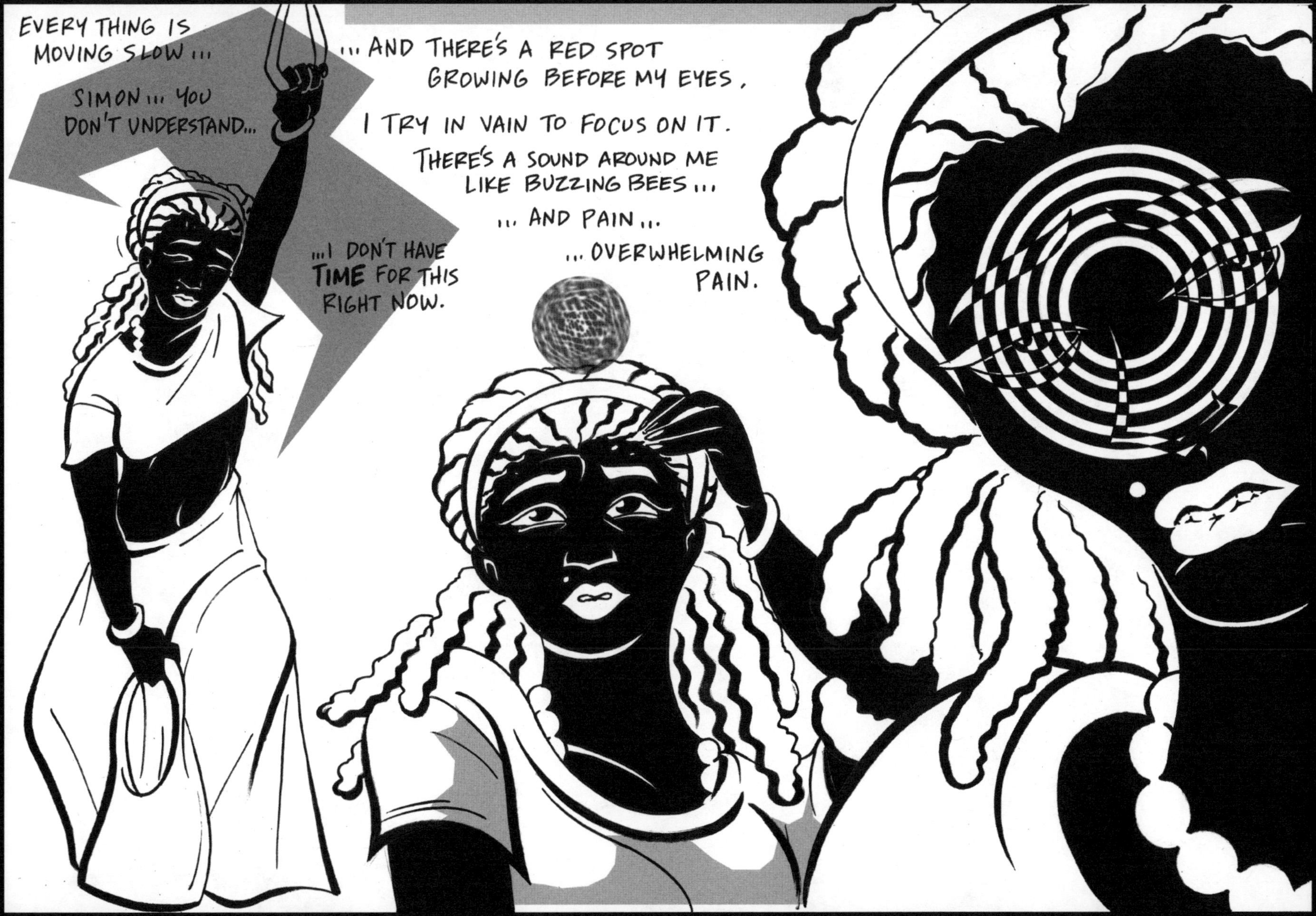
EVERY THING IS MOVING SLOW...
SIMON... YOU DON'T UNDERSTAND...
...I DON'T HAVE **TIME** FOR THIS RIGHT NOW.
...AND THERE'S A RED SPOT GROWING BEFORE MY EYES.
I TRY IN VAIN TO FOCUS ON IT.
THERE'S A SOUND AROUND ME LIKE BUZZING BEES...
...AND PAIN...
...OVERWHELMING PAIN.

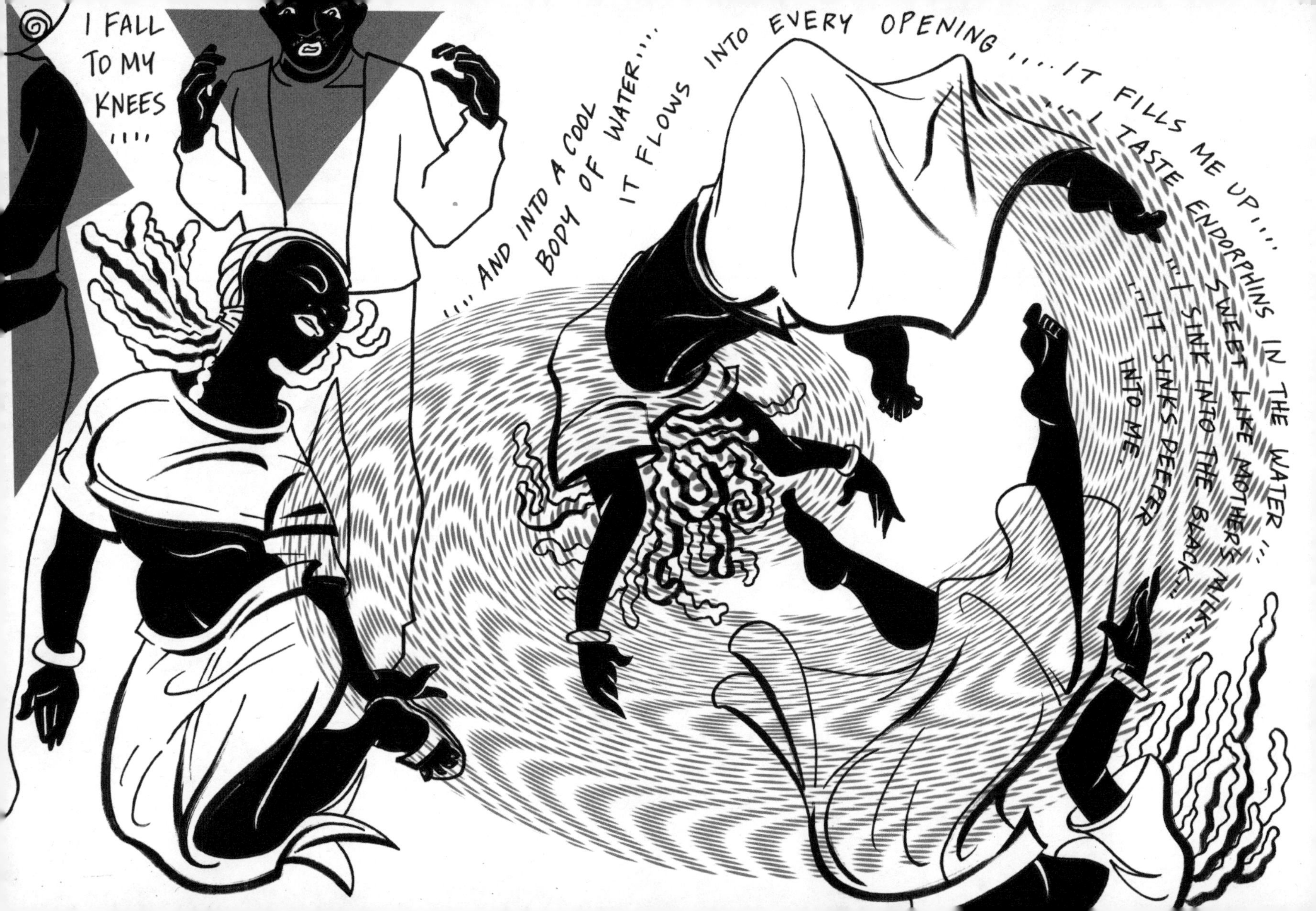
I FALL TO MY KNEES ''''
''''AND INTO A COOL BODY OF WATER''''
IT FLOWS INTO EVERY OPENING''''IT FILLS ME UP''''
''''I TASTE ENDORPHINS IN THE WATER
''''SWEET LIKE MOTHER'S MILK''''
''''I SINK INTO THE BLACK''''
''''IT SINKS DEEPER INTO ME.

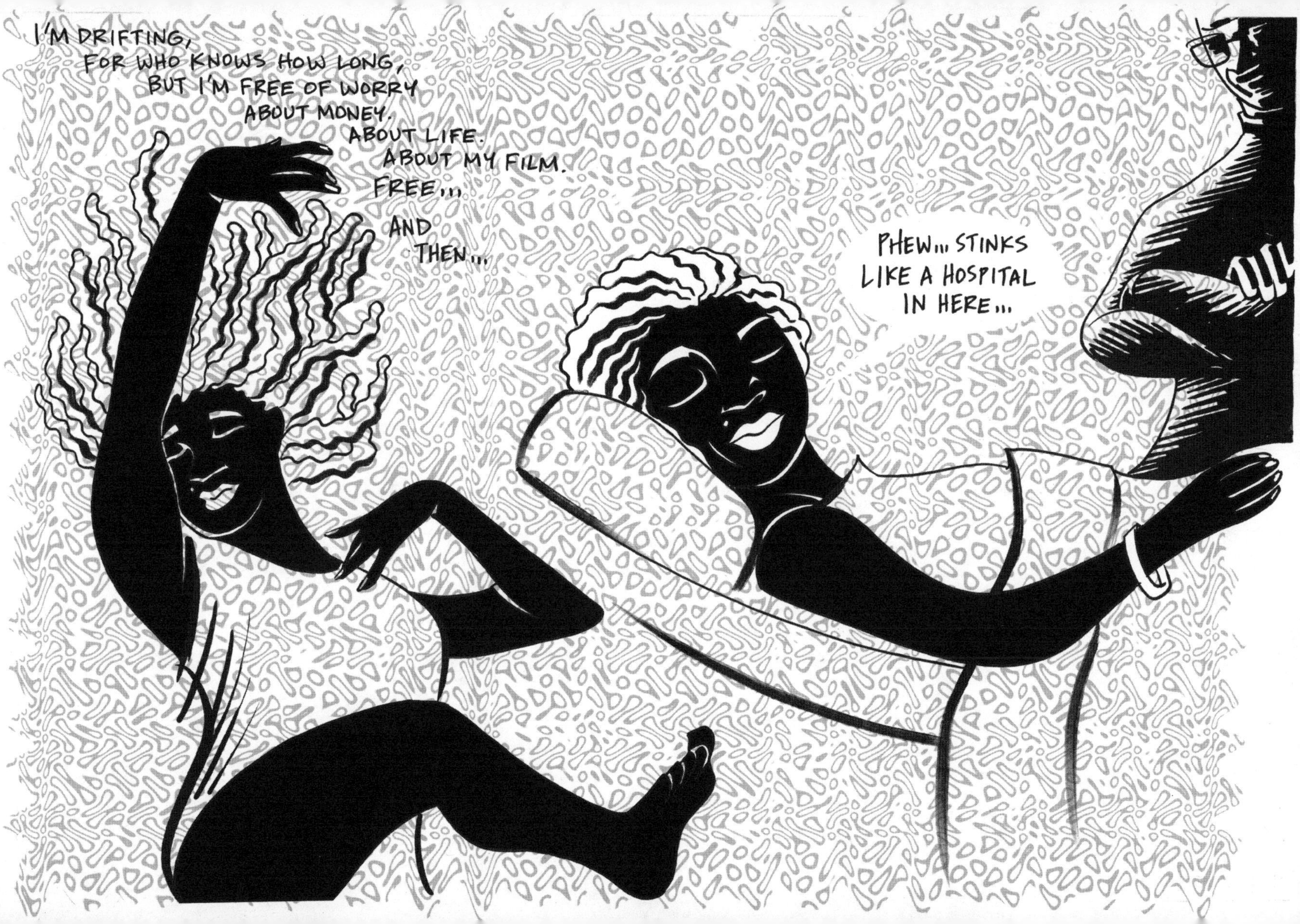
I'M DRIFTING,
FOR WHO KNOWS HOW LONG,
BUT I'M FREE OF WORRY
ABOUT MONEY.
ABOUT LIFE.
ABOUT MY FILM.
FREE...
AND
THEN...
PHEW... STINKS LIKE A HOSPITAL IN HERE...

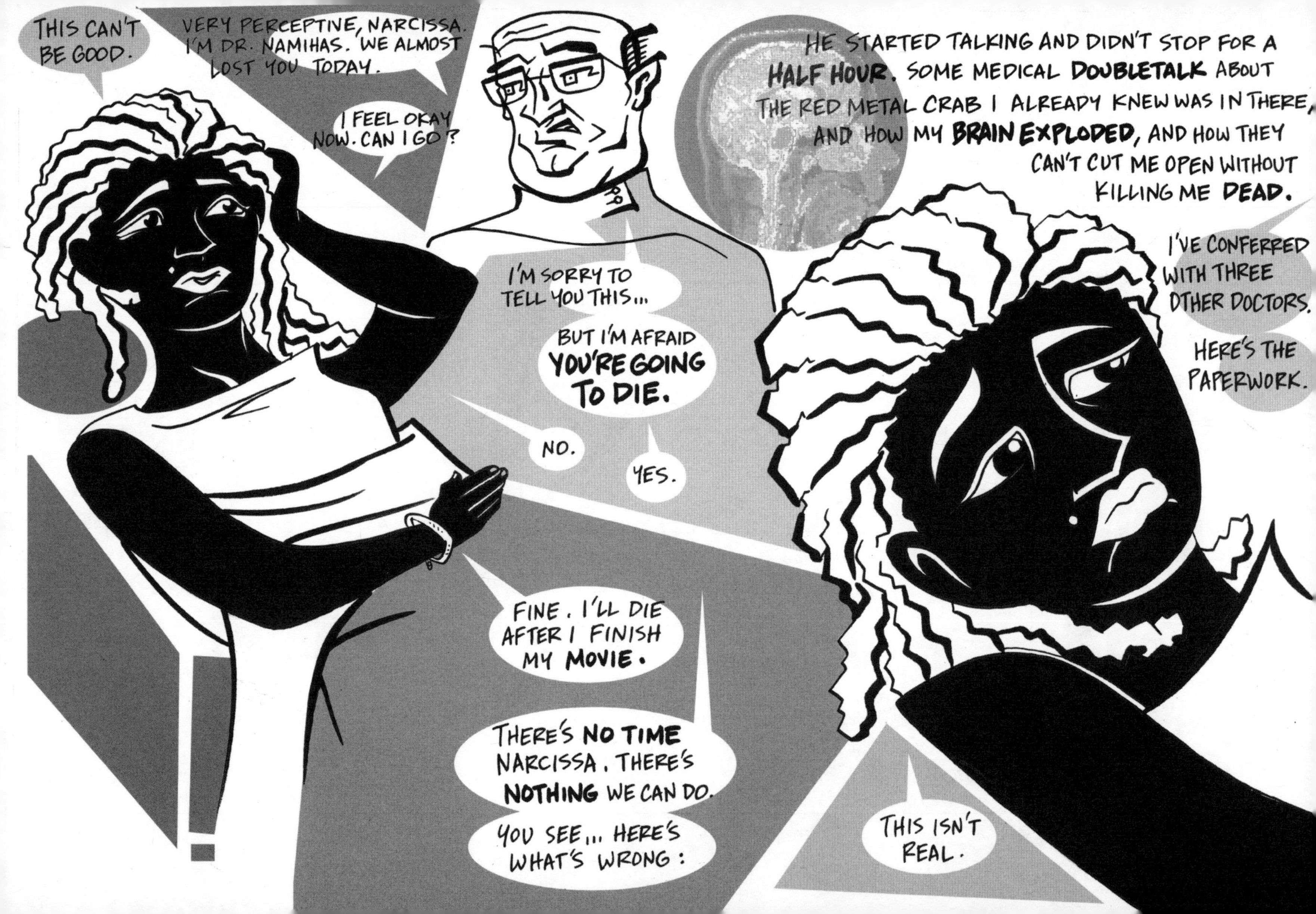
THIS CAN'T BE GOOD.
VERY PERCEPTIVE, NARCISSA. I'M DR. NAMIHAS. WE ALMOST LOST YOU TODAY.
I FEEL OKAY NOW. CAN I GO?
I'M SORRY TO TELL YOU THIS...
BUT I'M AFRAID **YOU'RE GOING TO DIE.**
NO.
YES.
FINE. I'LL DIE AFTER I FINISH MY **MOVIE**.
THERE'S **NO TIME** NARCISSA. THERE'S **NOTHING** WE CAN DO.
YOU SEE... HERE'S WHAT'S WRONG:
HE STARTED TALKING AND DIDN'T STOP FOR A **HALF HOUR**. SOME MEDICAL **DOUBLETALK** ABOUT THE RED METAL CRAB I ALREADY KNEW WAS IN THERE, AND HOW MY **BRAIN EXPLODED**, AND HOW THEY CAN'T CUT ME OPEN WITHOUT KILLING ME **DEAD**.
I'VE CONFERRED WITH THREE OTHER DOCTORS.
HERE'S THE PAPERWORK.
THIS ISN'T REAL.

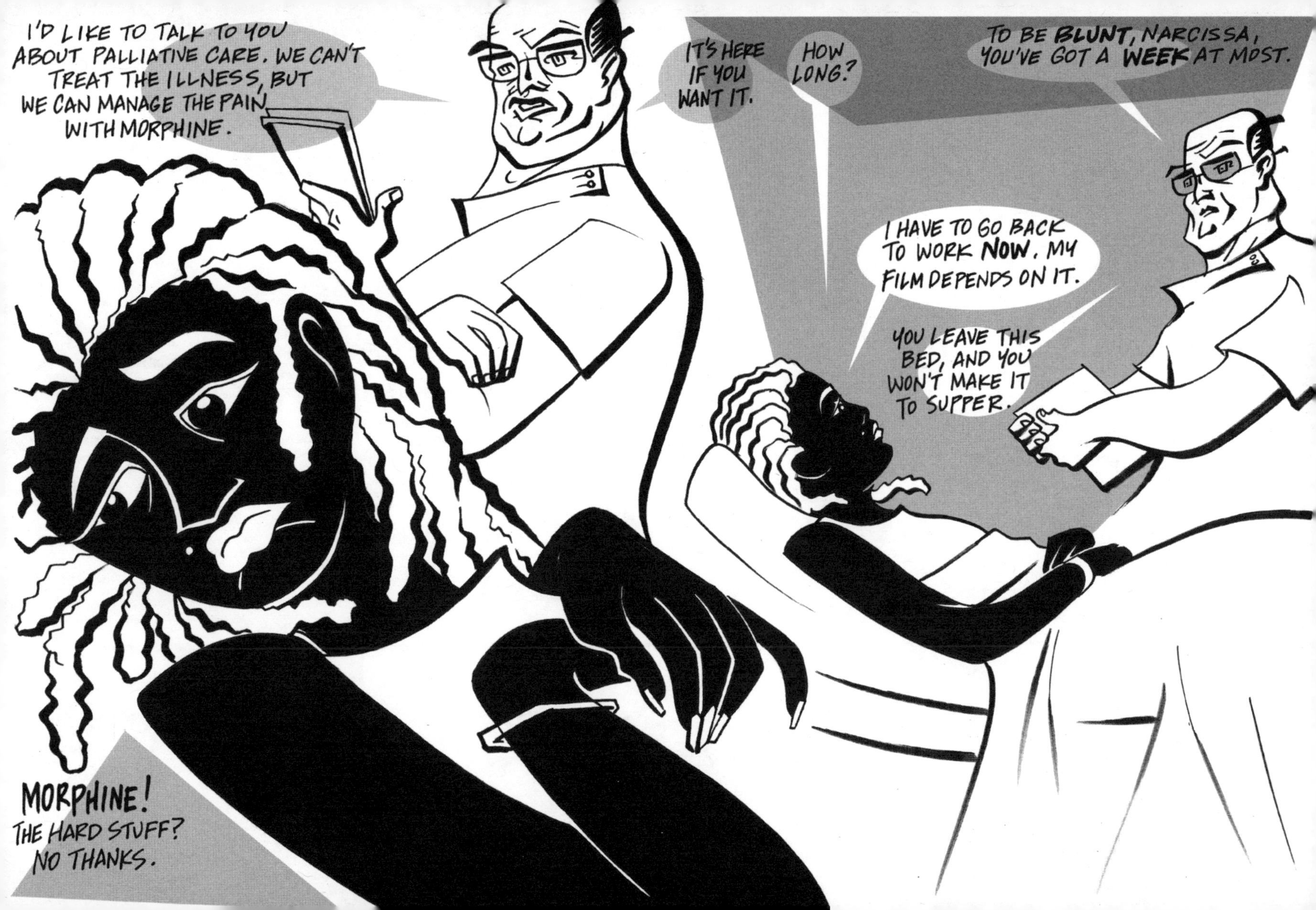
I'D LIKE TO TALK TO YOU ABOUT PALLIATIVE CARE. WE CAN'T TREAT THE ILLNESS, BUT WE CAN MANAGE THE PAIN WITH MORPHINE.
MORPHINE! THE HARD STUFF? NO THANKS.
IT'S HERE IF YOU WANT IT.
HOW LONG?
TO BE BLUNT, NARCISSA, YOU'VE GOT A WEEK AT MOST.
I HAVE TO GO BACK TO WORK NOW. MY FILM DEPENDS ON IT.
YOU LEAVE THIS BED, AND YOU WON'T MAKE IT TO SUPPER.

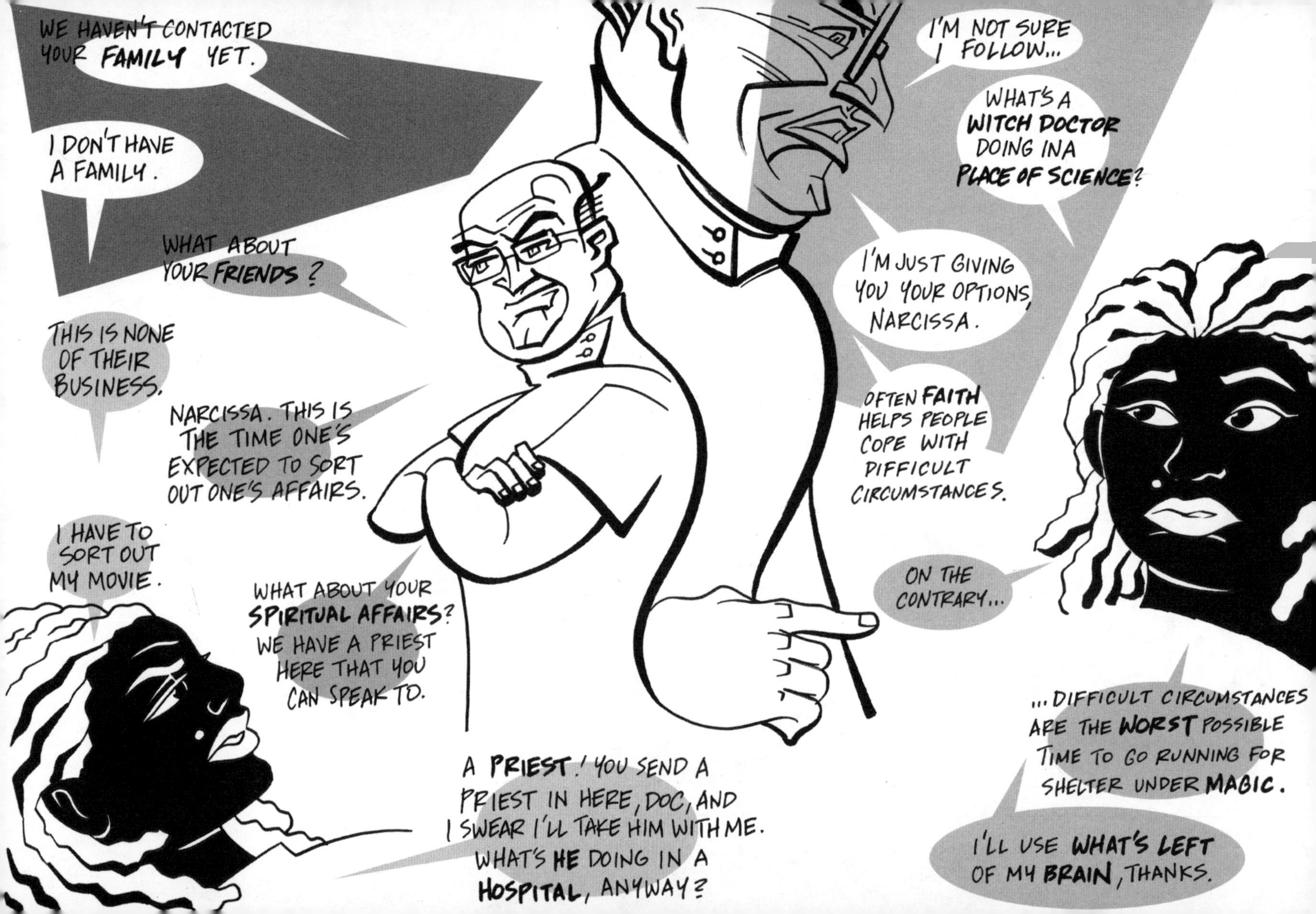

WE HAVEN'T CONTACTED YOUR FAMILY YET.
I DON'T HAVE A FAMILY.
WHAT ABOUT YOUR FRIENDS?
THIS IS NONE OF THEIR BUSINESS.
NARCISSA. THIS IS THE TIME ONE'S EXPECTED TO SORT OUT ONE'S AFFAIRS.
I HAVE TO SORT OUT MY MOVIE.
WHAT ABOUT YOUR SPIRITUAL AFFAIRS? WE HAVE A PRIEST HERE THAT YOU CAN SPEAK TO.
A PRIEST! YOU SEND A PRIEST IN HERE, DOC, AND I SWEAR I'LL TAKE HIM WITH ME. WHAT'S HE DOING IN A HOSPITAL, ANYWAY?
I'M NOT SURE I FOLLOW...
WHAT'S A WITCH DOCTOR DOING IN A PLACE OF SCIENCE?
I'M JUST GIVING YOU YOUR OPTIONS, NARCISSA.
OFTEN FAITH HELPS PEOPLE COPE WITH DIFFICULT CIRCUMSTANCES.
ON THE CONTRARY...
...DIFFICULT CIRCUMSTANCES ARE THE WORST POSSIBLE TIME TO GO RUNNING FOR SHELTER UNDER MAGIC.
I'LL USE WHAT'S LEFT OF MY BRAIN, THANKS.

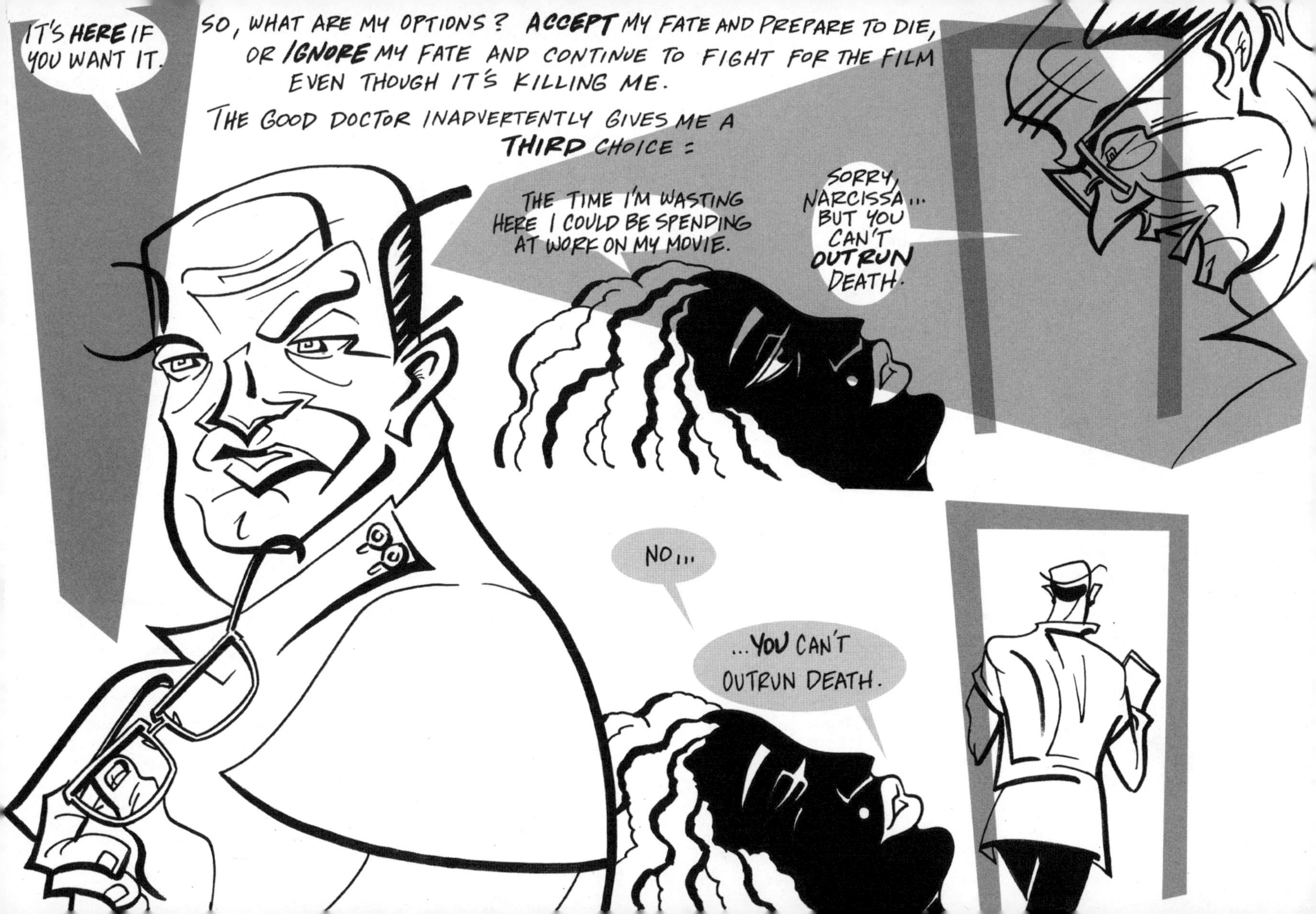
IT'S HERE IF YOU WANT IT.
SO, WHAT ARE MY OPTIONS? ACCEPT MY FATE AND PREPARE TO DIE, OR IGNORE MY FATE AND CONTINUE TO FIGHT FOR THE FILM EVEN THOUGH IT'S KILLING ME.
THE GOOD DOCTOR INADVERTENTLY GIVES ME A THIRD CHOICE:
THE TIME I'M WASTING HERE I COULD BE SPENDING AT WORK ON MY MOVIE.
SORRY, NARCISSA... BUT YOU CAN'T OUTRUN DEATH.
NO...
...YOU CAN'T OUTRUN DEATH.

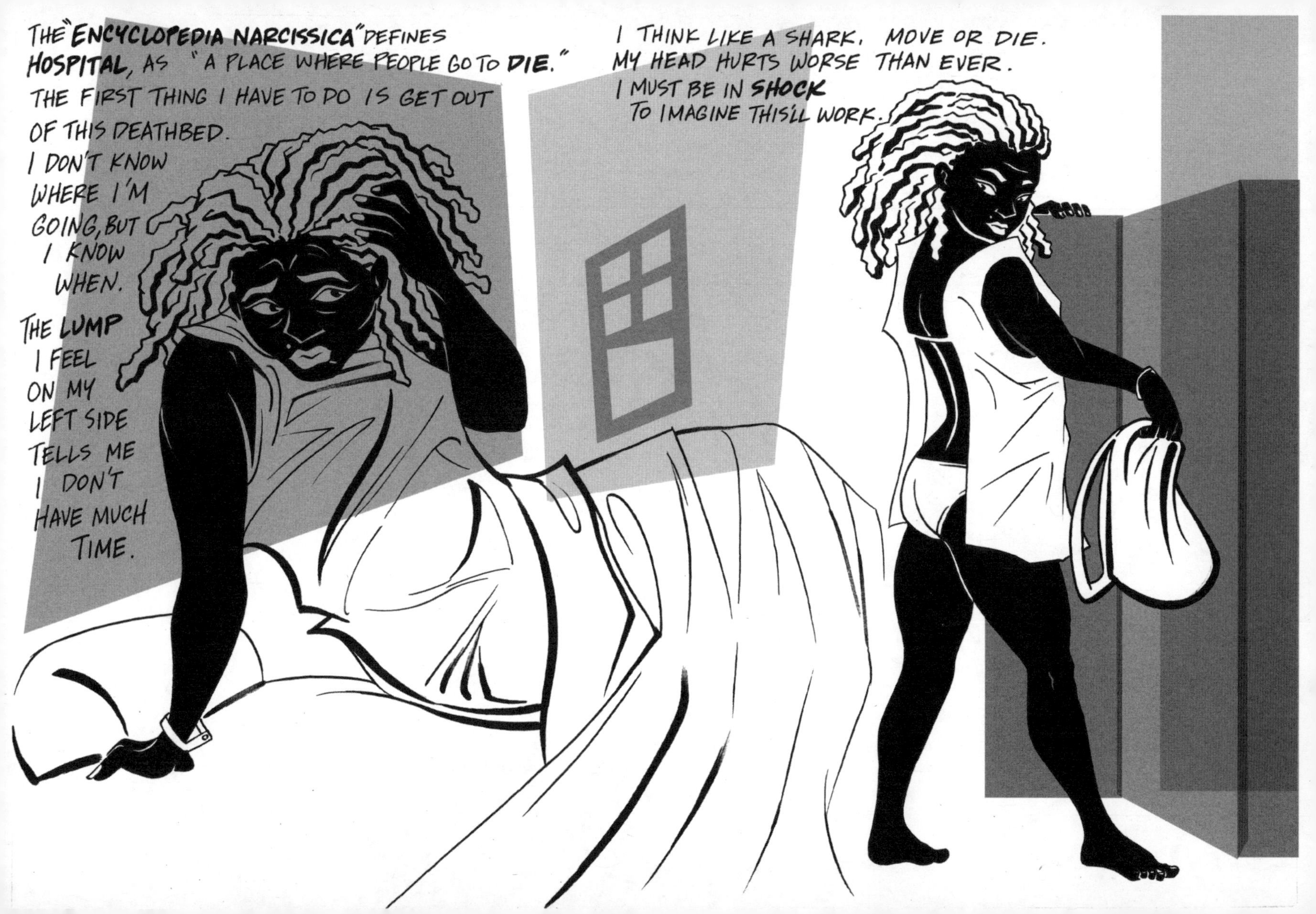
THE "ENCYCLOPEDIA NARCISSICA" DEFINES HOSPITAL, AS "A PLACE WHERE PEOPLE GO TO DIE."
THE FIRST THING I HAVE TO DO IS GET OUT OF THIS DEATHBED.
I DON'T KNOW WHERE I'M GOING, BUT I KNOW WHEN.
THE LUMP I FEEL ON MY LEFT SIDE TELLS ME I DON'T HAVE MUCH TIME.
I THINK LIKE A SHARK. MOVE OR DIE.
MY HEAD HURTS WORSE THAN EVER.
I MUST BE IN SHOCK TO IMAGINE THIS'LL WORK.

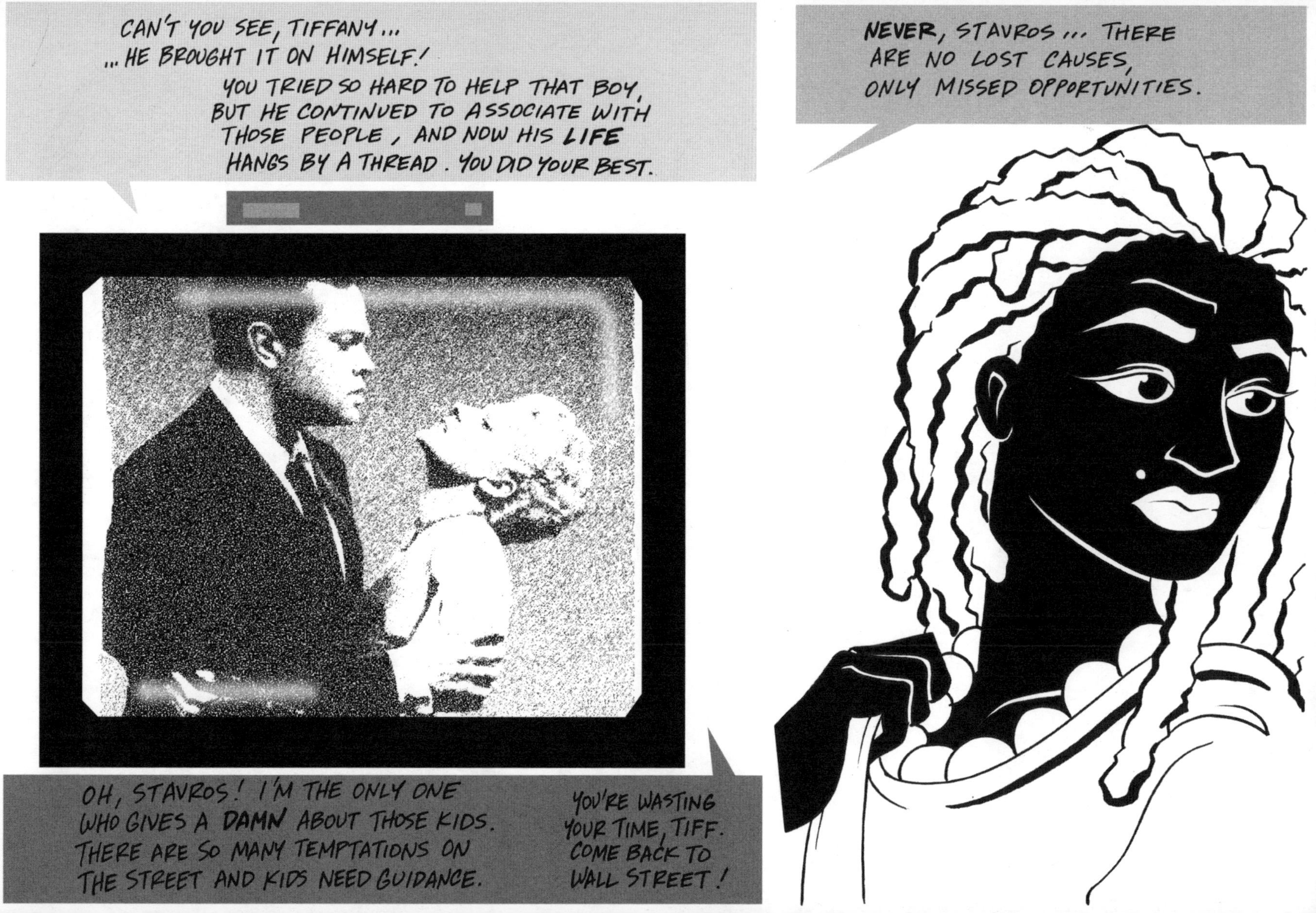
CAN'T YOU SEE, TIFFANY... ...HE BROUGHT IT ON HIMSELF!
YOU TRIED SO HARD TO HELP THAT BOY, BUT HE CONTINUED TO ASSOCIATE WITH THOSE PEOPLE, AND NOW HIS **LIFE** HANGS BY A THREAD. YOU DID YOUR BEST.
OH, STAVROS! I'M THE ONLY ONE WHO GIVES A **DAMN** ABOUT THOSE KIDS. THERE ARE SO MANY TEMPTATIONS ON THE STREET AND KIDS NEED GUIDANCE.
YOU'RE WASTING YOUR TIME, TIFF. COME BACK TO WALL STREET!
NEVER, STAVROS... THERE ARE NO LOST CAUSES, ONLY MISSED OPPORTUNITIES.

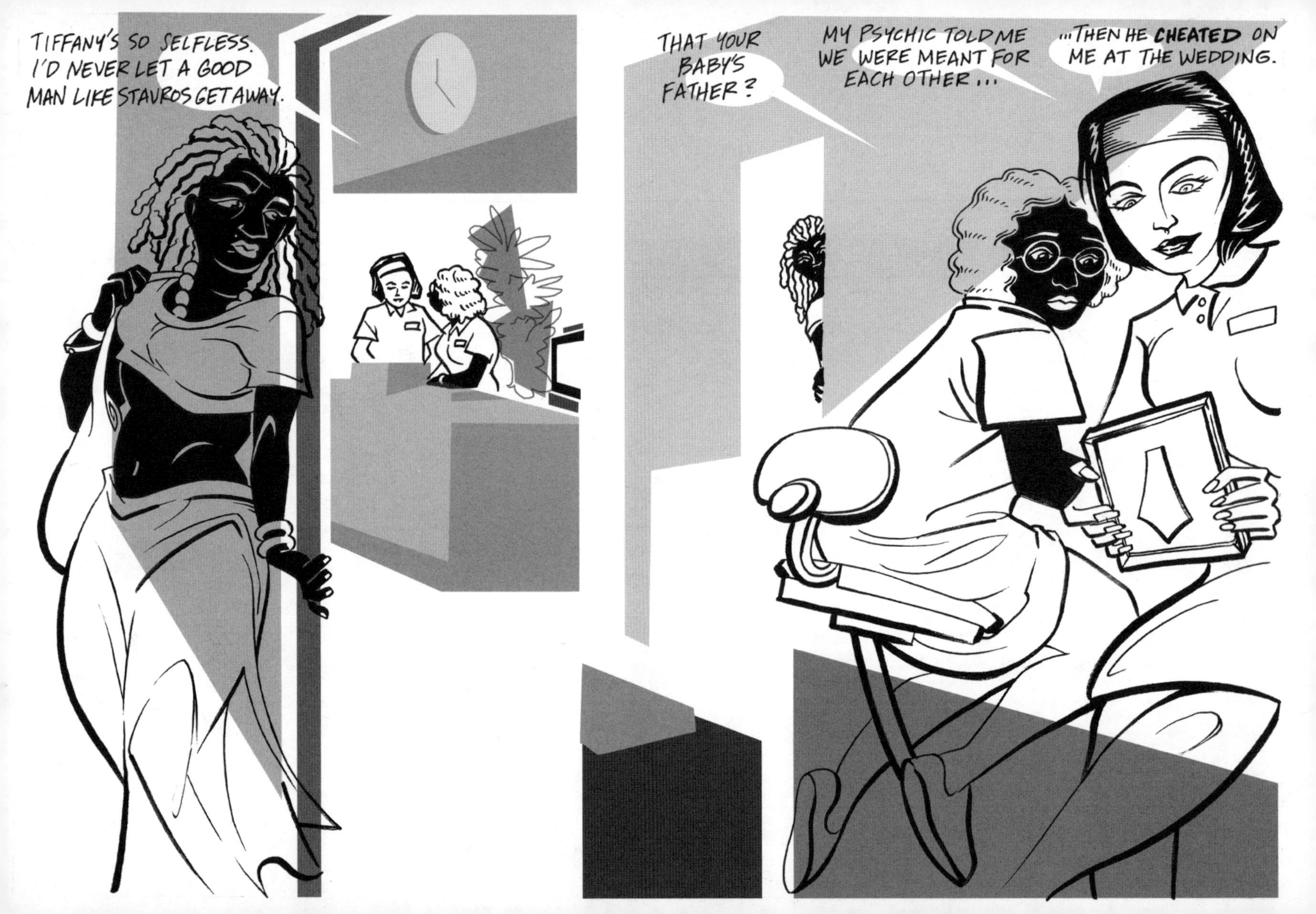
TIFFANY'S SO SELFLESS. I'D NEVER LET A GOOD MAN LIKE STAVROS GET AWAY.
THAT YOUR BABY'S FATHER?
MY PSYCHIC TOLD ME WE WERE MEANT FOR EACH OTHER...
...THEN HE **CHEATED** ON ME AT THE WEDDING.

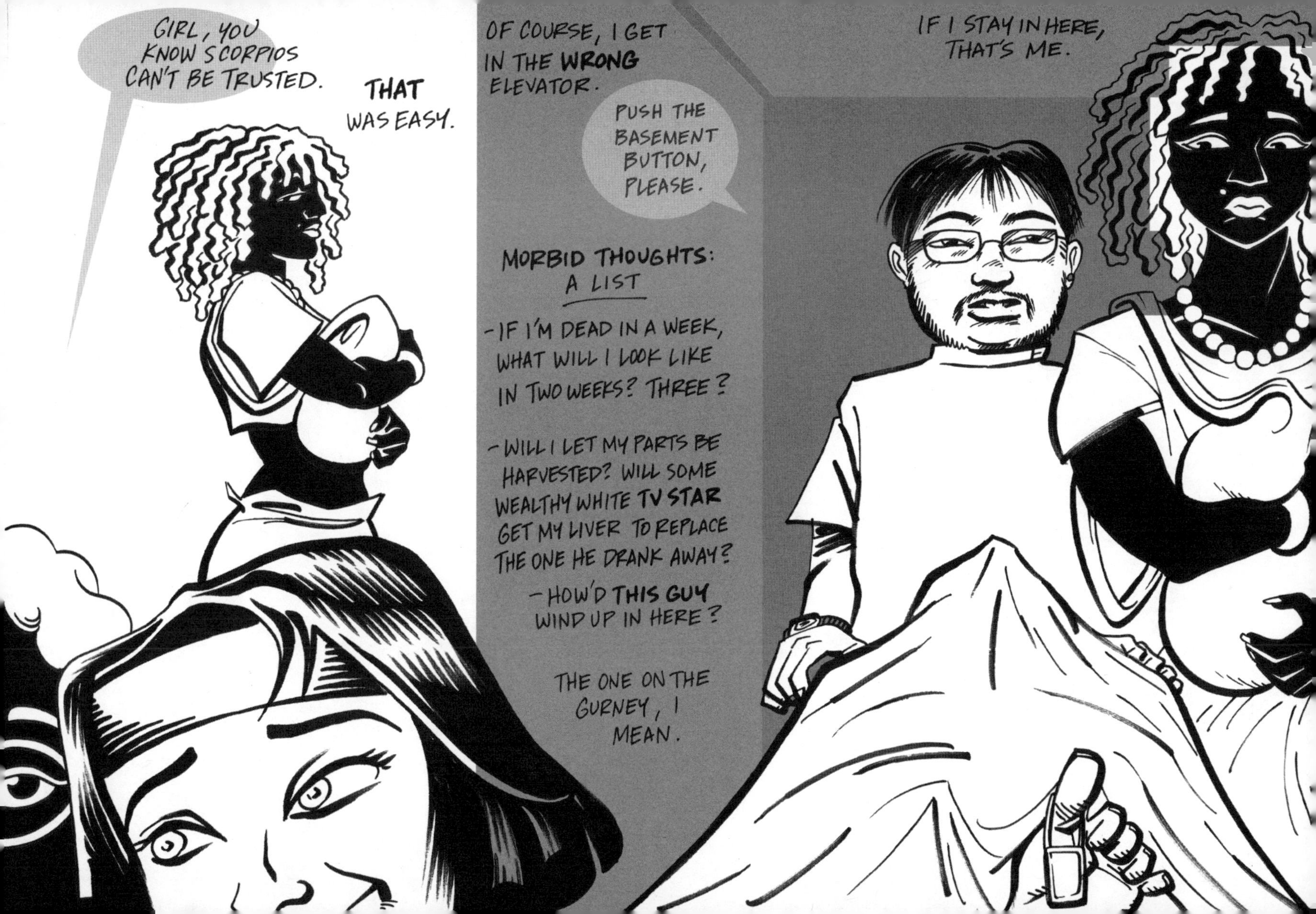
GIRL, YOU KNOW SCORPIOS CAN'T BE TRUSTED.
THAT WAS EASY.
OF COURSE, I GET IN THE WRONG ELEVATOR.
PUSH THE BASEMENT BUTTON, PLEASE.
MORBID THOUGHTS: A LIST
-IF I'M DEAD IN A WEEK, WHAT WILL I LOOK LIKE IN TWO WEEKS? THREE?
-WILL I LET MY PARTS BE HARVESTED? WILL SOME WEALTHY WHITE TV STAR GET MY LIVER TO REPLACE THE ONE HE DRANK AWAY?
-HOW'D THIS GUY WIND UP IN HERE?
THE ONE ON THE GURNEY, I MEAN.
IF I STAY IN HERE, THAT'S ME.

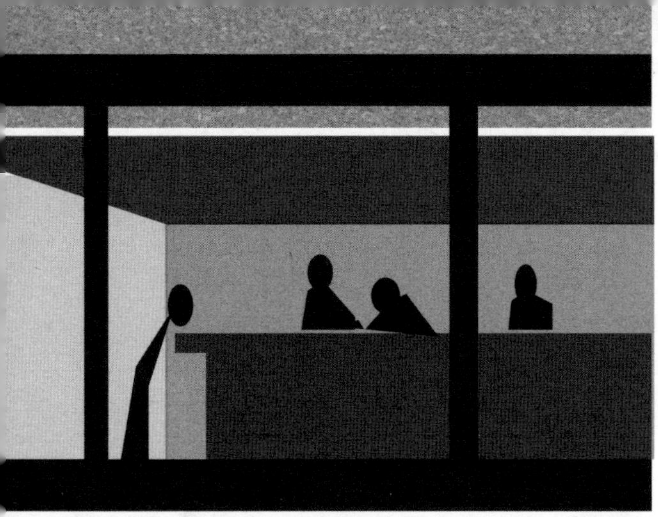
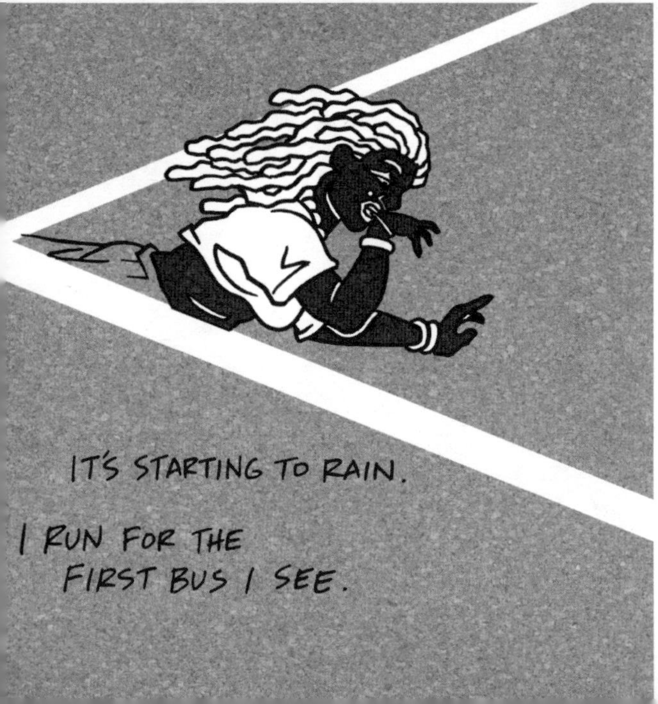
IT'S STARTING TO RAIN.
I RUN FOR THE FIRST BUS I SEE.
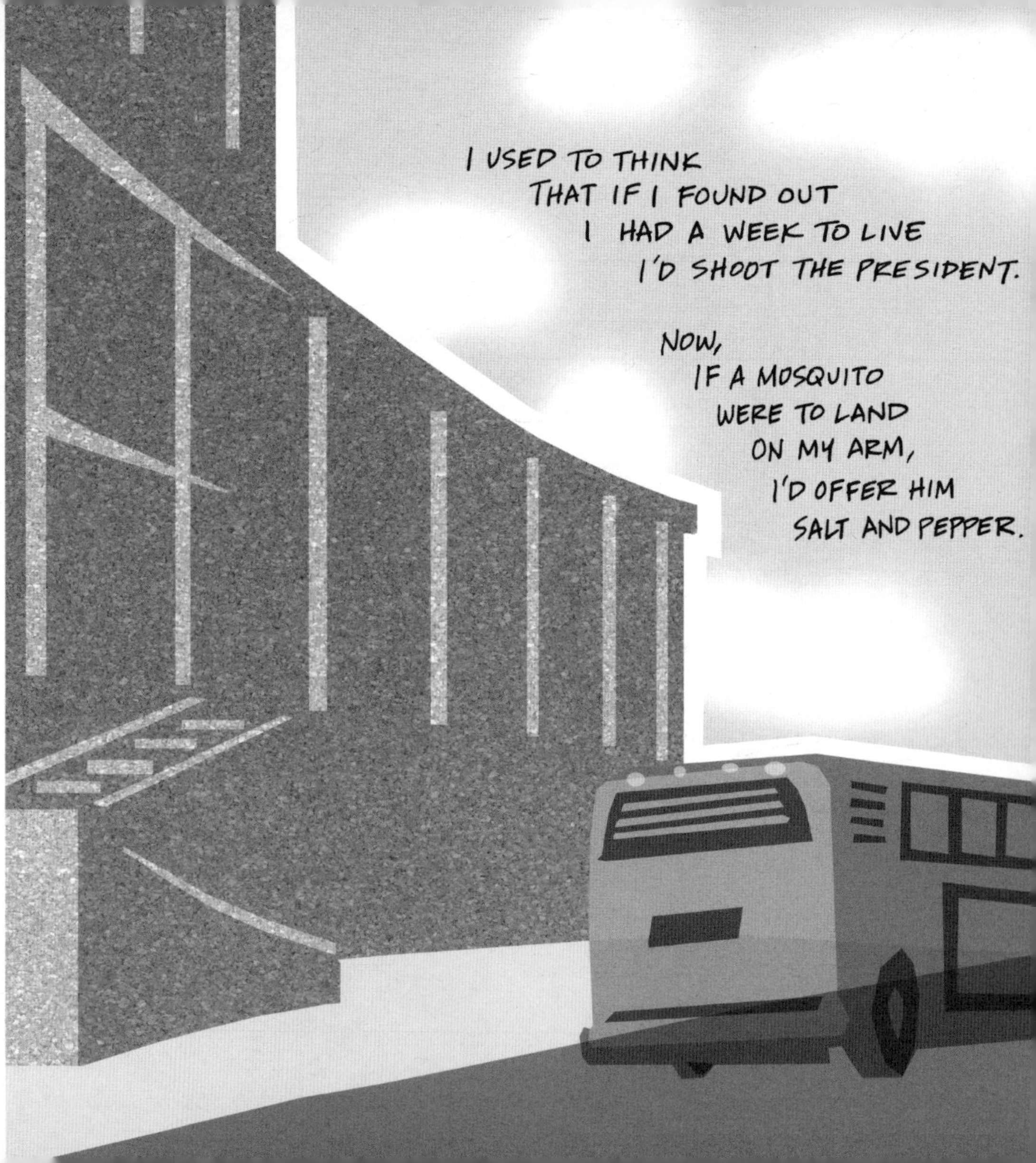
I USED TO THINK THAT IF I FOUND OUT I HAD A WEEK TO LIVE I'D SHOOT THE PRESIDENT.
NOW, IF A MOSQUITO WERE TO LAND ON MY ARM, I'D OFFER HIM SALT AND PEPPER.

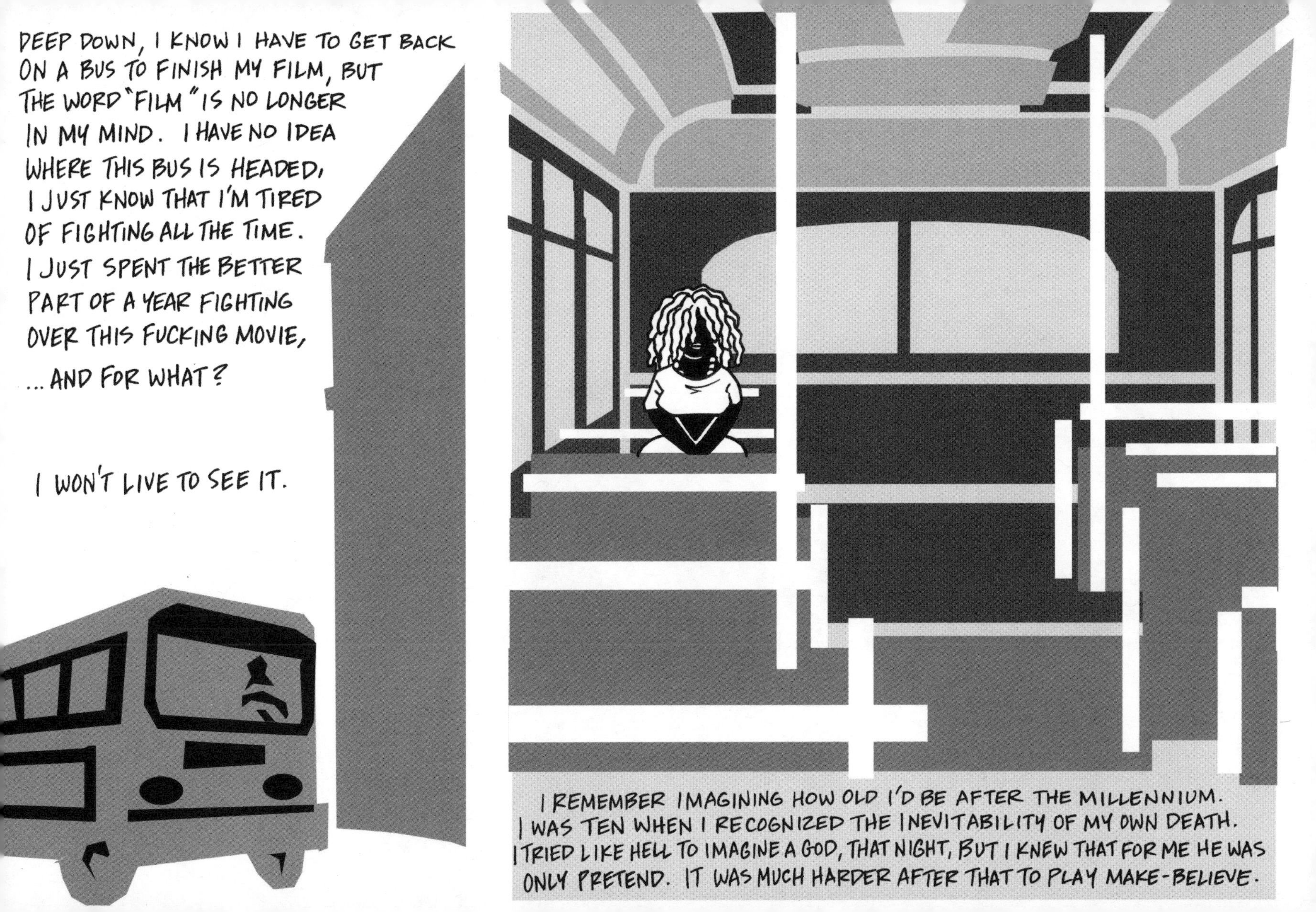
DEEP DOWN, I KNOW I HAVE TO GET BACK ON A BUS TO FINISH MY FILM, BUT THE WORD "FILM" IS NO LONGER IN MY MIND. I HAVE NO IDEA WHERE THIS BUS IS HEADED, I JUST KNOW THAT I'M TIRED OF FIGHTING ALL THE TIME. I JUST SPENT THE BETTER PART OF A YEAR FIGHTING OVER THIS FUCKING MOVIE,
... AND FOR WHAT?
I WON'T LIVE TO SEE IT.
I REMEMBER IMAGINING HOW OLD I'D BE AFTER THE MILLENNIUM. I WAS TEN WHEN I RECOGNIZED THE INEVITABILITY OF MY OWN DEATH. I TRIED LIKE HELL TO IMAGINE A GOD, THAT NIGHT, BUT I KNEW THAT FOR ME HE WAS ONLY PRETEND. IT WAS MUCH HARDER AFTER THAT TO PLAY MAKE-BELIEVE.

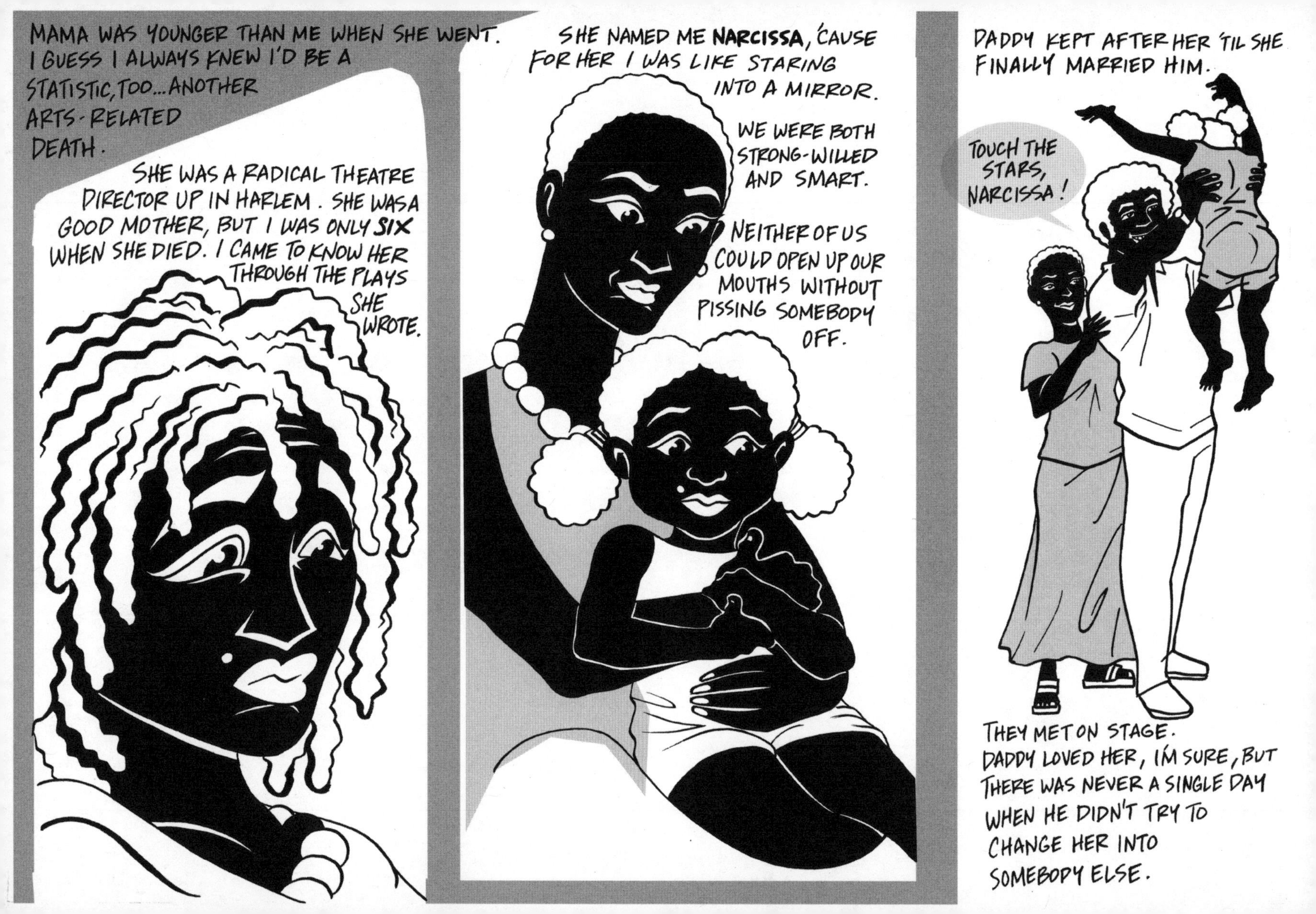
MAMA WAS YOUNGER THAN ME WHEN SHE WENT. I GUESS I ALWAYS KNEW I'D BE A STATISTIC, TOO... ANOTHER ARTS-RELATED DEATH.
SHE WAS A RADICAL THEATRE DIRECTOR UP IN HARLEM. SHE WAS A GOOD MOTHER, BUT I WAS ONLY **SIX** WHEN SHE DIED. I CAME TO KNOW HER THROUGH THE PLAYS SHE WROTE.
SHE NAMED ME **NARCISSA**, 'CAUSE FOR HER I WAS LIKE STARING INTO A MIRROR.
WE WERE BOTH STRONG-WILLED AND SMART.
NEITHER OF US COULD OPEN UP OUR MOUTHS WITHOUT PISSING SOMEBODY OFF.
DADDY KEPT AFTER HER 'TIL SHE FINALLY MARRIED HIM.
TOUCH THE STARS, NARCISSA!
THEY MET ON STAGE. DADDY LOVED HER, I'M SURE, BUT THERE WAS NEVER A SINGLE DAY WHEN HE DIDN'T TRY TO CHANGE HER INTO SOMEBODY ELSE.

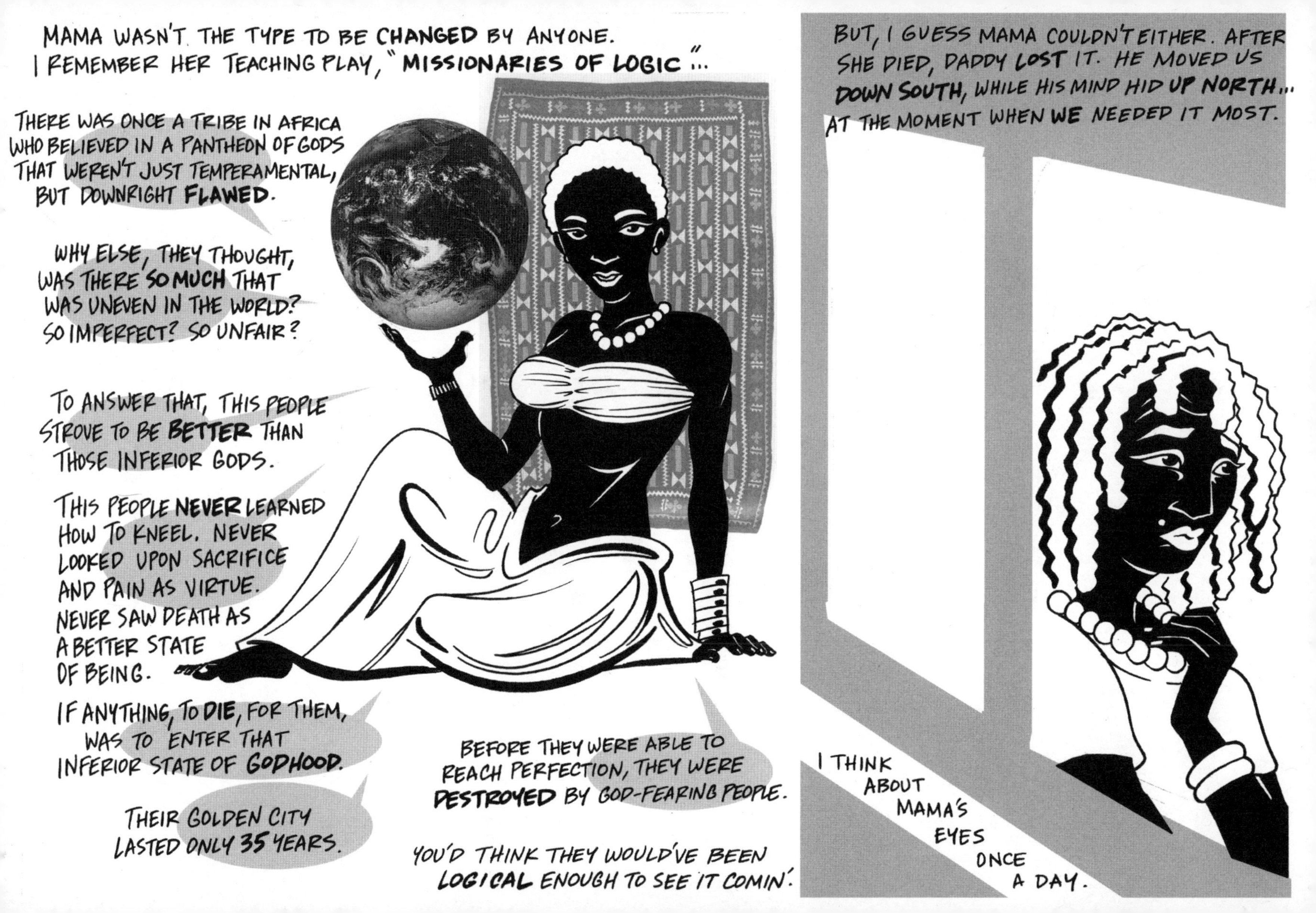
MAMA WASN'T THE TYPE TO BE CHANGED BY ANYONE. I REMEMBER HER TEACHING PLAY, "MISSIONARIES OF LOGIC"...
THERE WAS ONCE A TRIBE IN AFRICA WHO BELIEVED IN A PANTHEON OF GODS THAT WEREN'T JUST TEMPERAMENTAL, BUT DOWNRIGHT FLAWED.
WHY ELSE, THEY THOUGHT, WAS THERE SO MUCH THAT WAS UNEVEN IN THE WORLD? SO IMPERFECT? SO UNFAIR?
TO ANSWER THAT, THIS PEOPLE STROVE TO BE BETTER THAN THOSE INFERIOR GODS.
THIS PEOPLE NEVER LEARNED HOW TO KNEEL. NEVER LOOKED UPON SACRIFICE AND PAIN AS VIRTUE. NEVER SAW DEATH AS A BETTER STATE OF BEING.
IF ANYTHING, TO DIE, FOR THEM, WAS TO ENTER THAT INFERIOR STATE OF GODHOOD.
THEIR GOLDEN CITY LASTED ONLY 35 YEARS.
BEFORE THEY WERE ABLE TO REACH PERFECTION, THEY WERE DESTROYED BY GOD-FEARING PEOPLE.
YOU'D THINK THEY WOULD'VE BEEN LOGICAL ENOUGH TO SEE IT COMIN'.
BUT, I GUESS MAMA COULDN'T EITHER. AFTER SHE DIED, DADDY LOST IT. HE MOVED US DOWN SOUTH, WHILE HIS MIND HID UP NORTH... AT THE MOMENT WHEN WE NEEDED IT MOST.
I THINK ABOUT MAMA'S EYES ONCE A DAY.

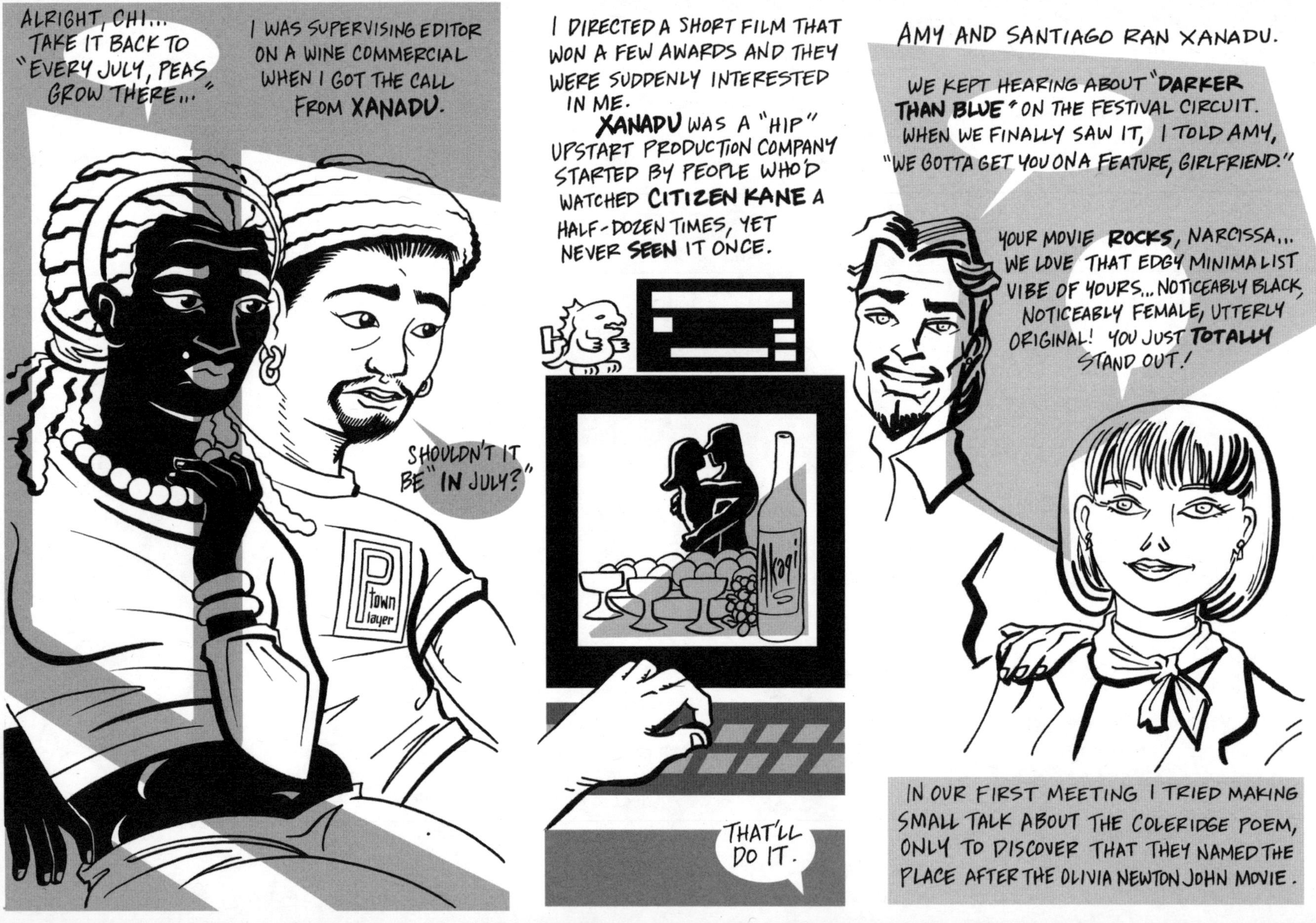
ALRIGHT, CHI... TAKE IT BACK TO "EVERY JULY, PEAS GROW THERE..."
I WAS SUPERVISING EDITOR ON A WINE COMMERCIAL WHEN I GOT THE CALL FROM XANADU.
SHOULDN'T IT BE "IN JULY?"
P town layer
I DIRECTED A SHORT FILM THAT WON A FEW AWARDS AND THEY WERE SUDDENLY INTERESTED IN ME.
XANADU WAS A "HIP" UPSTART PRODUCTION COMPANY STARTED BY PEOPLE WHO'D WATCHED CITIZEN KANE A HALF-DOZEN TIMES, YET NEVER SEEN IT ONCE.
Akagi
THAT'LL DO IT.
AMY AND SANTIAGO RAN XANADU.
WE KEPT HEARING ABOUT "DARKER THAN BLUE" ON THE FESTIVAL CIRCUIT. WHEN WE FINALLY SAW IT, I TOLD AMY, "WE GOTTA GET YOU ON A FEATURE, GIRLFRIEND."
YOUR MOVIE ROCKS, NARCISSA... WE LOVE THAT EDGY MINIMALIST VIBE OF YOURS... NOTICEABLY BLACK, NOTICEABLY FEMALE, UTTERLY ORIGINAL! YOU JUST TOTALLY STAND OUT!
IN OUR FIRST MEETING I TRIED MAKING SMALL TALK ABOUT THE COLERIDGE POEM, ONLY TO DISCOVER THAT THEY NAMED THE PLACE AFTER THE OLIVIA NEWTON JOHN MOVIE.

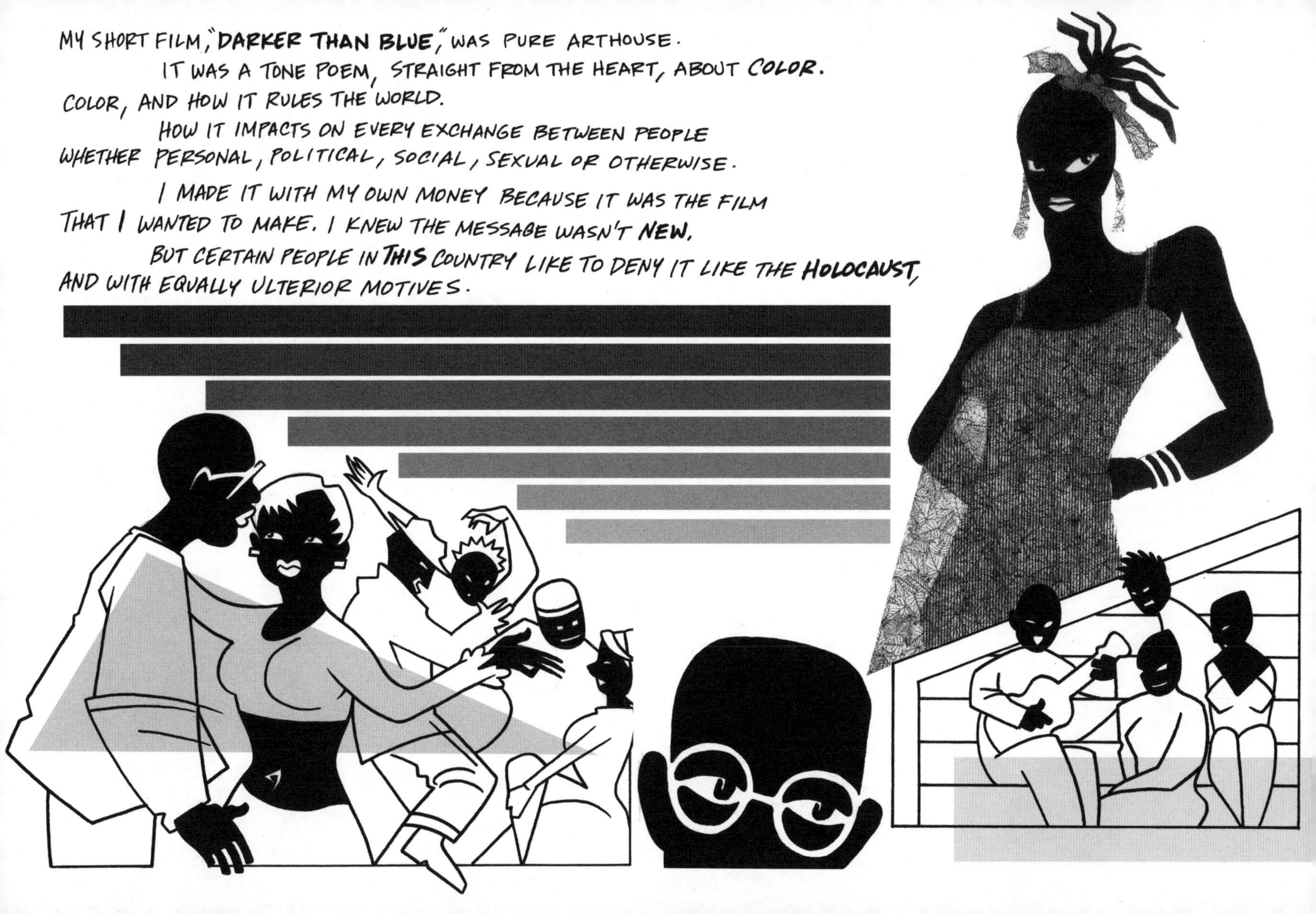
MY SHORT FILM, "DARKER THAN BLUE," WAS PURE ARTHOUSE.
IT WAS A TONE POEM, STRAIGHT FROM THE HEART, ABOUT COLOR.
COLOR, AND HOW IT RULES THE WORLD.
HOW IT IMPACTS ON EVERY EXCHANGE BETWEEN PEOPLE WHETHER PERSONAL, POLITICAL, SOCIAL, SEXUAL OR OTHERWISE.
I MADE IT WITH MY OWN MONEY BECAUSE IT WAS THE FILM THAT I WANTED TO MAKE. I KNEW THE MESSAGE WASN'T NEW.
BUT CERTAIN PEOPLE IN THIS COUNTRY LIKE TO DENY IT LIKE THE HOLOCAUST, AND WITH EQUALLY ULTERIOR MOTIVES.

IT'S BEEN MY EXPERIENCE IN A SHORT LIFETIME OF OBSERVING **CORPORATE FOLK**, THAT THEY WILL DO SOMETHING FOR YOU FOR ONLY ONE OF **TWO** REASONS:

EITHER YOU HAVE SOMETHING THAT THEY **WANT** OR SOMETHING THAT THEY'RE **AFRAID OF.**

SO **WHAT** DID "**XANADU**" WANT FROM **ME**?

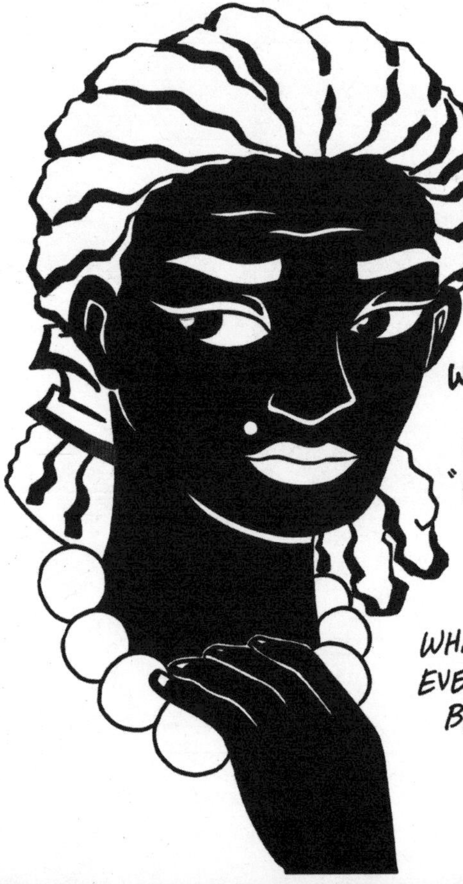

WELL... IT WAS A MATTER OF TIMING, REALLY. THE IDEA OF **MULTICULTURALISM** WAS, AT THAT MOMENT, A SALEABLE ONE IN AMERICAN BUSINESS.

THE CONCEPT OF **BLACK** OR "**NEGRO**" HAS ALWAYS BEEN USED TO SELL STUFF HERE, **WHITES**, OF COURSE, BEING THE TARGET MARKET. THEY WANT TO SEE PEOPLE WITH "**FEELINGS**" AND NO ONE "**FEELS**" LIKE A "**NEGRO**."

IN THE **NEW CENTURY** HOWEVER, WHAT'S SELLING IS "**OLD GLORY**" IN EVERY SENSE OF THE PHRASE. **XANADU** BELONGED TO THE TWENTIETH CENTURY AND THEY HADN'T YET SMELLED THE BOMBS BURSTING IN AIR. IF THEY HAD, THEY NEVER WOULD'VE MADE ME THE OFFER.

XANADU STARTED OUT IN THE NINETIES WITH A HORRORFILM, FOLLOWED BY A TEEN FILM. THEY MADE A HALF DOZEN VARIATIONS ON THE "WHITE GIRL AND WHITE BOY IN A RED CAR WITH A BLACK GUN" FILM, OR THE "WARM AND FUZZY WHITE FAMILY THAT KEEPS AN OLD BLACK WOMAN AS A PET" FILM.

THIS YEAR THEY WANTED TO PROJECT A MORE "**DIVERSE**" IDENTITY, SO THEY PUSHED FORWARD A LESBIAN FILM, AND ME. **WAY** BEHIND THE TIMES.

I'D HEARD IT **ALL** BEFORE. BY THE TIME THEY GOT TO THE PART OF THE SPEECH ABOUT "GIRLPOWER" AND "DIVERSITY" AND "SHAKING UP THE NATION", I'D HAD MY FILL.

I SURPRISED THEM BY SAYING **NO.**

THEY WANTED TO NEGOTIATE, SO I MADE THE MOST **OUTRAGEOUS** DEMANDS I COULD THINK OF FOR A FIRST-TIME DIRECTOR, FROM "GROSS POINTS" AND "PROFIT SHARES" TO "NAME ABOVE THE TITLE" AND "FINAL CUT", JUST TO MAKE THEM GO AWAY.

THEY SURPRISED **ME** BY SAYING **YES.**

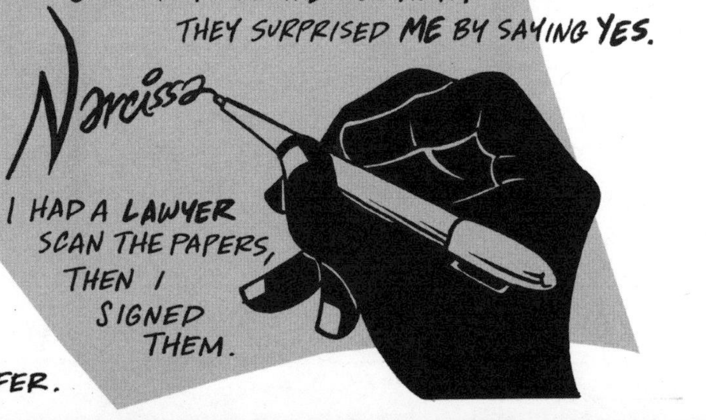
Narcissa

I HAD A **LAWYER** SCAN THE PAPERS, THEN I SIGNED THEM.

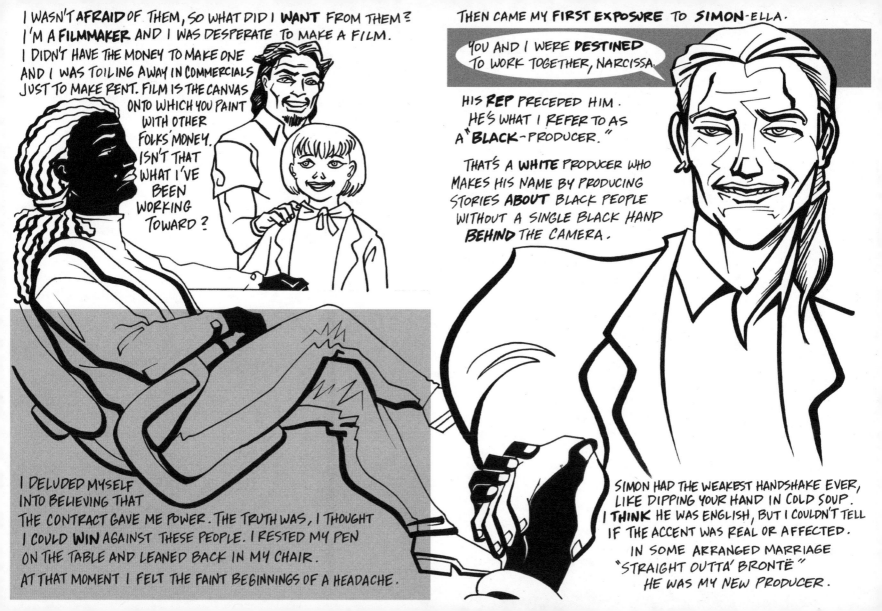

I WASN'T AFRAID OF THEM, SO WHAT DID I WANT FROM THEM? I'M A FILMMAKER AND I WAS DESPERATE TO MAKE A FILM. I DIDN'T HAVE THE MONEY TO MAKE ONE AND I WAS TOILING AWAY IN COMMERCIALS JUST TO MAKE RENT. FILM IS THE CANVAS ONTO WHICH YOU PAINT WITH OTHER FOLKS' MONEY. ISN'T THAT WHAT I'VE BEEN WORKING TOWARD?

I DELUDED MYSELF INTO BELIEVING THAT THE CONTRACT GAVE ME POWER. THE TRUTH WAS, I THOUGHT I COULD WIN AGAINST THESE PEOPLE. I RESTED MY PEN ON THE TABLE AND LEANED BACK IN MY CHAIR. AT THAT MOMENT I FELT THE FAINT BEGINNINGS OF A HEADACHE.

THEN CAME MY FIRST EXPOSURE TO SIMON-ELLA.

YOU AND I WERE DESTINED TO WORK TOGETHER, NARCISSA.

HIS REP PRECEDED HIM. HE'S WHAT I REFER TO AS A "BLACK-PRODUCER."

THAT'S A WHITE PRODUCER WHO MAKES HIS NAME BY PRODUCING STORIES ABOUT BLACK PEOPLE WITHOUT A SINGLE BLACK HAND BEHIND THE CAMERA.

SIMON HAD THE WEAKEST HANDSHAKE EVER, LIKE DIPPING YOUR HAND IN COLD SOUP. I THINK HE WAS ENGLISH, BUT I COULDN'T TELL IF THE ACCENT WAS REAL OR AFFECTED. IN SOME ARRANGED MARRIAGE "STRAIGHT OUTTA' BRONTË" HE WAS MY NEW PRODUCER.

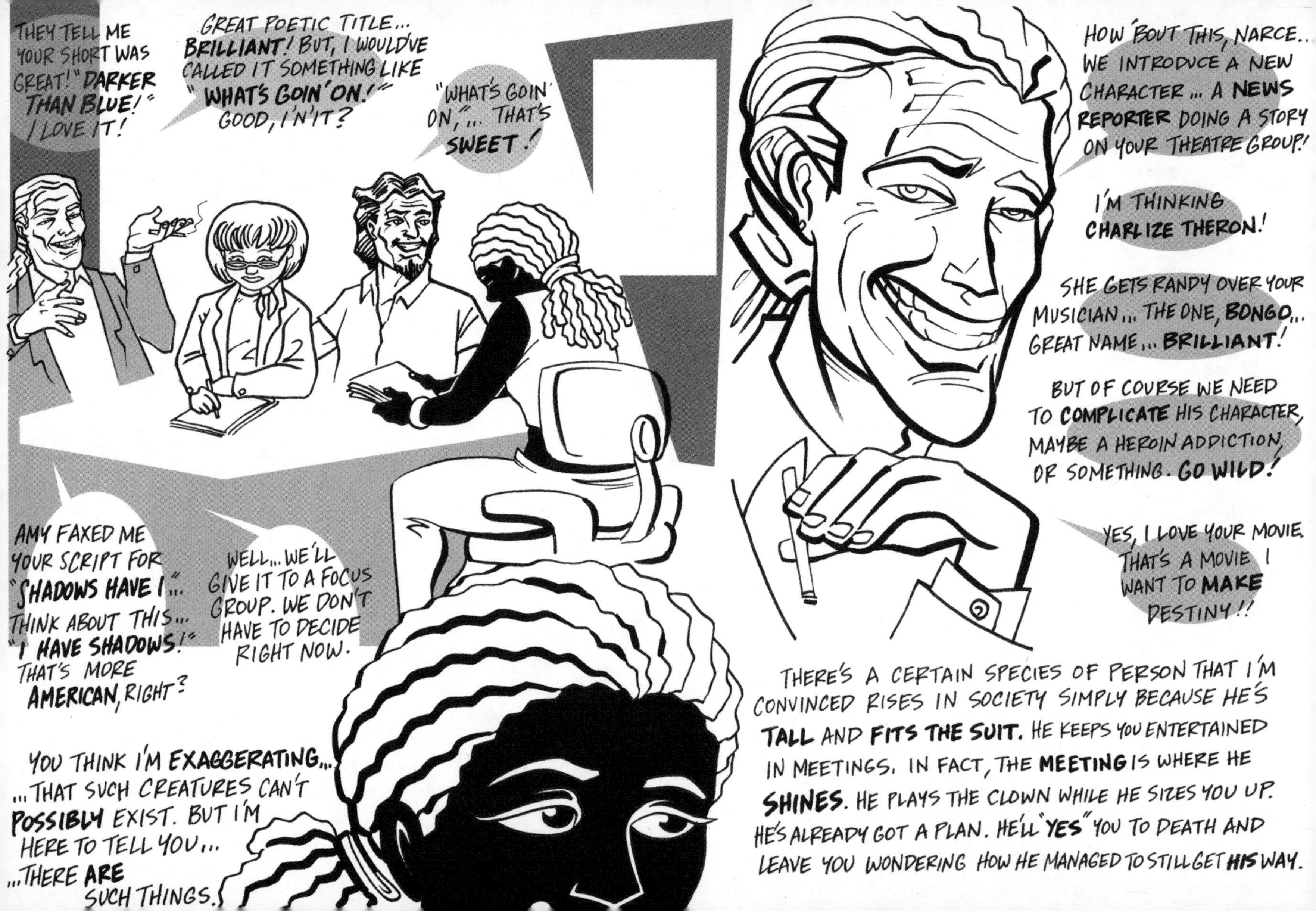
THEY TELL ME YOUR SHORT WAS GREAT! "DARKER THAN BLUE!" I LOVE IT!
GREAT POETIC TITLE... BRILLIANT! BUT, I WOULD'VE CALLED IT SOMETHING LIKE "WHAT'S GOIN' ON!" GOOD, I'N'IT?
"WHAT'S GOIN' ON,"... THAT'S SWEET!
AMY FAXED ME YOUR SCRIPT FOR "SHADOWS HAVE I"... THINK ABOUT THIS... "I HAVE SHADOWS!" THAT'S MORE AMERICAN, RIGHT?
WELL... WE'LL GIVE IT TO A FOCUS GROUP. WE DON'T HAVE TO DECIDE RIGHT NOW.
YOU THINK I'M EXAGGERATING... ...THAT SUCH CREATURES CAN'T POSSIBLY EXIST. BUT I'M HERE TO TELL YOU... ...THERE ARE SUCH THINGS.
HOW 'BOUT THIS, NARCE... WE INTRODUCE A NEW CHARACTER... A NEWS REPORTER DOING A STORY ON YOUR THEATRE GROUP!
I'M THINKING CHARLIZE THERON!
SHE GETS RANDY OVER YOUR MUSICIAN... THE ONE, BONGO... GREAT NAME... BRILLIANT!
BUT OF COURSE WE NEED TO COMPLICATE HIS CHARACTER, MAYBE A HEROIN ADDICTION, OR SOMETHING. GO WILD!
YES, I LOVE YOUR MOVIE. THAT'S A MOVIE I WANT TO MAKE DESTINY!!
THERE'S A CERTAIN SPECIES OF PERSON THAT I'M CONVINCED RISES IN SOCIETY SIMPLY BECAUSE HE'S TALL AND FITS THE SUIT. HE KEEPS YOU ENTERTAINED IN MEETINGS. IN FACT, THE MEETING IS WHERE HE SHINES. HE PLAYS THE CLOWN WHILE HE SIZES YOU UP. HE'S ALREADY GOT A PLAN. HE'LL "YES" YOU TO DEATH AND LEAVE YOU WONDERING HOW HE MANAGED TO STILL GET HIS WAY.

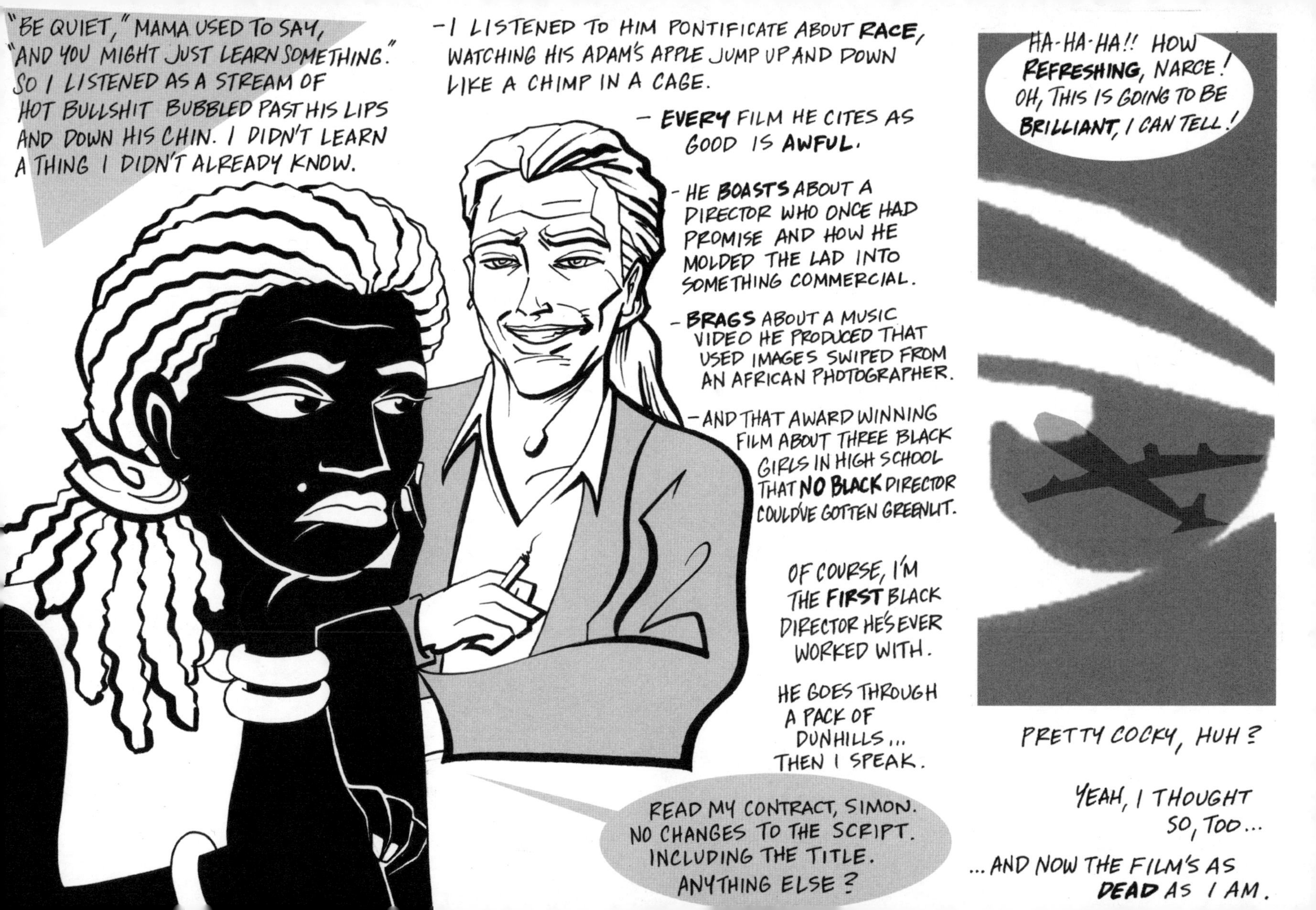
"BE QUIET," MAMA USED TO SAY, "AND YOU MIGHT JUST LEARN SOMETHING." SO I LISTENED AS A STREAM OF HOT BULLSHIT BUBBLED PAST HIS LIPS AND DOWN HIS CHIN. I DIDN'T LEARN A THING I DIDN'T ALREADY KNOW.
–I LISTENED TO HIM PONTIFICATE ABOUT **RACE**, WATCHING HIS ADAM'S APPLE JUMP UP AND DOWN LIKE A CHIMP IN A CAGE.
– **EVERY** FILM HE CITES AS GOOD IS **AWFUL**.
- HE **BOASTS** ABOUT A DIRECTOR WHO ONCE HAD PROMISE AND HOW HE MOLDED THE LAD INTO SOMETHING COMMERCIAL.
- **BRAGS** ABOUT A MUSIC VIDEO HE PRODUCED THAT USED IMAGES SWIPED FROM AN AFRICAN PHOTOGRAPHER.
–AND THAT AWARD WINNING FILM ABOUT THREE BLACK GIRLS IN HIGH SCHOOL THAT **NO BLACK** DIRECTOR COULD'VE GOTTEN GREENLIT.
OF COURSE, I'M THE **FIRST** BLACK DIRECTOR HE'S EVER WORKED WITH.
HE GOES THROUGH A PACK OF DUNHILLS... THEN I SPEAK.
READ MY CONTRACT, SIMON. NO CHANGES TO THE SCRIPT. INCLUDING THE TITLE. ANYTHING ELSE?
HA-HA-HA!! HOW **REFRESHING**, NARCE! OH, THIS IS GOING TO BE **BRILLIANT**, I CAN TELL!
PRETTY COCKY, HUH?
YEAH, I THOUGHT SO, TOO...
...AND NOW THE FILM'S AS **DEAD** AS I AM.

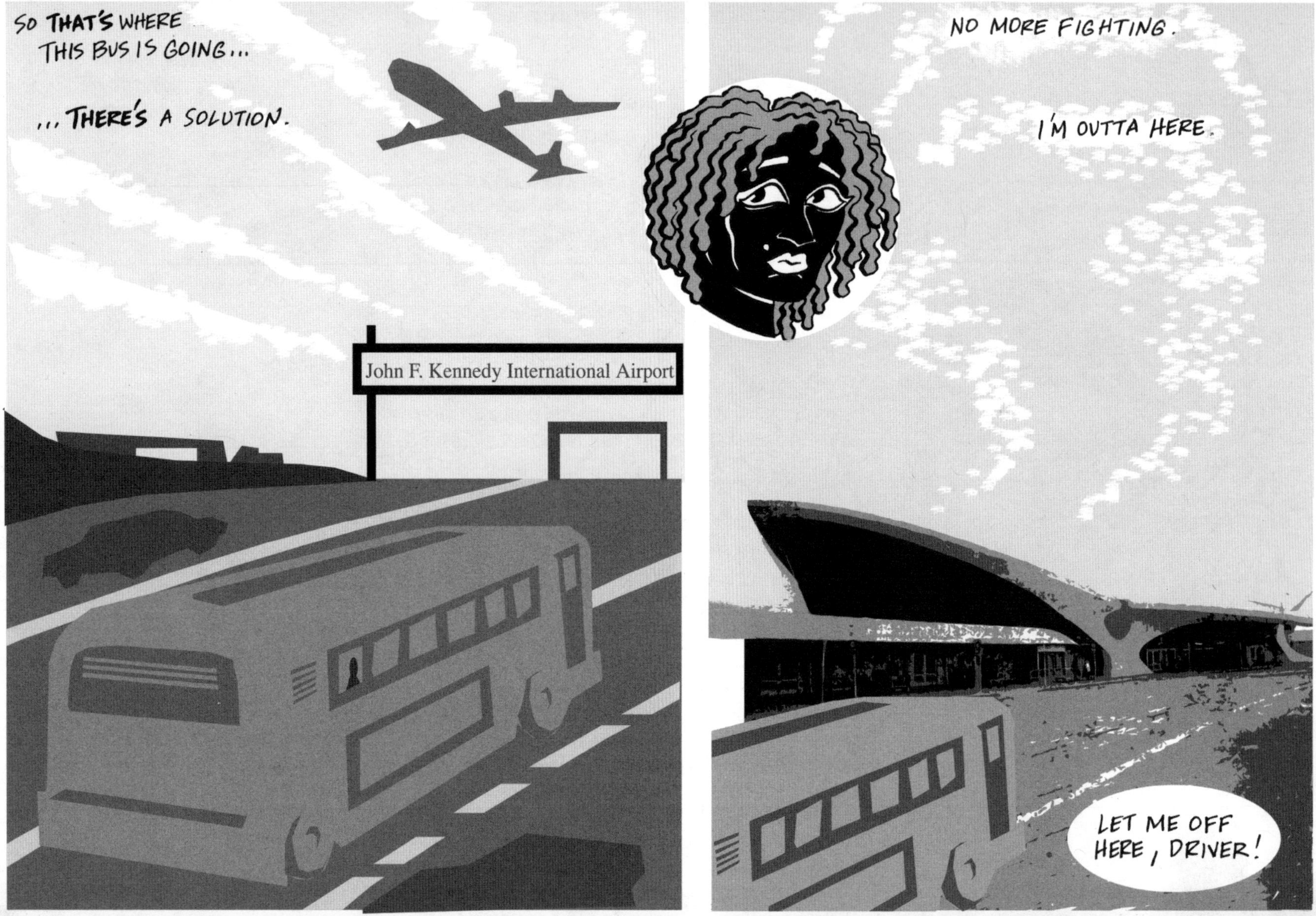
SO THAT'S WHERE THIS BUS IS GOING...
...THERE'S A SOLUTION.
John F. Kennedy International Airport
NO MORE FIGHTING.
I'M OUTTA HERE.
LET ME OFF HERE, DRIVER!

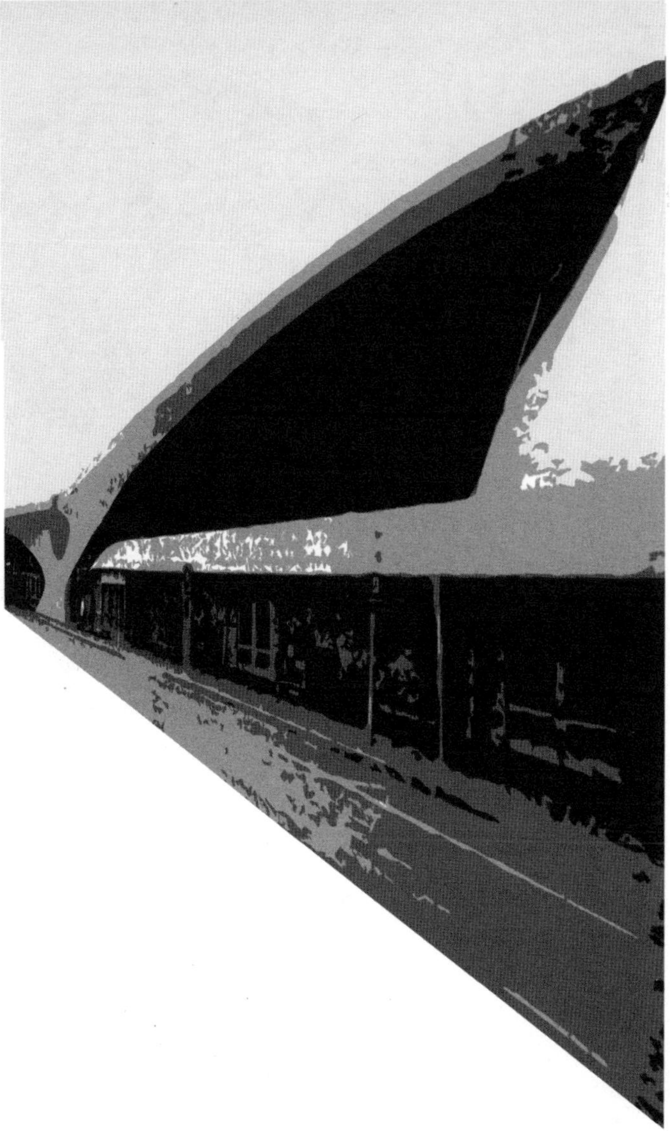

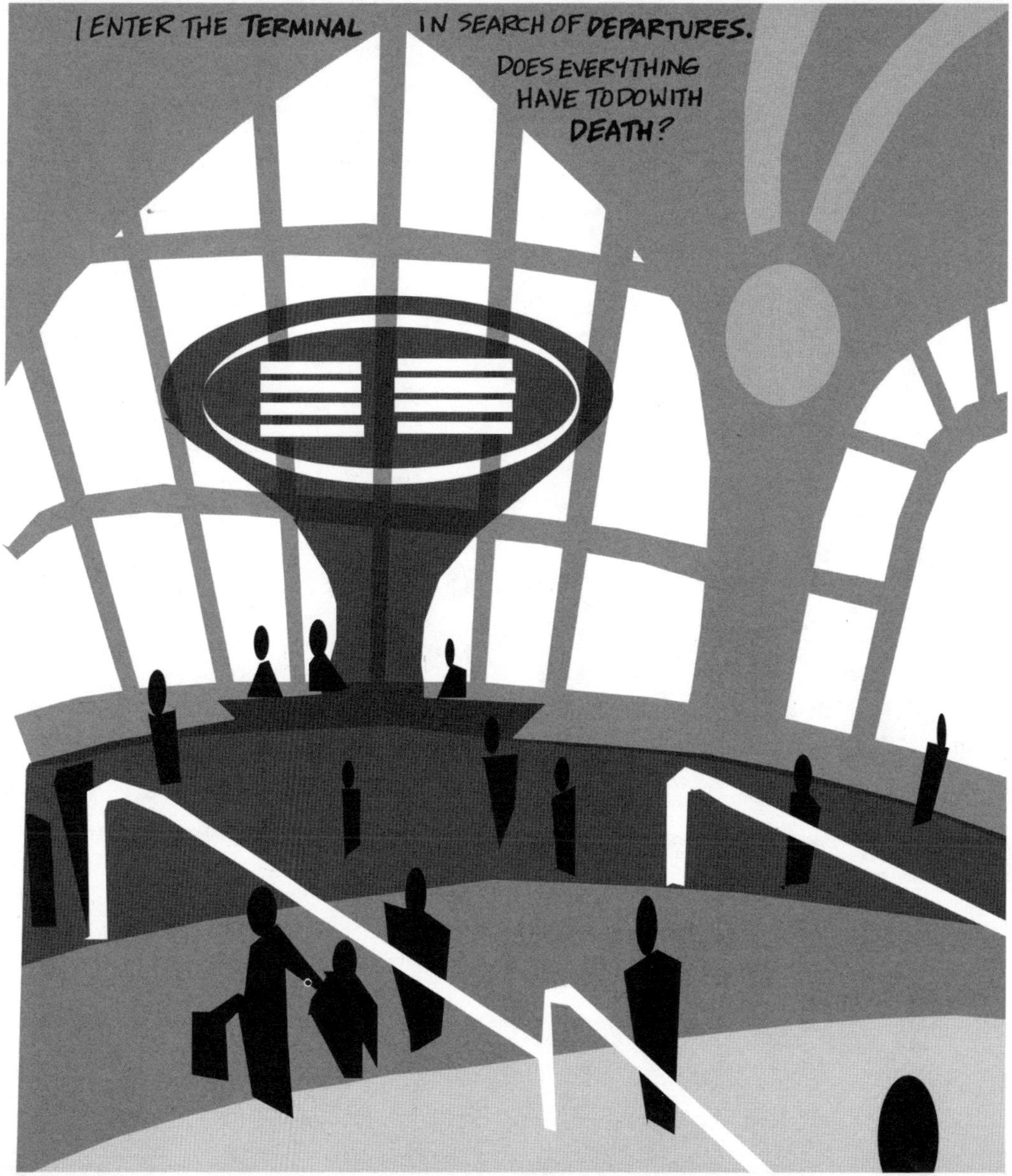
I ENTER THE TERMINAL IN SEARCH OF DEPARTURES.
DOES EVERYTHING HAVE TO DO WITH DEATH?

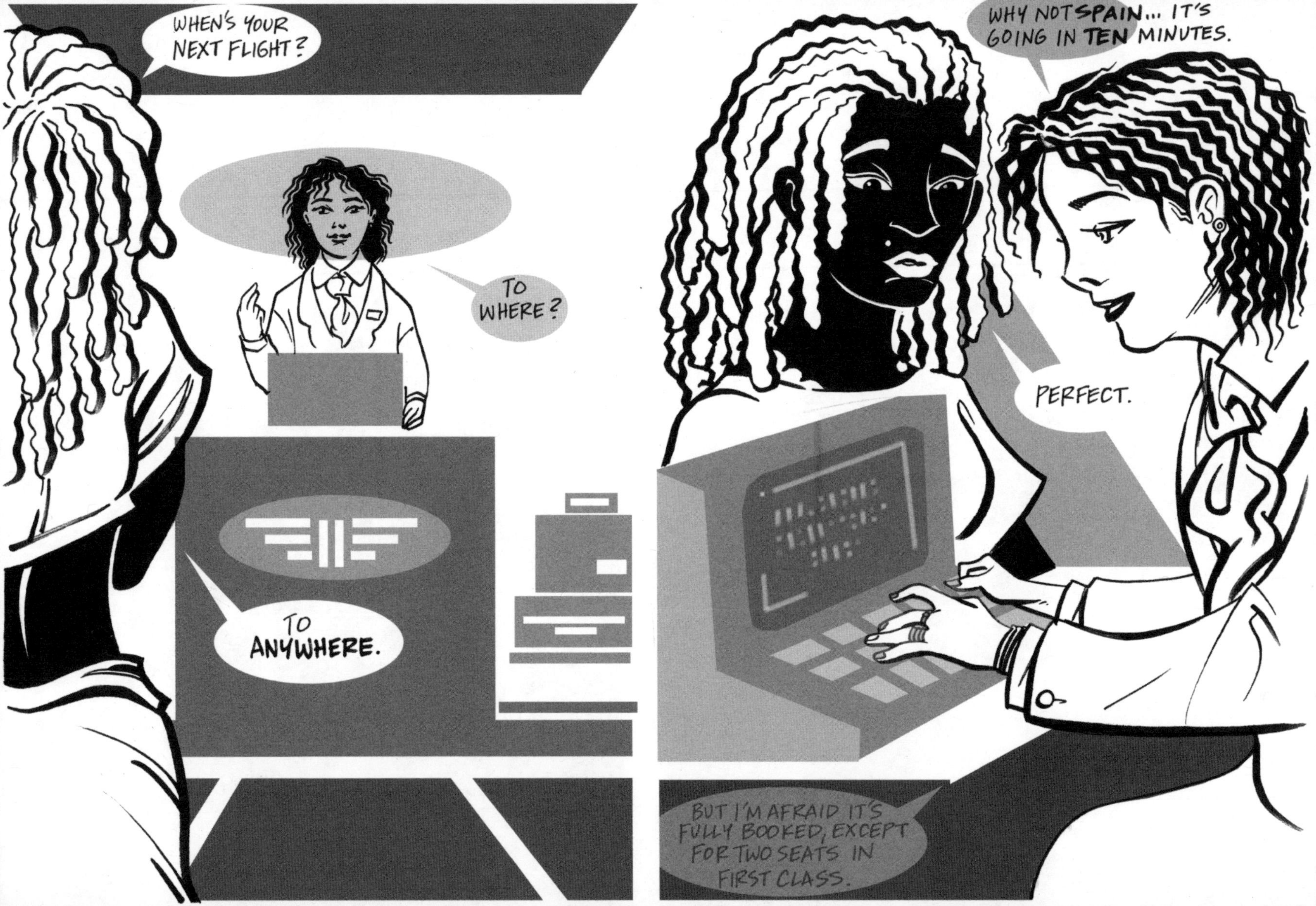
WHEN'S YOUR NEXT FLIGHT?
TO WHERE?
TO ANYWHERE.
WHY NOT SPAIN... IT'S GOING IN TEN MINUTES.
PERFECT.
BUT I'M AFRAID IT'S FULLY BOOKED, EXCEPT FOR TWO SEATS IN FIRST CLASS.

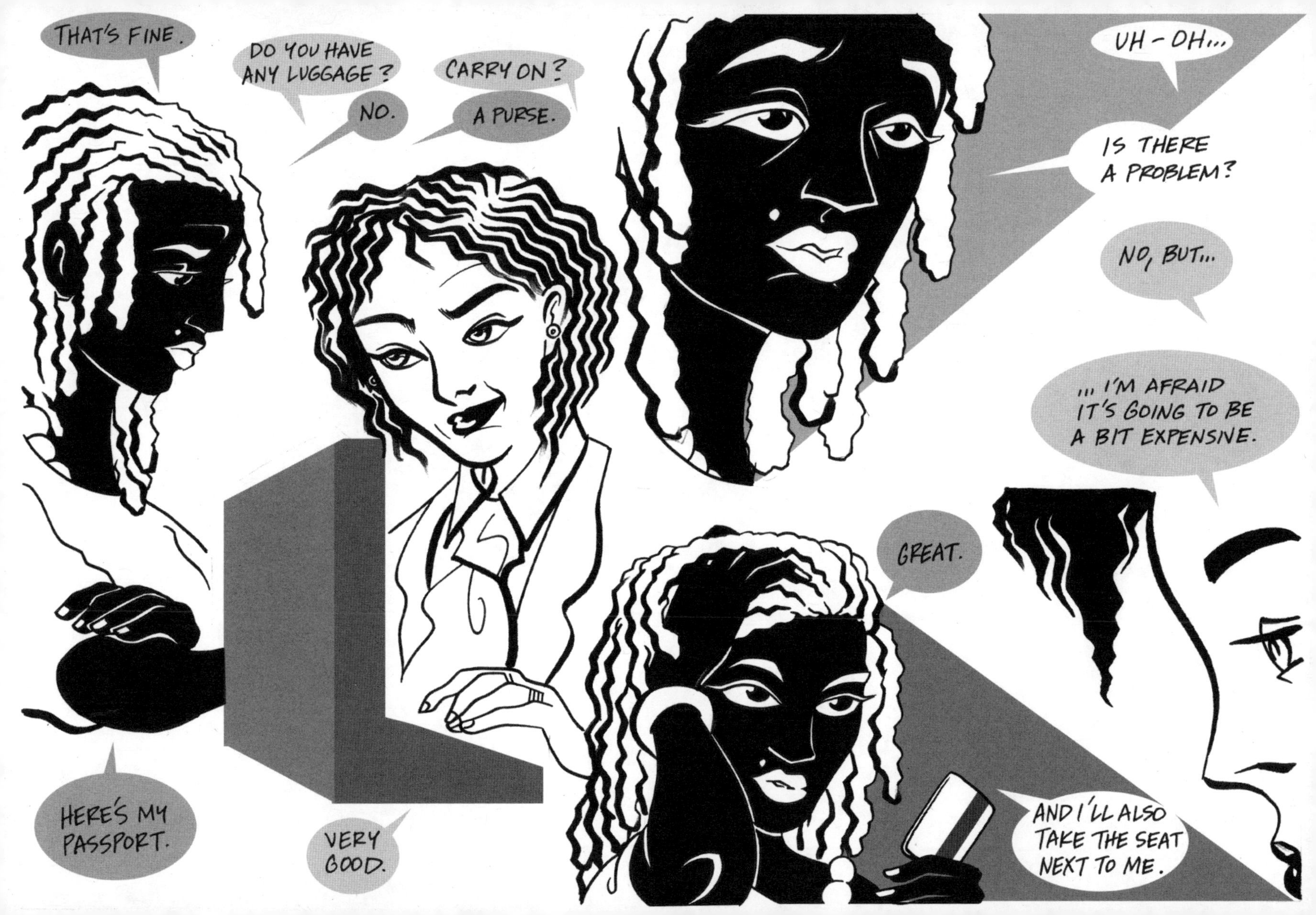
THAT'S FINE.
DO YOU HAVE ANY LUGGAGE?
NO.
CARRY ON?
A PURSE.
UH-OH...
IS THERE A PROBLEM?
NO, BUT...
... I'M AFRAID IT'S GOING TO BE A BIT EXPENSIVE.
GREAT.
AND I'LL ALSO TAKE THE SEAT NEXT TO ME.
HERE'S MY PASSPORT.
VERY GOOD.

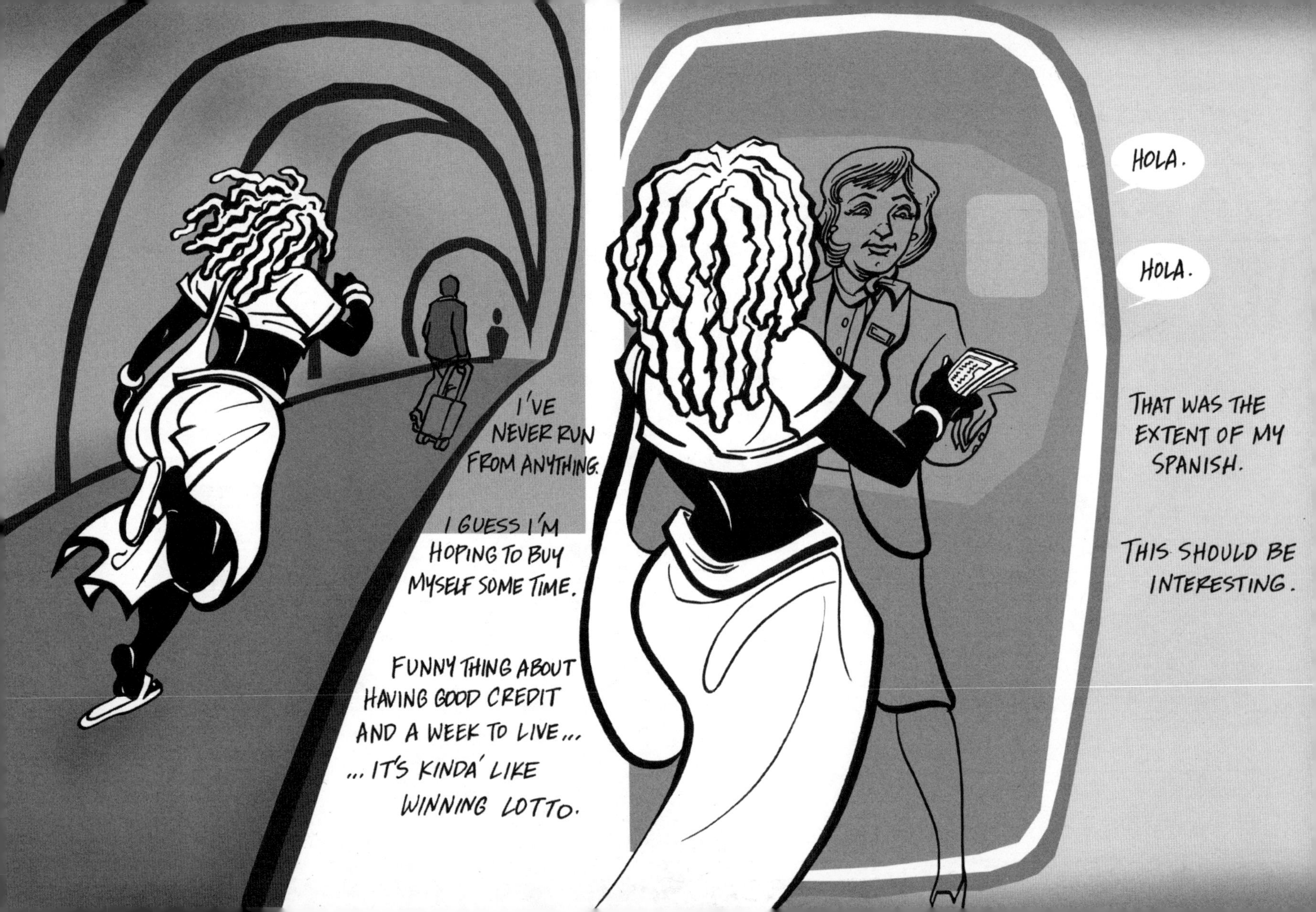
I'VE NEVER RUN FROM ANYTHING.
I GUESS I'M HOPING TO BUY MYSELF SOME TIME.
FUNNY THING ABOUT HAVING GOOD CREDIT AND A WEEK TO LIVE...
...IT'S KINDA' LIKE WINNING LOTTO.
HOLA.
HOLA.
THAT WAS THE EXTENT OF MY SPANISH.
THIS SHOULD BE INTERESTING.

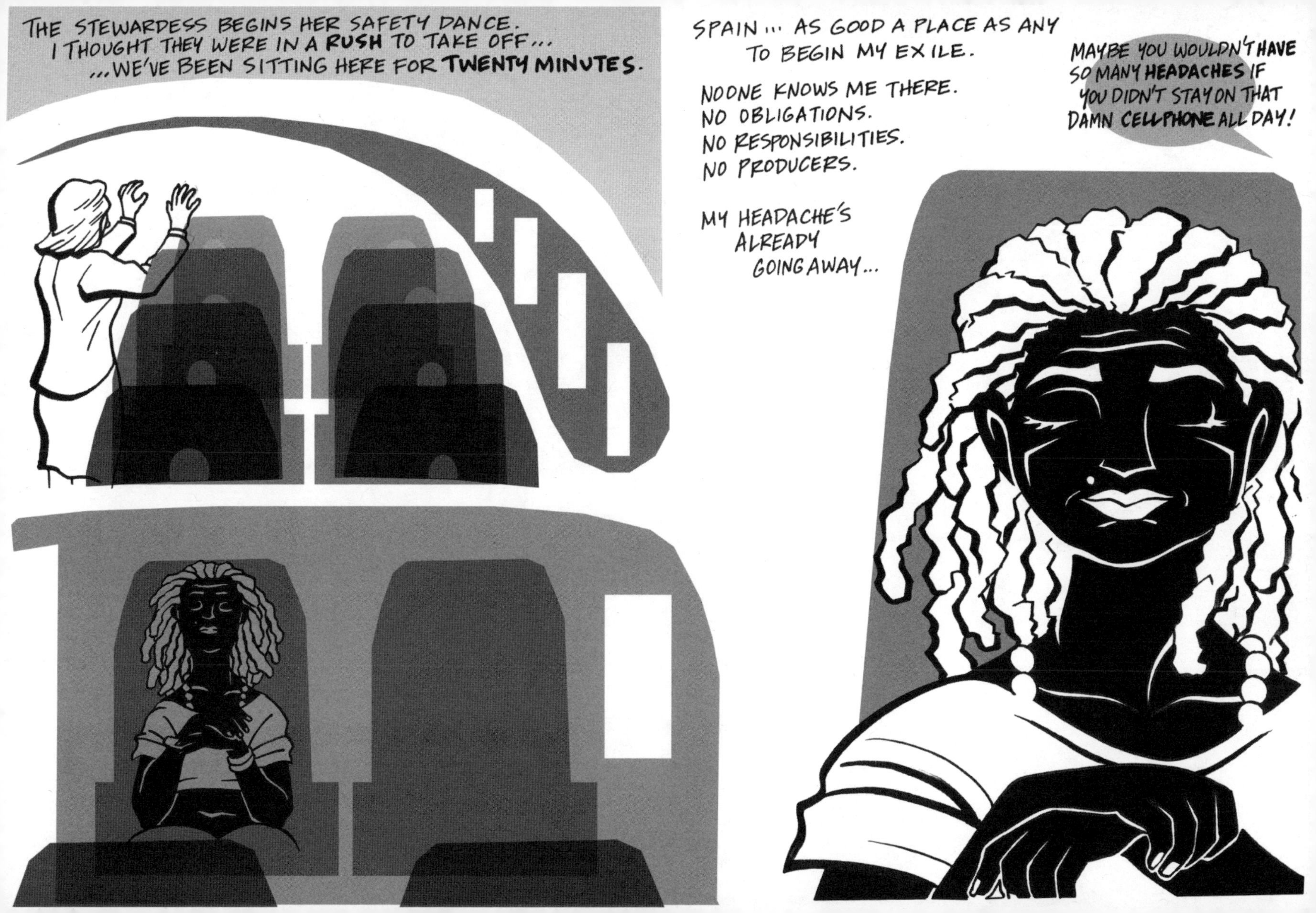
THE STEWARDESS BEGINS HER SAFETY DANCE. I THOUGHT THEY WERE IN A **RUSH** TO TAKE OFF... ...WE'VE BEEN SITTING HERE FOR **TWENTY MINUTES**.
SPAIN... AS GOOD A PLACE AS ANY TO BEGIN MY EXILE.
NOONE KNOWS ME THERE. NO OBLIGATIONS. NO RESPONSIBILITIES. NO PRODUCERS.
MY HEADACHE'S ALREADY GOING AWAY...
MAYBE YOU WOULDN'T **HAVE** SO MANY **HEADACHES** IF YOU DIDN'T STAY ON THAT DAMN **CELLPHONE** ALL DAY!

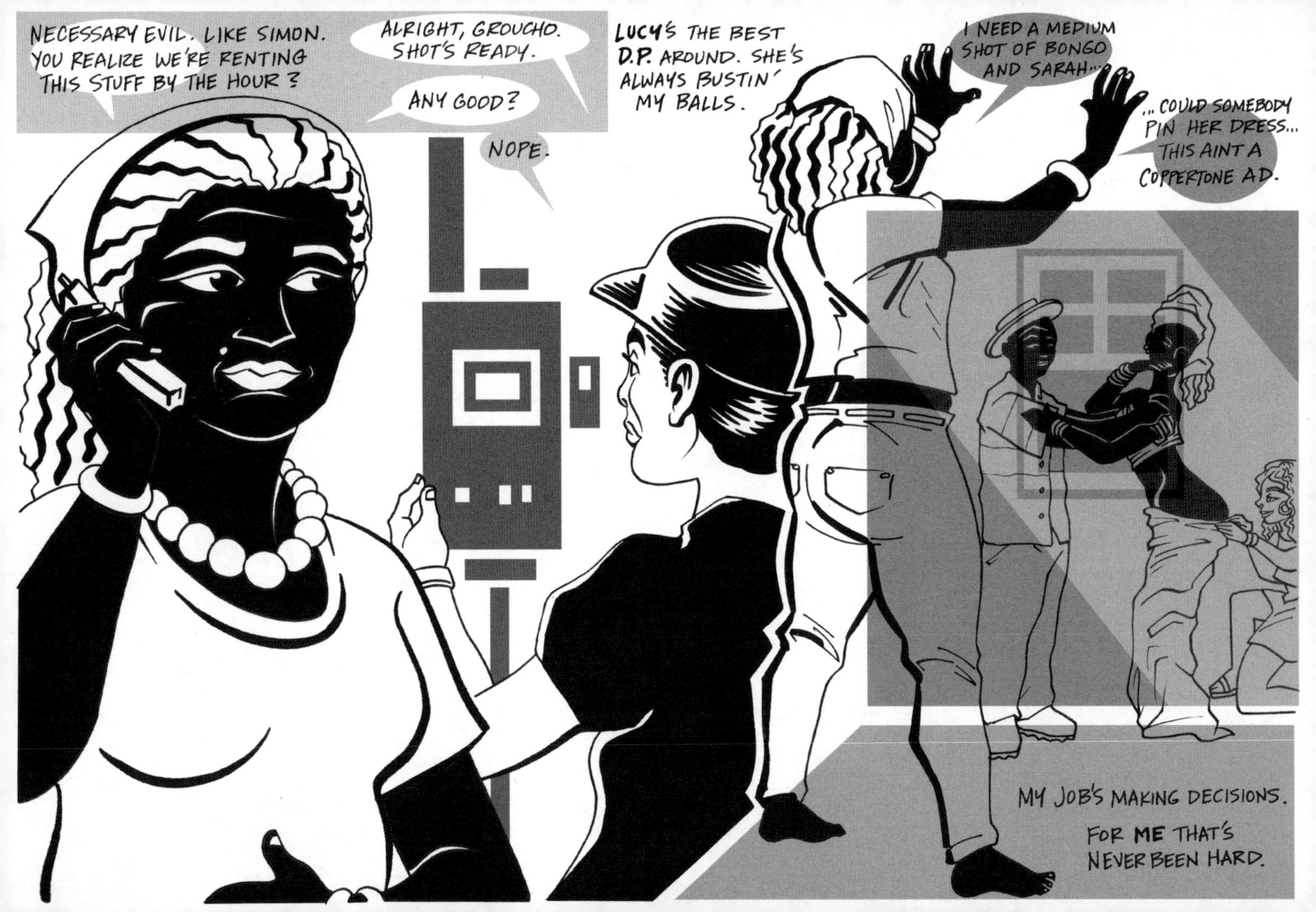

NECESSARY EVIL. LIKE SIMON. YOU REALIZE WE'RE RENTING THIS STUFF BY THE HOUR?
ALRIGHT, GROUCHO. SHOT'S READY.
ANY GOOD?
NOPE.
LUCY'S THE BEST D.P. AROUND. SHE'S ALWAYS BUSTIN' MY BALLS.
I NEED A MEDIUM SHOT OF BONGO AND SARAH...
...COULD SOMEBODY PIN HER DRESS... THIS AINT A COPPERTONE AD.
MY JOB'S MAKING DECISIONS.
FOR ME THAT'S NEVER BEEN HARD.

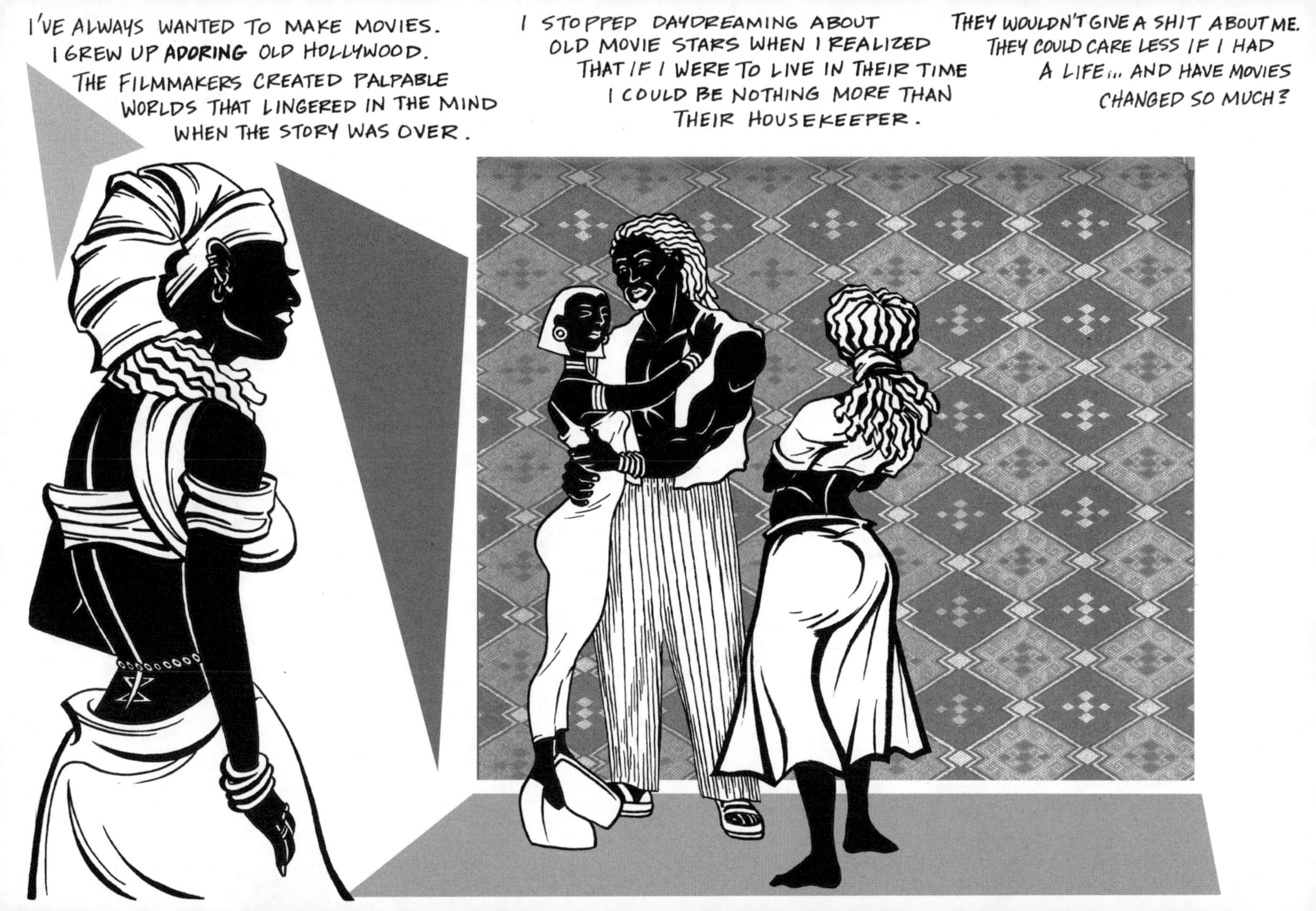
I'VE ALWAYS WANTED TO MAKE MOVIES. I GREW UP **ADORING** OLD HOLLYWOOD. THE FILMMAKERS CREATED PALPABLE WORLDS THAT LINGERED IN THE MIND WHEN THE STORY WAS OVER.
I STOPPED DAYDREAMING ABOUT OLD MOVIE STARS WHEN I REALIZED THAT IF I WERE TO LIVE IN THEIR TIME I COULD BE NOTHING MORE THAN THEIR HOUSEKEEPER.
THEY WOULDN'T GIVE A SHIT ABOUT ME. THEY COULD CARE LESS IF I HAD A LIFE... AND HAVE MOVIES CHANGED SO MUCH?

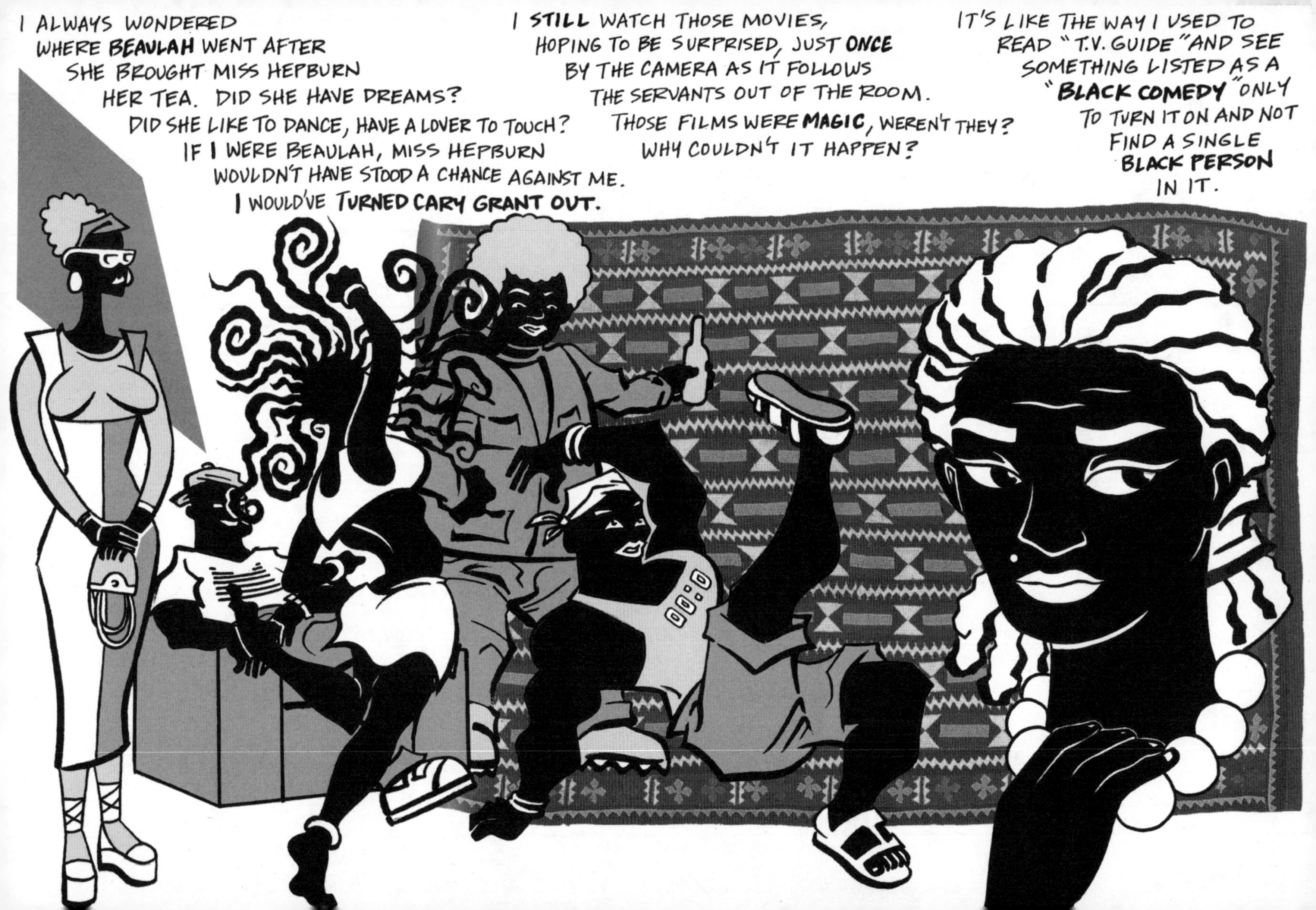
I ALWAYS WONDERED WHERE BEAULAH WENT AFTER SHE BROUGHT MISS HEPBURN HER TEA. DID SHE HAVE DREAMS? DID SHE LIKE TO DANCE, HAVE A LOVER TO TOUCH? IF I WERE BEAULAH, MISS HEPBURN WOULDN'T HAVE STOOD A CHANCE AGAINST ME. I WOULD'VE TURNED CARY GRANT OUT.
I STILL WATCH THOSE MOVIES, HOPING TO BE SURPRISED, JUST ONCE BY THE CAMERA AS IT FOLLOWS THE SERVANTS OUT OF THE ROOM. THOSE FILMS WERE MAGIC, WEREN'T THEY? WHY COULDN'T IT HAPPEN?
IT'S LIKE THE WAY I USED TO READ "T.V. GUIDE" AND SEE SOMETHING LISTED AS A "BLACK COMEDY" ONLY TO TURN IT ON AND NOT FIND A SINGLE BLACK PERSON IN IT.

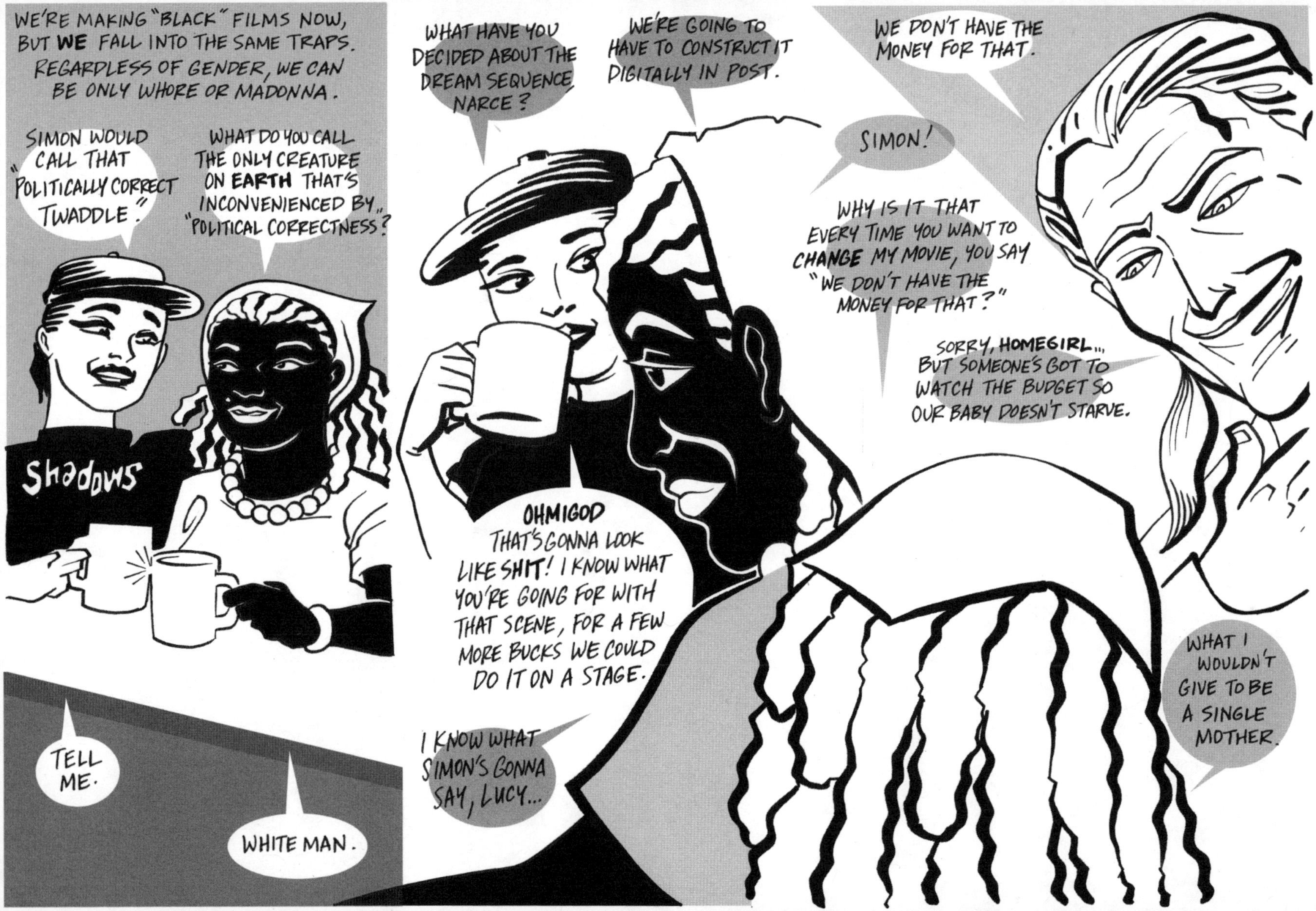
WE'RE MAKING "BLACK" FILMS NOW, BUT WE FALL INTO THE SAME TRAPS. REGARDLESS OF GENDER, WE CAN BE ONLY WHORE OR MADONNA.
SIMON WOULD CALL THAT "POLITICALLY CORRECT TWADDLE."
WHAT DO YOU CALL THE ONLY CREATURE ON EARTH THAT'S INCONVENIENCED BY "POLITICAL CORRECTNESS"?
TELL ME.
WHITE MAN.
SHADOWS
WHAT HAVE YOU DECIDED ABOUT THE DREAM SEQUENCE NARCE?
WE'RE GOING TO HAVE TO CONSTRUCT IT DIGITALLY IN POST.
WE DON'T HAVE THE MONEY FOR THAT.
SIMON!
WHY IS IT THAT EVERY TIME YOU WANT TO CHANGE MY MOVIE, YOU SAY "WE DON'T HAVE THE MONEY FOR THAT?"
SORRY, HOMEGIRL... BUT SOMEONE'S GOT TO WATCH THE BUDGET SO OUR BABY DOESN'T STARVE.
OHMIGOD THAT'S GONNA LOOK LIKE SHIT! I KNOW WHAT YOU'RE GOING FOR WITH THAT SCENE, FOR A FEW MORE BUCKS WE COULD DO IT ON A STAGE.
I KNOW WHAT SIMON'S GONNA SAY, LUCY...
WHAT I WOULDN'T GIVE TO BE A SINGLE MOTHER.

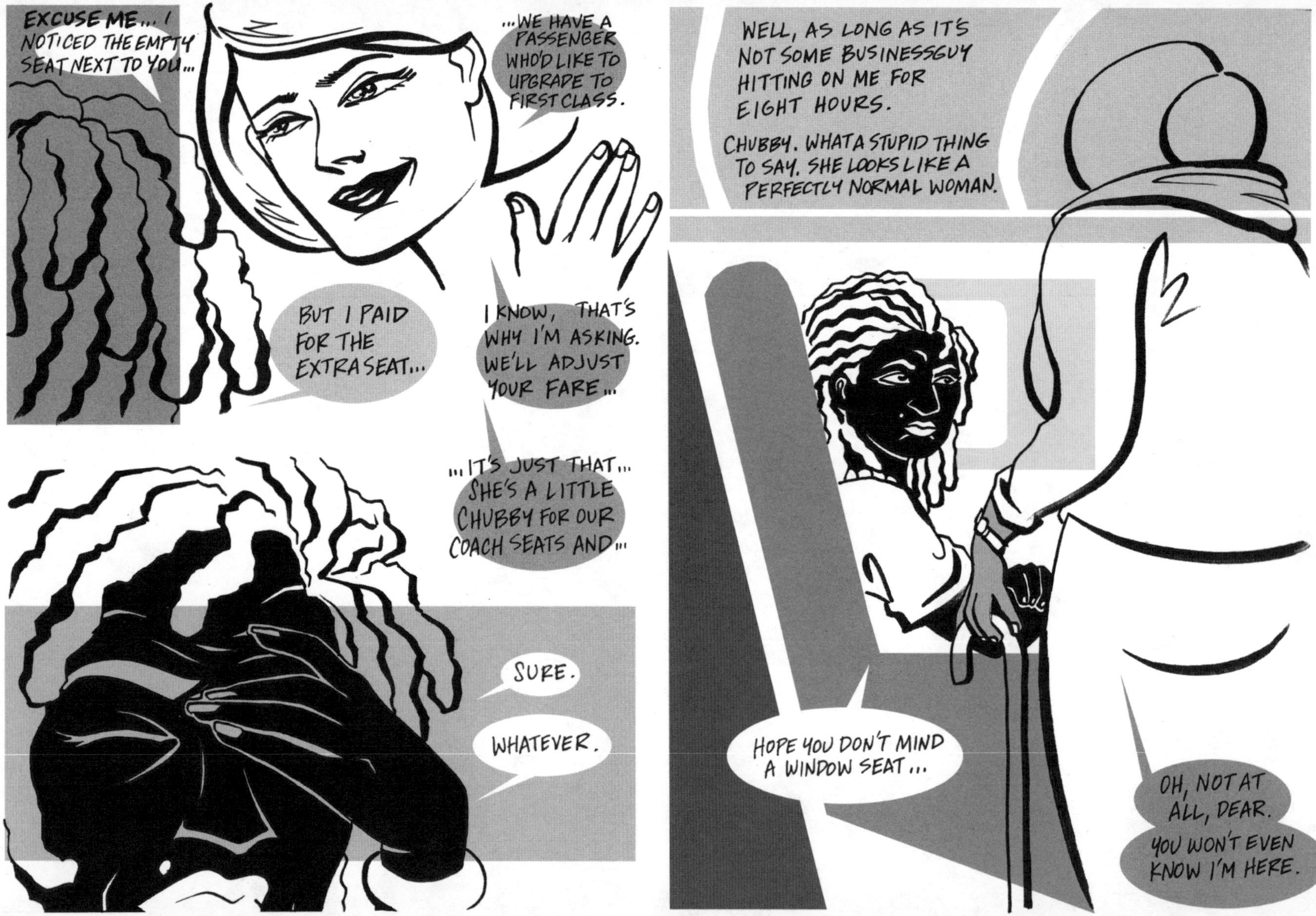
EXCUSE ME... I NOTICED THE EMPTY SEAT NEXT TO YOU...
...WE HAVE A PASSENGER WHO'D LIKE TO UPGRADE TO FIRST CLASS.
BUT I PAID FOR THE EXTRA SEAT...
I KNOW, THAT'S WHY I'M ASKING. WE'LL ADJUST YOUR FARE...
...IT'S JUST THAT... SHE'S A LITTLE CHUBBY FOR OUR COACH SEATS AND...
SURE.
WHATEVER.
WELL, AS LONG AS IT'S NOT SOME BUSINESSGUY HITTING ON ME FOR EIGHT HOURS.
CHUBBY. WHAT A STUPID THING TO SAY. SHE LOOKS LIKE A PERFECTLY NORMAL WOMAN.
HOPE YOU DON'T MIND A WINDOW SEAT...
OH, NOT AT ALL, DEAR.
YOU WON'T EVEN KNOW I'M HERE.

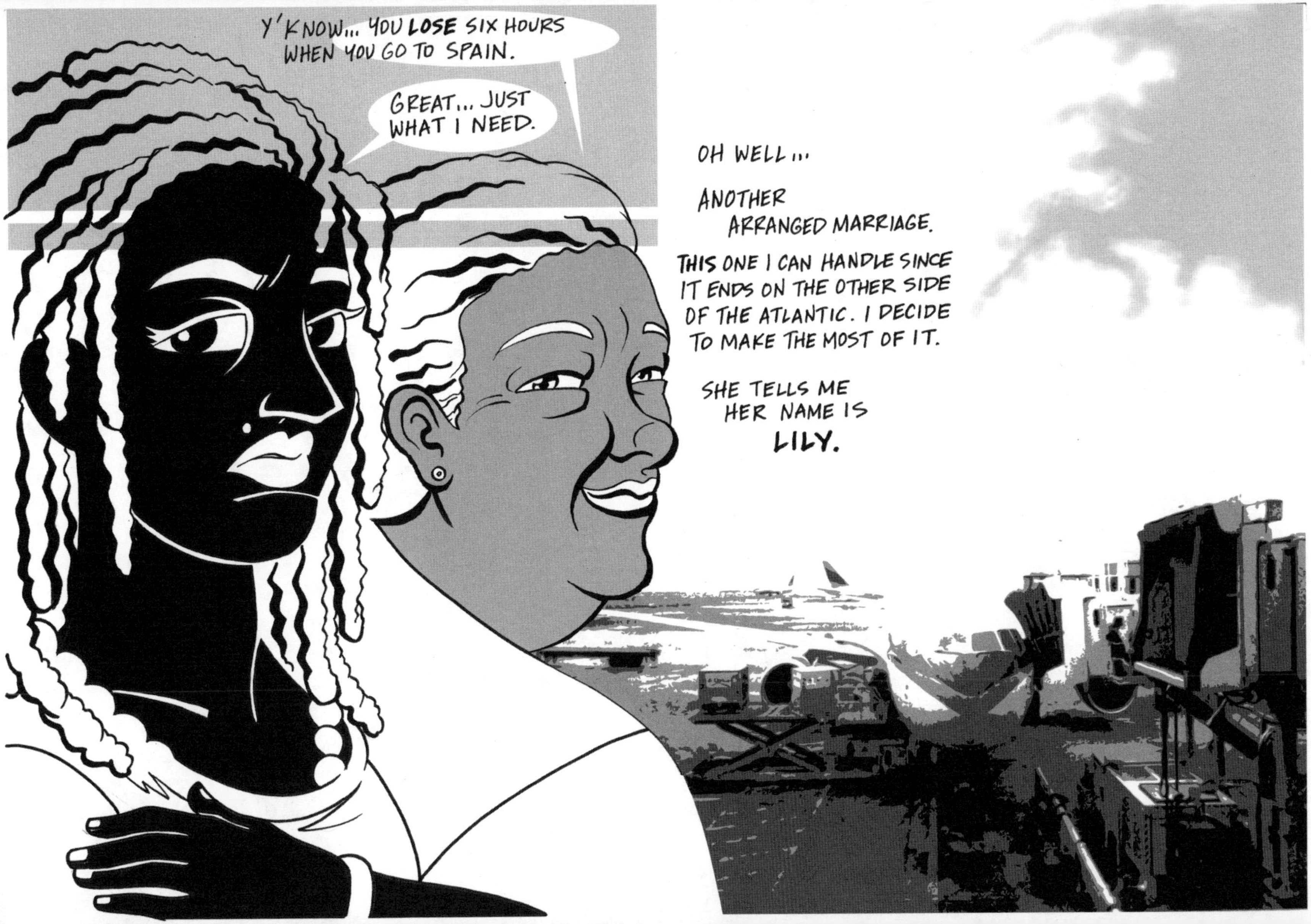
Y'KNOW... YOU LOSE SIX HOURS WHEN YOU GO TO SPAIN.
GREAT... JUST WHAT I NEED.
OH WELL...
ANOTHER ARRANGED MARRIAGE.
THIS ONE I CAN HANDLE SINCE IT ENDS ON THE OTHER SIDE OF THE ATLANTIC. I DECIDE TO MAKE THE MOST OF IT.
SHE TELLS ME HER NAME IS LILY.

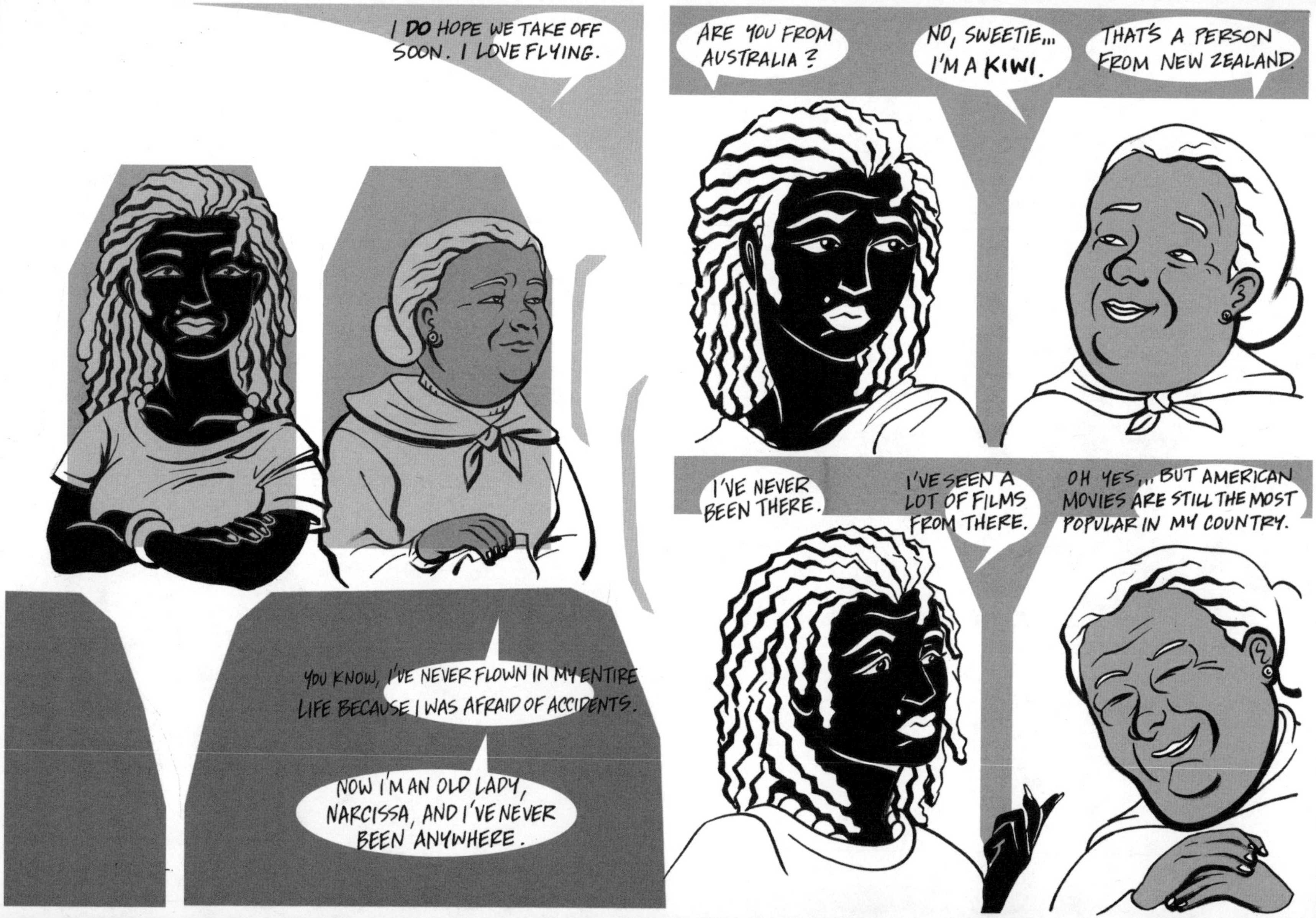
I DO HOPE WE TAKE OFF SOON. I LOVE FLYING.
YOU KNOW, I'VE NEVER FLOWN IN MY ENTIRE LIFE BECAUSE I WAS AFRAID OF ACCIDENTS.
NOW I'M AN OLD LADY, NARCISSA, AND I'VE NEVER BEEN ANYWHERE.
ARE YOU FROM AUSTRALIA?
NO, SWEETIE... I'M A KIWI.
THAT'S A PERSON FROM NEW ZEALAND.
I'VE NEVER BEEN THERE.
I'VE SEEN A LOT OF FILMS FROM THERE.
OH YES... BUT AMERICAN MOVIES ARE STILL THE MOST POPULAR IN MY COUNTRY.

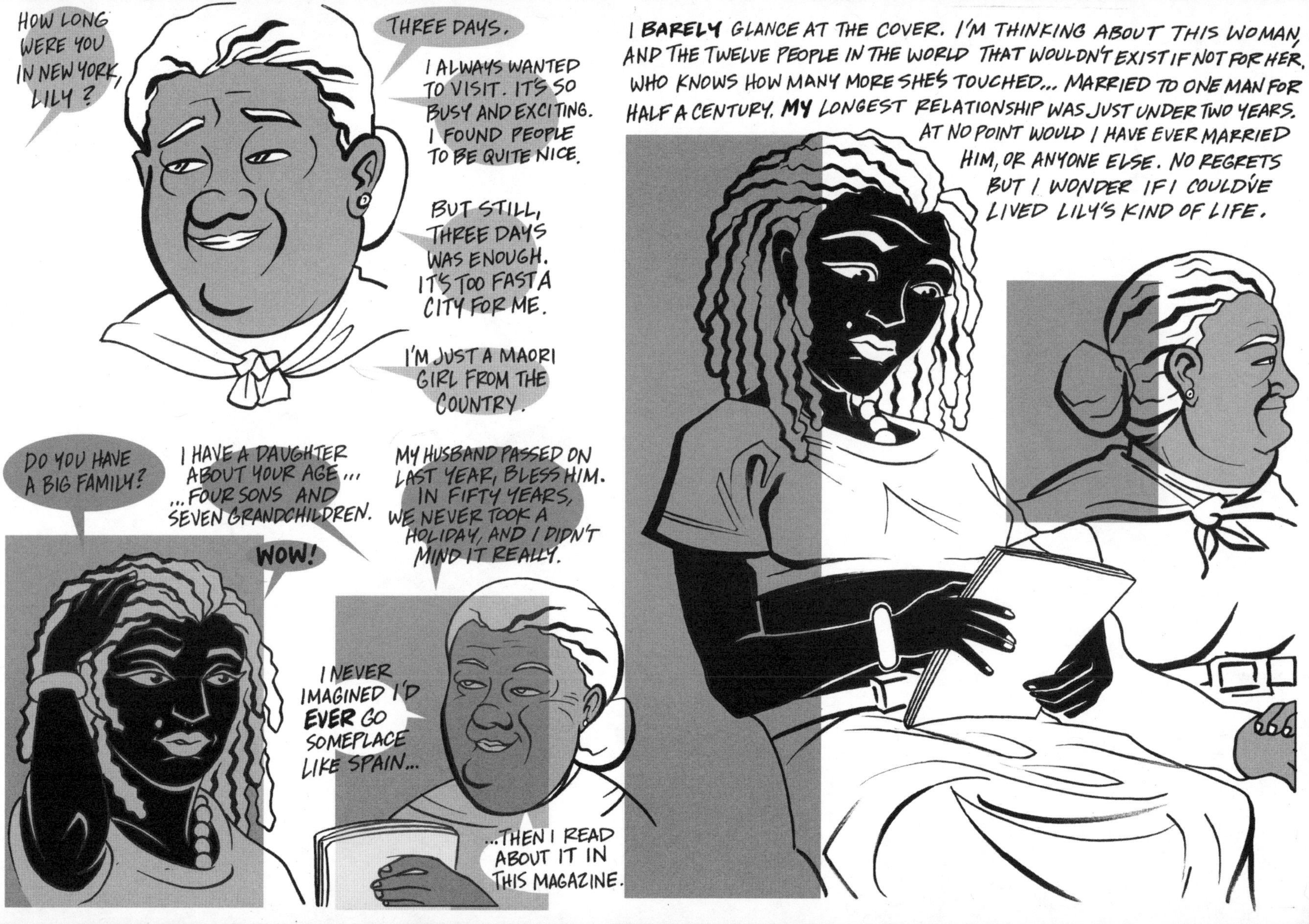

HOW LONG WERE YOU IN NEW YORK, LILY?
THREE DAYS.
I ALWAYS WANTED TO VISIT. IT'S SO BUSY AND EXCITING. I FOUND PEOPLE TO BE QUITE NICE.
BUT STILL, THREE DAYS WAS ENOUGH. IT'S TOO FAST A CITY FOR ME.
I'M JUST A MAORI GIRL FROM THE COUNTRY.
DO YOU HAVE A BIG FAMILY?
I HAVE A DAUGHTER ABOUT YOUR AGE... ...FOUR SONS AND SEVEN GRANDCHILDREN.
WOW!
MY HUSBAND PASSED ON LAST YEAR, BLESS HIM. IN FIFTY YEARS, WE NEVER TOOK A HOLIDAY, AND I DIDN'T MIND IT REALLY.
I NEVER IMAGINED I'D **EVER** GO SOMEPLACE LIKE SPAIN...
...THEN I READ ABOUT IT IN THIS MAGAZINE.
I **BARELY** GLANCE AT THE COVER. I'M THINKING ABOUT THIS WOMAN, AND THE TWELVE PEOPLE IN THE WORLD THAT WOULDN'T EXIST IF NOT FOR HER. WHO KNOWS HOW MANY MORE SHE'S TOUCHED... MARRIED TO ONE MAN FOR HALF A CENTURY. **MY** LONGEST RELATIONSHIP WAS JUST UNDER TWO YEARS. AT NO POINT WOULD I HAVE EVER MARRIED HIM, OR ANYONE ELSE. NO REGRETS BUT I WONDER IF I COULD'VE LIVED LILY'S KIND OF LIFE.

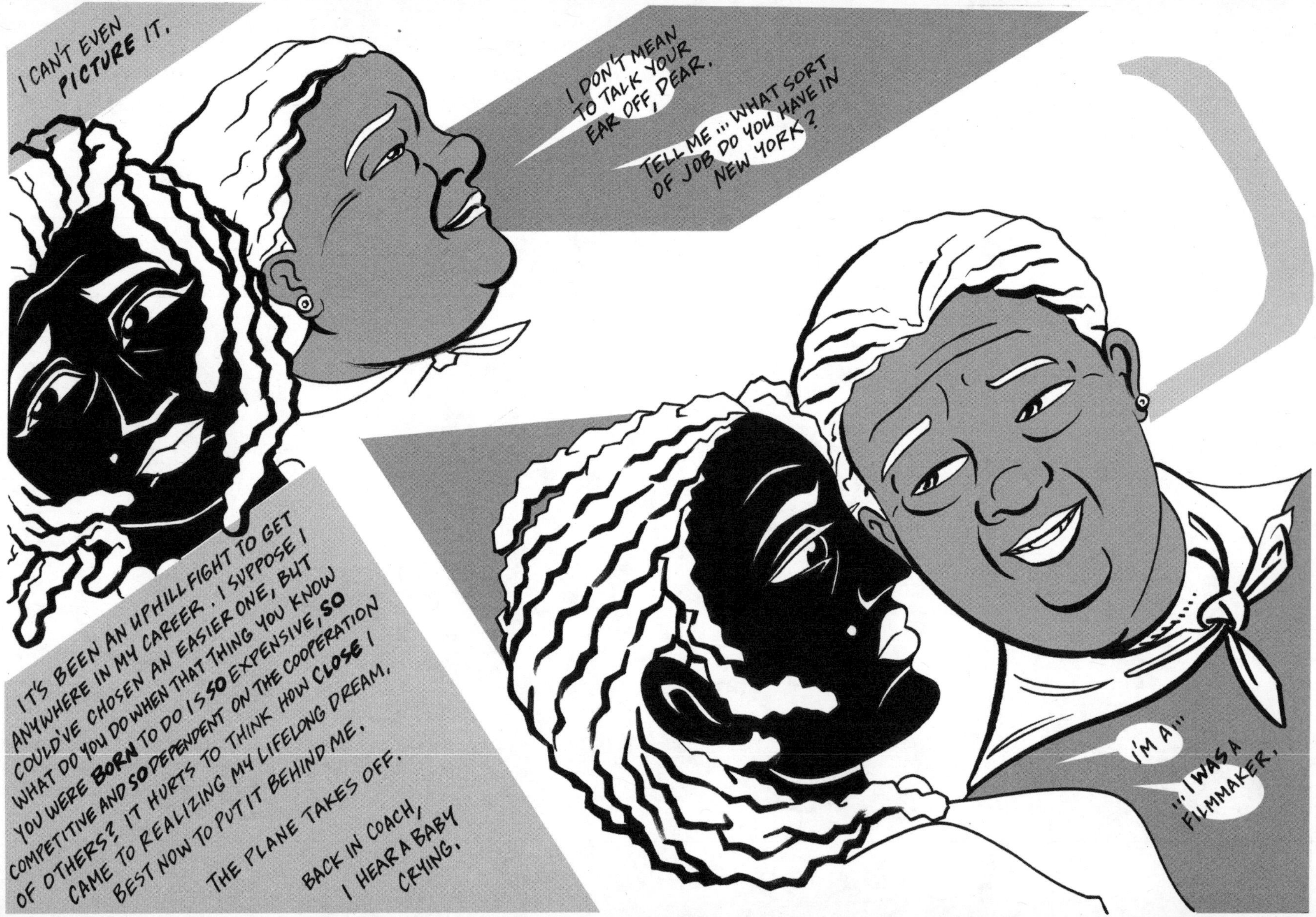
I CAN'T EVEN PICTURE IT.
I DON'T MEAN TO TALK YOUR EAR OFF, DEAR.
TELL ME ... WHAT SORT OF JOB DO YOU HAVE IN NEW YORK?
IT'S BEEN AN UPHILL FIGHT TO GET ANYWHERE IN MY CAREER. I SUPPOSE I COULD'VE CHOSEN AN EASIER ONE, BUT WHAT DO YOU DO WHEN THAT THING YOU KNOW YOU WERE BORN TO DO IS SO EXPENSIVE, SO COMPETITIVE AND SO DEPENDENT ON THE COOPERATION OF OTHERS? IT HURTS TO THINK HOW CLOSE I CAME TO REALIZING MY LIFELONG DREAM. BEST NOW TO PUT IT BEHIND ME.
THE PLANE TAKES OFF.
BACK IN COACH, I HEAR A BABY CRYING.
I'M A ...
... I WAS A FILMMAKER.

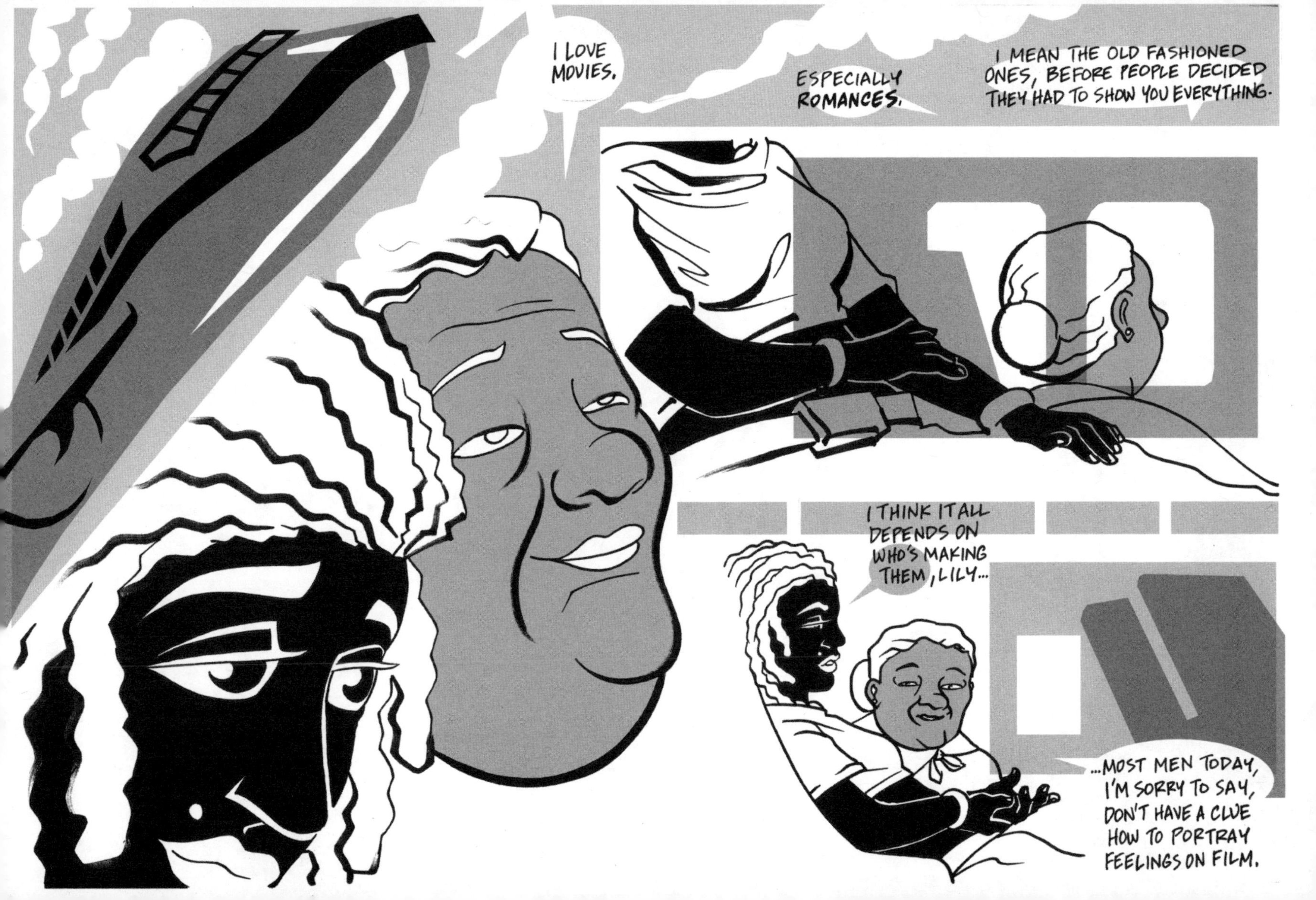
I LOVE MOVIES.
ESPECIALLY ROMANCES.
I MEAN THE OLD FASHIONED ONES, BEFORE PEOPLE DECIDED THEY HAD TO SHOW YOU EVERYTHING.
I THINK IT ALL DEPENDS ON WHO'S MAKING THEM, LILY...
...MOST MEN TODAY, I'M SORRY TO SAY, DON'T HAVE A CLUE HOW TO PORTRAY FEELINGS ON FILM.

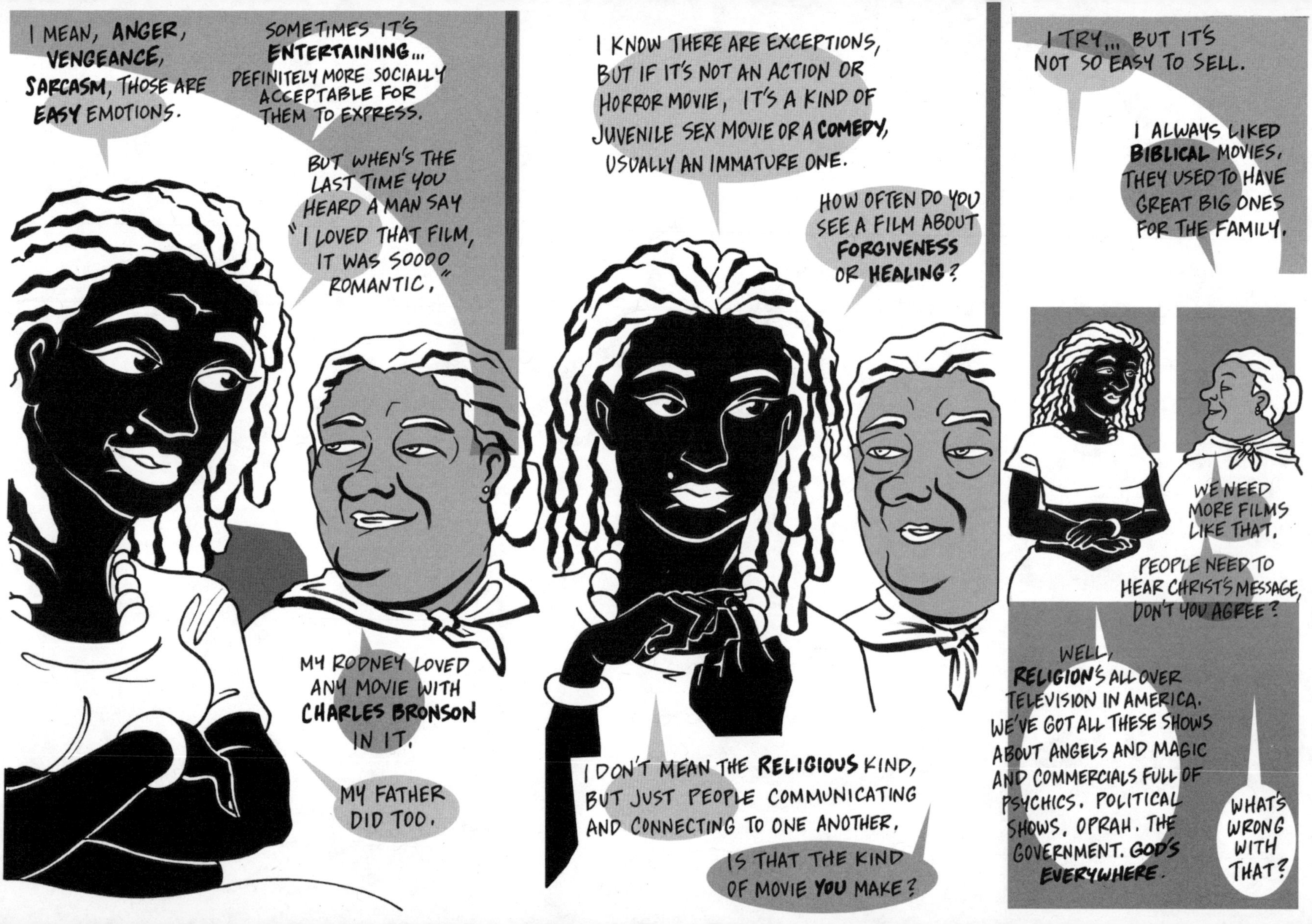

I MEAN, ANGER, VENGEANCE, SARCASM, THOSE ARE EASY EMOTIONS.
SOMETIMES IT'S ENTERTAINING... DEFINITELY MORE SOCIALLY ACCEPTABLE FOR THEM TO EXPRESS.
BUT WHEN'S THE LAST TIME YOU HEARD A MAN SAY "I LOVED THAT FILM, IT WAS SOOOO ROMANTIC."
MY RODNEY LOVED ANY MOVIE WITH CHARLES BRONSON IN IT.
MY FATHER DID TOO.
I KNOW THERE ARE EXCEPTIONS, BUT IF IT'S NOT AN ACTION OR HORROR MOVIE, IT'S A KIND OF JUVENILE SEX MOVIE OR A COMEDY, USUALLY AN IMMATURE ONE.
HOW OFTEN DO YOU SEE A FILM ABOUT FORGIVENESS OR HEALING?
I DON'T MEAN THE RELIGIOUS KIND, BUT JUST PEOPLE COMMUNICATING AND CONNECTING TO ONE ANOTHER.
IS THAT THE KIND OF MOVIE YOU MAKE?
I TRY... BUT IT'S NOT SO EASY TO SELL.
I ALWAYS LIKED BIBLICAL MOVIES, THEY USED TO HAVE GREAT BIG ONES FOR THE FAMILY.
WE NEED MORE FILMS LIKE THAT.
PEOPLE NEED TO HEAR CHRIST'S MESSAGE, DON'T YOU AGREE?
WELL, RELIGION'S ALL OVER TELEVISION IN AMERICA. WE'VE GOT ALL THESE SHOWS ABOUT ANGELS AND MAGIC AND COMMERCIALS FULL OF PSYCHICS. POLITICAL SHOWS. OPRAH. THE GOVERNMENT. GOD'S EVERYWHERE.
WHAT'S WRONG WITH THAT?

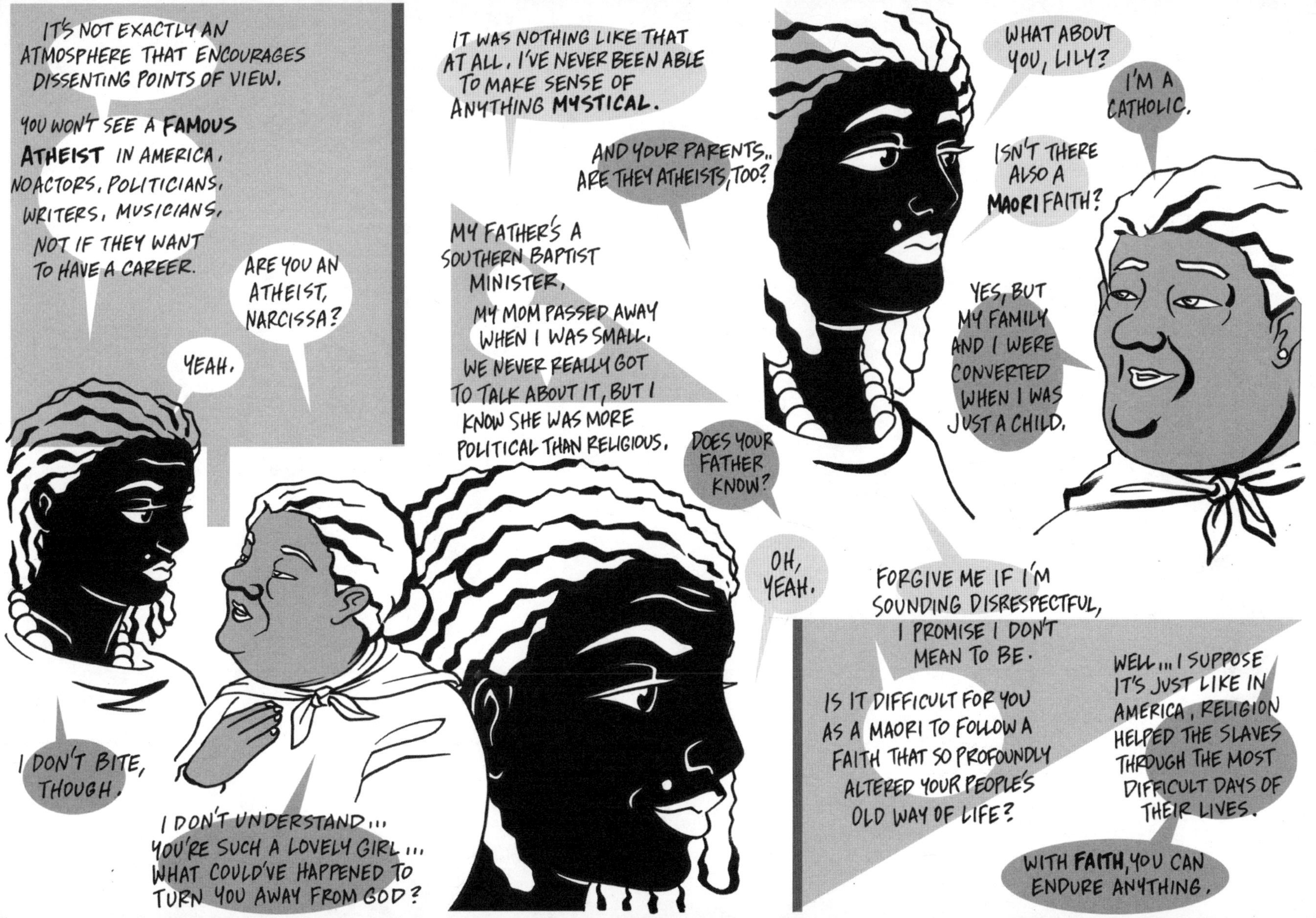

IT'S NOT EXACTLY AN ATMOSPHERE THAT ENCOURAGES DISSENTING POINTS OF VIEW.
YOU WON'T SEE A **FAMOUS ATHEIST** IN AMERICA. NO ACTORS. POLITICIANS, WRITERS, MUSICIANS, NOT IF THEY WANT TO HAVE A CAREER.
ARE YOU AN ATHEIST, NARCISSA?
YEAH.
I DON'T BITE, THOUGH.
I DON'T UNDERSTAND... YOU'RE SUCH A LOVELY GIRL... WHAT COULD'VE HAPPENED TO TURN YOU AWAY FROM GOD?
IT WAS NOTHING LIKE THAT AT ALL. I'VE NEVER BEEN ABLE TO MAKE SENSE OF ANYTHING **MYSTICAL**.
AND YOUR PARENTS.. ARE THEY ATHEISTS, TOO?
MY FATHER'S A SOUTHERN BAPTIST MINISTER.
MY MOM PASSED AWAY WHEN I WAS SMALL. WE NEVER REALLY GOT TO TALK ABOUT IT, BUT I KNOW SHE WAS MORE POLITICAL THAN RELIGIOUS.
DOES YOUR FATHER KNOW?
OH, YEAH.
WHAT ABOUT YOU, LILY?
I'M A CATHOLIC.
ISN'T THERE ALSO A **MAORI** FAITH?
YES, BUT MY FAMILY AND I WERE CONVERTED WHEN I WAS JUST A CHILD.
FORGIVE ME IF I'M SOUNDING DISRESPECTFUL, I PROMISE I DON'T MEAN TO BE.
IS IT DIFFICULT FOR YOU AS A MAORI TO FOLLOW A FAITH THAT SO PROFOUNDLY ALTERED YOUR PEOPLE'S OLD WAY OF LIFE?
WELL... I SUPPOSE IT'S JUST LIKE IN AMERICA. RELIGION HELPED THE SLAVES THROUGH THE MOST DIFFICULT DAYS OF THEIR LIVES.
WITH **FAITH**, YOU CAN ENDURE ANYTHING.

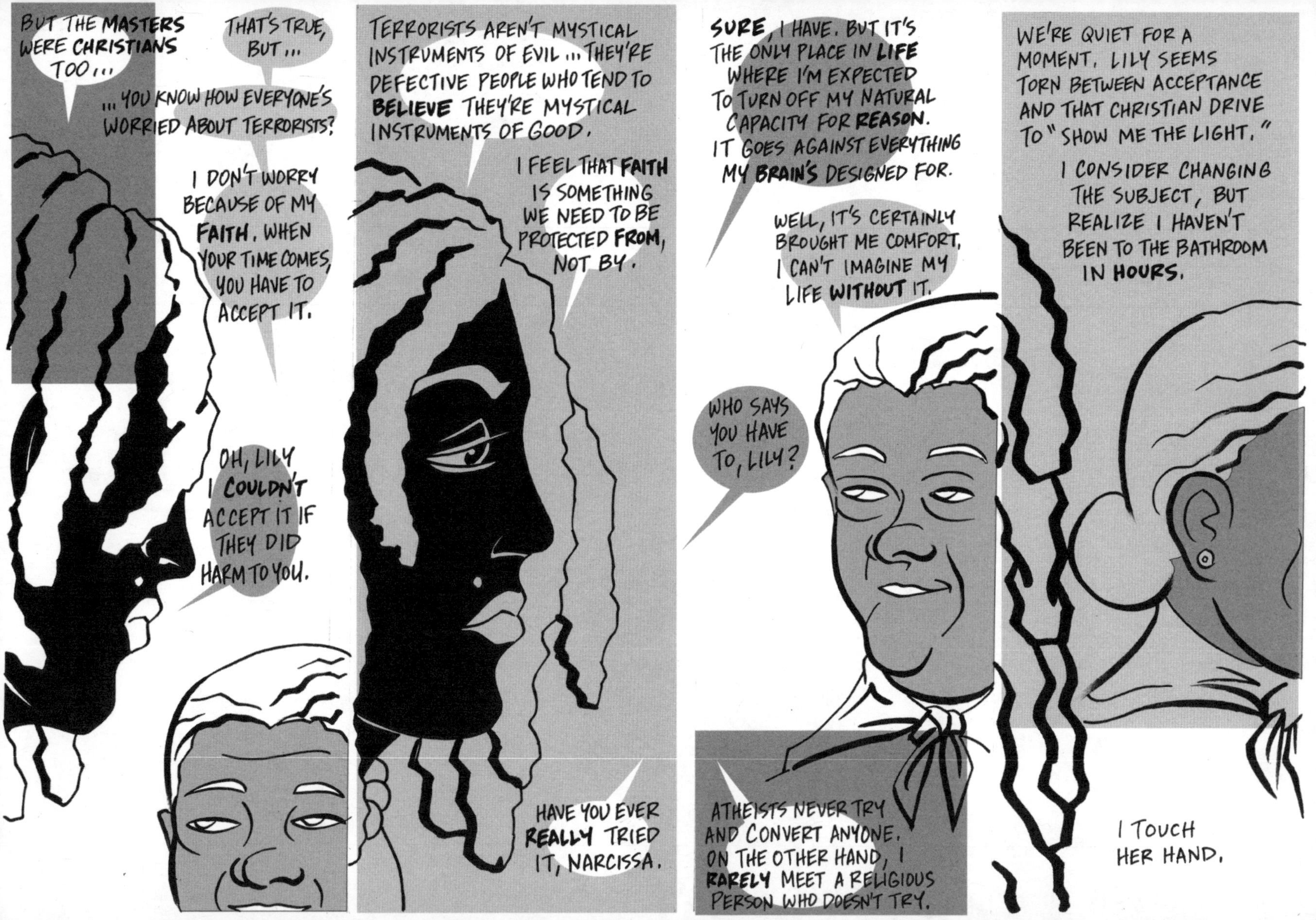
BUT THE MASTERS WERE CHRISTIANS TOO...
THAT'S TRUE, BUT...
...YOU KNOW HOW EVERYONE'S WORRIED ABOUT TERRORISTS?
I DON'T WORRY BECAUSE OF MY FAITH. WHEN YOUR TIME COMES, YOU HAVE TO ACCEPT IT.
OH, LILY I COULDN'T ACCEPT IT IF THEY DID HARM TO YOU.
TERRORISTS AREN'T MYSTICAL INSTRUMENTS OF EVIL... THEY'RE DEFECTIVE PEOPLE WHO TEND TO BELIEVE THEY'RE MYSTICAL INSTRUMENTS OF GOOD.
I FEEL THAT FAITH IS SOMETHING WE NEED TO BE PROTECTED FROM, NOT BY.
HAVE YOU EVER REALLY TRIED IT, NARCISSA.
SURE, I HAVE. BUT IT'S THE ONLY PLACE IN LIFE WHERE I'M EXPECTED TO TURN OFF MY NATURAL CAPACITY FOR REASON. IT GOES AGAINST EVERYTHING MY BRAIN'S DESIGNED FOR.
WELL, IT'S CERTAINLY BROUGHT ME COMFORT. I CAN'T IMAGINE MY LIFE WITHOUT IT.
WHO SAYS YOU HAVE TO, LILY?
ATHEISTS NEVER TRY AND CONVERT ANYONE. ON THE OTHER HAND, I RARELY MEET A RELIGIOUS PERSON WHO DOESN'T TRY.
WE'RE QUIET FOR A MOMENT. LILY SEEMS TORN BETWEEN ACCEPTANCE AND THAT CHRISTIAN DRIVE TO "SHOW ME THE LIGHT."
I CONSIDER CHANGING THE SUBJECT, BUT REALIZE I HAVEN'T BEEN TO THE BATHROOM IN HOURS.
I TOUCH HER HAND.

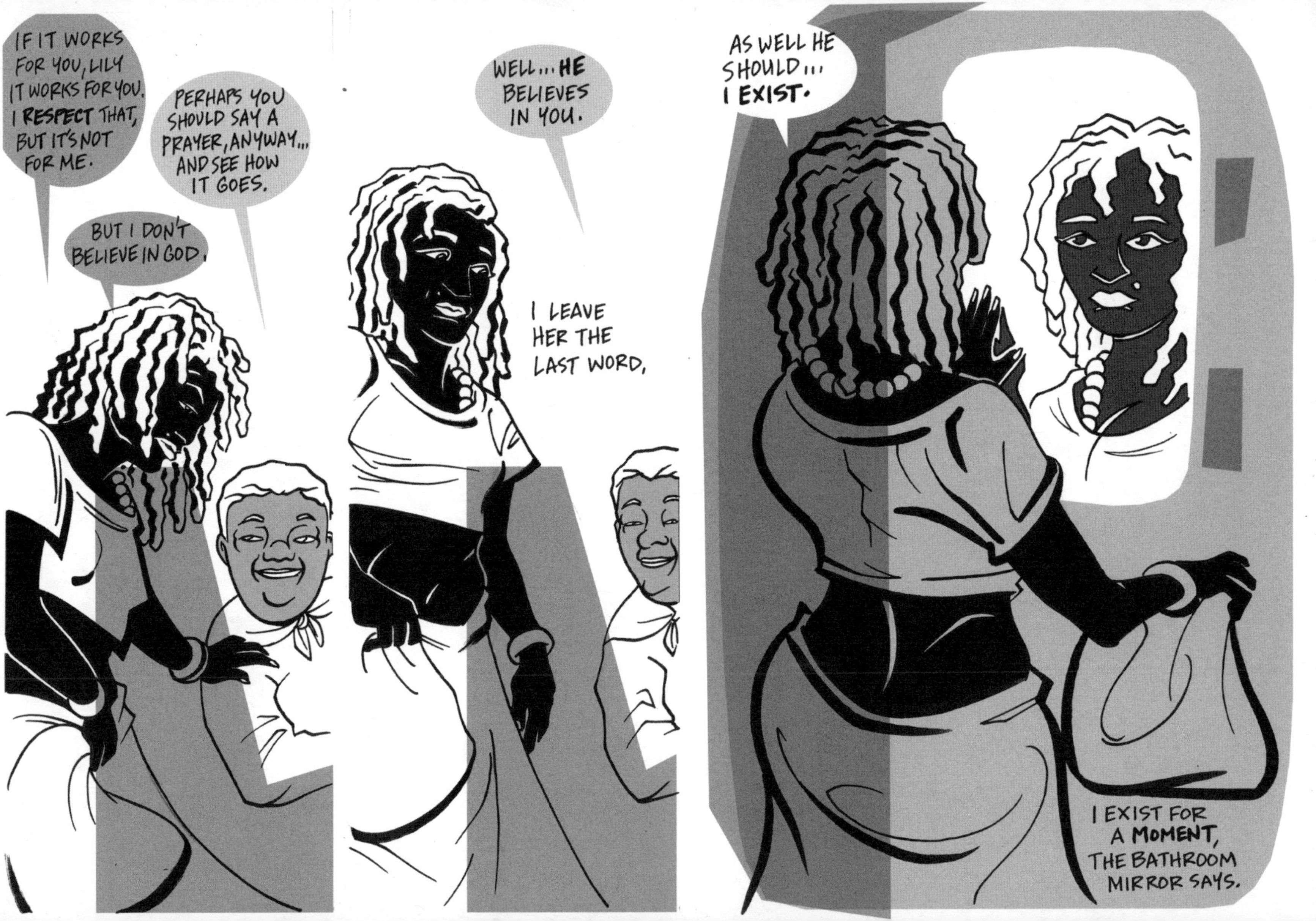
IF IT WORKS FOR YOU, LILY IT WORKS FOR YOU. I **RESPECT** THAT, BUT IT'S NOT FOR ME.
PERHAPS YOU SHOULD SAY A PRAYER, ANYWAY... AND SEE HOW IT GOES.
BUT I DON'T BELIEVE IN GOD.
WELL... **HE** BELIEVES IN YOU.
I LEAVE HER THE LAST WORD.
AS WELL HE SHOULD... I **EXIST.**
I EXIST FOR A **MOMENT**, THE BATHROOM MIRROR SAYS.

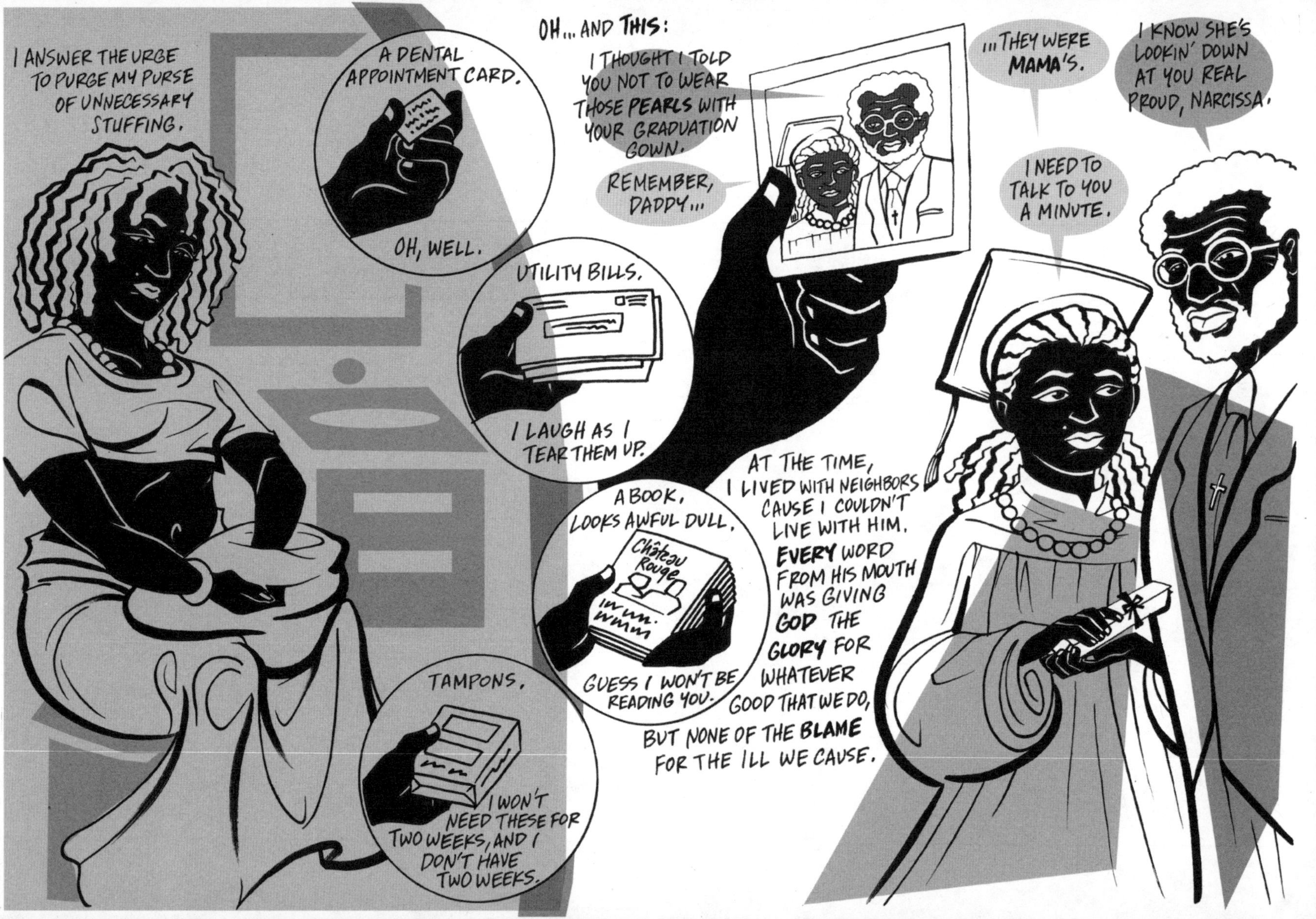
I ANSWER THE URGE TO PURGE MY PURSE OF UNNECESSARY STUFFING.
A DENTAL APPOINTMENT CARD.
OH, WELL.
UTILITY BILLS.
I LAUGH AS I TEAR THEM UP.
A BOOK, LOOKS AWFUL DULL.
Château Rouge
GUESS I WON'T BE READING YOU.
TAMPONS.
I WON'T NEED THESE FOR TWO WEEKS, AND I DON'T HAVE TWO WEEKS.
OH... AND THIS:
I THOUGHT I TOLD YOU NOT TO WEAR THOSE PEARLS WITH YOUR GRADUATION GOWN.
REMEMBER, DADDY...
...THEY WERE MAMA'S.
I KNOW SHE'S LOOKIN' DOWN AT YOU REAL PROUD, NARCISSA.
I NEED TO TALK TO YOU A MINUTE.
AT THE TIME, I LIVED WITH NEIGHBORS CAUSE I COULDN'T LIVE WITH HIM. EVERY WORD FROM HIS MOUTH WAS GIVING GOD THE GLORY FOR WHATEVER GOOD THAT WE DO, BUT NONE OF THE BLAME FOR THE ILL WE CAUSE.

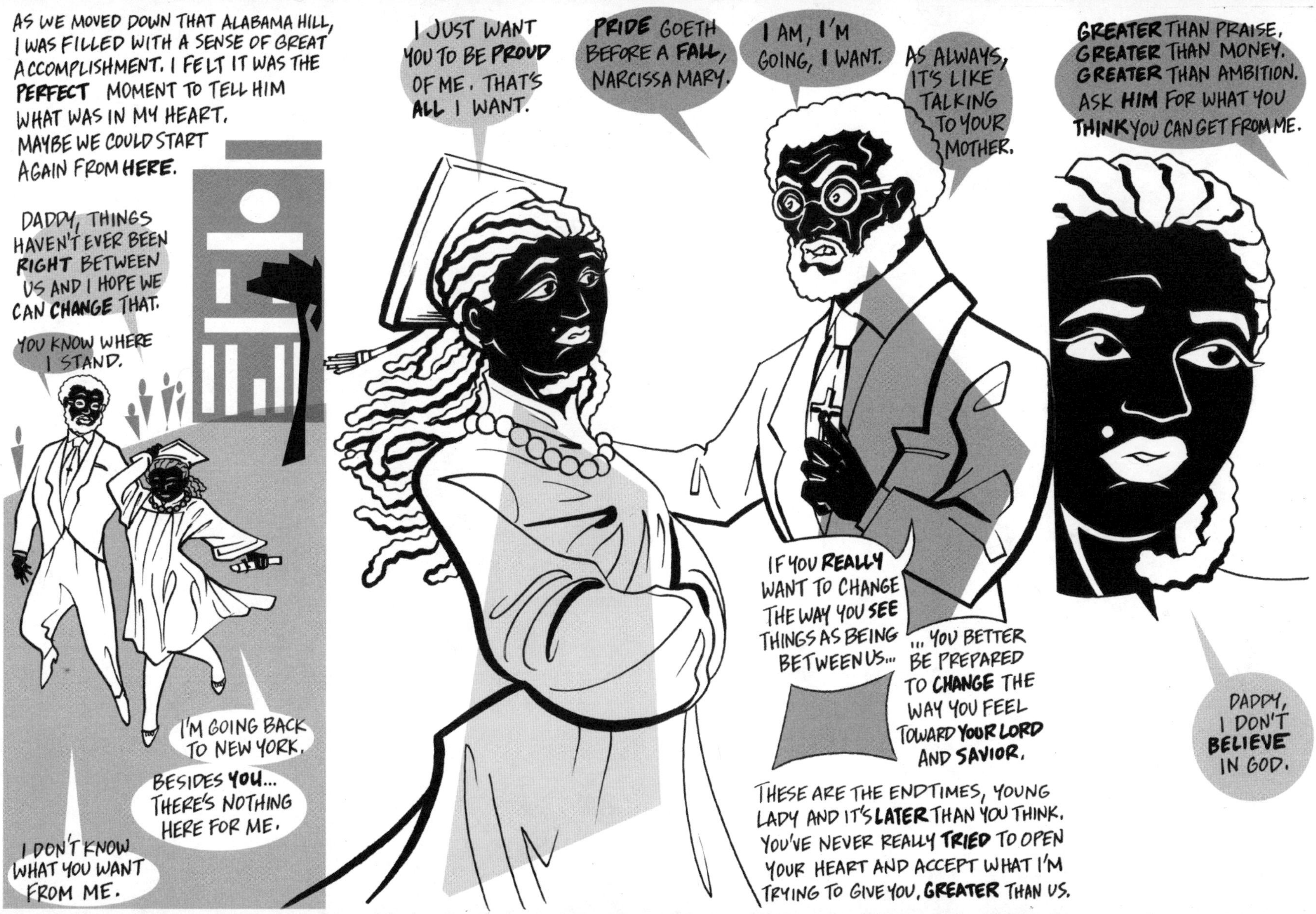

AS WE MOVED DOWN THAT ALABAMA HILL, I WAS FILLED WITH A SENSE OF GREAT ACCOMPLISHMENT. I FELT IT WAS THE PERFECT MOMENT TO TELL HIM WHAT WAS IN MY HEART. MAYBE WE COULD START AGAIN FROM HERE.
DADDY, THINGS HAVEN'T EVER BEEN RIGHT BETWEEN US AND I HOPE WE CAN CHANGE THAT.
YOU KNOW WHERE I STAND.
I'M GOING BACK TO NEW YORK.
BESIDES YOU... THERE'S NOTHING HERE FOR ME.
I DON'T KNOW WHAT YOU WANT FROM ME.
I JUST WANT YOU TO BE PROUD OF ME. THAT'S ALL I WANT.
PRIDE GOETH BEFORE A FALL, NARCISSA MARY.
I AM, I'M GOING, I WANT.
AS ALWAYS, IT'S LIKE TALKING TO YOUR MOTHER.
GREATER THAN PRAISE, GREATER THAN MONEY. GREATER THAN AMBITION. ASK HIM FOR WHAT YOU THINK YOU CAN GET FROM ME.
IF YOU REALLY WANT TO CHANGE THE WAY YOU SEE THINGS AS BEING BETWEEN US...
... YOU BETTER BE PREPARED TO CHANGE THE WAY YOU FEEL TOWARD YOUR LORD AND SAVIOR.
THESE ARE THE ENDTIMES, YOUNG LADY AND IT'S LATER THAN YOU THINK. YOU'VE NEVER REALLY TRIED TO OPEN YOUR HEART AND ACCEPT WHAT I'M TRYING TO GIVE YOU. GREATER THAN US.
DADDY, I DON'T BELIEVE IN GOD.

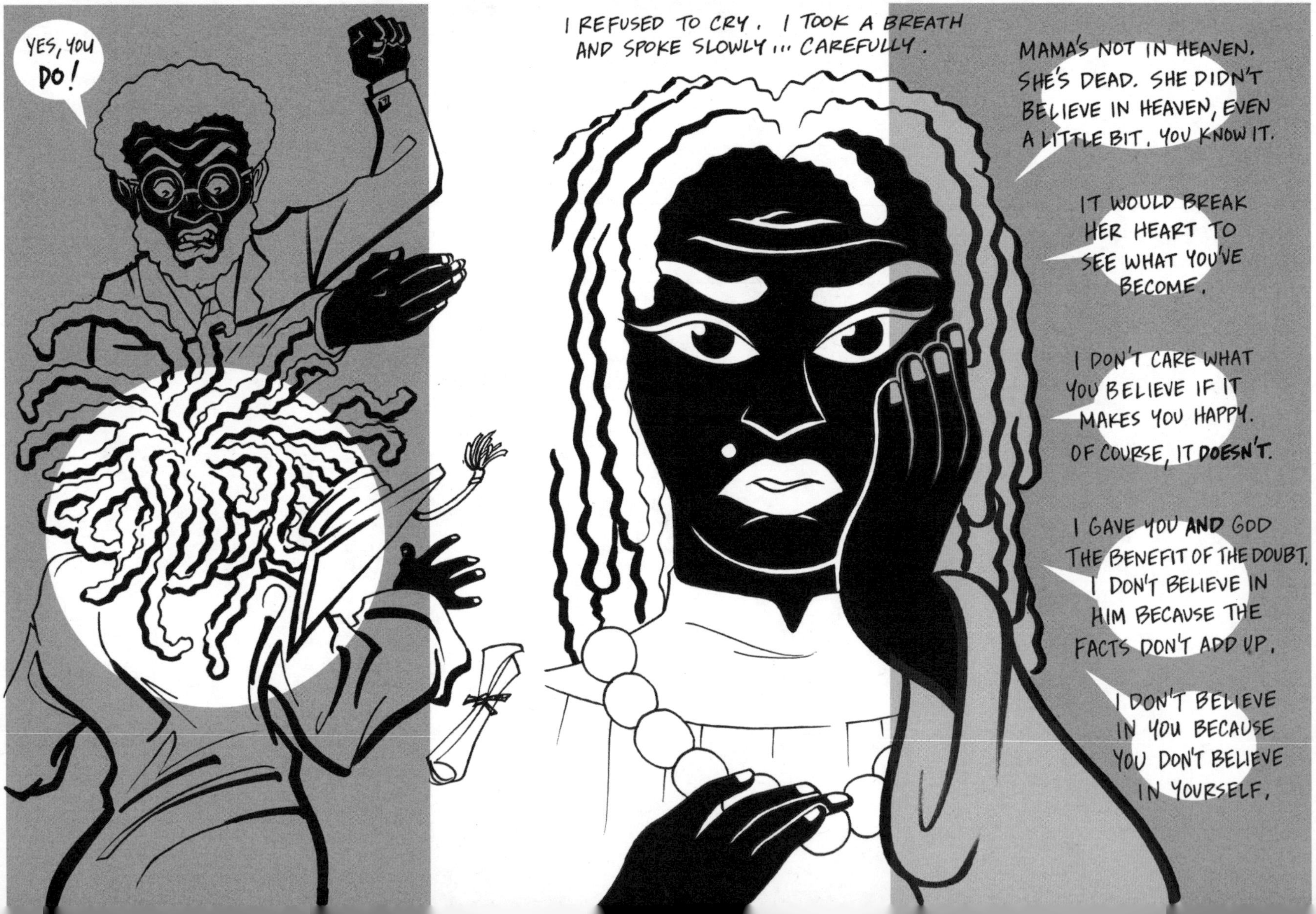
YES, YOU DO!
I REFUSED TO CRY. I TOOK A BREATH AND SPOKE SLOWLY... CAREFULLY.
MAMA'S NOT IN HEAVEN. SHE'S DEAD. SHE DIDN'T BELIEVE IN HEAVEN, EVEN A LITTLE BIT. YOU KNOW IT.
IT WOULD BREAK HER HEART TO SEE WHAT YOU'VE BECOME.
I DON'T CARE WHAT YOU BELIEVE IF IT MAKES YOU HAPPY. OF COURSE, IT DOESN'T.
I GAVE YOU AND GOD THE BENEFIT OF THE DOUBT. I DON'T BELIEVE IN HIM BECAUSE THE FACTS DON'T ADD UP.
I DON'T BELIEVE IN YOU BECAUSE YOU DON'T BELIEVE IN YOURSELF.

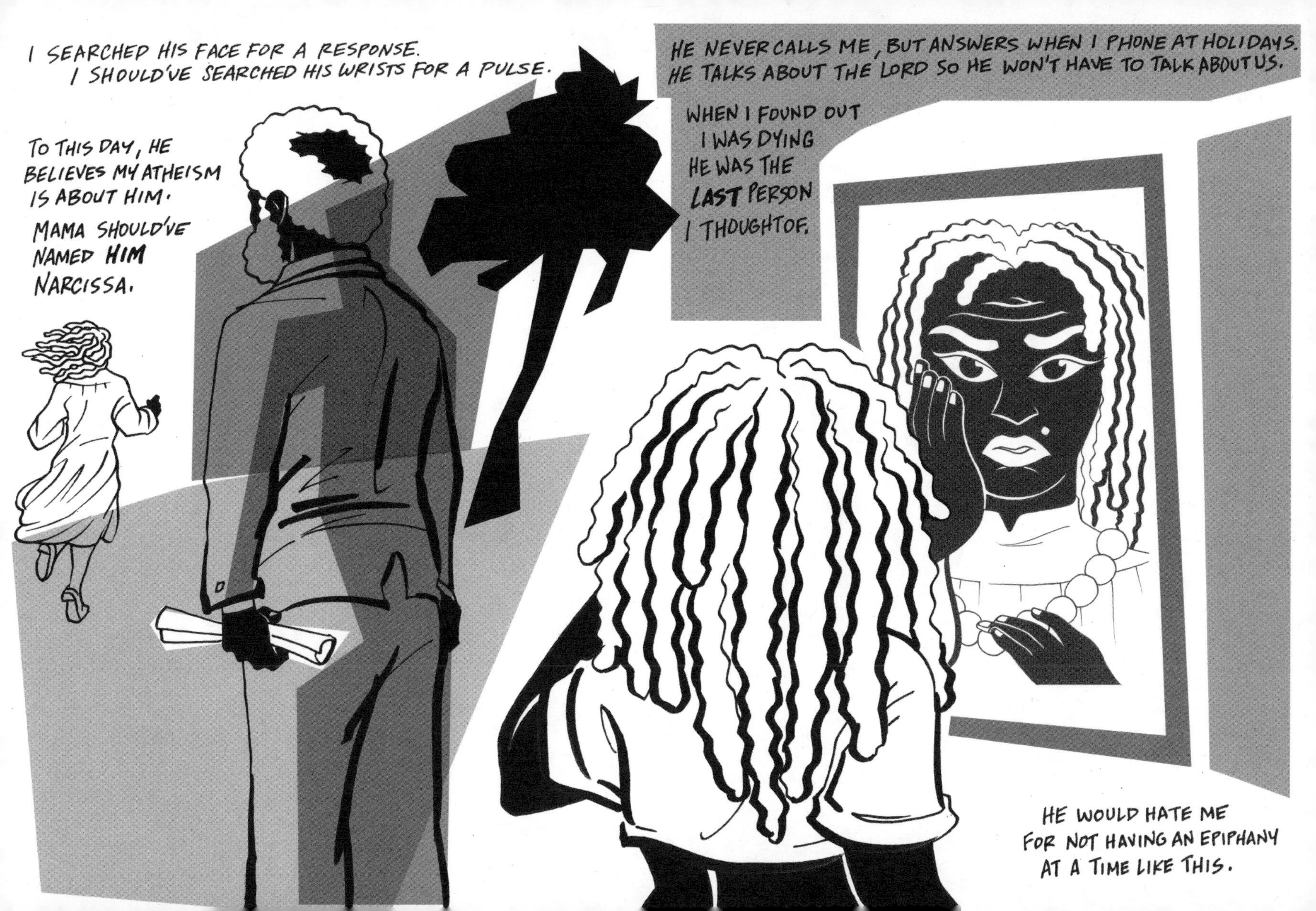

I SEARCHED HIS FACE FOR A RESPONSE. I SHOULD'VE SEARCHED HIS WRISTS FOR A PULSE.
TO THIS DAY, HE BELIEVES MY ATHEISM IS ABOUT HIM.
MAMA SHOULD'VE NAMED **HIM** NARCISSA.
HE NEVER CALLS ME, BUT ANSWERS WHEN I PHONE AT HOLIDAYS. HE TALKS ABOUT THE LORD SO HE WON'T HAVE TO TALK ABOUT US.
WHEN I FOUND OUT I WAS DYING HE WAS THE **LAST** PERSON I THOUGHT OF.
HE WOULD HATE ME FOR NOT HAVING AN EPIPHANY AT A TIME LIKE THIS.

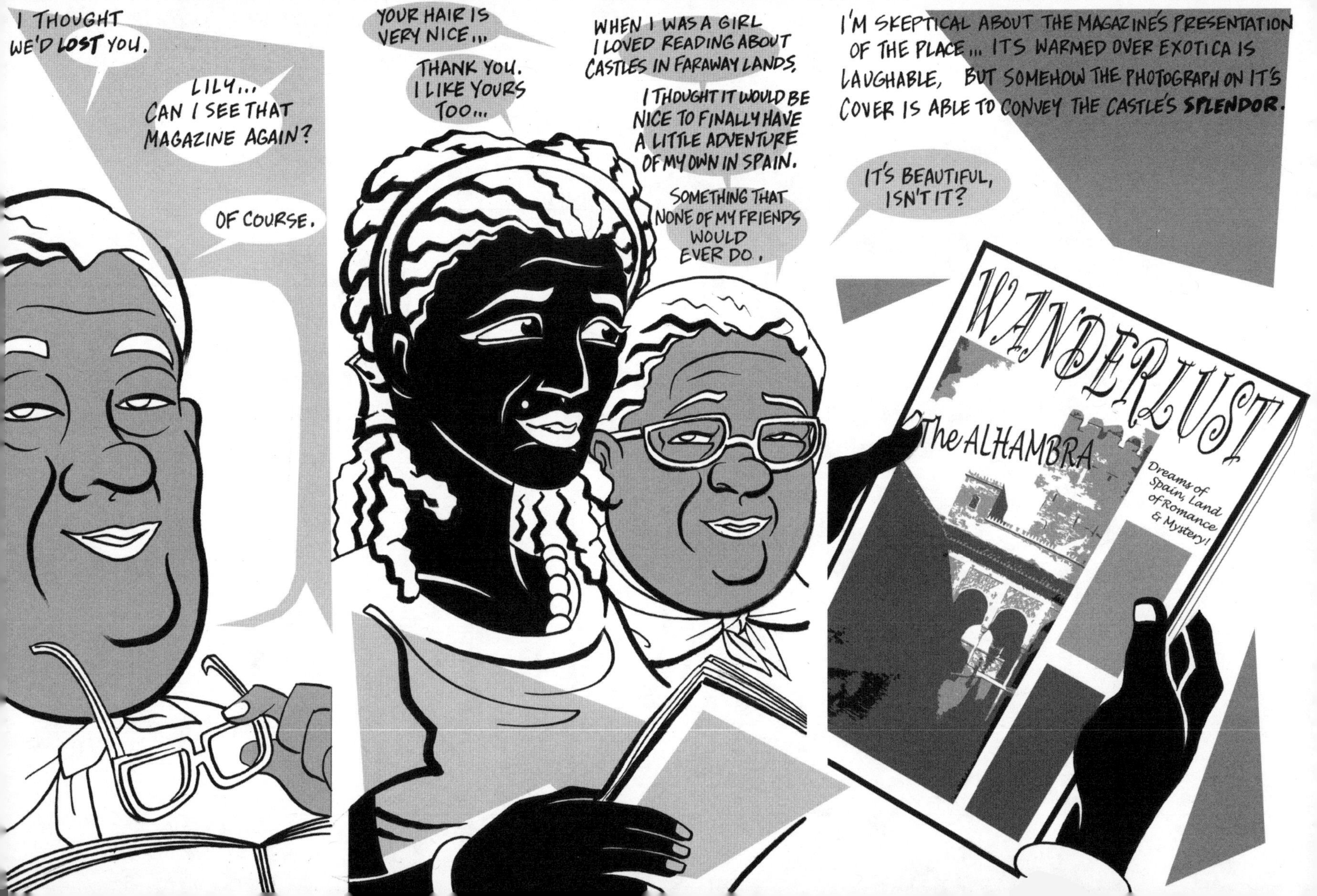
I THOUGHT WE'D **LOST** YOU.
LILY... CAN I SEE THAT MAGAZINE AGAIN?
OF COURSE.
YOUR HAIR IS VERY NICE...
THANK YOU. I LIKE YOURS TOO...
WHEN I WAS A GIRL I LOVED READING ABOUT CASTLES IN FARAWAY LANDS.
I THOUGHT IT WOULD BE NICE TO FINALLY HAVE A LITTLE ADVENTURE OF MY OWN IN SPAIN.
SOMETHING THAT NONE OF MY FRIENDS WOULD EVER DO.
I'M SKEPTICAL ABOUT THE MAGAZINE'S PRESENTATION OF THE PLACE... ITS WARMED OVER EXOTICA IS LAUGHABLE, BUT SOMEHOW THE PHOTOGRAPH ON IT'S COVER IS ABLE TO CONVEY THE CASTLE'S **SPLENDOR**.
IT'S BEAUTIFUL, ISN'T IT?
WANDERLUST
The ALHAMBRA
Dreams of Spain, Land of Romance & Mystery!

I IMAGINE THAT PEOPLE ARE DRAWN TO
THE ALHAMBRA FOR DIFFERENT REASONS.

MY REASONS AREN'T MYSTICAL... IT'S THE
SORT OF PLACE TO WHICH I'VE NEVER BEEN...
THE KIND OF SIGHT I WOULDN'T NORMALLY SEE.
I WON'T DIE WITHOUT VISITING
SUCH A GLORIOUS PLACE.

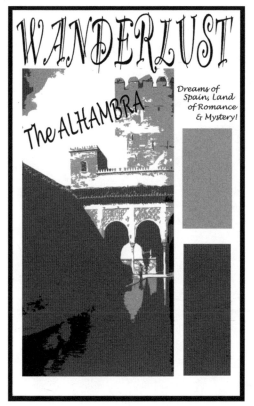

WANDERLUST

The ALHAMBRA

Dreams of
Spain, Land
of Romance
& Mystery!

I THINK BACK TO WHEN THE CASTLE
WAS NEW. PICTURE MYSELF BESIDE IT.

FEEL THE PRESENCE OF ITS BUILDERS
IN EVERY LINE AND CURVE AND ANGLE,

IT WOULD HAVE BEEN YET ANOTHER PLACE WHERE
A WOMAN'S ROLE WAS DECORATIVE AT BEST,
BUT I WOULD TRANSCEND ALL THAT
TO BECOME IT'S **MASTER**.

IT'S LOVELY,
ISN'T IT?

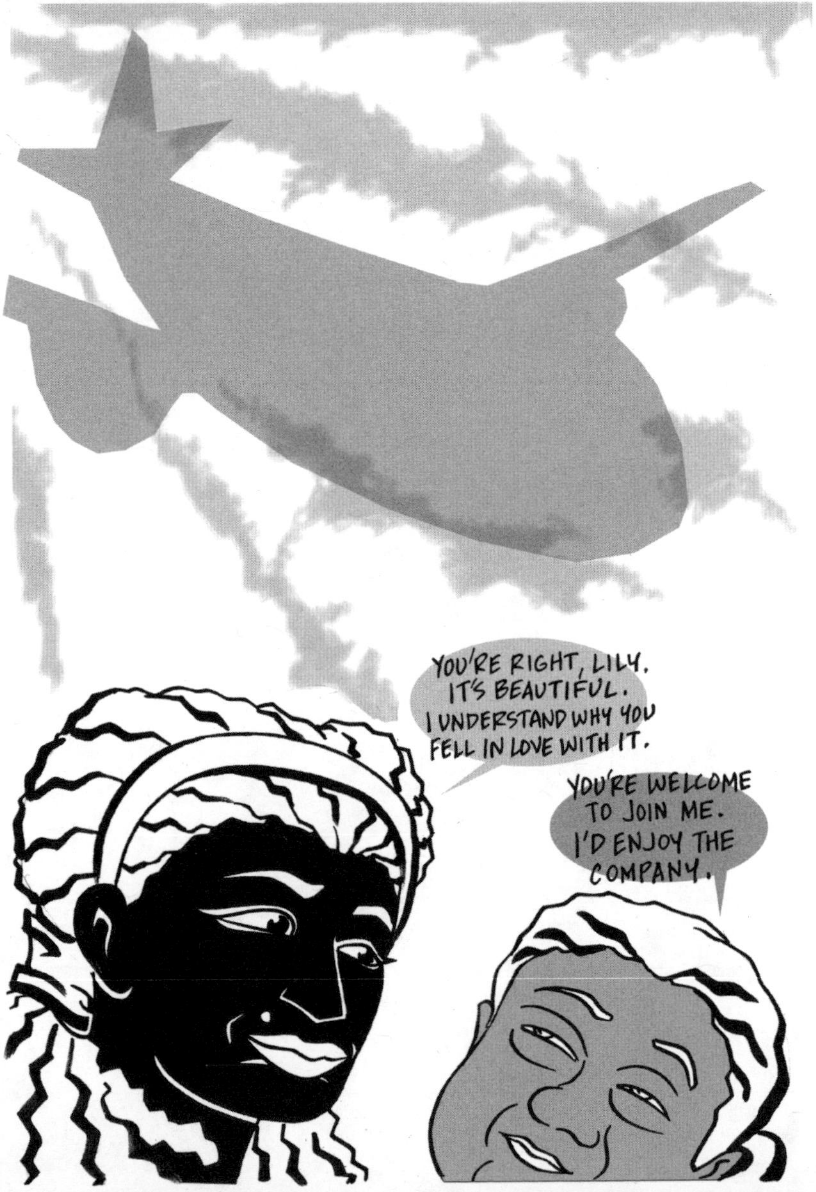
YOU'RE RIGHT, LILY. IT'S BEAUTIFUL. I UNDERSTAND WHY YOU FELL IN LOVE WITH IT.
YOU'RE WELCOME TO JOIN ME. I'D ENJOY THE COMPANY.

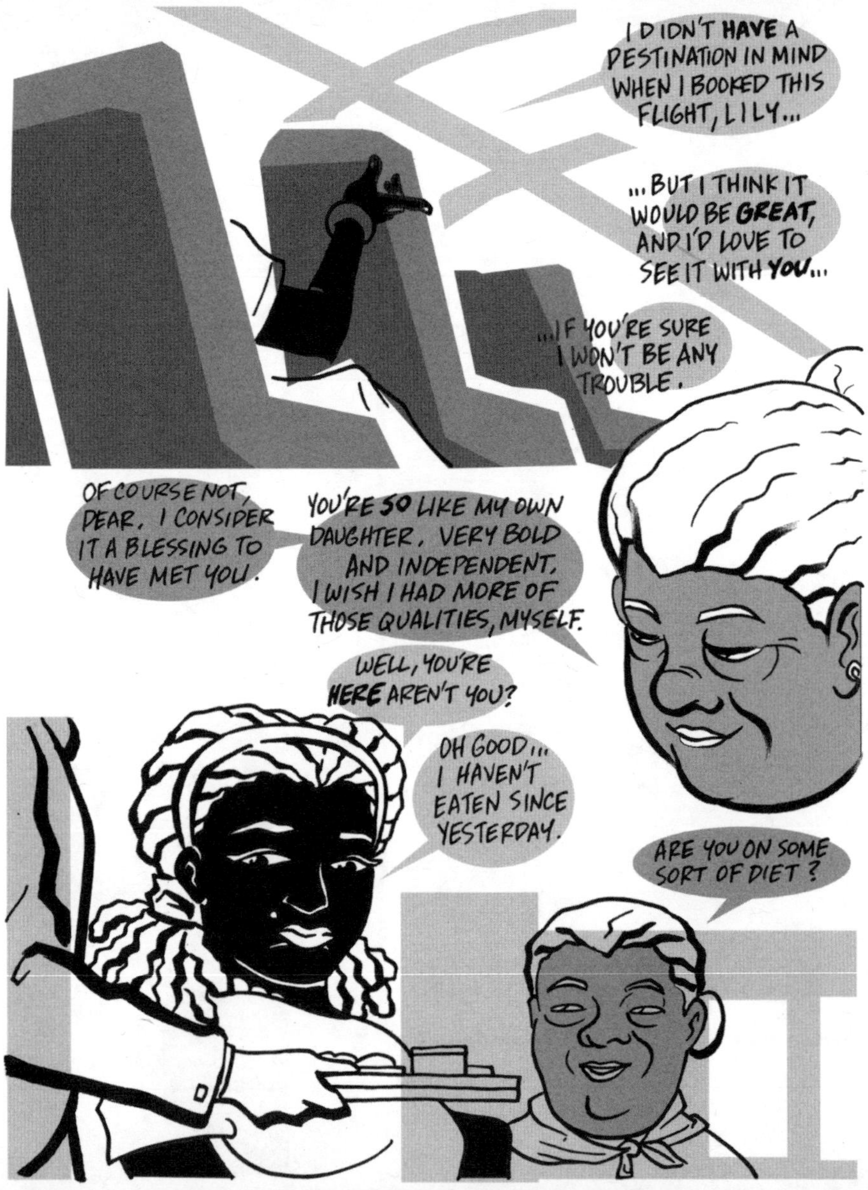
I DIDN'T **HAVE** A DESTINATION IN MIND WHEN I BOOKED THIS FLIGHT, LILY...
...BUT I THINK IT WOULD BE **GREAT**, AND I'D LOVE TO SEE IT WITH **YOU**...
...IF YOU'RE SURE I WON'T BE ANY TROUBLE.
OF COURSE NOT, DEAR. I CONSIDER IT A BLESSING TO HAVE MET YOU.
YOU'RE **SO** LIKE MY OWN DAUGHTER. VERY BOLD AND INDEPENDENT. I WISH I HAD MORE OF THOSE QUALITIES, MYSELF.
WELL, YOU'RE **HERE** AREN'T YOU?
OH GOOD... I HAVEN'T EATEN SINCE YESTERDAY.
ARE YOU ON SOME SORT OF DIET?

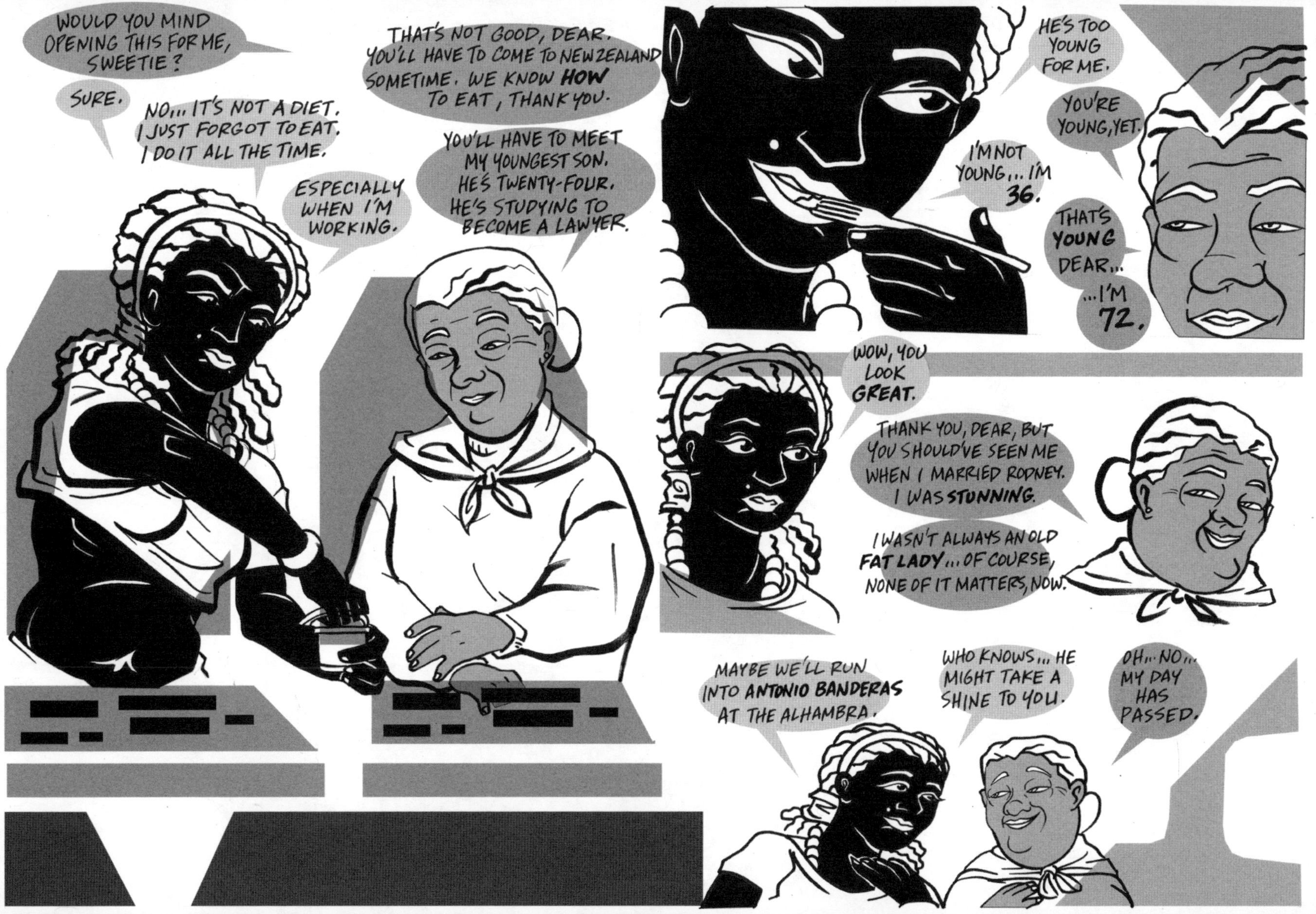

WOULD YOU MIND OPENING THIS FOR ME, SWEETIE?
SURE.
NO... IT'S NOT A DIET. I JUST FORGOT TO EAT. I DO IT ALL THE TIME.
ESPECIALLY WHEN I'M WORKING.
THAT'S NOT GOOD, DEAR. YOU'LL HAVE TO COME TO NEW ZEALAND SOMETIME. WE KNOW **HOW** TO EAT, THANK YOU.
YOU'LL HAVE TO MEET MY YOUNGEST SON. HE'S TWENTY-FOUR. HE'S STUDYING TO BECOME A LAWYER.
HE'S TOO YOUNG FOR ME.
YOU'RE YOUNG, YET.
I'M NOT YOUNG... I'M **36.**
THAT'S **YOUNG** DEAR...
...I'M **72.**
WOW, YOU LOOK **GREAT.**
THANK YOU, DEAR, BUT YOU SHOULD'VE SEEN ME WHEN I MARRIED RODNEY. I WAS **STUNNING.**
I WASN'T ALWAYS AN OLD **FAT LADY**... OF COURSE, NONE OF IT MATTERS, NOW.
MAYBE WE'LL RUN INTO **ANTONIO BANDERAS** AT THE ALHAMBRA.
WHO KNOWS... HE MIGHT TAKE A SHINE TO YOU.
OH... NO... MY DAY HAS PASSED.

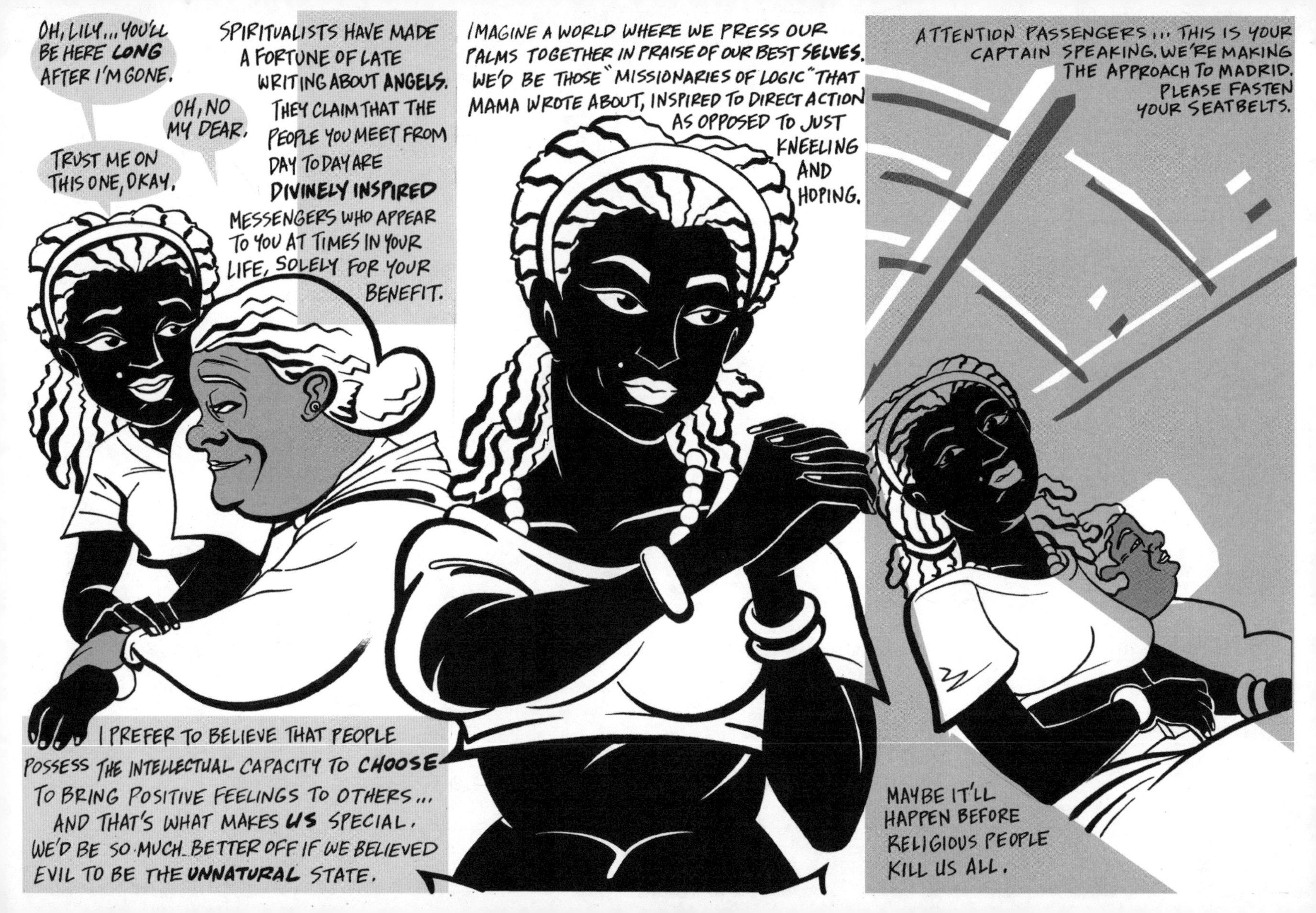

OH, LILY... YOU'LL BE HERE LONG AFTER I'M GONE.
TRUST ME ON THIS ONE, OKAY.
OH, NO MY DEAR.
SPIRITUALISTS HAVE MADE A FORTUNE OF LATE WRITING ABOUT ANGELS. THEY CLAIM THAT THE PEOPLE YOU MEET FROM DAY TO DAY ARE DIVINELY INSPIRED MESSENGERS WHO APPEAR TO YOU AT TIMES IN YOUR LIFE, SOLELY FOR YOUR BENEFIT.
I PREFER TO BELIEVE THAT PEOPLE POSSESS THE INTELLECTUAL CAPACITY TO CHOOSE TO BRING POSITIVE FEELINGS TO OTHERS... AND THAT'S WHAT MAKES US SPECIAL. WE'D BE SO MUCH BETTER OFF IF WE BELIEVED EVIL TO BE THE UNNATURAL STATE.
IMAGINE A WORLD WHERE WE PRESS OUR PALMS TOGETHER IN PRAISE OF OUR BEST SELVES. WE'D BE THOSE "MISSIONARIES OF LOGIC" THAT MAMA WROTE ABOUT, INSPIRED TO DIRECT ACTION AS OPPOSED TO JUST KNEELING AND HOPING.
ATTENTION PASSENGERS... THIS IS YOUR CAPTAIN SPEAKING. WE'RE MAKING THE APPROACH TO MADRID. PLEASE FASTEN YOUR SEATBELTS.
MAYBE IT'LL HAPPEN BEFORE RELIGIOUS PEOPLE KILL US ALL.

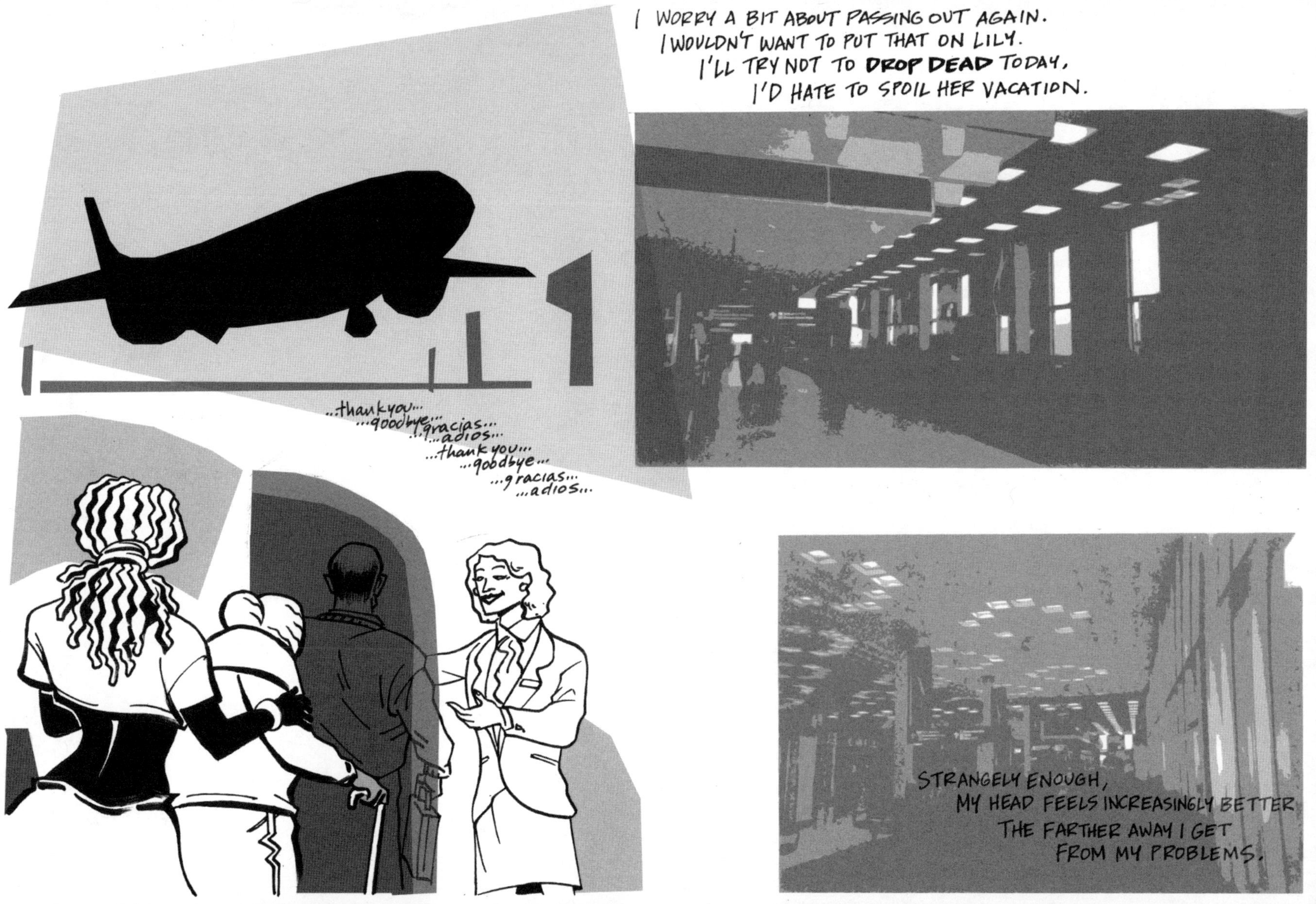
I WORRY A BIT ABOUT PASSING OUT AGAIN.
I WOULDN'T WANT TO PUT THAT ON LILY.
I'LL TRY NOT TO **DROP DEAD** TODAY,
I'D HATE TO SPOIL HER VACATION.
...thankyou...
...goodbye...
...gracias...
...adios...
...thank you...
...goodbye...
...gracias...
...adios...
STRANGELY ENOUGH,
MY HEAD FEELS INCREASINGLY BETTER
THE FARTHER AWAY I GET
FROM MY PROBLEMS.

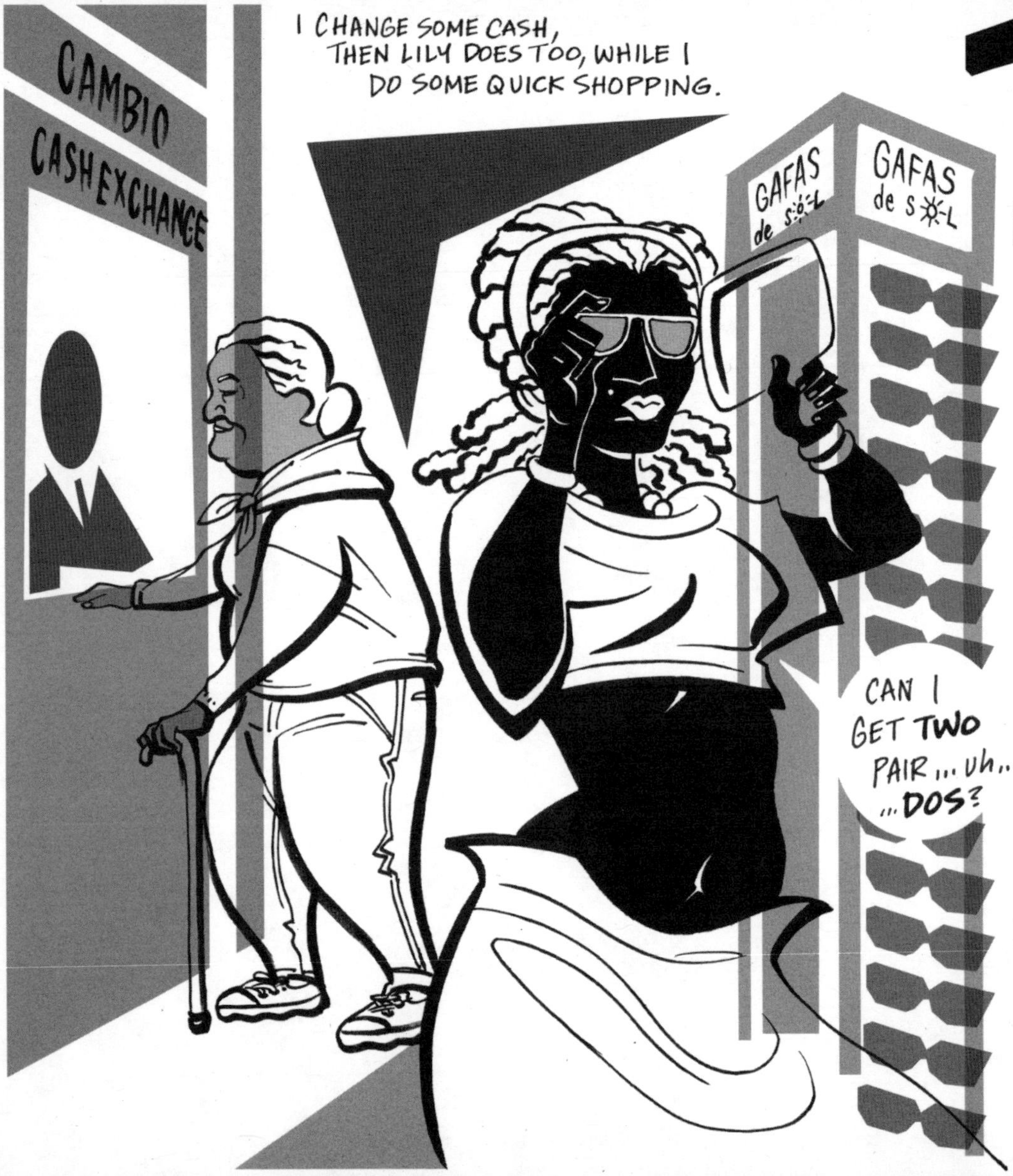

I CHANGE SOME CASH, THEN LILY DOES TOO, WHILE I DO SOME QUICK SHOPPING.
CAMBIO
CASH EXCHANGE
GAFAS de SOL
GAFAS de SOL
CAN I GET TWO PAIR... uh... ...DOS?

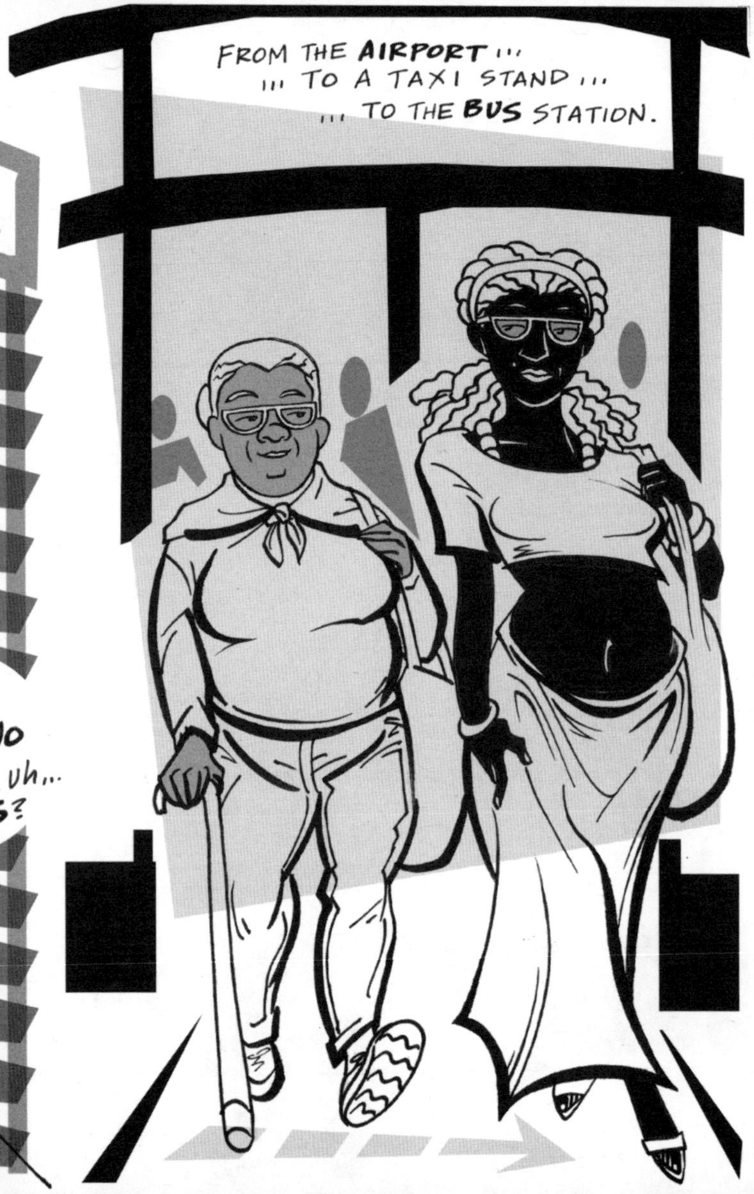

FROM THE AIRPORT... ...TO A TAXI STAND... ...TO THE BUS STATION.

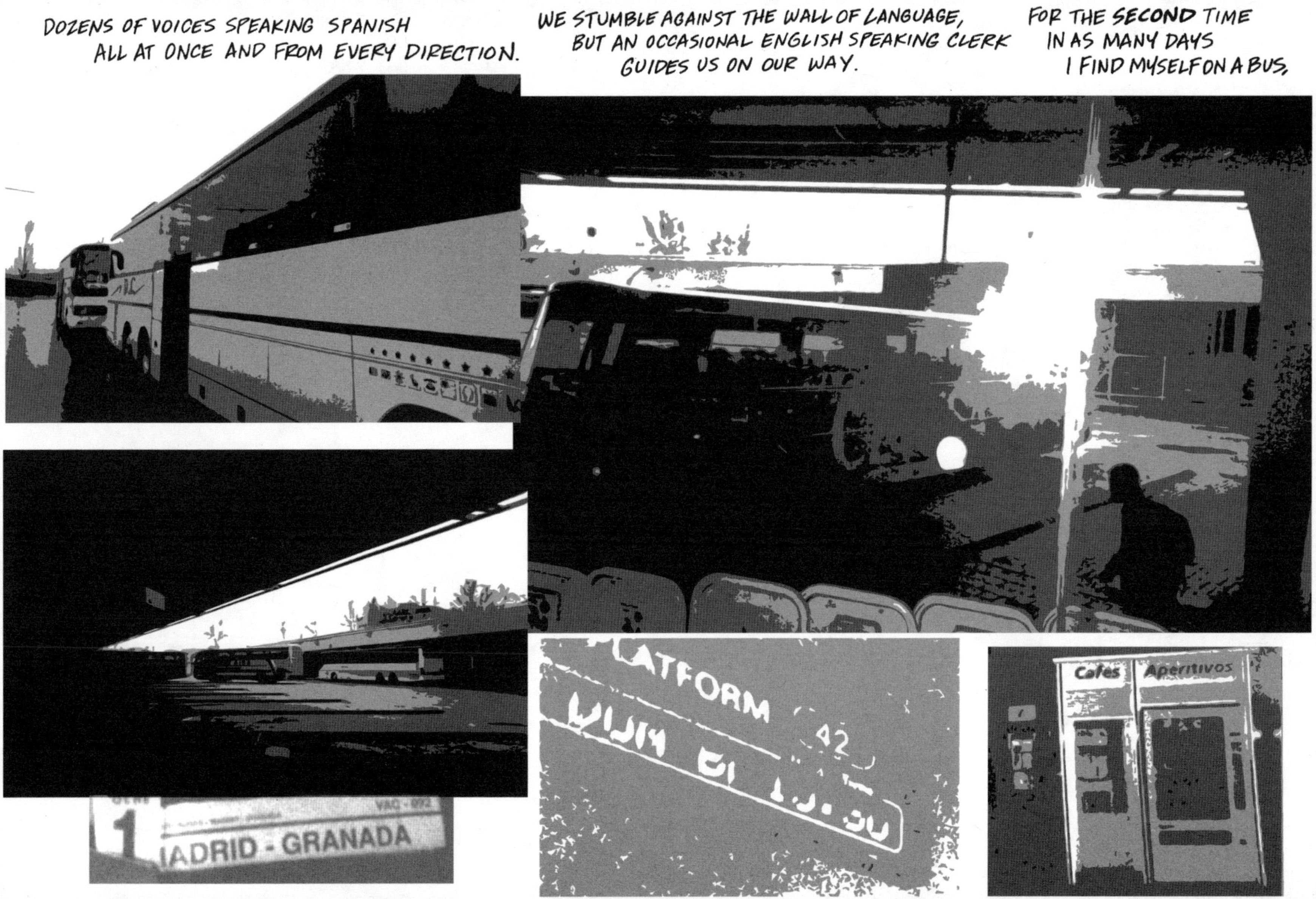
DOZENS OF VOICES SPEAKING SPANISH
ALL AT ONCE AND FROM EVERY DIRECTION.
WE STUMBLE AGAINST THE WALL OF LANGUAGE,
BUT AN OCCASIONAL ENGLISH SPEAKING CLERK
GUIDES US ON OUR WAY.
FOR THE SECOND TIME
IN AS MANY DAYS
I FIND MYSELF ON A BUS,
1
ADRID - GRANADA
LATFORM 42
Cafes
Aperitivos

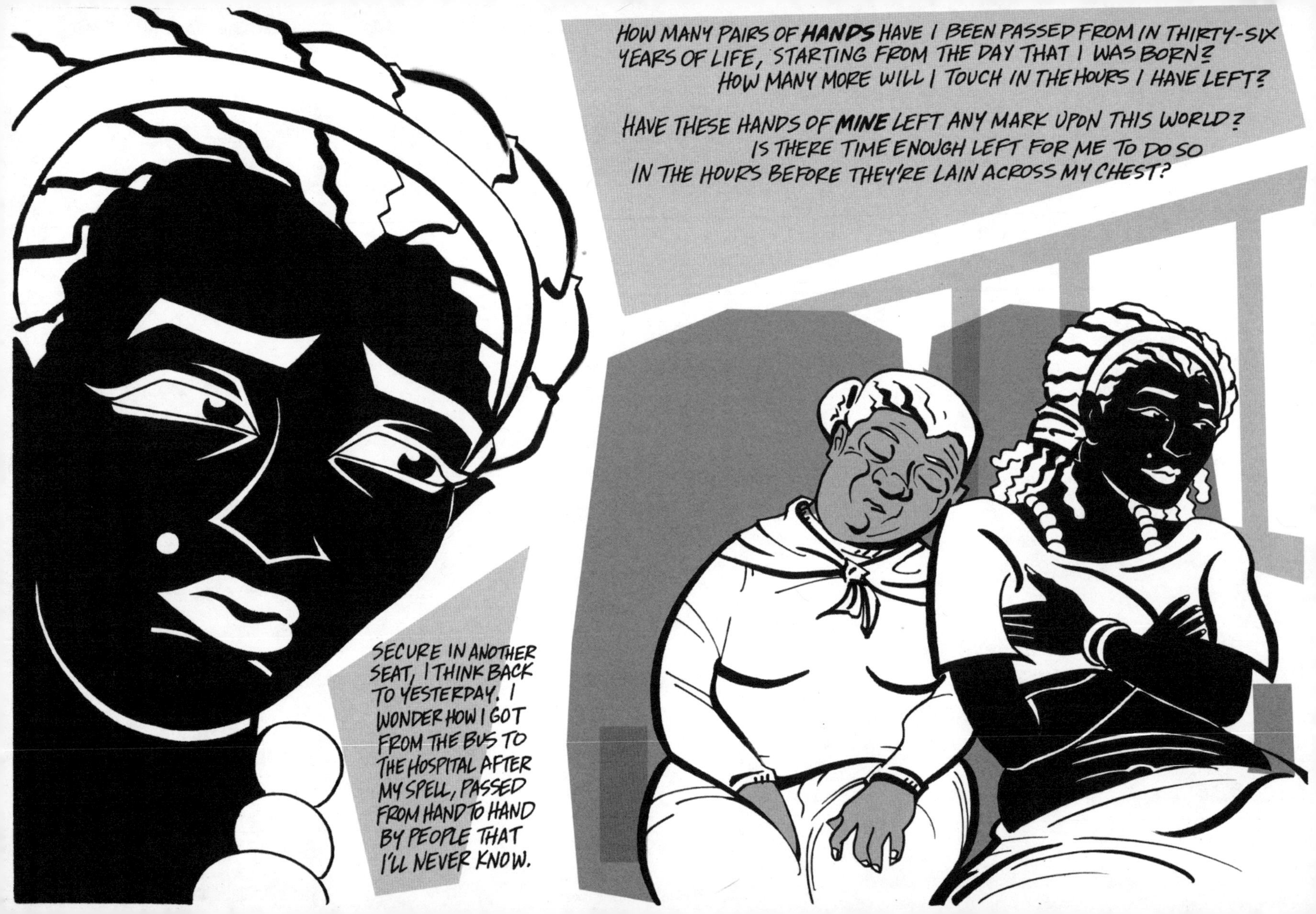
HOW MANY PAIRS OF HANDS HAVE I BEEN PASSED FROM IN THIRTY-SIX YEARS OF LIFE, STARTING FROM THE DAY THAT I WAS BORN? HOW MANY MORE WILL I TOUCH IN THE HOURS I HAVE LEFT?
HAVE THESE HANDS OF MINE LEFT ANY MARK UPON THIS WORLD? IS THERE TIME ENOUGH LEFT FOR ME TO DO SO IN THE HOURS BEFORE THEY'RE LAIN ACROSS MY CHEST?
SECURE IN ANOTHER SEAT, I THINK BACK TO YESTERDAY. I WONDER HOW I GOT FROM THE BUS TO THE HOSPITAL AFTER MY SPELL, PASSED FROM HAND TO HAND BY PEOPLE THAT I'LL NEVER KNOW.

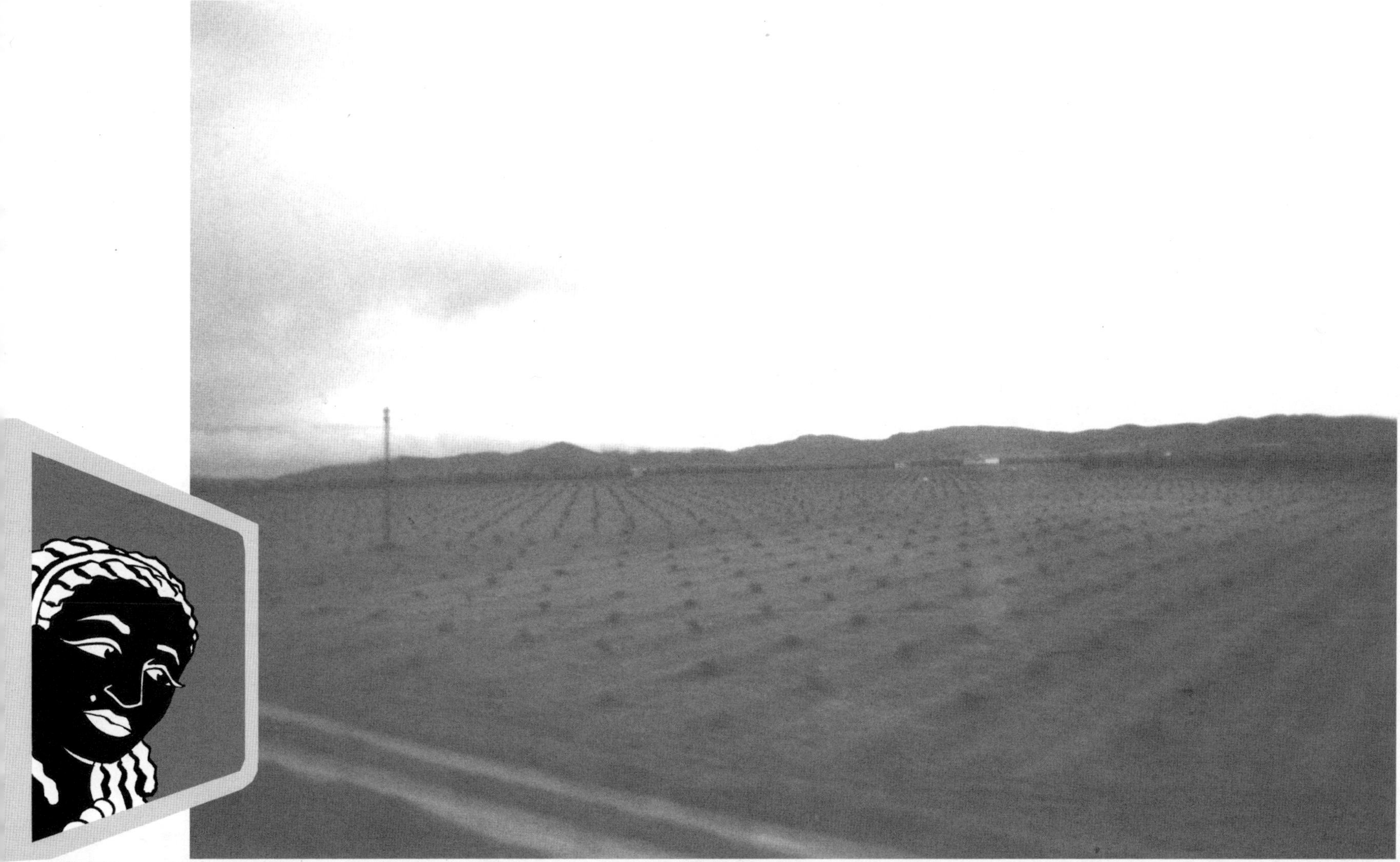

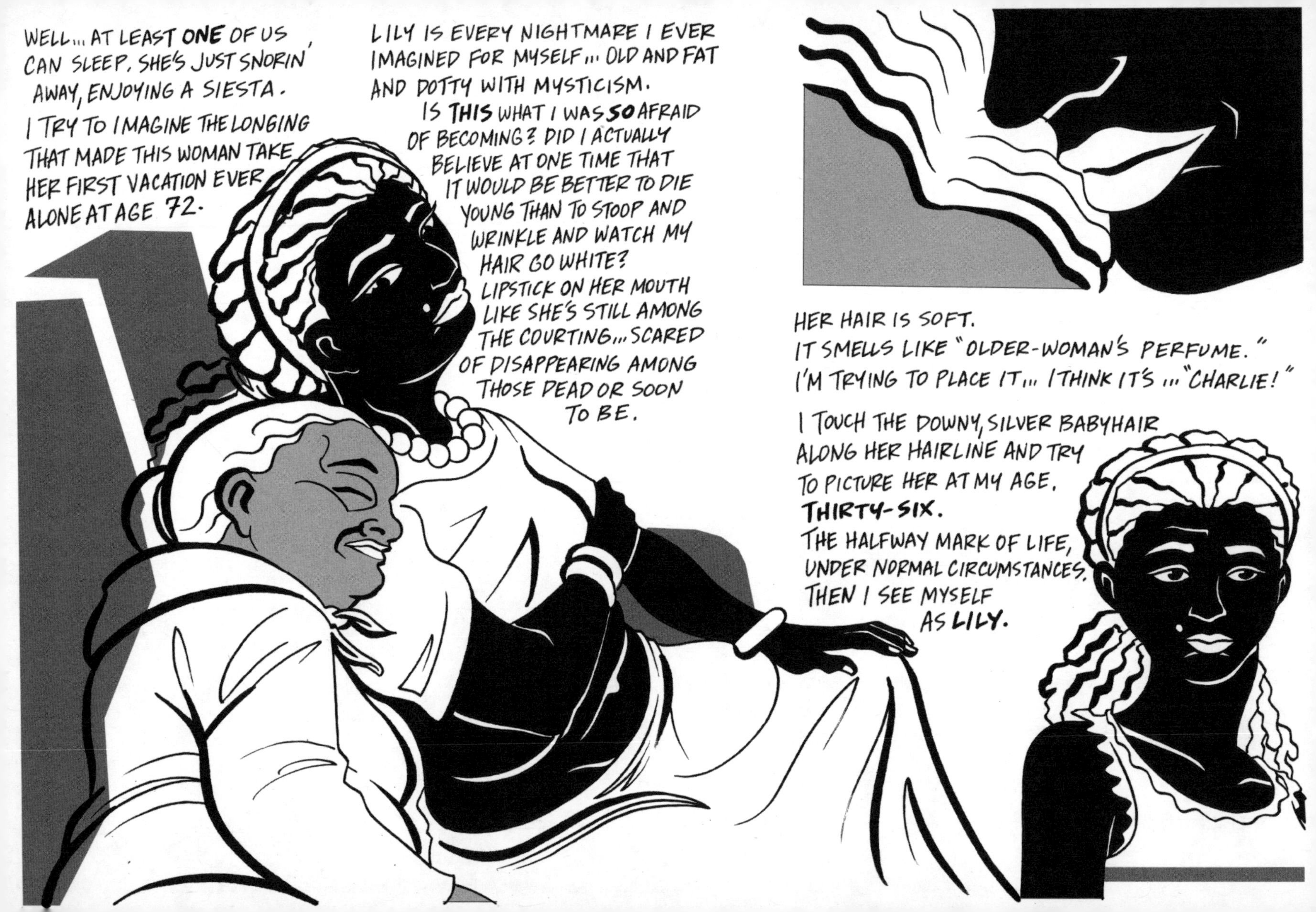
WELL... AT LEAST **ONE** OF US CAN SLEEP. SHE'S JUST SNORIN' AWAY, ENJOYING A SIESTA.
I TRY TO IMAGINE THE LONGING THAT MADE THIS WOMAN TAKE HER FIRST VACATION EVER ALONE AT AGE 72.
LILY IS EVERY NIGHTMARE I EVER IMAGINED FOR MYSELF... OLD AND FAT AND DOTTY WITH MYSTICISM.
IS **THIS** WHAT I WAS **SO** AFRAID OF BECOMING? DID I ACTUALLY BELIEVE AT ONE TIME THAT IT WOULD BE BETTER TO DIE YOUNG THAN TO STOOP AND WRINKLE AND WATCH MY HAIR GO WHITE?
LIPSTICK ON HER MOUTH LIKE SHE'S STILL AMONG THE COURTING... SCARED OF DISAPPEARING AMONG THOSE DEAD OR SOON TO BE.
HER HAIR IS SOFT.
IT SMELLS LIKE "OLDER-WOMAN'S PERFUME."
I'M TRYING TO PLACE IT... I THINK IT'S ... "CHARLIE!"
I TOUCH THE DOWNY, SILVER BABYHAIR ALONG HER HAIRLINE AND TRY TO PICTURE HER AT MY AGE.
THIRTY-SIX.
THE HALFWAY MARK OF LIFE, UNDER NORMAL CIRCUMSTANCES.
THEN I SEE MYSELF AS **LILY**.

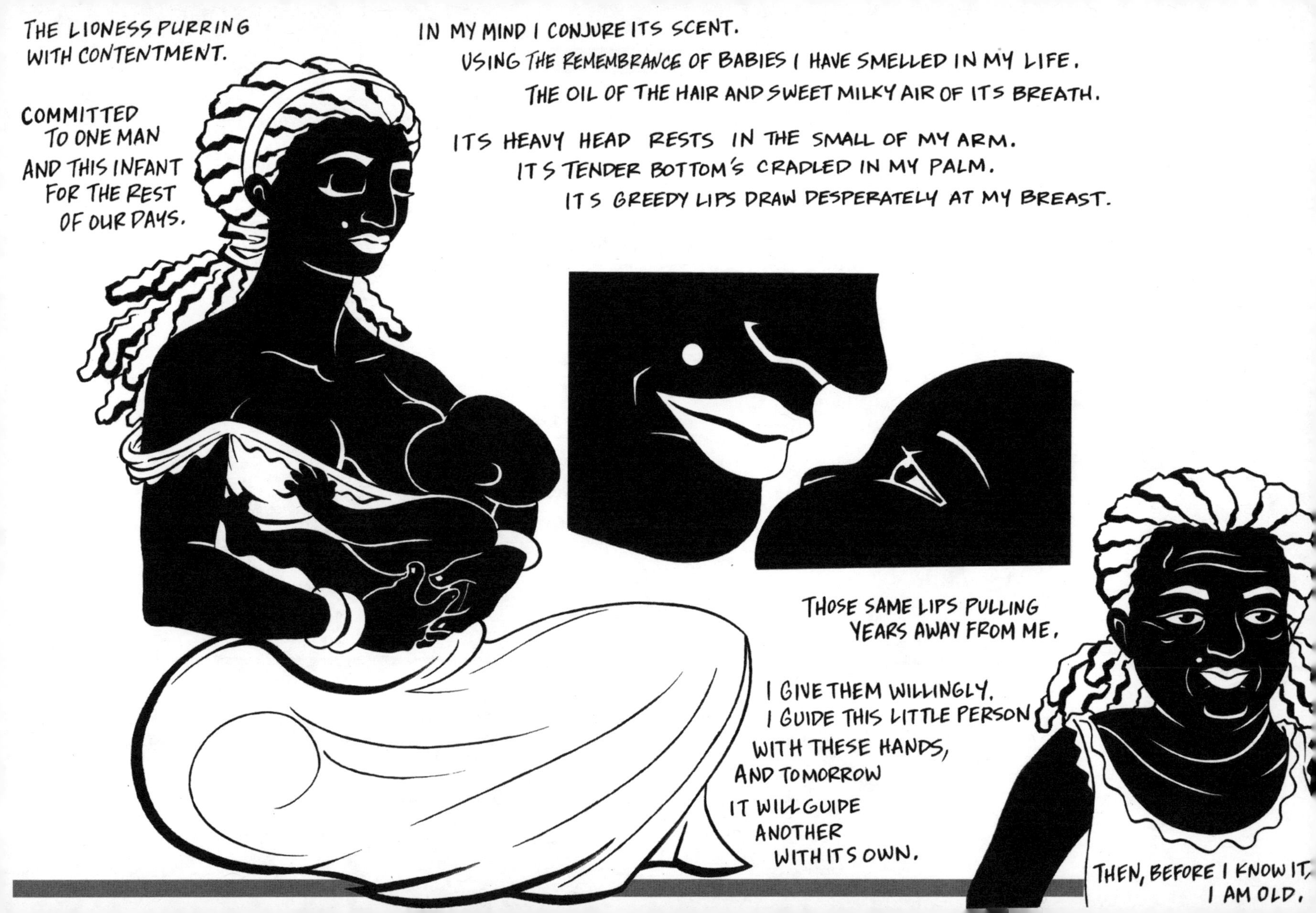
THE LIONESS PURRING WITH CONTENTMENT.
COMMITTED TO ONE MAN AND THIS INFANT FOR THE REST OF OUR DAYS.
IN MY MIND I CONJURE ITS SCENT.
USING THE REMEMBRANCE OF BABIES I HAVE SMELLED IN MY LIFE.
THE OIL OF THE HAIR AND SWEET MILKY AIR OF ITS BREATH.
ITS HEAVY HEAD RESTS IN THE SMALL OF MY ARM.
ITS TENDER BOTTOM'S CRADLED IN MY PALM.
ITS GREEDY LIPS DRAW DESPERATELY AT MY BREAST.
THOSE SAME LIPS PULLING YEARS AWAY FROM ME.
I GIVE THEM WILLINGLY.
I GUIDE THIS LITTLE PERSON WITH THESE HANDS,
AND TOMORROW IT WILL GUIDE ANOTHER WITH ITS OWN.
THEN, BEFORE I KNOW IT, I AM OLD.

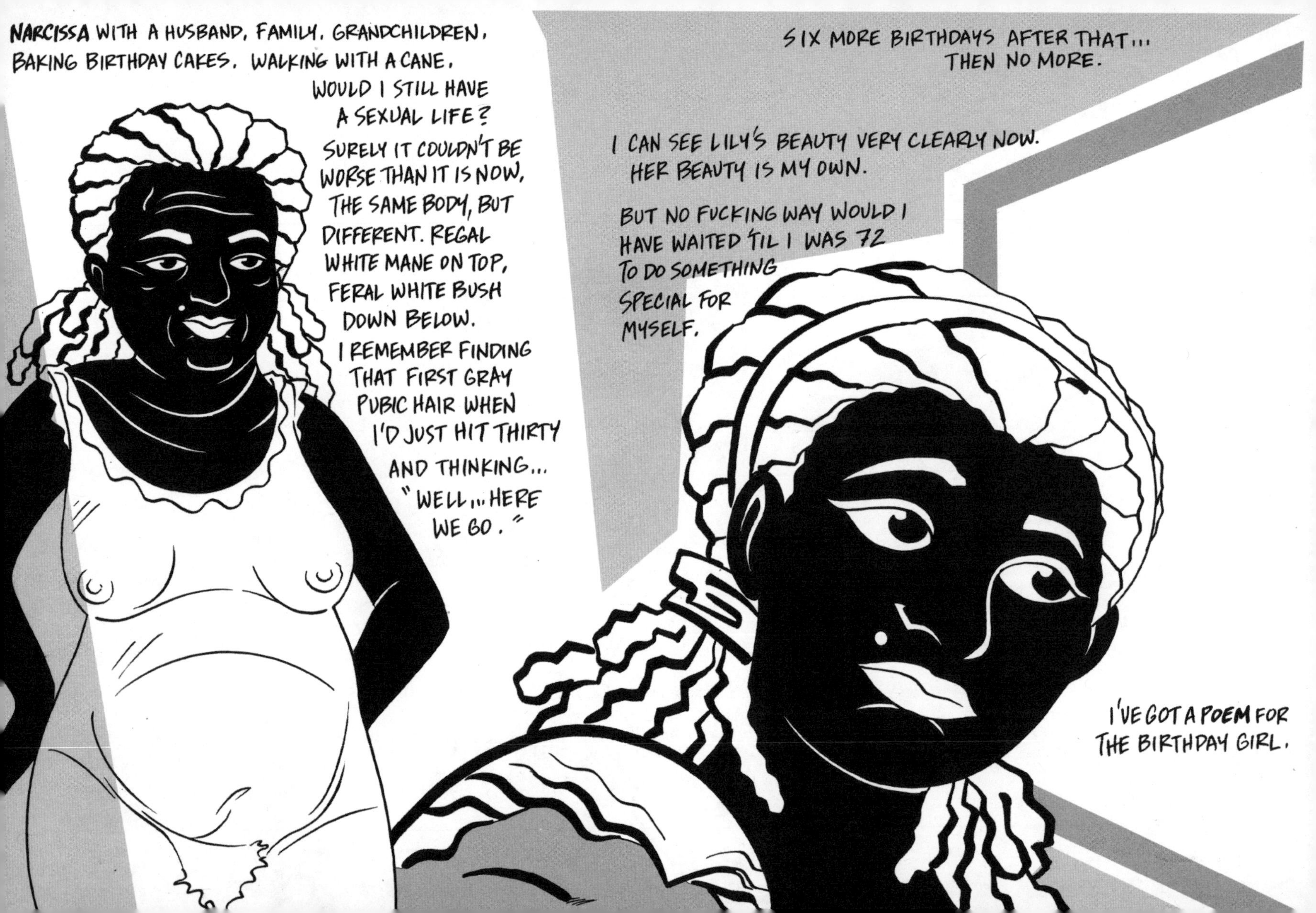
NARCISSA WITH A HUSBAND, FAMILY, GRANDCHILDREN, BAKING BIRTHDAY CAKES. WALKING WITH A CANE.
WOULD I STILL HAVE A SEXUAL LIFE?
SURELY IT COULDN'T BE WORSE THAN IT IS NOW, THE SAME BODY, BUT DIFFERENT. REGAL WHITE MANE ON TOP, FERAL WHITE BUSH DOWN BELOW.
I REMEMBER FINDING THAT FIRST GRAY PUBIC HAIR WHEN I'D JUST HIT THIRTY AND THINKING... "WELL... HERE WE GO."
SIX MORE BIRTHDAYS AFTER THAT... THEN NO MORE.
I CAN SEE LILY'S BEAUTY VERY CLEARLY NOW. HER BEAUTY IS MY OWN.
BUT NO FUCKING WAY WOULD I HAVE WAITED 'TIL I WAS 72 TO DO SOMETHING SPECIAL FOR MYSELF.
I'VE GOT A POEM FOR THE BIRTHDAY GIRL.

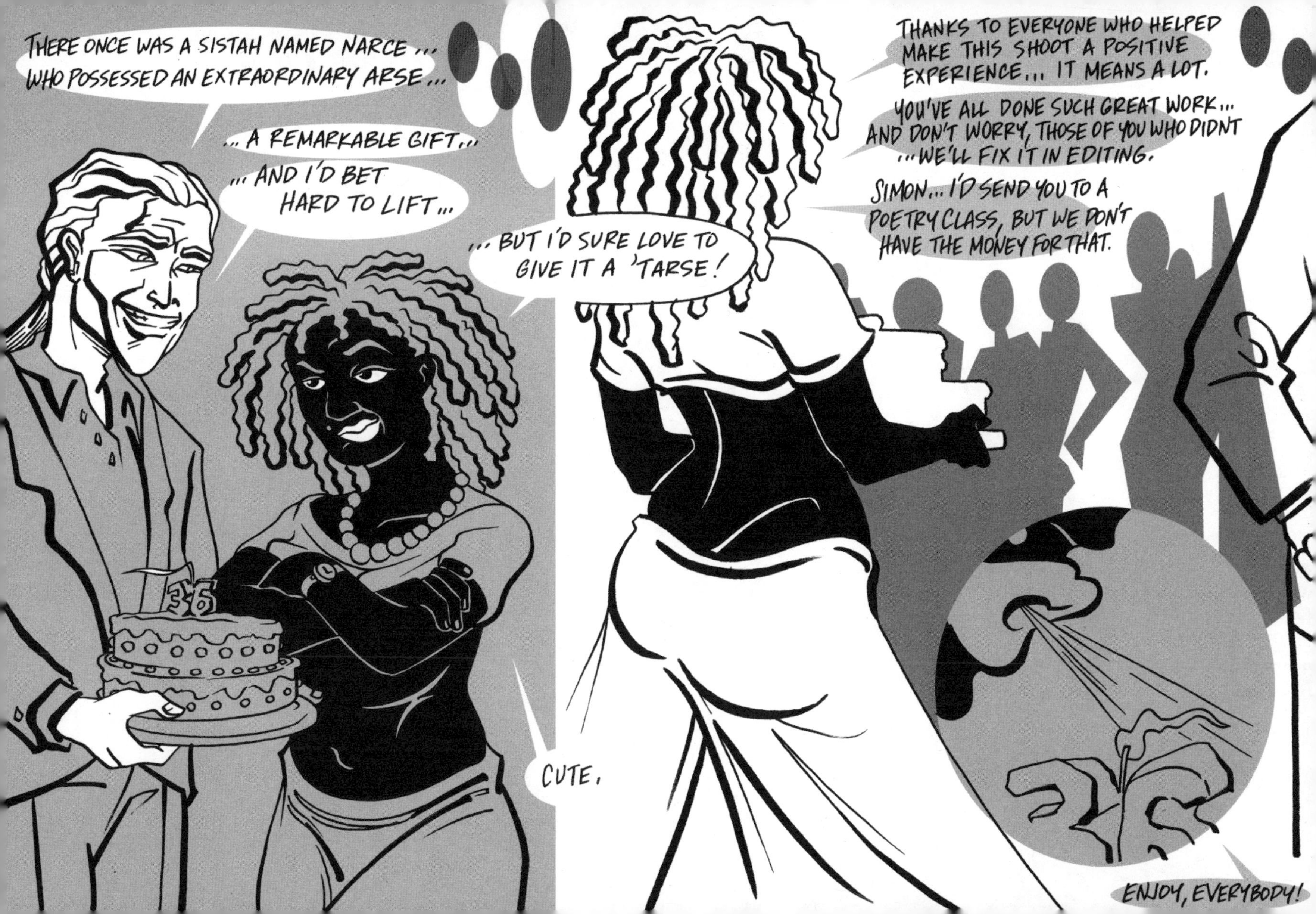
THERE ONCE WAS A SISTAH NAMED NARCE ... WHO POSSESSED AN EXTRAORDINARY ARSE ...
... A REMARKABLE GIFT ...
... AND I'D BET HARD TO LIFT ...
... BUT I'D SURE LOVE TO GIVE IT A 'TARSE!
CUTE.
THANKS TO EVERYONE WHO HELPED MAKE THIS SHOOT A POSITIVE EXPERIENCE ... IT MEANS A LOT.
YOU'VE ALL DONE SUCH GREAT WORK ... AND DON'T WORRY, THOSE OF YOU WHO DIDN'T ... WE'LL FIX IT IN EDITING.
SIMON ... I'D SEND YOU TO A POETRY CLASS, BUT WE DON'T HAVE THE MONEY FOR THAT.
ENJOY, EVERYBODY!

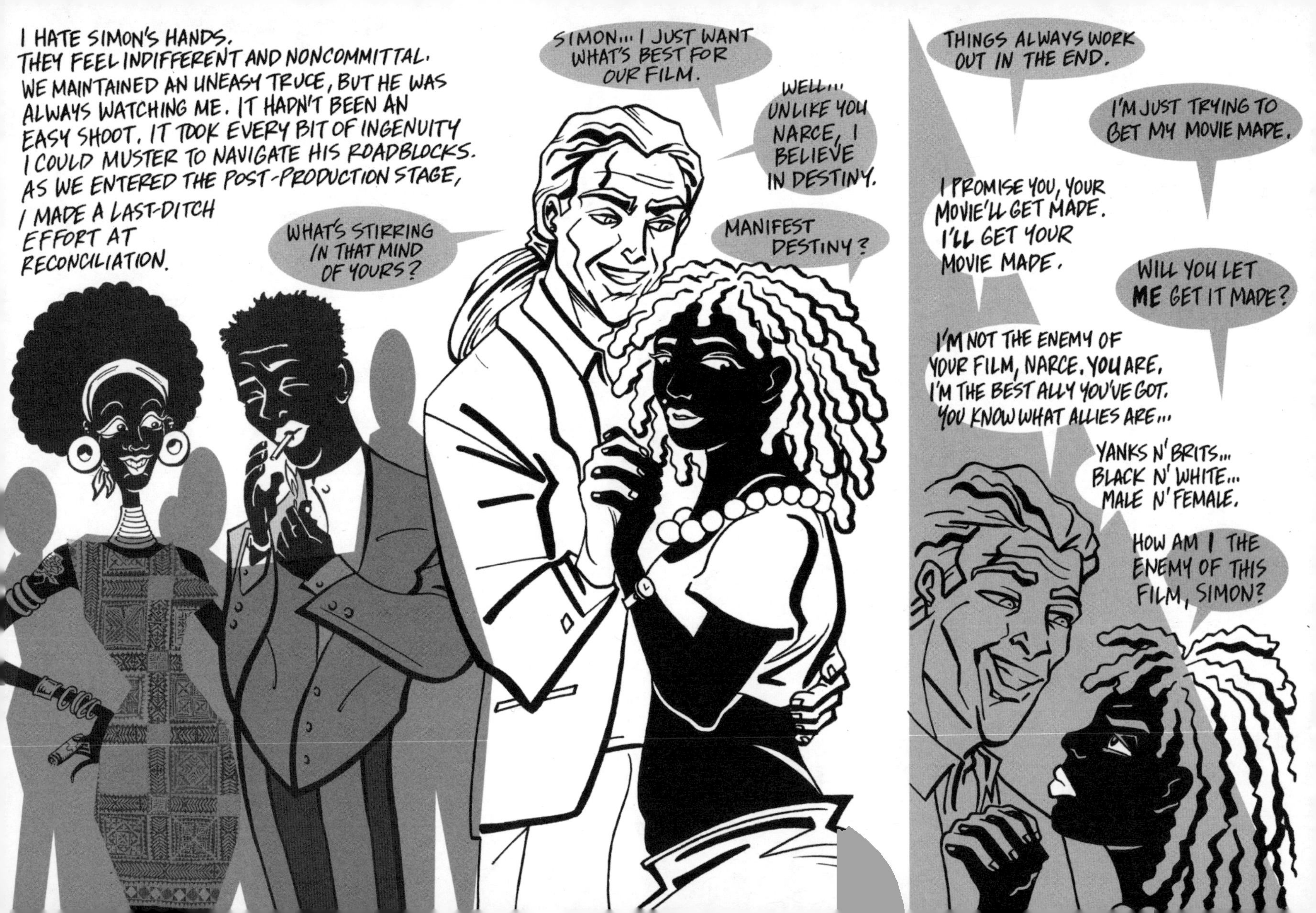
I HATE SIMON'S HANDS. THEY FEEL INDIFFERENT AND NONCOMMITTAL. WE MAINTAINED AN UNEASY TRUCE, BUT HE WAS ALWAYS WATCHING ME. IT HADN'T BEEN AN EASY SHOOT. IT TOOK EVERY BIT OF INGENUITY I COULD MUSTER TO NAVIGATE HIS ROADBLOCKS. AS WE ENTERED THE POST-PRODUCTION STAGE, I MADE A LAST-DITCH EFFORT AT RECONCILIATION.
WHAT'S STIRRING IN THAT MIND OF YOURS?
SIMON... I JUST WANT WHAT'S BEST FOR OUR FILM.
WELL... UNLIKE YOU NARCE, I BELIEVE IN DESTINY.
MANIFEST DESTINY?
THINGS ALWAYS WORK OUT IN THE END.
I'M JUST TRYING TO GET MY MOVIE MADE.
I PROMISE YOU, YOUR MOVIE'LL GET MADE. I'LL GET YOUR MOVIE MADE.
WILL YOU LET ME GET IT MADE?
I'M NOT THE ENEMY OF YOUR FILM, NARCE. YOU ARE. I'M THE BEST ALLY YOU'VE GOT. YOU KNOW WHAT ALLIES ARE...
YANKS N' BRITS... BLACK N' WHITE... MALE N' FEMALE.
HOW AM I THE ENEMY OF THIS FILM, SIMON?

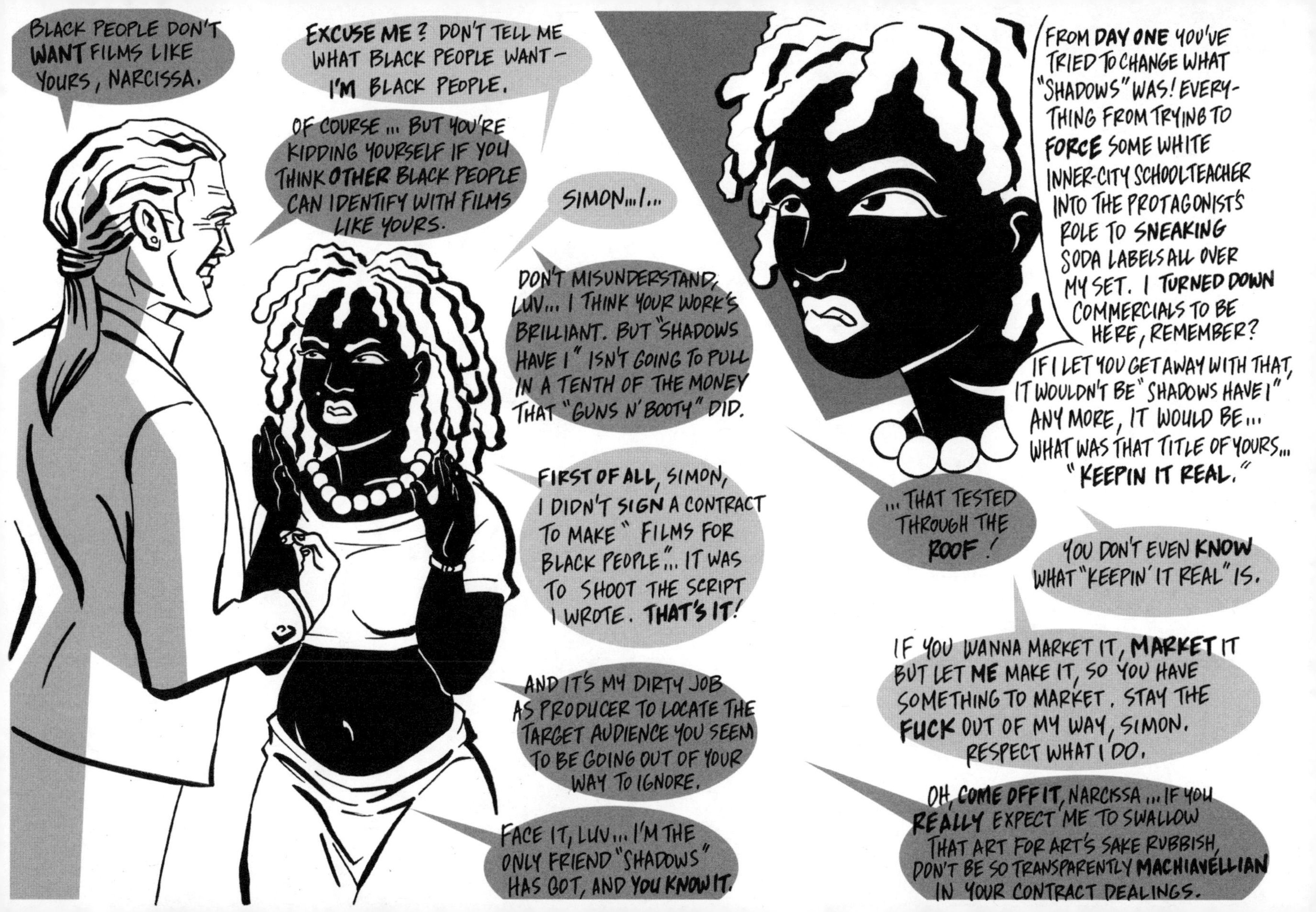

BLACK PEOPLE DON'T WANT FILMS LIKE YOURS, NARCISSA.
EXCUSE ME? DON'T TELL ME WHAT BLACK PEOPLE WANT— I'M BLACK PEOPLE.
OF COURSE ... BUT YOU'RE KIDDING YOURSELF IF YOU THINK OTHER BLACK PEOPLE CAN IDENTIFY WITH FILMS LIKE YOURS.
SIMON... I...
DON'T MISUNDERSTAND, LUV... I THINK YOUR WORK'S BRILLIANT. BUT "SHADOWS HAVE I" ISN'T GOING TO PULL IN A TENTH OF THE MONEY THAT "GUNS N' BOOTY" DID.
FIRST OF ALL, SIMON, I DIDN'T SIGN A CONTRACT TO MAKE "FILMS FOR BLACK PEOPLE"... IT WAS TO SHOOT THE SCRIPT I WROTE. THAT'S IT!
AND IT'S MY DIRTY JOB AS PRODUCER TO LOCATE THE TARGET AUDIENCE YOU SEEM TO BE GOING OUT OF YOUR WAY TO IGNORE.
FACE IT, LUV... I'M THE ONLY FRIEND "SHADOWS" HAS GOT, AND YOU KNOW IT.
FROM DAY ONE YOU'VE TRIED TO CHANGE WHAT "SHADOWS" WAS! EVERYTHING FROM TRYING TO FORCE SOME WHITE INNER-CITY SCHOOLTEACHER INTO THE PROTAGONIST'S ROLE TO SNEAKING SODA LABELS ALL OVER MY SET. I TURNED DOWN COMMERCIALS TO BE HERE, REMEMBER?
IF I LET YOU GET AWAY WITH THAT, IT WOULDN'T BE "SHADOWS HAVE I" ANY MORE, IT WOULD BE... WHAT WAS THAT TITLE OF YOURS... "KEEPIN IT REAL."
... THAT TESTED THROUGH THE ROOF!
YOU DON'T EVEN KNOW WHAT "KEEPIN' IT REAL" IS.
IF YOU WANNA MARKET IT, MARKET IT BUT LET ME MAKE IT, SO YOU HAVE SOMETHING TO MARKET. STAY THE FUCK OUT OF MY WAY, SIMON. RESPECT WHAT I DO.
OH, COME OFF IT, NARCISSA ... IF YOU REALLY EXPECT ME TO SWALLOW THAT ART FOR ART'S SAKE RUBBISH, DON'T BE SO TRANSPARENTLY MACHIAVELLIAN IN YOUR CONTRACT DEALINGS.

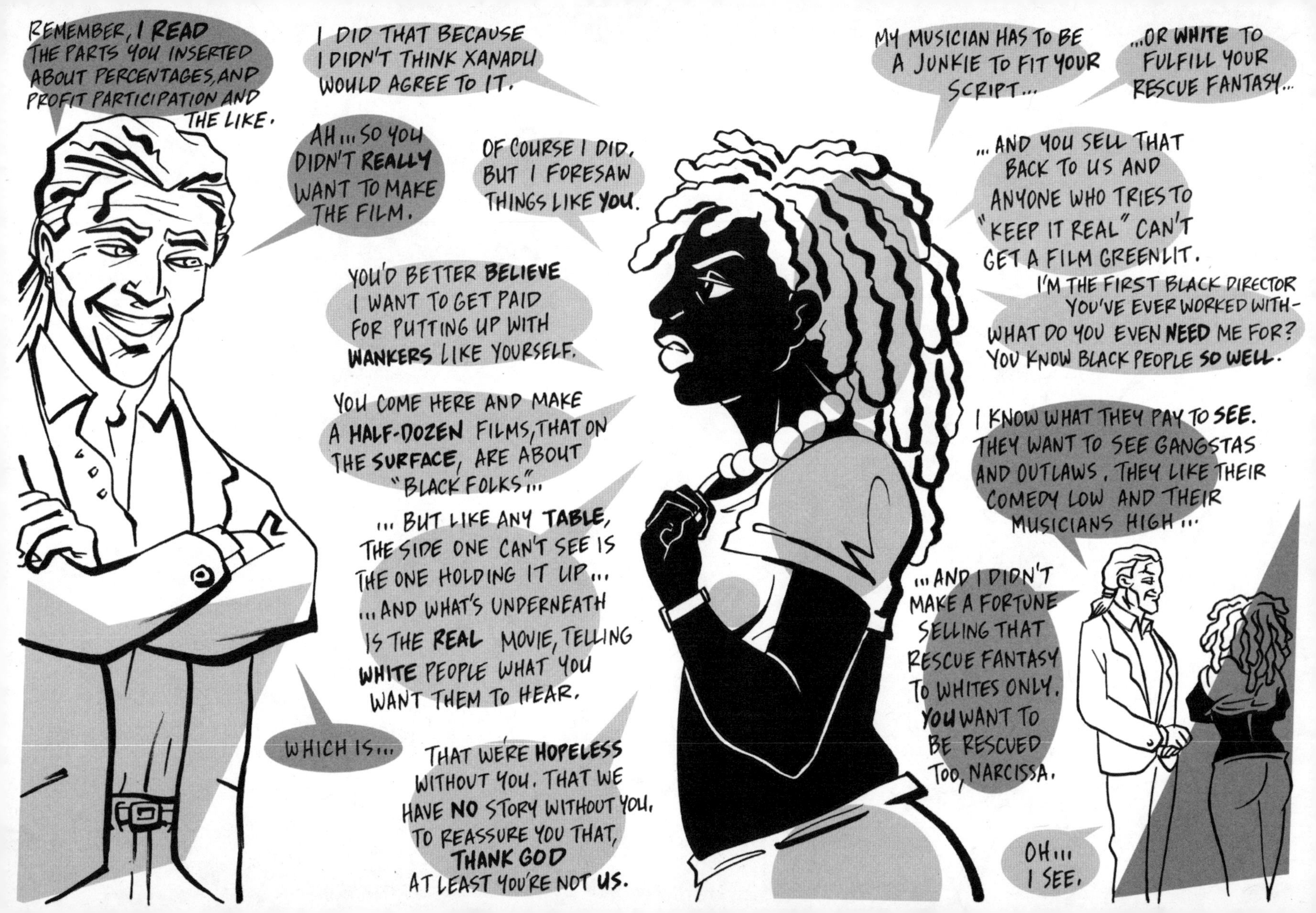
REMEMBER, I READ THE PARTS YOU INSERTED ABOUT PERCENTAGES, AND PROFIT PARTICIPATION AND THE LIKE.
I DID THAT BECAUSE I DIDN'T THINK XANADU WOULD AGREE TO IT.
AH... SO YOU DIDN'T REALLY WANT TO MAKE THE FILM.
OF COURSE I DID. BUT I FORESAW THINGS LIKE YOU.
YOU'D BETTER BELIEVE I WANT TO GET PAID FOR PUTTING UP WITH WANKERS LIKE YOURSELF.
YOU COME HERE AND MAKE A HALF-DOZEN FILMS, THAT ON THE SURFACE, ARE ABOUT "BLACK FOLKS"...
... BUT LIKE ANY TABLE, THE SIDE ONE CAN'T SEE IS THE ONE HOLDING IT UP... ...AND WHAT'S UNDERNEATH IS THE REAL MOVIE, TELLING WHITE PEOPLE WHAT YOU WANT THEM TO HEAR.
WHICH IS...
THAT WE'RE HOPELESS WITHOUT YOU. THAT WE HAVE NO STORY WITHOUT YOU. TO REASSURE YOU THAT, THANK GOD AT LEAST YOU'RE NOT US.
MY MUSICIAN HAS TO BE A JUNKIE TO FIT YOUR SCRIPT...
...OR WHITE TO FULFILL YOUR RESCUE FANTASY...
...AND YOU SELL THAT BACK TO US AND ANYONE WHO TRIES TO "KEEP IT REAL" CAN'T GET A FILM GREENLIT.
I'M THE FIRST BLACK DIRECTOR YOU'VE EVER WORKED WITH- WHAT DO YOU EVEN NEED ME FOR? YOU KNOW BLACK PEOPLE SO WELL.
I KNOW WHAT THEY PAY TO SEE. THEY WANT TO SEE GANGSTAS AND OUTLAWS. THEY LIKE THEIR COMEDY LOW AND THEIR MUSICIANS HIGH...
...AND I DIDN'T MAKE A FORTUNE SELLING THAT RESCUE FANTASY TO WHITES ONLY. YOU WANT TO BE RESCUED TOO, NARCISSA.
OH... I SEE.

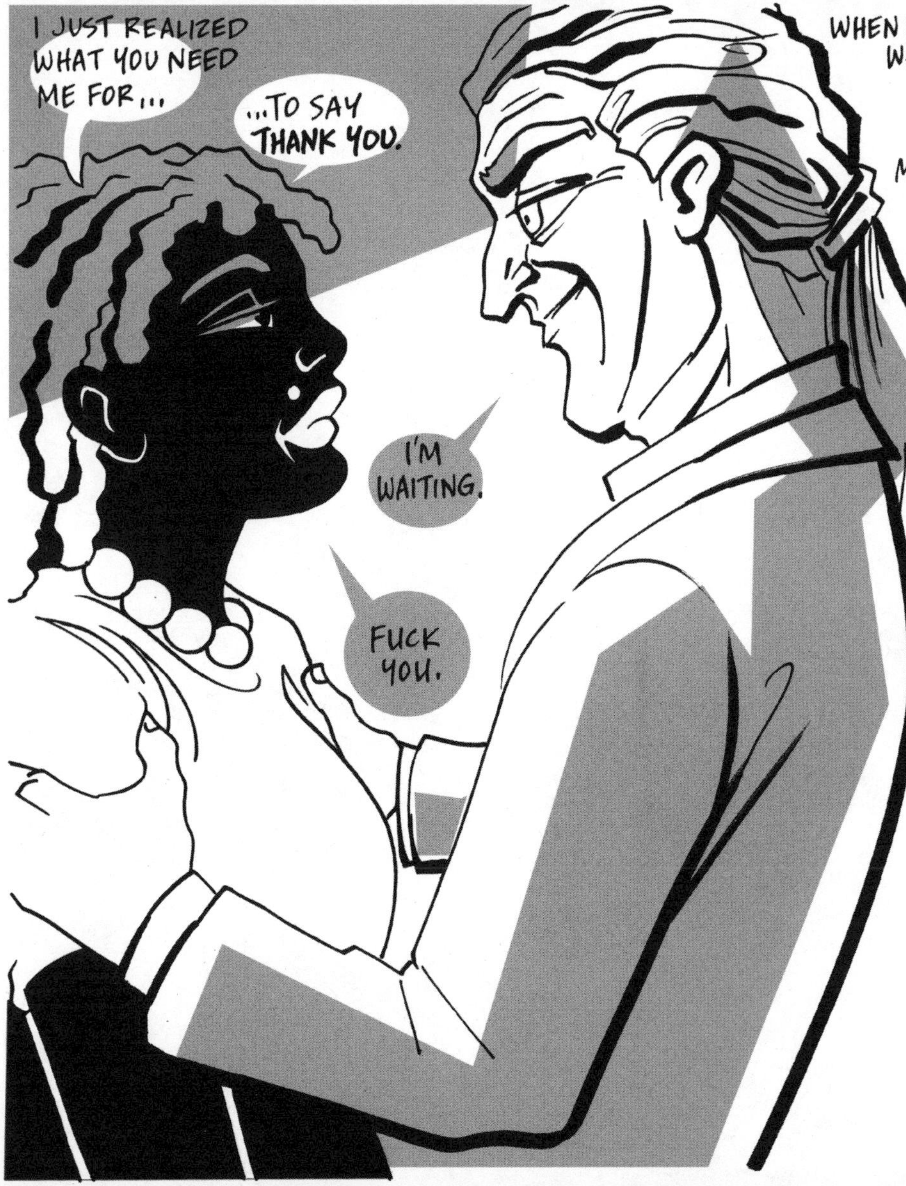
I JUST REALIZED WHAT YOU NEED ME FOR...
...TO SAY THANK YOU.
I'M WAITING.
FUCK YOU.

WHEN DOES A BLACK PERSON BECOME **USELESS** TO A WHITE LIBERAL? WHEN SHE OPENS HER MOUTH. I THOUGHT... AT LEAST **SIMON** COMES AT YOU FROM THE FRONT. I UNDERSTAND NOW, THAT HE'LL COME AT YOU **ANYWAY** THAT WORKS.

MAMA WOULD SAY TO NEVER GIVE OUT MORE INFO IN A FIGHT THAN YOU GET. SIMON GOT ME ANGRY AND I FORGOT.

NOW THE RACE WAS ON TO FINISH THE MOVIE MY WAY. I ADJUSTED MY SLEEP SCHEDULE FROM A COUPLE OF HOURS A WEEK TO NONE AT ALL. SIMON APPEARED TO BE PULLING BACK. HAD OUR LITTLE ROW DONE US GOOD?

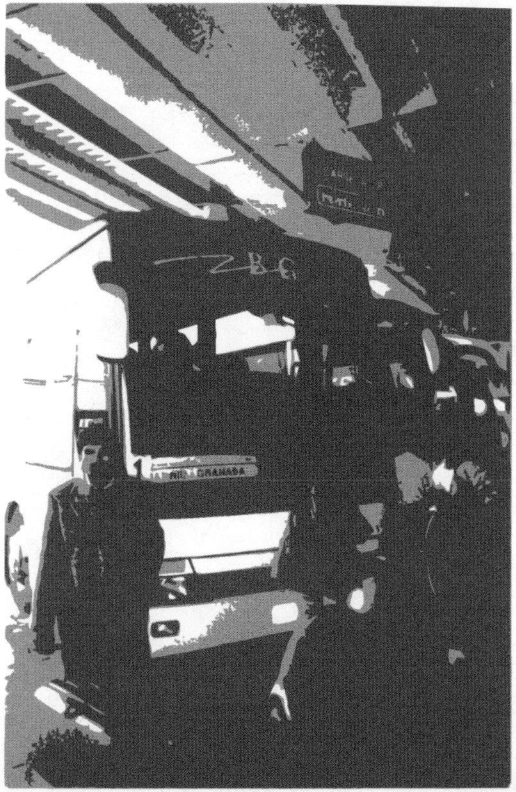

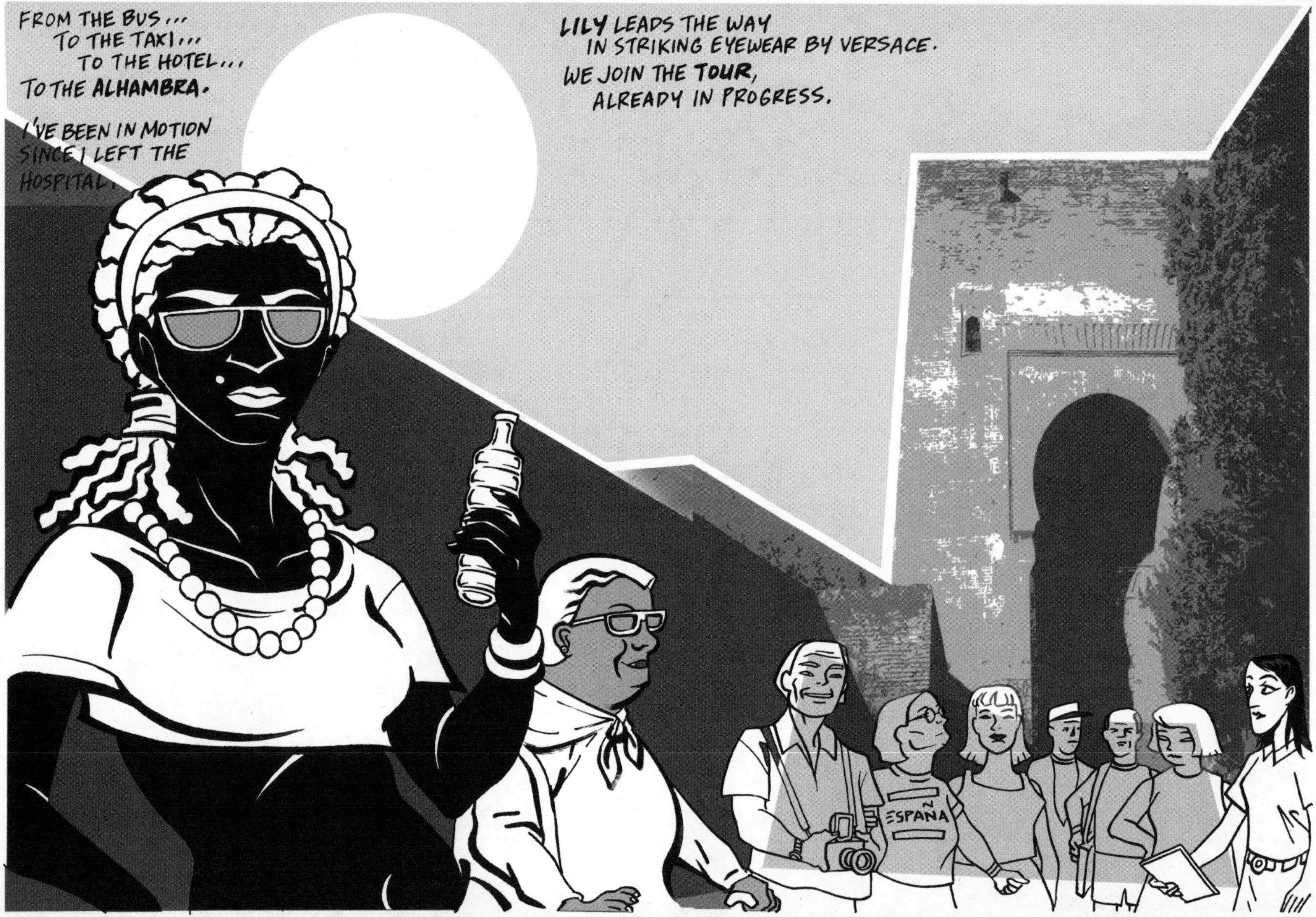
FROM THE BUS...
TO THE TAXI...
TO THE HOTEL...
TO THE ALHAMBRA.
I'VE BEEN IN MOTION SINCE I LEFT THE HOSPITAL.
LILY LEADS THE WAY IN STRIKING EYEWEAR BY VERSACE.
WE JOIN THE TOUR, ALREADY IN PROGRESS.
ESPAÑA

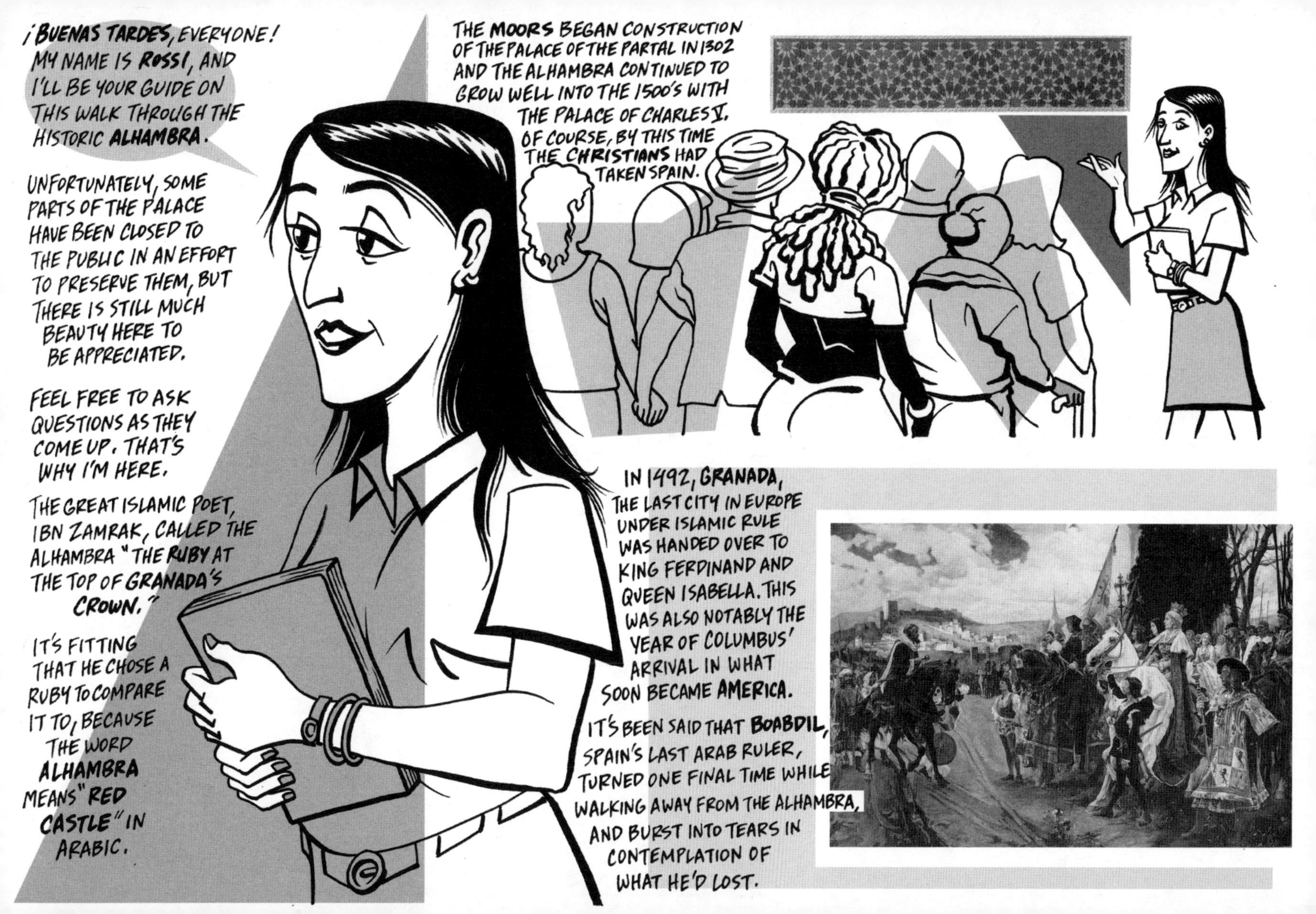

¡BUENAS TARDES, EVERYONE! MY NAME IS ROSSI, AND I'LL BE YOUR GUIDE ON THIS WALK THROUGH THE HISTORIC ALHAMBRA.
UNFORTUNATELY, SOME PARTS OF THE PALACE HAVE BEEN CLOSED TO THE PUBLIC IN AN EFFORT TO PRESERVE THEM, BUT THERE IS STILL MUCH BEAUTY HERE TO BE APPRECIATED.
FEEL FREE TO ASK QUESTIONS AS THEY COME UP. THAT'S WHY I'M HERE.
THE GREAT ISLAMIC POET, IBN ZAMRAK, CALLED THE ALHAMBRA "THE RUBY AT THE TOP OF GRANADA'S CROWN."
IT'S FITTING THAT HE CHOSE A RUBY TO COMPARE IT TO, BECAUSE THE WORD ALHAMBRA MEANS "RED CASTLE" IN ARABIC.
THE MOORS BEGAN CONSTRUCTION OF THE PALACE OF THE PARTAL IN 1302 AND THE ALHAMBRA CONTINUED TO GROW WELL INTO THE 1500'S WITH THE PALACE OF CHARLES V. OF COURSE, BY THIS TIME THE CHRISTIANS HAD TAKEN SPAIN.
IN 1492, GRANADA, THE LAST CITY IN EUROPE UNDER ISLAMIC RULE WAS HANDED OVER TO KING FERDINAND AND QUEEN ISABELLA. THIS WAS ALSO NOTABLY THE YEAR OF COLUMBUS' ARRIVAL IN WHAT SOON BECAME AMERICA.
IT'S BEEN SAID THAT BOABDIL, SPAIN'S LAST ARAB RULER, TURNED ONE FINAL TIME WHILE WALKING AWAY FROM THE ALHAMBRA, AND BURST INTO TEARS IN CONTEMPLATION OF WHAT HE'D LOST.

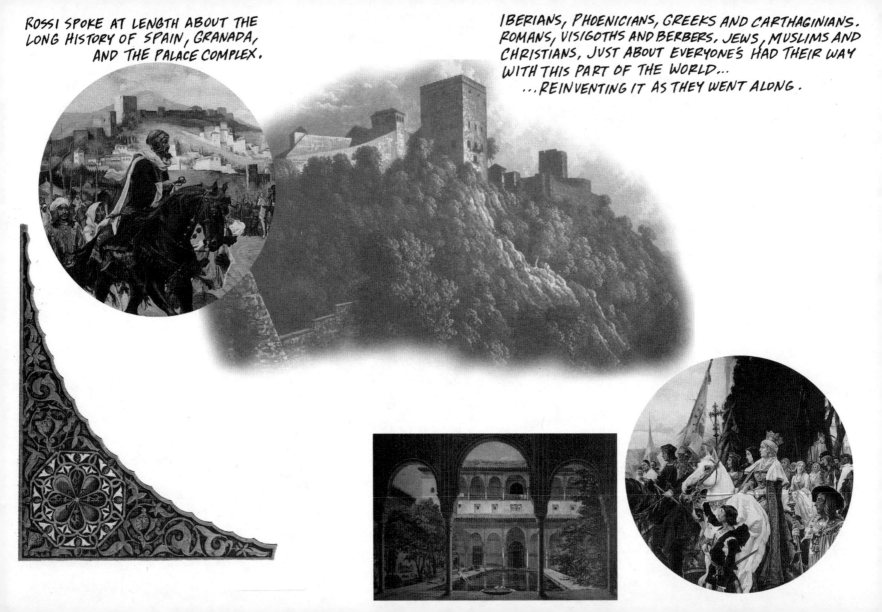

ROSSI SPOKE AT LENGTH ABOUT THE LONG HISTORY OF SPAIN, GRANADA, AND THE PALACE COMPLEX.

IBERIANS, PHOENICIANS, GREEKS AND CARTHAGINIANS. ROMANS, VISIGOTHS AND BERBERS. JEWS, MUSLIMS AND CHRISTIANS, JUST ABOUT EVERYONE'S HAD THEIR WAY WITH THIS PART OF THE WORLD...
...REINVENTING IT AS THEY WENT ALONG.

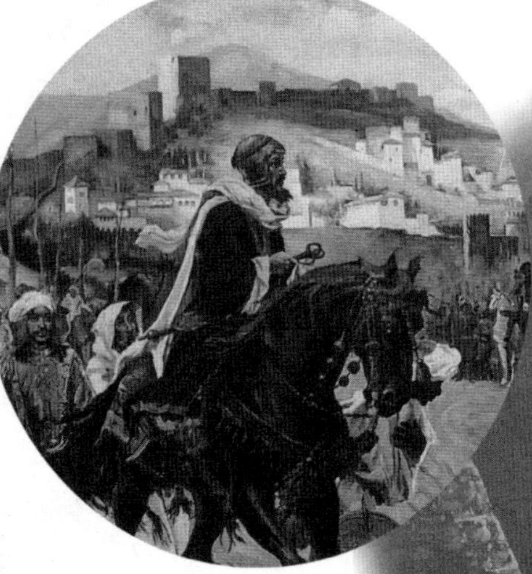

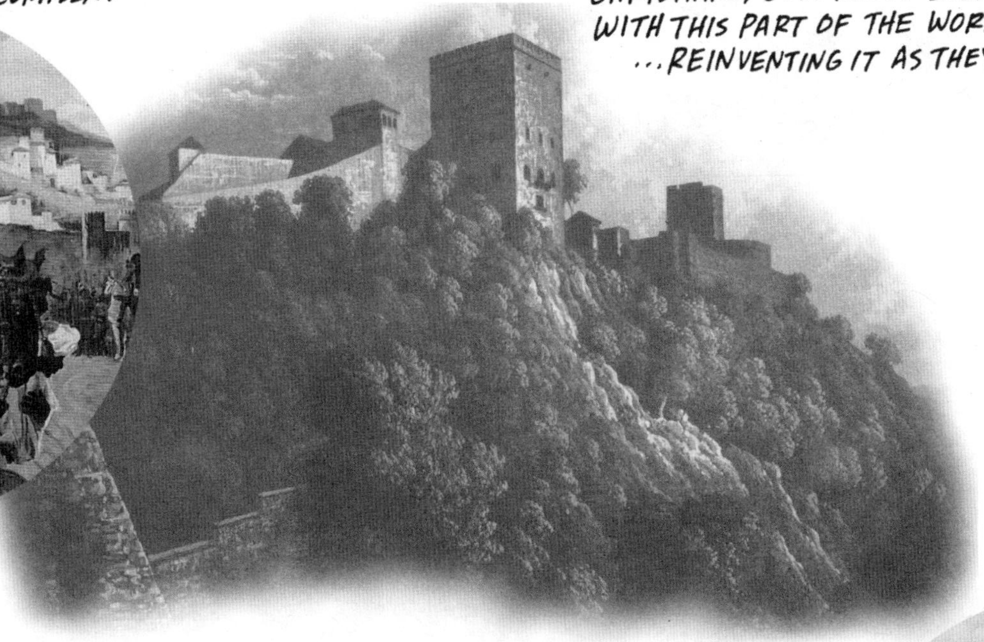

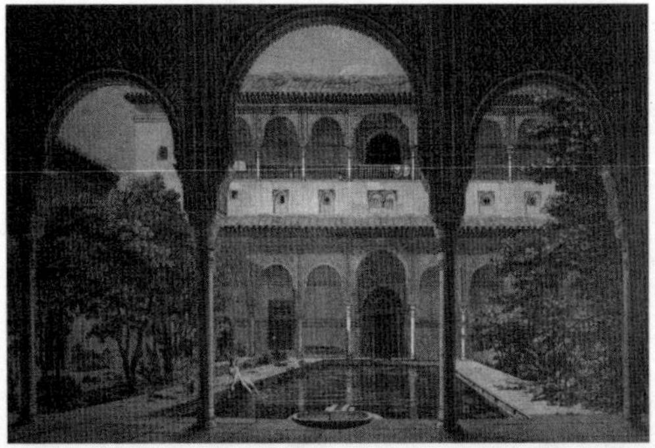

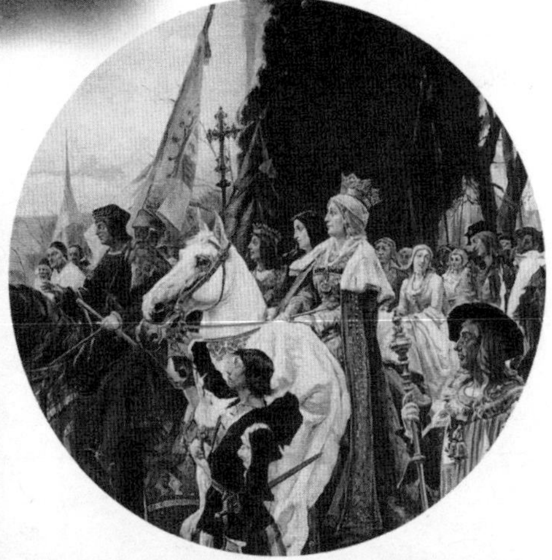

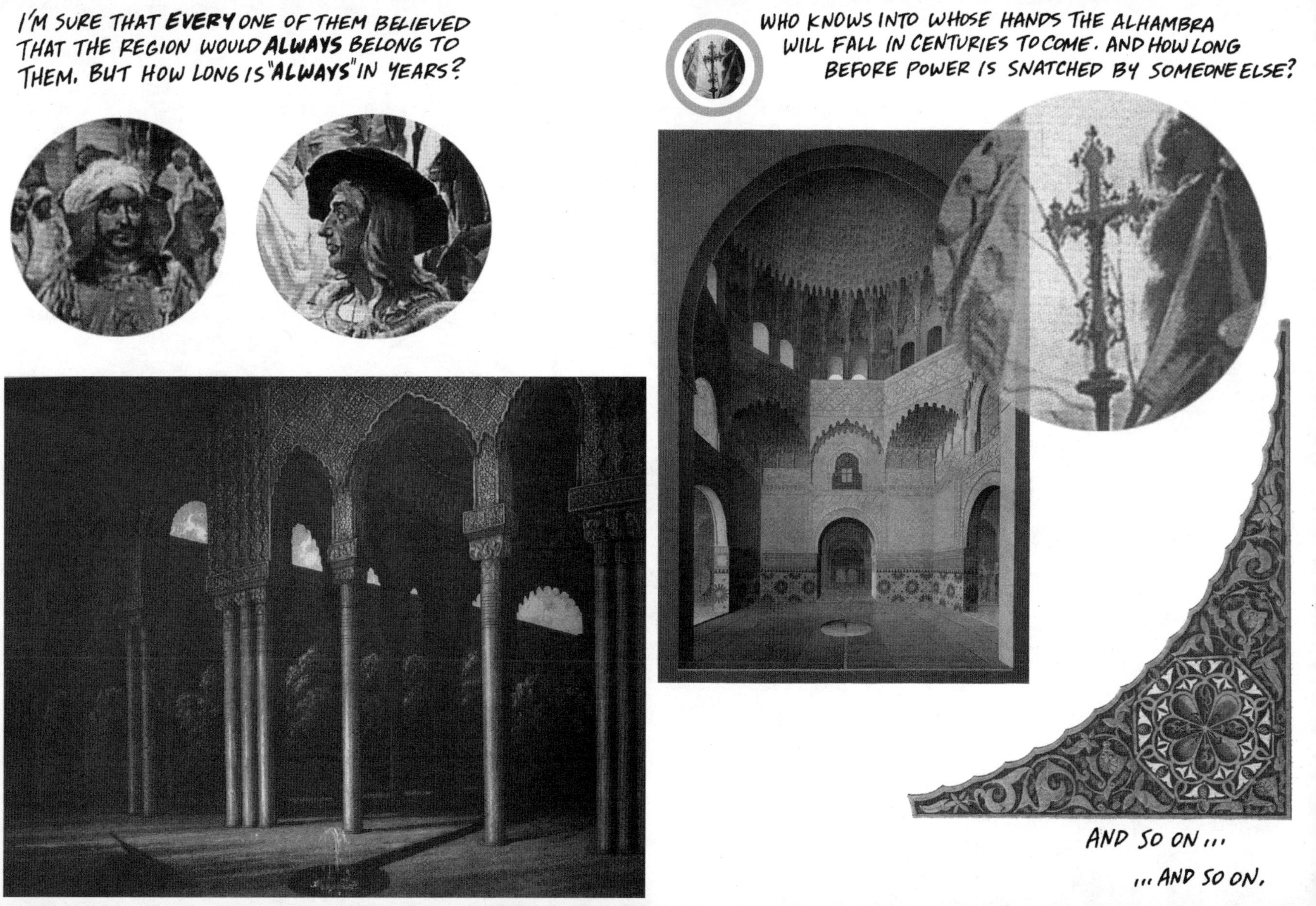
I'M SURE THAT **EVERY** ONE OF THEM BELIEVED THAT THE REGION WOULD **ALWAYS** BELONG TO THEM. BUT HOW LONG IS "**ALWAYS**" IN YEARS?
WHO KNOWS INTO WHOSE HANDS THE ALHAMBRA WILL FALL IN CENTURIES TO COME. AND HOW LONG BEFORE POWER IS SNATCHED BY SOMEONE ELSE?
AND SO ON...
...AND SO ON.

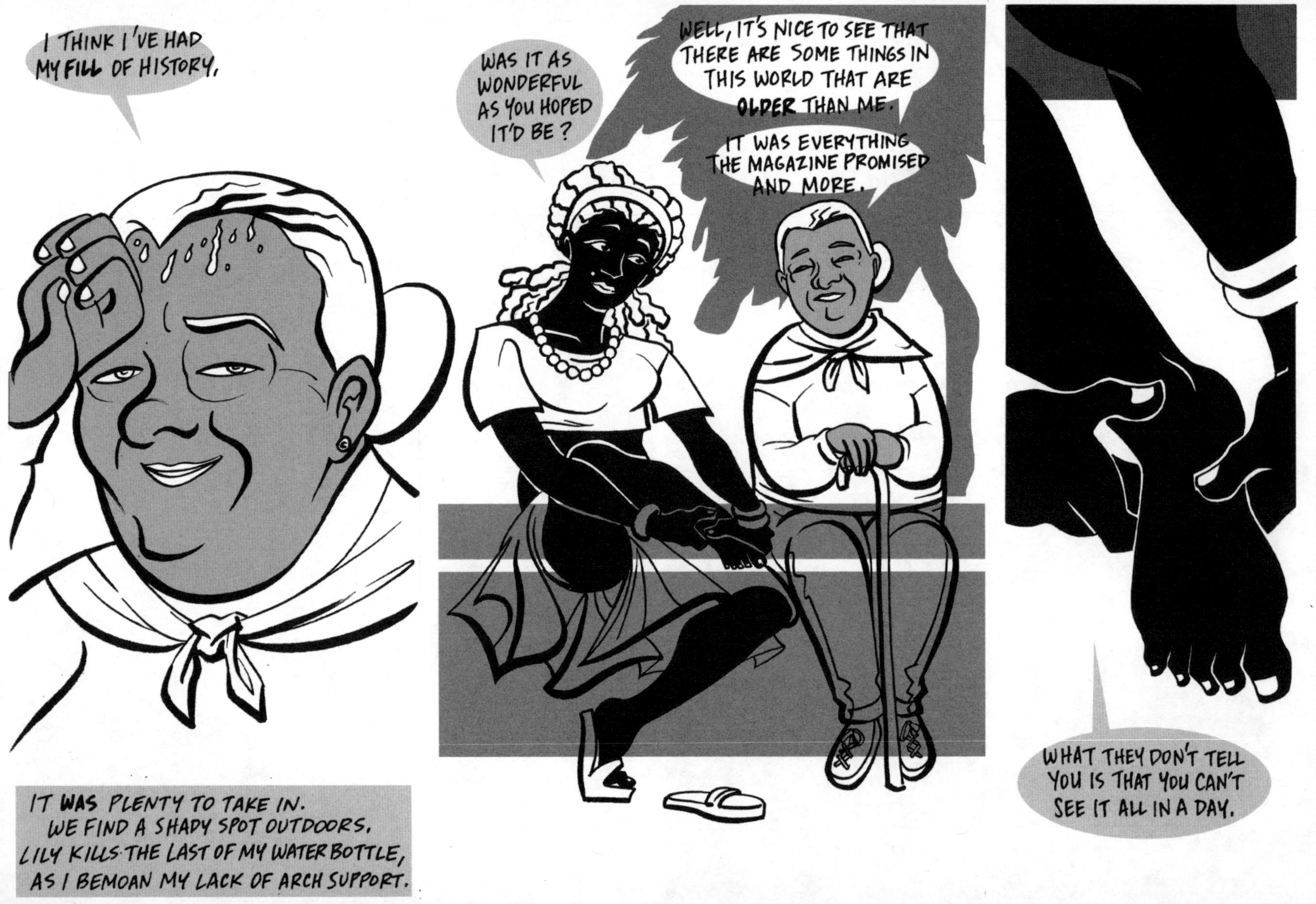

I THINK I'VE HAD MY FILL OF HISTORY,
IT WAS PLENTY TO TAKE IN. WE FIND A SHADY SPOT OUTDOORS. LILY KILLS THE LAST OF MY WATER BOTTLE, AS I BEMOAN MY LACK OF ARCH SUPPORT.
WAS IT AS WONDERFUL AS YOU HOPED IT'D BE?
WELL, IT'S NICE TO SEE THAT THERE ARE SOME THINGS IN THIS WORLD THAT ARE OLDER THAN ME.
IT WAS EVERYTHING THE MAGAZINE PROMISED AND MORE.
WHAT THEY DON'T TELL YOU IS THAT YOU CAN'T SEE IT ALL IN A DAY.

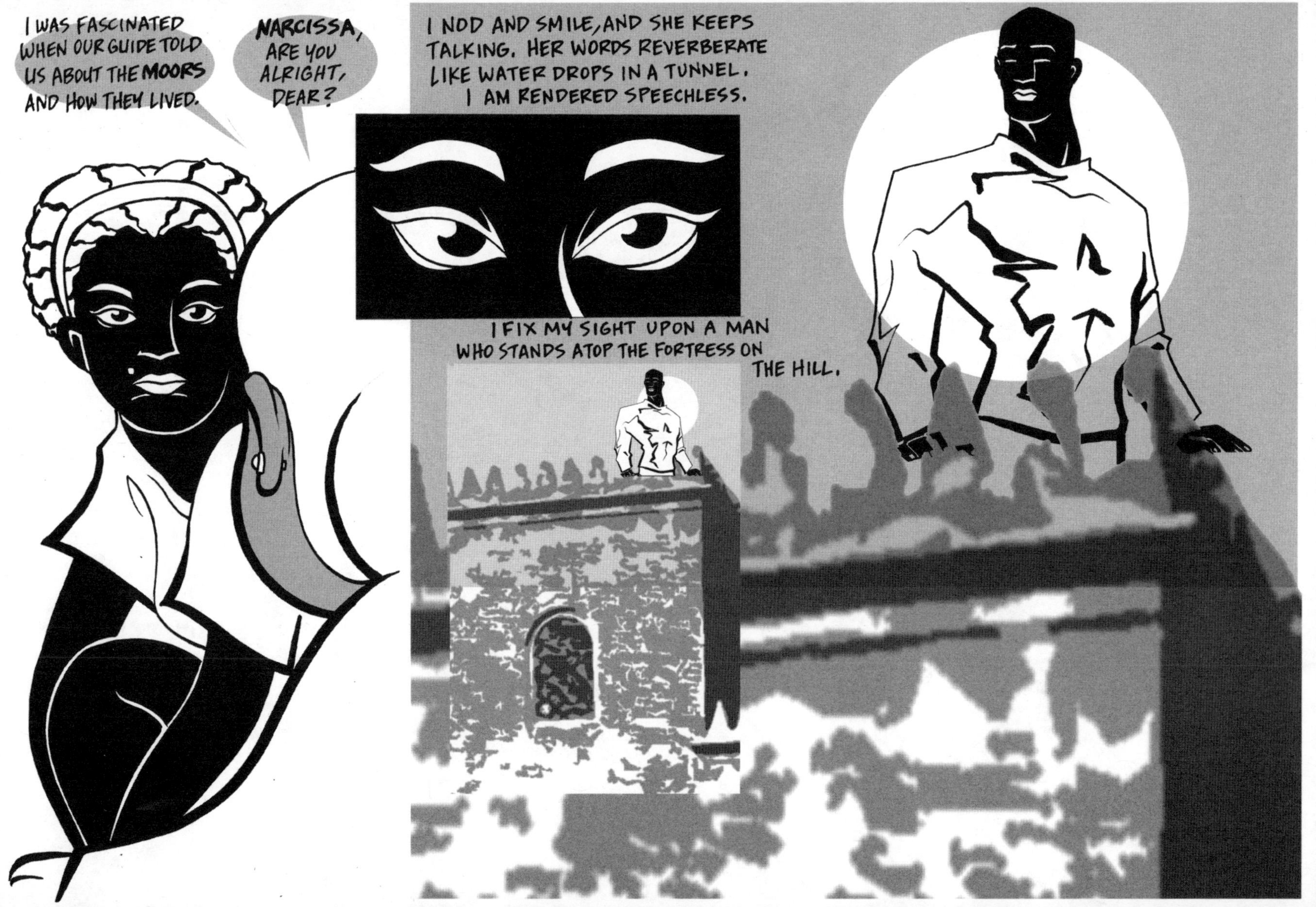
I WAS FASCINATED WHEN OUR GUIDE TOLD US ABOUT THE MOORS AND HOW THEY LIVED.
NARCISSA, ARE YOU ALRIGHT, DEAR?
I NOD AND SMILE, AND SHE KEEPS TALKING. HER WORDS REVERBERATE LIKE WATER DROPS IN A TUNNEL. I AM RENDERED SPEECHLESS.
I FIX MY SIGHT UPON A MAN WHO STANDS ATOP THE FORTRESS ON THE HILL.

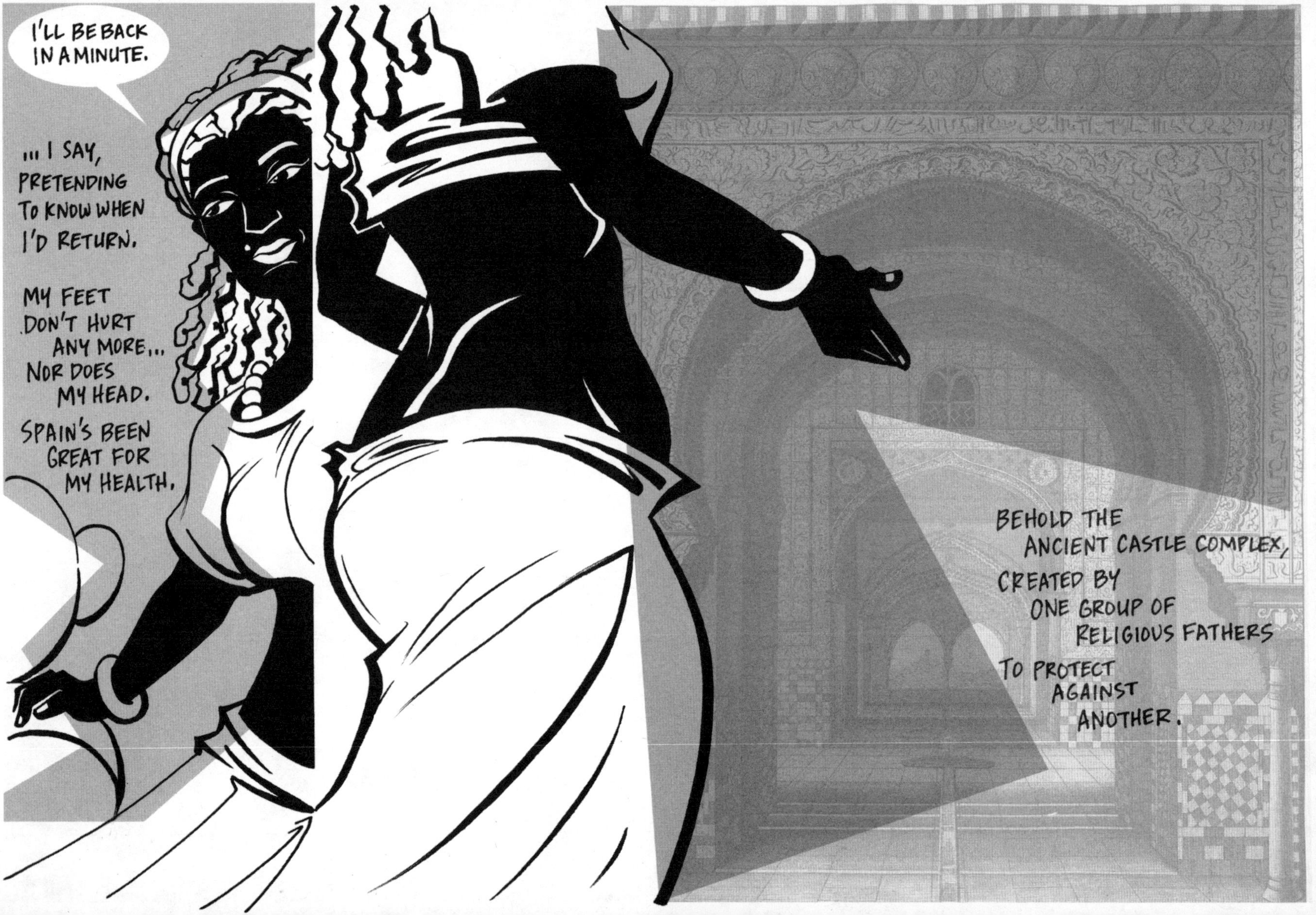
I'LL BE BACK IN A MINUTE.
... I SAY, PRETENDING TO KNOW WHEN I'D RETURN.
MY FEET DON'T HURT ANY MORE... NOR DOES MY HEAD.
SPAIN'S BEEN GREAT FOR MY HEALTH.
BEHOLD THE ANCIENT CASTLE COMPLEX, CREATED BY ONE GROUP OF RELIGIOUS FATHERS
TO PROTECT AGAINST ANOTHER.

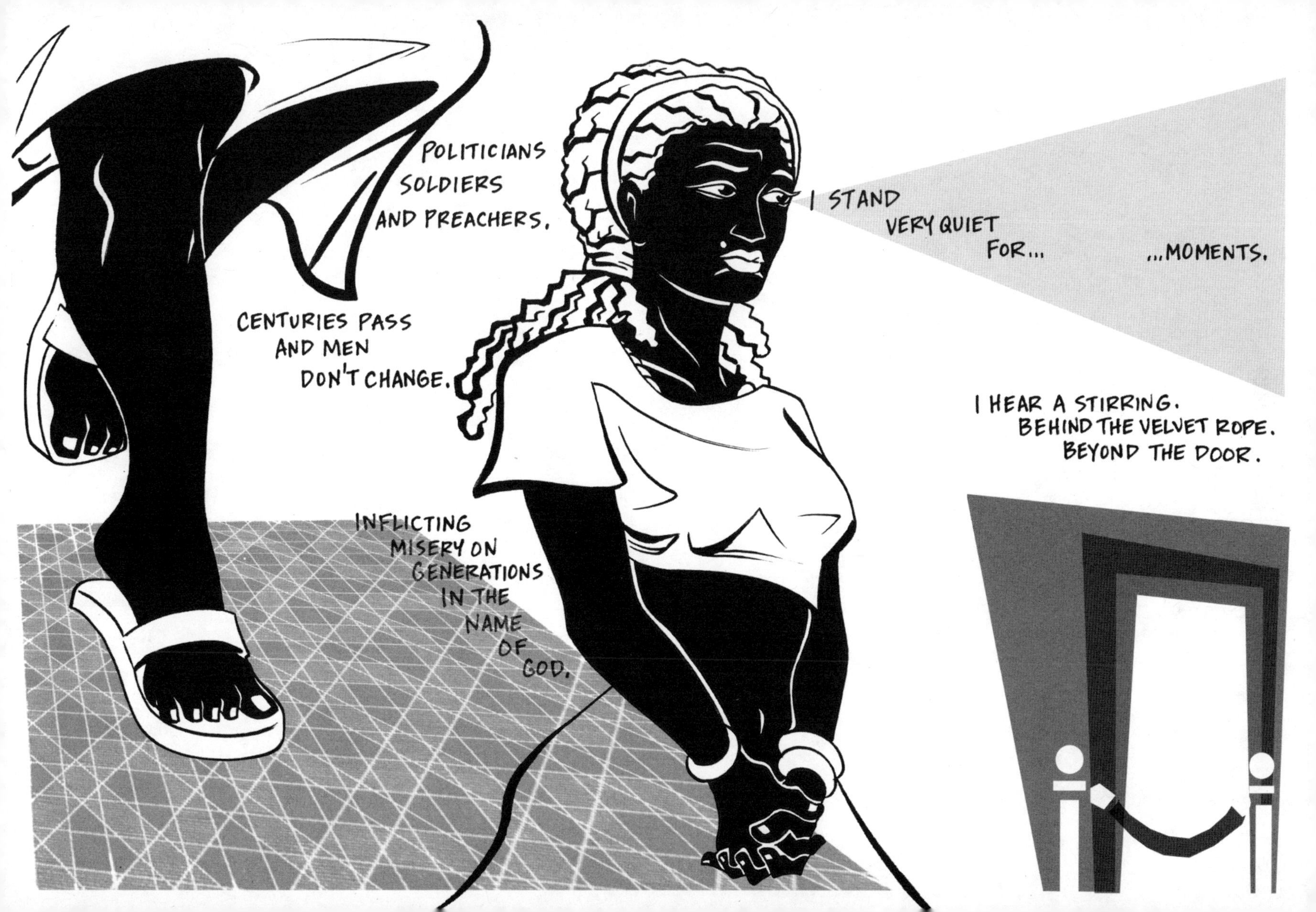
POLITICIANS
SOLDIERS
AND PREACHERS.
I STAND
VERY QUIET
FOR...
...MOMENTS.
CENTURIES PASS
AND MEN
DON'T CHANGE.
I HEAR A STIRRING.
BEHIND THE VELVET ROPE.
BEYOND THE DOOR.
INFLICTING
MISERY ON
GENERATIONS
IN THE
NAME
OF
GOD.

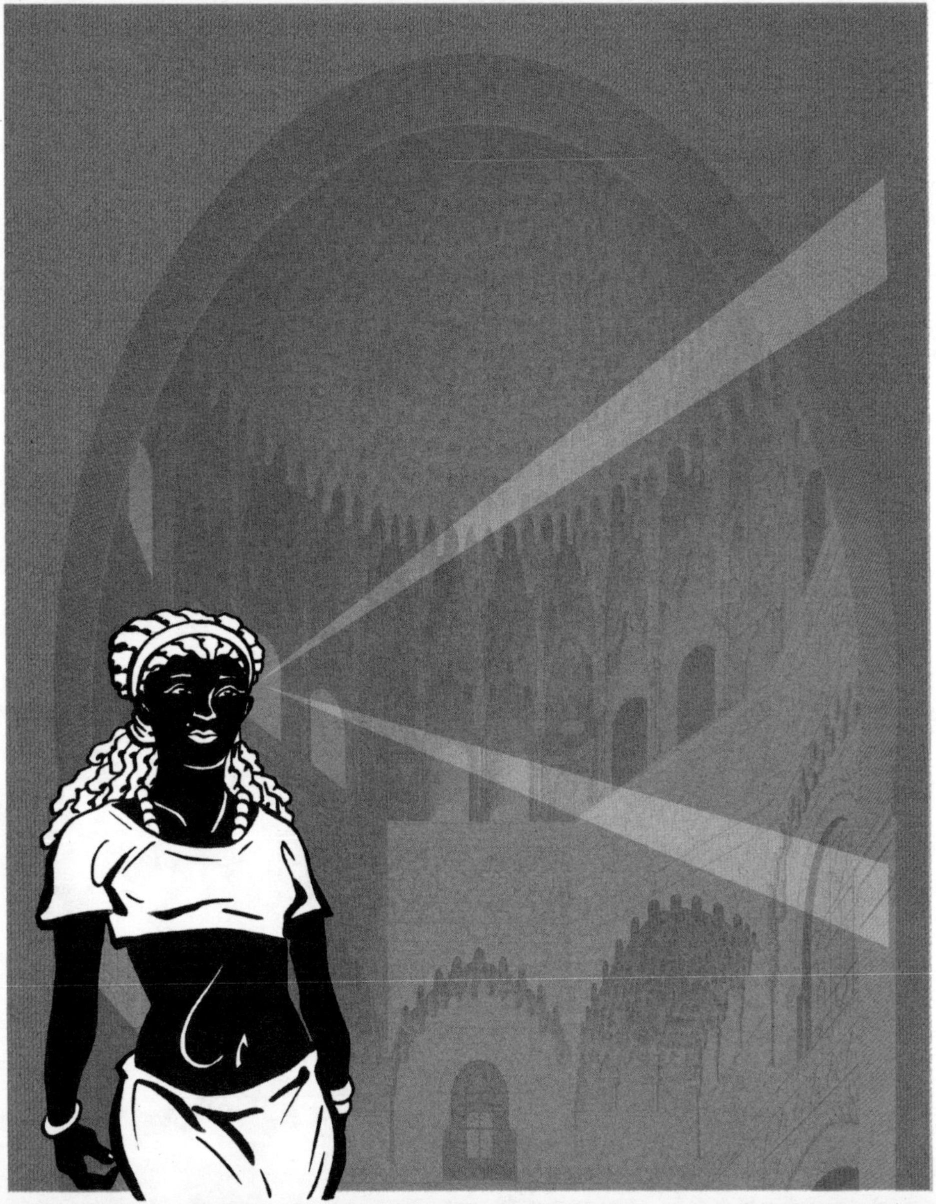

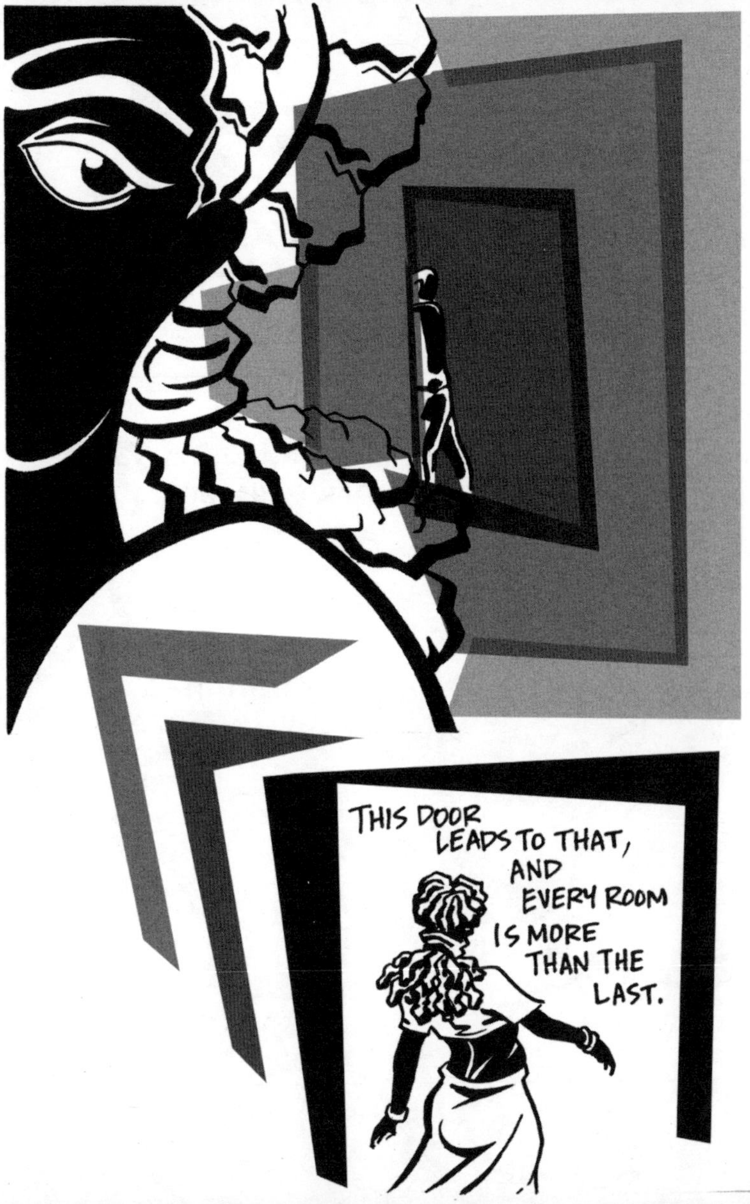
THIS DOOR
LEADS TO THAT,
AND
EVERY ROOM
IS MORE
THAN THE
LAST.

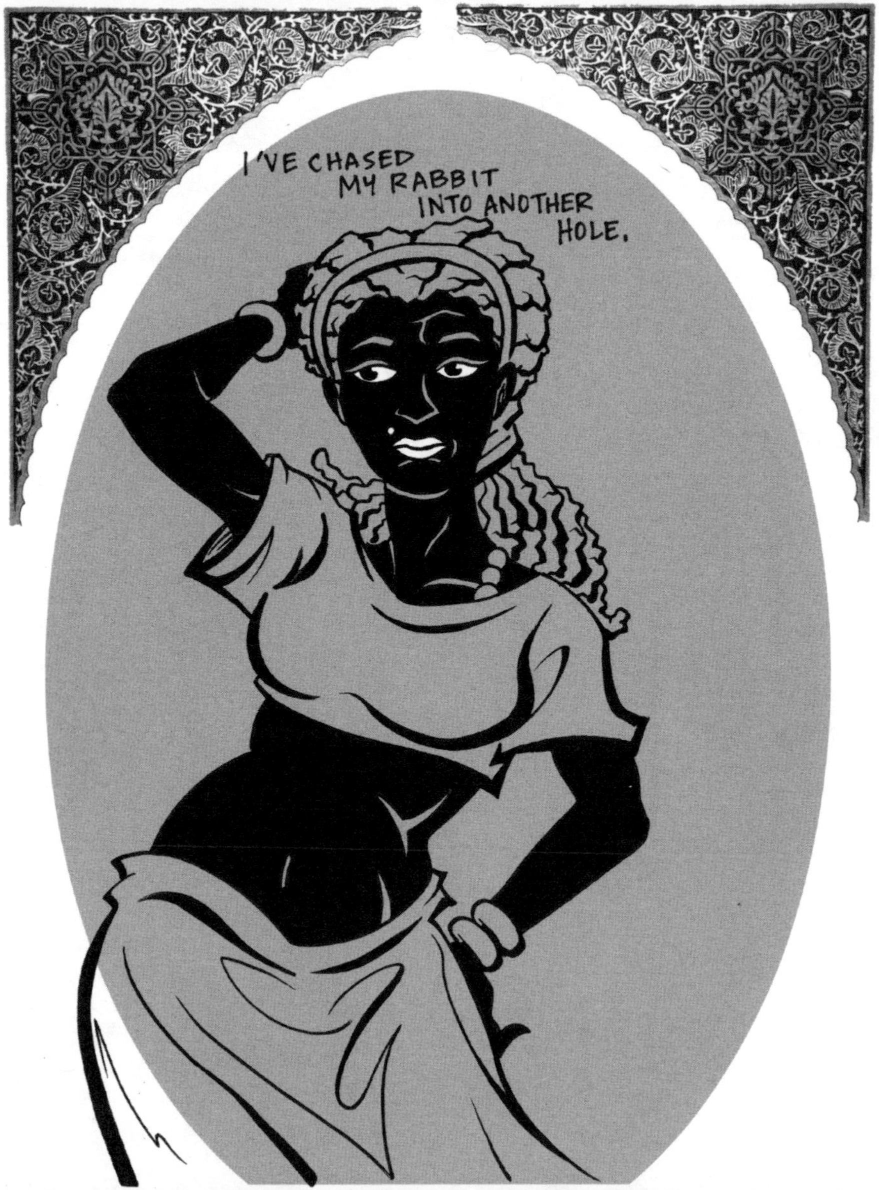
I'VE CHASED MY RABBIT INTO ANOTHER HOLE.

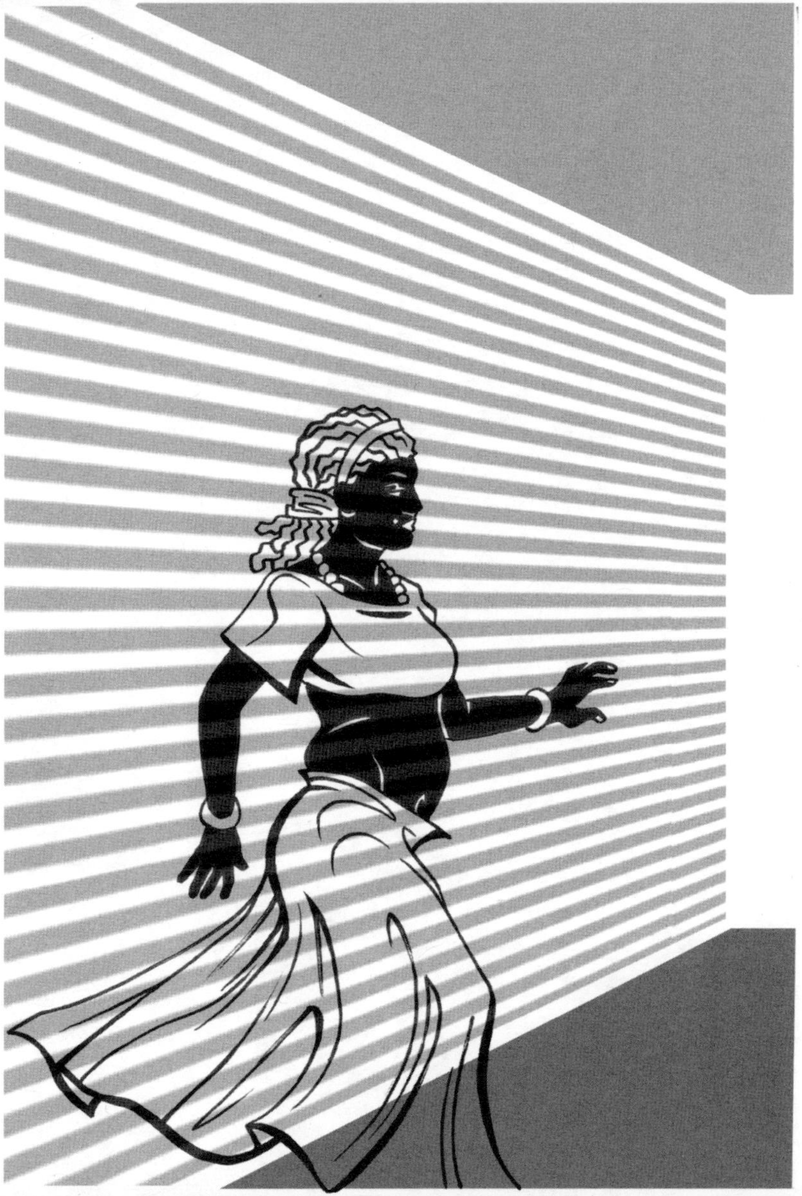

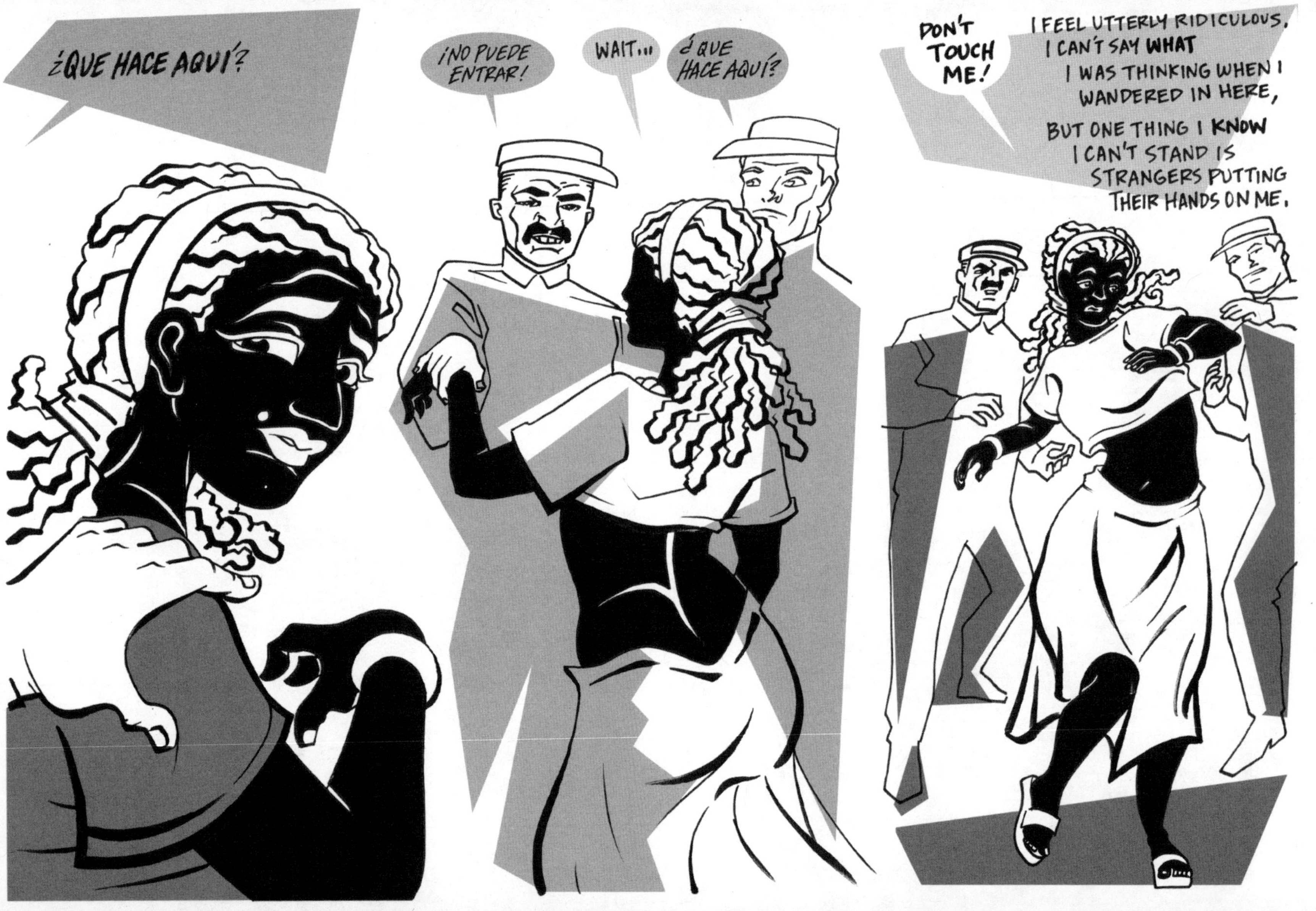
¿QUE HACE AQUI?
¡NO PUEDE ENTRAR!
WAIT...
¿QUE HACE AQUI?
DON'T TOUCH ME!
I FEEL UTTERLY RIDICULOUS. I CAN'T SAY WHAT I WAS THINKING WHEN I WANDERED IN HERE,
BUT ONE THING I KNOW I CAN'T STAND IS STRANGERS PUTTING THEIR HANDS ON ME.

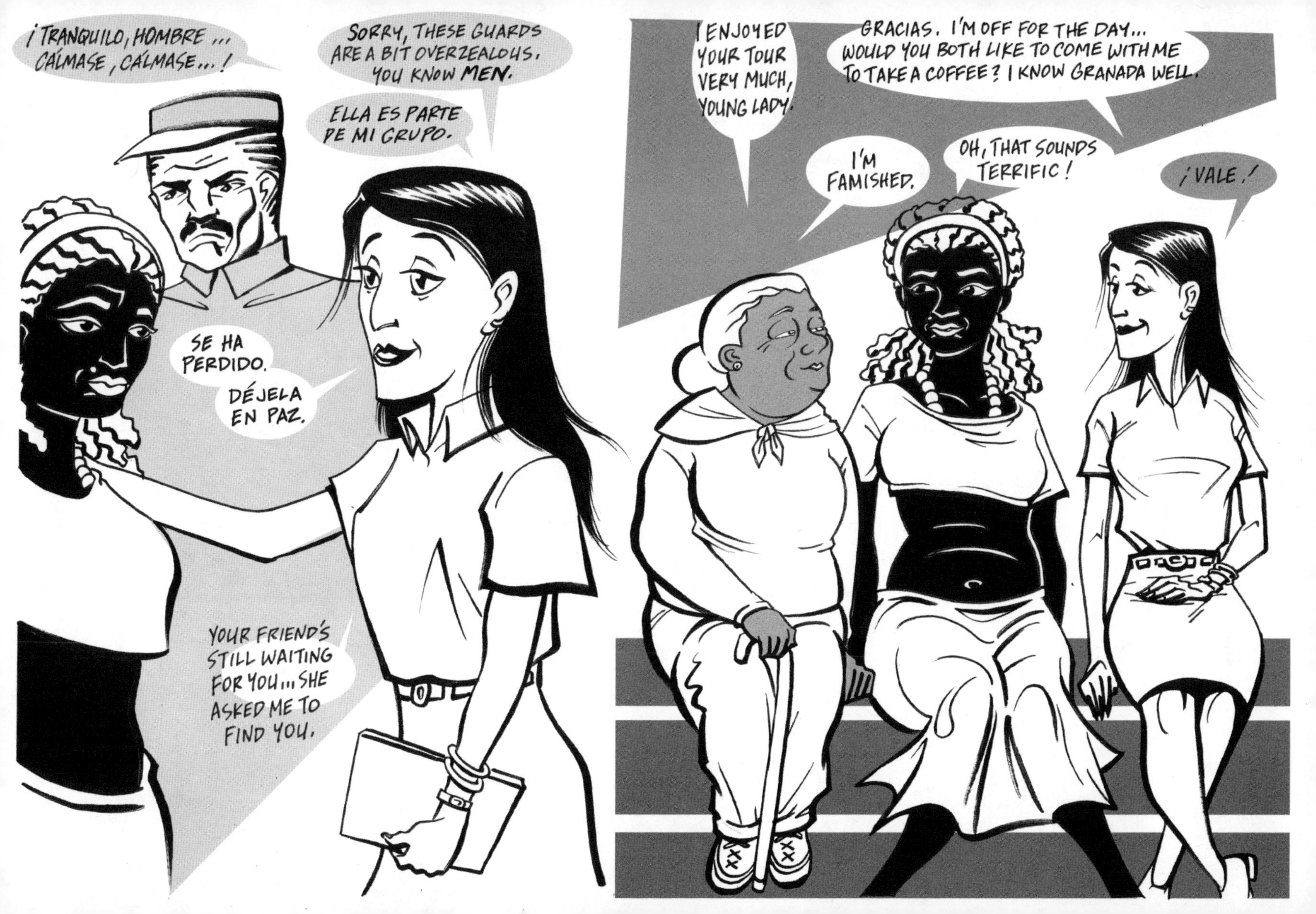
¡TRANQUILO, HOMBRE ...
CÁLMASE, CÁLMASE... !
SORRY, THESE GUARDS ARE A BIT OVERZEALOUS. YOU KNOW MEN.
ELLA ES PARTE DE MI GRUPO.
SE HA PERDIDO.
DÉJELA EN PAZ.
YOUR FRIEND'S STILL WAITING FOR YOU... SHE ASKED ME TO FIND YOU.
I ENJOYED YOUR TOUR VERY MUCH, YOUNG LADY.
GRACIAS. I'M OFF FOR THE DAY... WOULD YOU BOTH LIKE TO COME WITH ME TO TAKE A COFFEE? I KNOW GRANADA WELL.
I'M FAMISHED.
OH, THAT SOUNDS TERRIFIC!
¡VALE.!

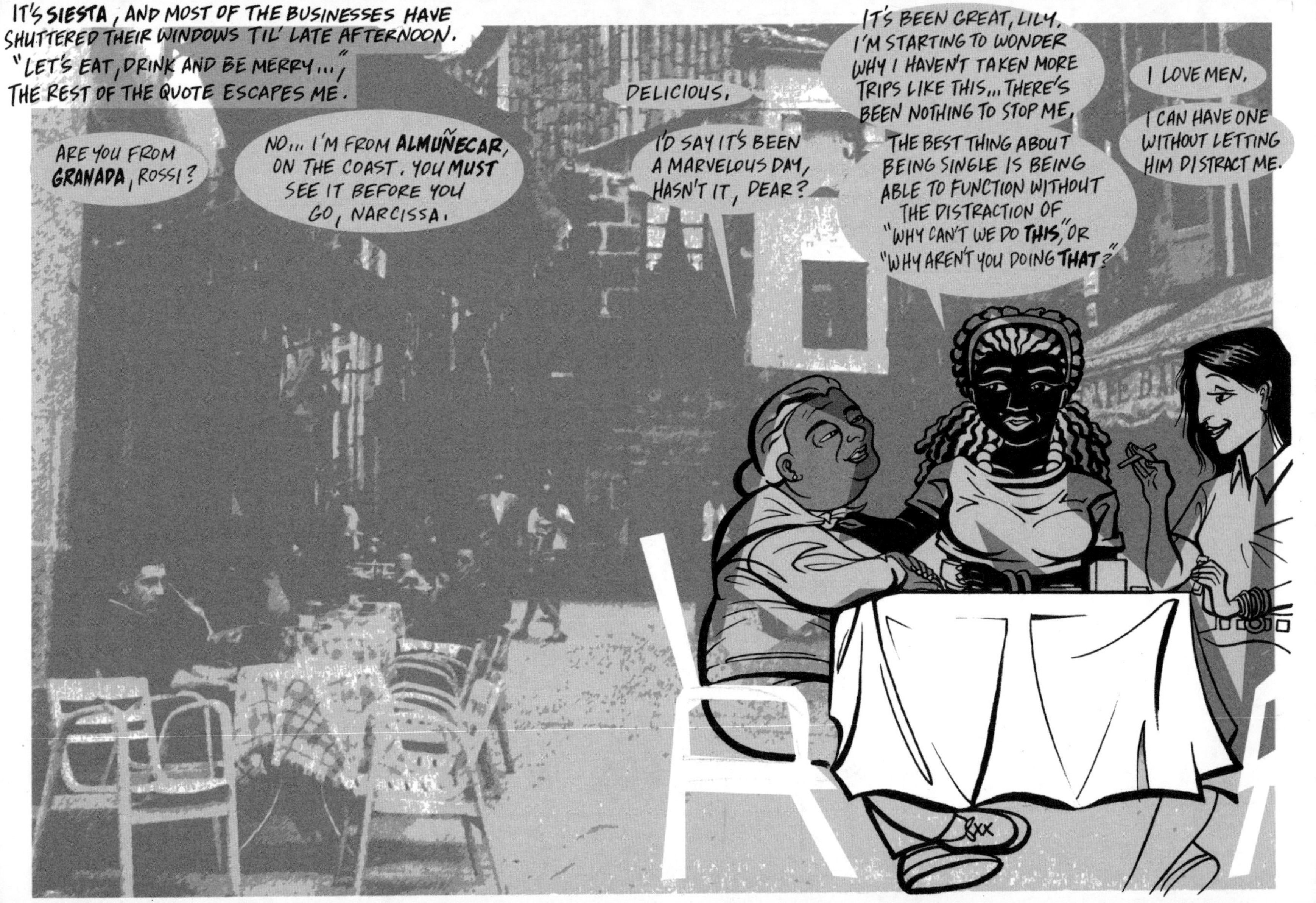
IT'S SIESTA, AND MOST OF THE BUSINESSES HAVE SHUTTERED THEIR WINDOWS TIL' LATE AFTERNOON. "LET'S EAT, DRINK AND BE MERRY...," THE REST OF THE QUOTE ESCAPES ME.
ARE YOU FROM GRANADA, ROSSI?
NO... I'M FROM ALMUÑECAR, ON THE COAST. YOU MUST SEE IT BEFORE YOU GO, NARCISSA.
DELICIOUS.
I'D SAY IT'S BEEN A MARVELOUS DAY, HASN'T IT, DEAR?
IT'S BEEN GREAT, LILY. I'M STARTING TO WONDER WHY I HAVEN'T TAKEN MORE TRIPS LIKE THIS... THERE'S BEEN NOTHING TO STOP ME.
THE BEST THING ABOUT BEING SINGLE IS BEING ABLE TO FUNCTION WITHOUT THE DISTRACTION OF "WHY CAN'T WE DO THIS," OR "WHY AREN'T YOU DOING THAT?"
I LOVE MEN.
I CAN HAVE ONE WITHOUT LETTING HIM DISTRACT ME.

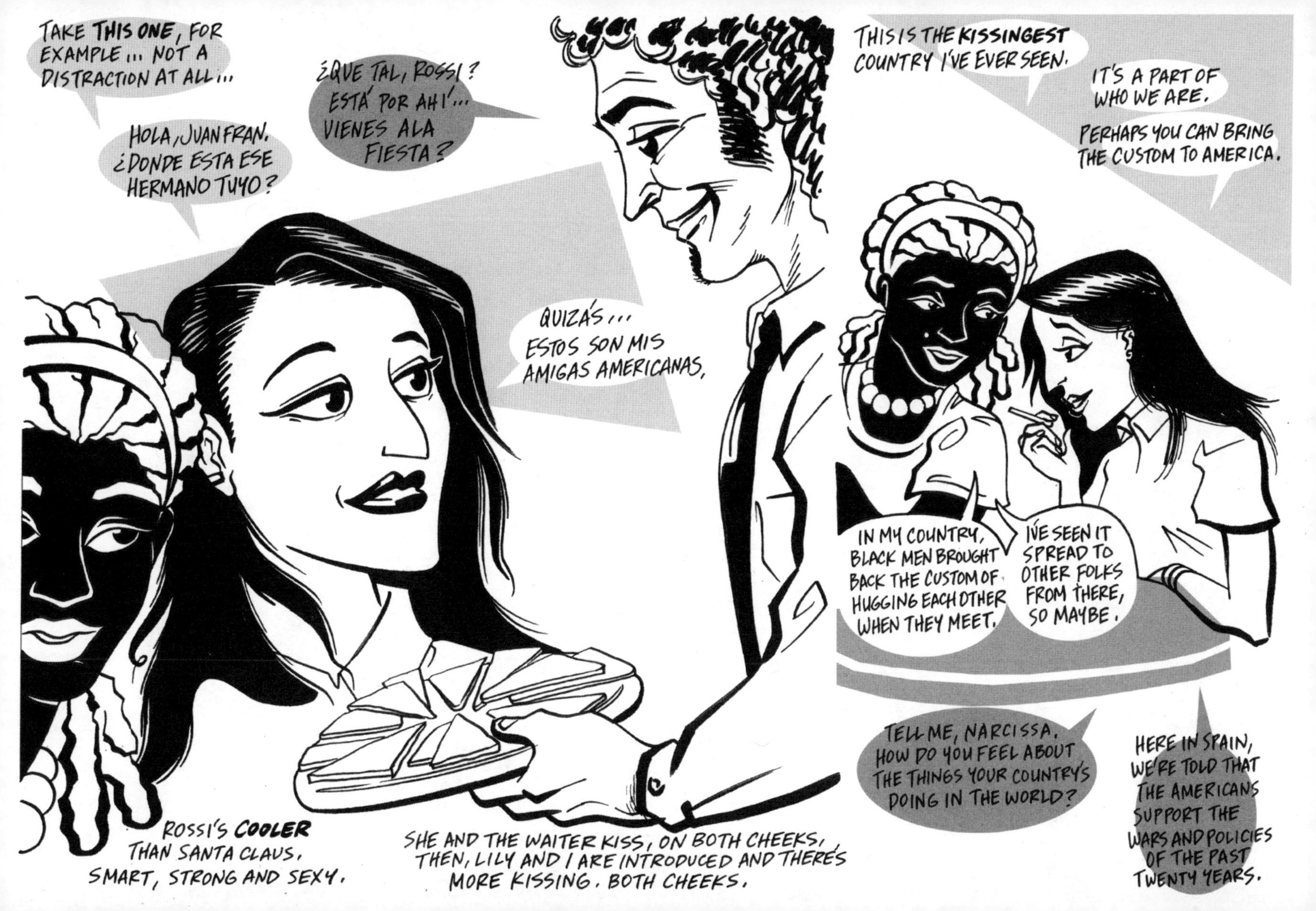
TAKE THIS ONE, FOR EXAMPLE... NOT A DISTRACTION AT ALL...
HOLA, JUAN FRAN. ¿DONDE ESTA ESE HERMANO TUYO?
¿QUE TAL, ROSSI? ESTÁ POR AHÍ... VIENES ALA FIESTA?
QUIZÁS... ESTOS SON MIS AMIGAS AMERICANAS.
ROSSI'S COOLER THAN SANTA CLAUS, SMART, STRONG AND SEXY.
SHE AND THE WAITER KISS, ON BOTH CHEEKS, THEN, LILY AND I ARE INTRODUCED AND THERE'S MORE KISSING. BOTH CHEEKS.
THIS IS THE KISSINGEST COUNTRY I'VE EVER SEEN.
IT'S A PART OF WHO WE ARE.
PERHAPS YOU CAN BRING THE CUSTOM TO AMERICA.
IN MY COUNTRY, BLACK MEN BROUGHT BACK THE CUSTOM OF HUGGING EACH OTHER WHEN THEY MEET.
I'VE SEEN IT SPREAD TO OTHER FOLKS FROM THERE, SO MAYBE.
TELL ME, NARCISSA. HOW DO YOU FEEL ABOUT THE THINGS YOUR COUNTRY'S DOING IN THE WORLD?
HERE IN SPAIN, WE'RE TOLD THAT THE AMERICANS SUPPORT THE WARS AND POLICIES OF THE PAST TWENTY YEARS.

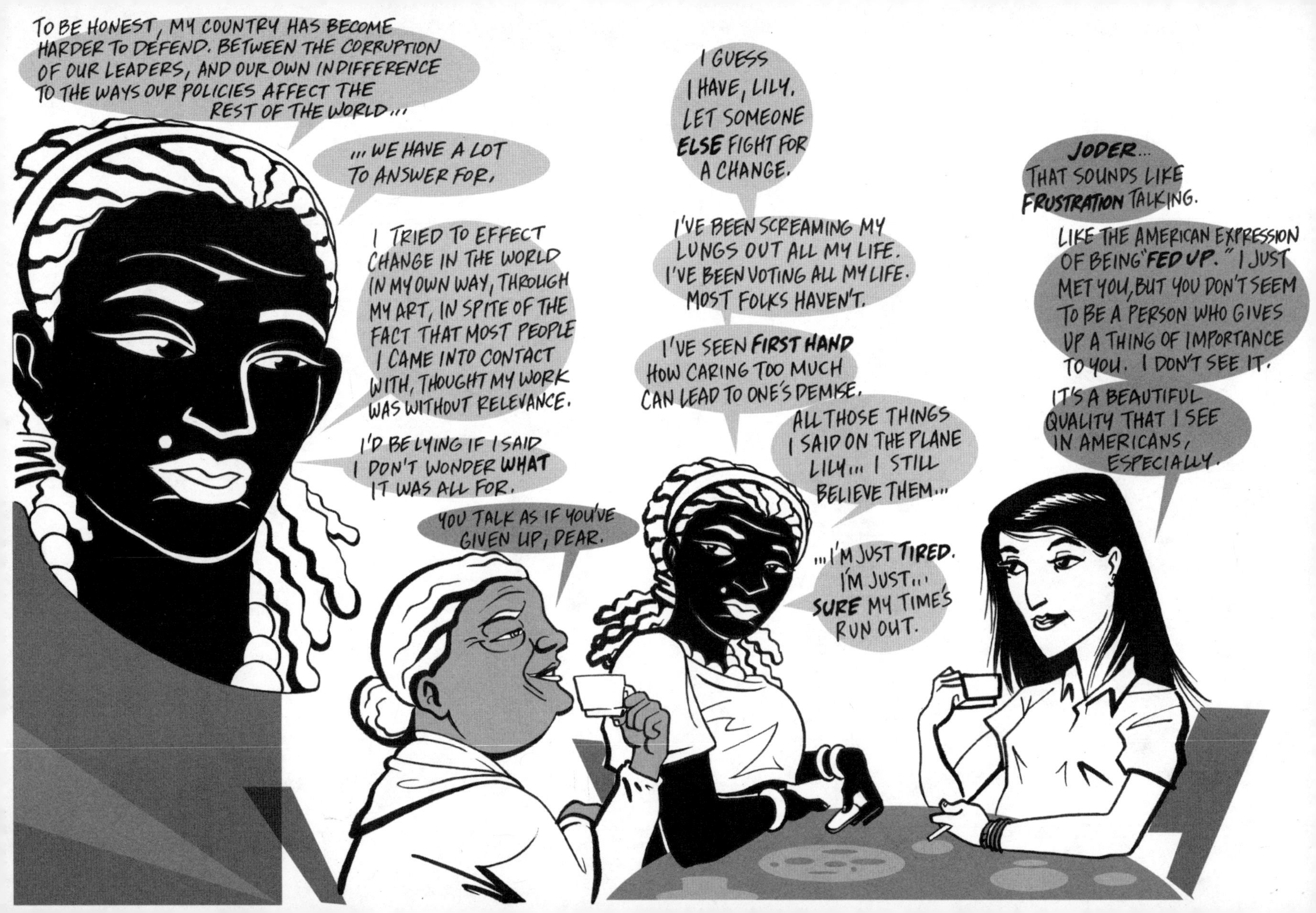
TO BE HONEST, MY COUNTRY HAS BECOME HARDER TO DEFEND. BETWEEN THE CORRUPTION OF OUR LEADERS, AND OUR OWN INDIFFERENCE TO THE WAYS OUR POLICIES AFFECT THE REST OF THE WORLD...
...WE HAVE A LOT TO ANSWER FOR.
I TRIED TO EFFECT CHANGE IN THE WORLD IN MY OWN WAY, THROUGH MY ART, IN SPITE OF THE FACT THAT MOST PEOPLE I CAME INTO CONTACT WITH, THOUGHT MY WORK WAS WITHOUT RELEVANCE.
I'D BE LYING IF I SAID I DON'T WONDER WHAT IT WAS ALL FOR.
YOU TALK AS IF YOU'VE GIVEN UP, DEAR.
I GUESS I HAVE, LILY. LET SOMEONE ELSE FIGHT FOR A CHANGE.
I'VE BEEN SCREAMING MY LUNGS OUT ALL MY LIFE. I'VE BEEN VOTING ALL MY LIFE. MOST FOLKS HAVEN'T.
I'VE SEEN FIRST HAND HOW CARING TOO MUCH CAN LEAD TO ONE'S DEMISE.
ALL THOSE THINGS I SAID ON THE PLANE LILY... I STILL BELIEVE THEM...
...I'M JUST TIRED. I'M JUST... SURE MY TIME'S RUN OUT.
JODER... THAT SOUNDS LIKE FRUSTRATION TALKING.
LIKE THE AMERICAN EXPRESSION OF BEING "FED UP." I JUST MET YOU, BUT YOU DON'T SEEM TO BE A PERSON WHO GIVES UP A THING OF IMPORTANCE TO YOU. I DON'T SEE IT.
IT'S A BEAUTIFUL QUALITY THAT I SEE IN AMERICANS, ESPECIALLY.

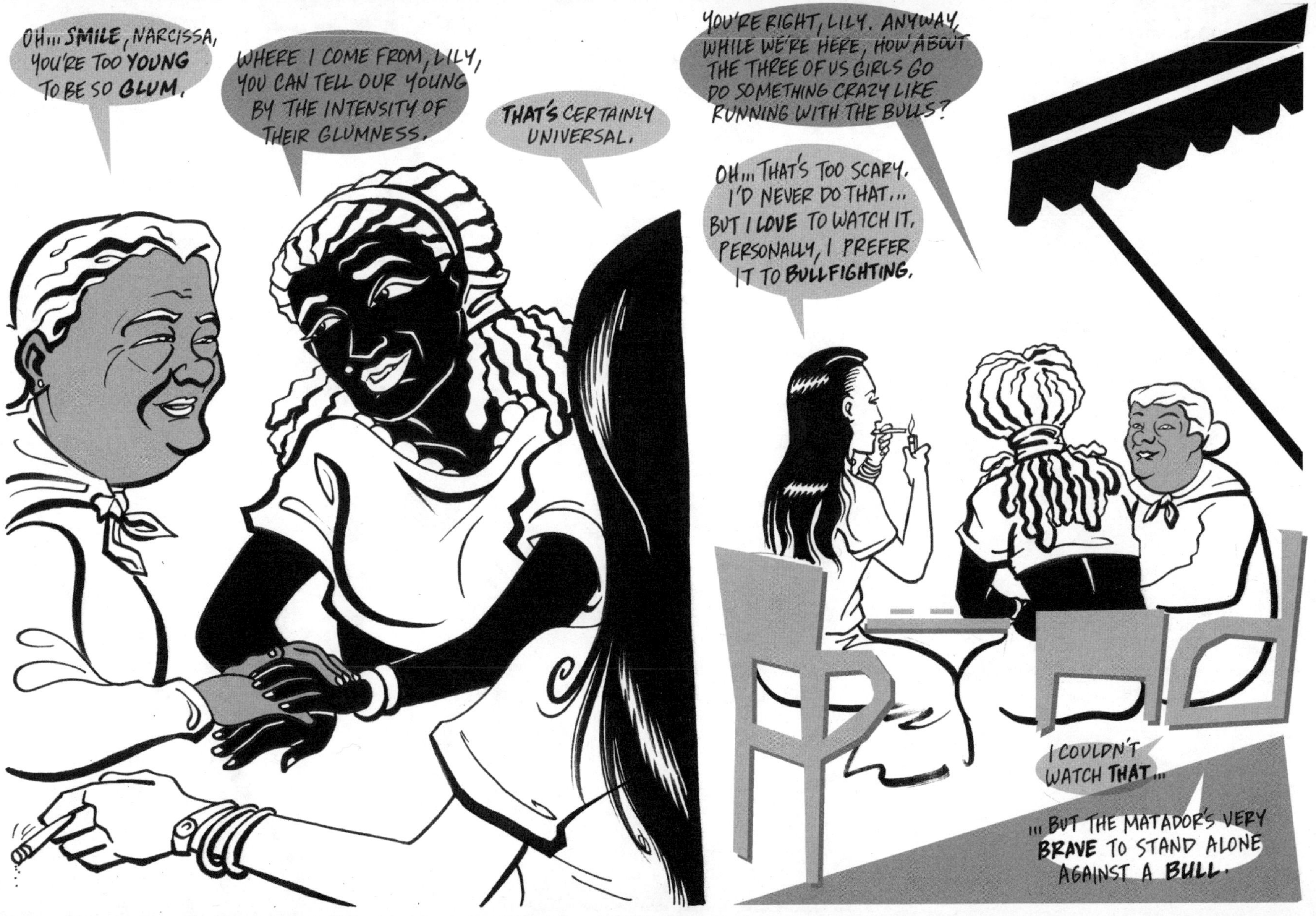

OH... SMILE, NARCISSA, YOU'RE TOO YOUNG TO BE SO GLUM.
WHERE I COME FROM, LILY, YOU CAN TELL OUR YOUNG BY THE INTENSITY OF THEIR GLUMNESS.
THAT'S CERTAINLY UNIVERSAL.
YOU'RE RIGHT, LILY. ANYWAY, WHILE WE'RE HERE, HOW ABOUT THE THREE OF US GIRLS GO DO SOMETHING CRAZY LIKE RUNNING WITH THE BULLS?
OH... THAT'S TOO SCARY. I'D NEVER DO THAT... BUT I LOVE TO WATCH IT. PERSONALLY, I PREFER IT TO BULLFIGHTING.
I COULDN'T WATCH THAT...
...BUT THE MATADOR'S VERY BRAVE TO STAND ALONE AGAINST A BULL.

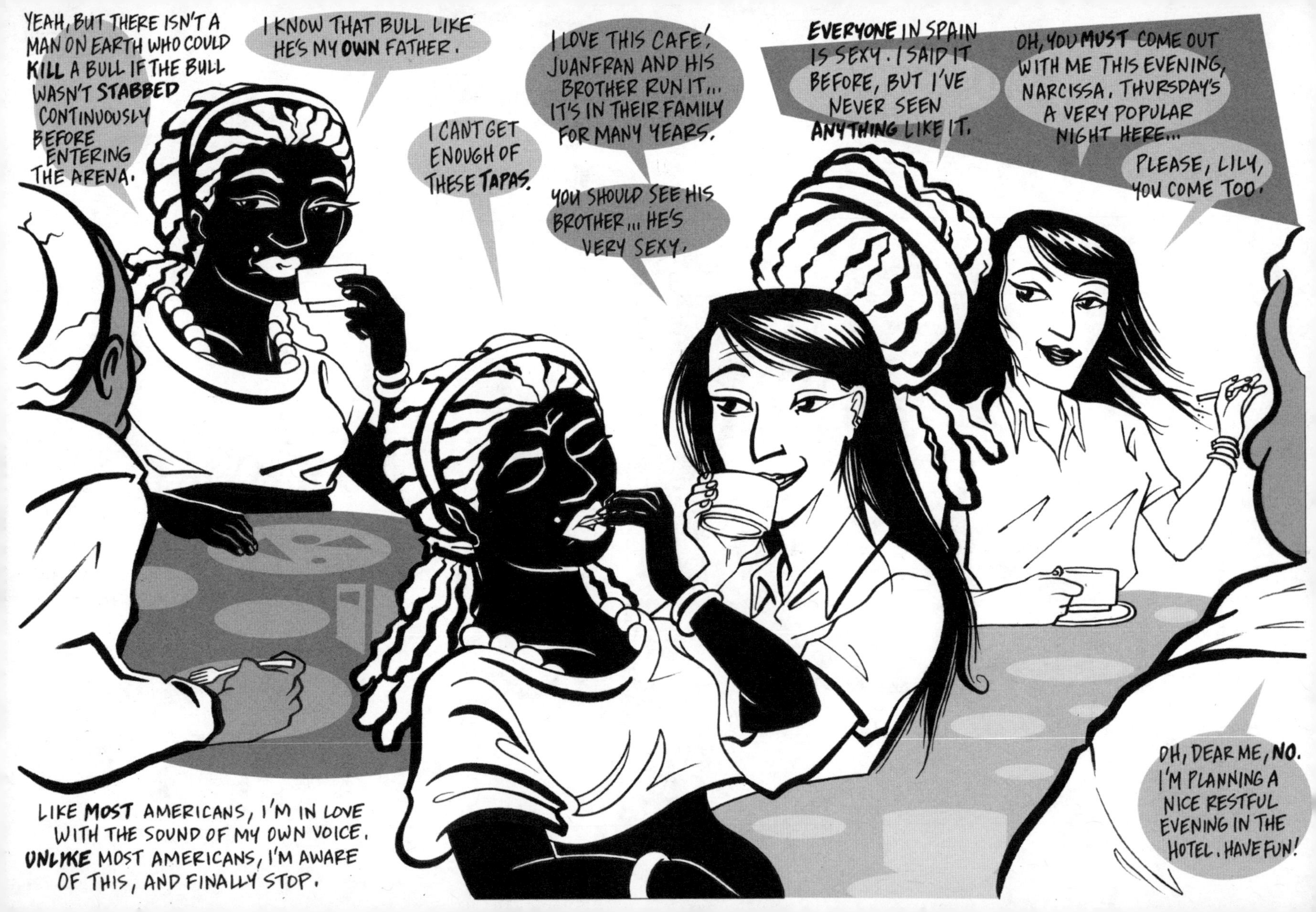
YEAH, BUT THERE ISN'T A MAN ON EARTH WHO COULD **KILL** A BULL IF THE BULL WASN'T **STABBED** CONTINUOUSLY BEFORE ENTERING THE ARENA.
I KNOW THAT BULL LIKE HE'S MY **OWN** FATHER.
I CANT GET ENOUGH OF THESE **TAPAS**.
I LOVE THIS CAFE! JUANFRAN AND HIS BROTHER RUN IT... IT'S IN THEIR FAMILY FOR MANY YEARS.
YOU SHOULD SEE HIS BROTHER... HE'S VERY SEXY.
EVERYONE IN SPAIN IS SEXY. I SAID IT BEFORE, BUT I'VE NEVER SEEN **ANYTHING** LIKE IT.
OH, YOU **MUST** COME OUT WITH ME THIS EVENING, NARCISSA. THURSDAY'S A VERY POPULAR NIGHT HERE...
PLEASE, LILY, YOU COME TOO.
OH, DEAR ME, **NO**. I'M PLANNING A NICE RESTFUL EVENING IN THE HOTEL. HAVE FUN!
LIKE **MOST** AMERICANS, I'M IN LOVE WITH THE SOUND OF MY OWN VOICE. **UNLIKE** MOST AMERICANS, I'M AWARE OF THIS, AND FINALLY STOP.

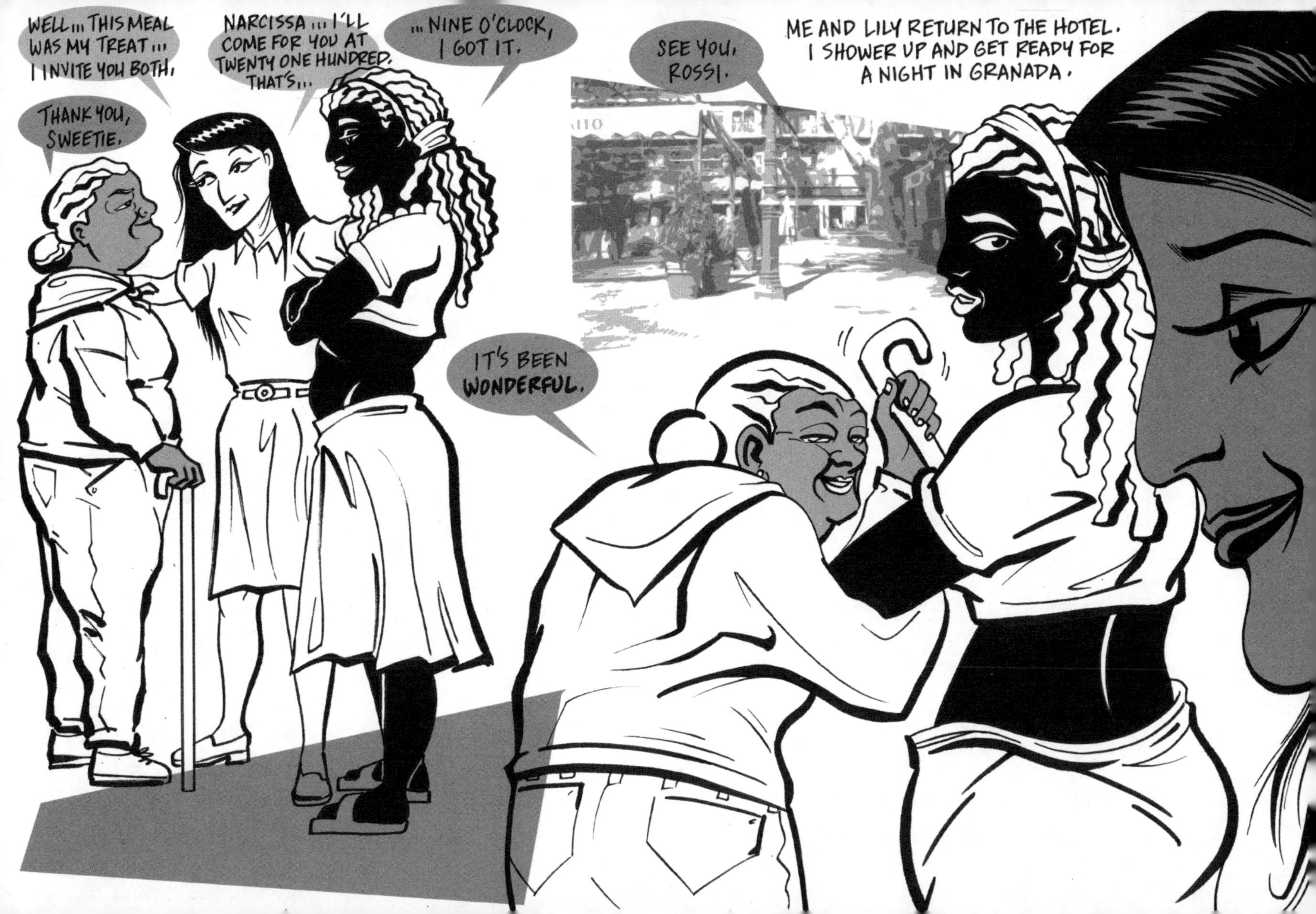
WELL... THIS MEAL WAS MY TREAT... I INVITE YOU BOTH.
THANK YOU, SWEETIE.
NARCISSA... I'LL COME FOR YOU AT TWENTY ONE HUNDRED. THAT'S...
...NINE O'CLOCK, I GOT IT.
IT'S BEEN WONDERFUL.
SEE YOU, ROSSI.
ME AND LILY RETURN TO THE HOTEL. I SHOWER UP AND GET READY FOR A NIGHT IN GRANADA.

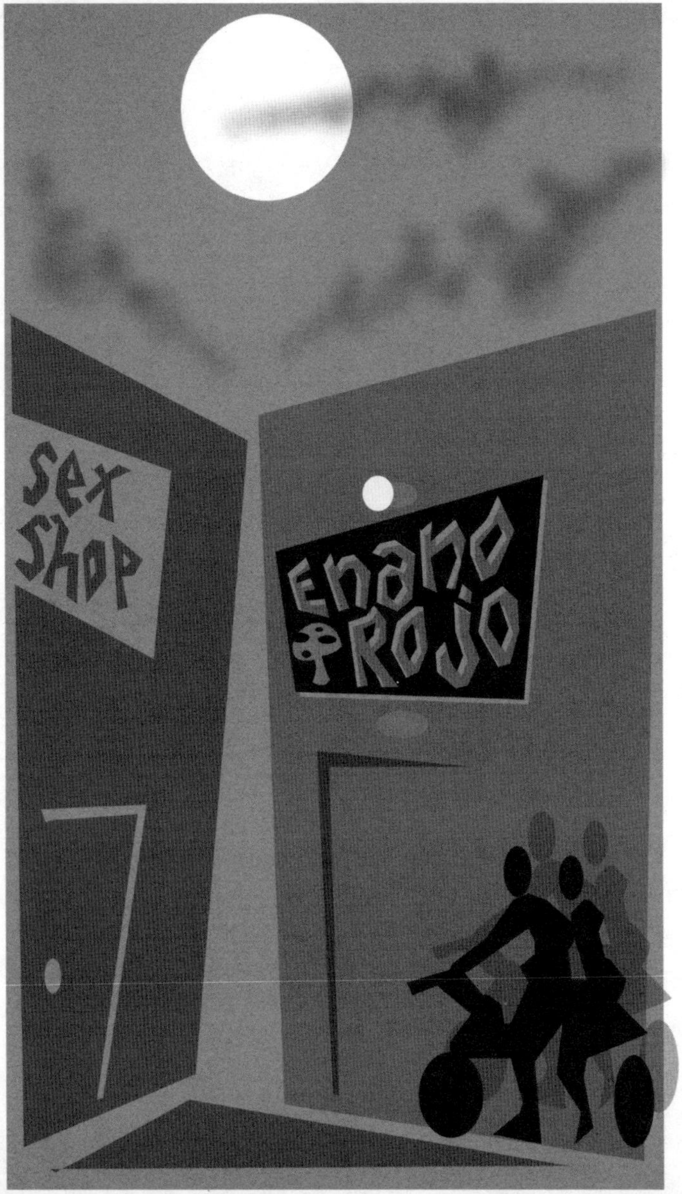
SEX SHOP
ENANO ROJO

AFTER DARK. THE ROOM'S FILLED TO THE RAFTERS WITH BODIES AND SMOKE, BUT WE RULE IT JUST THE SAME. ROSSI IS KILLER WITH HER WHITEWHITE SKIN AND RED RED LIPS, AS AM I WITH MY BLACKBLACK SKIN AND BLUEBLUE MIND.

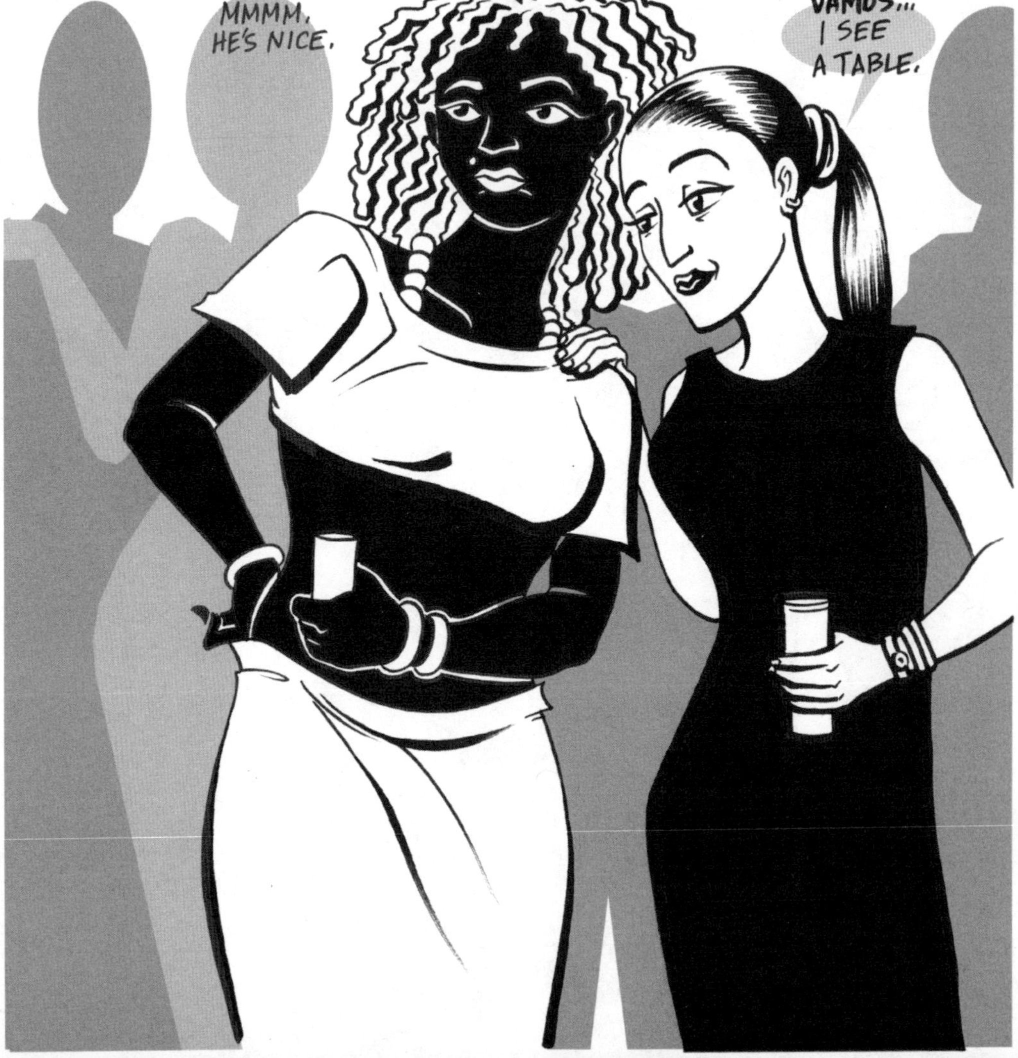
MMMM. HE'S NICE.
VAMOS... I SEE A TABLE.

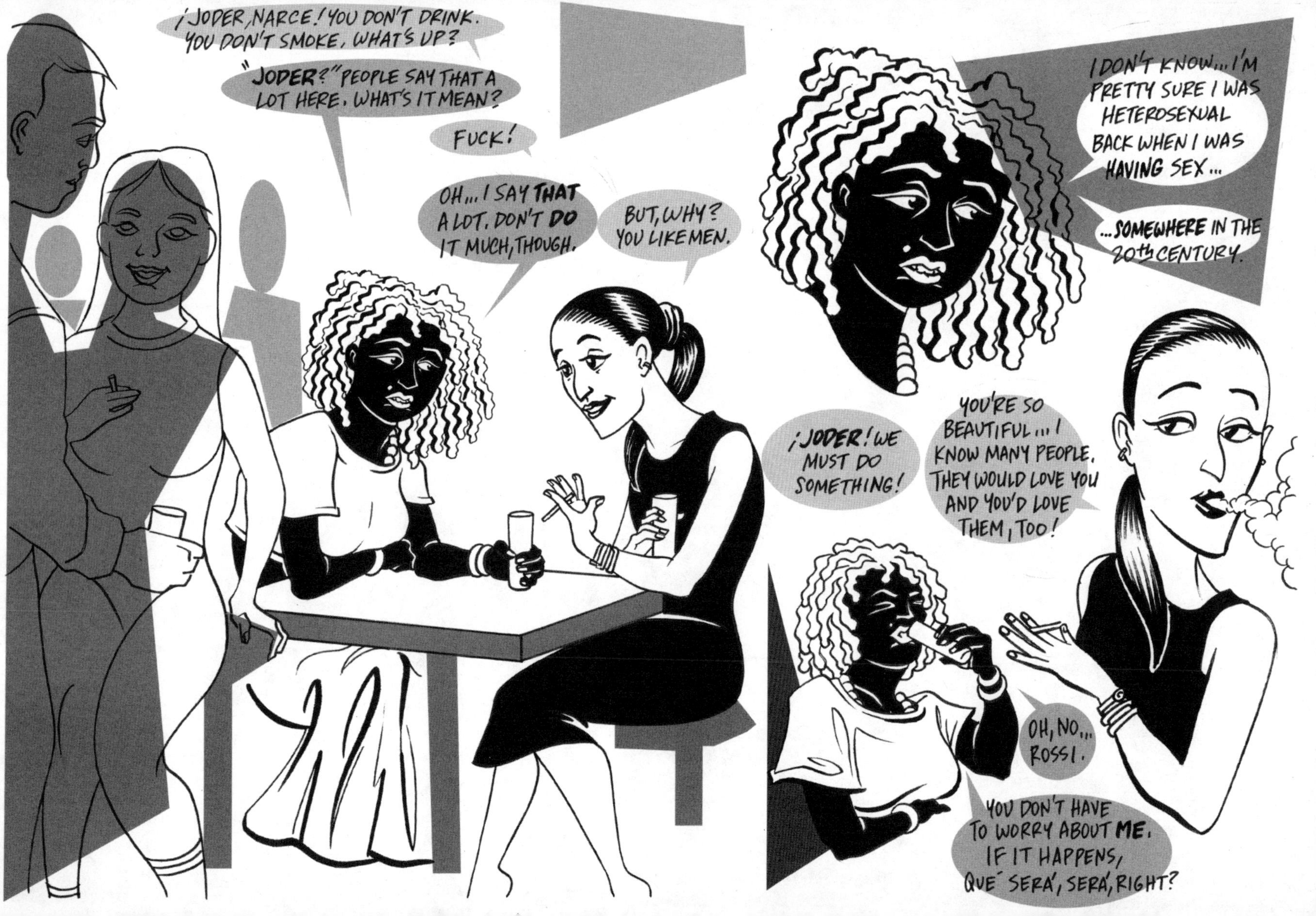
¡JODER, NARCE! YOU DON'T DRINK. YOU DON'T SMOKE, WHAT'S UP?
"JODER?" PEOPLE SAY THAT A LOT HERE. WHAT'S IT MEAN?
FUCK!
OH... I SAY THAT A LOT. DON'T DO IT MUCH, THOUGH.
BUT, WHY? YOU LIKE MEN.
I DON'T KNOW... I'M PRETTY SURE I WAS HETEROSEXUAL BACK WHEN I WAS HAVING SEX...
...SOMEWHERE IN THE 20th CENTURY.
¡JODER! WE MUST DO SOMETHING!
YOU'RE SO BEAUTIFUL... I KNOW MANY PEOPLE. THEY WOULD LOVE YOU AND YOU'D LOVE THEM, TOO!
OH, NO... ROSSI.
YOU DON'T HAVE TO WORRY ABOUT ME. IF IT HAPPENS, QUÉ SERÁ, SERÁ, RIGHT?

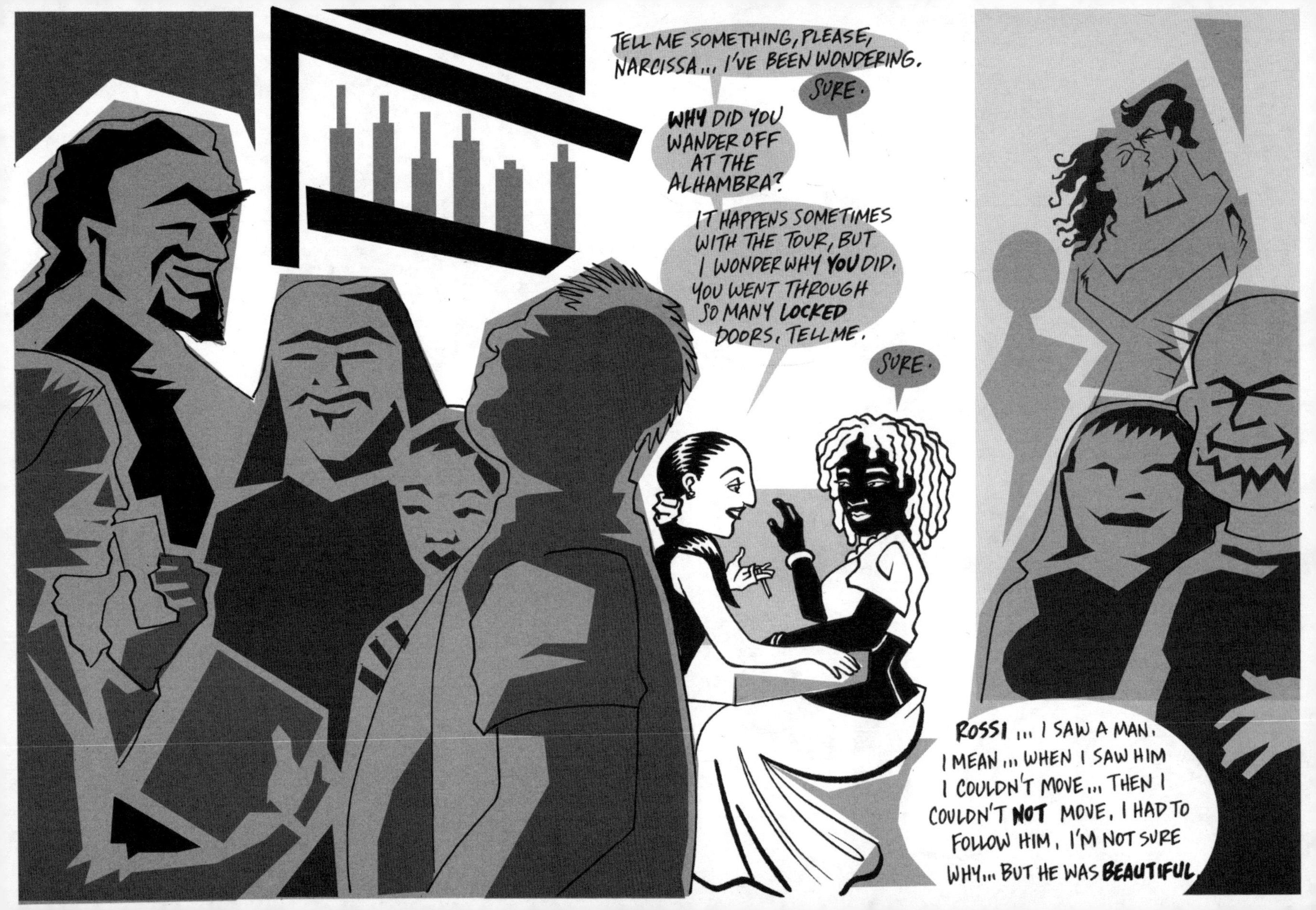
TELL ME SOMETHING, PLEASE, NARCISSA... I'VE BEEN WONDERING.
SURE.
WHY DID YOU WANDER OFF AT THE ALHAMBRA?
IT HAPPENS SOMETIMES WITH THE TOUR, BUT I WONDER WHY YOU DID. YOU WENT THROUGH SO MANY LOCKED DOORS. TELL ME.
SURE.
ROSSI ... I SAW A MAN. I MEAN ... WHEN I SAW HIM I COULDN'T MOVE ... THEN I COULDN'T NOT MOVE. I HAD TO FOLLOW HIM. I'M NOT SURE WHY... BUT HE WAS BEAUTIFUL.

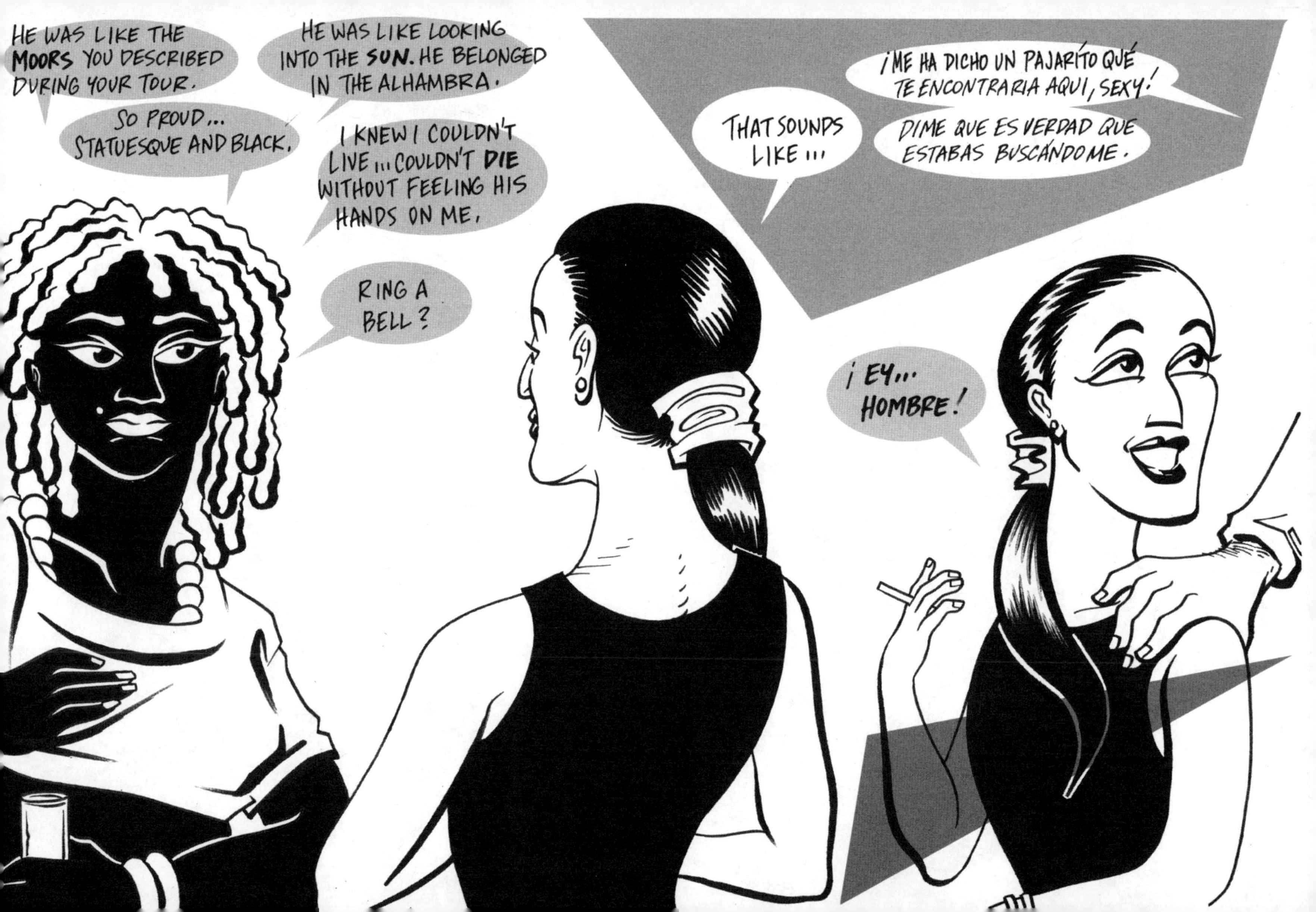
HE WAS LIKE THE **MOORS** YOU DESCRIBED DURING YOUR TOUR.
SO PROUD... STATUESQUE AND BLACK.
HE WAS LIKE LOOKING INTO THE **SUN**. HE BELONGED IN THE ALHAMBRA.
I KNEW I COULDN'T LIVE... COULDN'T **DIE** WITHOUT FEELING HIS HANDS ON ME.
RING A BELL?
THAT SOUNDS LIKE...
¡ME HA DICHO UN PAJARITO QUÉ TE ENCONTRARIA AQUI, SEXY!
DIME QUE ES VERDAD QUE ESTABAS BUSCÁNDOME.
¡EY... HOMBRE!

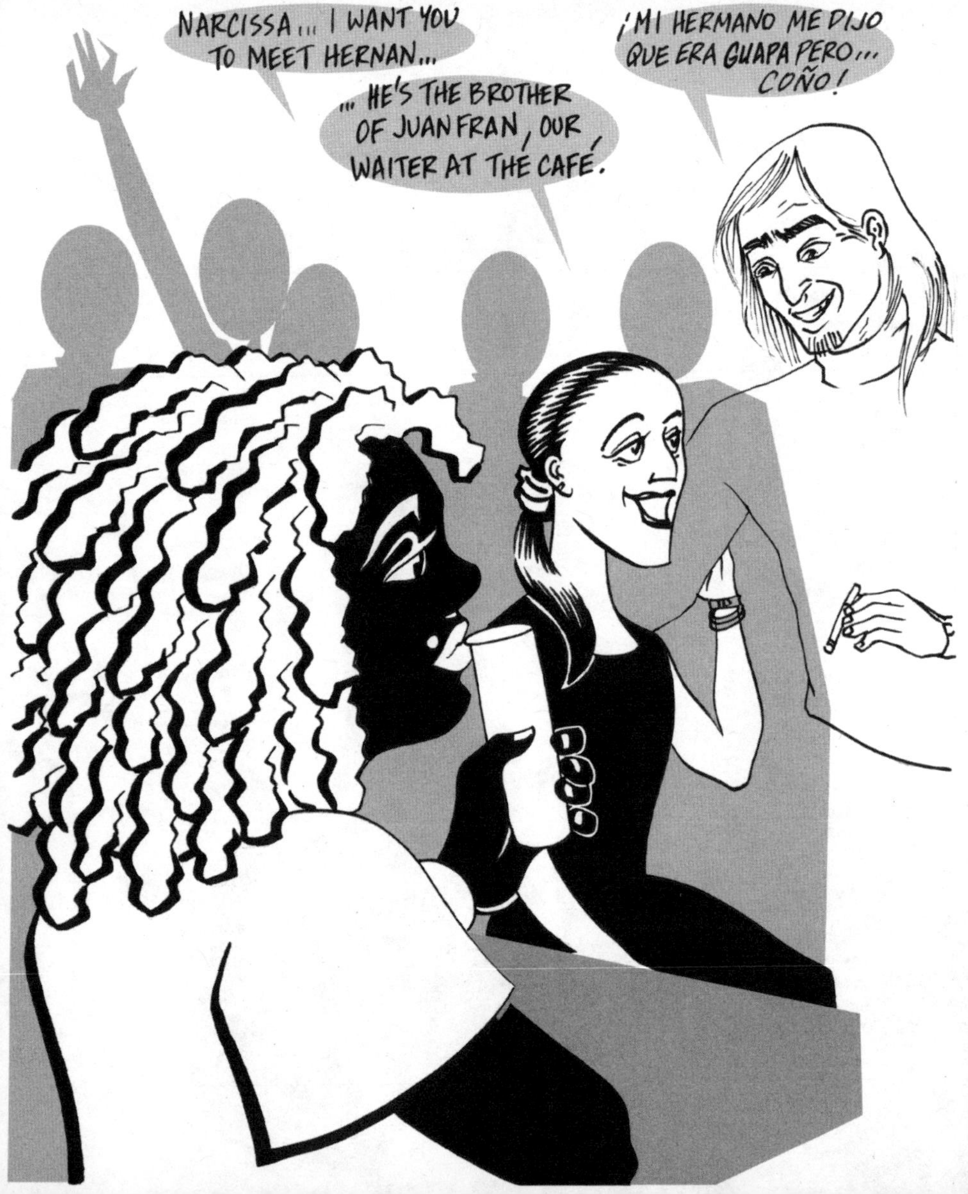
NARCISSA... I WANT YOU TO MEET HERNAN...
... HE'S THE BROTHER OF JUAN FRAN, OUR WAITER AT THE CAFÉ.
¡MI HERMANO ME DIJO QUE ERA GUAPA PERO... COÑO!

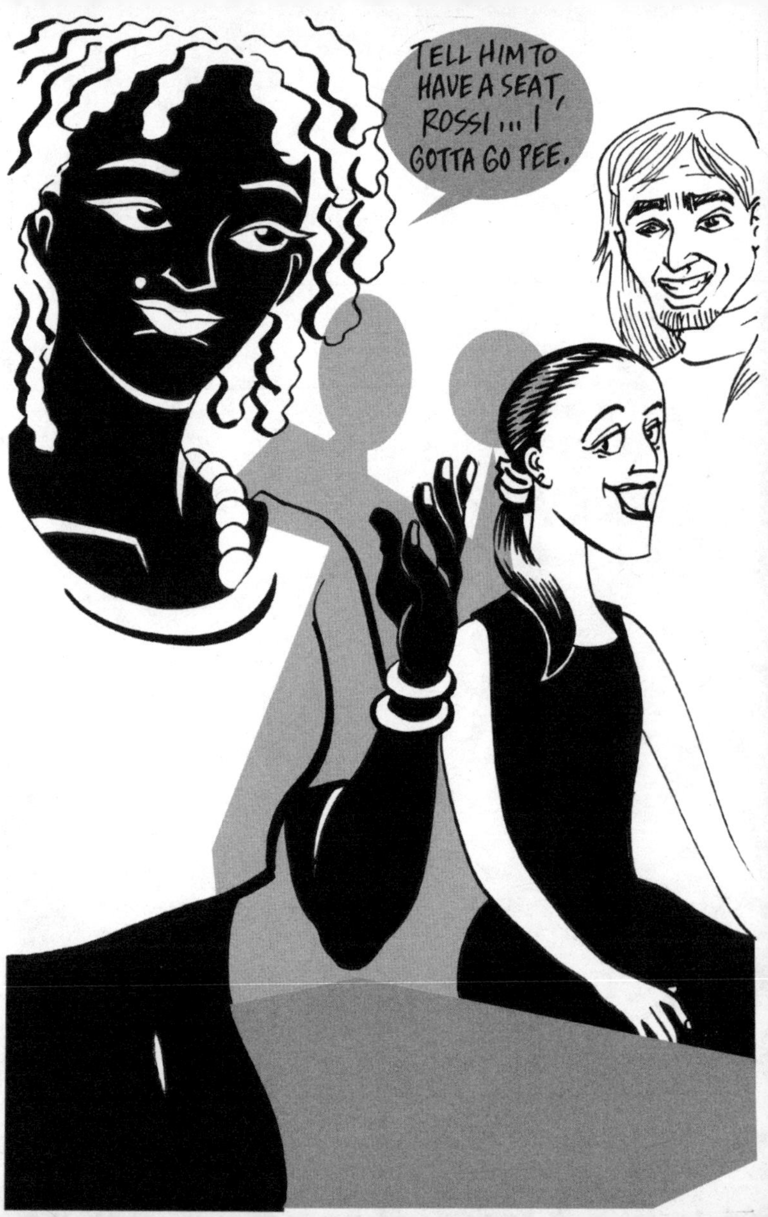
TELL HIM TO HAVE A SEAT, ROSSI... I GOTTA GO PEE.

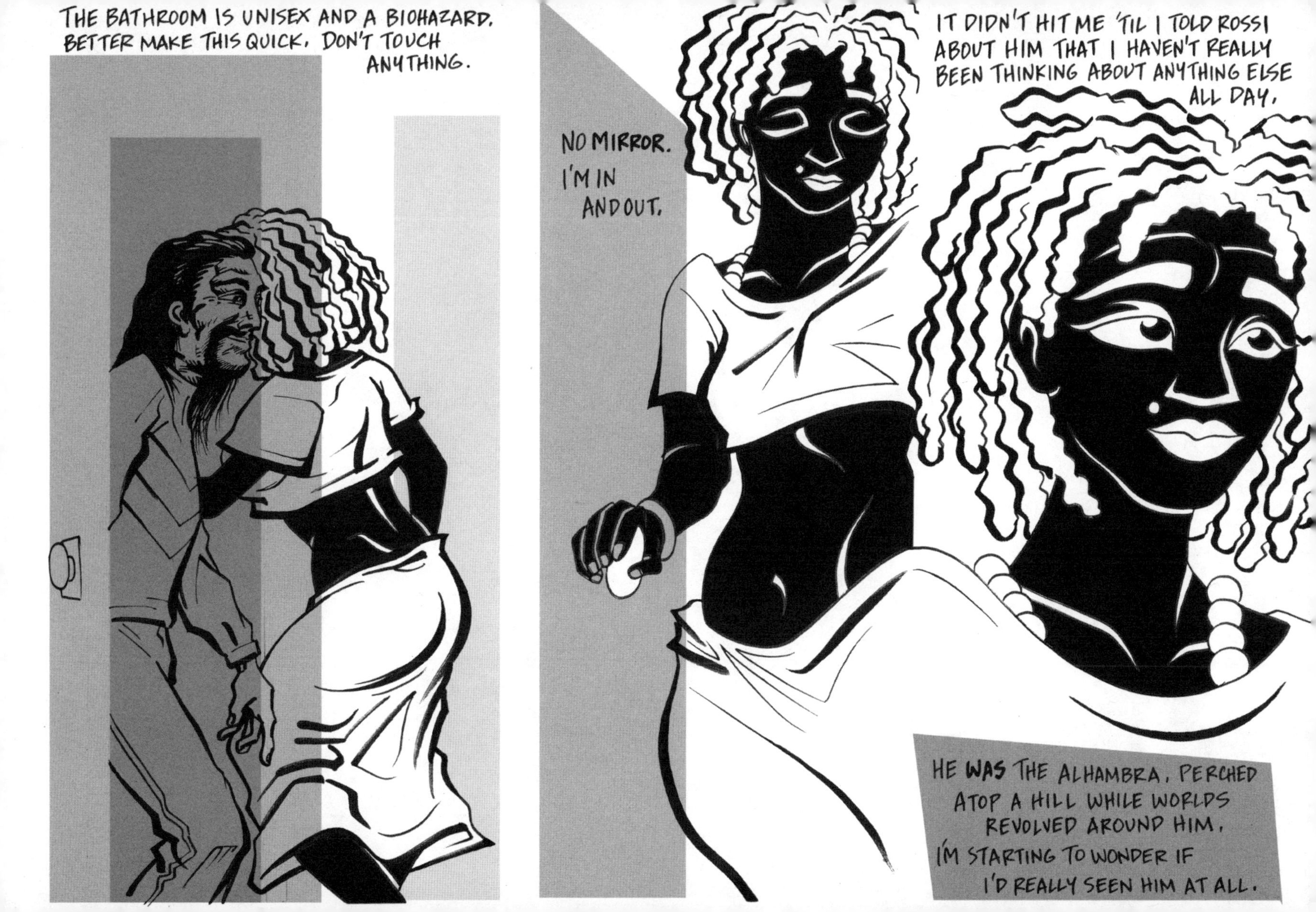

THE BATHROOM IS UNISEX AND A BIOHAZARD. BETTER MAKE THIS QUICK. DON'T TOUCH ANYTHING.
NO MIRROR.
I'M IN AND OUT.
IT DIDN'T HIT ME 'TIL I TOLD ROSSI ABOUT HIM THAT I HAVEN'T REALLY BEEN THINKING ABOUT ANYTHING ELSE ALL DAY.
HE **WAS** THE ALHAMBRA, PERCHED ATOP A HILL WHILE WORLDS REVOLVED AROUND HIM.
I'M STARTING TO WONDER IF I'D REALLY SEEN HIM AT ALL.

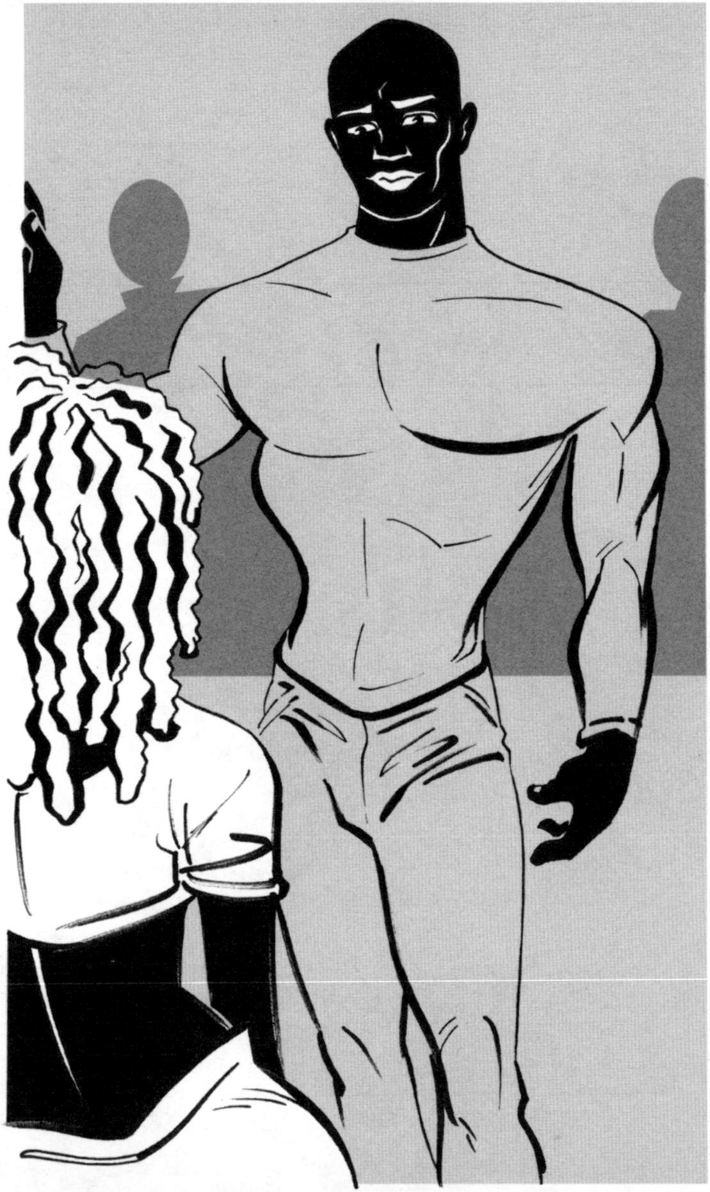

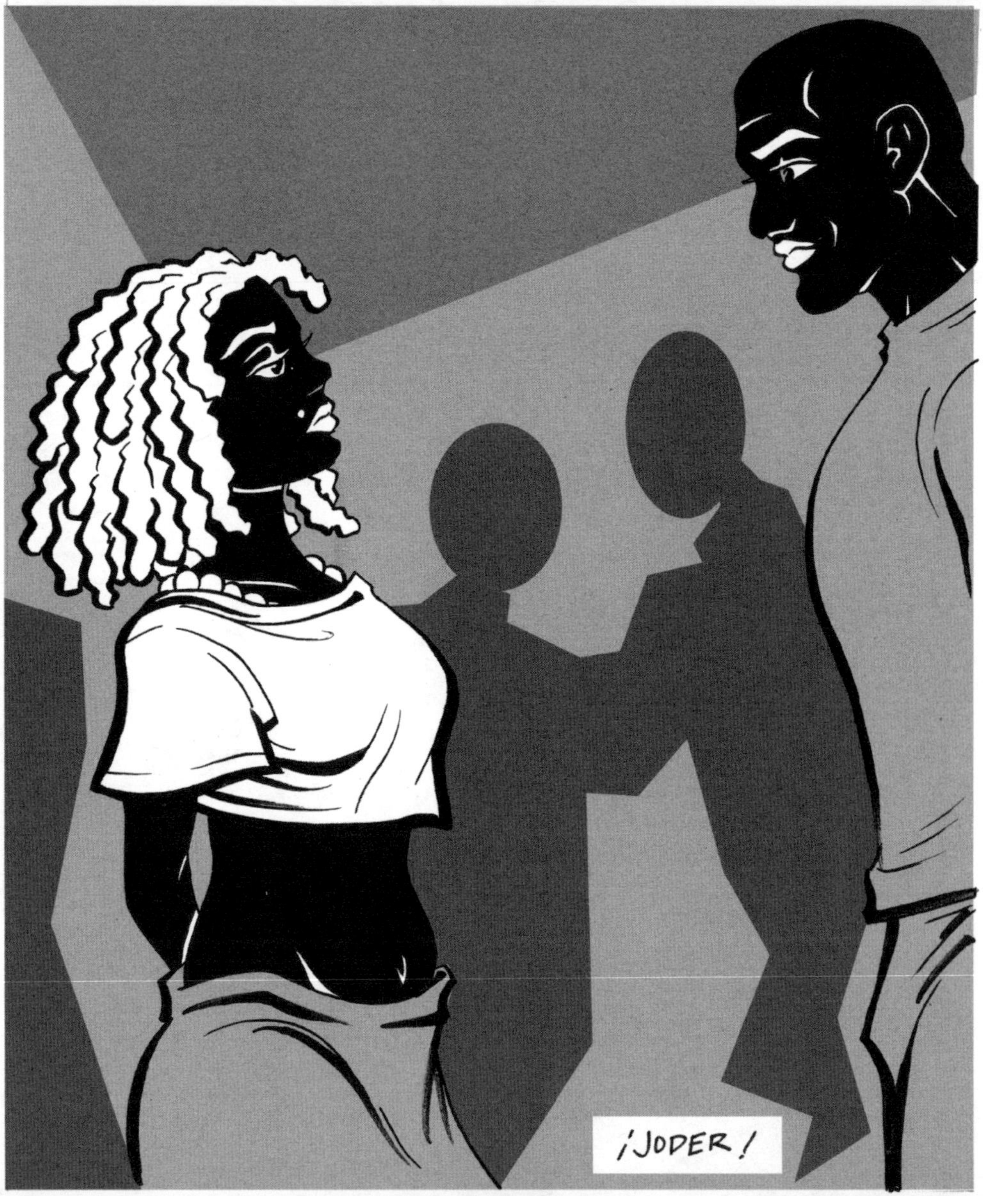
¡JODER!

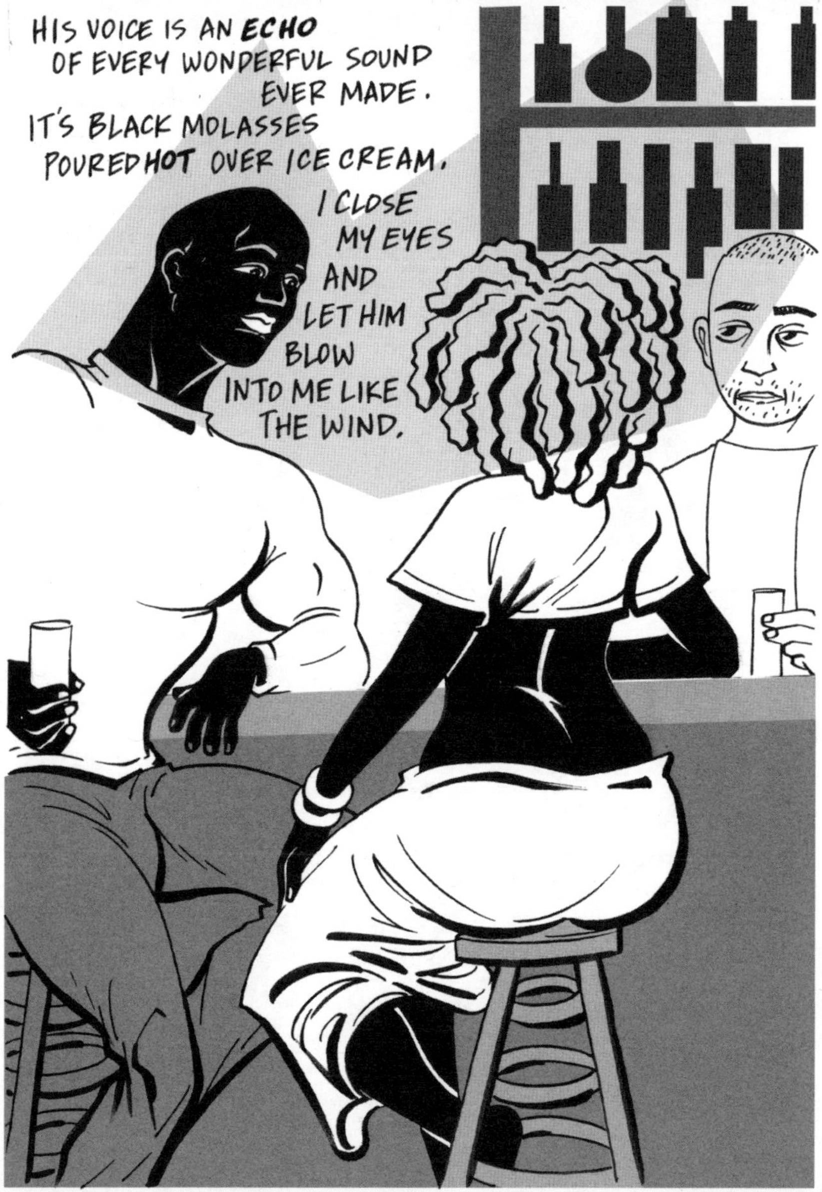
HIS VOICE IS AN **ECHO** OF EVERY WONDERFUL SOUND EVER MADE.
IT'S BLACK MOLASSES POURED **HOT** OVER ICE CREAM.
I CLOSE MY EYES AND LET HIM BLOW INTO ME LIKE THE WIND.

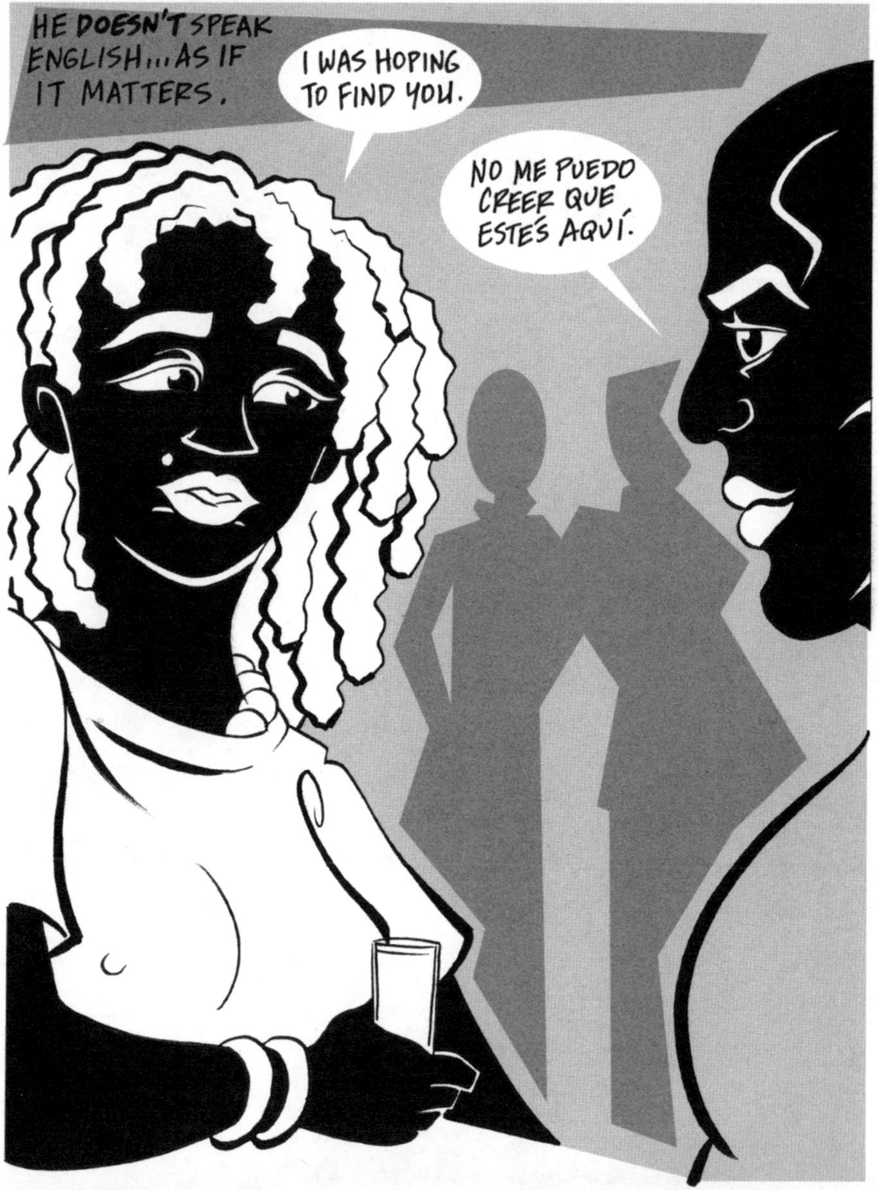
HE **DOESN'T** SPEAK ENGLISH...AS IF IT MATTERS.
I WAS HOPING TO FIND YOU.
NO ME PUEDO CREER QUE ESTÉS AQUÍ.

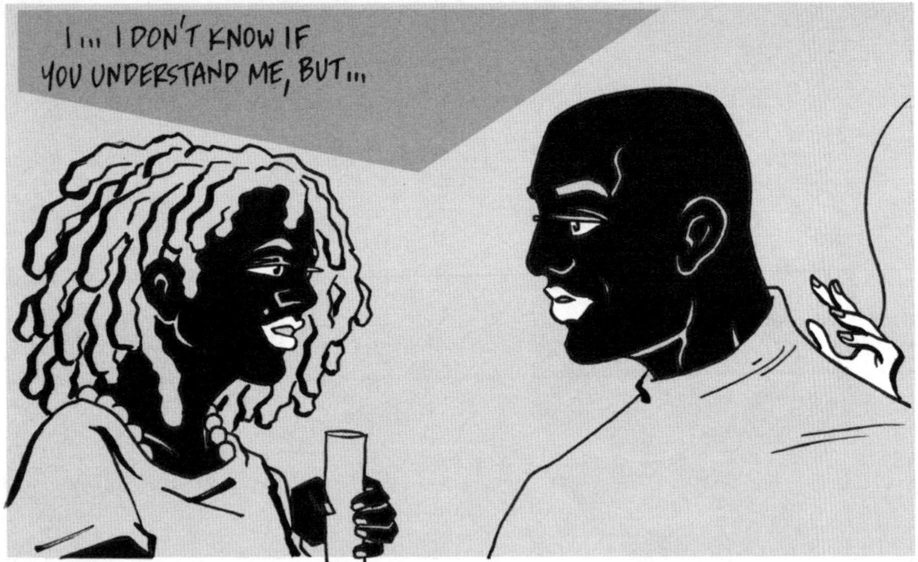

I... I DON'T KNOW IF YOU UNDERSTAND ME, BUT...

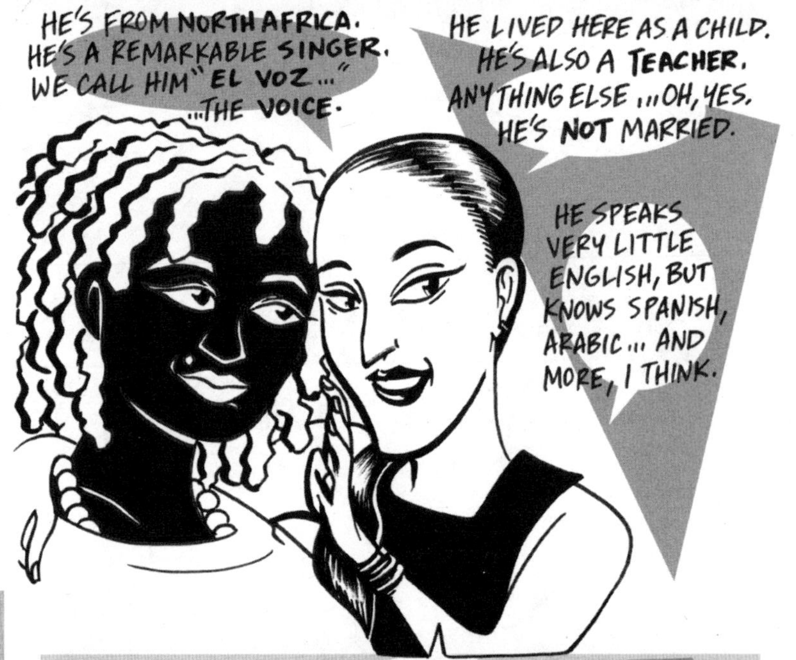

HE'S FROM NORTH AFRICA. HE'S A REMARKABLE SINGER. WE CALL HIM "EL VOZ..." ...THE VOICE.
HE LIVED HERE AS A CHILD. HE'S ALSO A TEACHER. ANYTHING ELSE ...OH, YES. HE'S NOT MARRIED.
HE SPEAKS VERY LITTLE ENGLISH, BUT KNOWS SPANISH, ARABIC... AND MORE, I THINK.

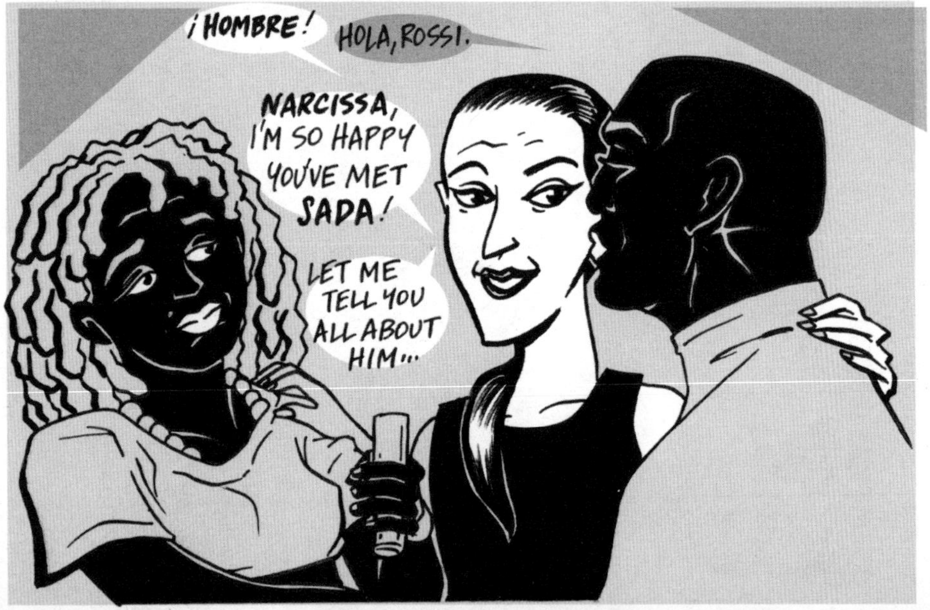

¡HOMBRE!
HOLA, ROSSI.
NARCISSA, I'M SO HAPPY YOU'VE MET SADA!
LET ME TELL YOU ALL ABOUT HIM...

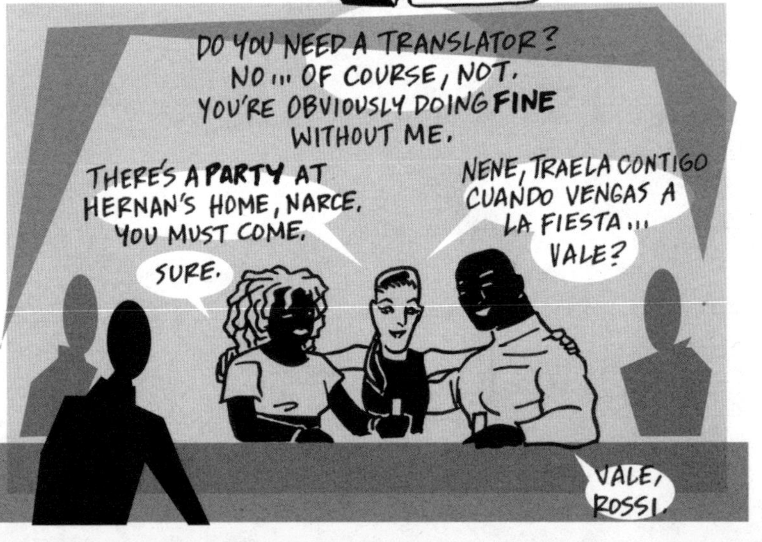

DO YOU NEED A TRANSLATOR? NO... OF COURSE, NOT. YOU'RE OBVIOUSLY DOING FINE WITHOUT ME.
THERE'S A PARTY AT HERNAN'S HOME, NARCE. YOU MUST COME.
SURE.
NENE, TRAELA CONTIGO CUANDO VENGAS A LA FIESTA... VALE?
VALE, ROSSI.

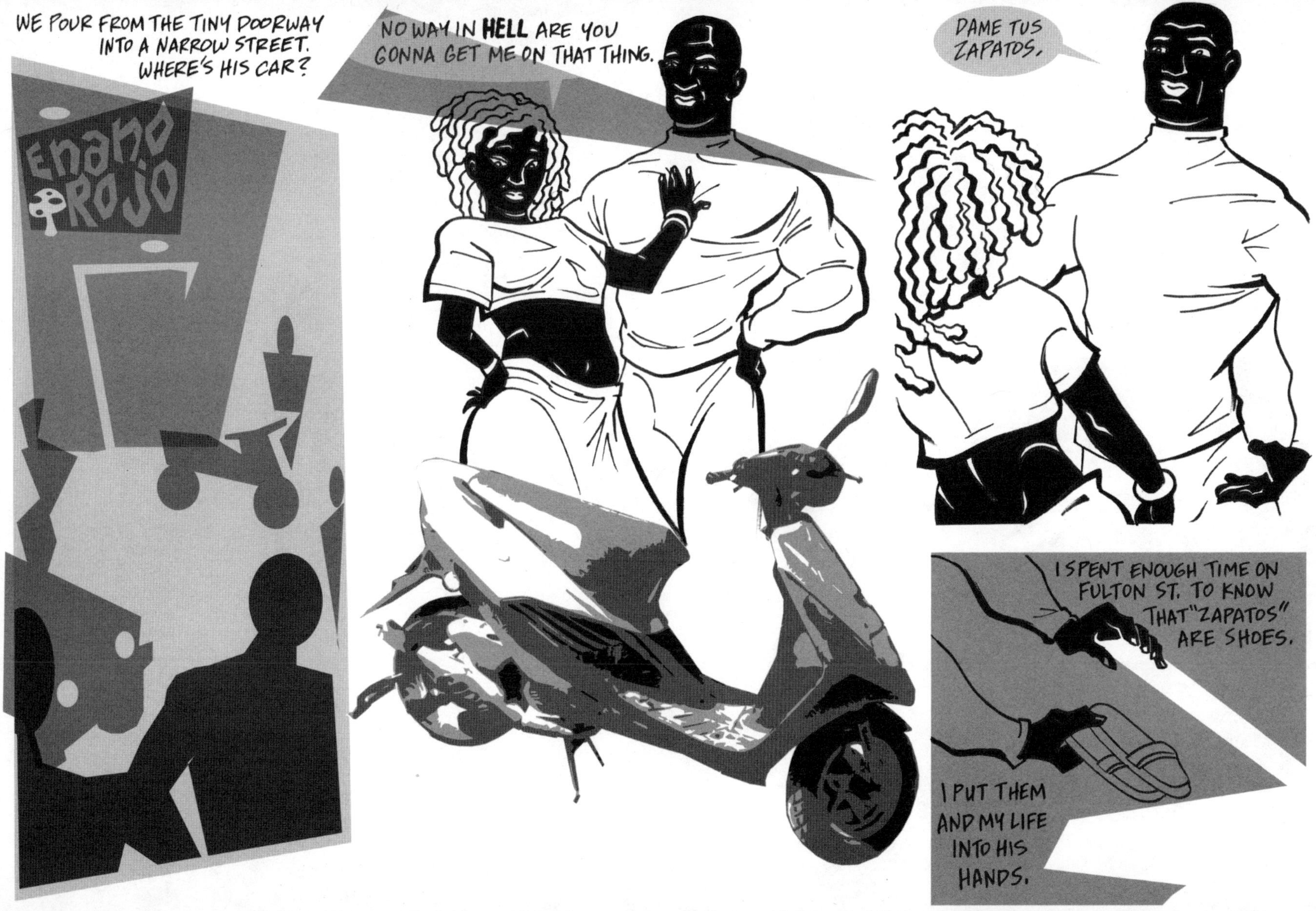
WE POUR FROM THE TINY DOORWAY INTO A NARROW STREET. WHERE'S HIS CAR?
ENANO ROJO
NO WAY IN **HELL** ARE YOU GONNA GET ME ON THAT THING.
DAME TUS ZAPATOS.
I SPENT ENOUGH TIME ON FULTON ST. TO KNOW THAT "ZAPATOS" ARE SHOES.
I PUT THEM AND MY LIFE INTO HIS HANDS.

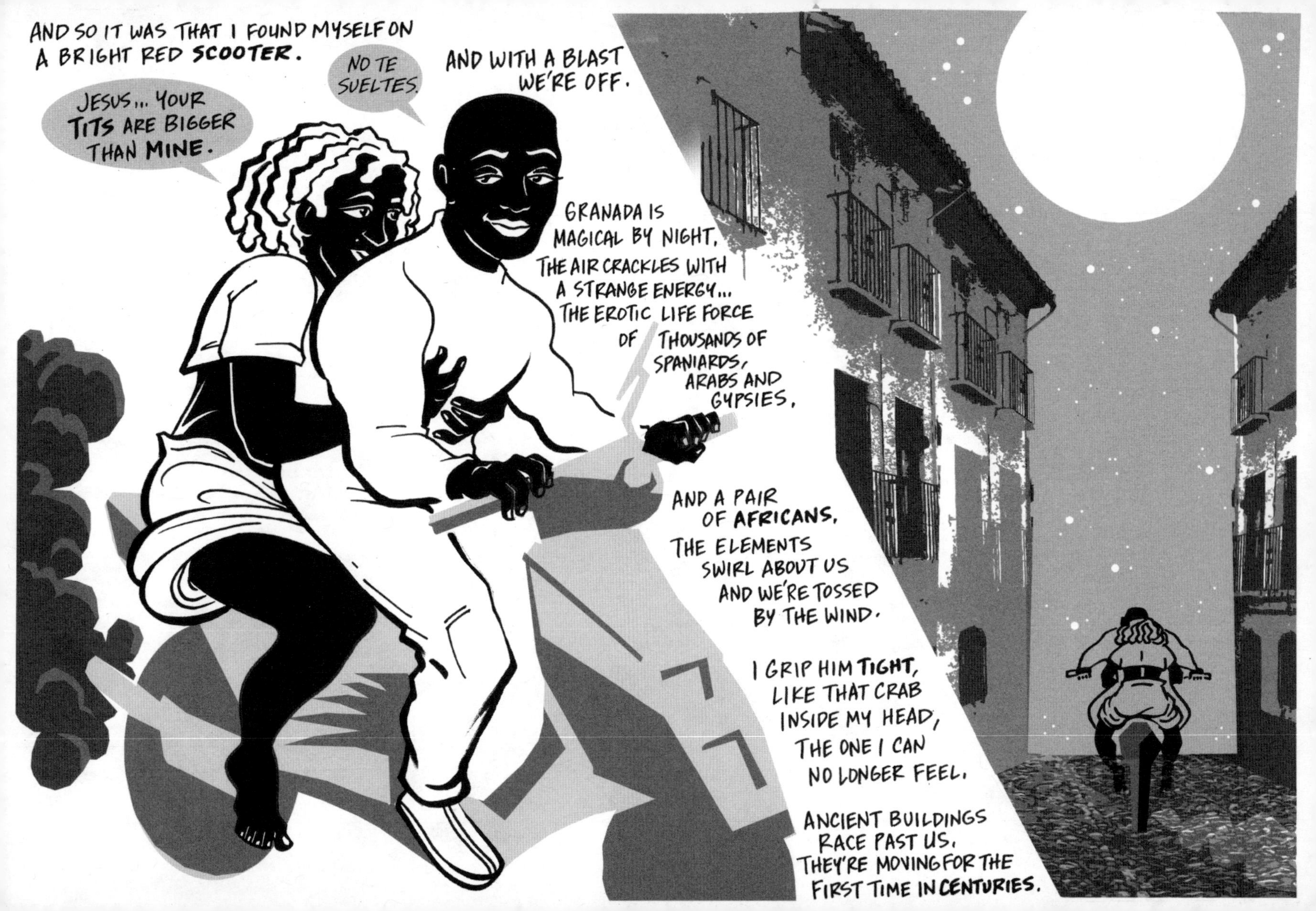

AND SO IT WAS THAT I FOUND MYSELF ON A BRIGHT RED SCOOTER.
JESUS... YOUR TITS ARE BIGGER THAN MINE.
NO TE SUELTES.
AND WITH A BLAST WE'RE OFF.
GRANADA IS MAGICAL BY NIGHT. THE AIR CRACKLES WITH A STRANGE ENERGY... THE EROTIC LIFE FORCE OF THOUSANDS OF SPANIARDS, ARABS AND GYPSIES,
AND A PAIR OF AFRICANS. THE ELEMENTS SWIRL ABOUT US AND WE'RE TOSSED BY THE WIND.
I GRIP HIM TIGHT, LIKE THAT CRAB INSIDE MY HEAD, THE ONE I CAN NO LONGER FEEL.
ANCIENT BUILDINGS RACE PAST US. THEY'RE MOVING FOR THE FIRST TIME IN CENTURIES.

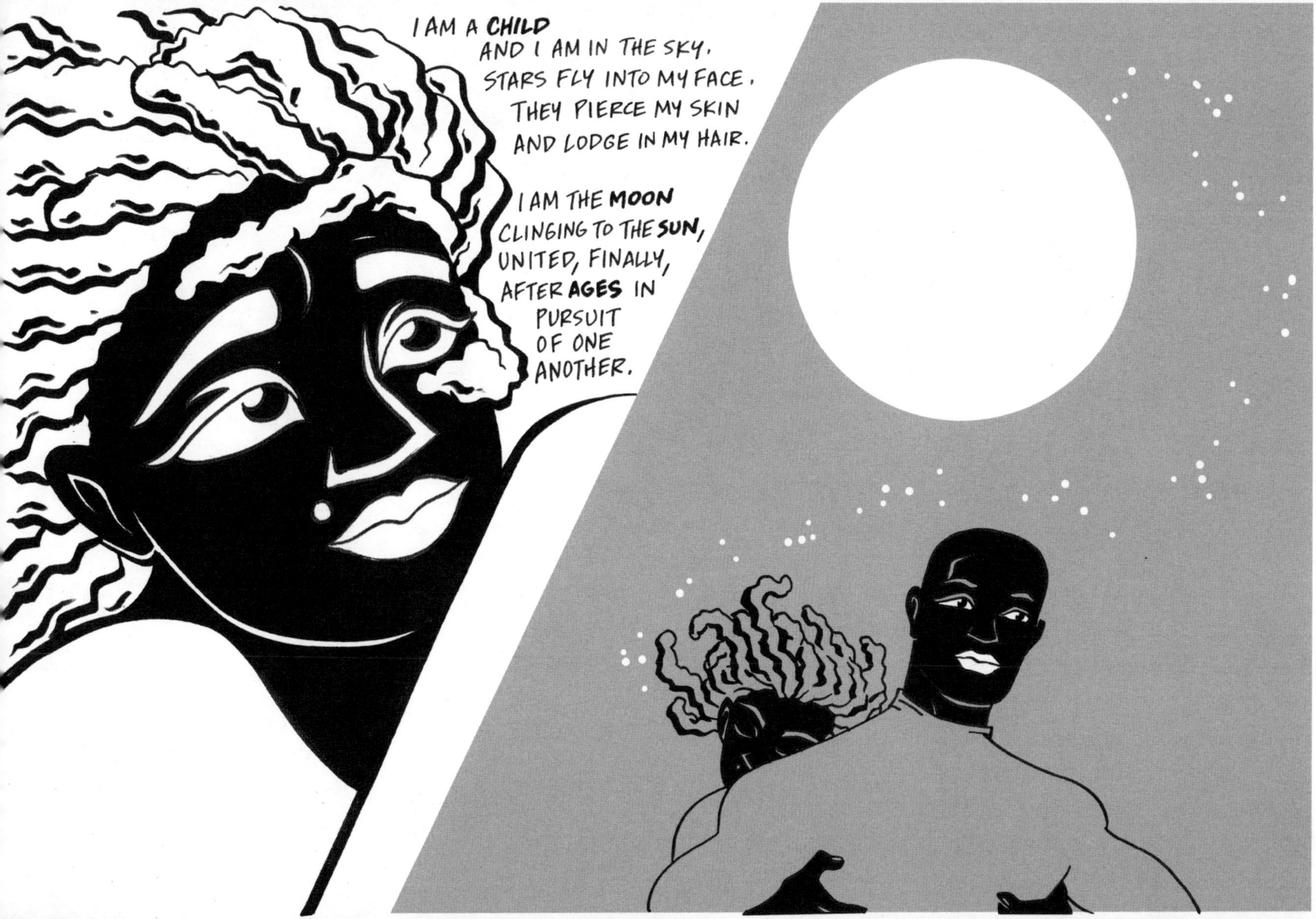
I AM A **CHILD**
AND I AM IN THE SKY.
STARS FLY INTO MY FACE.
THEY PIERCE MY SKIN
AND LODGE IN MY HAIR.
I AM THE **MOON**
CLINGING TO THE **SUN**,
UNITED, FINALLY,
AFTER **AGES** IN
PURSUIT
OF ONE
ANOTHER.

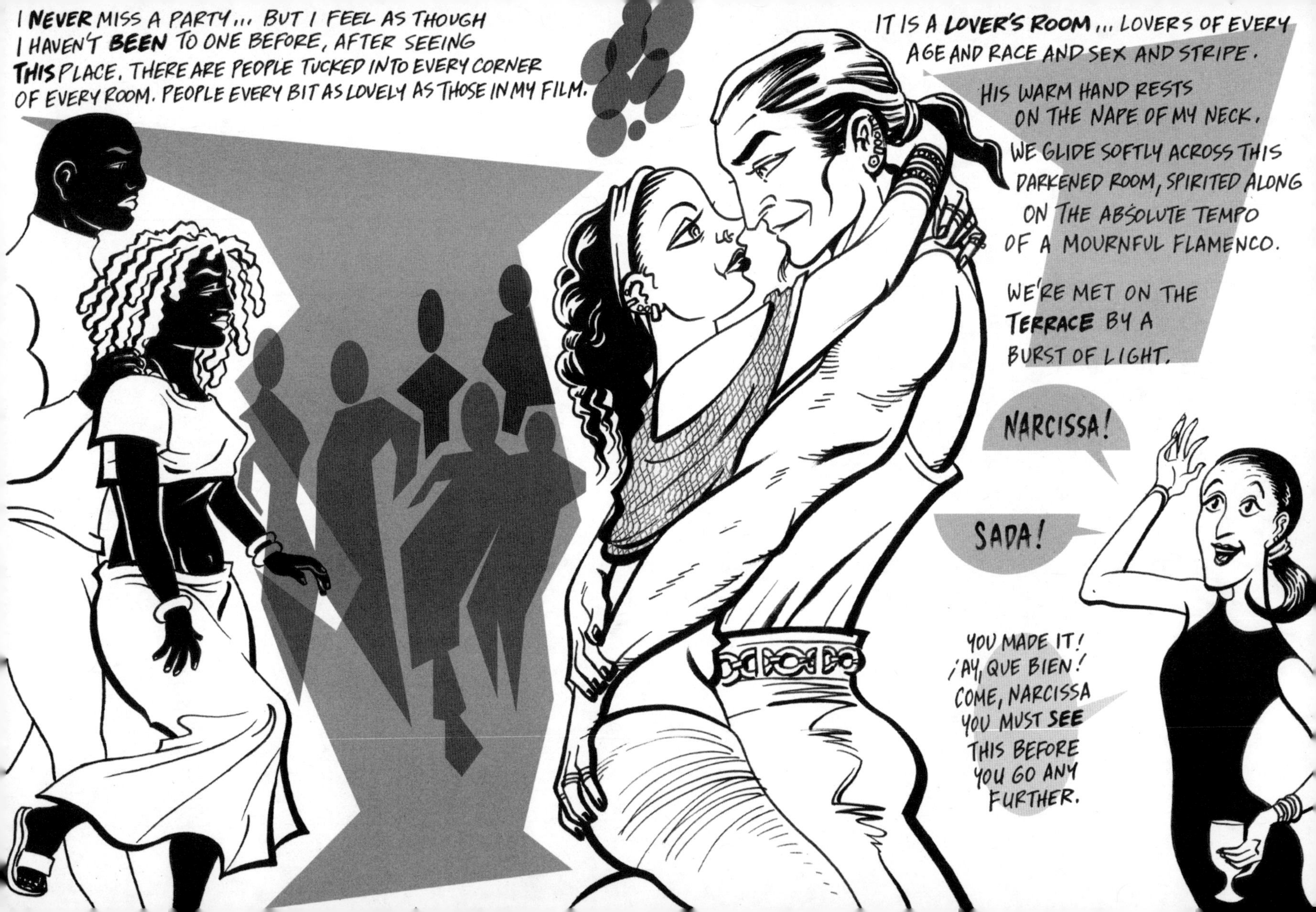
I NEVER MISS A PARTY... BUT I FEEL AS THOUGH I HAVEN'T BEEN TO ONE BEFORE, AFTER SEEING THIS PLACE. THERE ARE PEOPLE TUCKED INTO EVERY CORNER OF EVERY ROOM. PEOPLE EVERY BIT AS LOVELY AS THOSE IN MY FILM.
IT IS A LOVER'S ROOM... LOVERS OF EVERY AGE AND RACE AND SEX AND STRIPE.
HIS WARM HAND RESTS ON THE NAPE OF MY NECK.
WE GLIDE SOFTLY ACROSS THIS DARKENED ROOM, SPIRITED ALONG ON THE ABSOLUTE TEMPO OF A MOURNFUL FLAMENCO.
WE'RE MET ON THE TERRACE BY A BURST OF LIGHT.
NARCISSA!
SADA!
YOU MADE IT! ¡AY, QUE BIEN! COME, NARCISSA YOU MUST SEE THIS BEFORE YOU GO ANY FURTHER.

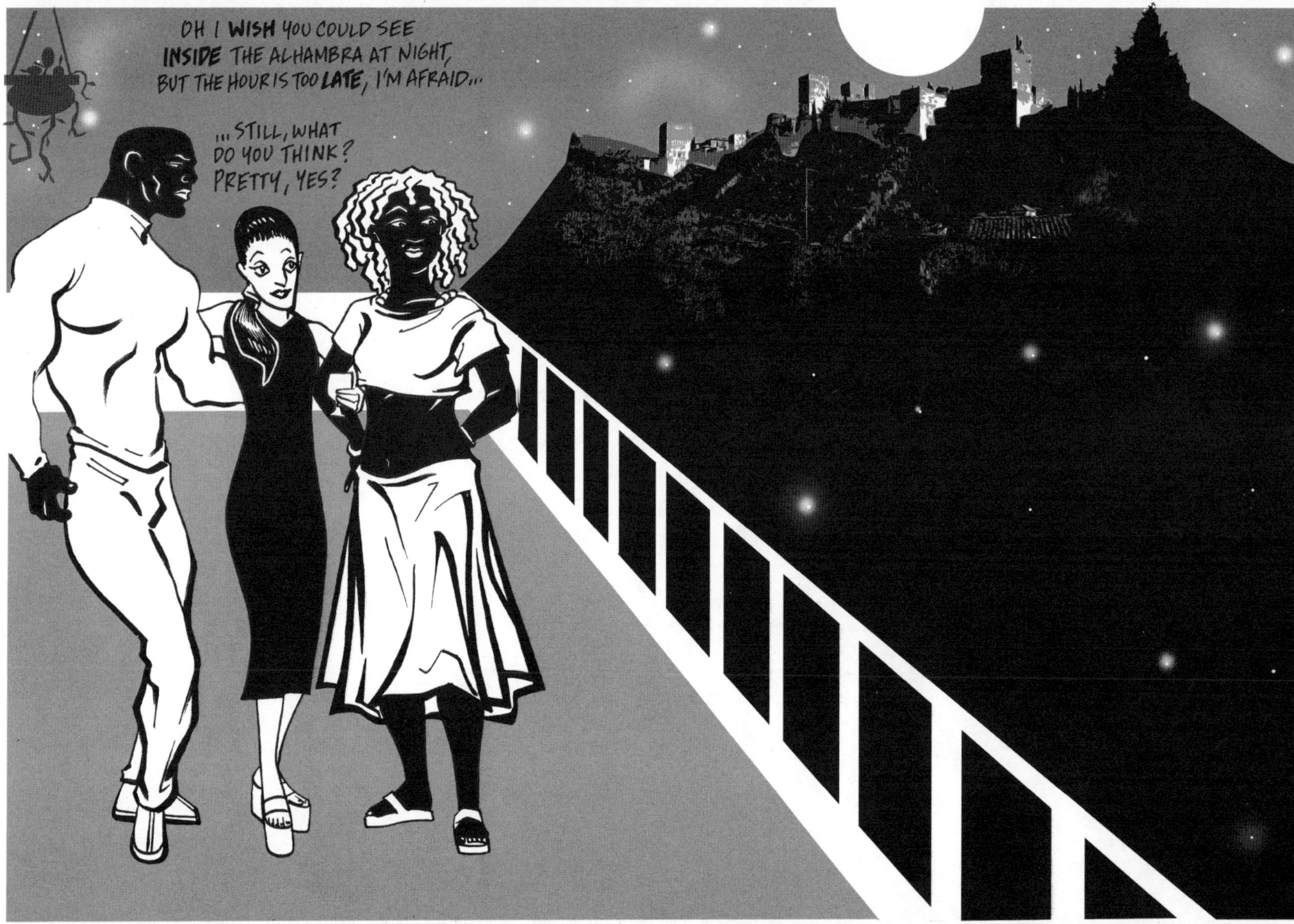
OH I **WISH** YOU COULD SEE **INSIDE** THE ALHAMBRA AT NIGHT, BUT THE HOUR IS TOO **LATE**, I'M AFRAID...
...STILL, WHAT DO YOU THINK? PRETTY, YES?

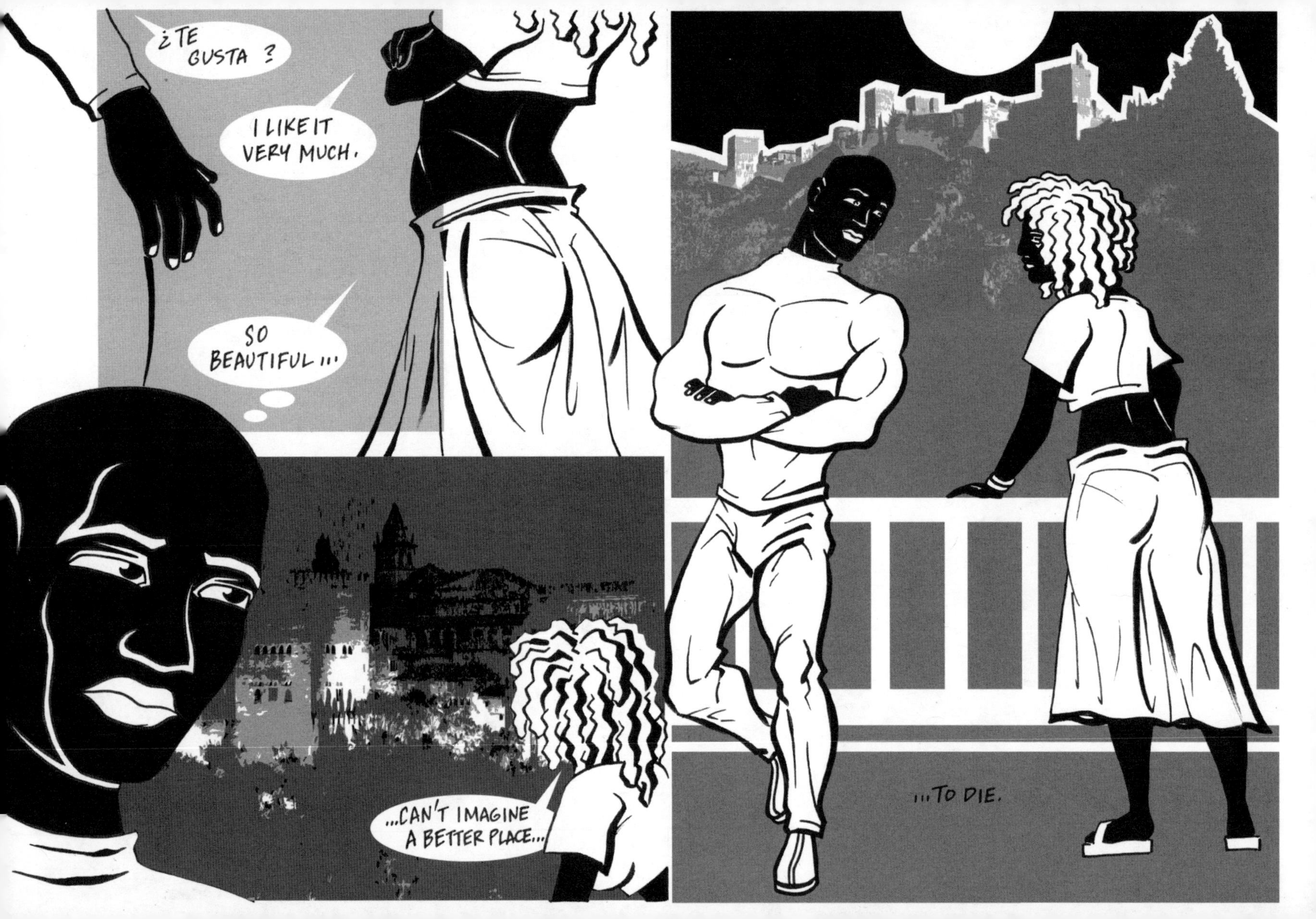
¿TE GUSTA ?
I LIKE IT VERY MUCH.
SO BEAUTIFUL...
...CAN'T IMAGINE A BETTER PLACE...
...TO DIE.

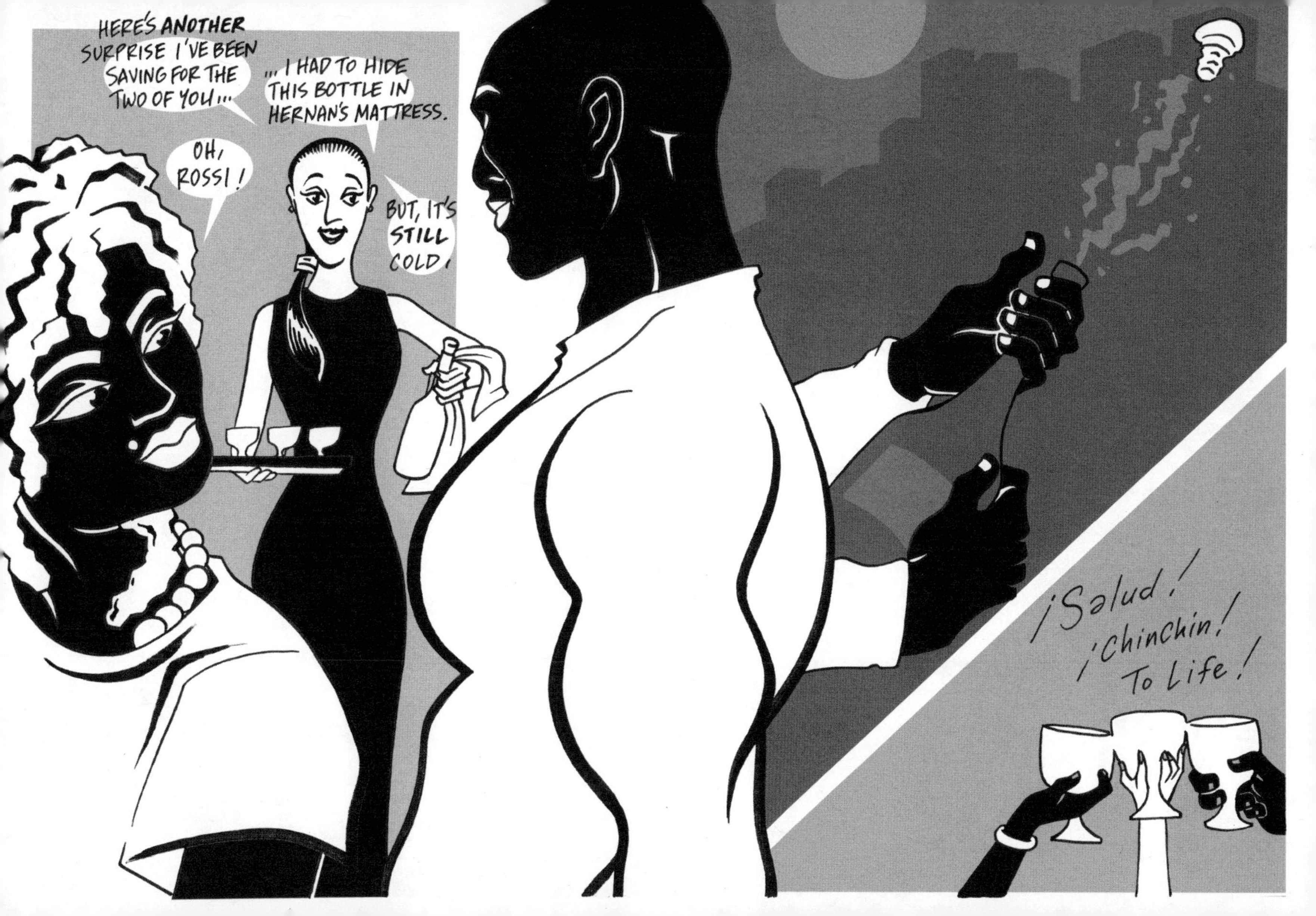
HERE'S ANOTHER SURPRISE I'VE BEEN SAVING FOR THE TWO OF YOU...
... I HAD TO HIDE THIS BOTTLE IN HERNAN'S MATTRESS.
OH, ROSSI!
BUT, IT'S STILL COLD!
¡Salud!
¡Chinchin!
To Life!

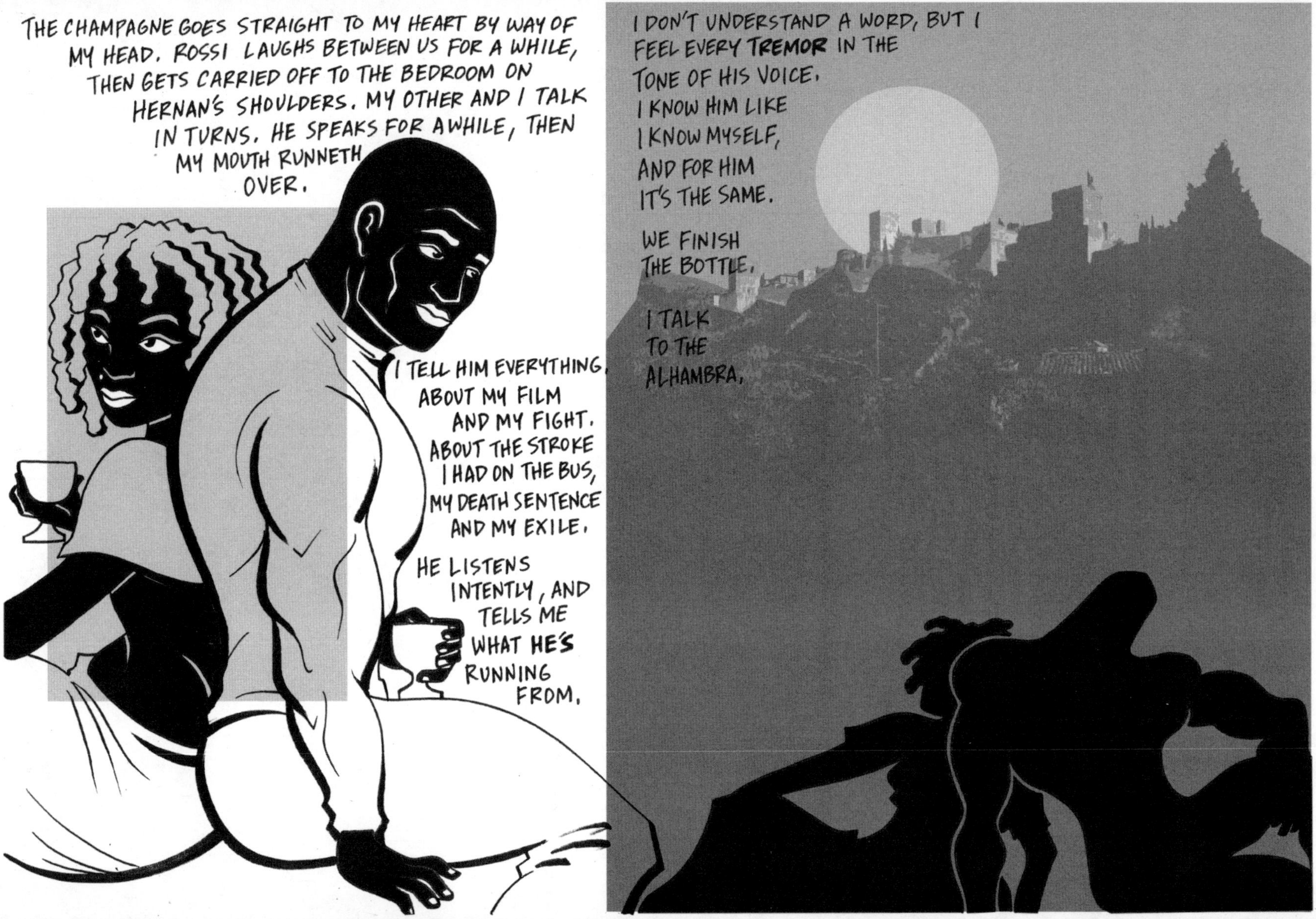
THE CHAMPAGNE GOES STRAIGHT TO MY HEART BY WAY OF MY HEAD. ROSSI LAUGHS BETWEEN US FOR A WHILE, THEN GETS CARRIED OFF TO THE BEDROOM ON HERNAN'S SHOULDERS. MY OTHER AND I TALK IN TURNS. HE SPEAKS FOR AWHILE, THEN MY MOUTH RUNNETH OVER.
I TELL HIM EVERYTHING, ABOUT MY FILM AND MY FIGHT. ABOUT THE STROKE I HAD ON THE BUS, MY DEATH SENTENCE AND MY EXILE.
HE LISTENS INTENTLY, AND TELLS ME WHAT **HE'S** RUNNING FROM.
I DON'T UNDERSTAND A WORD, BUT I FEEL EVERY **TREMOR** IN THE TONE OF HIS VOICE.
I KNOW HIM LIKE I KNOW MYSELF, AND FOR HIM IT'S THE SAME.
WE FINISH THE BOTTLE.
I TALK TO THE ALHAMBRA.

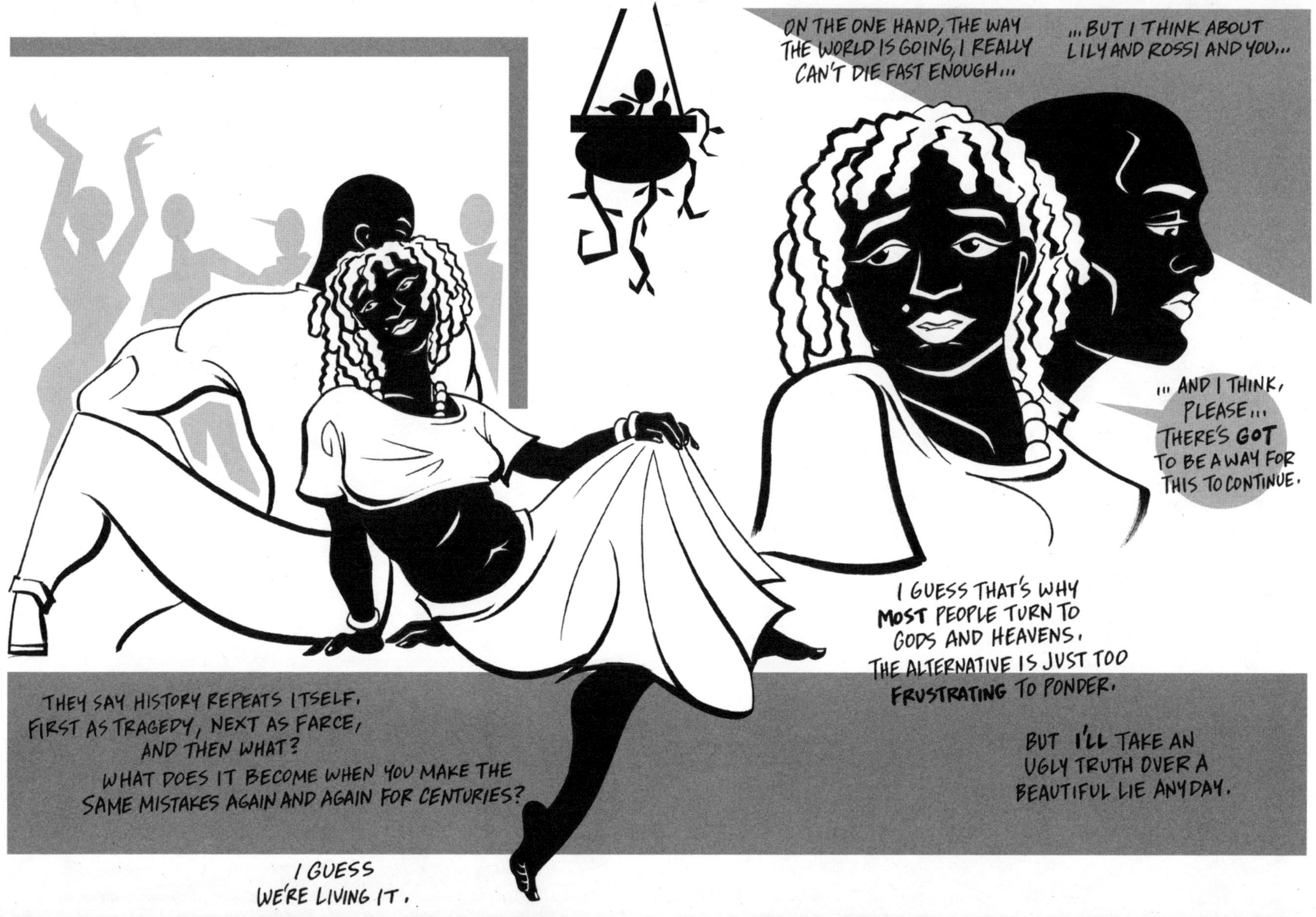

ON THE ONE HAND, THE WAY THE WORLD IS GOING, I REALLY CAN'T DIE FAST ENOUGH...
...BUT I THINK ABOUT LILY AND ROSSI AND YOU...
... AND I THINK, PLEASE... THERE'S **GOT** TO BE A WAY FOR THIS TO CONTINUE.
I GUESS THAT'S WHY **MOST** PEOPLE TURN TO GODS AND HEAVENS. THE ALTERNATIVE IS JUST TOO **FRUSTRATING** TO PONDER.
BUT **I'LL** TAKE AN UGLY TRUTH OVER A BEAUTIFUL LIE ANYDAY.
THEY SAY HISTORY REPEATS ITSELF. FIRST AS TRAGEDY, NEXT AS FARCE, AND THEN WHAT?
WHAT DOES IT BECOME WHEN YOU MAKE THE SAME MISTAKES AGAIN AND AGAIN FOR CENTURIES?
I GUESS WE'RE LIVING IT.

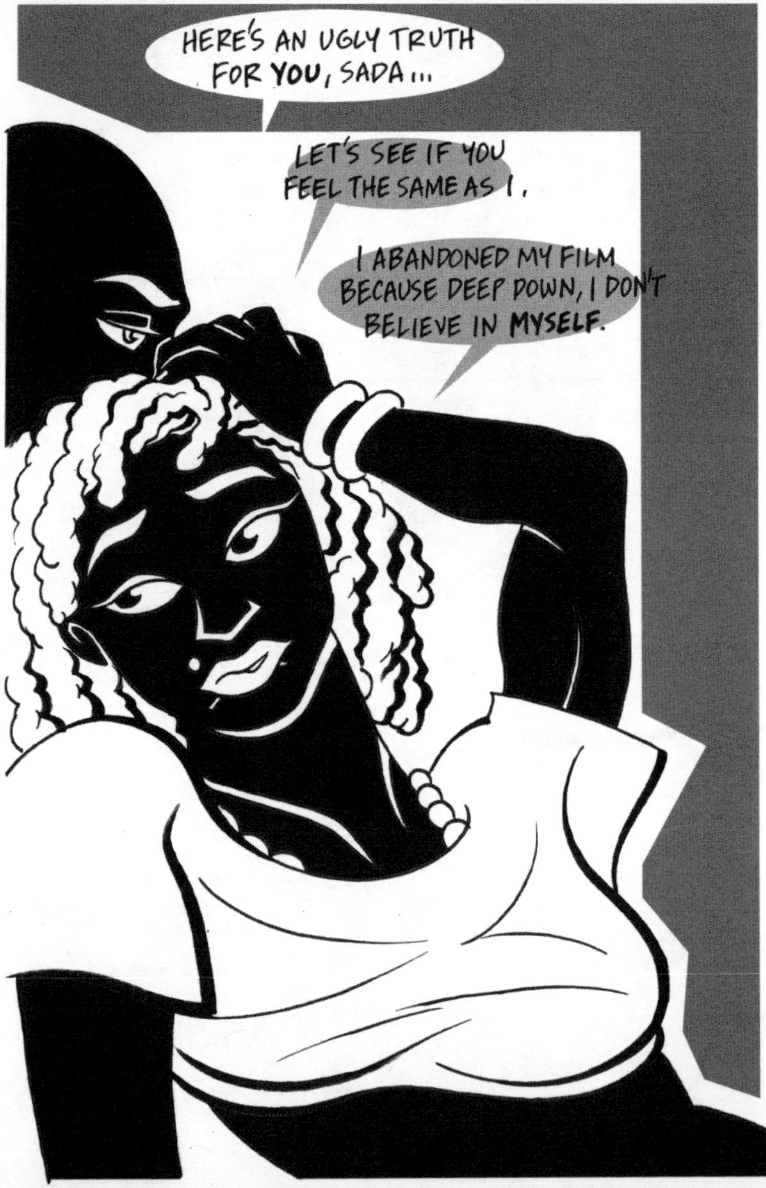
HERE'S AN UGLY TRUTH FOR **YOU**, SADA...
LET'S SEE IF YOU FEEL THE SAME AS I.
I ABANDONED MY FILM BECAUSE DEEP DOWN, I DON'T BELIEVE IN **MYSELF**.

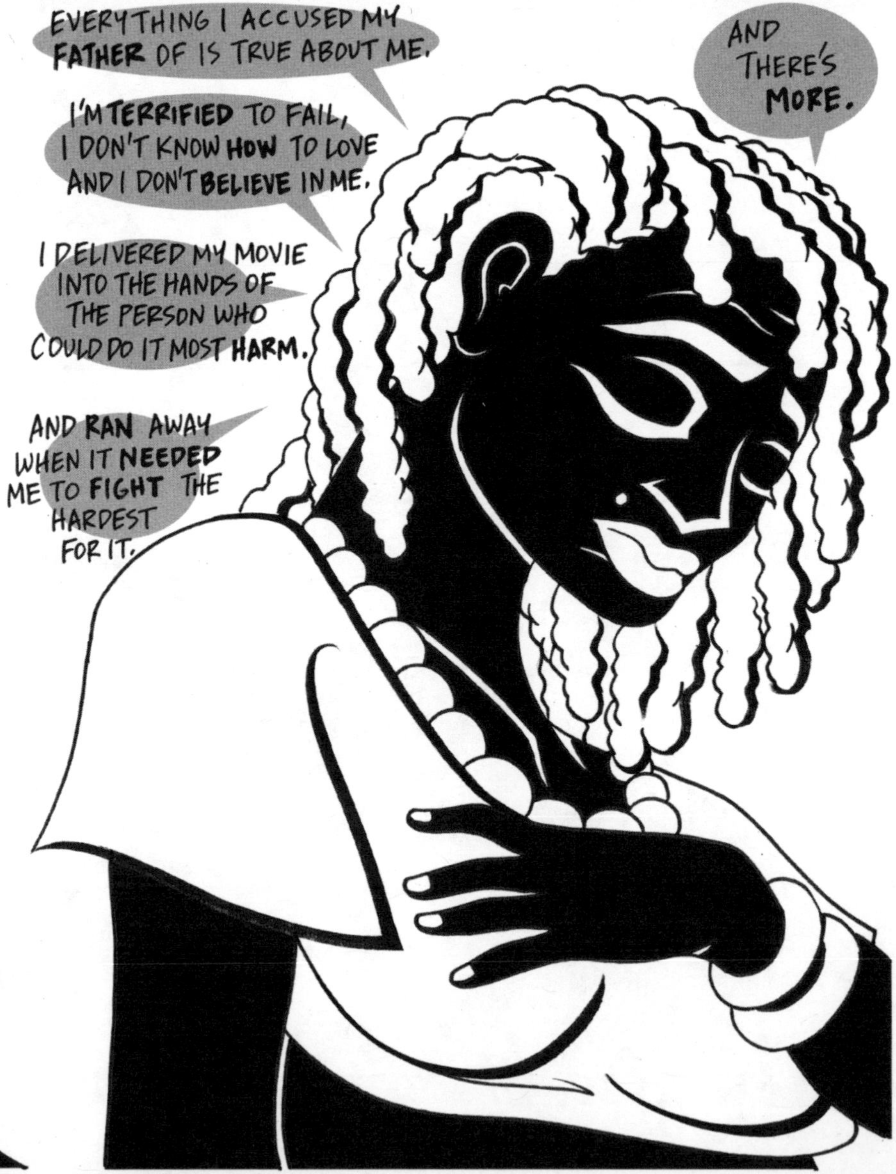
EVERYTHING I ACCUSED MY **FATHER** OF IS TRUE ABOUT ME.
I'M **TERRIFIED** TO FAIL, I DON'T KNOW **HOW** TO LOVE AND I DON'T **BELIEVE** IN ME.
I DELIVERED MY MOVIE INTO THE HANDS OF THE PERSON WHO COULD DO IT MOST **HARM**.
AND **RAN** AWAY WHEN IT **NEEDED** ME TO **FIGHT** THE HARDEST FOR IT.
AND THERE'S **MORE**.

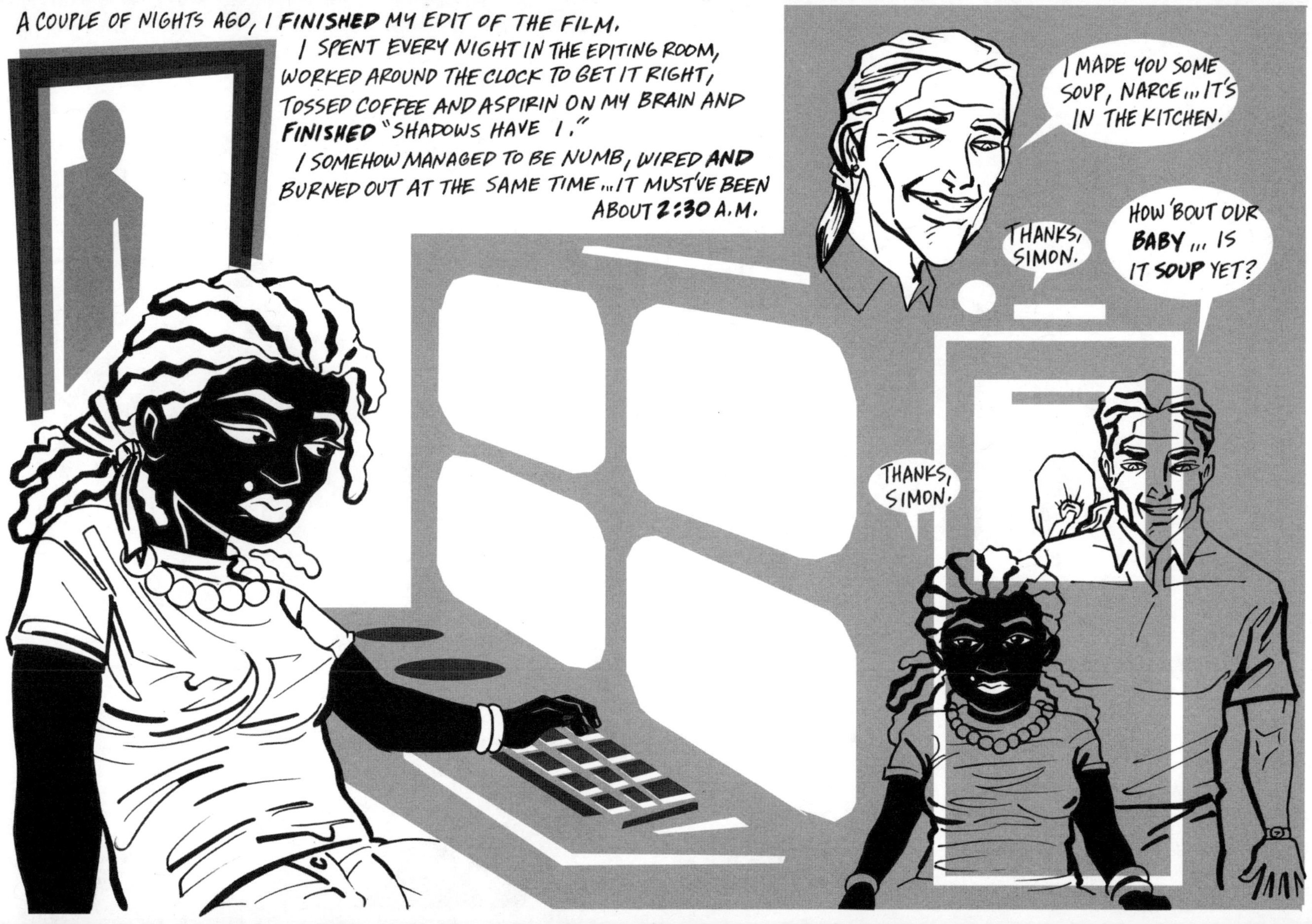
A COUPLE OF NIGHTS AGO, I **FINISHED** MY EDIT OF THE FILM.
I SPENT EVERY NIGHT IN THE EDITING ROOM, WORKED AROUND THE CLOCK TO GET IT RIGHT, TOSSED COFFEE AND ASPIRIN ON MY BRAIN AND **FINISHED** "SHADOWS HAVE I."
I SOMEHOW MANAGED TO BE NUMB, WIRED **AND** BURNED OUT AT THE SAME TIME... IT MUST'VE BEEN ABOUT **2:30** A.M.
I MADE YOU SOME SOUP, NARCE... IT'S IN THE KITCHEN.
THANKS, SIMON.
HOW 'BOUT OUR **BABY**... IS IT **SOUP** YET?
THANKS, SIMON.

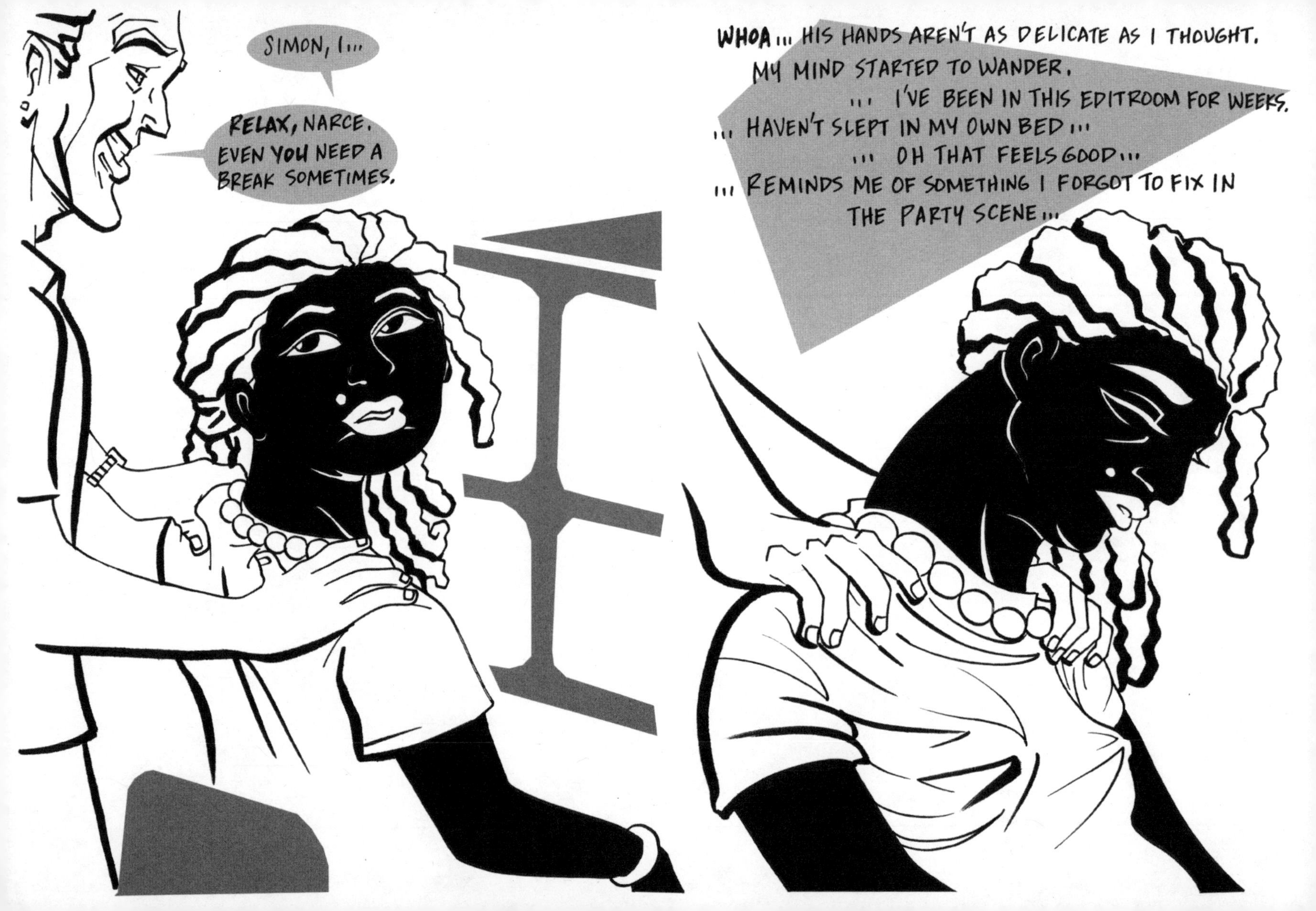

SIMON, I...
RELAX, NARCE. EVEN YOU NEED A BREAK SOMETIMES.
WHOA... HIS HANDS AREN'T AS DELICATE AS I THOUGHT.
MY MIND STARTED TO WANDER.
... I'VE BEEN IN THIS EDITROOM FOR WEEKS.
... HAVEN'T SLEPT IN MY OWN BED...
... OH THAT FEELS GOOD...
... REMINDS ME OF SOMETHING I FORGOT TO FIX IN THE PARTY SCENE...

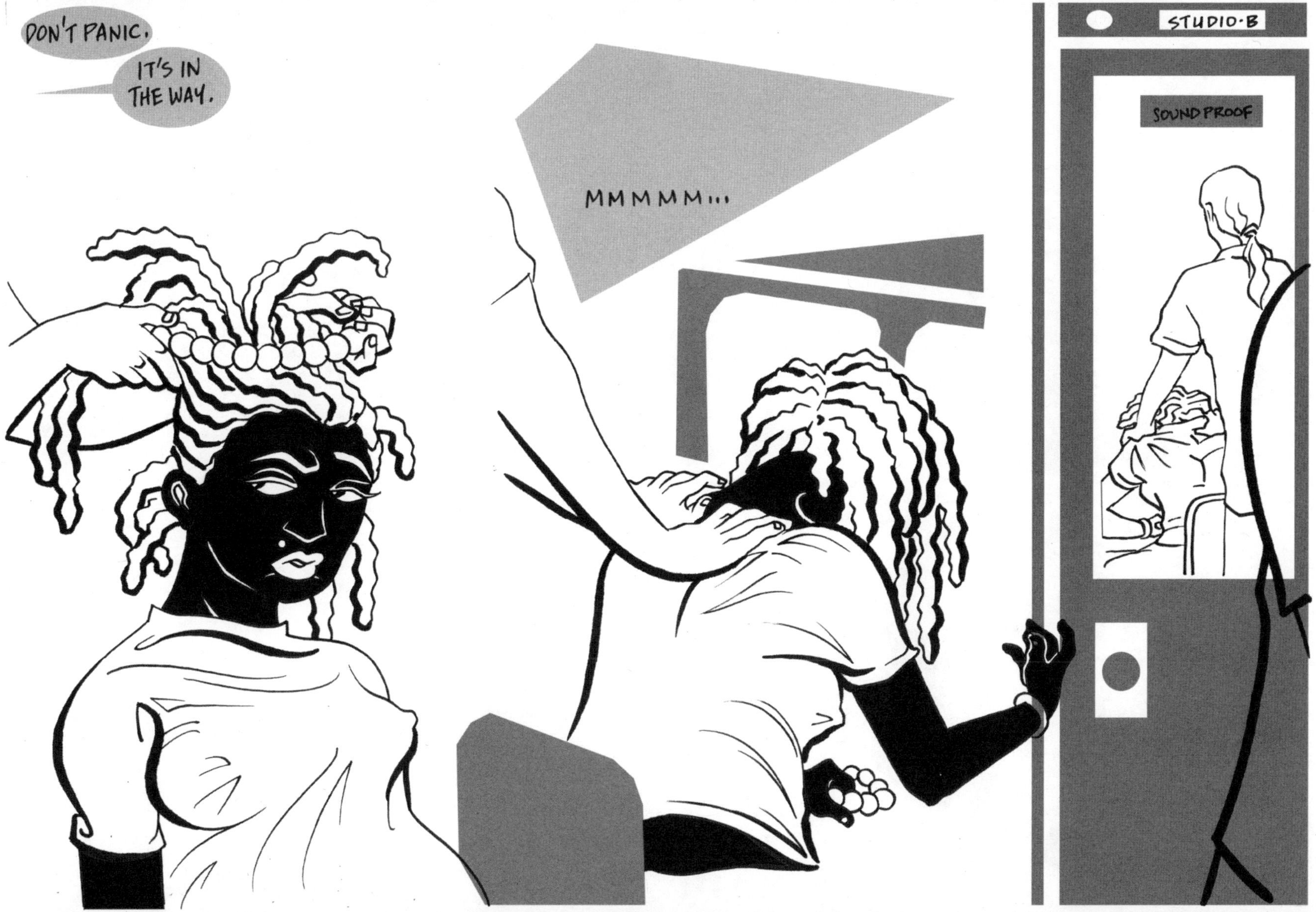
DON'T PANIC.
IT'S IN THE WAY.
MMMMM...
STUDIO·B
SOUND PROOF

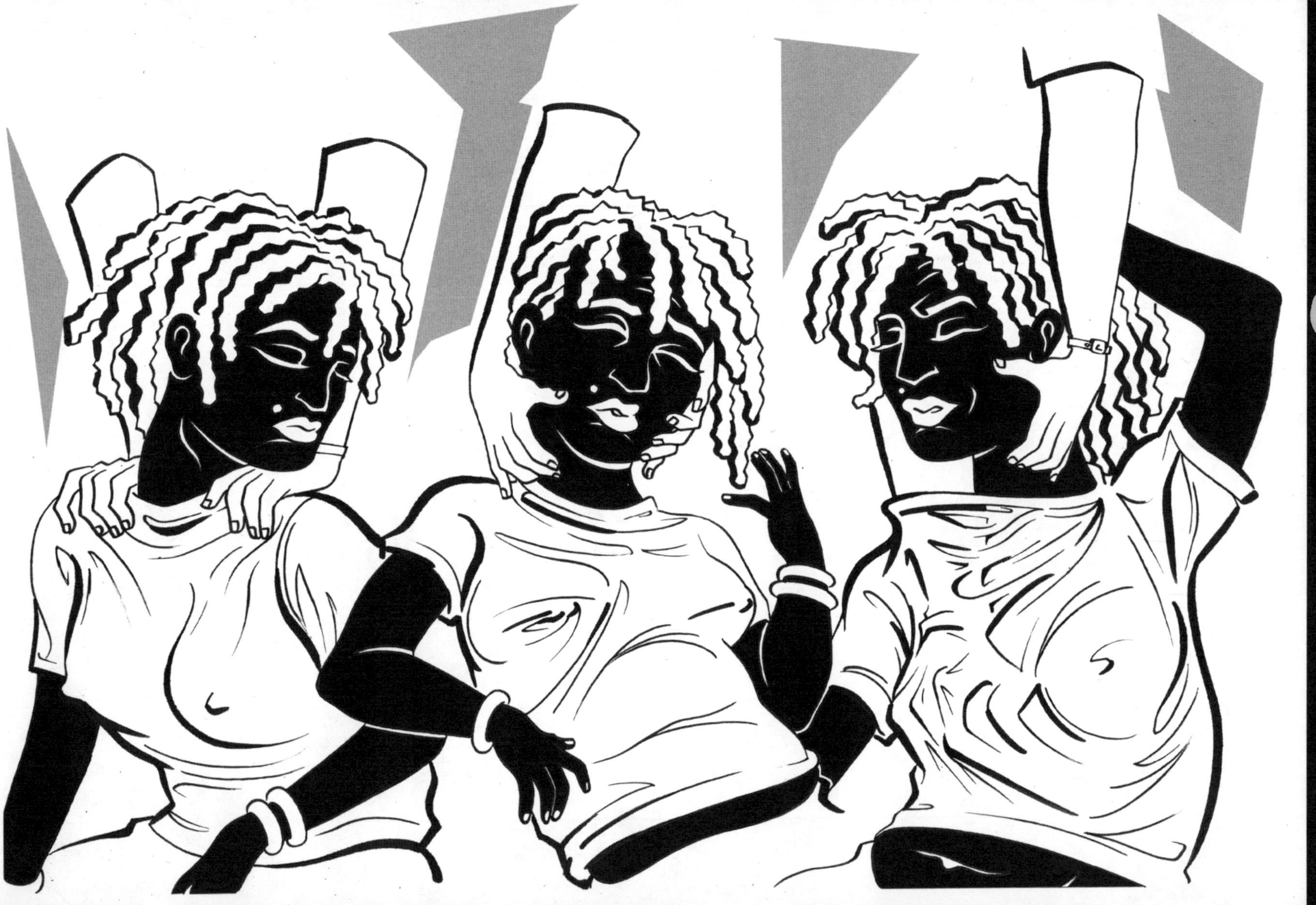

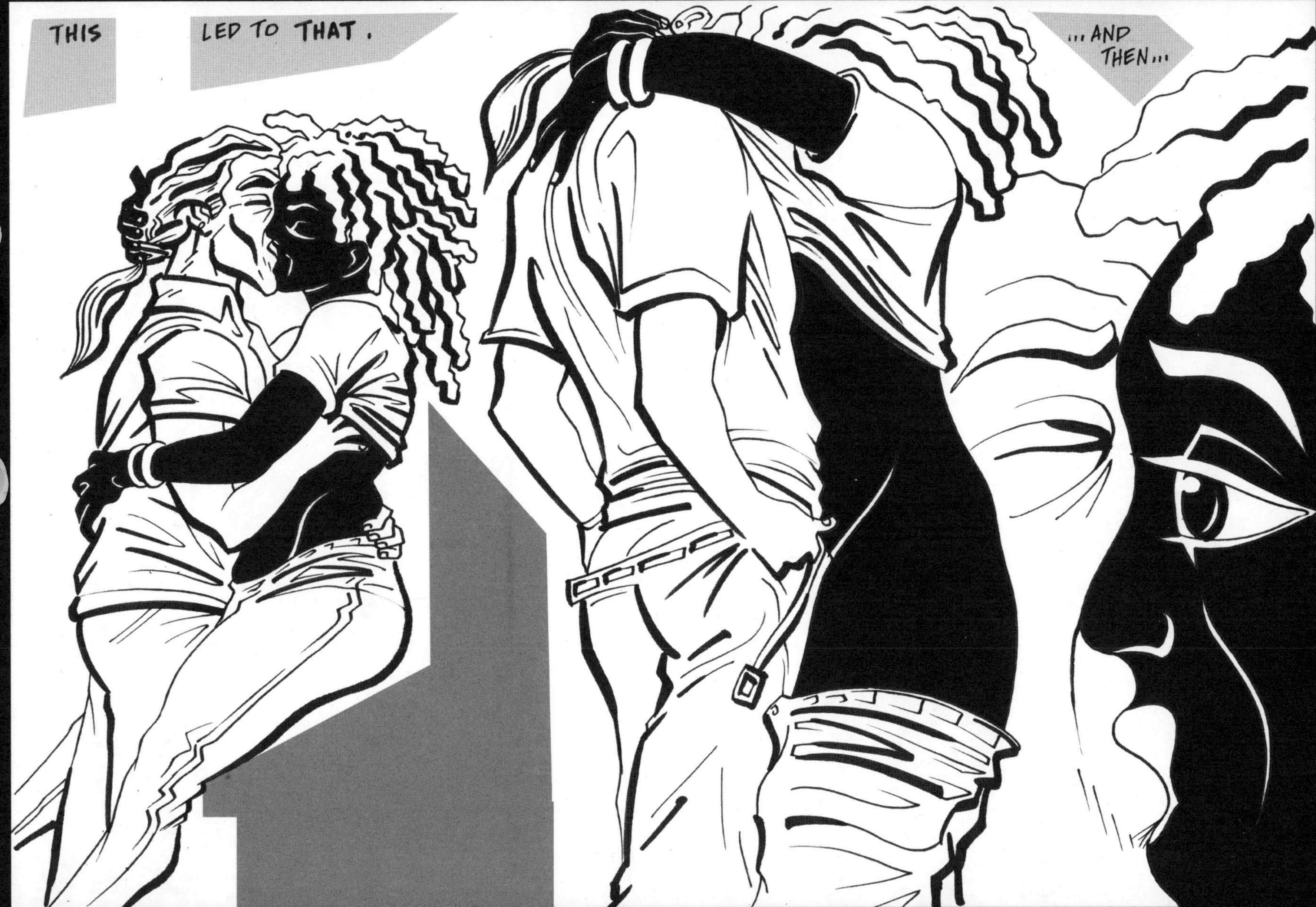
THIS
LED TO THAT.
...AND THEN...

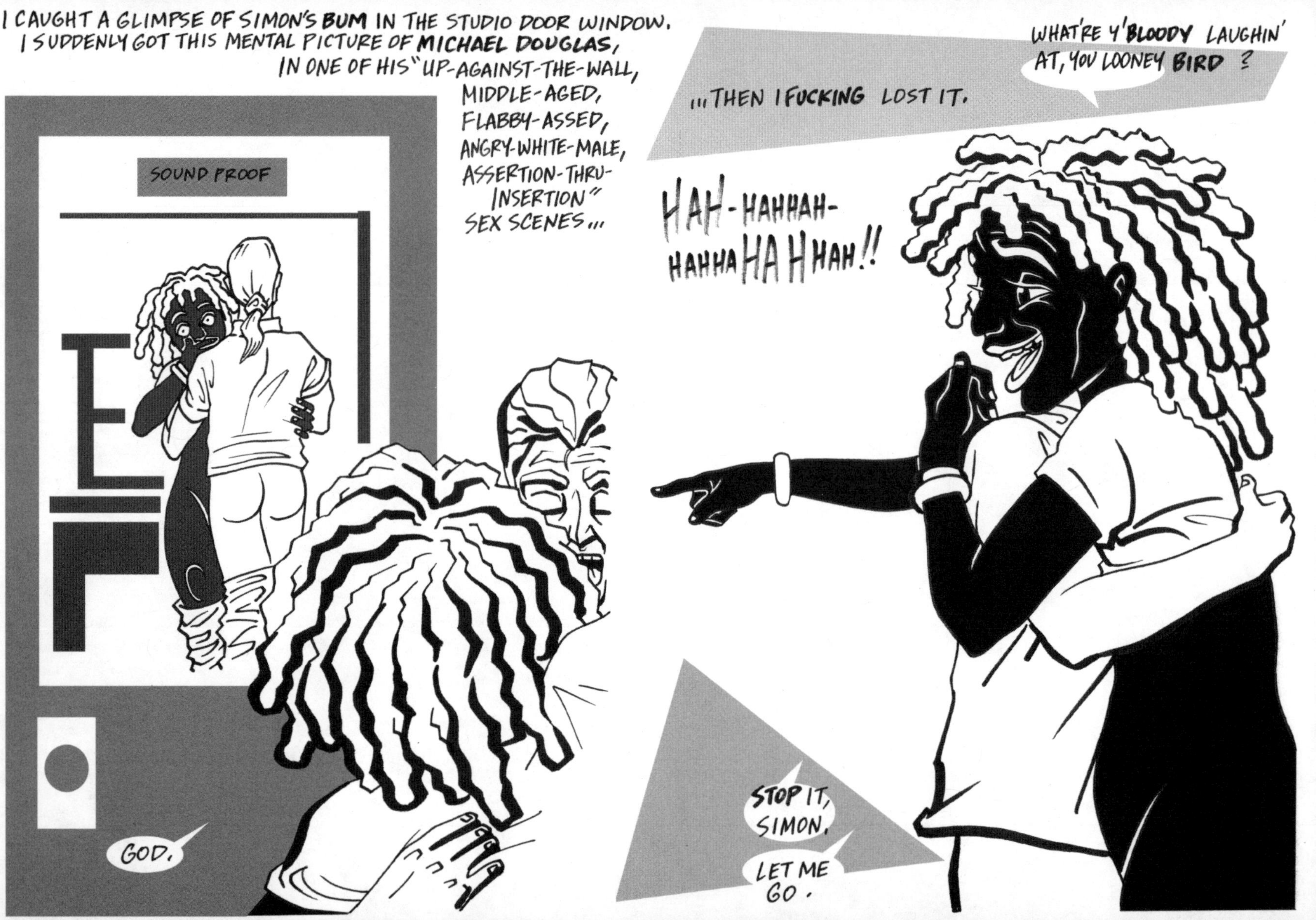
I CAUGHT A GLIMPSE OF SIMON'S **BUM** IN THE STUDIO DOOR WINDOW. I SUDDENLY GOT THIS MENTAL PICTURE OF **MICHAEL DOUGLAS**, IN ONE OF HIS "UP-AGAINST-THE-WALL, MIDDLE-AGED, FLABBY-ASSED, ANGRY-WHITE-MALE, ASSERTION-THRU-INSERTION" SEX SCENES...
SOUND PROOF
GOD.
...THEN I **FUCKING** LOST IT.
WHAT'RE Y'**BLOODY** LAUGHIN' AT, YOU LOONEY **BIRD** ?
HAH-HAHHAH-HAHHAHAHHAH!!
STOP IT, SIMON.
LET ME GO.

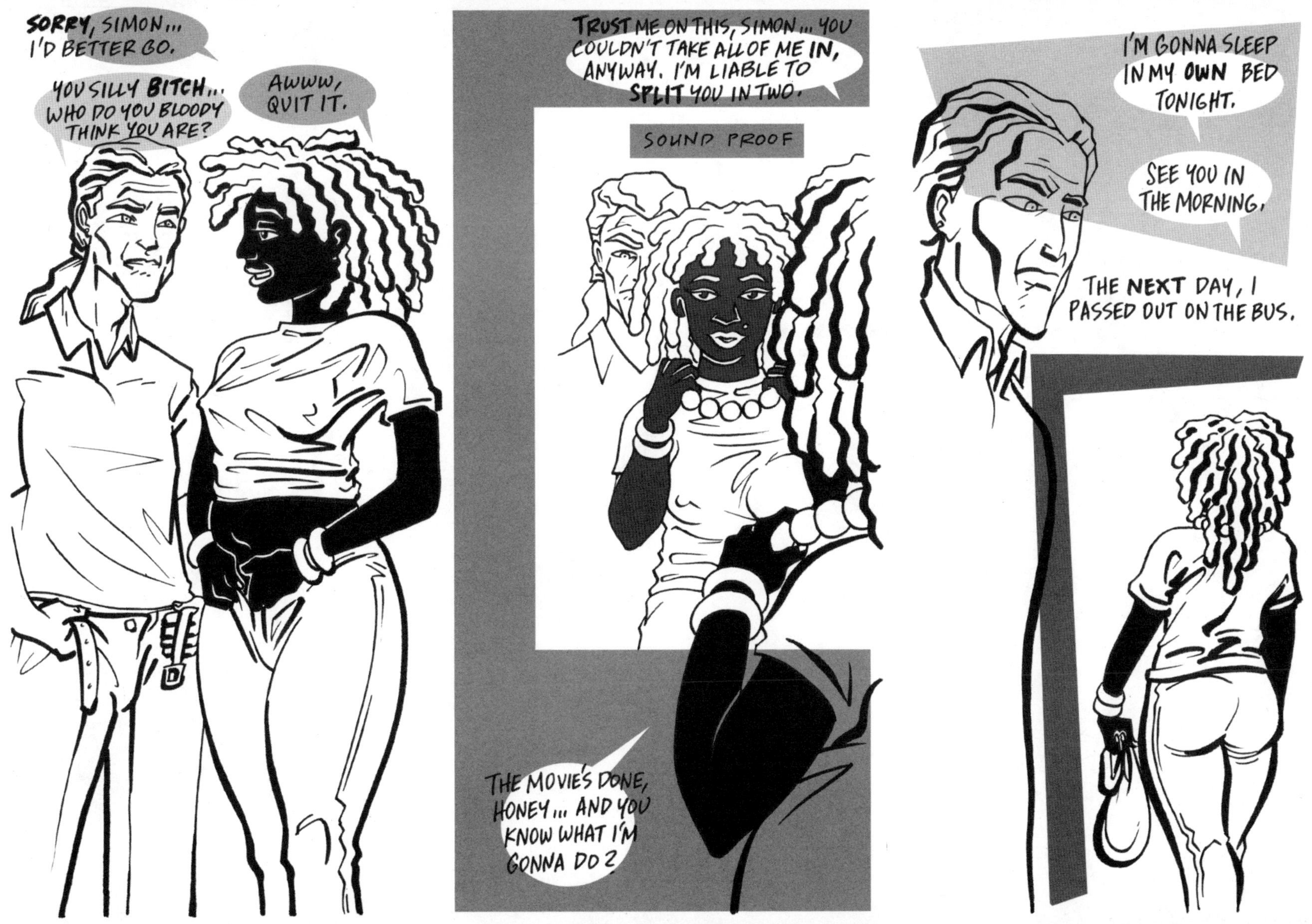
SORRY, SIMON... I'D BETTER GO.
YOU SILLY BITCH... WHO DO YOU BLOODY THINK YOU ARE?
AWWW, QUIT IT.
TRUST ME ON THIS, SIMON... YOU COULDN'T TAKE ALL OF ME IN, ANYWAY. I'M LIABLE TO SPLIT YOU IN TWO.
SOUND PROOF
THE MOVIE'S DONE, HONEY... AND YOU KNOW WHAT I'M GONNA DO?
I'M GONNA SLEEP IN MY OWN BED TONIGHT.
SEE YOU IN THE MORNING.
THE NEXT DAY, I PASSED OUT ON THE BUS.

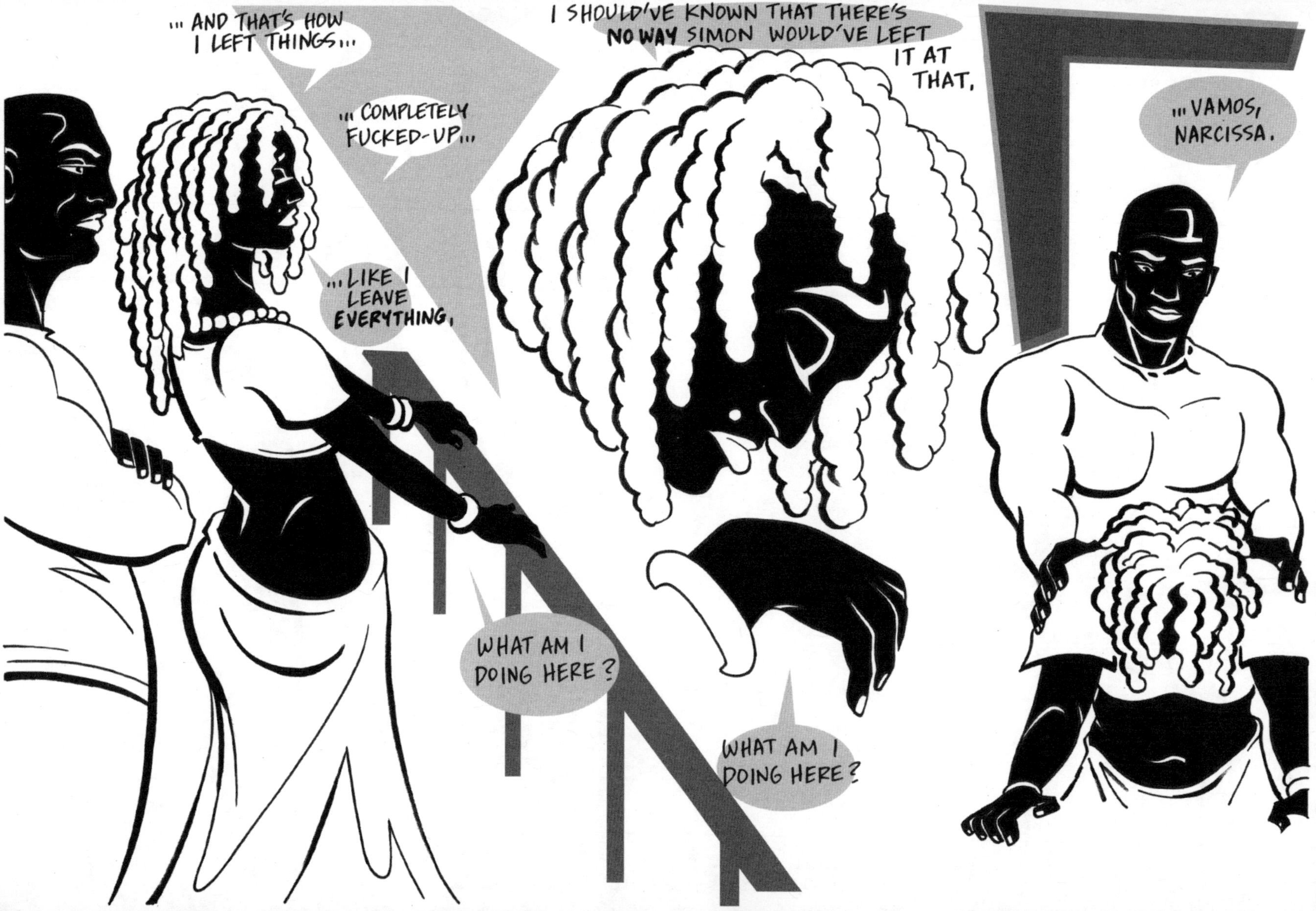
... AND THAT'S HOW I LEFT THINGS...
... COMPLETELY FUCKED-UP...
... LIKE I LEAVE EVERYTHING.
WHAT AM I DOING HERE?
I SHOULD'VE KNOWN THAT THERE'S NO WAY SIMON WOULD'VE LEFT IT AT THAT.
WHAT AM I DOING HERE?
... VAMOS, NARCISSA.

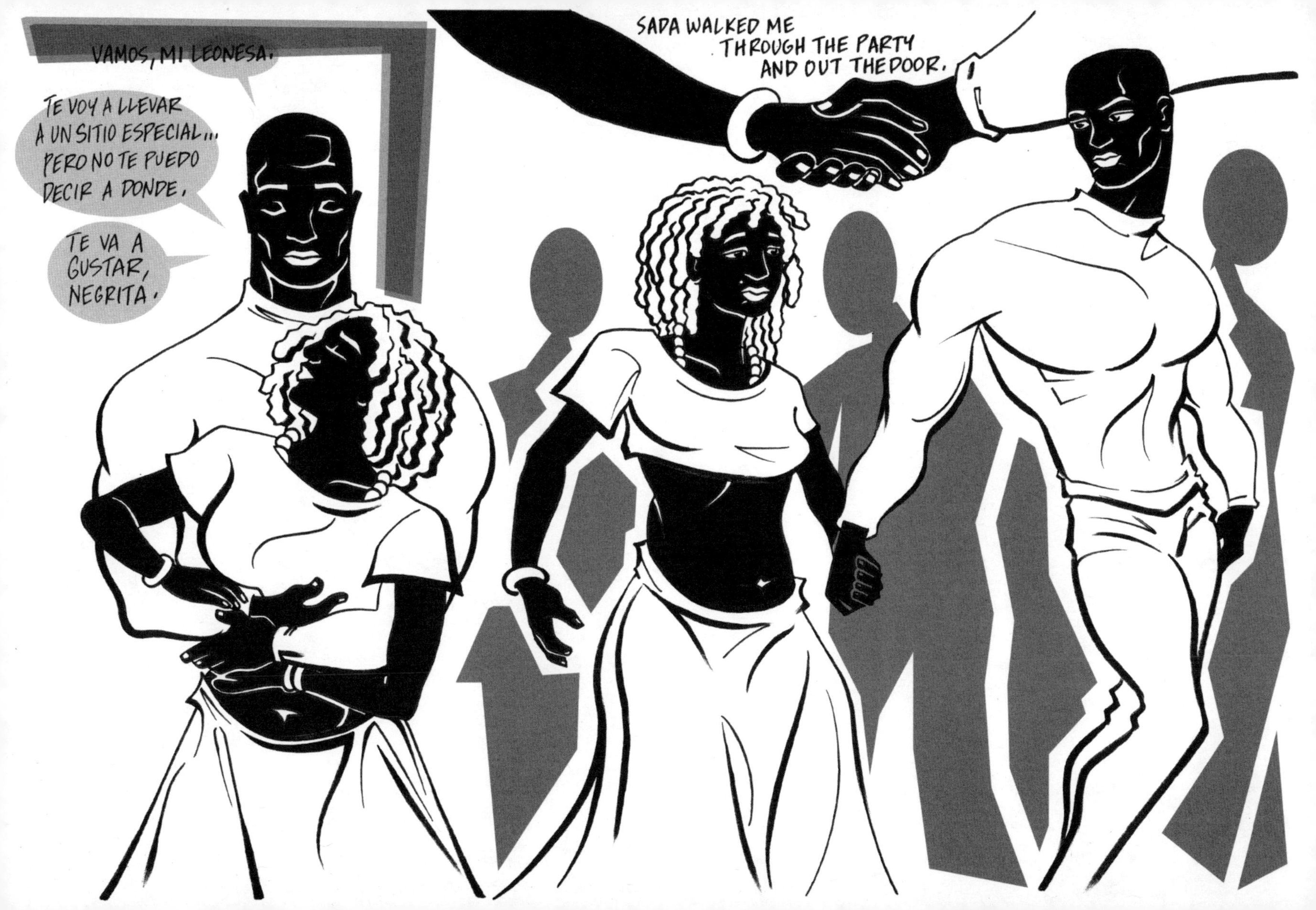
VAMOS, MI LEONESA.
TE VOY A LLEVAR A UN SITIO ESPECIAL... PERO NO TE PUEDO DECIR A DONDE.
TE VA A GUSTAR, NEGRITA.
SADA WALKED ME THROUGH THE PARTY AND OUT THE DOOR.

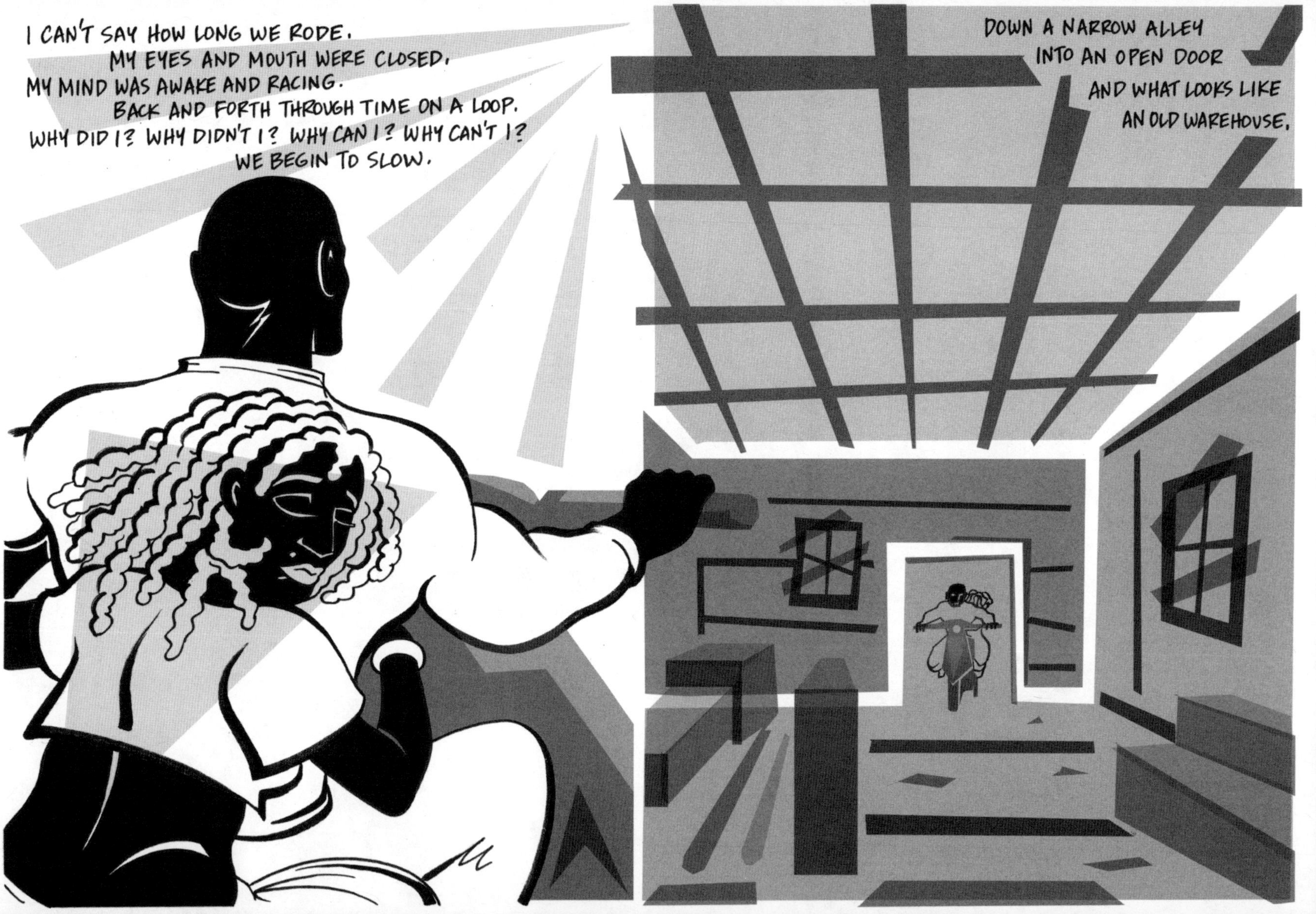
I CAN'T SAY HOW LONG WE RODE.
MY EYES AND MOUTH WERE CLOSED.
MY MIND WAS AWAKE AND RACING.
BACK AND FORTH THROUGH TIME ON A LOOP.
WHY DID I? WHY DIDN'T I? WHY CAN I? WHY CAN'T I?
WE BEGIN TO SLOW.
DOWN A NARROW ALLEY
INTO AN OPEN DOOR
AND WHAT LOOKS LIKE
AN OLD WAREHOUSE.

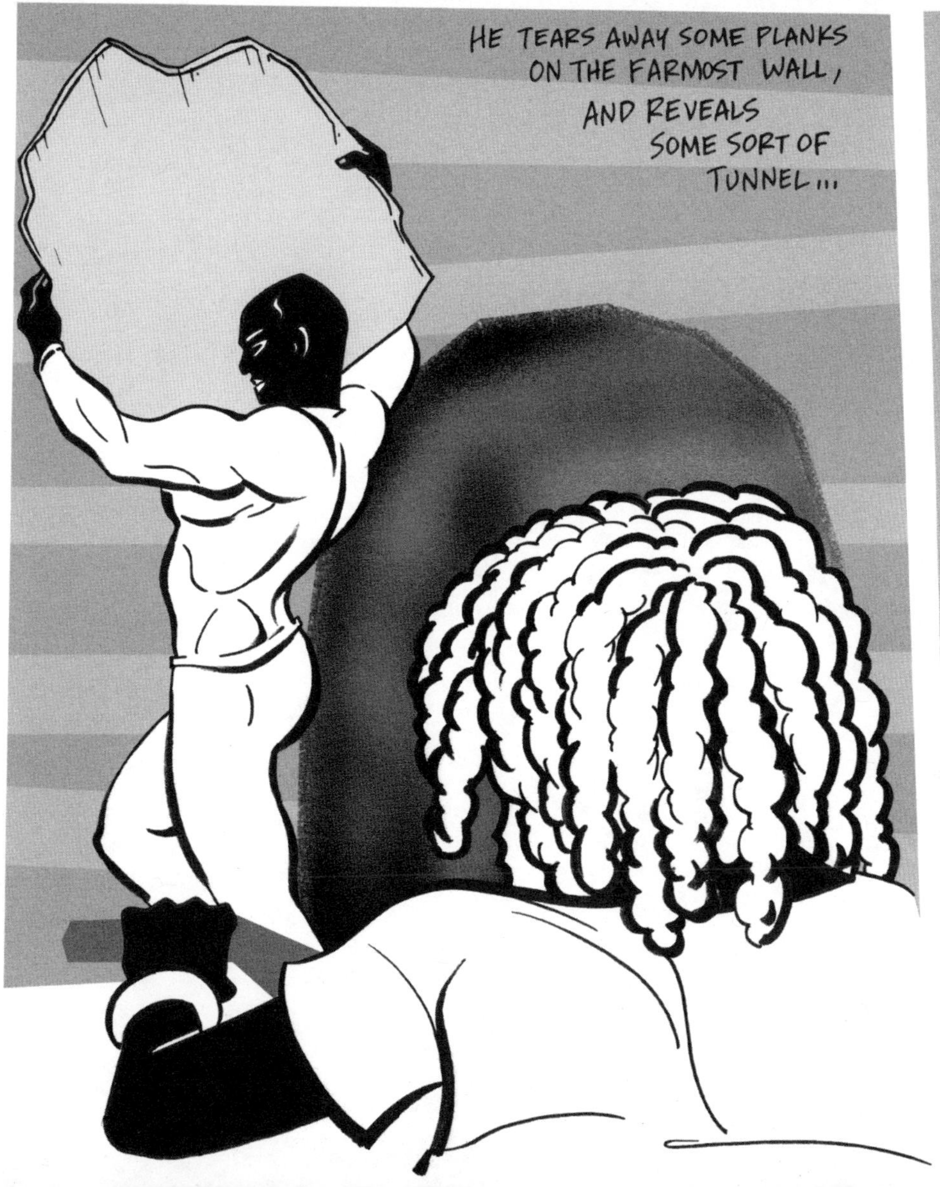
HE TEARS AWAY SOME PLANKS ON THE FARMOST WALL,
AND REVEALS SOME SORT OF TUNNEL...

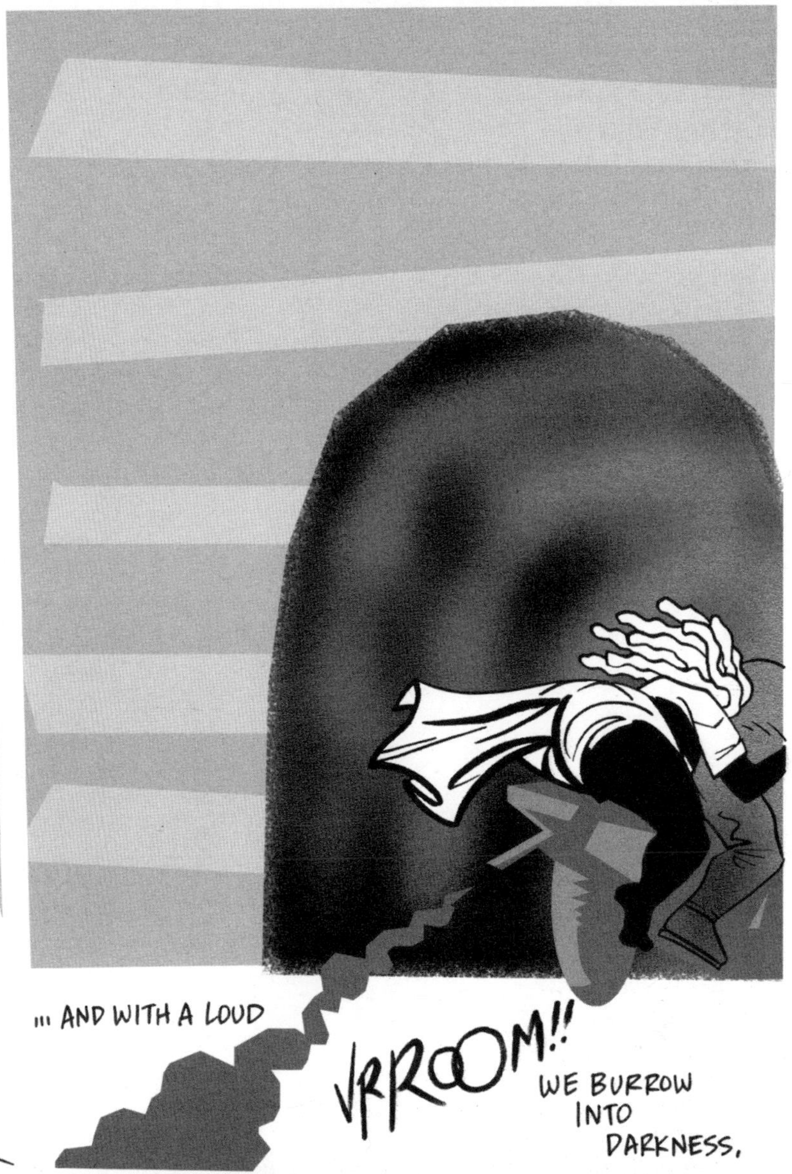
... AND WITH A LOUD
VRROOM!!
WE BURROW INTO DARKNESS.

I NO LONGER FEEL
THE EXHILARATION
I FELT BEFORE.

I'M NUMB INSIDE,
AND MORE AWARE OF
TIME THAN EVER.

WE MOVE SWIFTLY
THROUGH THE RED TUNNEL,
THE WAY AHEAD
ILLUMINATED BY A
SINGLE HEADLIGHT.

THE DARK LEAPS FORWARD
TO SWALLOW UP THE
SPACE BEHIND US.

THE SMELL OF EARTH
GROWS SWEETER
AND STRONGER
AS WE
DESCEND.

HE KNOWS EVERY TURN
BY HEART.
WE MOVE TOGETHER,
SPLASHING THROUGH
PUDDLES OF WATER.

I CATCH GLIMPSES
TO THE SIDES...
OTHER TUNNELS,
OTHER PATHS
THAT LEAD TO...
...WHERE?

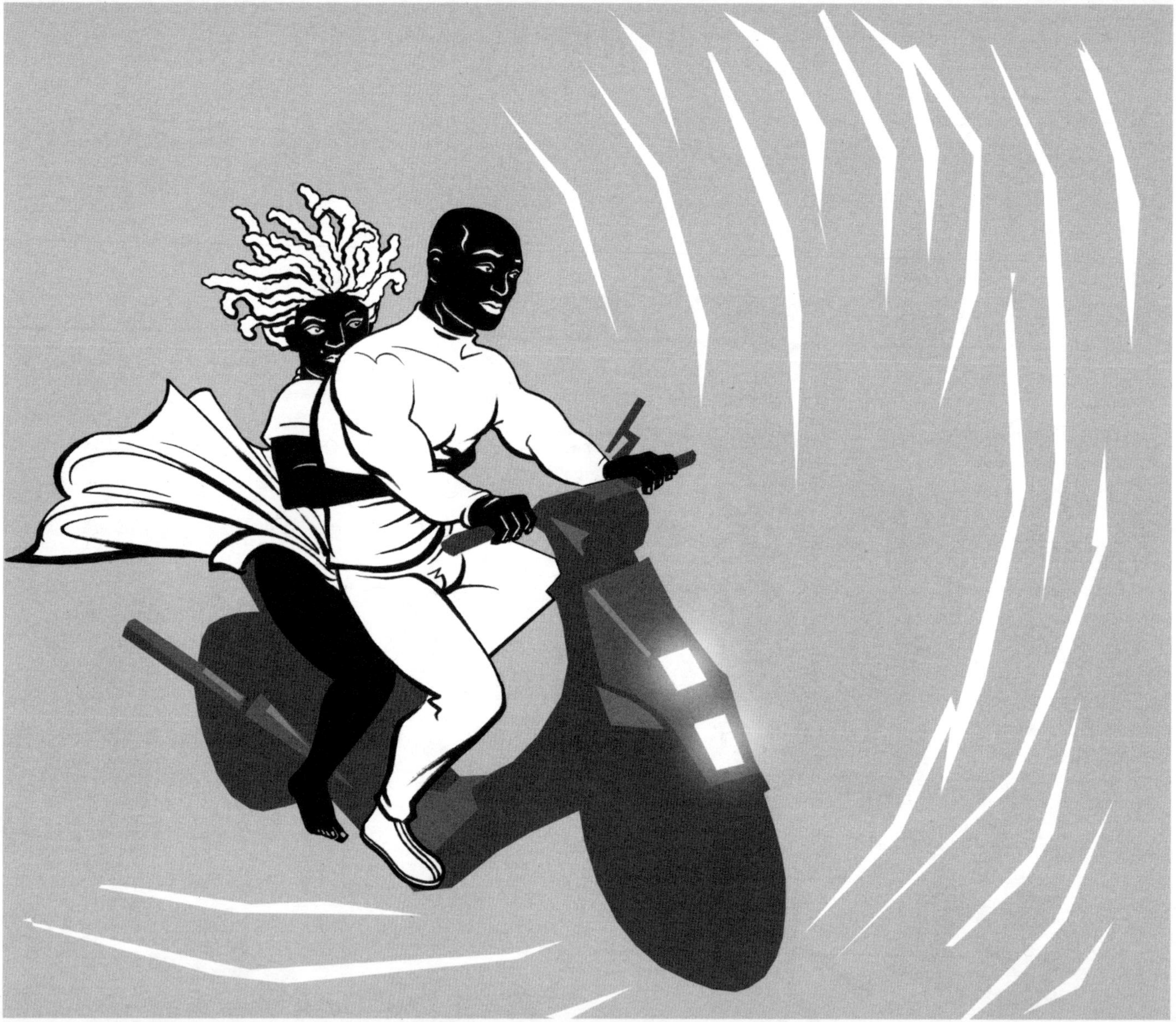

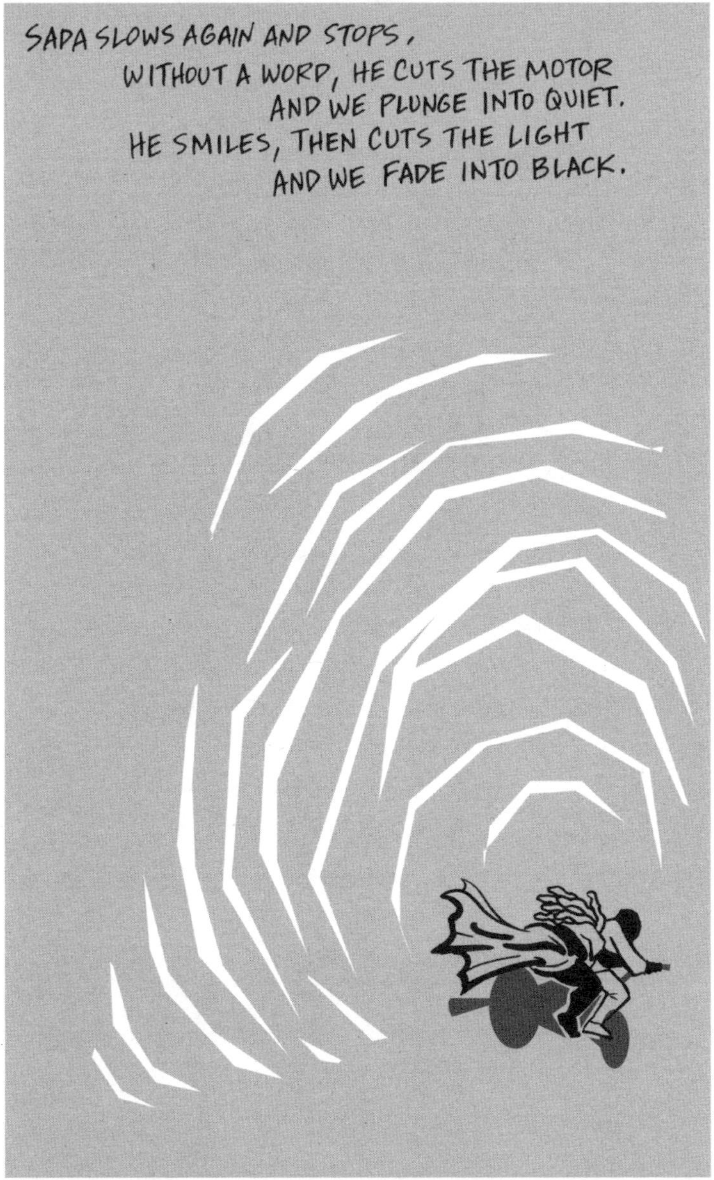
SADA SLOWS AGAIN AND STOPS,
WITHOUT A WORD, HE CUTS THE MOTOR
AND WE PLUNGE INTO QUIET.
HE SMILES, THEN CUTS THE LIGHT
AND WE FADE INTO BLACK.

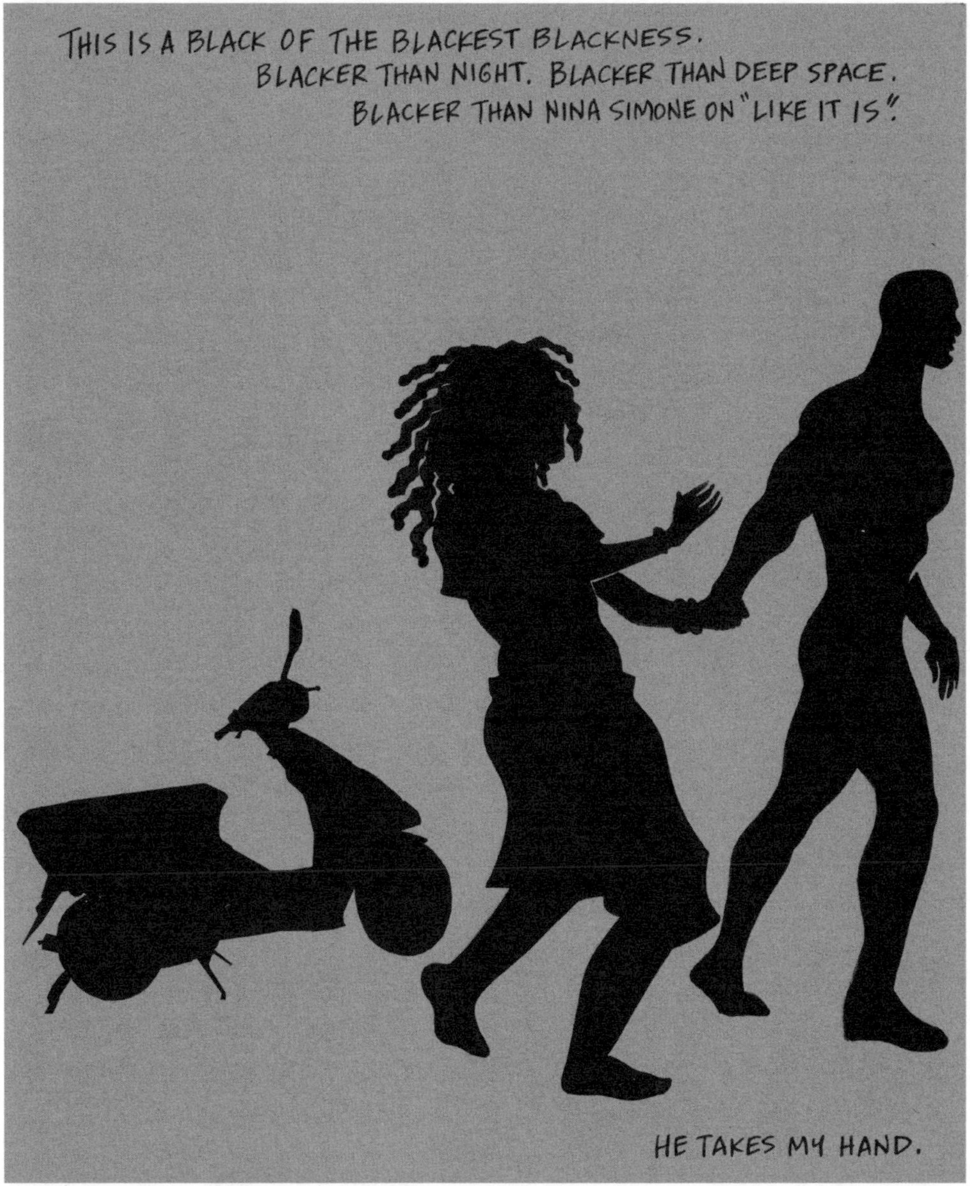
THIS IS A BLACK OF THE BLACKEST BLACKNESS.
BLACKER THAN NIGHT. BLACKER THAN DEEP SPACE.
BLACKER THAN NINA SIMONE ON "LIKE IT IS".
HE TAKES MY HAND.

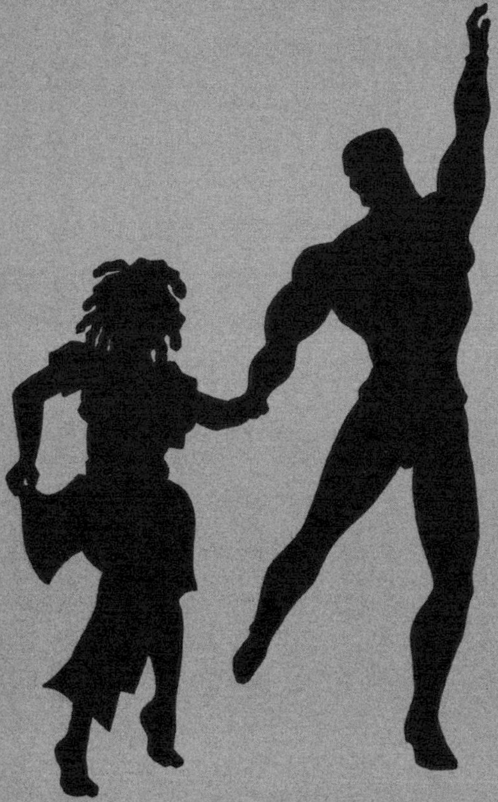

I FEEL THE COOL WET MUD
BETWEEN MY TOES.
I STEP INTO A NARROW POCKET
FILLED WITH WATER.
A STARTLED SHIVER MOVES UP MY LEG
AND INSIDE ME.

HIS SCENT MIXES WITH
THE SCENT OF EARTH.
ALL I CAN HEAR IS HIS BREATHING,
AND THE SOUND OF
WATER FLOWING.
I AM BEYOND FEAR
WITH HIS HAND IN MINE
AND BEYOND TRUST.

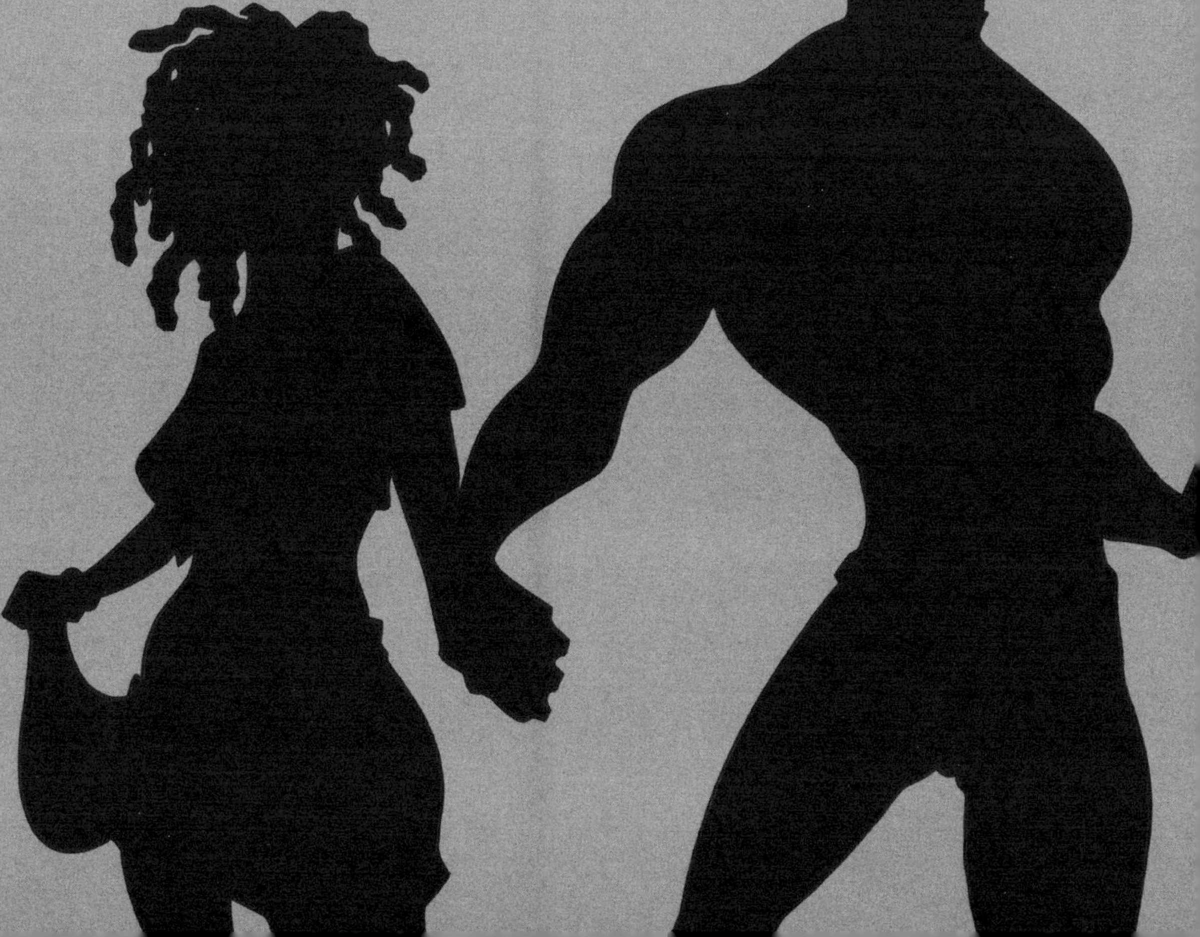

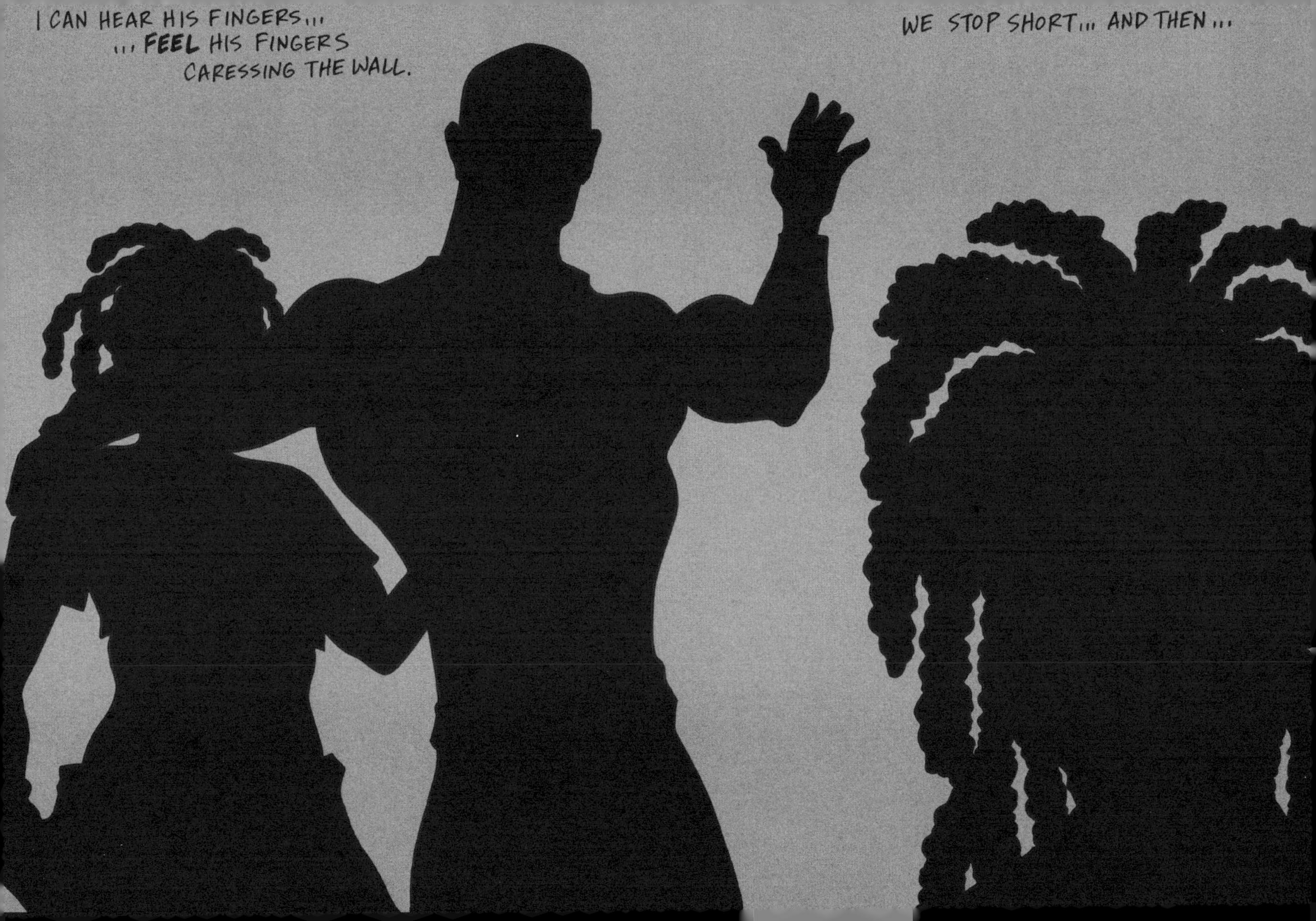
I CAN HEAR HIS FINGERS...
...**FEEL** HIS FINGERS
CARESSING THE WALL.
WE STOP SHORT... AND THEN...

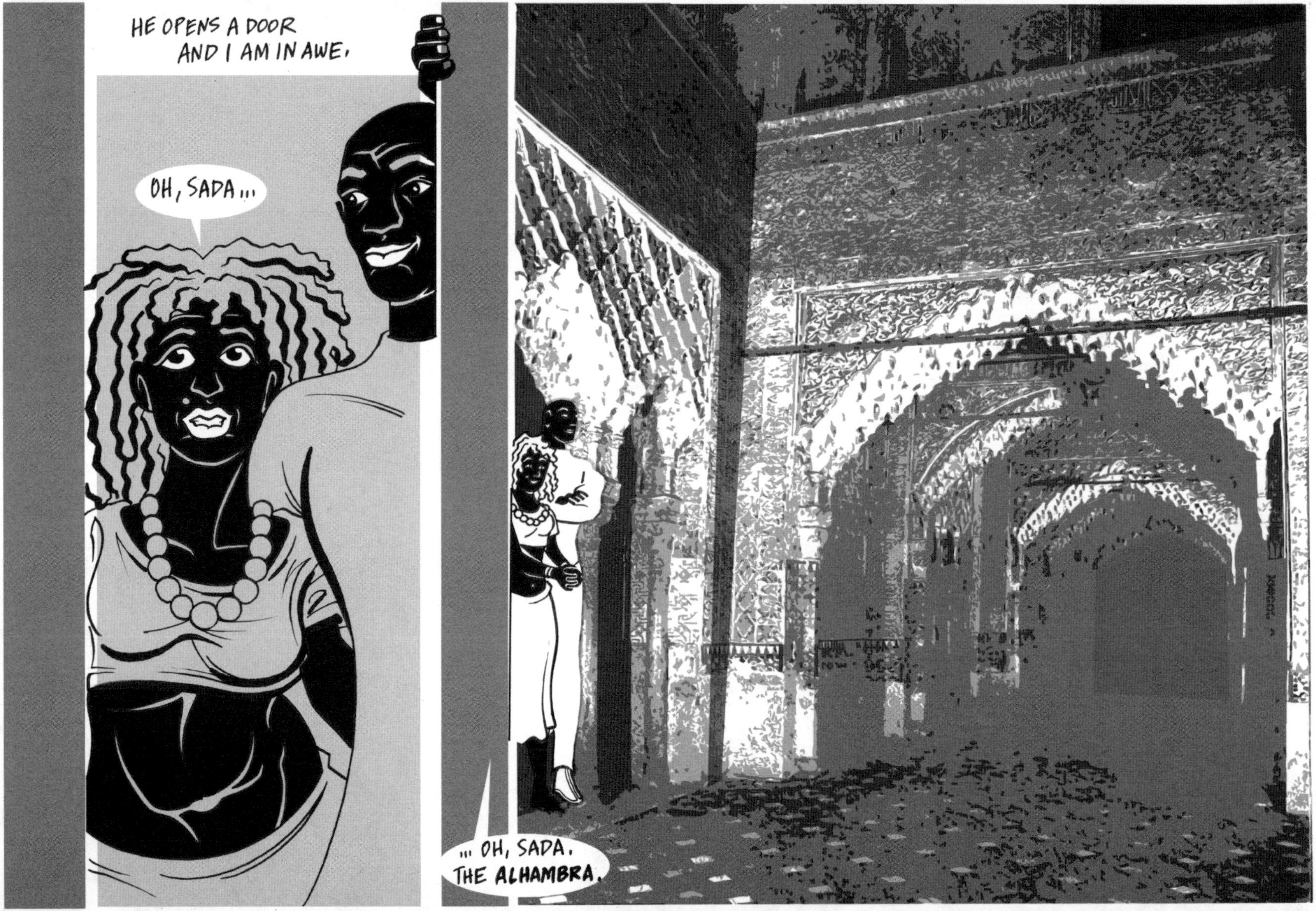
HE OPENS A DOOR AND I AM IN AWE.
OH, SADA...
... OH, SADA. THE ALHAMBRA.

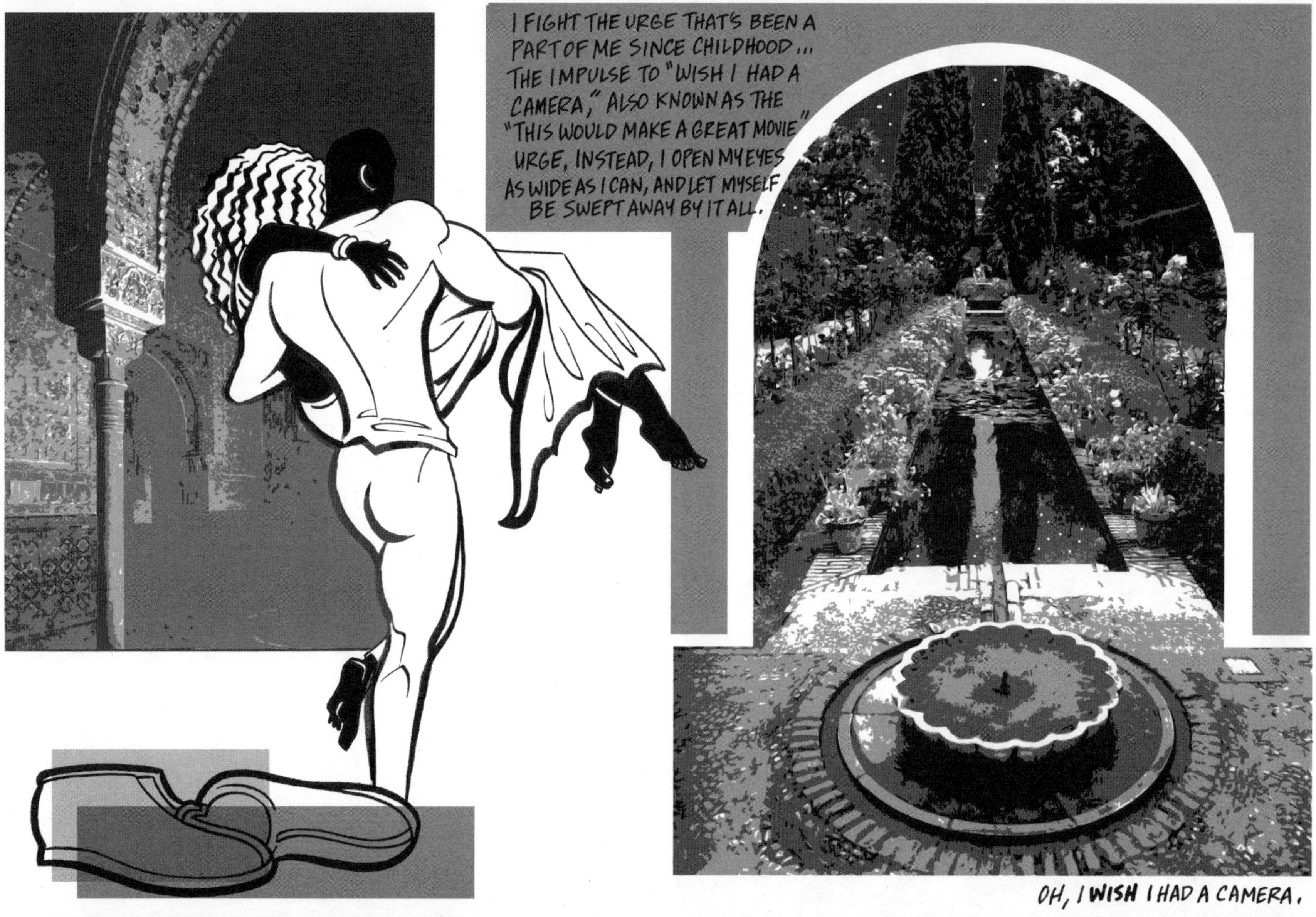
I FIGHT THE URGE THAT'S BEEN A PART OF ME SINCE CHILDHOOD... THE IMPULSE TO "WISH I HAD A CAMERA," ALSO KNOWN AS THE "THIS WOULD MAKE A GREAT MOVIE" URGE. INSTEAD, I OPEN MY EYES AS WIDE AS I CAN, AND LET MYSELF BE SWEPT AWAY BY IT ALL.
OH, I **WISH** I HAD A CAMERA.

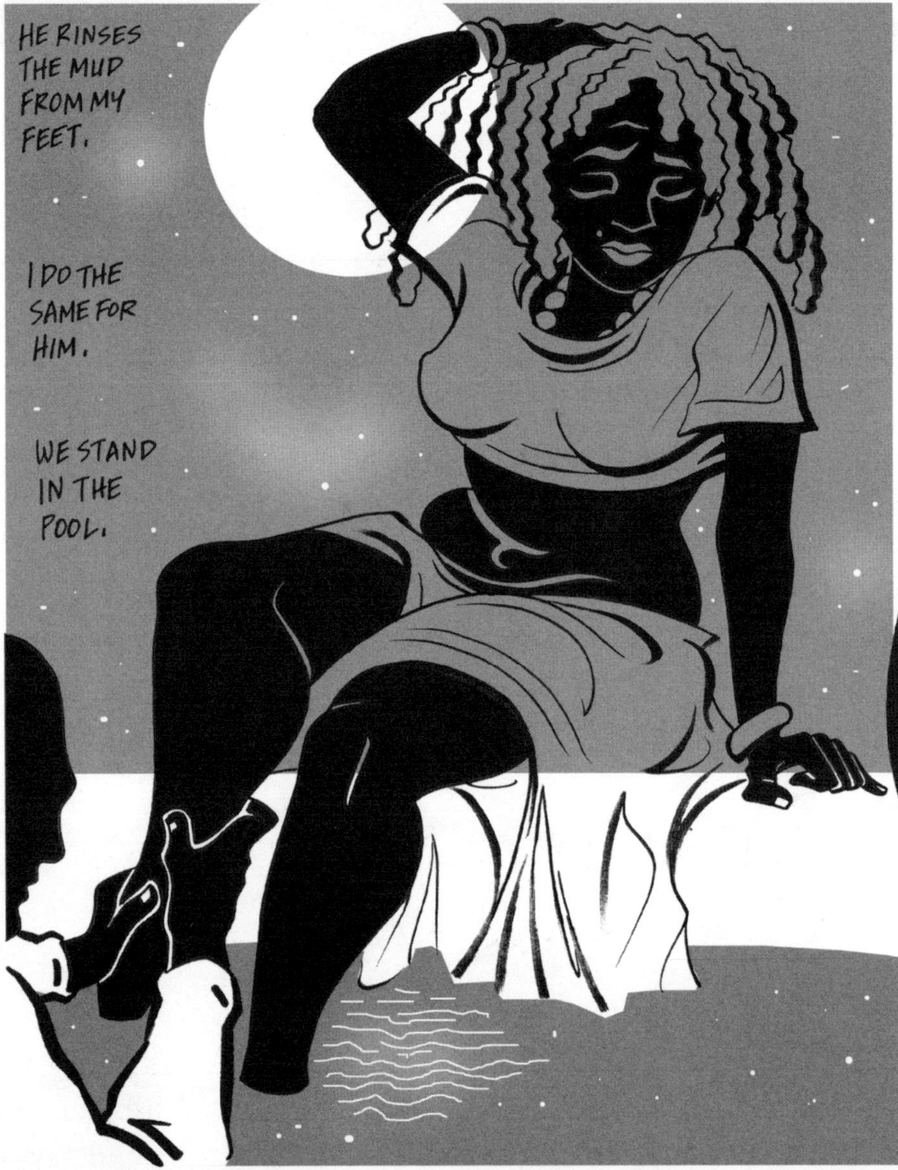
HE RINSES THE MUD FROM MY FEET.
I DO THE SAME FOR HIM.
WE STAND IN THE POOL.

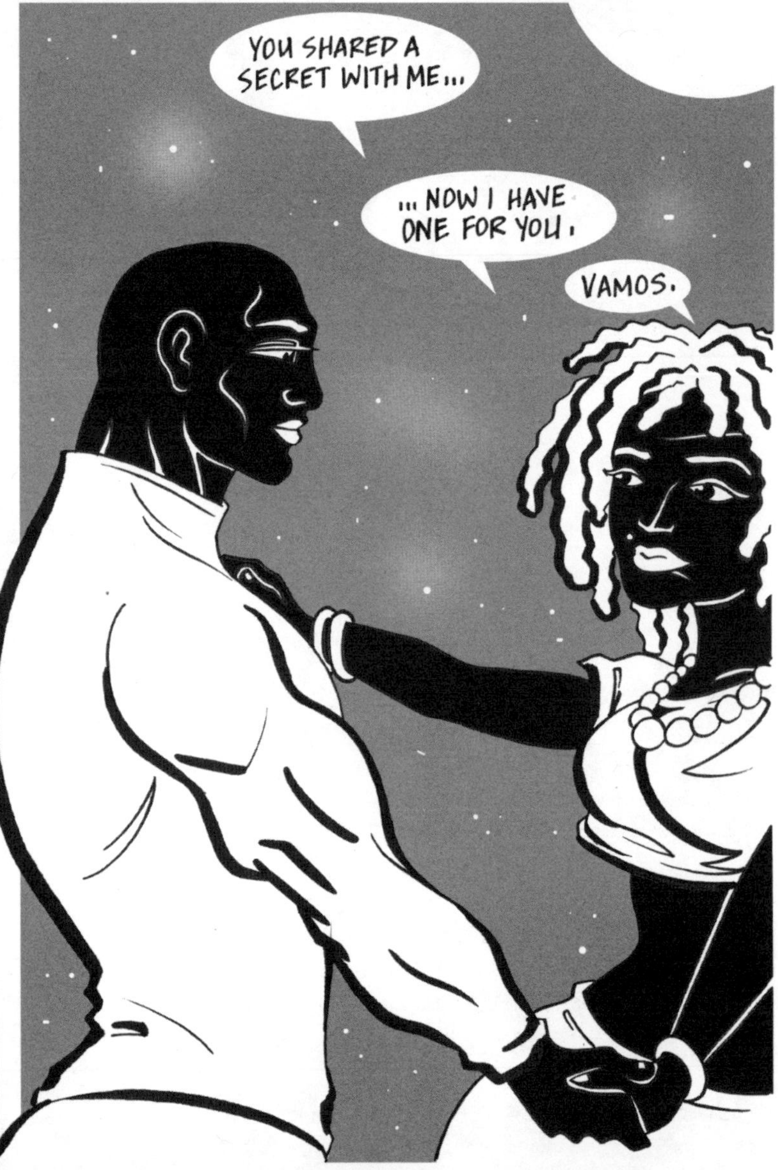
YOU SHARED A SECRET WITH ME...
...NOW I HAVE ONE FOR YOU.
VAMOS.

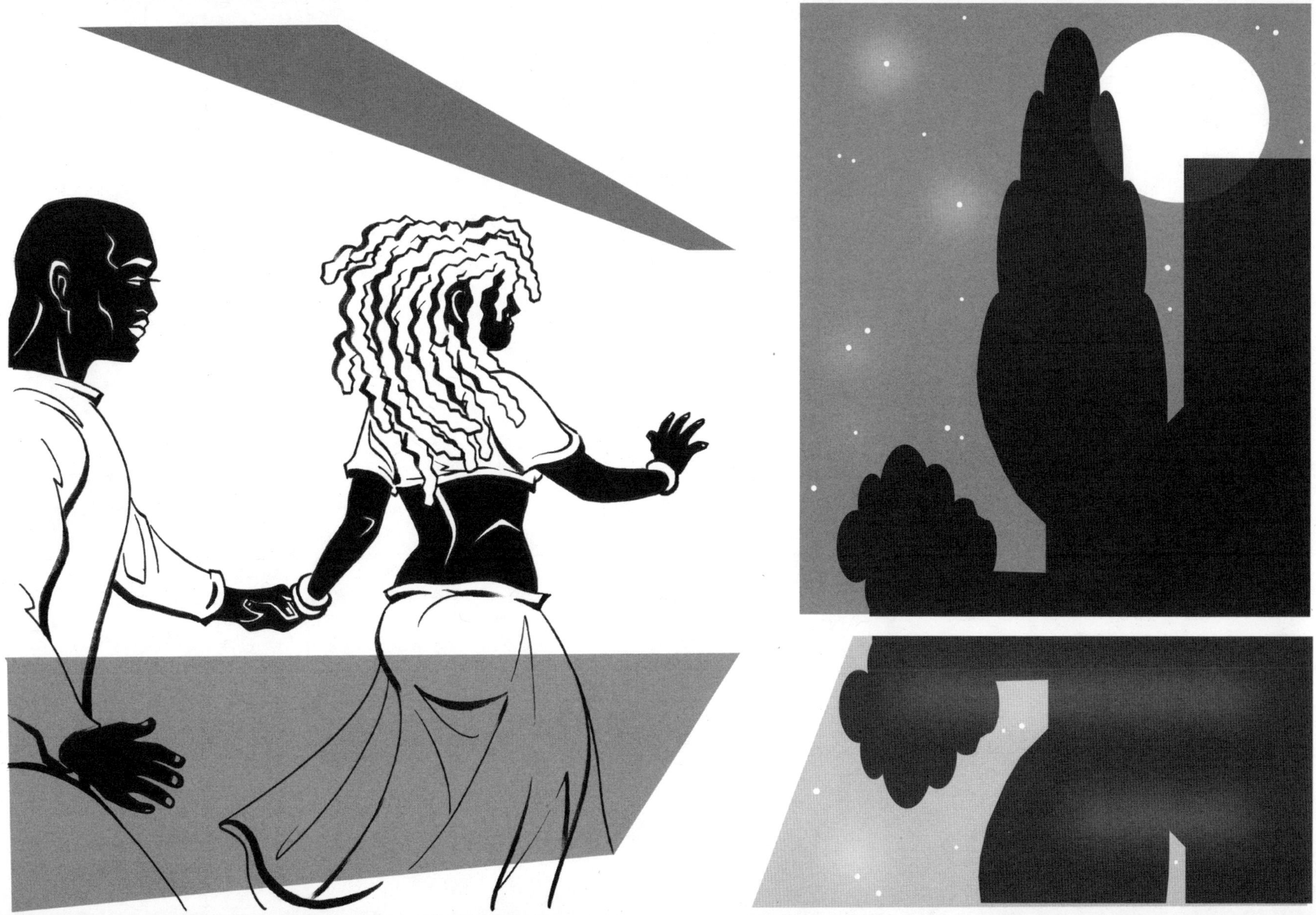

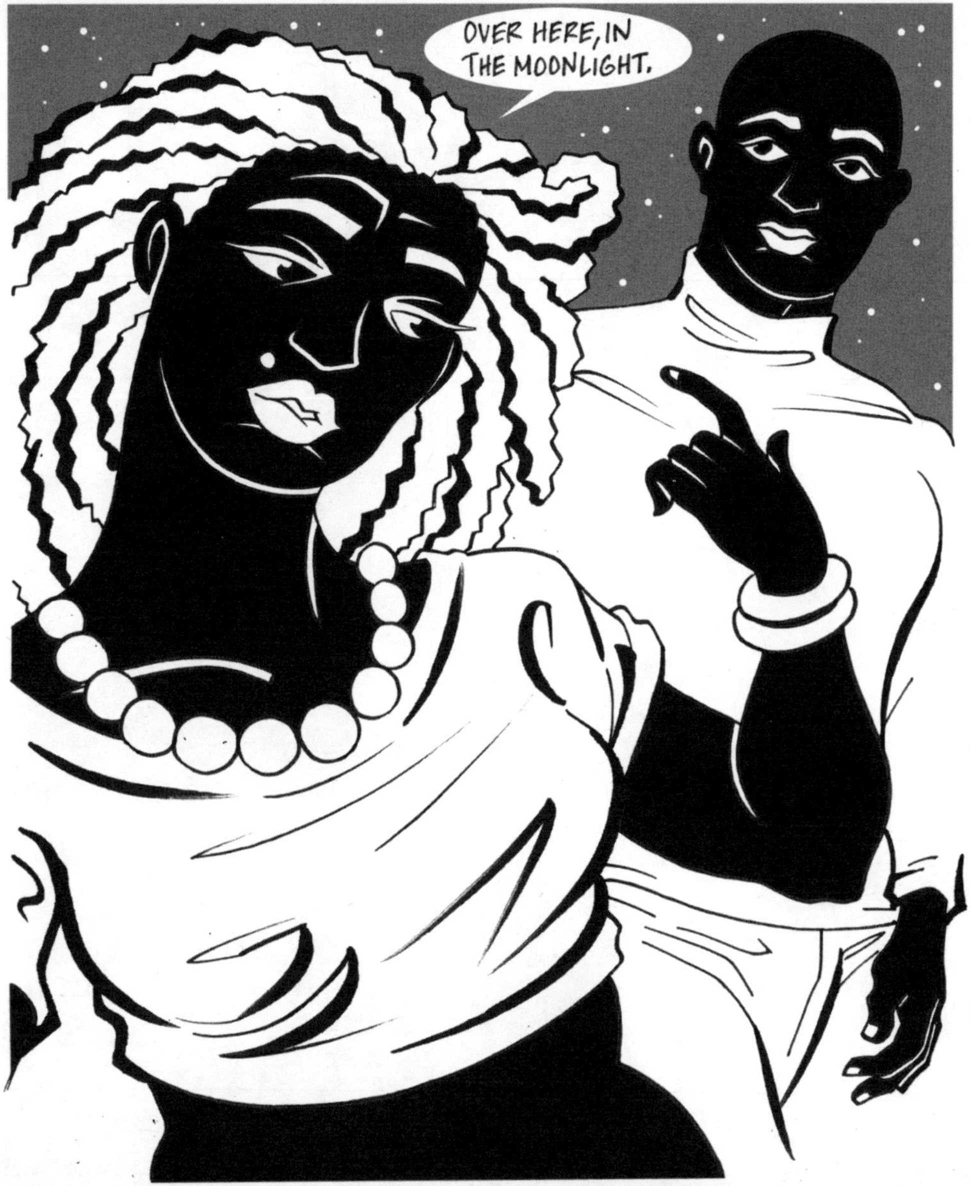
OVER HERE, IN THE MOONLIGHT.

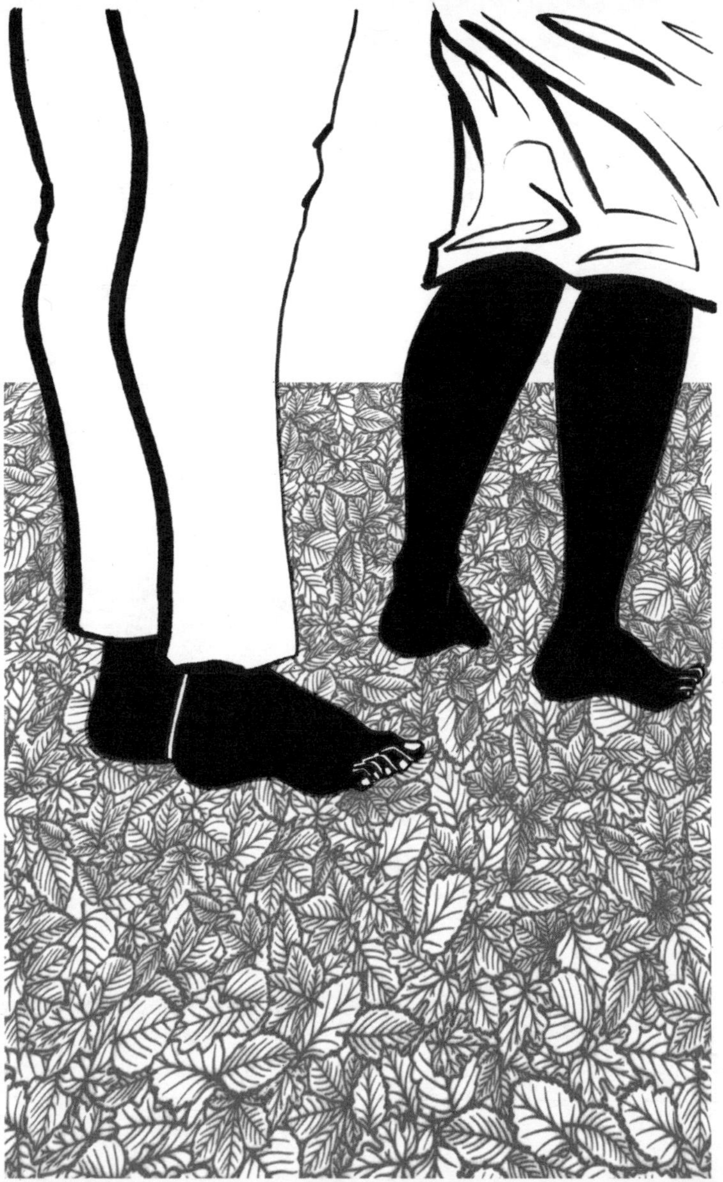

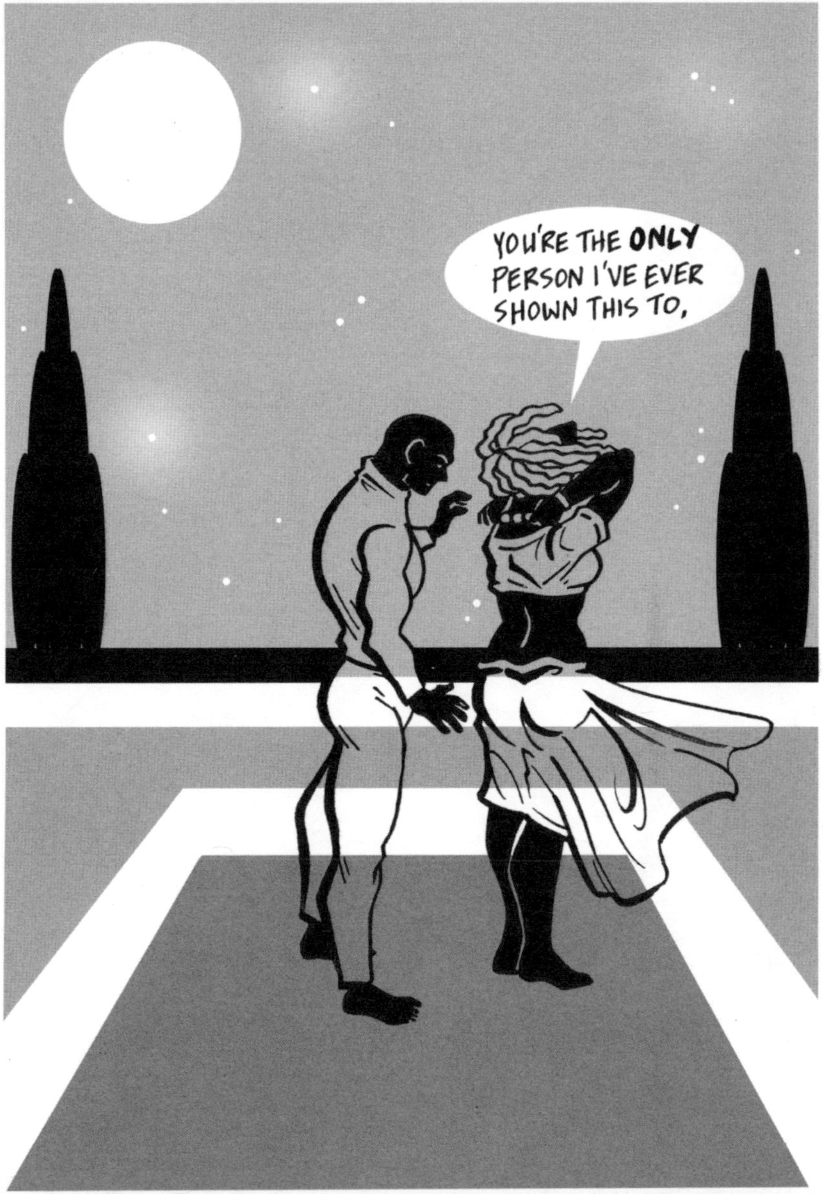
YOU'RE THE **ONLY** PERSON I'VE EVER SHOWN THIS TO,

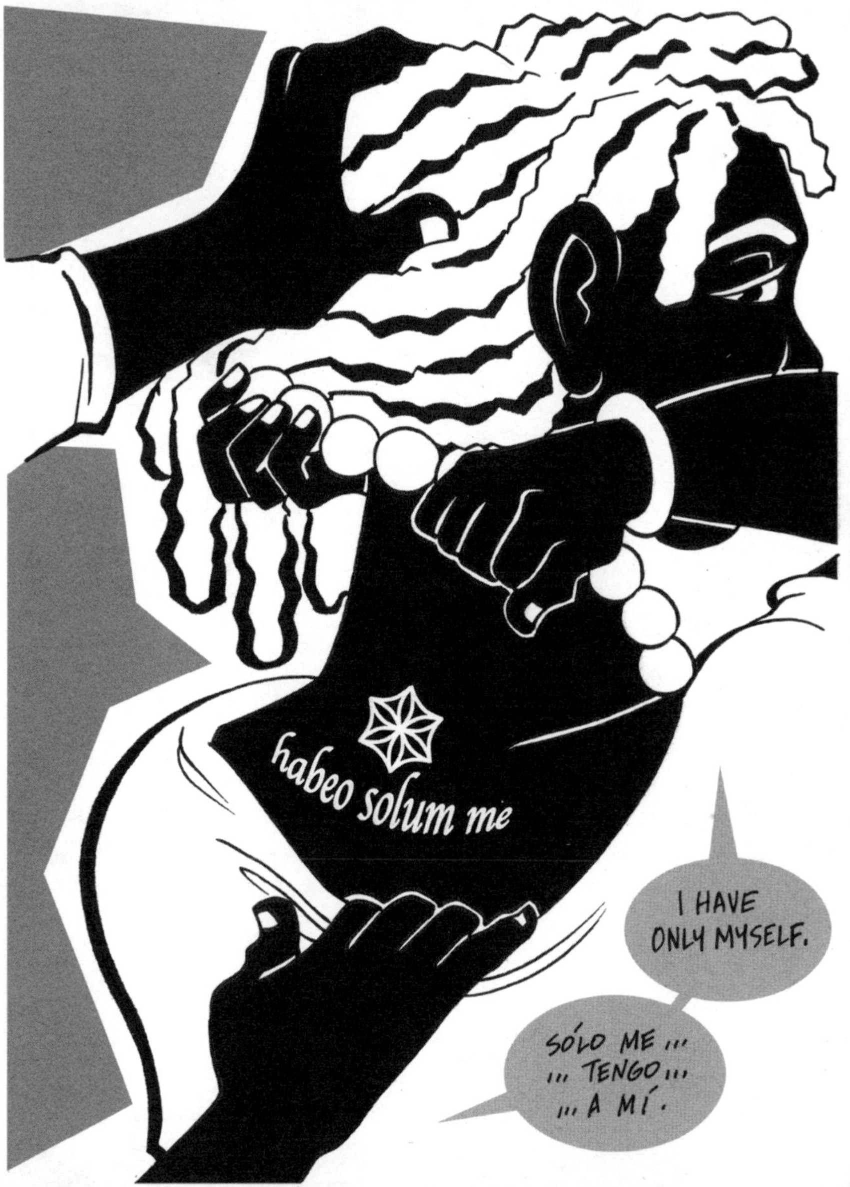
habeo solum me
I HAVE ONLY MYSELF.
SÓLO ME ... ... TENGO ... ... A MÍ.

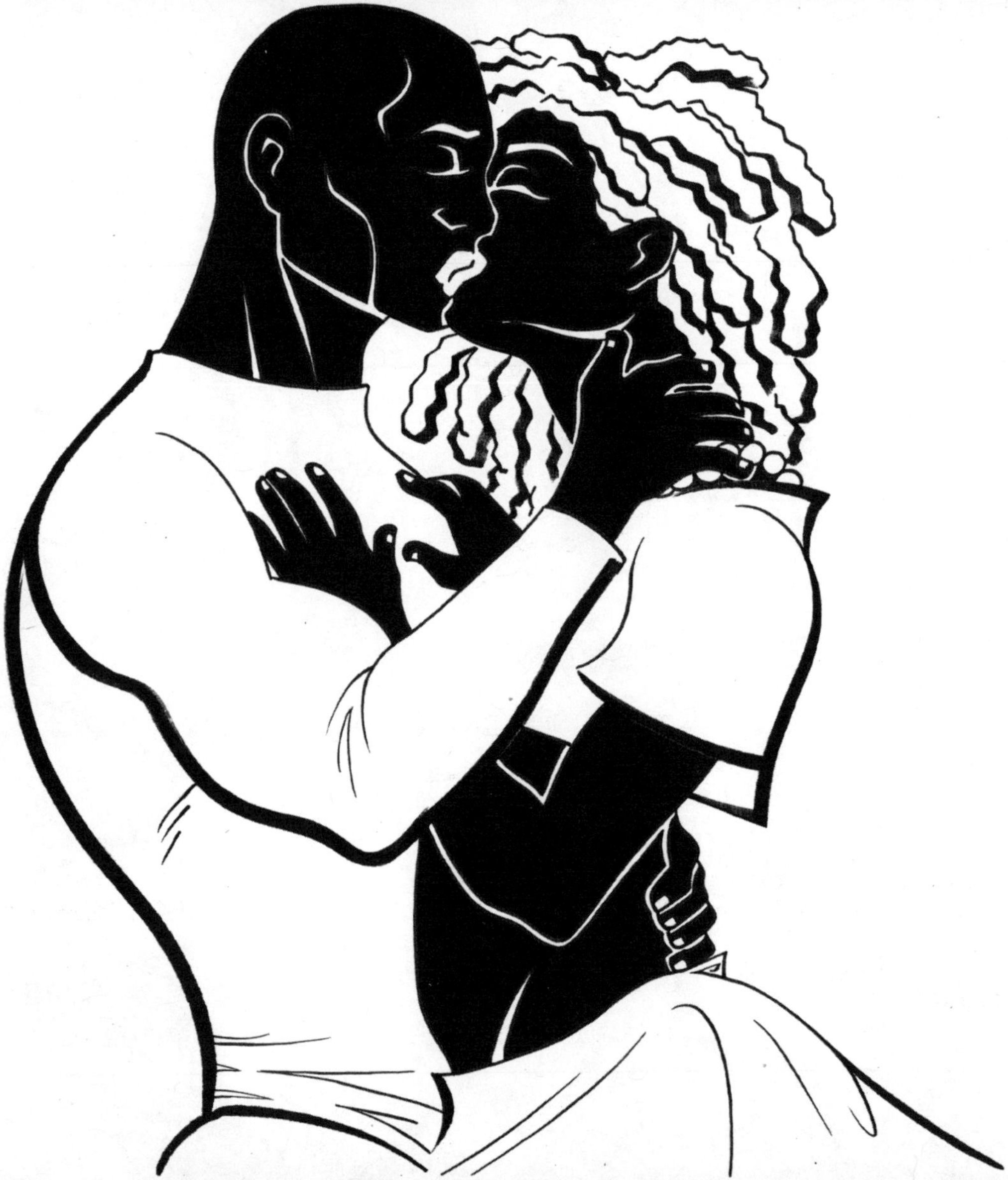

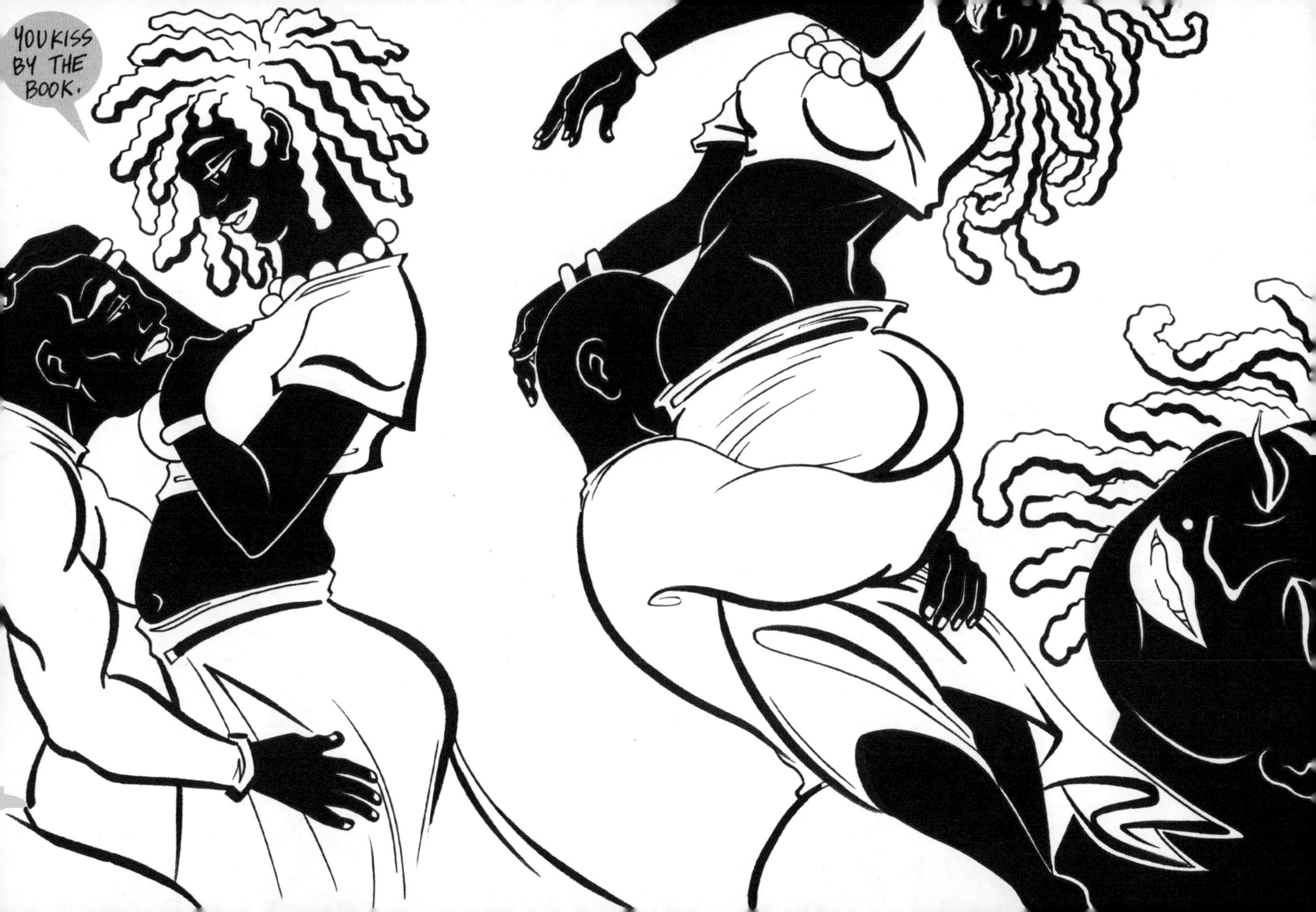
YOU KISS BY THE BOOK.

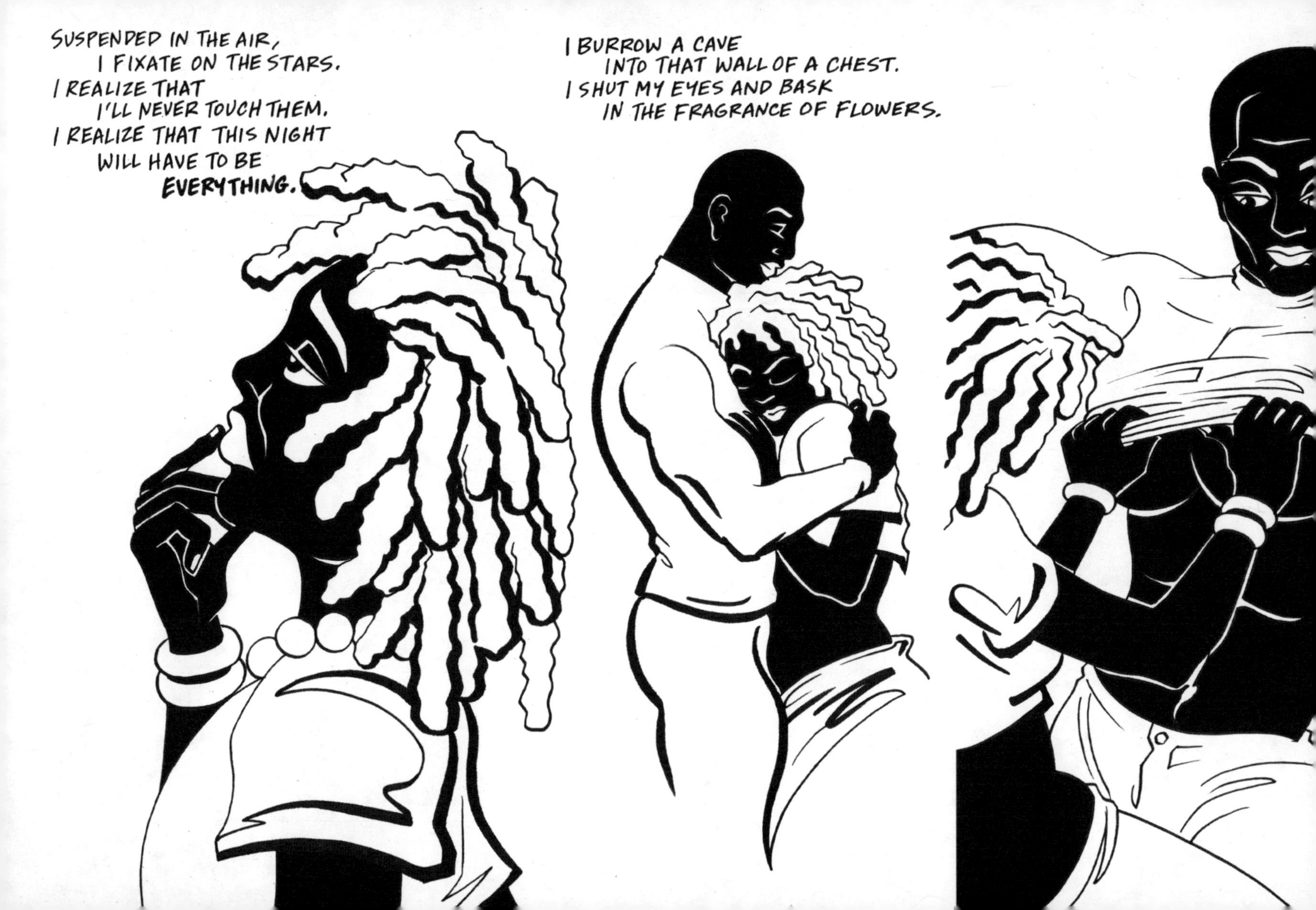
SUSPENDED IN THE AIR,
I FIXATE ON THE STARS.
I REALIZE THAT
I'LL NEVER TOUCH THEM.
I REALIZE THAT THIS NIGHT
WILL HAVE TO BE
EVERYTHING.
I BURROW A CAVE
INTO THAT WALL OF A CHEST.
I SHUT MY EYES AND BASK
IN THE FRAGRANCE OF FLOWERS.

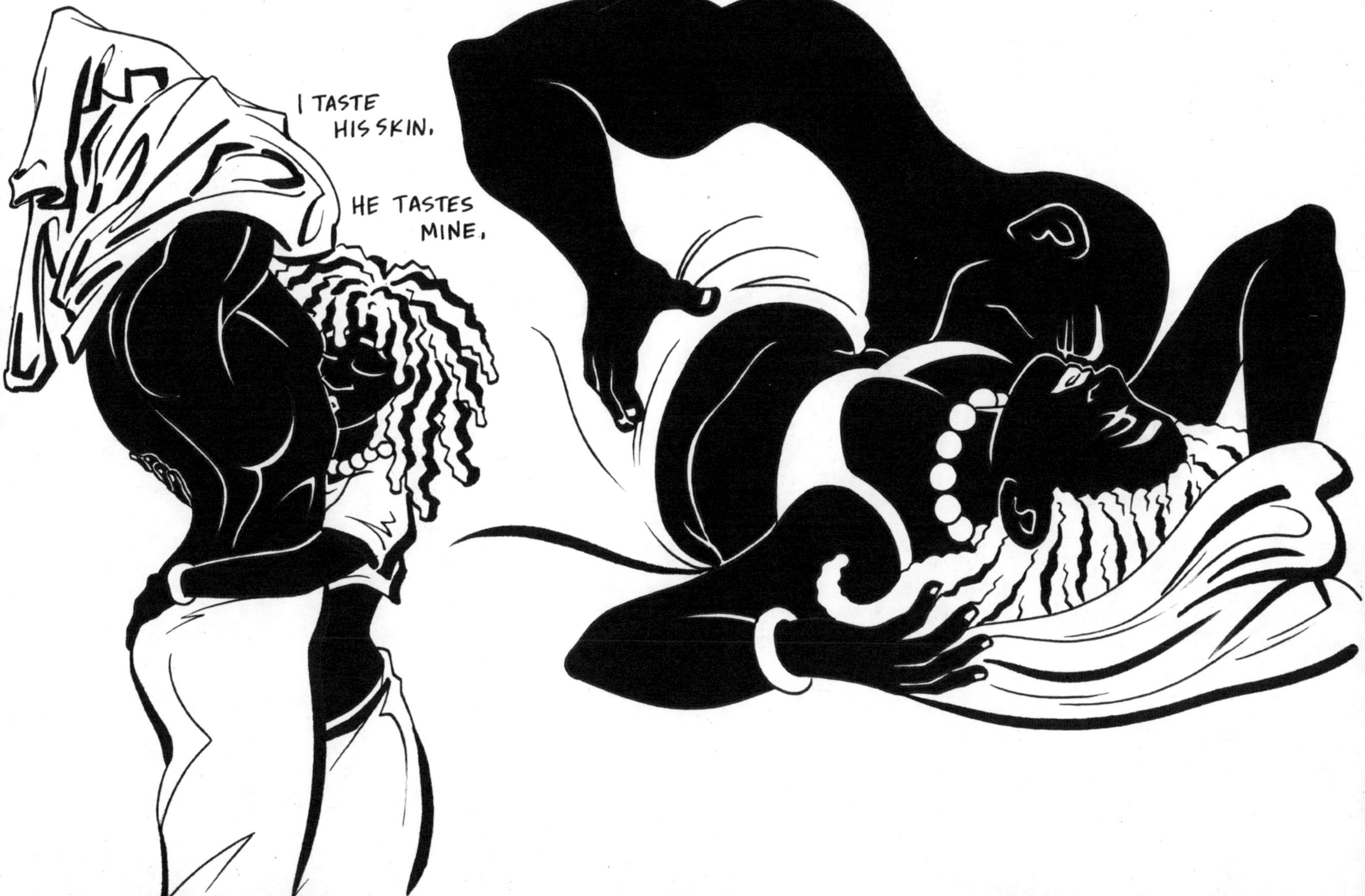
I TASTE HIS SKIN.
HE TASTES MINE.

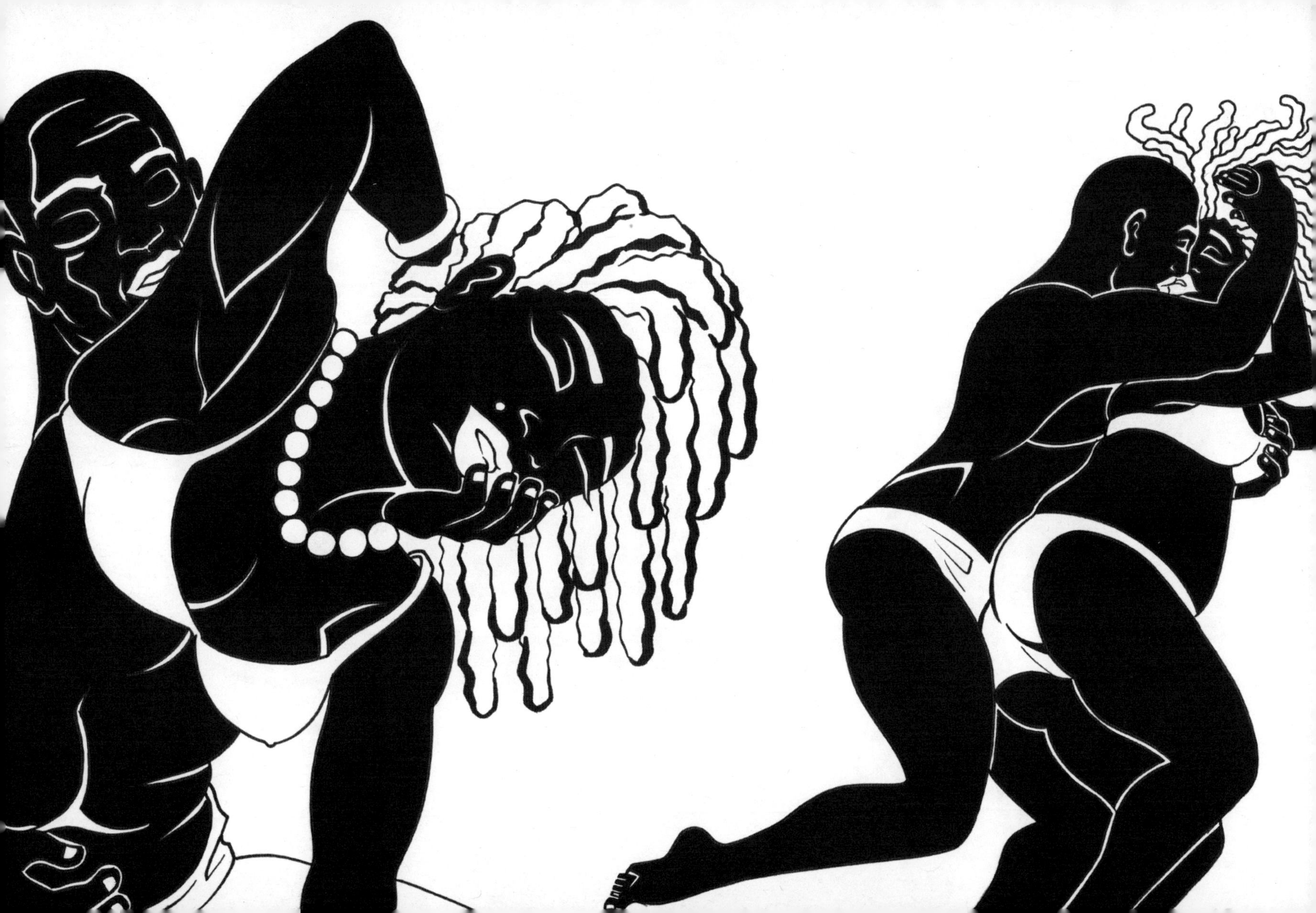

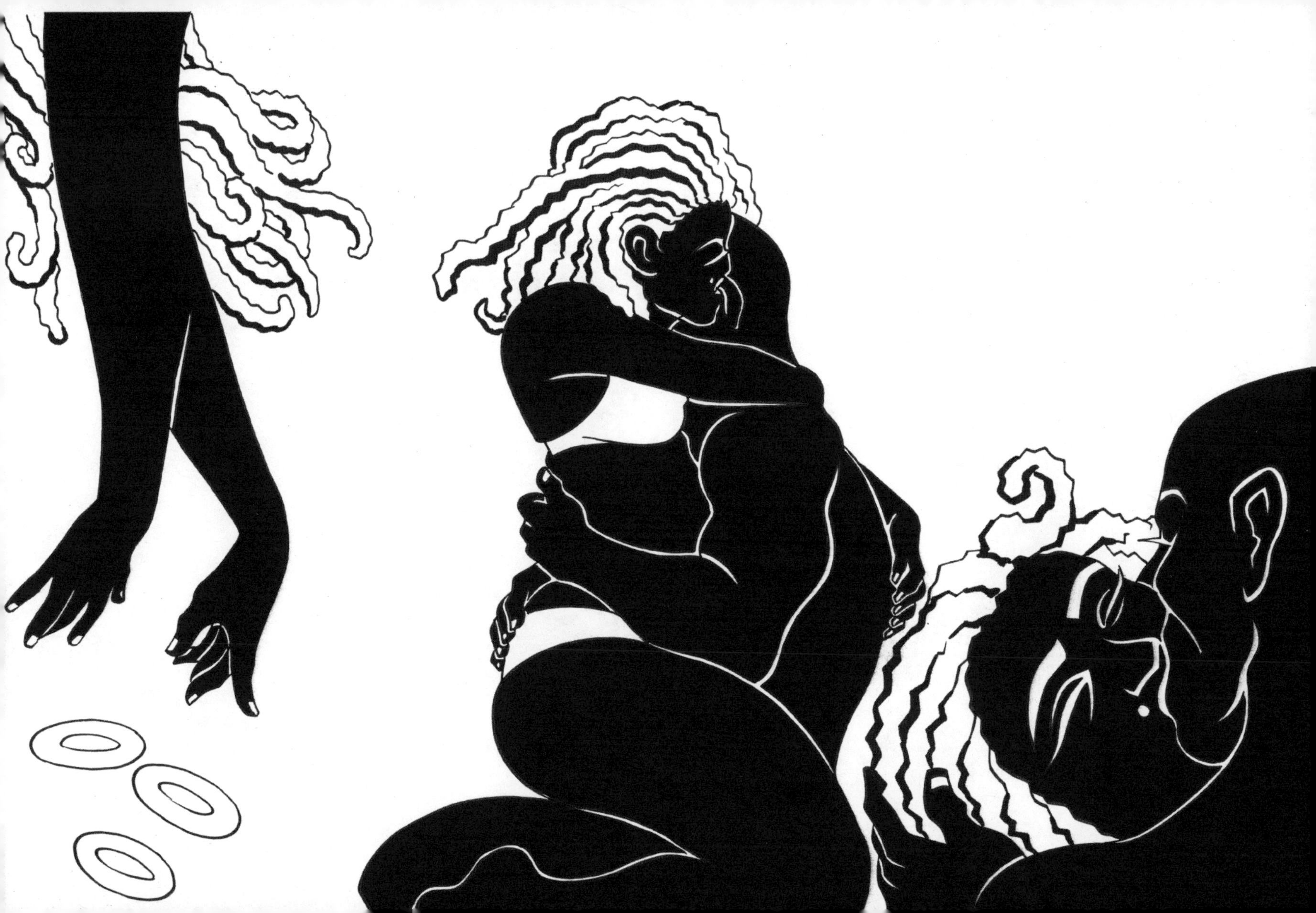

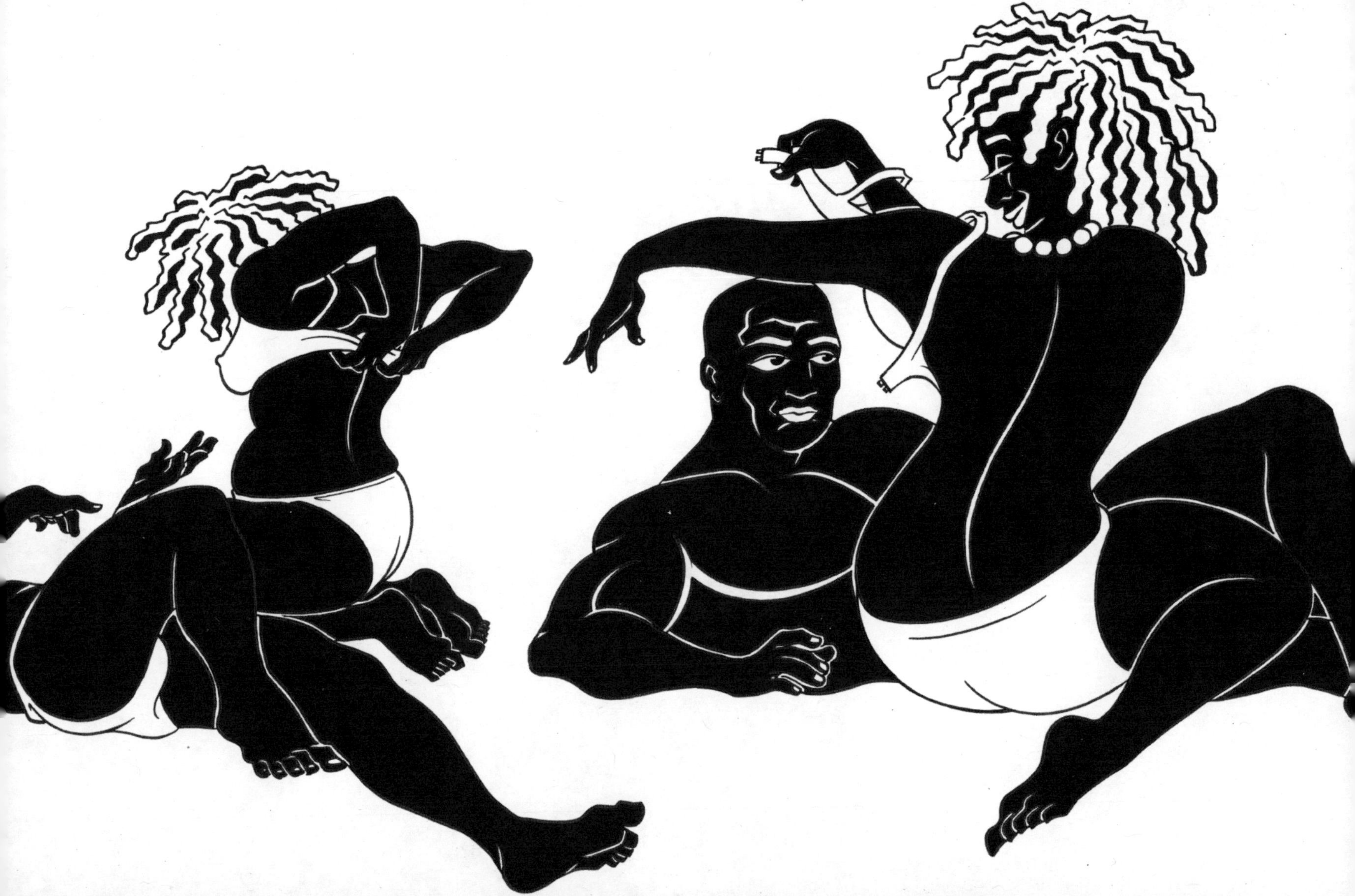

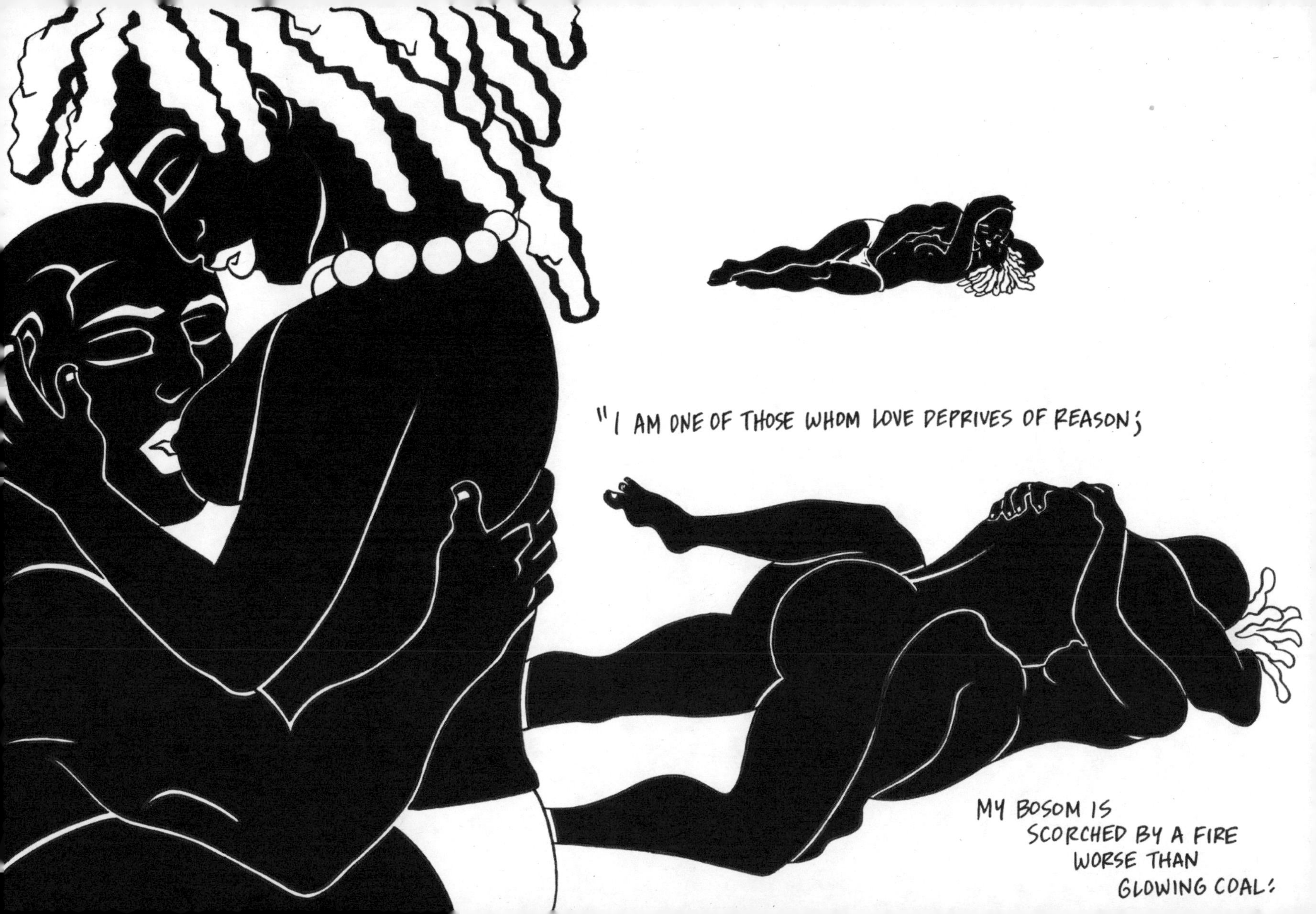
"I AM ONE OF THOSE WHOM LOVE DEPRIVES OF REASON;
MY BOSOM IS SCORCHED BY A FIRE WORSE THAN GLOWING COAL:

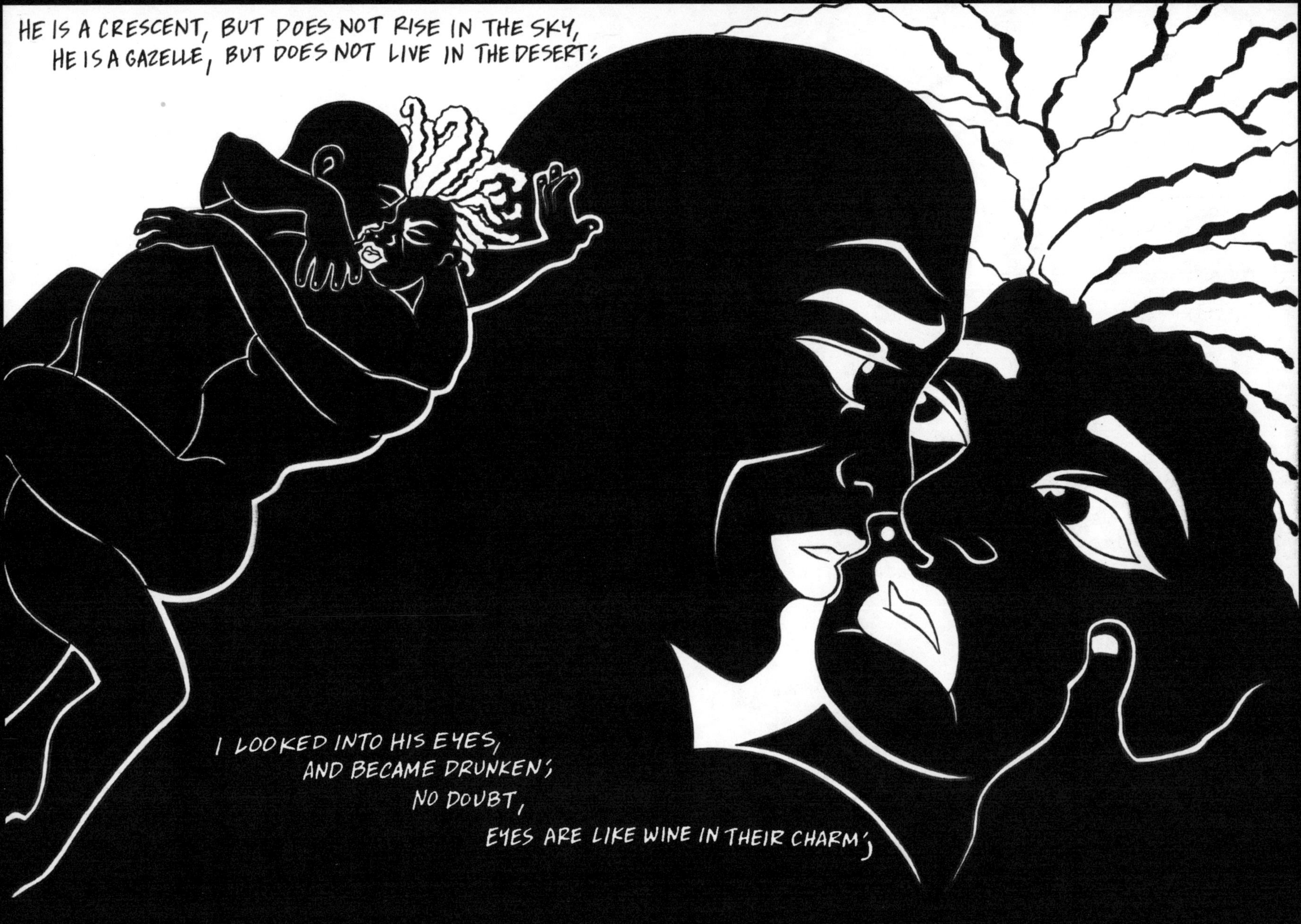
HE IS A CRESCENT, BUT DOES NOT RISE IN THE SKY,
HE IS A GAZELLE, BUT DOES NOT LIVE IN THE DESERT:
I LOOKED INTO HIS EYES,
AND BECAME DRUNKEN;
NO DOUBT,
EYES ARE LIKE WINE IN THEIR CHARM;

I TALK TO HIM SO THAT HE WILL ANSWER ME, BUT I
DO SO ON PURPOSE TO HEAR HIM SCATTER PEARLS:
I AM HIS SLAVE, HE IS THE LORD, JUST LIKE HIS NAME:
I'LL HAVE A FULL SHARE OF HIS COMPANY,
AND HE OF MINE."

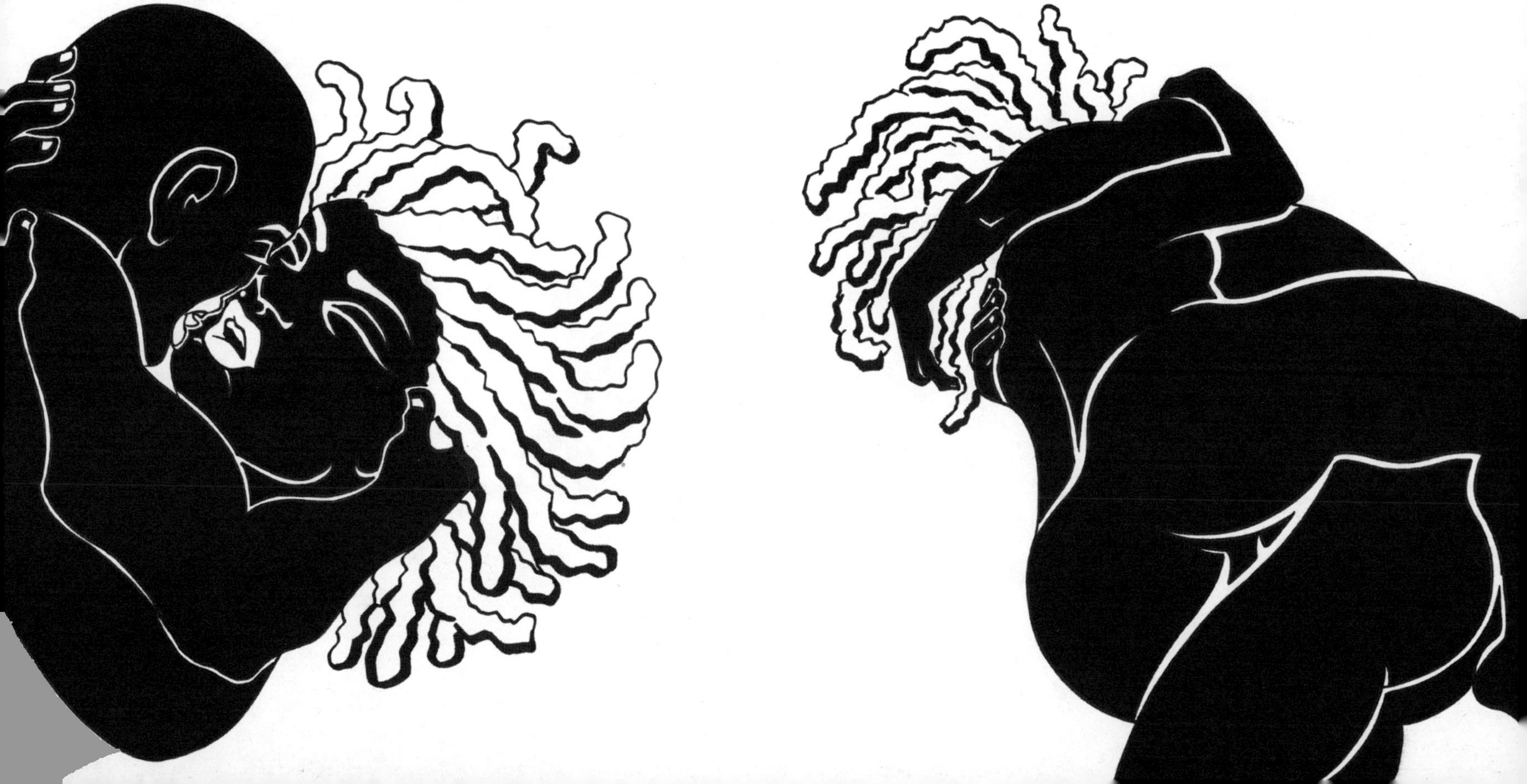

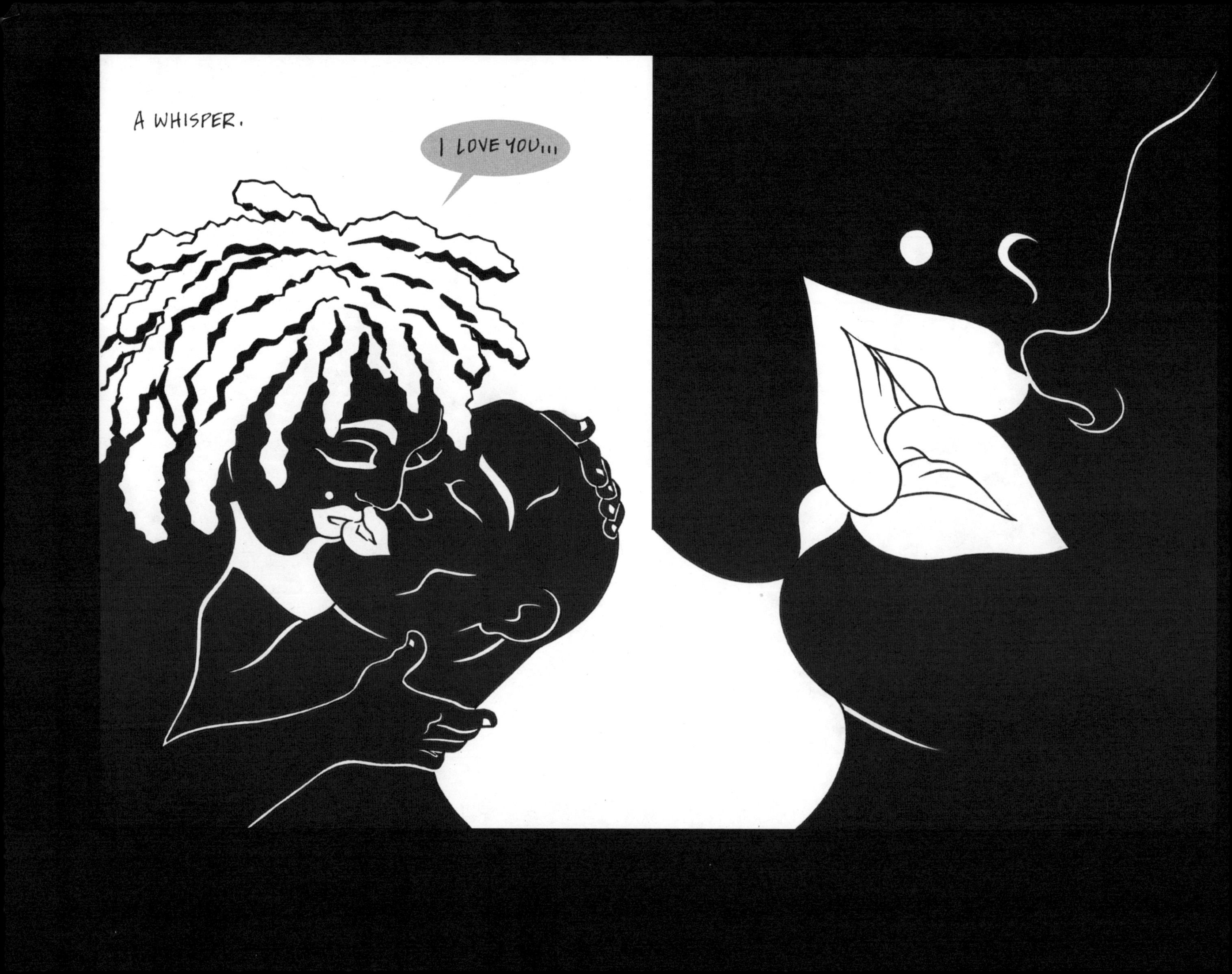
A WHISPER.
I LOVE YOU...

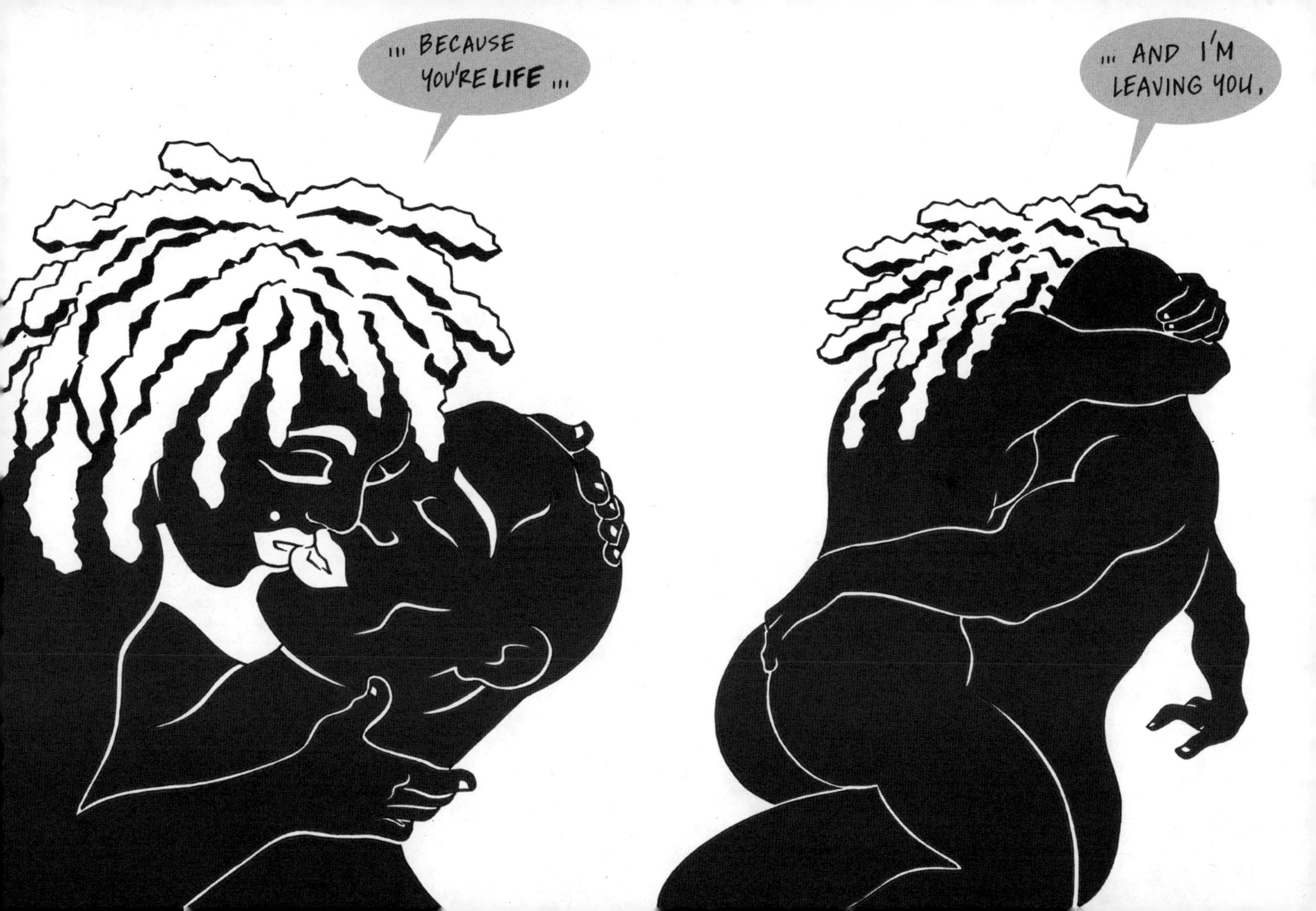
... BECAUSE YOU'RE LIFE ...
... AND I'M LEAVING YOU.

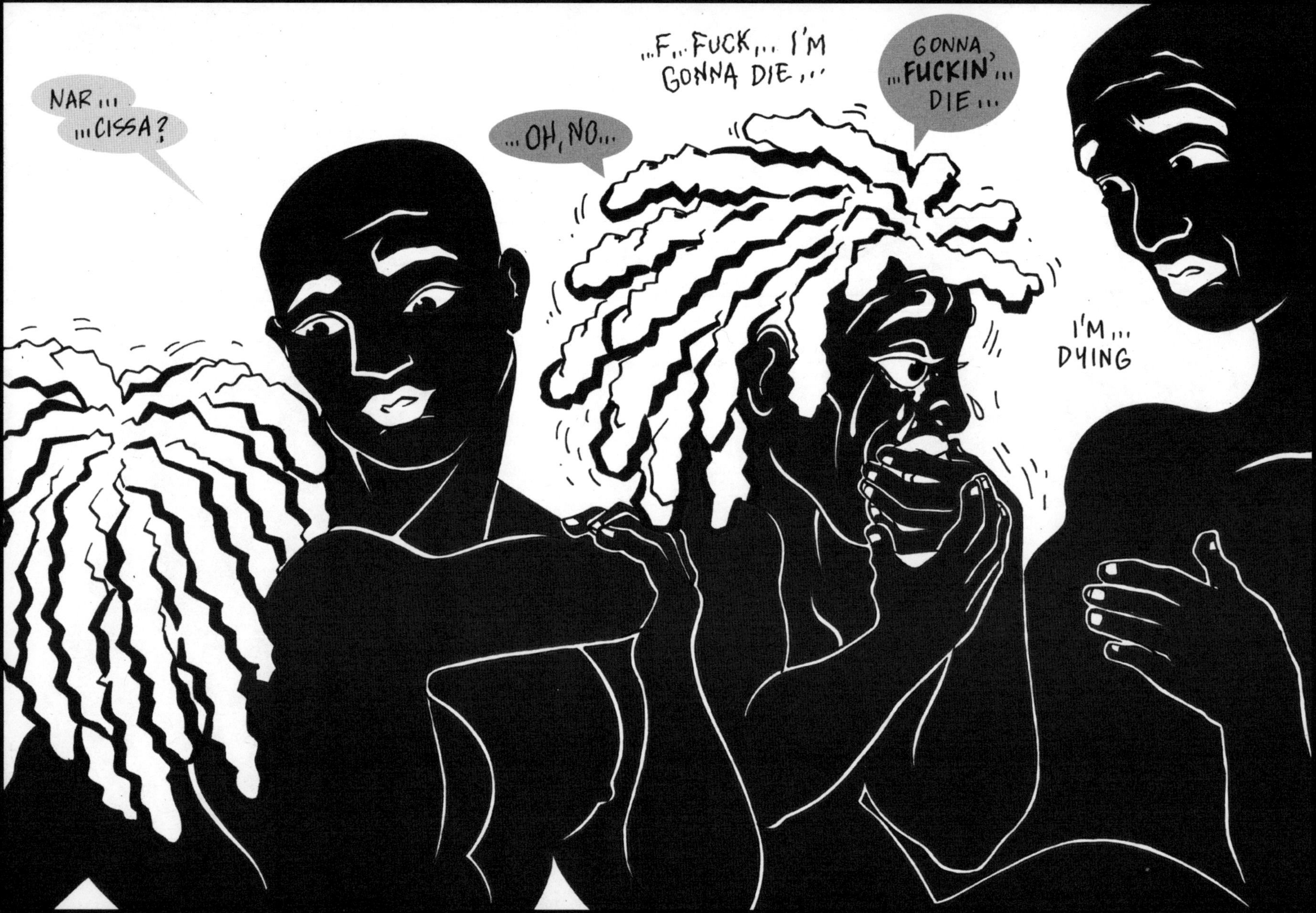
NAR... ...CISSA?
...OH, NO...
...F... FUCK,... I'M GONNA DIE,...
GONNA ...FUCKIN'... DIE...
I'M... DYING

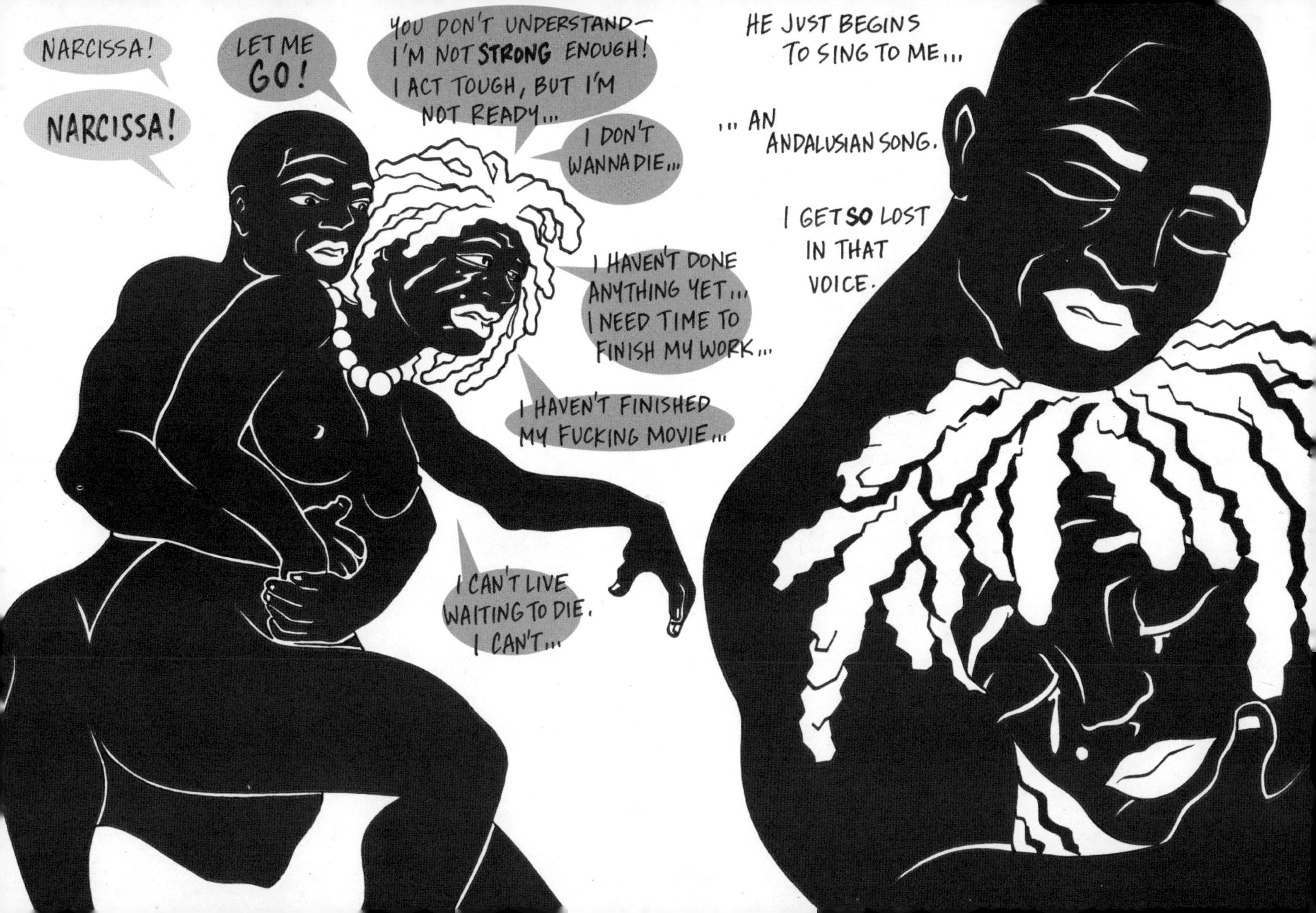
NARCISSA!
NARCISSA!
LET ME GO!
YOU DON'T UNDERSTAND— I'M NOT STRONG ENOUGH! I ACT TOUGH, BUT I'M NOT READY...
I DON'T WANNA DIE...
I HAVEN'T DONE ANYTHING YET... I NEED TIME TO FINISH MY WORK...
I HAVEN'T FINISHED MY FUCKING MOVIE...
I CAN'T LIVE WAITING TO DIE. I CAN'T...
HE JUST BEGINS TO SING TO ME...
... AN ANDALUSIAN SONG.
I GET SO LOST IN THAT VOICE.

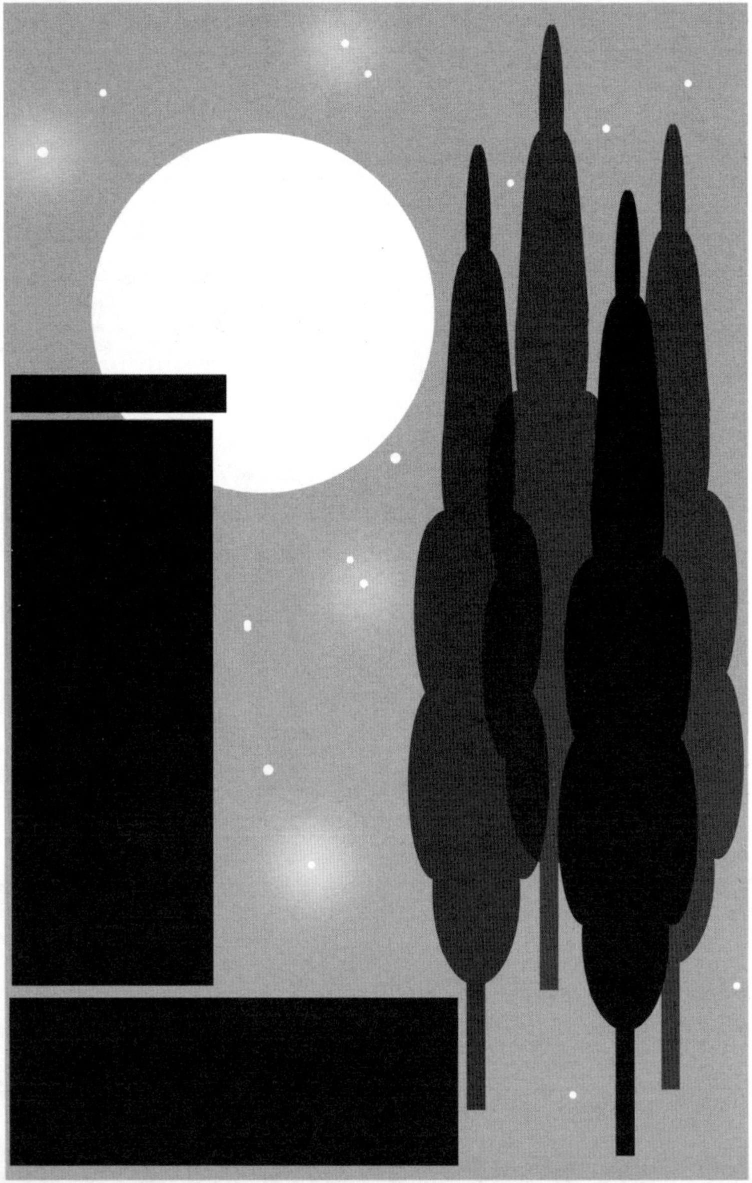

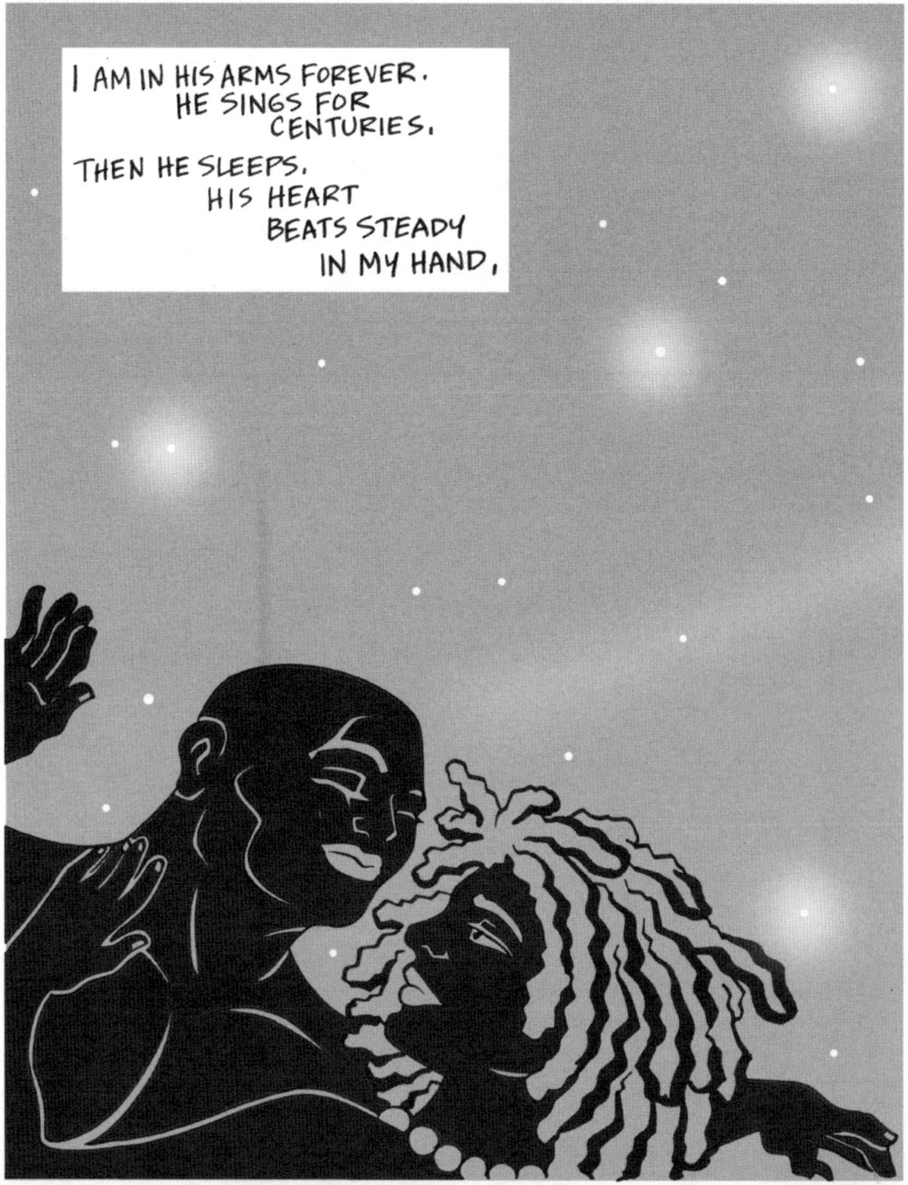
I AM IN HIS ARMS FOREVER. HE SINGS FOR CENTURIES.
THEN HE SLEEPS. HIS HEART BEATS STEADY IN MY HAND.

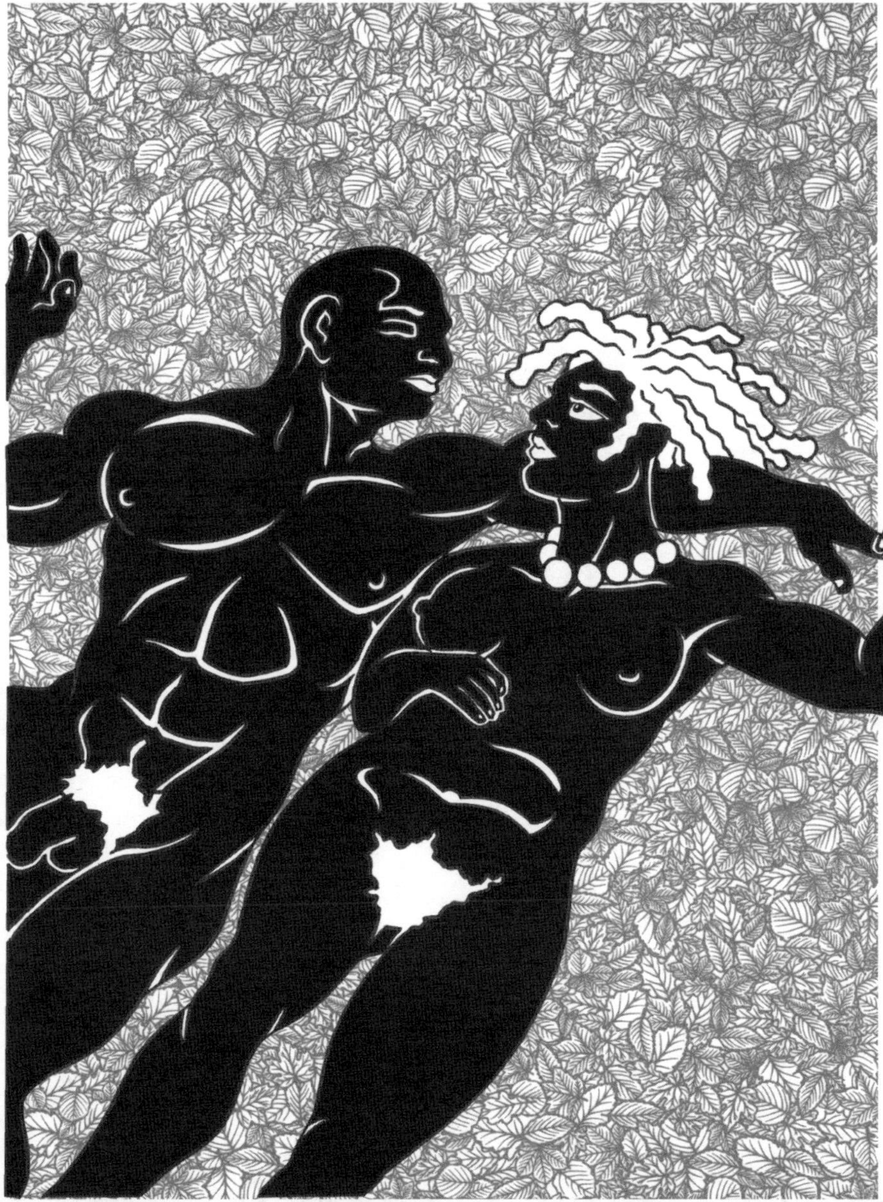

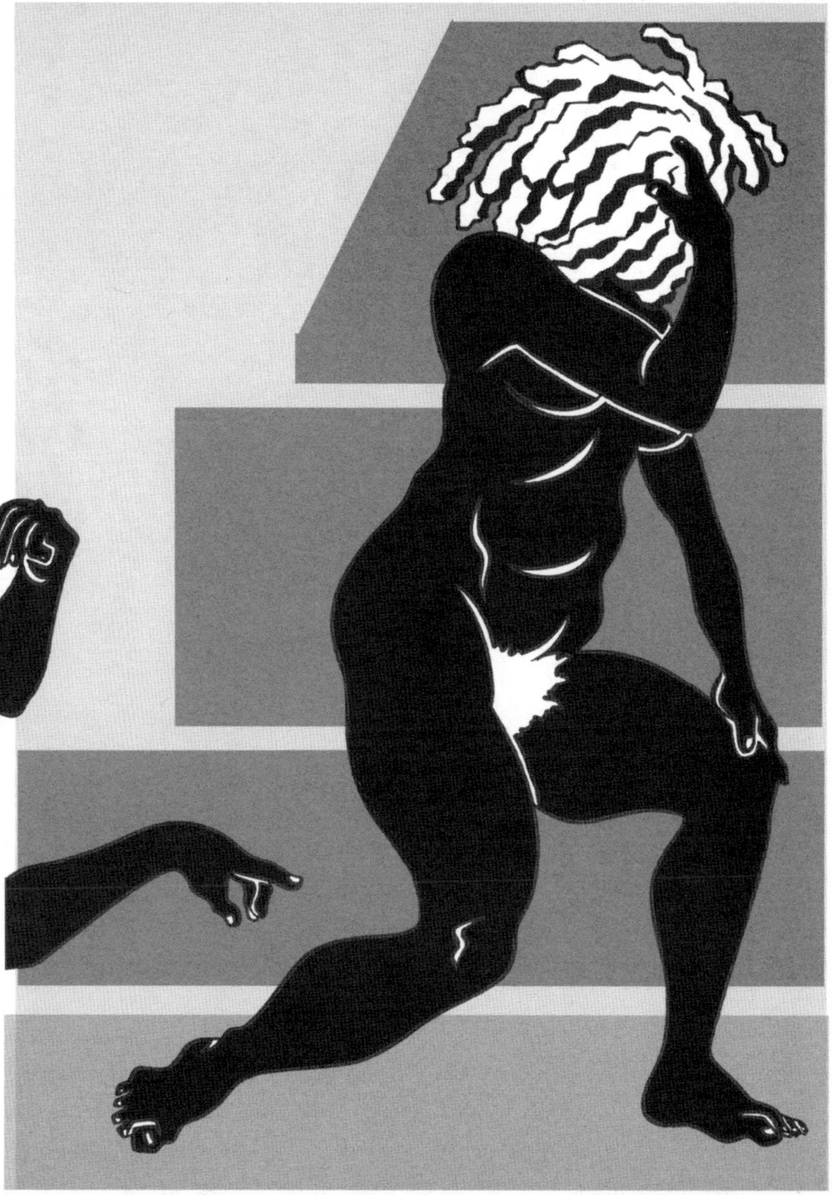

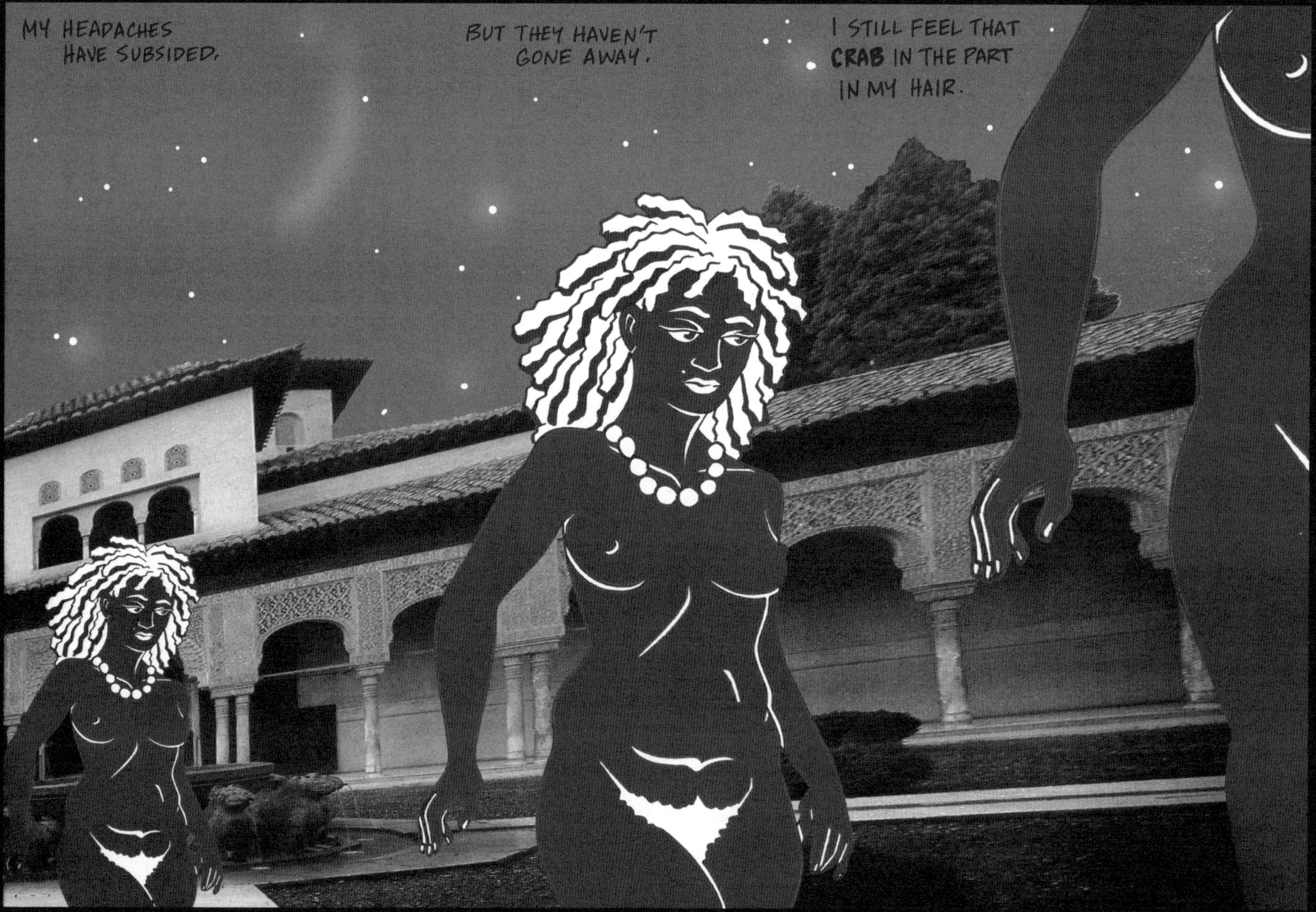
MY HEADACHES HAVE SUBSIDED.
BUT THEY HAVEN'T GONE AWAY.
I STILL FEEL THAT **CRAB** IN THE PART IN MY HAIR.

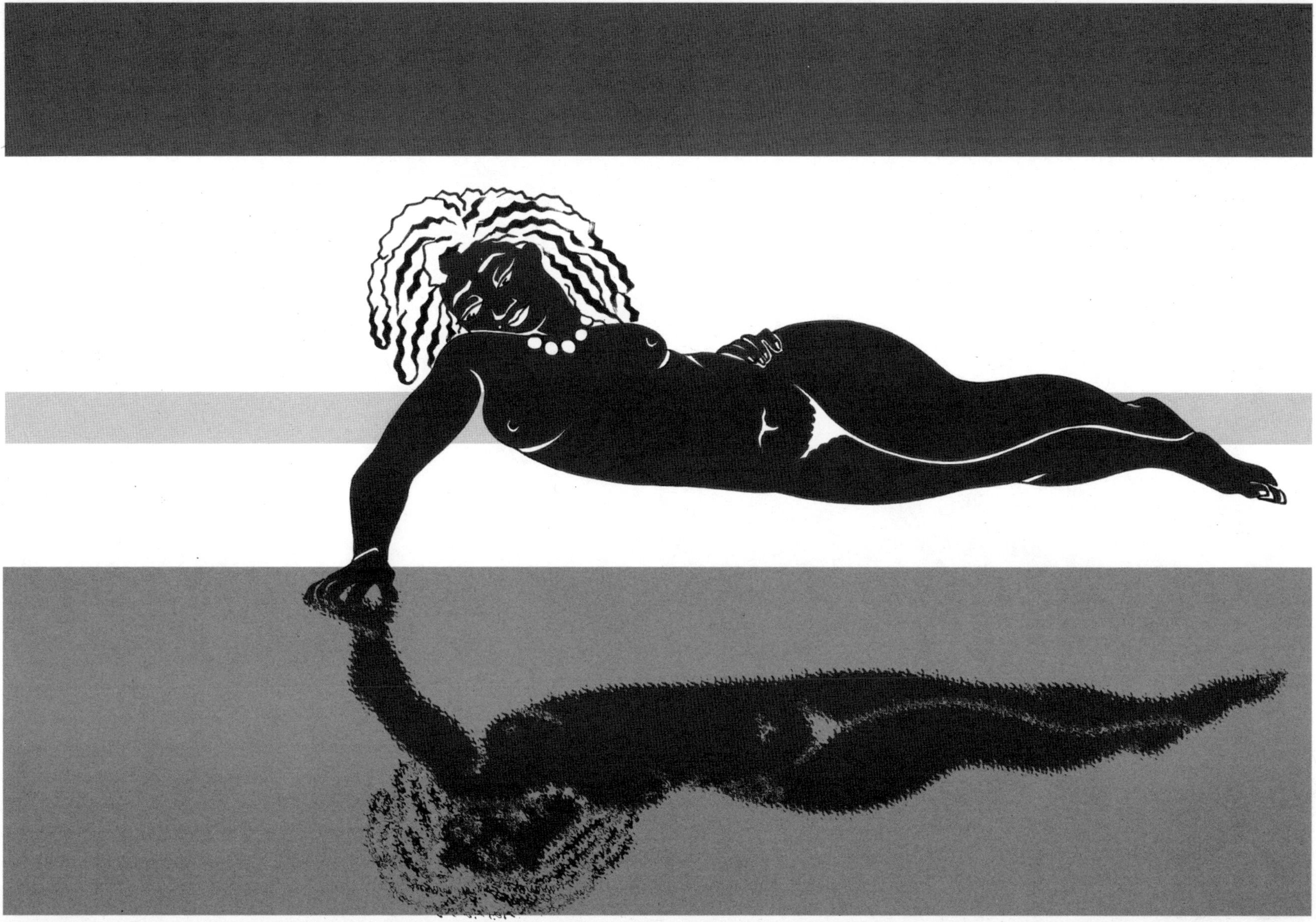

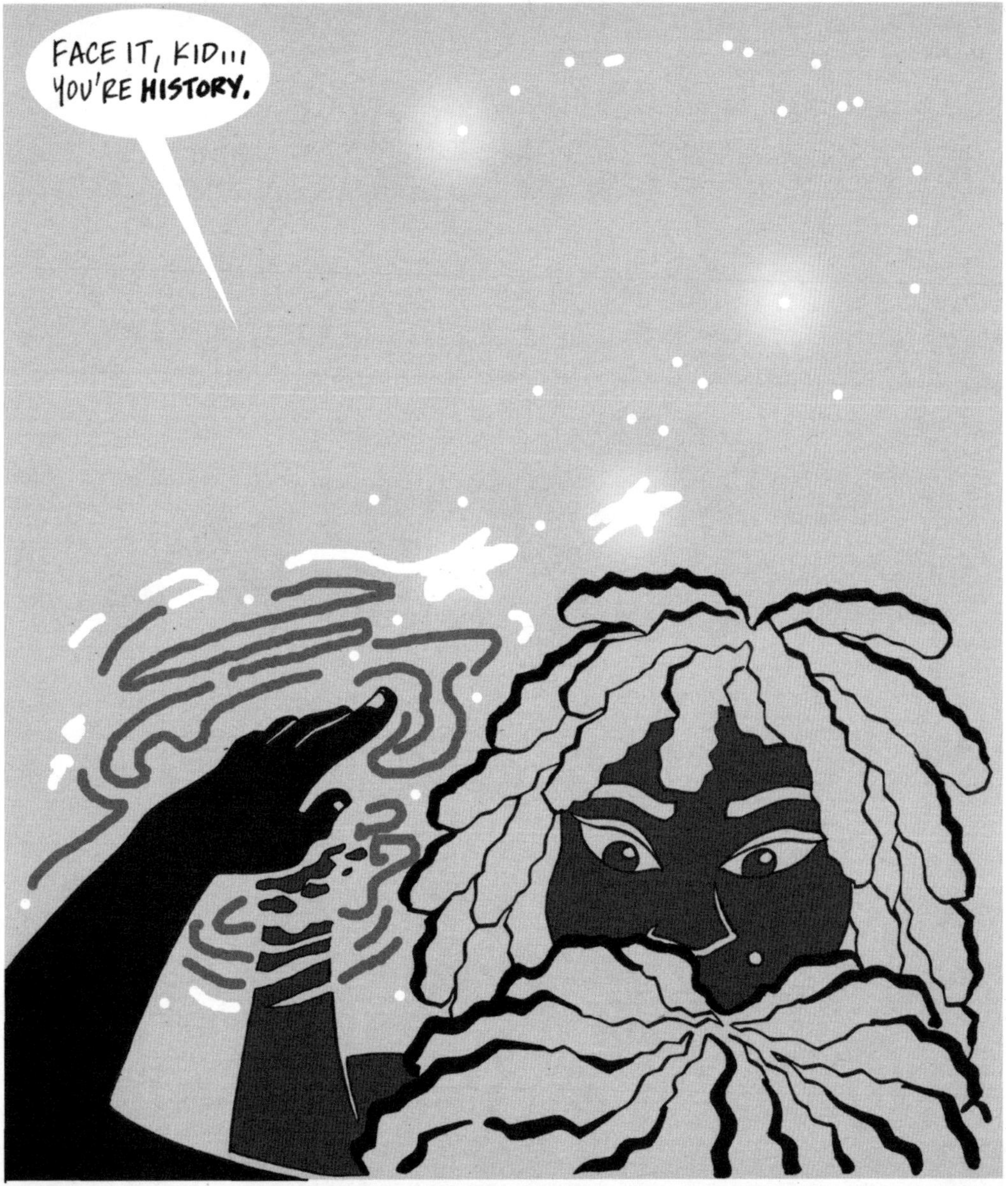
FACE IT, KID...
YOU'RE **HISTORY.**

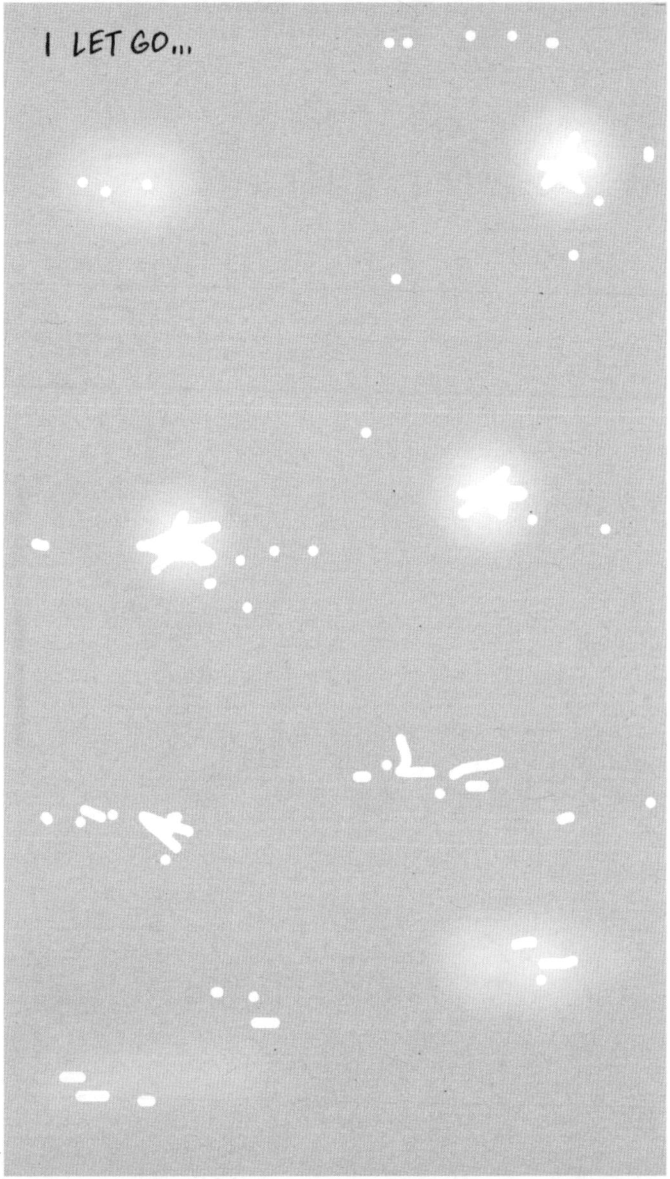
I LET GO...

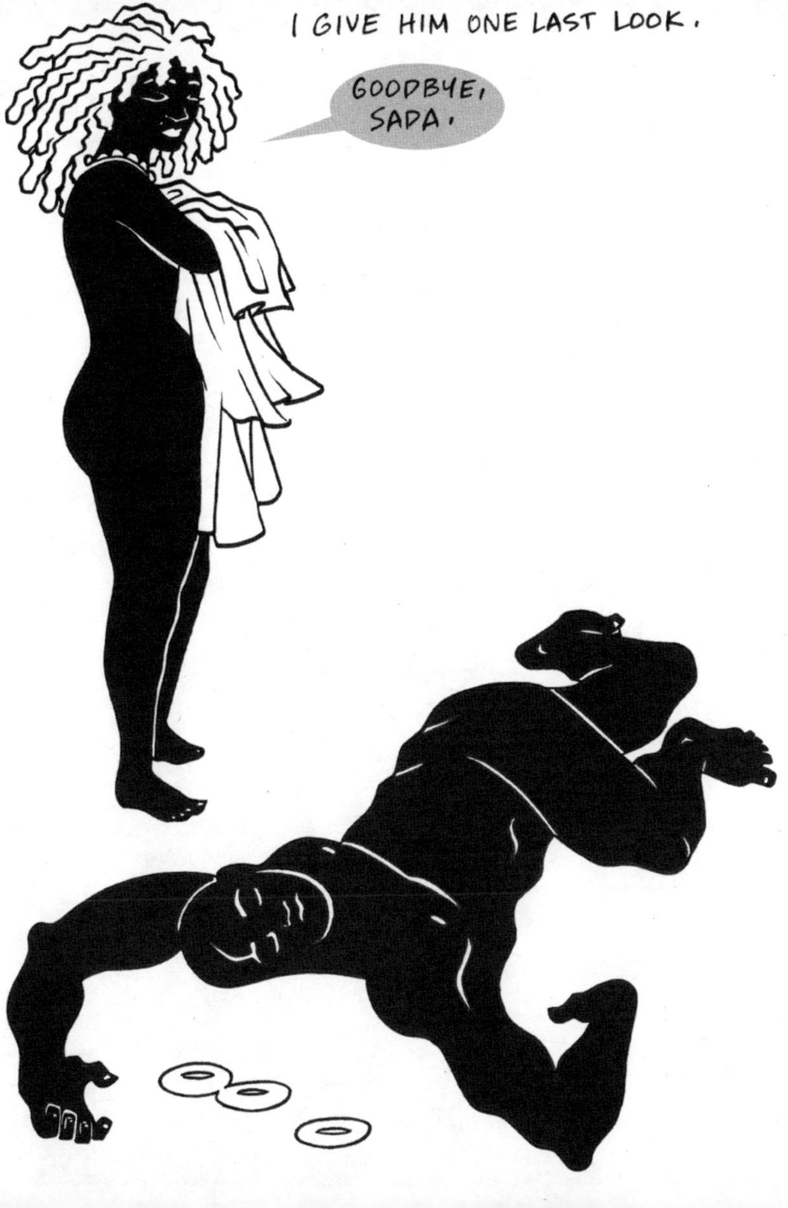
I GIVE HIM ONE LAST LOOK.
GOODBYE, SADA.

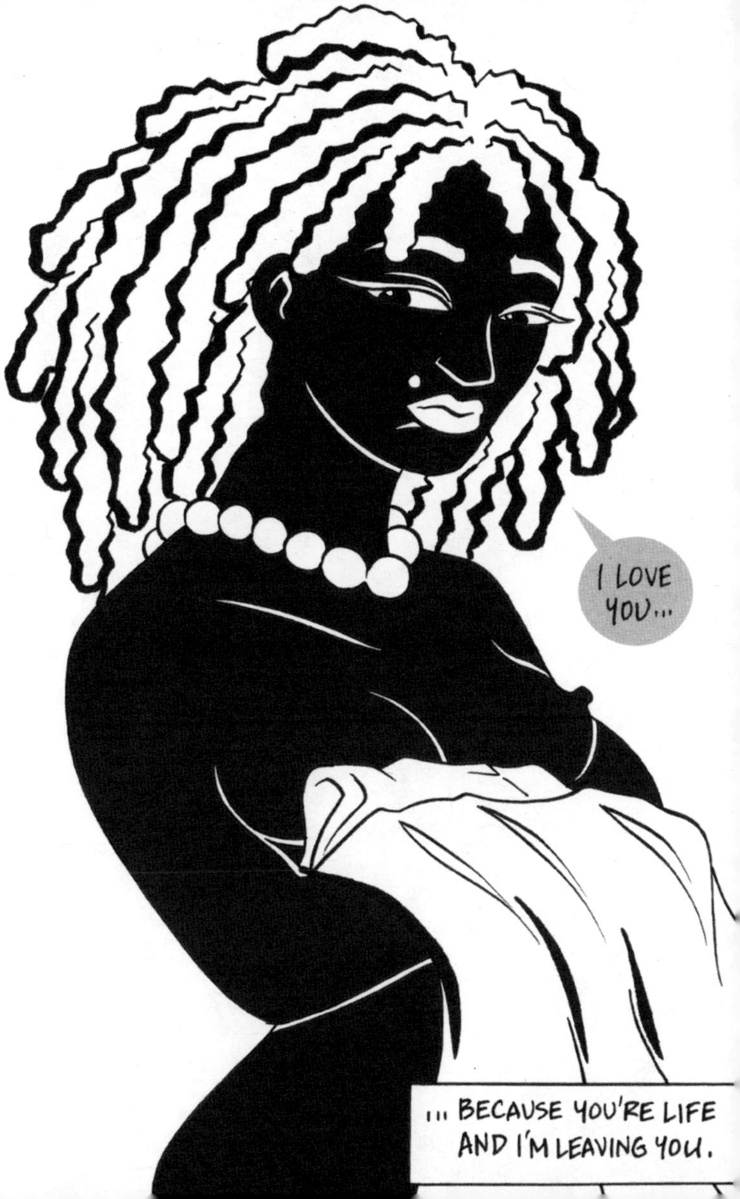
I LOVE YOU...
... BECAUSE YOU'RE LIFE AND I'M LEAVING YOU.

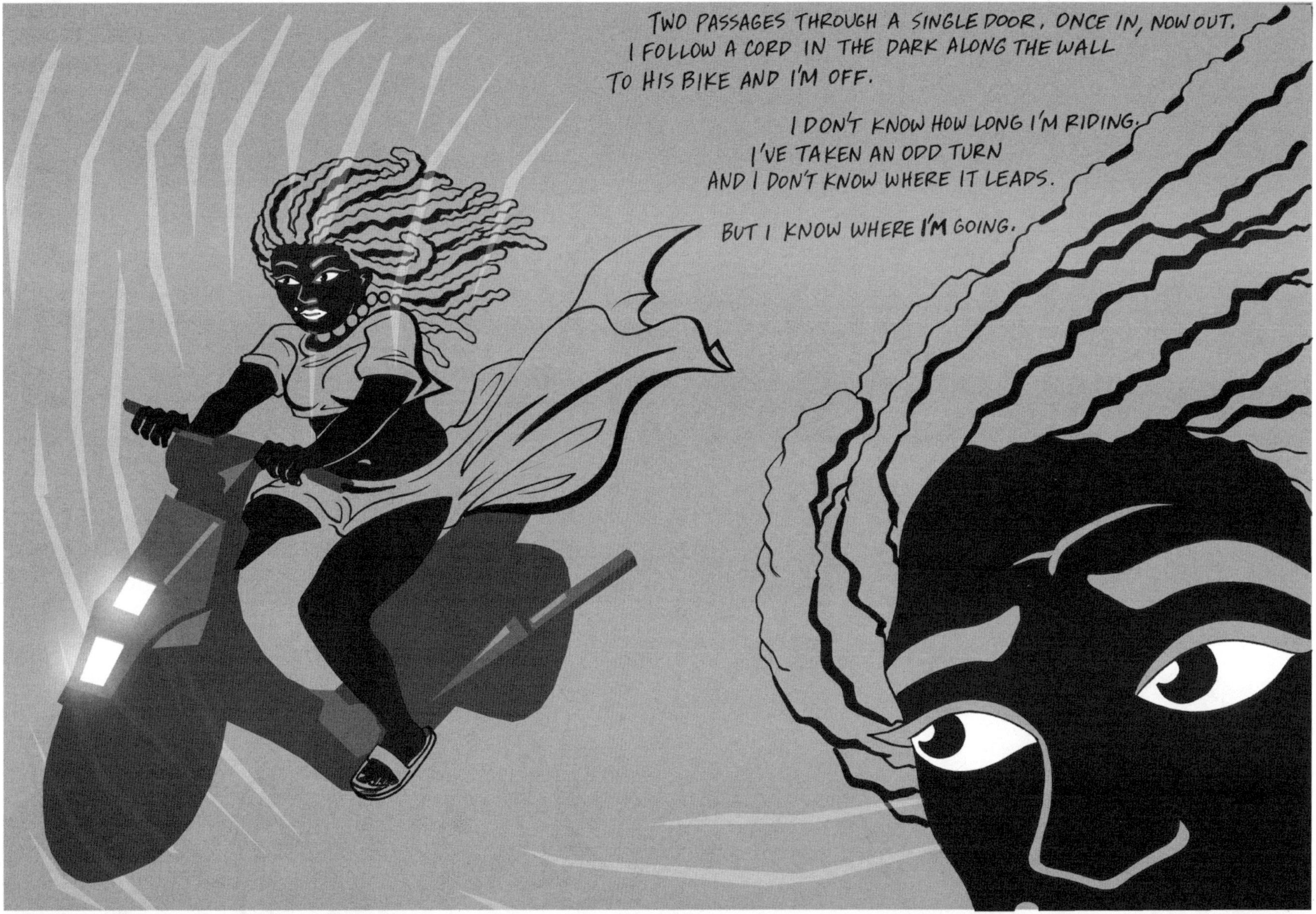
TWO PASSAGES THROUGH A SINGLE DOOR, ONCE IN, NOW OUT.
I FOLLOW A CORD IN THE DARK ALONG THE WALL
TO HIS BIKE AND I'M OFF.
I DON'T KNOW HOW LONG I'M RIDING.
I'VE TAKEN AN ODD TURN
AND I DON'T KNOW WHERE IT LEADS.
BUT I KNOW WHERE **I'M** GOING.

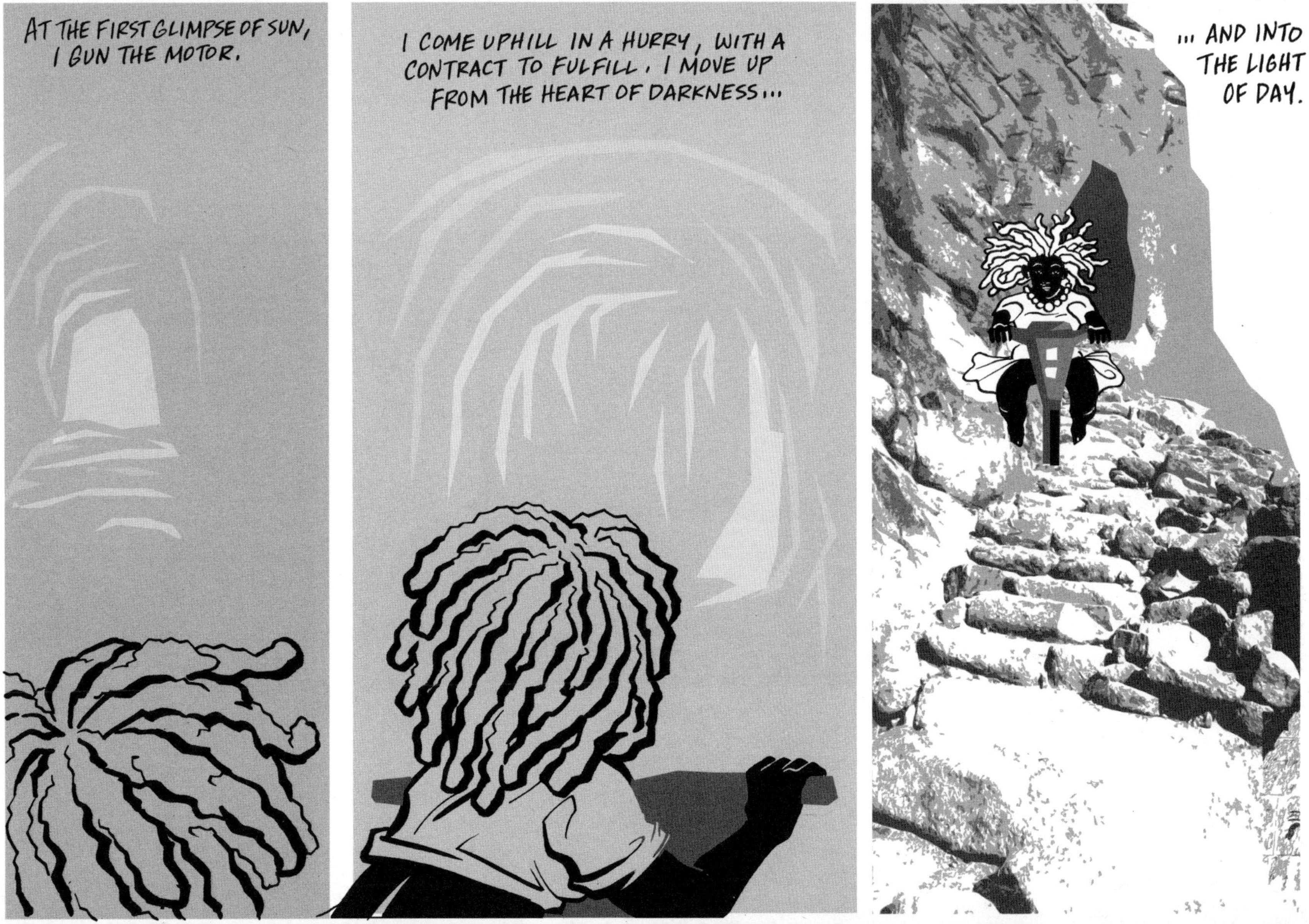
AT THE FIRST GLIMPSE OF SUN, I GUN THE MOTOR.
I COME UPHILL IN A HURRY, WITH A CONTRACT TO FULFILL. I MOVE UP FROM THE HEART OF DARKNESS...
... AND INTO THE LIGHT OF DAY.

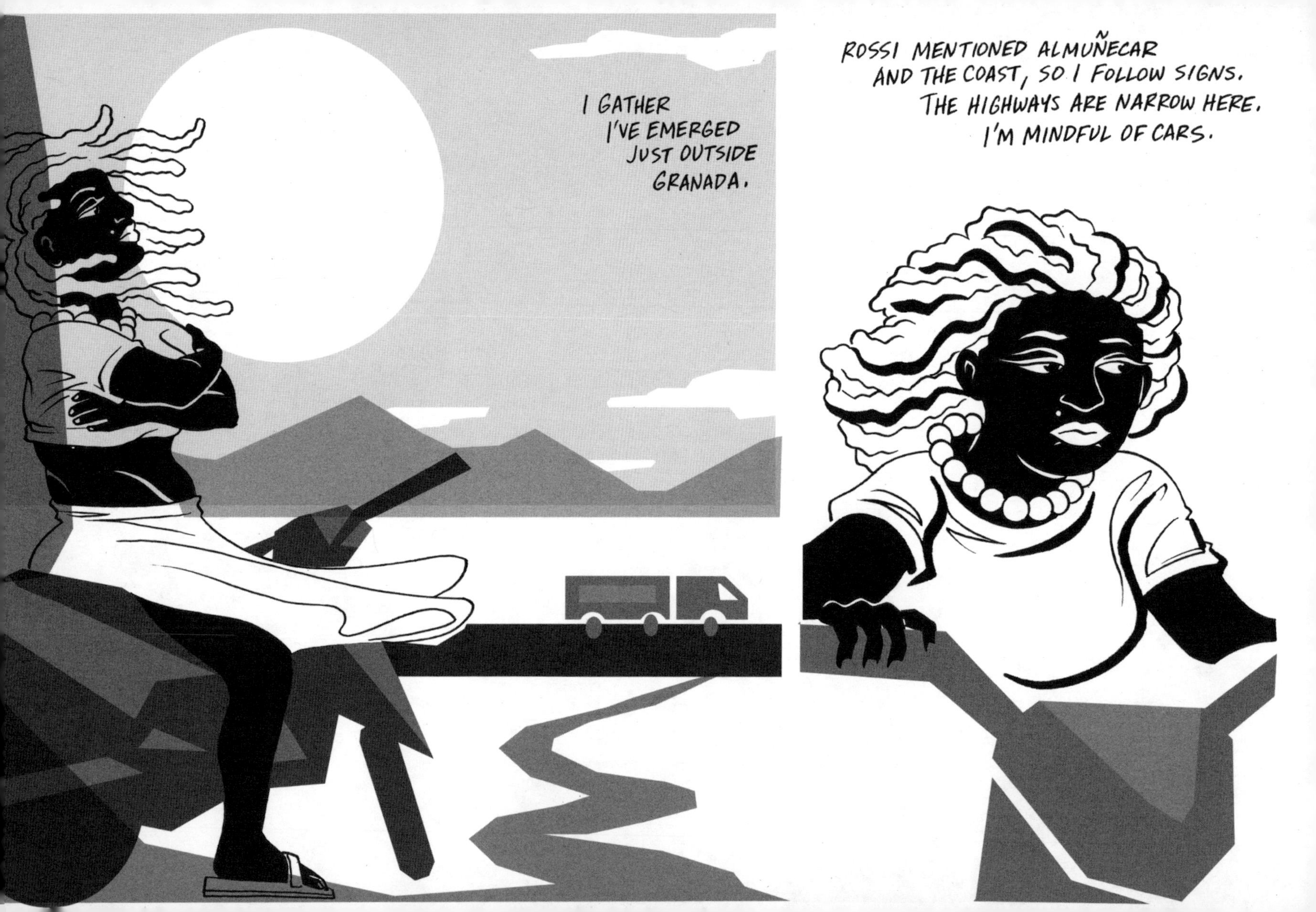
I GATHER I'VE EMERGED JUST OUTSIDE GRANADA.
ROSSI MENTIONED ALMUÑECAR AND THE COAST, SO I FOLLOW SIGNS. THE HIGHWAYS ARE NARROW HERE. I'M MINDFUL OF CARS.

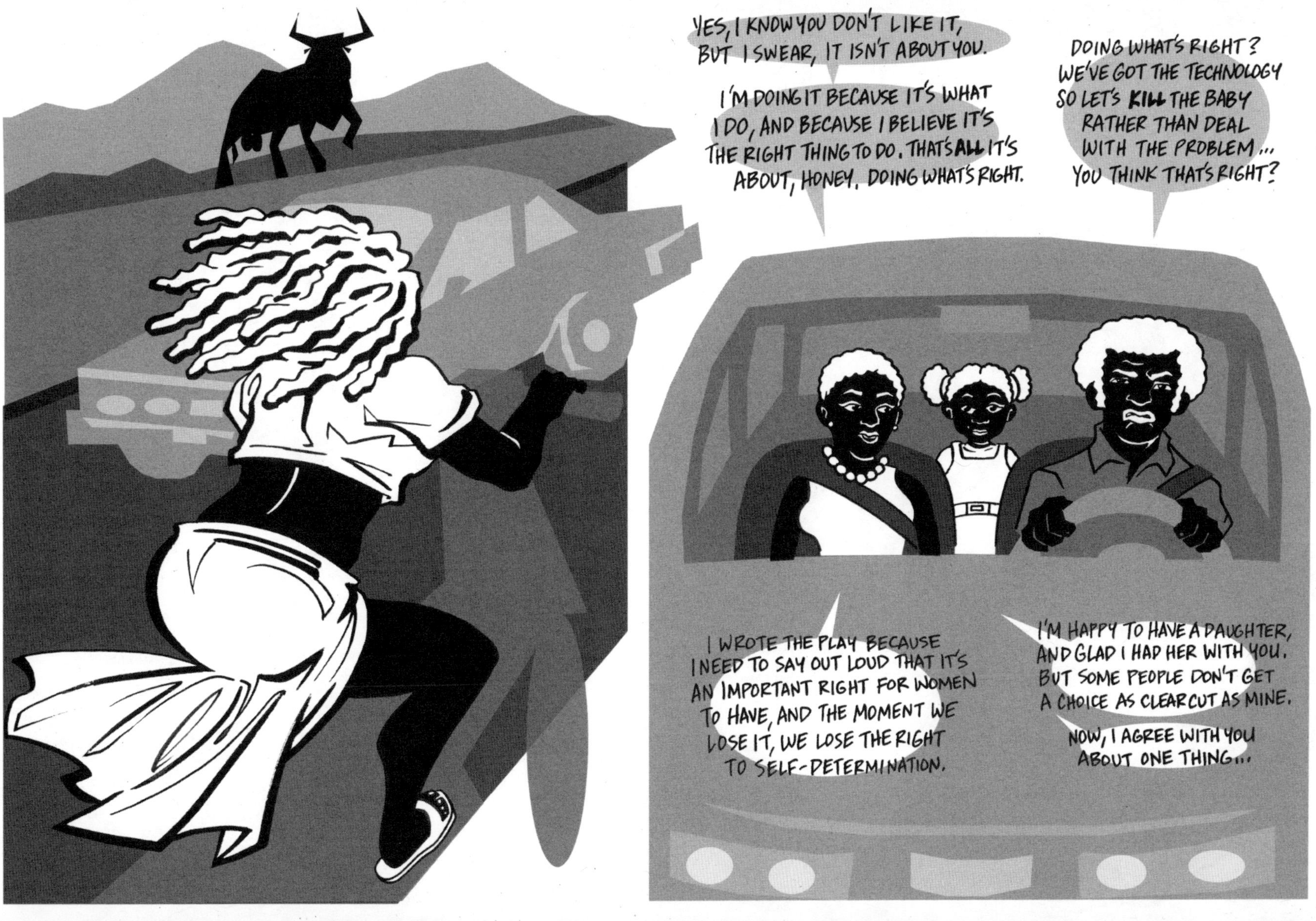
YES, I KNOW YOU DON'T LIKE IT, BUT I SWEAR, IT ISN'T ABOUT YOU.
I'M DOING IT BECAUSE IT'S WHAT I DO, AND BECAUSE I BELIEVE IT'S THE RIGHT THING TO DO. THAT'S ALL IT'S ABOUT, HONEY. DOING WHAT'S RIGHT.
DOING WHAT'S RIGHT? WE'VE GOT THE TECHNOLOGY SO LET'S KILL THE BABY RATHER THAN DEAL WITH THE PROBLEM... YOU THINK THAT'S RIGHT?
I WROTE THE PLAY BECAUSE I NEED TO SAY OUT LOUD THAT IT'S AN IMPORTANT RIGHT FOR WOMEN TO HAVE, AND THE MOMENT WE LOSE IT, WE LOSE THE RIGHT TO SELF-DETERMINATION.
I'M HAPPY TO HAVE A DAUGHTER, AND GLAD I HAD HER WITH YOU. BUT SOME PEOPLE DON'T GET A CHOICE AS CLEARCUT AS MINE.
NOW, I AGREE WITH YOU ABOUT ONE THING...

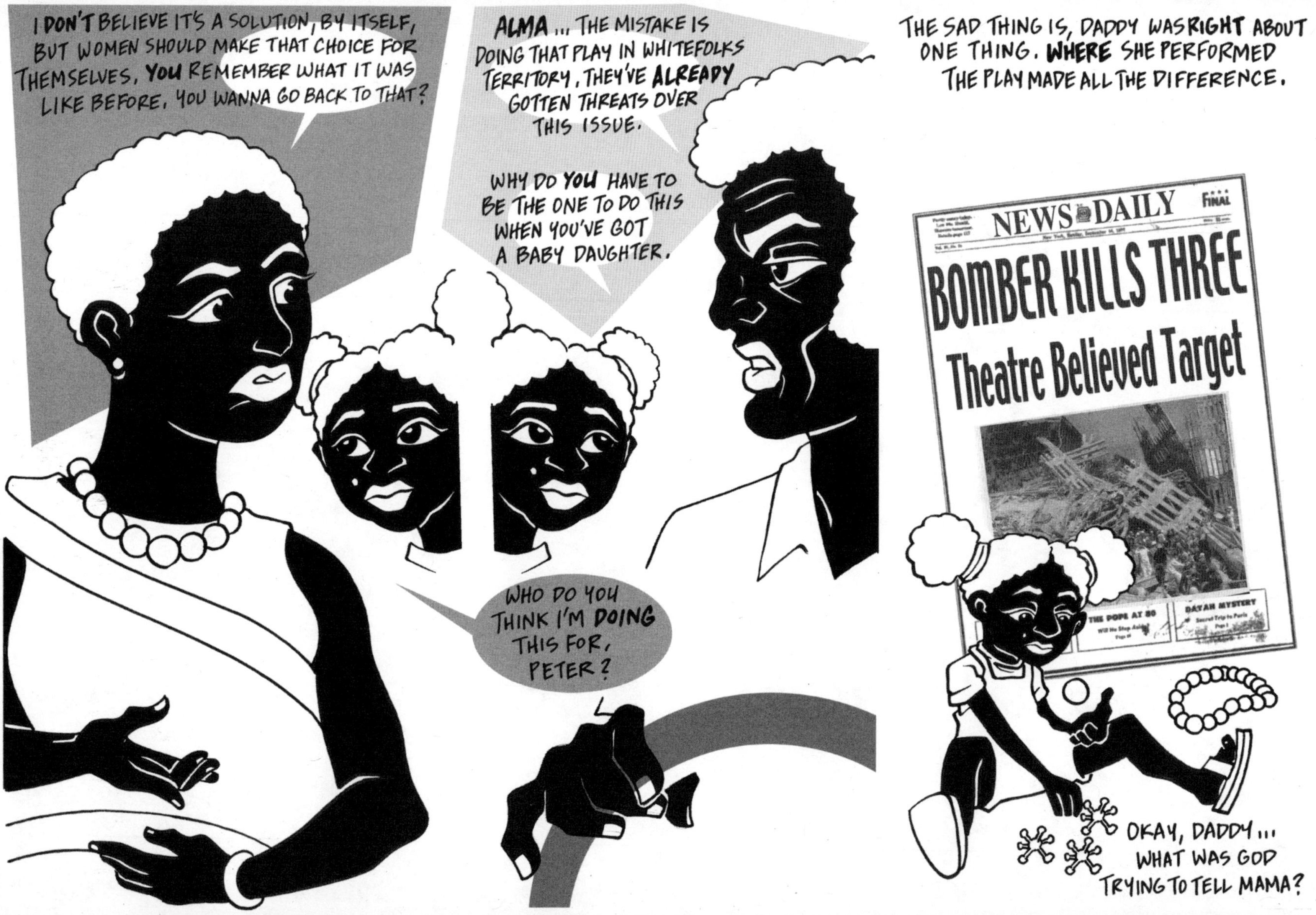

I DON'T BELIEVE IT'S A SOLUTION, BY ITSELF, BUT WOMEN SHOULD MAKE THAT CHOICE FOR THEMSELVES. YOU REMEMBER WHAT IT WAS LIKE BEFORE. YOU WANNA GO BACK TO THAT?
ALMA ... THE MISTAKE IS DOING THAT PLAY IN WHITEFOLKS TERRITORY. THEY'VE ALREADY GOTTEN THREATS OVER THIS ISSUE.
WHY DO YOU HAVE TO BE THE ONE TO DO THIS WHEN YOU'VE GOT A BABY DAUGHTER.
WHO DO YOU THINK I'M DOING THIS FOR, PETER?
THE SAD THING IS, DADDY WAS RIGHT ABOUT ONE THING. WHERE SHE PERFORMED THE PLAY MADE ALL THE DIFFERENCE.
NEWS DAILY
FINAL
BOMBER KILLS THREE
Theatre Believed Target
THE POPE AT 80
DAYAN MYSTERY
OKAY, DADDY ... WHAT WAS GOD TRYING TO TELL MAMA?

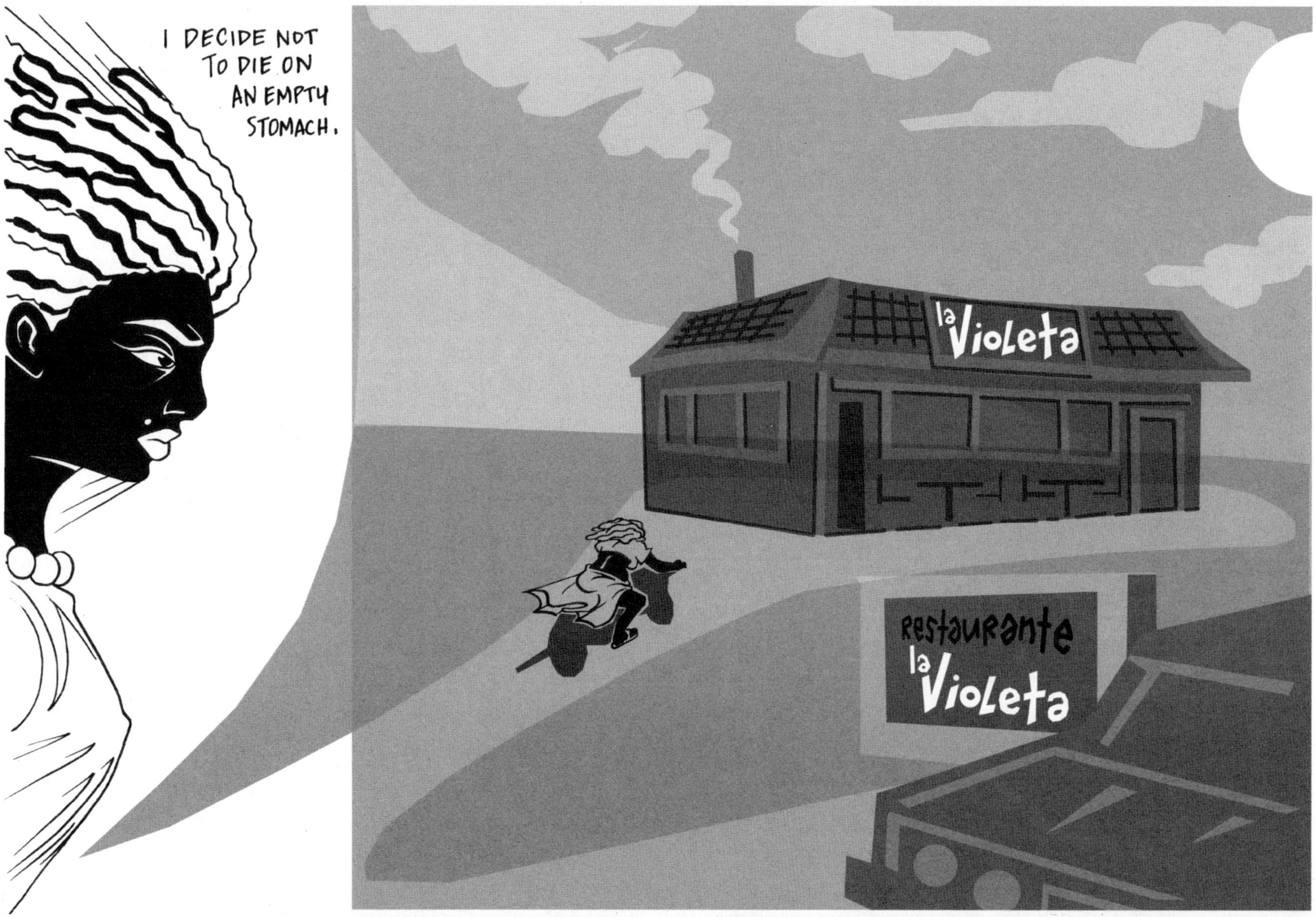
I DECIDE NOT TO DIE ON AN EMPTY STOMACH.
la Violeta
Restaurante la Violeta

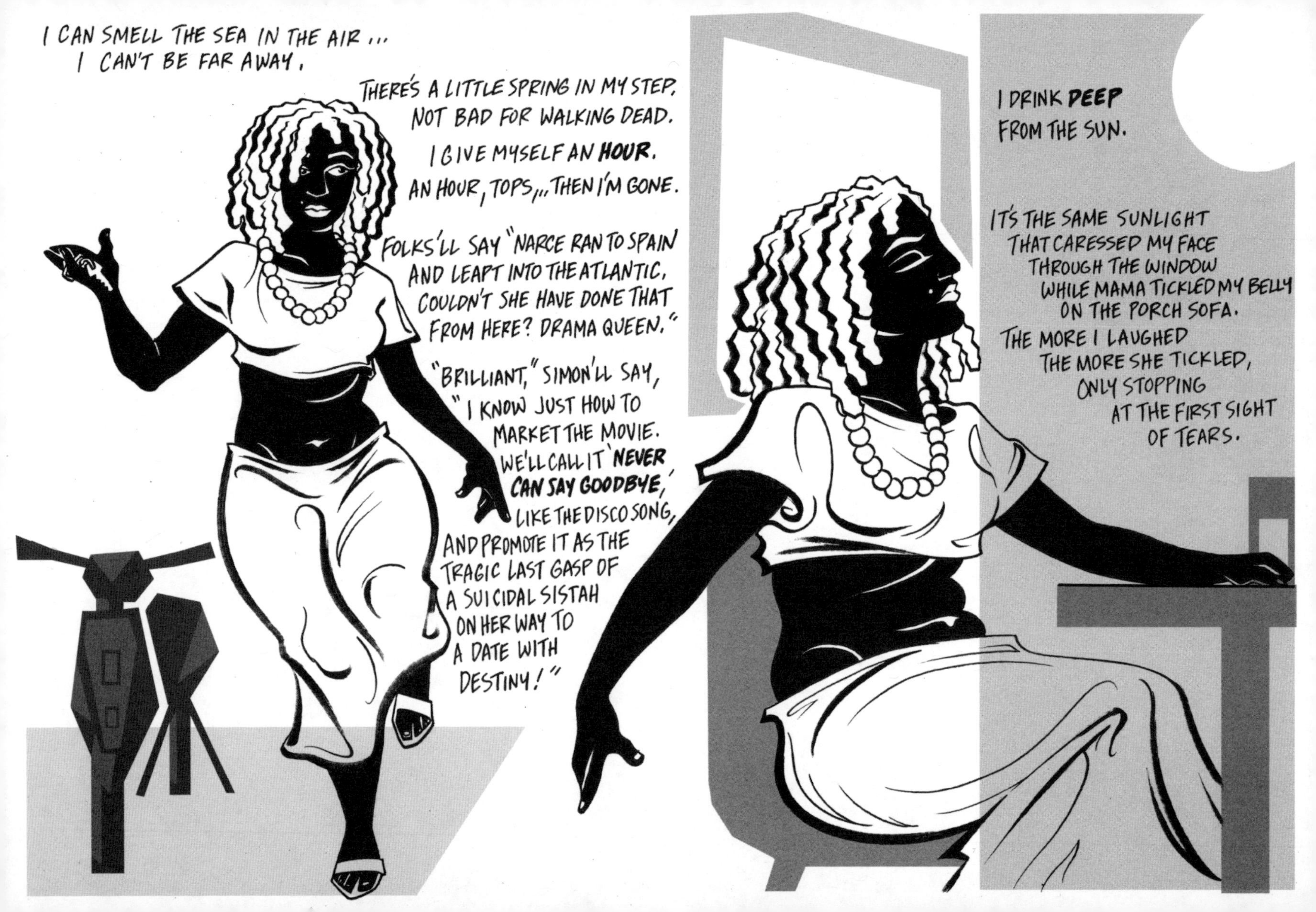
I CAN SMELL THE SEA IN THE AIR ...
I CAN'T BE FAR AWAY.
THERE'S A LITTLE SPRING IN MY STEP, NOT BAD FOR WALKING DEAD.
I GIVE MYSELF AN **HOUR**.
AN HOUR, TOPS,,, THEN I'M GONE.
FOLKS'LL SAY "NARCE RAN TO SPAIN AND LEAPT INTO THE ATLANTIC, COULDN'T SHE HAVE DONE THAT FROM HERE? DRAMA QUEEN."
"BRILLIANT," SIMON'LL SAY, "I KNOW JUST HOW TO MARKET THE MOVIE. WE'LL CALL IT '**NEVER CAN SAY GOODBYE**,' LIKE THE DISCO SONG, AND PROMOTE IT AS THE TRAGIC LAST GASP OF A SUICIDAL SISTAH ON HER WAY TO A DATE WITH DESTINY!"
I DRINK **DEEP** FROM THE SUN.
IT'S THE SAME SUNLIGHT THAT CARESSED MY FACE THROUGH THE WINDOW WHILE MAMA TICKLED MY BELLY ON THE PORCH SOFA.
THE MORE I LAUGHED THE MORE SHE TICKLED, ONLY STOPPING AT THE FIRST SIGHT OF TEARS.

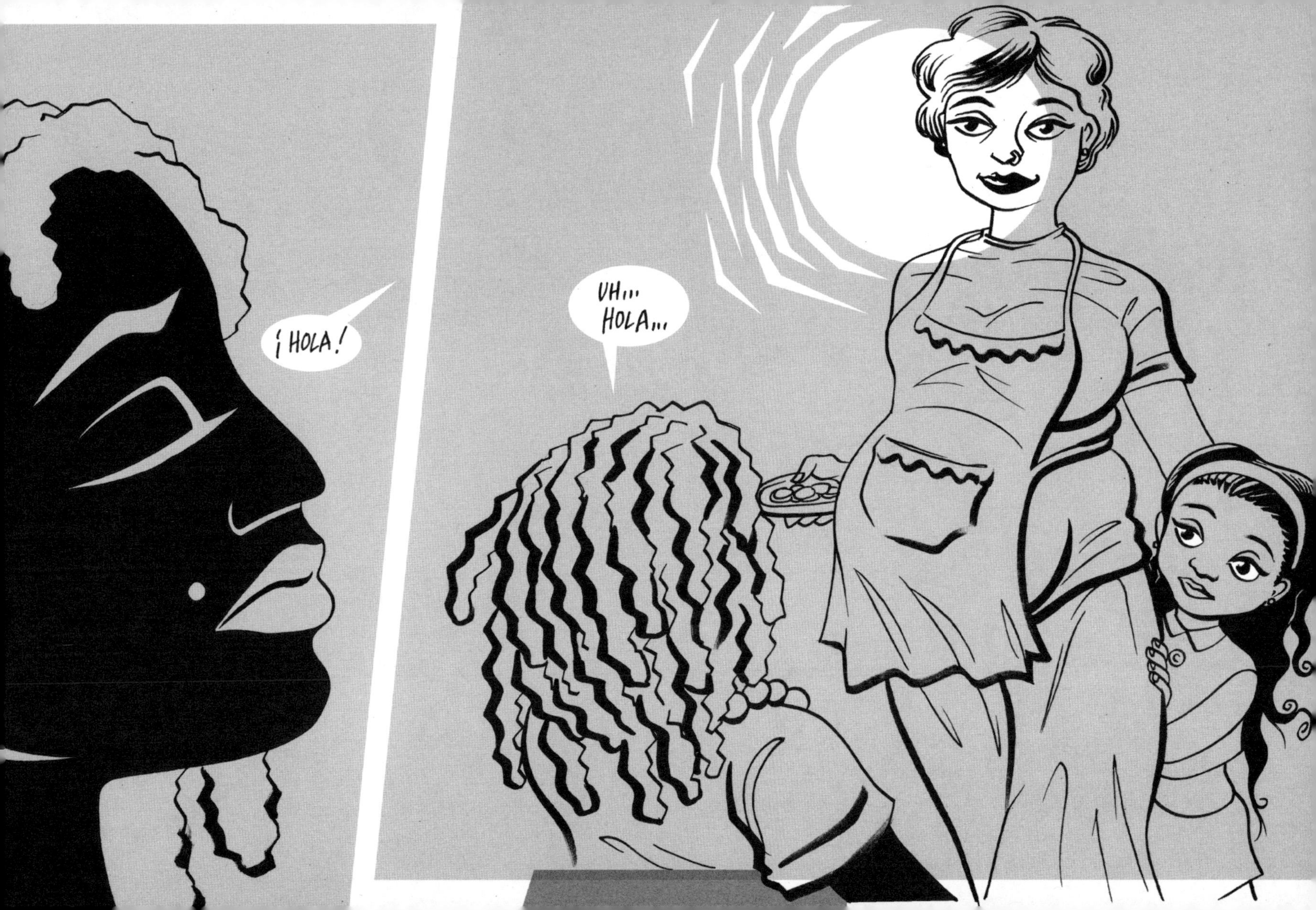
¡HOLA!
UH... HOLA...

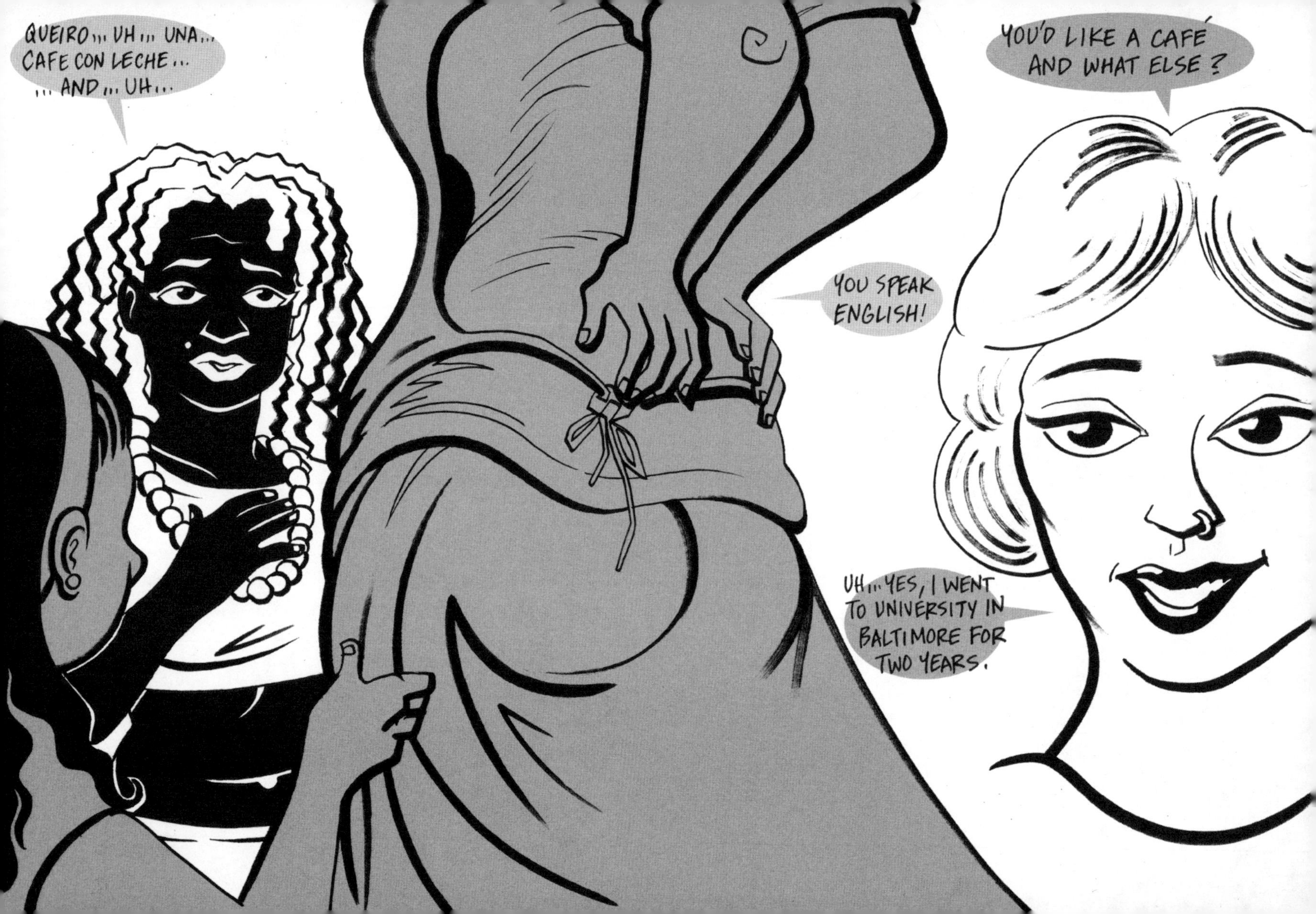
QUEIRO... UH... UNA... CAFE CON LECHE... ... AND... UH...
YOU'D LIKE A CAFÉ AND WHAT ELSE?
YOU SPEAK ENGLISH!
UH... YES, I WENT TO UNIVERSITY IN BALTIMORE FOR TWO YEARS.

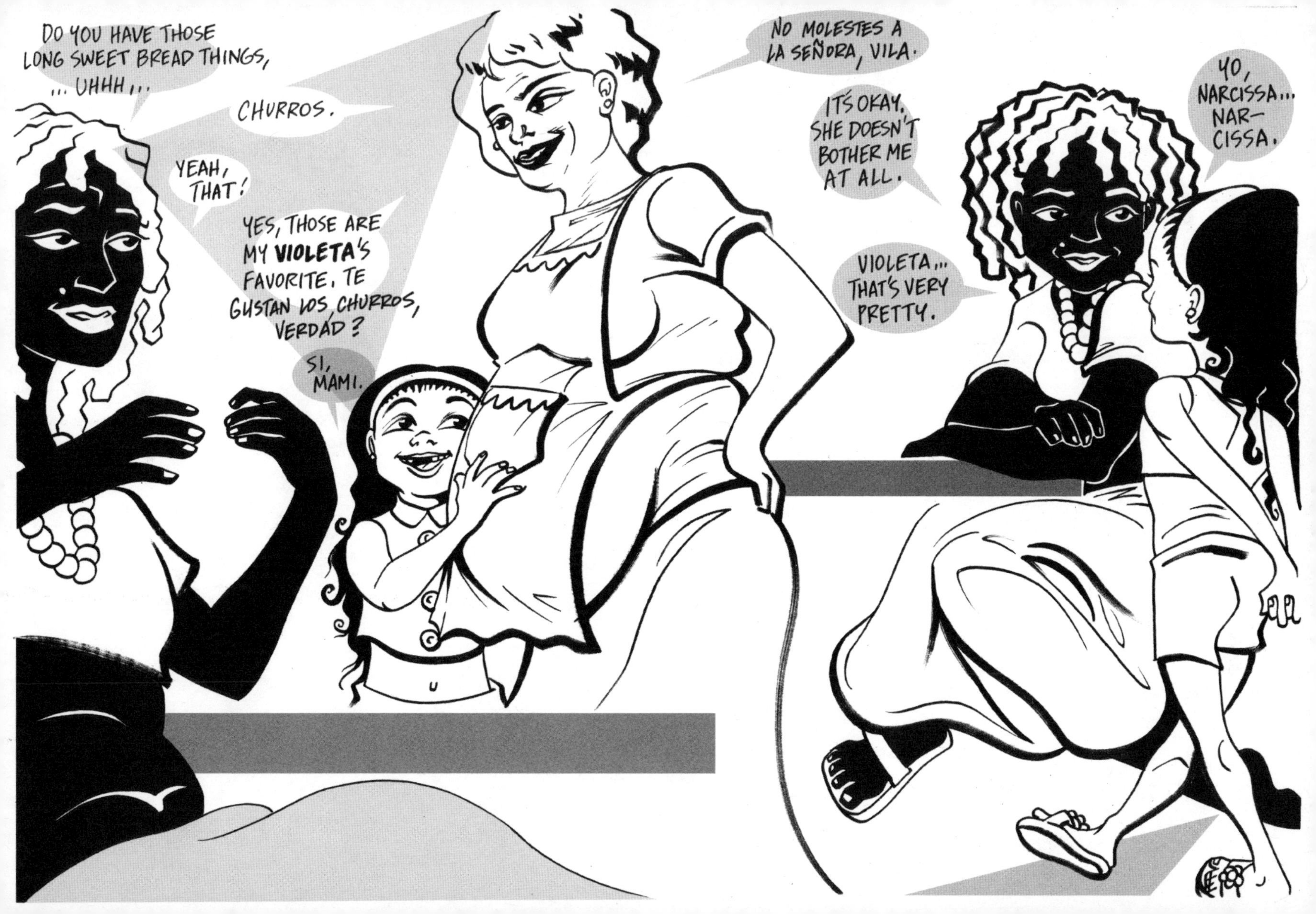
DO YOU HAVE THOSE LONG SWEET BREAD THINGS, ... UHHH ...
CHURROS.
YEAH, THAT!
YES, THOSE ARE MY **VIOLETA**'S FAVORITE. TE GUSTAN LOS CHURROS, VERDÁD?
SI, MAMI.
NO MOLESTES A LA SEÑORA, VILA.
IT'S OKAY. SHE DOESN'T BOTHER ME AT ALL.
YO, NARCISSA... NAR-CISSA.
VIOLETA... THAT'S VERY PRETTY.

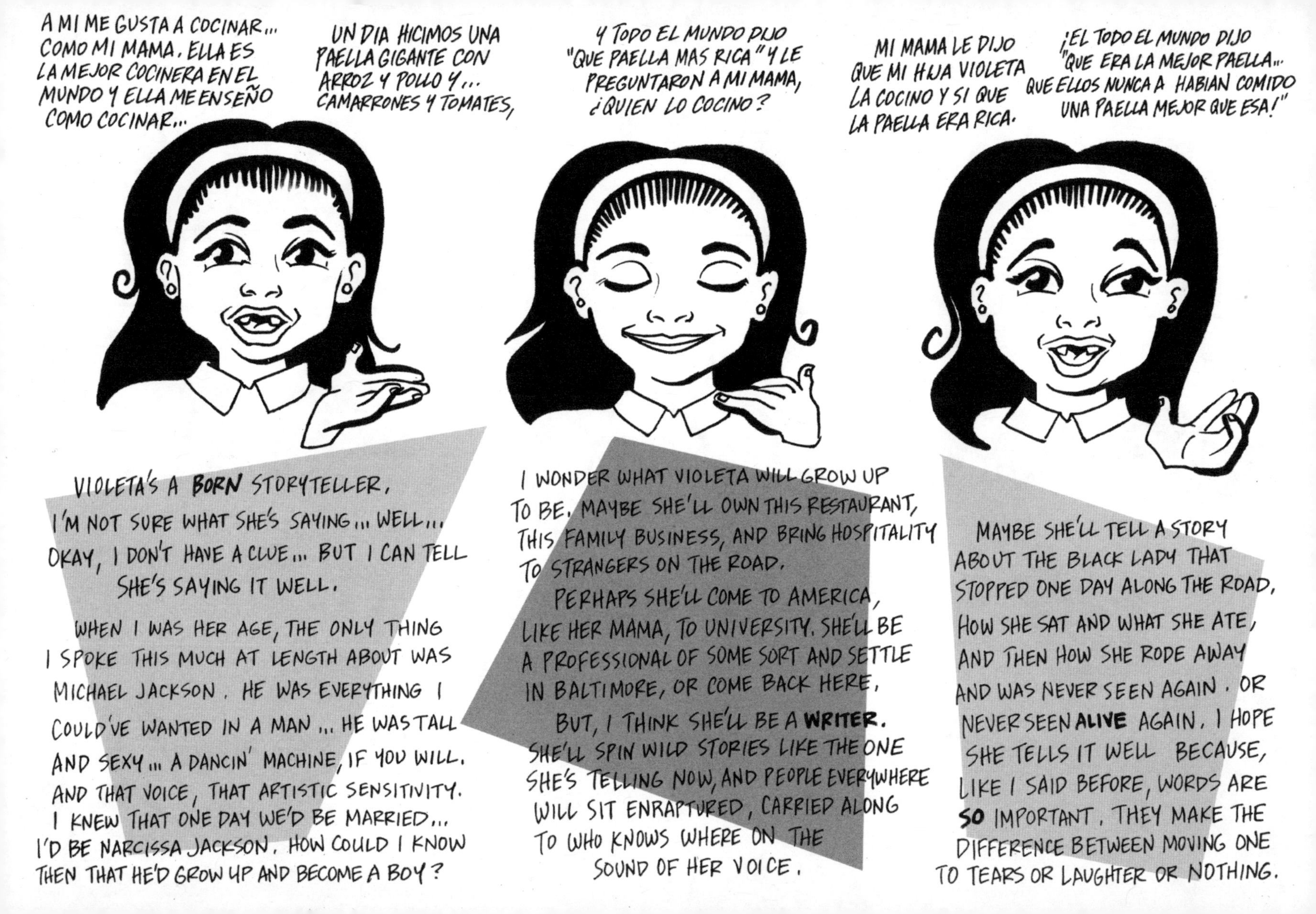

A MI ME GUSTA A COCINAR... COMO MI MAMA. ELLA ES LA MEJOR COCINERA EN EL MUNDO Y ELLA ME ENSEÑO COMO COCINAR...
UN DIA HICIMOS UNA PAELLA GIGANTE CON ARROZ Y POLLO Y... CAMARRONES Y TOMATES,
VIOLETA'S A **BORN** STORYTELLER. I'M NOT SURE WHAT SHE'S SAYING... WELL... OKAY, I DON'T HAVE A CLUE... BUT I CAN TELL SHE'S SAYING IT WELL.
WHEN I WAS HER AGE, THE ONLY THING I SPOKE THIS MUCH AT LENGTH ABOUT WAS MICHAEL JACKSON. HE WAS EVERYTHING I COULD'VE WANTED IN A MAN... HE WAS TALL AND SEXY... A DANCIN' MACHINE, IF YOU WILL. AND THAT VOICE, THAT ARTISTIC SENSITIVITY. I KNEW THAT ONE DAY WE'D BE MARRIED... I'D BE NARCISSA JACKSON. HOW COULD I KNOW THEN THAT HE'D GROW UP AND BECOME A BOY?
Y TODO EL MUNDO DIJO "QUE PAELLA MAS RICA" Y LE PREGUNTARON A MI MAMA, ¿QUIEN LO COCINO?
I WONDER WHAT VIOLETA WILL GROW UP TO BE. MAYBE SHE'LL OWN THIS RESTAURANT, THIS FAMILY BUSINESS, AND BRING HOSPITALITY TO STRANGERS ON THE ROAD.
PERHAPS SHE'LL COME TO AMERICA, LIKE HER MAMA, TO UNIVERSITY. SHE'LL BE A PROFESSIONAL OF SOME SORT AND SETTLE IN BALTIMORE, OR COME BACK HERE.
BUT, I THINK SHE'LL BE A **WRITER**. SHE'LL SPIN WILD STORIES LIKE THE ONE SHE'S TELLING NOW, AND PEOPLE EVERYWHERE WILL SIT ENRAPTURED, CARRIED ALONG TO WHO KNOWS WHERE ON THE SOUND OF HER VOICE.
MI MAMA LE DIJO QUE MI HIJA VIOLETA LA COCINO Y SI QUE LA PAELLA ERA RICA.
¡EL TODO EL MUNDO DIJO "QUE ERA LA MEJOR PAELLA... QUE ELLOS NUNCA A HABIAN COMIDO UNA PAELLA MEJOR QUE ESA!"
MAYBE SHE'LL TELL A STORY ABOUT THE BLACK LADY THAT STOPPED ONE DAY ALONG THE ROAD, HOW SHE SAT AND WHAT SHE ATE, AND THEN HOW SHE RODE AWAY AND WAS NEVER SEEN AGAIN. OR NEVER SEEN **ALIVE** AGAIN. I HOPE SHE TELLS IT WELL BECAUSE, LIKE I SAID BEFORE, WORDS ARE **SO** IMPORTANT. THEY MAKE THE DIFFERENCE BETWEEN MOVING ONE TO TEARS OR LAUGHTER OR NOTHING.

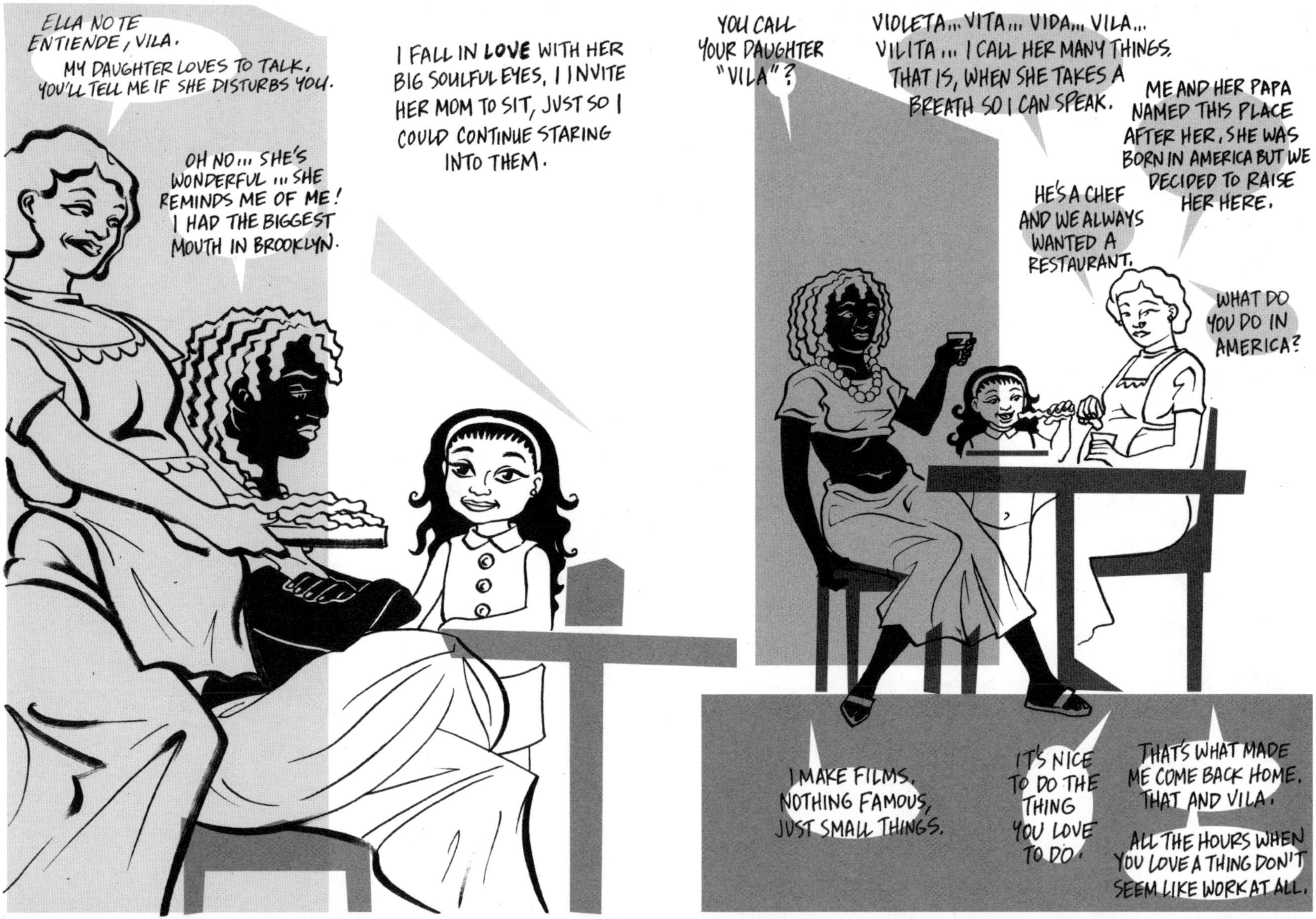
ELLA NO TE ENTIENDE, VILA.
MY DAUGHTER LOVES TO TALK. YOU'LL TELL ME IF SHE DISTURBS YOU.
OH NO... SHE'S WONDERFUL... SHE REMINDS ME OF ME! I HAD THE BIGGEST MOUTH IN BROOKLYN.
I FALL IN LOVE WITH HER BIG SOULFUL EYES. I INVITE HER MOM TO SIT, JUST SO I COULD CONTINUE STARING INTO THEM.
YOU CALL YOUR DAUGHTER "VILA"?
VIOLETA... VITA... VIDA... VILA... VILITA... I CALL HER MANY THINGS. THAT IS, WHEN SHE TAKES A BREATH SO I CAN SPEAK.
ME AND HER PAPA NAMED THIS PLACE AFTER HER. SHE WAS BORN IN AMERICA BUT WE DECIDED TO RAISE HER HERE.
HE'S A CHEF AND WE ALWAYS WANTED A RESTAURANT.
WHAT DO YOU DO IN AMERICA?
I MAKE FILMS. NOTHING FAMOUS, JUST SMALL THINGS.
IT'S NICE TO DO THE THING YOU LOVE TO DO.
THAT'S WHAT MADE ME COME BACK HOME. THAT AND VILA.
ALL THE HOURS WHEN YOU LOVE A THING DON'T SEEM LIKE WORK AT ALL.

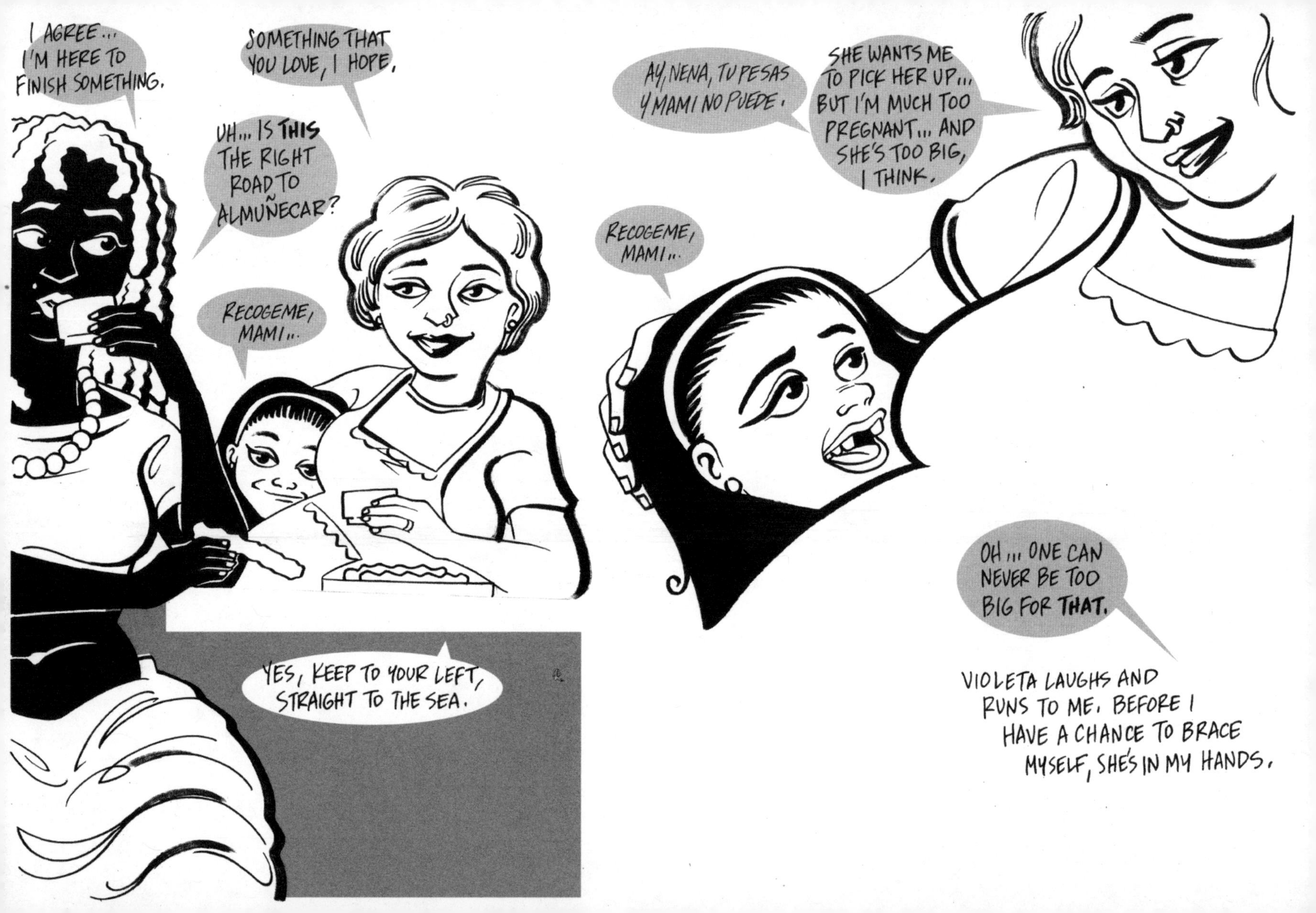
I AGREE... I'M HERE TO FINISH SOMETHING.
SOMETHING THAT YOU LOVE, I HOPE.
UH... IS **THIS** THE RIGHT ROAD TO ALMUÑECAR?
RECOGEME, MAMI...
YES, KEEP TO YOUR LEFT, STRAIGHT TO THE SEA.
AY, NENA, TU PESAS Y MAMI NO PUEDE.
SHE WANTS ME TO PICK HER UP... BUT I'M MUCH TOO PREGNANT... AND SHE'S TOO BIG, I THINK.
RECOGEME, MAMI...
OH... ONE CAN NEVER BE TOO BIG FOR **THAT.**
VIOLETA LAUGHS AND RUNS TO ME. BEFORE I HAVE A CHANCE TO BRACE MYSELF, SHE'S IN MY HANDS.

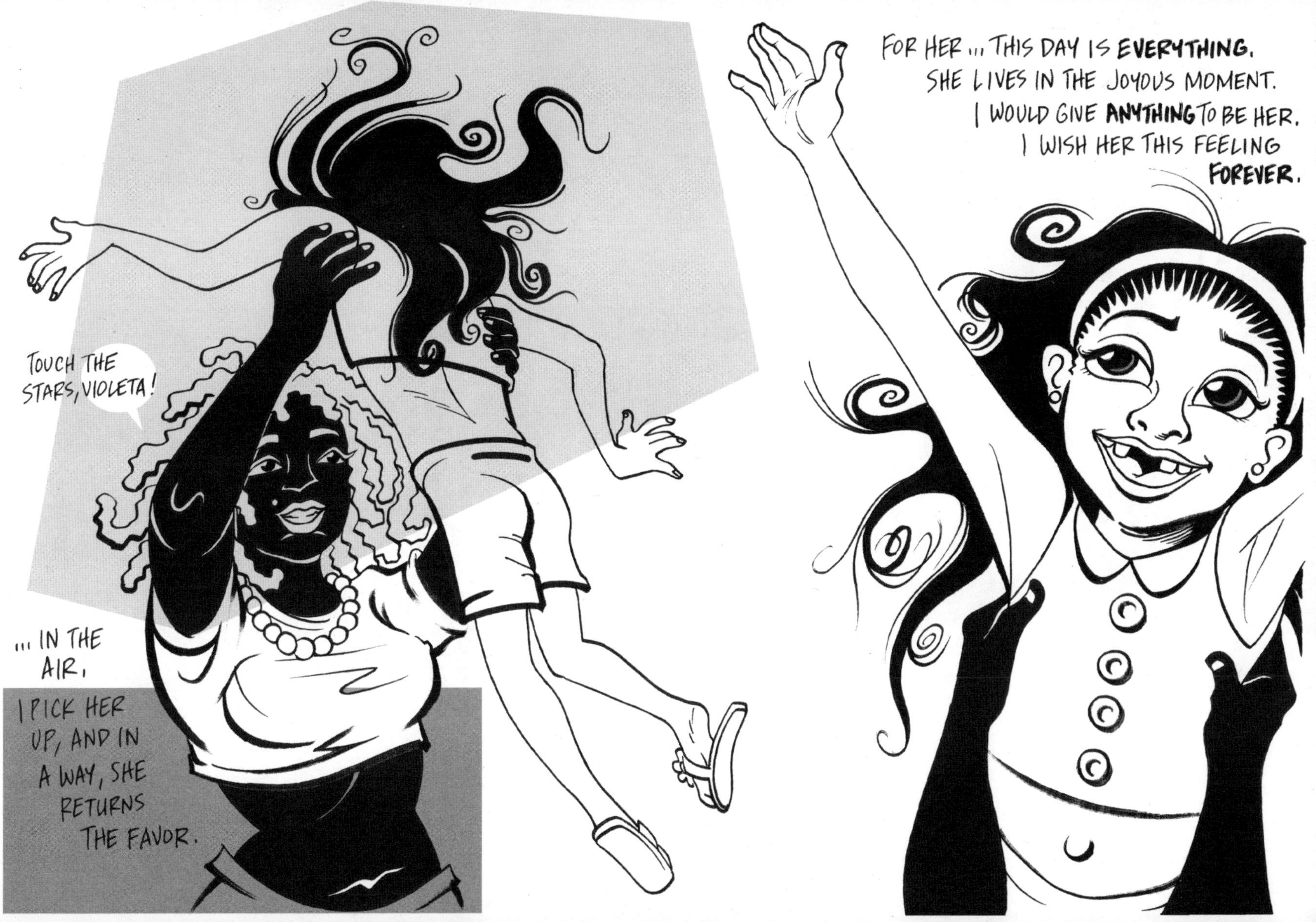
TOUCH THE STARS, VIOLETA!
... IN THE AIR.
I PICK HER UP, AND IN A WAY, SHE RETURNS THE FAVOR.
FOR HER ... THIS DAY IS **EVERYTHING.** SHE LIVES IN THE JOYOUS MOMENT. I WOULD GIVE **ANYTHING** TO BE HER. I WISH HER THIS FEELING **FOREVER.**

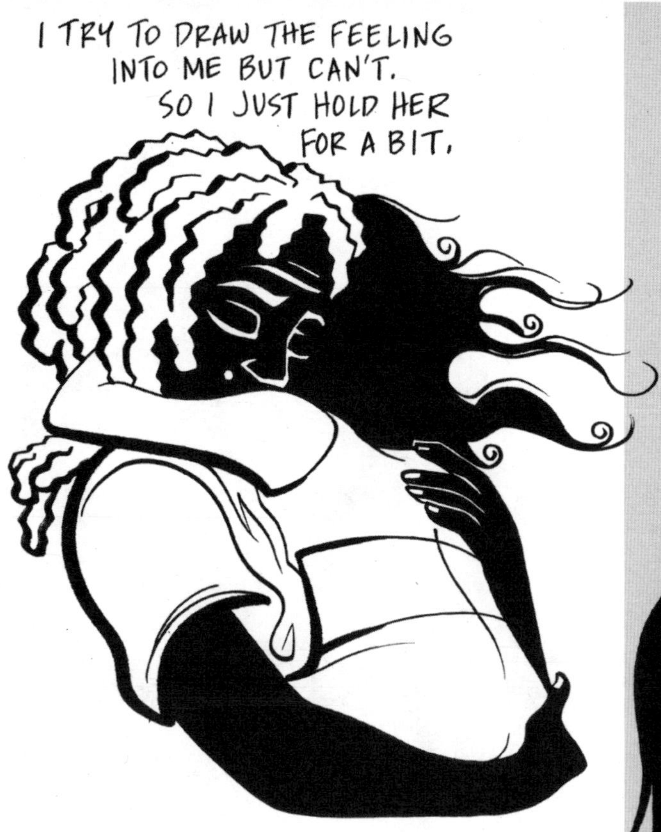
I TRY TO DRAW THE FEELING
INTO ME BUT CAN'T.
SO I JUST HOLD HER
FOR A BIT.

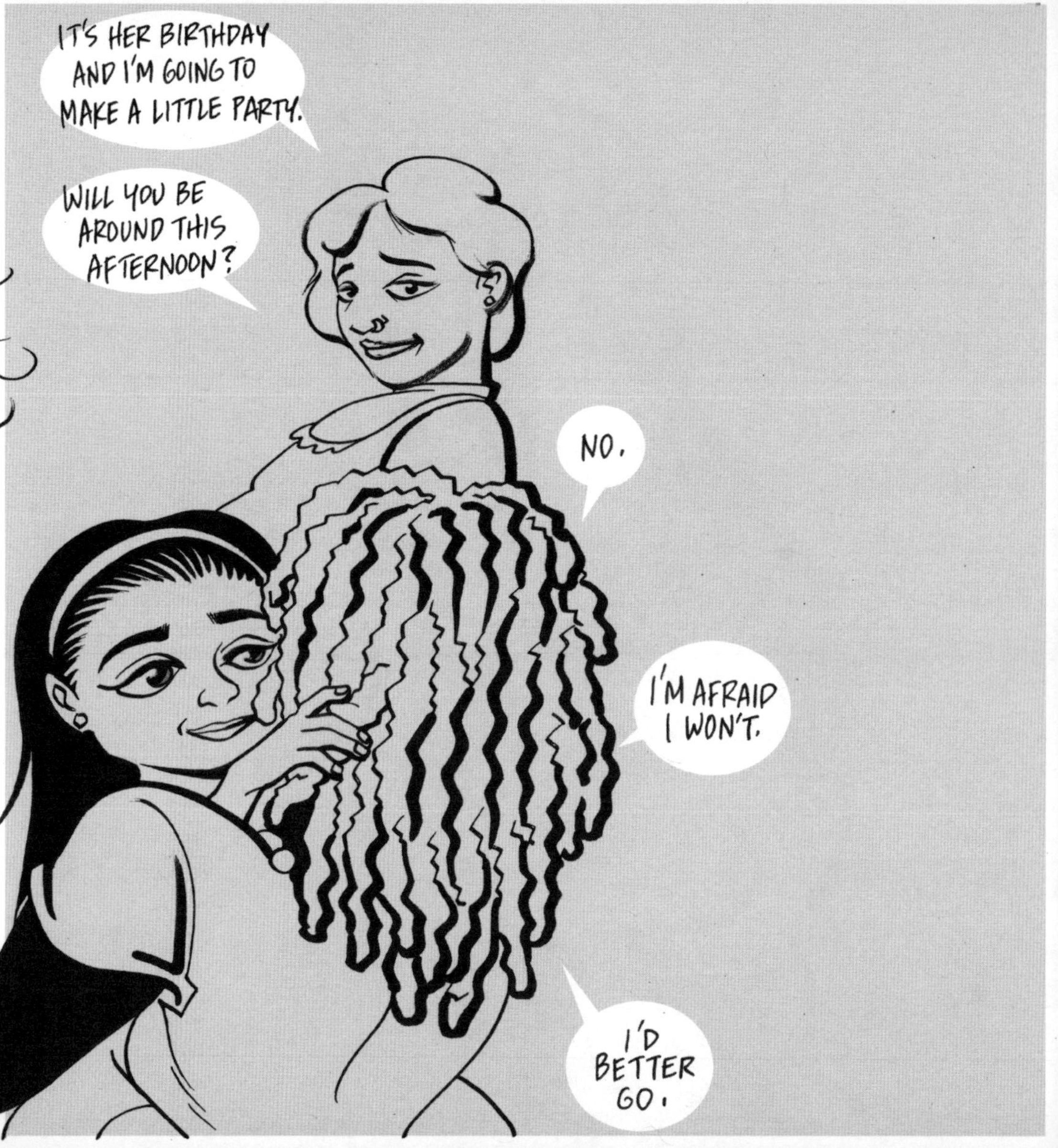
IT'S HER BIRTHDAY
AND I'M GOING TO
MAKE A LITTLE PARTY.
WILL YOU BE
AROUND THIS
AFTERNOON?
NO.
I'M AFRAID
I WON'T.
I'D
BETTER
GO.

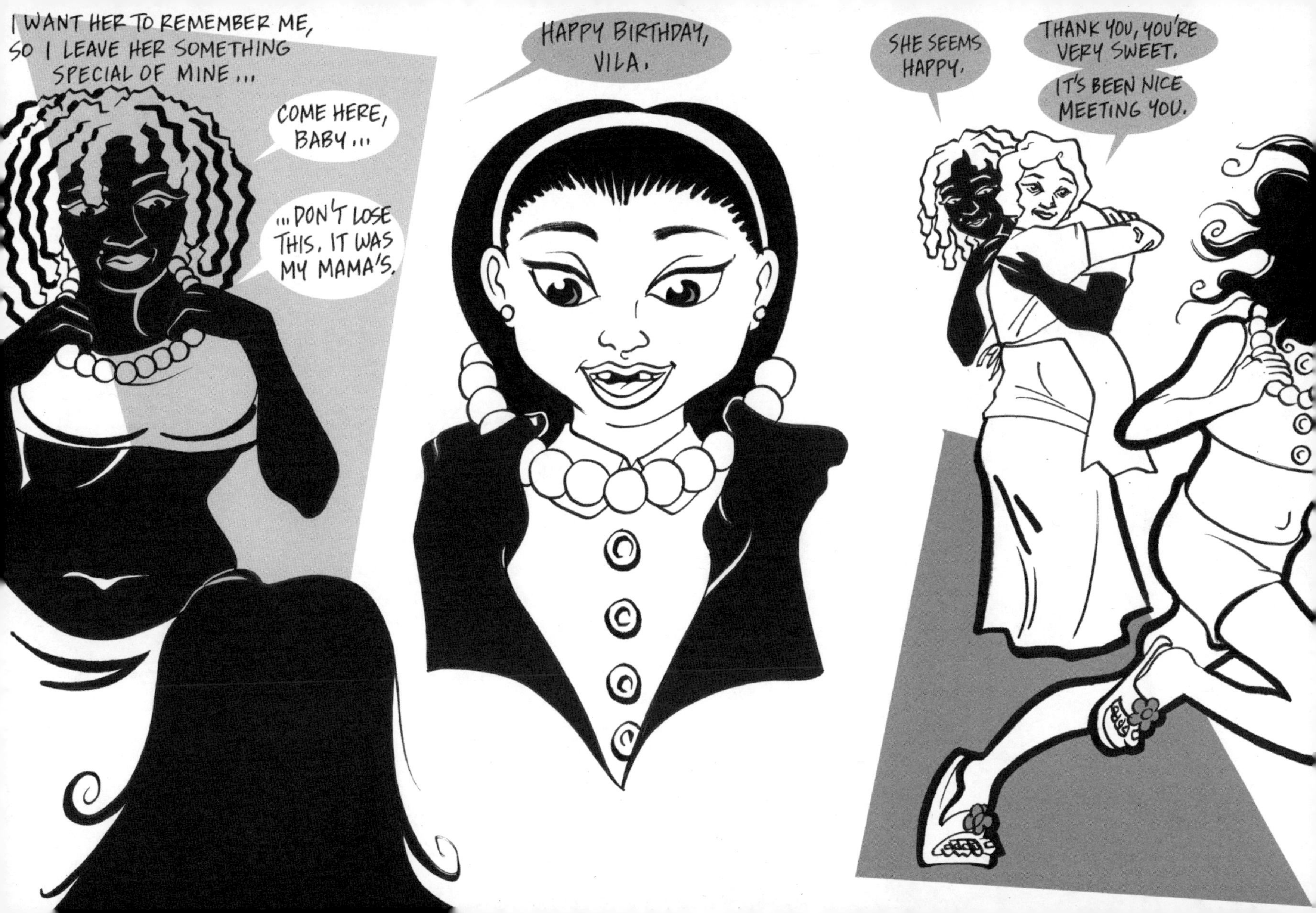

I WANT HER TO REMEMBER ME, SO I LEAVE HER SOMETHING SPECIAL OF MINE...
COME HERE, BABY...
...DON'T LOSE THIS. IT WAS MY MAMA'S.
HAPPY BIRTHDAY, VILA.
SHE SEEMS HAPPY.
THANK YOU, YOU'RE VERY SWEET.
IT'S BEEN NICE MEETING YOU.

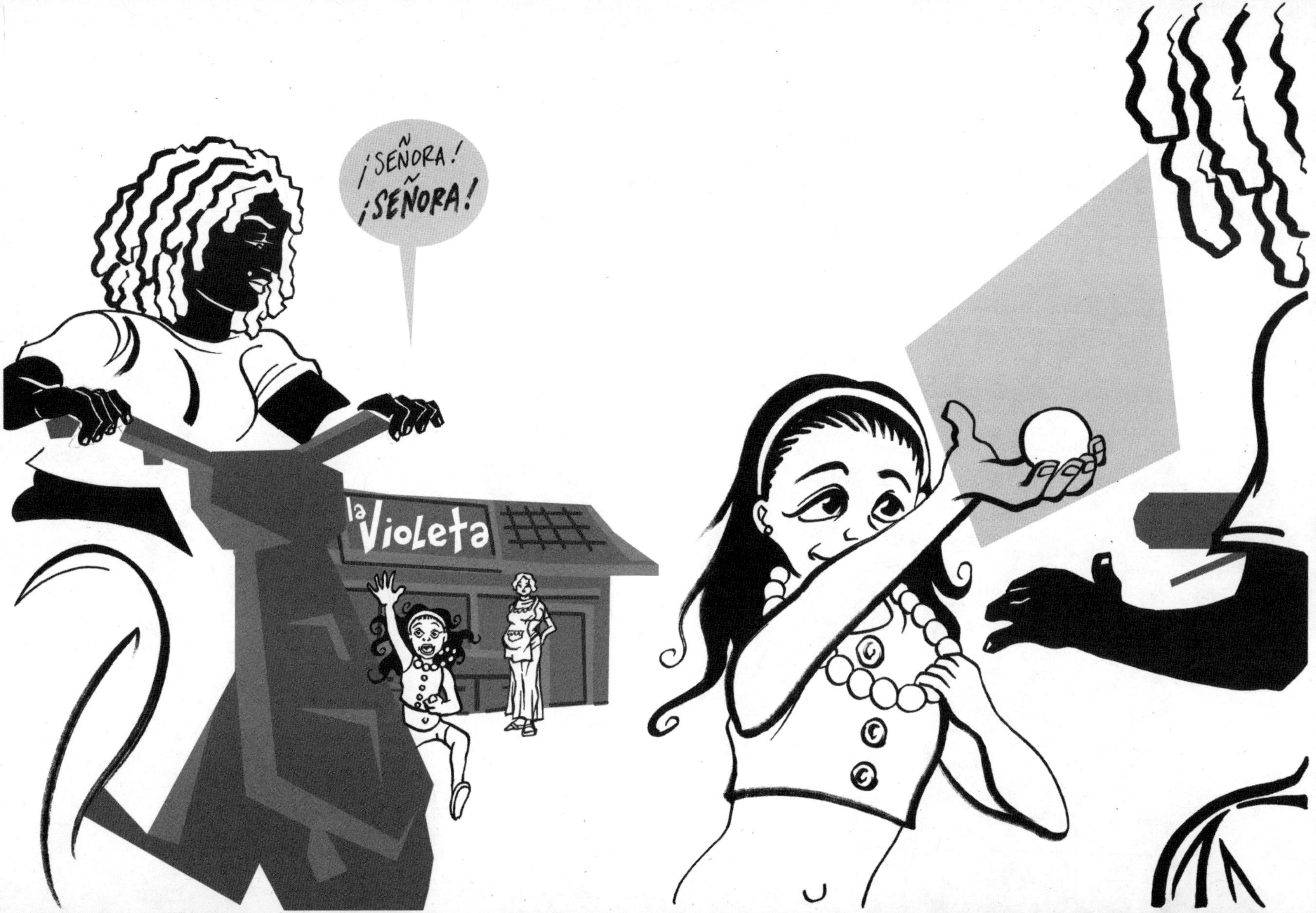
¡SEÑORA!
¡SEÑORA!
la Violeta

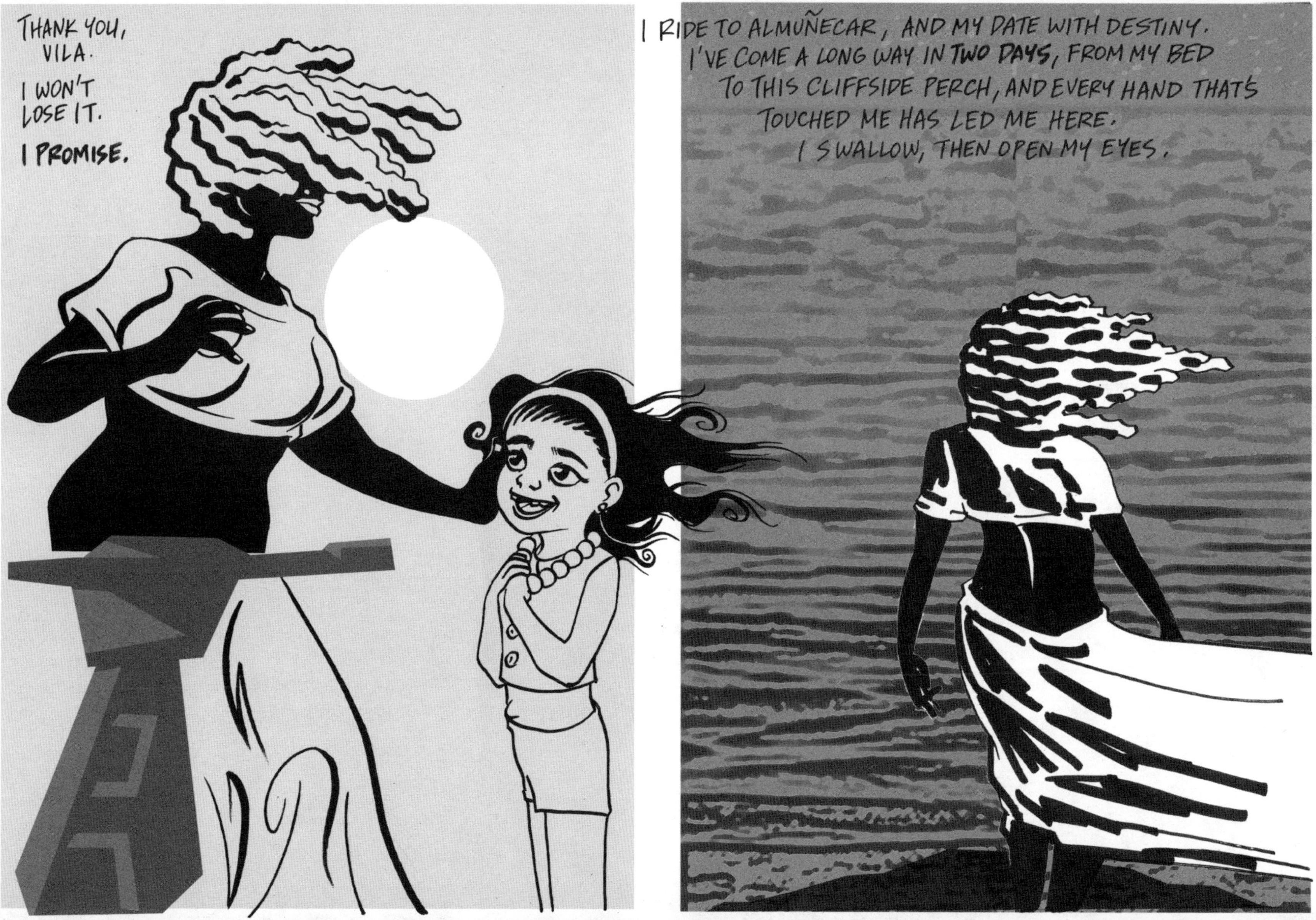
THANK YOU, VILA.
I WON'T LOSE IT.
I PROMISE.
I RIDE TO ALMUÑECAR, AND MY DATE WITH DESTINY. I'VE COME A LONG WAY IN TWO DAYS, FROM MY BED TO THIS CLIFFSIDE PERCH, AND EVERY HAND THAT'S TOUCHED ME HAS LED ME HERE. I SWALLOW, THEN OPEN MY EYES.

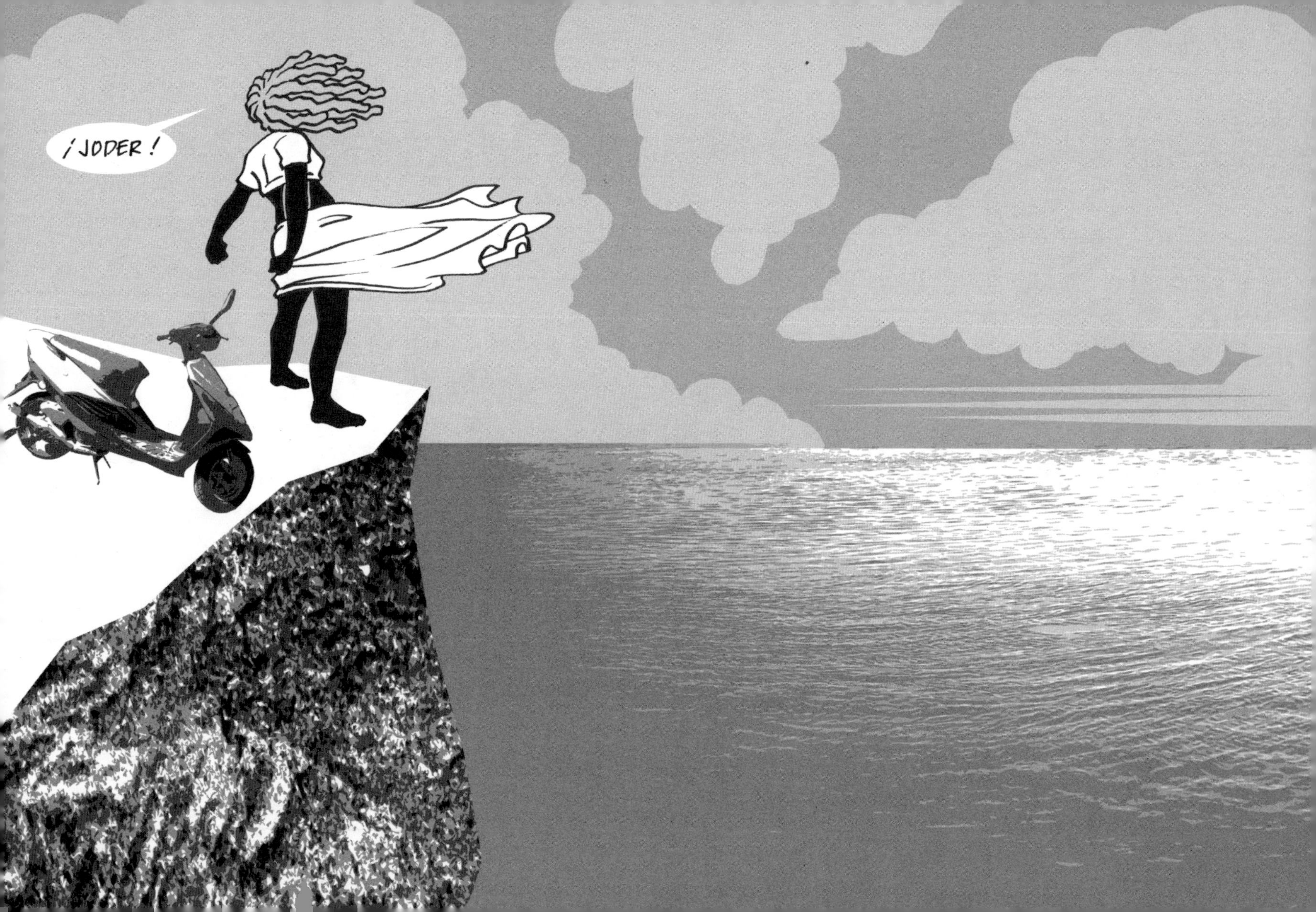
¡JODER!

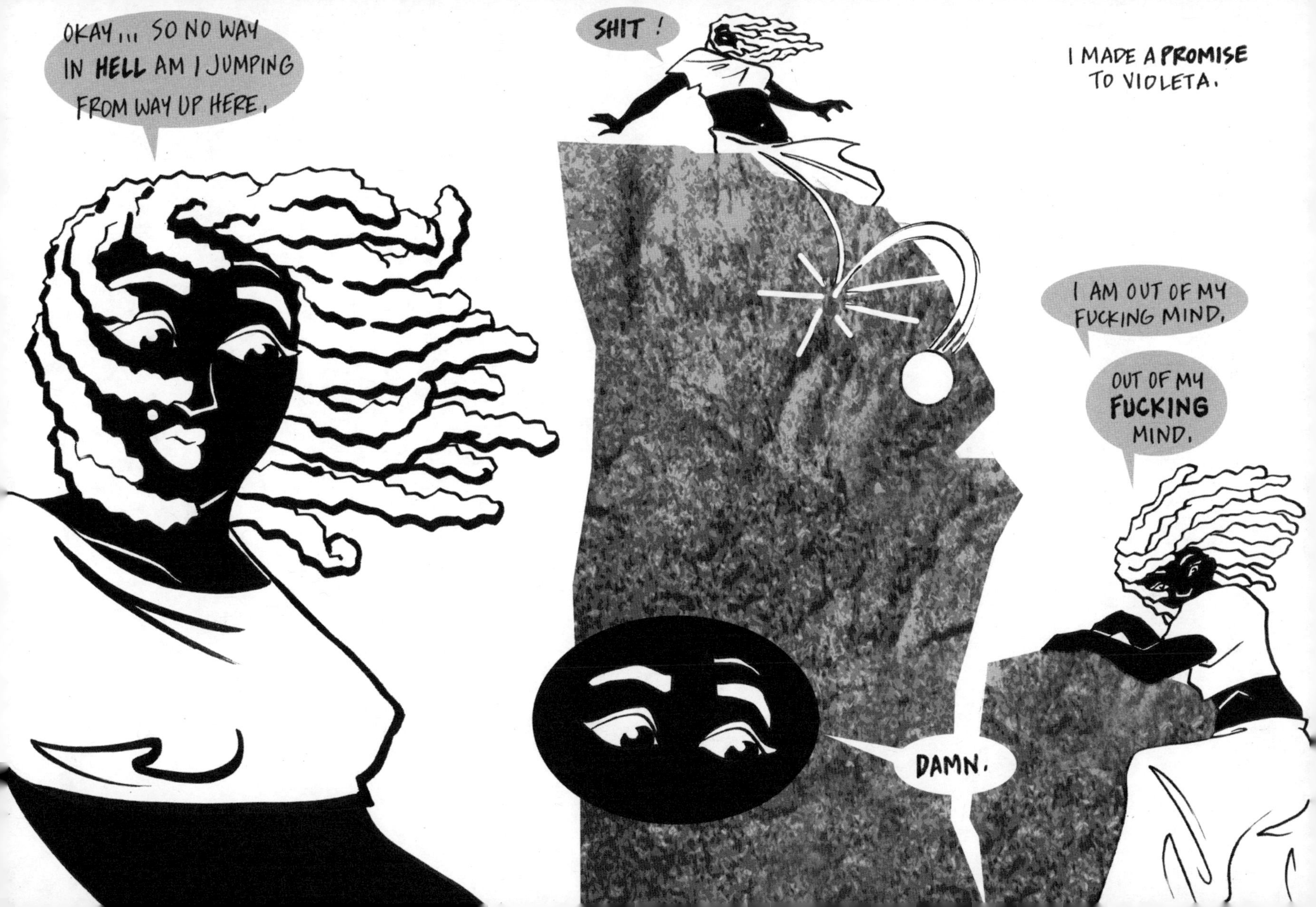
OKAY... SO NO WAY IN HELL AM I JUMPING FROM WAY UP HERE.
SHIT!
DAMN.
I MADE A PROMISE TO VIOLETA.
I AM OUT OF MY FUCKING MIND.
OUT OF MY FUCKING MIND.

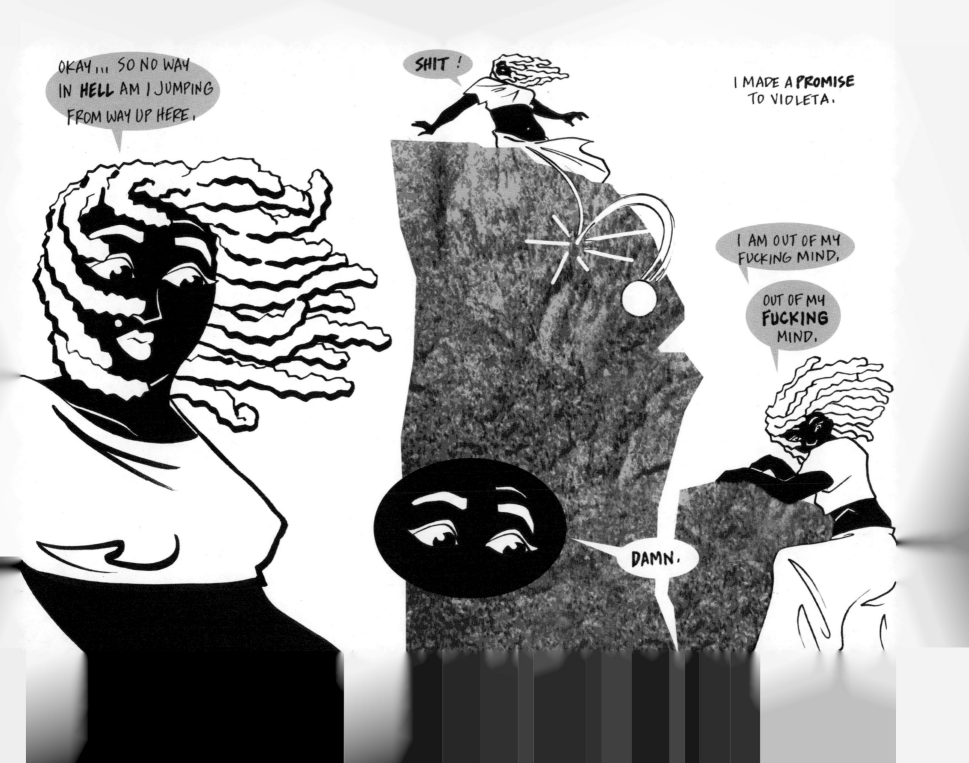

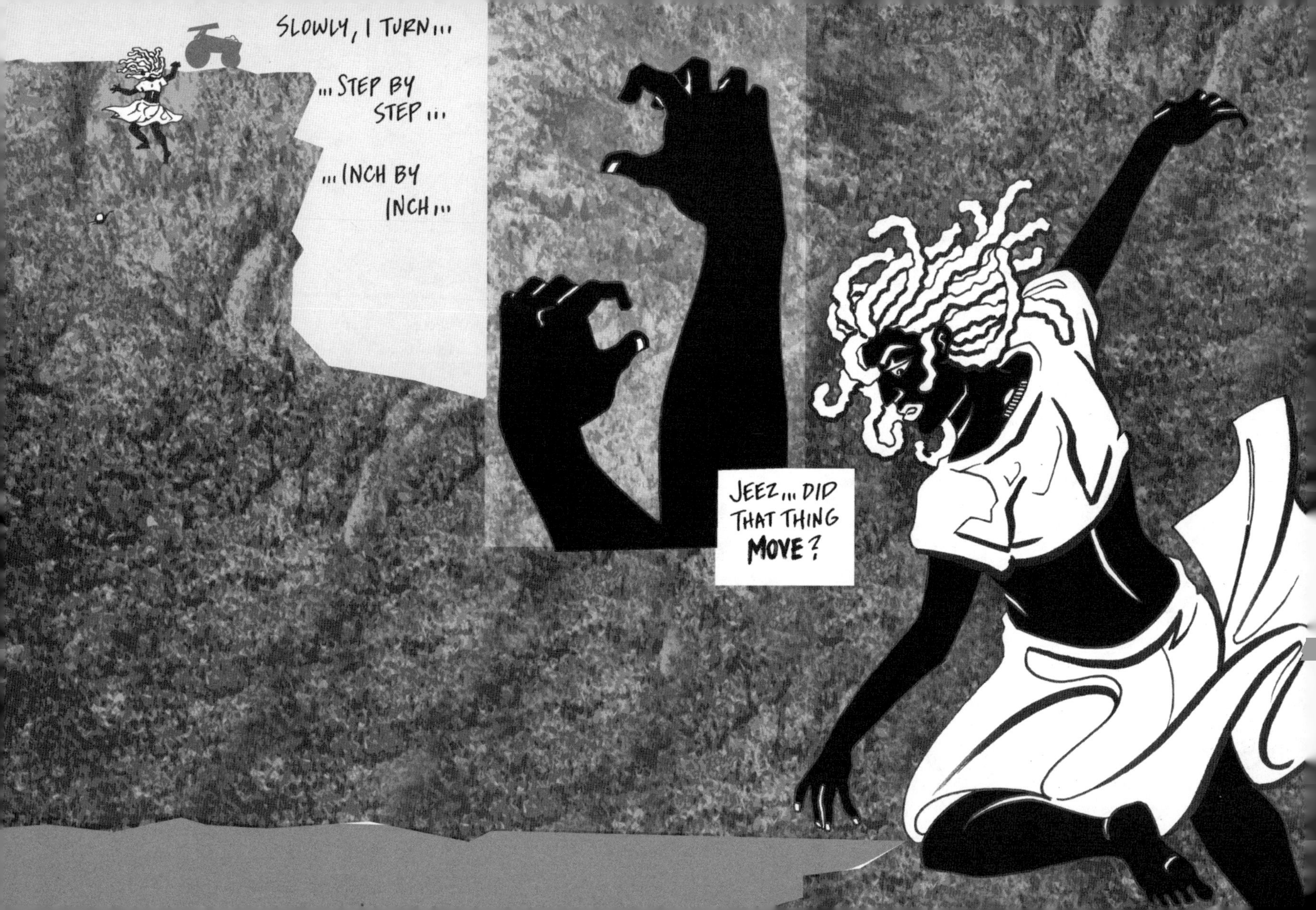
SLOWLY, I TURN...
...STEP BY STEP...
...INCH BY INCH...
JEEZ... DID THAT THING MOVE?

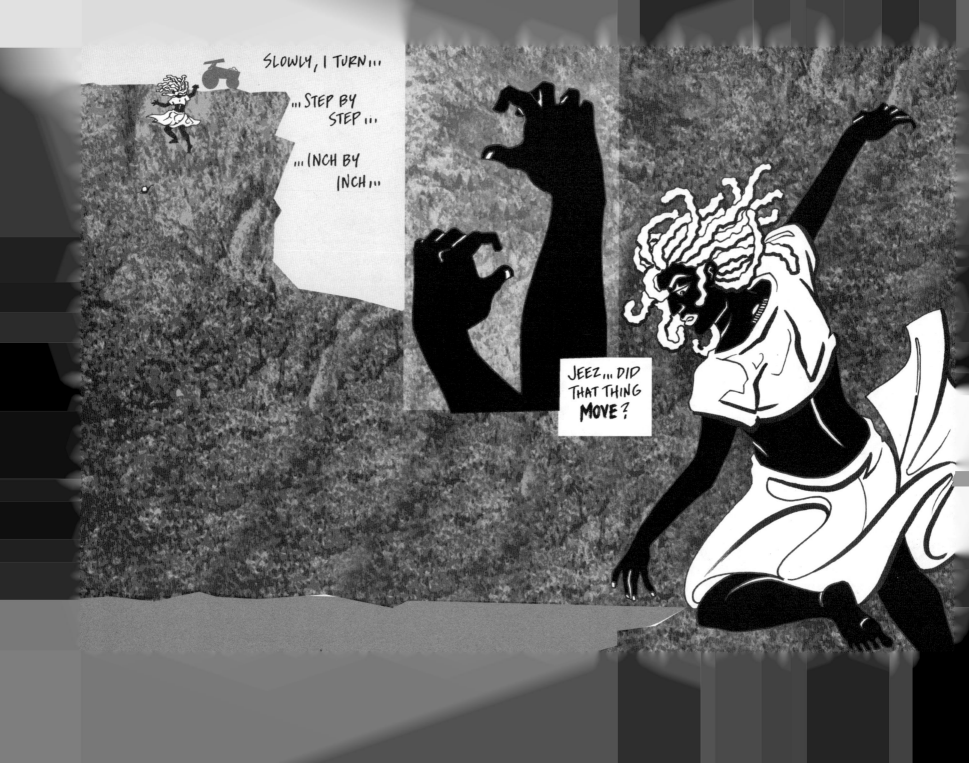

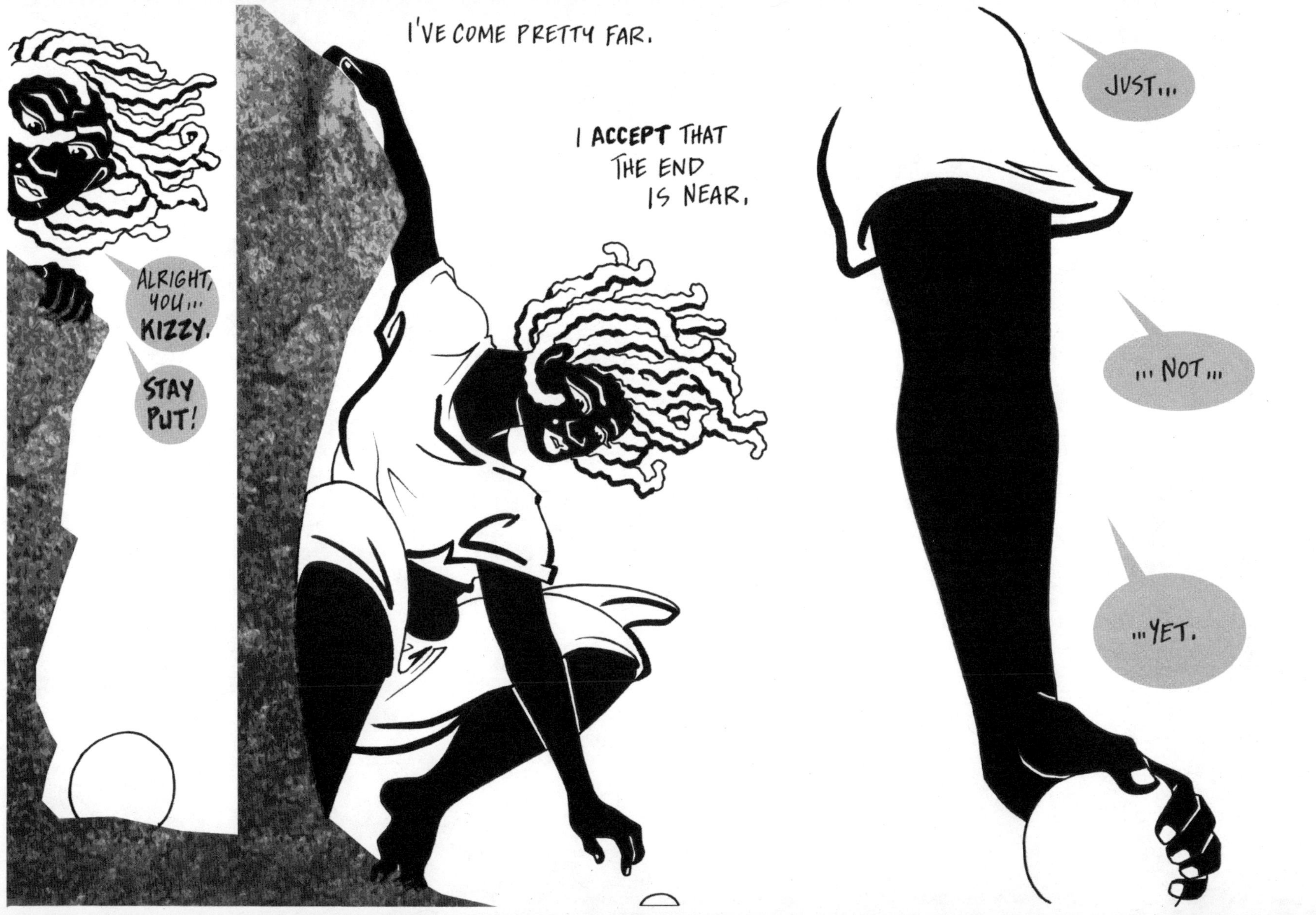

ALRIGHT, YOU... KIZZY.
STAY PUT!
I'VE COME PRETTY FAR.
I ACCEPT THAT THE END IS NEAR.
JUST...
... NOT...
...YET.

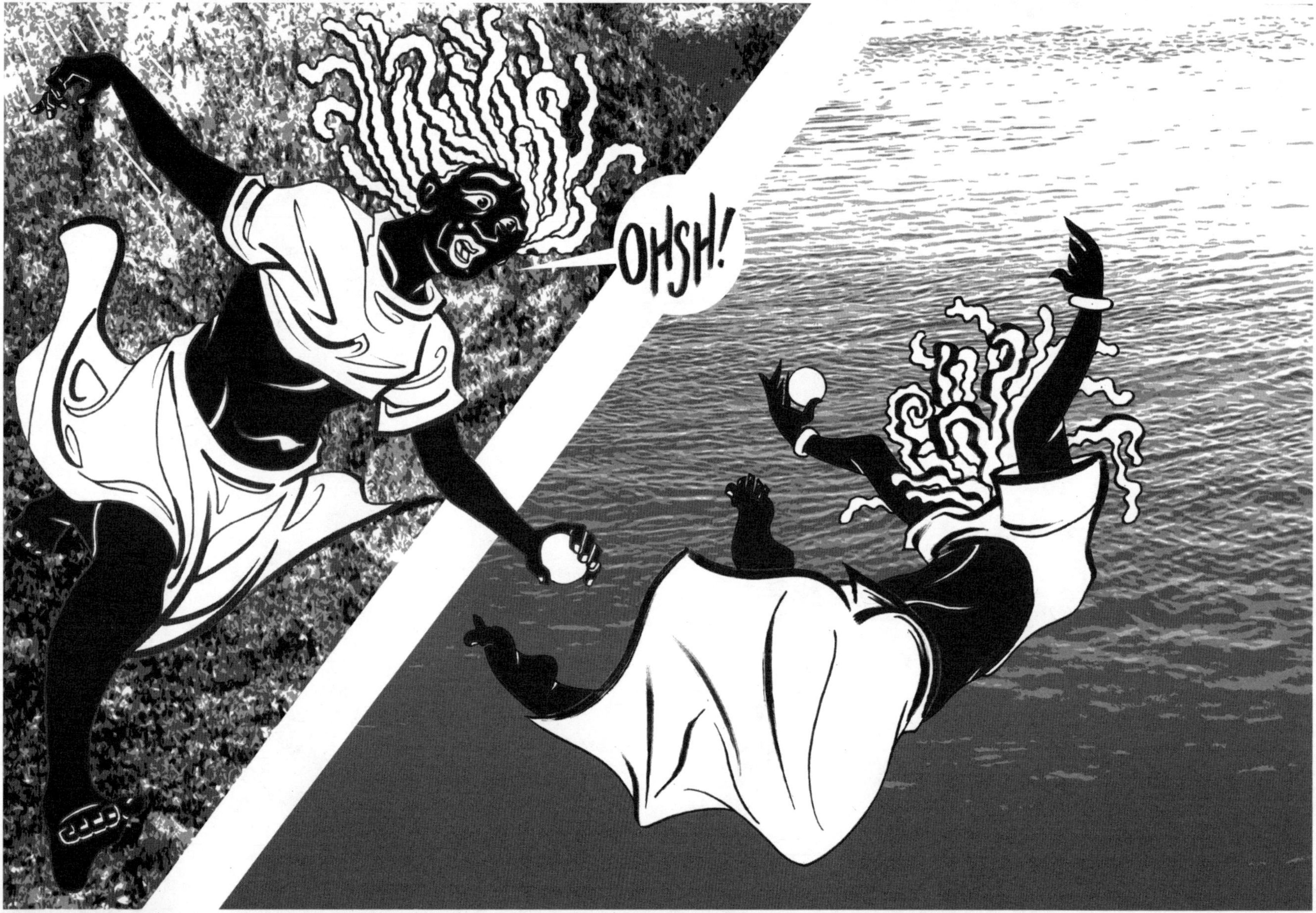
OHSH!

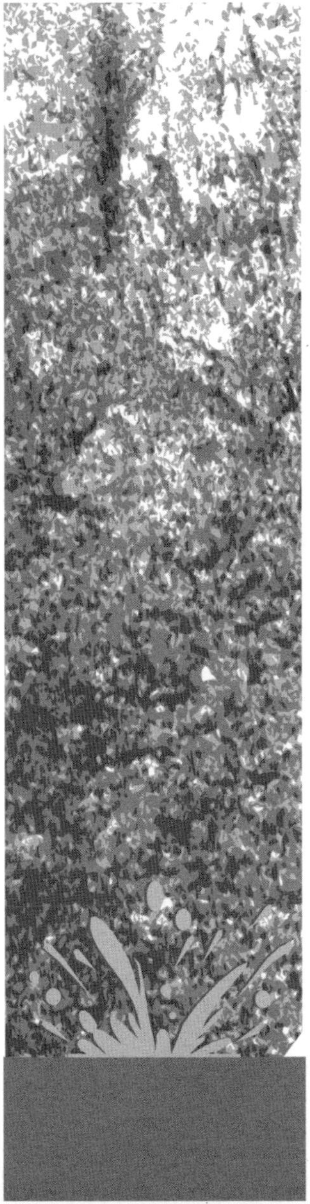

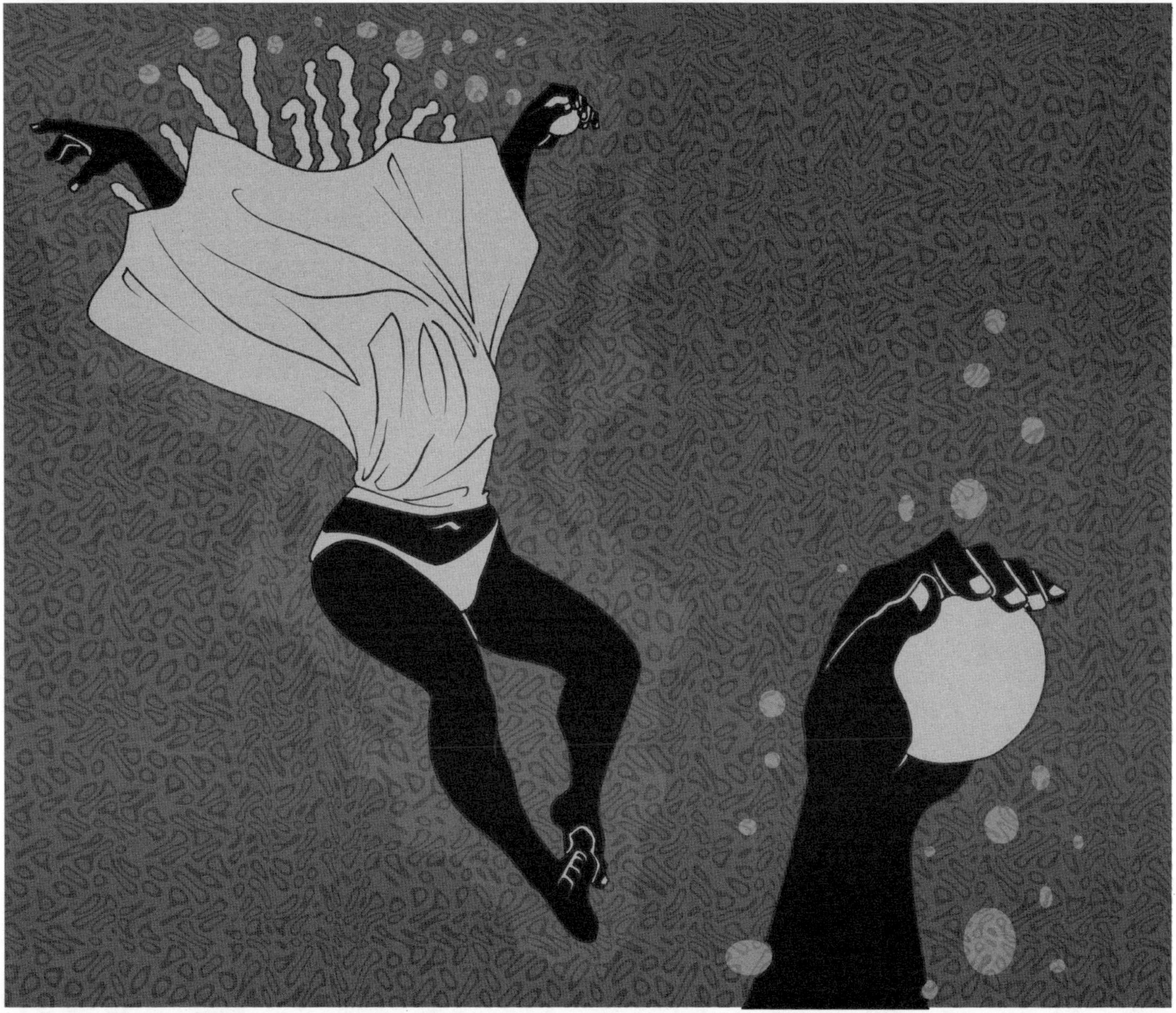

I'LL **DIE** IF I HAVE TO...

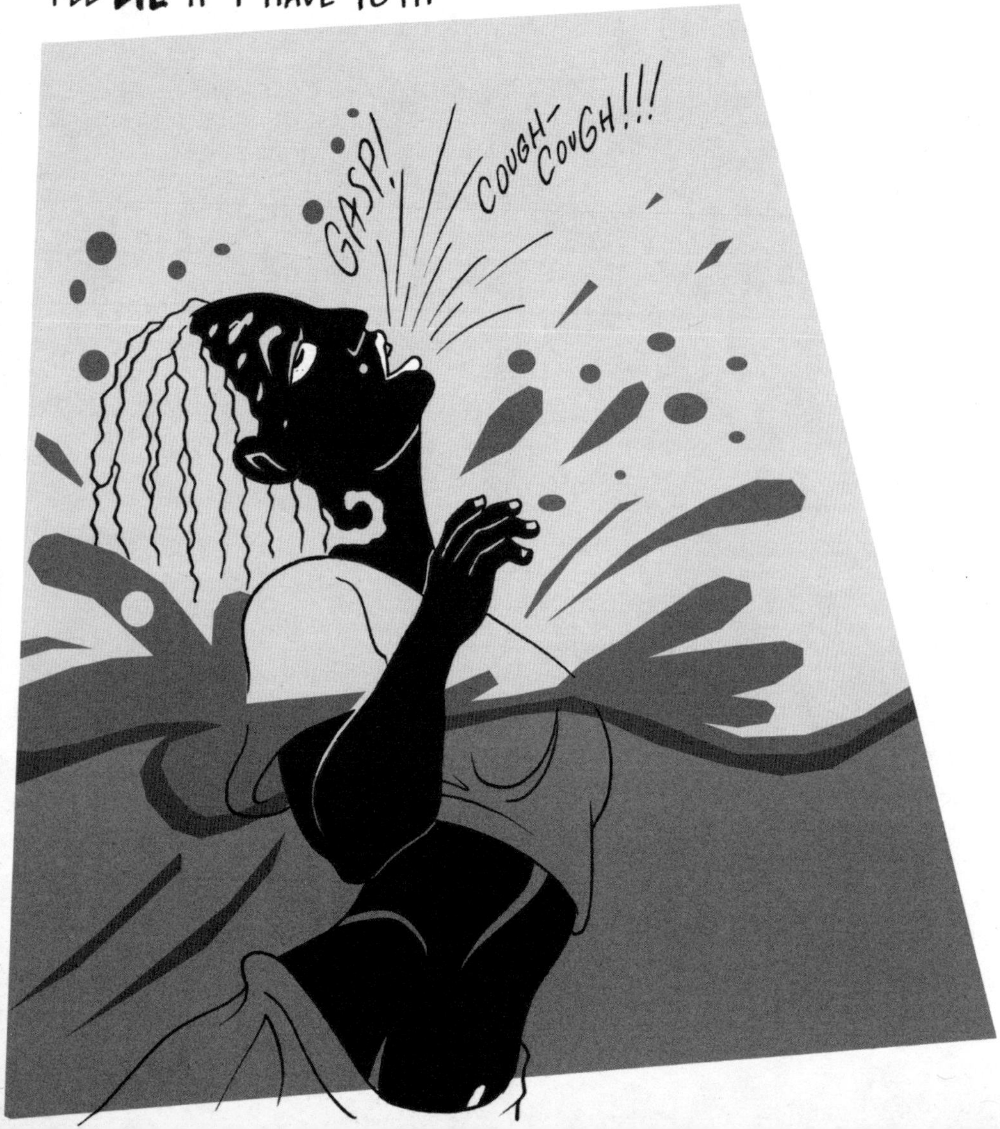
GASP!
COUGH-COUGH!!!

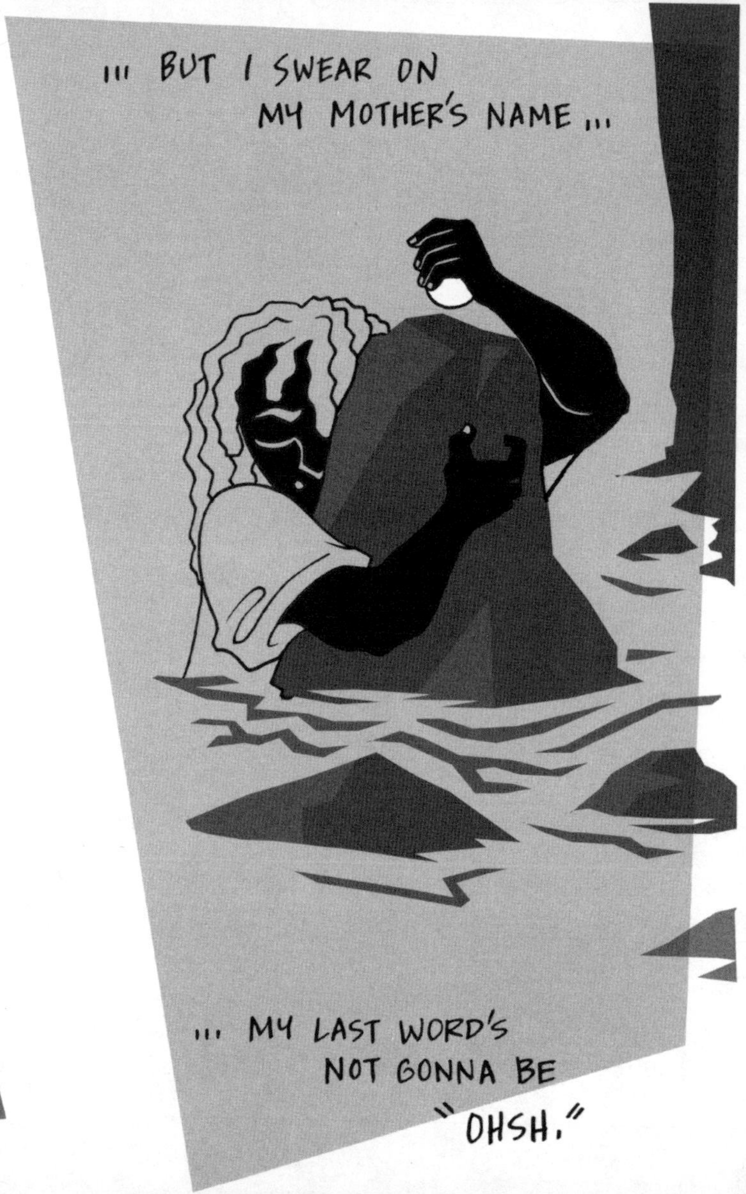
... BUT I SWEAR ON MY MOTHER'S NAME...
... MY LAST WORD'S NOT GONNA BE "OHSH."

I FEEL THE GROUND UNDER MY FEET AS I WALK, EACH STEP BRINGS ME CLOSER TO LAND.

I'M GONNA CALL MY DAD, TOUCH BASE WITH SADA... ..., AND RETURN HIS BIKE, AND KISS MY FRIEND, LILY GOODBYE.

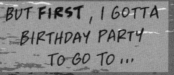

BUT **FIRST**, I GOTTA BIRTHDAY PARTY TO GO TO ...

... AND NARCISSA **NEVER** MISSES A PARTY.

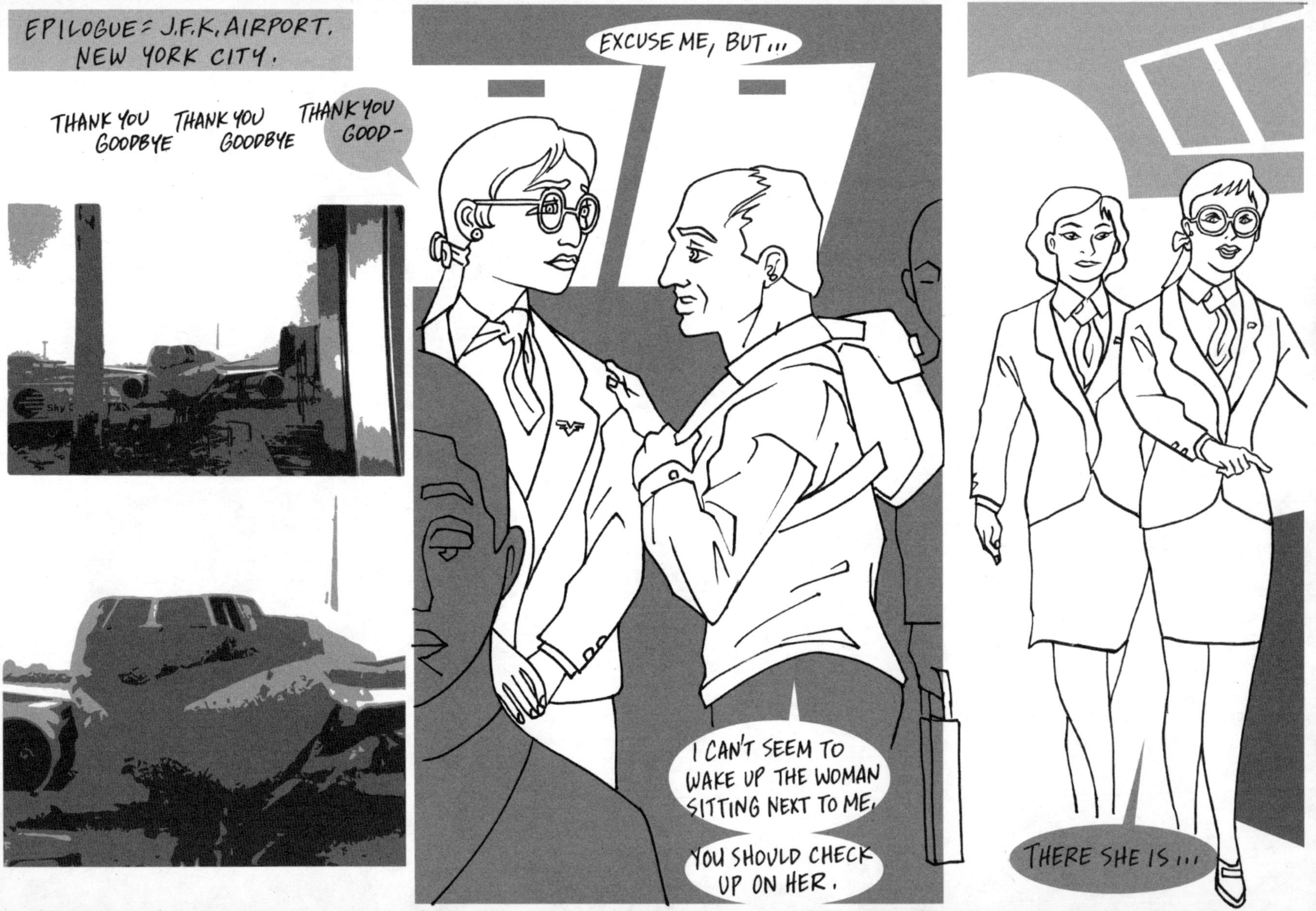

EPILOGUE: J.F.K. AIRPORT. NEW YORK CITY.
THANK YOU GOODBYE
THANK YOU GOODBYE
THANK YOU GOOD-
EXCUSE ME, BUT...
I CAN'T SEEM TO WAKE UP THE WOMAN SITTING NEXT TO ME.
YOU SHOULD CHECK UP ON HER.
THERE SHE IS...

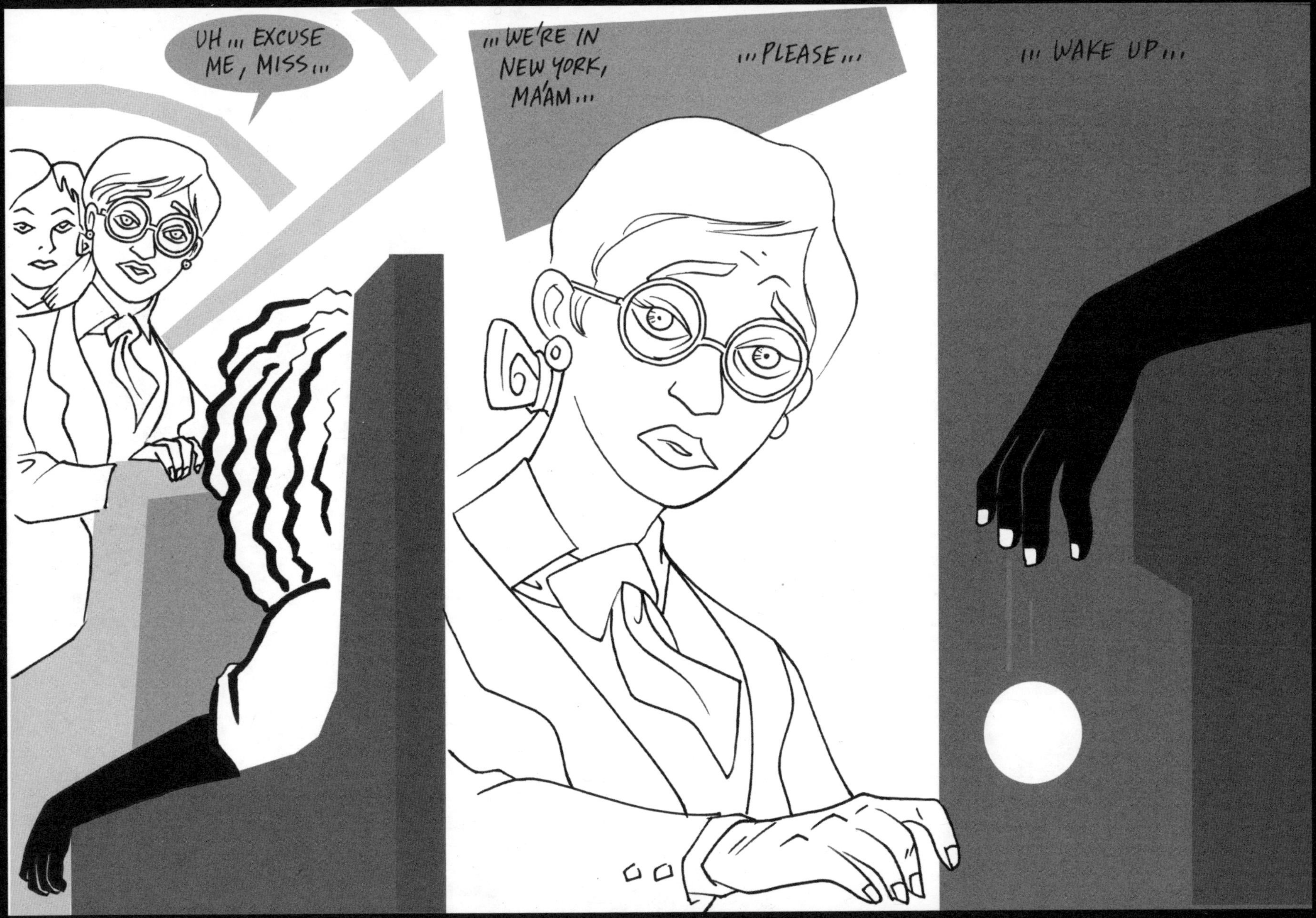
UH... EXCUSE ME, MISS...
...WE'RE IN NEW YORK, MA'AM...
...PLEASE...
...WAKE UP...

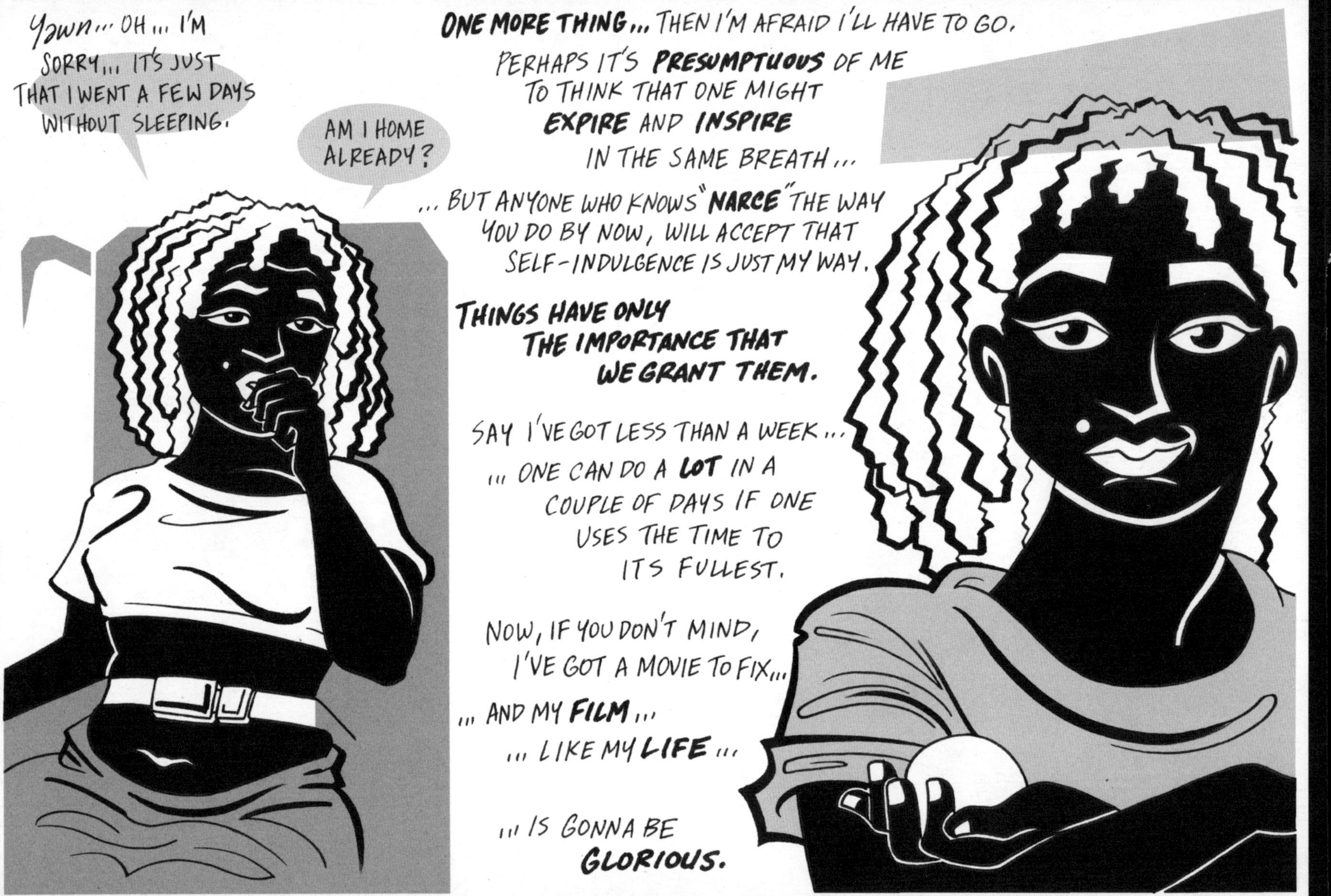
Yawn... OH... I'M SORRY... IT'S JUST THAT I WENT A FEW DAYS WITHOUT SLEEPING.
AM I HOME ALREADY?
ONE MORE THING... THEN I'M AFRAID I'LL HAVE TO GO.
PERHAPS IT'S PRESUMPTUOUS OF ME TO THINK THAT ONE MIGHT EXPIRE AND INSPIRE IN THE SAME BREATH...
... BUT ANYONE WHO KNOWS "NARCE" THE WAY YOU DO BY NOW, WILL ACCEPT THAT SELF-INDULGENCE IS JUST MY WAY.
THINGS HAVE ONLY THE IMPORTANCE THAT WE GRANT THEM.
SAY I'VE GOT LESS THAN A WEEK...
... ONE CAN DO A LOT IN A COUPLE OF DAYS IF ONE USES THE TIME TO ITS FULLEST.
NOW, IF YOU DON'T MIND, I'VE GOT A MOVIE TO FIX...
... AND MY FILM...
... LIKE MY LIFE...
... IS GONNA BE GLORIOUS.

I would like to thank Harry Candelario, "Mac Doctor," for his support both technical and moral.

Thanks to Eric Tooks & Stephania Baptiste, Titus Thomas & Sharon Joseph, Randy DuBurke & Olivia Wolff, Sean M. Taggart, Jason Little, Isabella Bannerman, Syr Ivan & Kikelomo Bennett, Barbara Lehman, Geoffrey Johnson, and Kevin J. Taylor for lookin' out, above and beyond.

To Adam Osterfeld and family I dedicate page 25 with respect.

Thanks to Gilbert Giles, for being a great sounding board. I promise to return the favor someday.

Gracias a la familia Tavera para todos. Thanks to George "Circling Eagle" Tooks, Ed Tooks, Rosalyn Arnold, Sean Tooks, Thomas Emery, and my family in Sunflower.

Thanks to Liz Sample, you'll know why. Thanks also to David Bastian, Nina Ross, Geoff Mosher, Dave Savage, and the ZipGun Posse.

Thanks to JuanFran de Granada for his answers to Alhambra questions.

Thanks to those at Doubleday who helped. Thanks also to Stuart Rees Esq. and Ernie Villany Sr. & Jr.

The poem during Narcissa & Sada's love scene was written over six hundred years ago by the Sevillan Moor Al Rahman.

Finally, thanks to Lucille & Phyliss. I love you.